THE AUTHOR

A A Hasker was born in the poorer part of Birmingham in the early 'twenties. He spent his childhood in the dreary slums of Birmingham during the depression. Hasker attended Rea Street School, a tough place where "survival of the fittest" easily could have been the school motto. He left school at fourteen and worked in a factory, first on the machines and then as a blacksmith striker.

Also at this time, he joined the Territorial Army - altering his birth certificate to show he was seventeen. A year later, at fifteen, Hasker transferred to Man Service, Royal Army Medical Corps and trained at Royal Victoria Hospital on the shores of Southampton Water.

When war was declared two years later, Hasker saw service in northern Norway and was evacuated from the Narvik area; served in South Africa and Madagascar; posted to North Africa and joined the Desert Rats. For the invasion of Salerno, Hasker was attached to the American 5th Army. He returned to England in the middle of January 1944 to train for the Normandy landings. He was eventually invalided home and underwent major surgery.

In 1948 Hasker started his own business and after seven years went to Australia, where he had a variety of jobs including working on a sheep station. He returned to England three years later, settling once again in Portsmouth and restarting the family business with his wife and two sons.

His hobbies include writing and travelling. He has written many short stories. *Eternity Must Wait* is his first novel to be published, another is completed and one is currently under way.

A A Hasker

ETERNITY MUST WAIT

DEDICATION

This novel is dedicated to the officers and men of the Second Light Field Ambulance, Seventh Armoured Division (original Desert Rats), both to the survivors and those who never made it back home. There are far too many people to list here but I feel I must mention my driver and friend, Ernie, killed in 1944.

CHAPTER 1

Harry sat hunched up in his usual corner seat in the front of the ambulance. The wind whistled through the inadequate, ill-fitting canvas sides, biting through his thick clothing and cutting into the exposed parts of his face. Ahead the sky was constantly lit by the brilliant flashes of heavy artillery, while behind them dawn was creeping over the horizon. He moved uncomfortably on the hard seat, lifting first one buttock and rubbing it vigorously until he felt it tingle its way back into life, then he lifted the other repeating the treatment, continuing this exercise several times before settling down again. Taking two cigarettes from a battered tobacco tin, he lit both, then without a word, passed one to his driver who grunted in acknowledgement. There was no word of thanks, although it didn't offend Harry. They had been together for three years and like an old married couple knew each others ways, habits and mannerisms, and Harry knew that Charlie never uttered a word before his hot mug of tea.

The road was rough and bumpy, like most of the secondary roads that crisscrossed France. On either side a grass verge stretched for ten or twelve yards. A hedge, interspersed with tall poplars every few yards, separated the verge from the fields of crops beyond and a pale mist hung a couple of feet above the sodden grass covering it like a ghostly shroud.

Harry suddenly broke one of their unwritten laws. He gasped, smacked his dry lips and said, "Bloody hell, Charlie, my mouth feels like the undercarriage of a shite hawk."

Charlie didn't answer. Harry hadn't expected him to. He just grunted, blew the ash from the tip of his cigarette and pointed towards the grass verge. Barely readable in the early morning light every few yards a notice in German read 'MINEN' with, below the writing, a picture of a red skull and crossbones.

They had left their parent unit a couple of hours before without breakfast or brew, replacing another ambulance crew attached to a regiment of Hussars, whose own ambulance had been hit and both crew members killed.

A farmhouse loomed before them, a victim of the fighting - but then this area was no stranger to war. Devastated in the Great War it had been damaged in the retreat of the B.E.F. in 1940, and occupied by the Germans for four wearying years. Forlorn, the farmhouse's blackened rafters stood out like a giant spider web stretched across the pale early morning sky. The front of the house had fallen away leaving the rooms exposed like a gigantic doll's house. Beds were unmade in the rooms above and the kitchen table was littered with dishes and part of an unfinished

1

meal, now being devoured by a horde of hungry rats. Over the fireplace - the fire long since dead - a large pot curtsied in the faint breeze. On one side of the fireplace there was a large photograph of an elderly woman who sat with a white apron across her knees and hands clasped in her lap, glaring sternly into space. On the other side was a photograph of a French soldier from the Great War, a rifle laid across his knees. Four medals in a glass case hung beneath it.

In the adjoining field, cattle lay with misshapen legs pointing skywards, death gas extending their stomachs to bursting. Others that had escaped, or only been slightly wounded, wandered aimlessly about the farmyard, overfilled udders dragging over the shiny cobbles. Poultry pecked fruitlessly between the stones.

"Poor bastards," Charlie muttered.

Harry nodded his head in agreement. Then he stepped carefully down after the ambulance had come to a halt. He adjusted the collar of his greatcoat and after carefully inspecting the gate for hidden booby traps kicked it open and made his way towards the great barn at the side of the farmhouse. Following his usual cautious pattern of searching out booby traps he carefully opened the barn door, but jumped and flattened himself against the wall as a large, half wild cat came screaming out followed by several terrified kittens.

Pulse racing he broke out in a cold sweat, still trembling as he lifted a sack of corn and tipped it in the yard. The starving chickens descended on the corn like locusts settling on the African plains. Then he lifted several bales of hay into the yard. A large antique galvanised bath, long since dry, stood under an old fashioned pump. He quickly filled it, opened the gates into the adjoining fields and yelled,

"That's it, Charlie. They should be fine now. Pity we don't have time to milk them. The poor sods are in agony."

Charlie eased the ambulance into gear and had hardly covered a hundred yards when there was a deafening explosion just ahead. Great clods of earth rose and scattered across the road and verges in a wide circle. Charlie reacted by slamming down his foot brake.

"What the fuck was that?" Charlie bawled, as the ambulance screeched to a halt. Unfastening the side screen, he poked his head outside the cab as it filled with the acrid stench of explosives.

"Sounded like an 88 to me," Harry replied.

"I know that, you prick! But where the hell did it come from? Jerry is supposed to be at least half a mile in front of those guns up ahead!" Charlie snorted, his sentence trailing off as another

2

shell screamed over, much nearer this time. Clods of earth and stones slammed against the front of the ambulance, and a piece of shrapnel removed the metal circle with its red cross from the top of the cab.

"So much for the bleeding Geneva Convention," Harry muttered as Charlie slammed the ambulance into gear and it shot forward. "That's all I need," he grumbled. "I very nearly shat myself when that bloody cat and her family scrambled out of that barn like their arses were on fire. I saw you, you bastard, laughing your bloody head off."

Charlie was far from amused now. For the past couple of hours the only thing on his mind had been getting his first brew and a breakfast of tinned bacon and eggs. Now it was obvious they were being singled out for artillery practice. The only explanation was a small suicide unit left behind to try and slow down the Allied advance - and they weren't novices at the game. They were good experienced artillery men. There was nothing for it but to run the gauntlet. The unit needed Charlie and Harry, but first Charlie would try and locate the gun, or guns.

"They came from the right of us, Harry," Charlie said and pulling up behind a clump of trees that hid them from view, he took an old German bayonet from behind his seat and a pair of German binoculars. With the bayonet he prodded the earth at a steep angle and gingerly made his way towards a tree. Two more shells screamed overhead, falling well clear of them, and the two men were certain they were hidden from view of the gunners for the moment.

Charlie scanned the countryside with the binoculars, but his attention kept returning to a small dense copse, the ideal place for artillery. There was a small puff of white smoke and a bullet slammed into the branch of the tree Charlie was lying across. He scrambled down and almost fell from the branch screaming in pain. Harry believed that the sniper had found his target, but Charlie was holding his crutch and wincing in agony in between sucking air through his clenched teeth.

"God, Harry," he gasped. "I scratched my goolies climbing down that tree. The Jerries are in that copse alright, although it's difficult to see clearly with all those patches of mist hanging around."

"That bleeding sniper saw you alright, Charlie. I don't think I ever saw you move so quickly," Harry replied.

"You needn't rub it in," moaned Charlie. He'd taken his penis in his hand and was examining it closely.

"Ah, put it away, Charlie. It's not a pretty sight first thing in the morning," Harry grumbled, pulling a face. A moment later

3

another shell screamed over and, instinctively, they both flattened themselves on the damp ground. The explosion deafened them, the hot blast taking their breath away. Shrapnel pierced the air with a metallic hiss and thudded into the ground around them.

Being under shell fire was nothing new to either of them but being singled out as a prime target was a new experience. On a couple of occasions they had been targeted by a dive bomber, but this was frightening. The gun or guns were at short range and it was impossible to miss. Harry and Charlie were left with two choices: abandon the ambulance and make a run for it, or take a chance with the ambulance, relying on speed and Charlie's driving. The first choice was instantly dismissed from both their minds.

"Come on, Harry. Put on your helmet and grab your balls. Let's make a dash for it."

Charlie's dash however was reduced to a painful limp. The mist had all but vanished, evaporated by a watery sun. Still wincing with pain as the rough serge of his battle dress sand-papered his genitals, Charlie slipped the engine into gear.

"She'll have to go like she's never gone before, Harry," he told his companion and fortunately the ambulance maintained it's reputation. Harry held his breath expecting at any minute to hear the morbid whine of shells around them. They swerved round a hairpin bend, Harry clutching the side of the ambulance as the offside wheels left the ground and then fell back, thudding him down in his seat.

"Hold it, Charlie," he gasped and pointed ahead to a small scout car, half on its side, being held up by a tall poplar tree. He grabbed his medical satchel and before Charlie had brought the ambulance to a stop, made his way across the mined grass verge, relying on the tracks made by the scout car. Charlie found a spot to hide the ambulance from the view of the trigger happy gunners.

Harry was taking no chances. According to the wet tracks the scout car couldn't have passed by long before. He held his breath every step of the way and although the scout car was less then fifty yards away it took him a good ten minutes to reach it. His shirt was saturated with cold sweat and his bottom lip trembled. The steel body of the car was ice cold and wet with dew. Gingerly he hauled himself aboard. A corporal hung out of the small turret. He felt the man's neck, but there was no pulse although the body was still warm. He pulled the corporal upright. A piece of shrapnel had hit the man under the chin and passed through the top of his head leaving a large gaping hole. His steel helmet

4

lay by the side of the scout car. It was filled with the contents of his skull - a mass of grey slime and blood.

Harry slid over the car and peered through the driver's slits. A face, teeth bared in a perpetual grin leered back at him silently accusing him of intruding on the death scene.

"Oh, Christ," gasped Harry, his voice just a whisper. He wanted to be sick and retched, but all that came up from his stomach was green bile. He reached for his water bottle and lifted it to his lips, his face distorted with pain. He'd forgotten that he'd filled it with cheap French wine and the burning liquid bit into his raw, chapped lips.

"Dead?"

Harry jumped. "Christ, Charlie, I wish you wouldn't do that!" Harry rinsed his mouth out with the wine. "Poor bastards didn't know what hit them. Shell must have dropped right in front of their car. Hardly a mark on the car itself." He had his back to his driver and stared into space not moving for at least five minutes, his water bottle still in his hand.

"How much longer is this bloody carnage going to go on for, Charlie? Don't the Jerries realise they're finished?"

Charlie shrugged his shoulders, his six foot frame out of place in the small scout car.

"Like us in 1940, Harry. Everyone gave us up as a lost cause. Even the American Ambassador, Joe Kennedy, said we were finished and not worth helping out. I suppose until we go through Berlin and flatten Germany in the process, Jerries will hold out some kind of hope. Hitler and his cronies keep telling their people they're coming up with some kind of secret weapon and the stupid sods believe them." He lit two cigarettes and passed one to his mate.

"Get their I.D.'s and let's get cracking Harry. It'll be tougher this time. That hairpin bend must have brought us at least fifty yards nearer those guns. It's going to be tough," he repeated.

Harry cut away the identity tags from the corporal's neck and fished around inside his pockets for his pay book and papers. He slipped his hand inside the driver's slits and felt around blindly for his tags, his finger catching a jagged end of bone. He found the string and gave it a tug. The man's head pitched forward and hit the metal with a sickening thud. Then Harry cut the string away.

"Let's piss off," he said.

Harry sat dejected on the back step of the ambulance while Charlie ran the engine for a few minutes. He wanted to get off to a fast start and didn't want the engine stalling at the crucial moment. He joined his mate while they finished their smoke.

5

"Just think, Charlie, at this very minute we're the only two people in the world that knows those two men are dead. You can imagine at home now, their parents, wives, perhaps girlfriends are boasting about them swanning around France in that small scout car. Some poor sods are in for a real shock. What a sodding war this is. Before they start the next one they should get every politician, arms manufacturer and weapons designer, put them way out in the desert with every diabolical weapon ever invented - flame throwers, shells, phosphorous bombs, gas, mortars and everything that can be thought of - and let them fight it out. I bet it wouldn't last twenty four hours and there would certainly never be another one. You can just imagine all those arms barons rubbing their hands with glee whenever they hear of a big battle going on, wondering how many shells'll be fired and tanks need replacing. I bet there was great jubilation when they heard of D. Day in the board rooms, wondering how they could increase output in the national interest. What a load of crap. Don't mind the poor sods wiped off the face of the earth or maimed for life."

"Bloody hell, Harry, you're in a right shitty mood today. We're trying to stuff a dictator who wants to take over the world, and getting it right, thank God ... Getting cheesed off or just cracking up?"

Harry sighed. "I dunno, Charlie. I suppose meeting Kim and her family gave me a different slant on life. Her mum and dad treated me as one of the family. I never knew what family life was like before I met her. Seeing the effect the death of her brother had on the family really got to me. He was only twenty when he was killed in the desert. For the first time I witnessed what that did to a family. You know, her mother gave me a key to the house. One day I went in, but she hadn't heard me open the door. She was sobbing, tears flooding down her face. Believe me, it's something I'll never forget."

They ground their cigarettes into the dust with the heels of their boots and returned to their seats.

The shelling had stopped and the two men moved on. The ambulance, like the ones they had driven in North Africa and Italy, had taken a similar battering but never once had the engine let them down, thanks to Charlie. For there were two things Charlie was expert in - women and engines.

"Hang onto your balls, Harry. Here we go!"

How many times Harry had heard that expression in the last six months he'd lost count, but it never failed to bring a smile to his face. The ambulance shot forward and instantly a shell landed a few yards in front of them.

"They're good, Harry, bloody good..."

6

These were the last words Charlie ever uttered.

The ambulance bumped over the small crater the shell left behind and they never heard the shell which hit the back wheel. Charlie fought with the steering wheel. The ambulance slewed round and ran onto the grass verge. Another louder explosion lifted the rear of the vehicle off the ground. Evidently they had hit a land mine. The back of the ambulance fell away. The front dragged along a few yards and with another muffled explosion the remainder disintegrated as they hit a second mine.

Charlie was flung from the ambulance in a complete arc, the front of his stomach ripped away and his intestines trailing like a gigantic silver snake. He slid along the opposite verge on the dew soaked grass leaving a trail of slime and blood. He was dead before he hit the ground.

Harry was hurled in the other direction landing flat on his back and sliding along for ten yards before coming to a rest below a tall poplar tree.

The watery sun was filtering through the tremulous leaves of a slender poplar when he opened his eyes. His lids felt heavy and he could hardly open or close them. Then, gradually, the realisation of what had happened came to him. God, it must be midday. He must have been here about four hours. He tried to lick his lips but his tongue felt like a lump of misshapen putty. His breathing was difficult, as if a weight was pressing on his chest. His arms felt leaden and wouldn't move, nor would his hands. Not even one finger would react to the commands of his brain. He tried one limb after another, but his head remained stationary.

Panic set in. 'My God, I'm paralysed,' he thought. His pulse thumped against his temple as if his brain was about to burst and he tried to yell for Charlie, but no sound left his lips. Then his throat muscles knotted as he remembered what had happened. Charlie had been right above the first mine and if Charlie were alive he'd have searched for and found him.

From out of the corner of one eye he could see the mudguard of the ambulance with the Divisional sign plainly visible. He made another round of his limbs: a toe, a leg, first one then the other and finally the upper limbs. His whole body felt as if it was being weighed down by a slab of lead moulded to his body and he couldn't turn his head a fraction of an inch. There was simply no response. Slowly a shadow fell across him as he sank into oblivion. The will to live was gone. No way did he want to return home and be a burden to anyone, least of all dear Kim. A face danced before his eyes, which was at first a distorted blur.

7

It gradually sharpened and he recognised her, tears falling down her beautiful, childlike face. Reaching out to him with one hand she ran her delicate fingers around the contours of his face. Her mother stood behind her. She, too, was crying and held out her hand towards him. She placed her arm around her daughter's shoulders, no sound coming from their mouths, but they were pleading with him to live. They turned and walked away, turning back twice to look at him before fading from view... He felt calmer.

Now Charlie stood at his feet, and about time too. Charlie grinned and winked as he read Harry's thoughts. His fair stubbly hair stood on end. He was wearing khaki shorts and that old bush shirt he'd worn when they first met. There was someone standing beside him. As first Harry couldn't recognise who it was, but gradually he realised he'd seen many pictures of this young man around Kim's house. It was her dead brother. Charlie and Kim's brother stood staring down at Harry for what seemed hours, but in reality could only have been a long strange moment somewhere in time... Was he dreaming, Harry wondered, or had they come to take him off into eternity?

A wet spot trickled down his face. Was it Kim's tear or just a rain drop? He looked up at the tree above him and smacked his dry lips. The swollen tongue had subsided. His spit tasted salty and blood trickled from the side of his mouth. He wiped it away with his hand and several seconds elapsed before he realised that movement had returned to his body. He tried one arm after the other. They felt heavy but moved. Yet there was no movement from the waist down and Harry knew at once that his spine was severed somewhere in the lumbar region. He tried to pull himself into a sitting position, but a bolt of pain shot through his whole body and lights flashed before his eyes. He wanted to scream. His mouth filled with green bile from his stomach and mixed with blood, and as he turned his head to one side it dribbled out. He was face to face with death and knew it, but didn't want to choke to death. He slid into unconsciousness.

He opened his eyes and in the distance could hear faint voices. All fear vanished as, with relief, he knew that Charlie had returned for him, although from his signs and symptoms Harry realised he would be paralysed from the waist down for life. Someone was kneeling beside him.

"That you, Charlie?" Harry whispered.

"Found one, sarge. He's still alive - just," the kneeling figure shouted. He gently wiped his hand across Harry's forehead. "Follow the white tape, sarge. It's clear of mines. Know him?" the sapper asked.

8

"Know him! Of course I know him. One of the best medics in the divi. Been with us since the desert. Saved my life and my marriage. Tell you, sapper, Harry here and his mate could tell you some stories that would make your hair curl." He took a towel from his haversack and cleaned Harry's face.

"Go and get a stretcher and blankets."

Harry put a restraining hand on the sergeant's arm and shook his head. His mouth worked and the sergeant moved nearer.

"Don't bother, sarge," he gasped. "Waste of time. Can't be moved." The sergeant tenderly lifted his head and placed it on a folded piece of scorched blanket. Then he covered him with his overcoat.

"You'll be alright, Harry, as soon as we get you to a dressing station."

Harry made signs for the sergeant to lower his head.

"See Kim... Tell her I love her... and she's not to shed any tears. Tell her she made me happy ..." Every word was an effort. "Stay with me, sarge," he pleaded laboriously. The sergeant clenched Harry's wrist in a reassuring grip.

"Bleeding hell, sarge, you're crying," the sapper said.

"Why don't you fuck off and get on with your mine clearing, you stupid prat?" the sergeant sniffed angrily.

A golden smudge became visible on the horizon the next morning when Harry stopped breathing, a peaceful smile on his lips. The sergeant took his identity tags, pay book and what few possessions he could find including the heavy silver watch Kim had given Harry just before he'd left for Normandy. Then the sergeant lifted Harry onto his shoulder and carrying him to the side of the lonely French country road placed him in a grave beside Charlie and the two other members of the British Army from the scout car. The graves were filled in that afternoon. Alongside each other in death Harry and Charlie would lie forever. Two brave men who had been through so much together, fighting for democracy in a crazed dictator's ugly war over three eventful years ...

CHAPTER 2

The three tonner trundled over the uneven sand track. Barrel track they called it, so named after the fifty gallon, white painted oil drums positioned every five hundred to a thousand yards according to whether they were visible from their nearest neighbour. Apart from the tell-tale barrels, there was little else to distinguish the track from any other part of the desert. Maybe there was an occasional tyre track where a vehicle hit a soft spot, but more often a burnt out tank or lorry, and now and again a solitary white painted cross - a true indication the war had passed this way.

The lorry was packed with men returning from hospital or convalescence. Others, like Harry, were new reinforcements from the holding depot joining their regiments for the first time. Harry wiped the sweat from his forehead and armpits, his hair wet through as if he had just stepped from under a shower. He would dearly have loved to take a long drag from a cigarette but the minute he touched one it became soggy with his sweat. The sun showed no mercy as it tore through the flimsy sand-blasted canvas sheet covering the lorry.

"God," said Harry to the man sitting beside him, "it's like one of those Turkish baths back home. I must have shed at least two stone since we left the depot at El Quasassin. I'm sitting in a pool of sweat. Feels like I just pissed myself!"

"Join the club, mate. It would have been a damn sight better if this stupid driver stopped occasionally to let us stretch our legs." In the limited space there was little room to stretch an elbow never mind a leg.

"Been out long, medic?"

Harry shook his head. "Just a couple of weeks in North Africa. Been on the Abyssinian campaign then came up through the Sudan. Christ, I thought that was bad enough but this place is sheer hell. I suppose I'm lucky to be here, though. The unit I was with was disbanded after the Sudan. Most of the men went out to Burma. Didn't fancy that much."

"It's not so bad here once you get used to the flies and scorpions, bully beef and hard tack, salinated water and your mates so sunburned you can't tell them apart from the Arabs. And you have to fight hard against lust. Even the sergeant major starts to look sexy - that's when you really know the strain is getting to you! But Jerry livens things up occasionally, sending a few Stukas over. Get used to that and life isn't too bad."

Harry's companion sighed, shrugged his shoulders and took a long swig from his water bottle. "Just watch you don't dehydrate," he warned and stared blankly at the canvas cover. "I suppose there are worse places."

Two young infantrymen just out from home were suffering the pangs of motion sickness and hung their heads over the tailboard, at the same time trying hard to listen to the conversation. They were getting no sympathy from the other occupants, especially the sergeant. He sat on the tailgate along side them, hanging on to the metal crossbar supporting the canvas cover oblivious to the red hot metal tearing at his hands.

"What you two need is a tin of bully and a couple of hard tack biscuits, washed down with a mug or two of strong tea," the sergeant said, poking one of the recruits with a stumpy finger.

They stared at him impassively, struggling to keep down what little food and drink remained in their stomachs. It was okay for the sergeant - he was an old desert campaigner.

The stench from a dozen or more sweating bodies fouled the air adding to the discomfort and constantly fraying tempers were kept in check by the sergeant.

"Sarge, can't we open the canvas front? The stink is terrible down this end," a voice shouted from the gloomy interior.

The sergeant shook his head. "Open that and the flies and sand will torment you to death. Better put up with the smell, laddie." He had a detectable Scottish brogue and Harry figured he came from the Borders.

"This bastard isn't making it any easier, sarge. He's got his boots off and his feet stink like an open cess pit." A gunner aimed a kick into the middle of a prostrate form laying across the full width of the lorry. "He's a lance corporal, sarge, and he's been pissed since we left the depot. It's not only his feet, sarge - the filthy bastard hasn't stopped farting since he got on the lorry."

"Don't know how he got a stripe. I wouldn't have him as a shit house wallah in our mob. Met him up the Blue couple of months ago and he looked half pissed then. Matter of fact for the few days we spent at the depot he was walking round in a daze with half a bottle of whisky sticking out of his pocket. Why the hell they put up with him I don't know," the sergeant spat out contemptuously.

One of the men from the corporal's unit riding in the lorry came to his defence. "Best sniper in the regiment when he's sober. They reckon he's accounted for more Iteys and Jerries than the average man has had hot dinners." The man laughed. "The old man rations him to one beer a day when the N.A.A.F.I. truck gets in and heaven help anyone who gives him their ration. The old man's threatened to court martial anybody who does. He's not a bad bloke when he's sober though."

11

"He's a stinking pain in the arse when he's pissed and that's for sure," replied the sergeant.

The corporal raised his head with some effort, as a sloppy dog might when he suspects his owners are discussing him in derogatory terms. His watery eyes gazed around the crowded lorry mournfully.

"What's going on? Where the hell are we?" he mumbled, staggering up onto his feet. Then, amidst a chorus of curses, he elbowed his way to the back of the vehicle. "Got to have a piss," he insisted, pushing one of the recruits to one side, and stumbling he grabbed the red hot cross bar. He swore loudly at everyone and everything. "Fucking desert," he finally concluded, gasping for breath after his strenuous efforts at damning all and everything to hell. "Let the bleeding Arabs have the God forsaken hole." He knelt down and fumbled with the brass buttons on his shorts and as the lorry bounced over the sand track he lost control of his penis and it fell on the hot metal of the tailgate. He screamed, pulling back sharply, his penis slipped back into his shorts dribbling urine and he muttered a long drawn out, "Jees..." followed by a string of oaths.

"You disgusting bastard," the sergeant yelled at him and looked as if he were exerting extreme self control not to lash out at the corporal. "You stink. Your breath stinks. Your feet stink. In fact you stink like a mobile shit house. Jesus Christ!" The sergeant was purple in the face as he blinked back the sweat streaming down his face from his eyes and bared his teeth and hissed through them. "That piss... When it dries... God help any man within five feet of you." He took a deep breath. "Now, put your boots on before you do Jerry's job and gas us all - and get the hell back to your place, for Christ's sake!"

"Balls. Man's got to pee, ain't he? Couldn't help pissing myself. I burnt my prick on that hot metal."

"Don't you balls me, you filthy drunken bastard, or you might just find yourself grovelling in a sand bath out there." Grimly he jerked a meaty thumb out of the back towards the desert.

Through bloodshot eyes the corporal looked the sergeant up and down, but didn't bother to pursue the matter further. The sergeant was head and shoulders taller than him and twice as broad. The corporal might be the best shot in his regiment but he was no match for the hefty sergeant's fists. The corporal struggled to the rear, knocking over a table four men had made with their packs. They were trying to play cards and cursed him in unison. He answered with the only word he seemed to know, "Balls!" Then he sat down and pulled another bottle of whisky from his side pack, took a generous gulp, belched and shuddered. Harry gazed on astonished. Half that amount of booze and he would be flat on his back. The corporal lay down and belched again, bringing a comment from his nearest neighbour, "If it's not one foul end, it's t'other."

The card players gave up with a moan, "Didn't want to play anyway. Cards are too sticky."

Silence settled over the crowded lorry again, while the sun beat down on the flimsy canvas. The men were physically drained, talking was an effort and only the noise of the engine and the heavy tyres churning up the sand disturbed the peace. The landscape was barren with patches of dried scrub defying nature and pushing up through the hard ground. The horizon met the sky in a torrid dance of flimsy gauze, nothing was still and yet it seemed the whole planet was dead. The temperature was well above one hundred and twenty degrees with no shade to be seen. Everyone cursed silently at the driver for not stopping to brew and allowing them to stretch their aching muscles. It was through no fault of his. He was on a tight schedule. Every man must be dropped off at their units and he wanted to be well on his way back before sunset.

They were a mixed bag: four gunners including the sergeant, four tankies, six infantrymen and two signalmen. Harry was the only medic there. They all had one thing in common. They all belonged to the same armoured division, which had earned it's name the hard way. It was called the "Desert Rats." Harry was thankful he wasn't taller than his five feet ten as his legs were so cramped they felt like lead and ached from his thighs to the tips of his toes. He was thick set and his face tanned dark after two years in some of the hottest areas of Africa. His face resembled a dried prune and like the rest of the men in the lorry he was covered in a fine film of sand which gave him a clownish appearance.

Going to a new unit always caused him some concern. This was a new experience. He had never been with the tanks before. The division had been in constant action since the desert war began and in their last retreat to Alamein had taken a hammering, with his new unit taking more than its' fair share of casualties. There were new friends to be made and old contacts renewed. Five years as a regular in the army, three of them in the war service and constantly moving from one unit to another, there had to be someone who'd crossed his path in the past.

Brought up in a Quaker orphanage from infancy, he'd no knowledge of his parents and could only assume he'd been abandoned. At fifteen he realised there was another world outside the orphanage walls. He ran away to London and

13

wandered round aimlessly for days. Then his eye had caught the recruiting posters. Cold and hungry he'd walked into the recruiting office and picked up an illustrated book.

At Boy Service he was entitled to one shilling a day and at Man Service it started at two shillings. The Medical Corps sounded interesting and the pay was good once you qualified. Looking a lot older than his fifteen years he talked the sergeant into accepting him. Three days later found him at the depot, well fed on three good meals a day and dressed in nice warm clothing, so that never once did he regret his decision.

When the matron at the orphanage heard he'd enlisted she was terribly upset. A strong pacifist, she'd not only taught the children pacifism but practised it herself. With Harry she considered herself a failure. His music teacher was livid as well. She was convinced he had a great future at the piano, perhaps one day becoming a concert pianist.

Harry had neither relatives nor friends outside service life and hardly received mail. Occasionally the matron would write but her letters were full of do's and don'ts. While doing a training course at one of the great London teaching hospitals, Harry became friendly with one or two nurses. One became serious and put on the pressure, but from the start he made it clear that he didn't want a serious relationship with any girl while the war was still on.

He looked at the barren wilderness unfolding itself from the back of the lorry. A burnt out tank came into view. He couldn't tell whether it was an enemy tank or one of their own. All that was clear to him was the three white crosses by the side of it, standing out proud against the blackened background, as if conveying a message to him. He shuddered. No one would know he was out here if anything happened to him. In weeks, days perhaps, he would be entirely forgotten.

It was over a year since the matron last wrote and almost as long since one of the nurses sent a letter. Victoria sent a carton of cigarettes but that had been eighteen months ago and he hadn't had the decency to acknowledge them. Perhaps he deserved to be forgotten. That was one thing he was certain of, his being forgotten, for his pay book registered 'No next of kin.' This thought jolted his senses. Once he was settled into his new unit he would write to everyone with whom he had the slightest acquaintance. A wave of depression swept through his whole body as he stared at the three white crosses and the burnt out tank.

They all disappeared from view, and he reflected on happier times. Victoria, that lovely blue eyed blonde, in her third year and studying hard. She also played hard, he recalled, his memory resting fondly on that time she took him home on leave to her parents who lived in the heart of Devon. He smiled to himself recalling every tiny detail. Very nearly shit himself, he had, when she'd tiptoed to his bedroom after her parents were asleep. Fortunately it was a very large house, more in the way of a small mansion, and their bedroom was well away from the one he had occupied. All the same it had been a nerve racking experience - even more so when he discovered her father had been a major in his own corps in the Great War. He sired her very late in life and thought she was the reincarnation of a vestal virgin. Overawed and uneasy in the retired Major's presence Harry decided he would never go to her home again, although Victoria's parents were never snobbish and had made him feel very welcome. She had urged him to visit again but he'd always declined. He'd felt uncomfortable - out of his class. But that didn't stop him from taking her to their favourite hotel just off Sloane Square. It would do no harm to drop her a few lines.

He was interrupted from his day dreams when the lorry jolted and stopped suddenly, throwing them all forward. The driver ran to the back.

"Come on, two of you infantry wallahs." The two recruits went towards the tailgate, but he pushed them back. "Not you two," he told them and winked at the sergeant. "You'll soon get used to sitting in the back of lorries by the time you've flapped up and down this bleeding place a few times. You'll welcome a ride in one of these. You lads getting off, don't forget to tip the driver."

"Bollocks," someone inside shouted. "How about a brew and let us stretch our legs?"

One of the new men looked at him, his face ashen. "When do we get off, driver? I can't stand much more of this."

The driver assessed him dispassionately and blew half an inch of ash from the cigarette gripped firmly between his lips. "In about twenty minutes, providing there's no hold ups." He raised his voice. "The rest of you shower can get over to the cookhouse and see if the cook can rustle up some tea. It'll give you a chance to stretch your legs, but don't hang around I have a tight schedule."

Grabbing their mugs the men flung themselves from the rear of the lorry sending the two recruits flying. Hitting the sand they didn't move further, quite content to spread themselves out on it.

"Mind a scorpion doesn't get up your shorts and sting your knackers," a gunner shouted as he passed them.

"Ah, fuck you and fuck the scorpions," one of the recruits answered as he tried yet again to vomit.

15

"Oh yes? You believe me, mate, if one does get up there you won't be fucking anyone for a bloody long time. You'll think an elephant's kicked you," the gunner hooted with laughter.

The drunken corporal never moved, quite content to lie prostrate sipping at his bottle. The sergeant opened a tin of bully and sliced great lumps of it into his mouth, washing it down with gulps of strong tea. A gunner squatted down on his haunches beside him.

"Pity we couldn't get rid of that booze artist, sarge. The lorry would smell a lot sweeter. Can't we leave him on the side of the track with his kit?"

The thought brought a roar of laughter. "Good idea, laddie, but no chance. Pity really. He's the last to be dropped."

The gunner offered the two men a drink from his mug. The recruits turned a shade greener and one let out a dull moan.

"Please yourself." The gunner gulped it down and then burped loudly.

"Right," the driver shouted, "let's get mounted. Signalmen next drop, not long - ten minutes at the most. Get your gear ready. No time to waste. The officer up front gets off next stop, sarge," he went on, "come up front if you like. The stuck up prick has hardly uttered a word since we left the depot."

The sergeant nodded and added to the discomfort of the two men by filling a filthy pipe with rough shag tobacco on which he puffed away without a care in the world.

They had barely covered a half mile when the lorry ground to a halt and sank up to its back axle in soft sand.

"All out!"

The driver banged on the metal side of the lorry with a shovel. The sergeant vaulted over the tailboard and examined the wheels. He unstrapped the metal sand runners from the side of the lorry and soon had a digging out party organised. "Alright, you shower, you know the drill." He handed one of the recruits a shovel. "Here, laddie, here starteth your very first lesson. Dig hard. Just imagine you're digging a grave for your R.S.M. back in Blighty."

A channel some six feet long and two feet deep was soon dug out in front of the two rear wheels and the metal sand runners put in place.

"Now, everyone, shoulders to the lorry and push!" He stopped barking orders and glanced around at the men with their shoulders to the lorry. "Where the hell is that drunken corporal?"

"Still in the lorry and fast asleep," said the gunner.

The sergeant's face reddened behind the mask of fine sand and the corners of his mouth turned up in a sickening, foam-flecked grin, his voice when he spoke some long and weighty seconds afterwards, an agitated croak.

"He is, is he?" He vaulted back into the lorry, caught the corporal by the neck of his bush shirt and dragged him along the metal floor not bothering to stop at the end, the corporal hitting the sand with a thud.

"What the fuck is going on?" he groaned, staring up at the sergeant's face glaring down at him.

"You drunken bastard! Even you, in your perpetual drunken daze, should know when a vehicle is bedded down. Now get behind that lorry and when I say push, you push with all your might or so help me I'll ram this shovel right up your ring piece. Side on!"

There was a chorus of agonised whistles from the gathering. Twenty minutes later they stood around the lorry gasping and sweating, but the lorry was on firm ground once again.

"Hard work, sarge," a man said wiping his forearm across his sweaty brow. "I feel like a pedigree bull that's just served a herd of cows."

The sergeant offered the two recruits a swig from his water bottle as they lay across the sand their travel sickness temporarily forgotten, but within minutes they retched up a dirty green slime.

"That's right, waste water," the sergeant snorted. "It's bloody hard enough to get where you're going."

"That's buggered my schedule up," said the driver. "When I say get off next time do it as quick as you can, no poncing about, lads."

The driver tried to make up for lost time; the lorry swaying from side to side, sand rearing up in clouds cutting off any view from the outside. Ten minutes later the lorry came to an abrupt halt, but the driver didn't bother to get out. He just opened the door and yelled, "Right, you signal wallahs, out you get, pronto! I haven't got all day."

Back and side packs flew out, followed by kit bags and rolled blankets, making a huge pile. While they put on their webbing and adjusted their packs, one of the recruits vomited again and covered the pyramid of equipment with green slime. The signalman snarled at him, drawing his arm backwards and clenching his fist. Luckily the lorry pulled away just in time and the fist made contact with the metal.

"You dirty little bastard!" he shouted at the departing truck. "I hope you get fucking shot!"

There was more room now in the lorry for the remaining men to spread out. Not for long, though, for within ten minutes they were up to their axles in soft sand again.

"All out! Don't forget that drunken sod in there!"

The corporal rose unsteadily to his feet and made his way to the rear grumbling. "I'm supposed to be on light duties, sarge. I was wounded and told to take it easy."

"Wounded," snorted the sergeant. "That is great, that is. You have more change of cutting yourself on one of those whisky bottles than stopping a Jerry bullet. Come on, shift yourself, you stinking lazy shithead."

They eventually continued on their way to the next stop without any further mishaps and the driver ran round the back.

"Right, you two, we part company here," he shouted. A look of relief spread across the recruits' faces as they stumbled to the ground but it soon turned to horror as they scanned the desolate scene. Apart from a burned out Italian lorry half a mile away, before them lay a barren landscape.

"Where the hell are we, sarge?"

The sergeant looked at the driver with a broad grin on his face, and they both pointed to the far horizon. There, just discernible to the naked eye, a few distorted blobs danced in the heat haze. The recruits' hearts joyful a few minutes ago sank once again.

"How are we supposed to get there?"

"Well, you don't want me to give you a chucky back, do you? The driver can't take the lorry across there. You've just seen what it's like when we hit a patch of soft sand."

They adjusted their packs and lifted their kit bags across their shoulders and the sergeant checked to make sure their water bottles were filled.

"It's not that far really. Five miles at the most. Distances are very deceiving in this heat." He gave them a long drink from his water bottle.

"Don't puke up this time and take it easy with your own water. Don't drink until you have to, but make certain you don't dehydrate. Make for that lorry and have a rest in the shade. You have about five hours of daylight left but there'll be no moon till three or four in the morning, before that it will be as black as pitch."

The driver bought out a jerry can of water and a tin of condensed milk. Between them they managed to find enough tea and sugar and soon they had a brew going.

"I'll make an early start at first light," the sergeant said and as they waited for the water to boil they watched the two men struggling across the desert loaded down like a pair of pack animals.

18

"Poor sods," the sergeant muttered to himself. It wouldn't do to show the others he was getting soft. Aloud he said, "At least they should get their bloody knees brown."

They sat around in what little shade the lorry had to offer, sipping at their mugs of scalding tea.

The sergeant turned to Harry. "Been out long?"

"Couple of years, mostly in East Africa, Abyssinia and the Sudan."

"Should be used to the heat. You a regular?"

Harry nodded.

"Worked in one of those big military hospitals have you, laddie? God, man, those hospitals in Cairo..." He sucked his breath in between his teeth with a hissing sound. "Gorgeous sisters. There was this little blonde nurse... I would tell her my bum was sore, always when there was no orderly about or if they were busy. She would come and rub cold meths all over my ring. It was sheer heaven. One day she gave me a blanket bath and she washed all round my goolies. I swear she hesitated with them in her hand. Then she rubbed my arse again with cold meths and dusted round the family jewels with this talc. I don't know how I controlled myself. I had a hard on for three days."

While the men listened to this tale their mouths hung half open taking in every word. Harry smiled to himself. He'd heard similar stories many times. The men were all under the illusion that the orderlies worked in the wards all day and screwed all night. Nothing could be further from the truth. His own experiences with sisters were far from happy.

"Never had much to do with them myself. Just worked and kept my mouth shut. I'm not saying they don't do a decent job, but up here in the desert suits me. After the war I'll have had quite enough of them," Harry said.

"Bleeding sex maniacs, you lot. That's all you ever talk about. Your minds don't rise above your navels," the corporal grunted, taking another swig from his bottle, some of its contents dribbling from the corners of his mouth.

Putting his hand to his ear the sergeant said, "What was that remark, my inebriated friend? Why, you drunken bastard, you couldn't raise a beat if you wanted to. Your genitals must be pickled. You were rattled because I said the sister washed my ring with meths. You thought it was wasted. You would have drunk the bloody stuff. I know I would rather have a good woman any time than a bottle of that gut rot. Just take a shufti at yourself, you can't get the stuff down quick enough. It's dribbled all down the front of you. I drink and screw for pleasure. Free booze and fags... It's bastards like you that will be sorry when this war is over. If you live through it, and if a bullet doesn't get you, your liver will probably pack in before long."

He stood up and threw the dregs of his tea into the cooling fire where it hissed and spluttered.

"Come on. Let's get cracking," he ordered.

Three stops later Harry saw the tell-tale red crosses scattered around the vehicles in open leaguer. A closer scrutiny and he could see the background of the crosses were no longer white, but a dirty stone colour. The sand and the sun had wreaked a devastating vengeance over the years. He felt a rush of excitement grip him.

CHAPTER 3

Harry stood a few minutes outside the canvas lean-to and gazed round, taking in the desolate scene. Ambulances and vehicles were scattered over a vast area, some of them just discernible in the heat haze. Two hundred yards from the lean-to was the kitchen, only distinguishable from the other vehicles by the two blackened soya stoves outside and a deal table scrubbed and bleached white by the sun.

He dropped his kit outside the lean-to, adjusted his bush shirt and shorts, lifted back the canvas flap and stood inside, pausing for several seconds while his eyes adjusted to the gloom. A man sat shirtless at a table tapping away with one finger at an ancient typewriter. His back was a mass of inflamed pimples and spots that rose from the belt of his shorts and straddled each side of his spine and spread out over his shoulders. It was no cooler in the lean-to than out in the blast furnace outside. Harry's cough caused the man at the typewriter to pause, his finger a few inches above the keys.

"What do you want?" His voice was brisk and tarnished with a deep north country accent. He didn't bother to look around.

"Just joining the unit, mate."

"Mate!" snarled the pimple-backed man. "Corporal to you." He adjusted his shirt which was draped over the back of his chair to show off the one single stripe. There was something about this man that sent alarm bells ringing through Harry's system. He tried to shrug it off. After all it was a new unit and he wanted to make a decent impression, but God help him if all the N.C.O.s were like that.

Harry snapped to attention. "Sorry, corporal."

"Alright, hand me your papers."

Harry handed the buff coloured envelope over. The corporal held it to the light trying to make out the contents but didn't dare open it.

"How many men did they send?" he asked, trying to sound more important than the one stripe warranted.

Harry frowned, the question taking him by surprise. "Just me, corporal. How many did you expect?"

The corporal swivelled round in his chair. Just as Harry thought, his face like his back was covered in unsightly spots, and a large festering pimple stood out on his neck like a volcano about to erupt.

"One," snarled the corporal, "just one. There'll be hell to play when the old man gets to know. We were expecting at least four but eight would have been better."

21

There was movement from the darkened corner of the lean-to. A stretcher was raised on four old ammo boxes, and a fly stained mosquito net hung from the roof covering the make-shift bed. The net parted and two bare feet shot out. They fiddled around for a few seconds and then they found a pair of plimsolls to dive into.

"What the hell is going on, Sykes?" someone enquired moodily. The rest of the body appeared and, like Sykes, was naked from the waist. This man was about the same size as Harry although Harry was much broader and heavier. The man wore a khaki band around his wrist but instead of a watch there was the R.S.M.'s insignia. Harry snapped to attention for a second time. The R.S.M. looked him up and down a few times and then barked, "Who the hell are you?"

"Private Jackson, sir."

The R.S.M. opened the buff envelope. "A regular, eh?" It was a statement rather than a question. The thought of a regular pleased him. "I see you're a first class nursing orderly and a second class operating room attendant. What the hell are you doing up here with those qualifications? Got a reputation for being a naughty boy, have you? Been in the glass house? With your qualifications you could have found yourself a cushy number back in Cairo or Alex."

"Couldn't stand the idea of a base job, sir," said Harry. But what he would have preferred to say was that he couldn't stand working for army sisters. They were a hard-boiled bunch who enjoyed bullying him unmercifully.

"You must be bloody bonkers," answered the R.S.M. whilst studying Harry's record. "I see you were at Dunkirk and you've been in the East African campaign and in the Sudan." He walked around Harry studying him as if he were a statue by a famous sculptor. "They only sent you, did they?" He threw down the papers in disgust. "I asked for at least four men. My lads here are working their arses off." He turned his attention towards the corporal. "For heavens sake, Sykes, how many times do I have to tell you to wear that bloody shirt while you're in the company office. That back of yours is puke making, not that your face is any improvement. Take Jackson over to Williams. He needs a medic."

Sykes tried to smother a smile.

"What's the matter, Sykes? Did I say something funny?"

"No, sir," snapped the corporal, slipping on his bush shirt.

They prepared to leave the lean-to as the R.S.M. added, "Williams is a good driver, Jackson, but unfortunately he has some very bad habits. You being a regular may be able to instil

22

some discipline in him. Don't let him lead you astray. Knowing Williams he'll have his ambulance parked well away from here so dump your kit by the lean-to. He can bring the ambulance over to collect it later."

Outside, well away from the company office, Sykes burst out laughing. "That's a beaut, that is, you with Williams. Teach him some discipline? He's the most reckless driver in the unit. See that blob on the horizon?" He pointed to a misshapen mess just discernible in the heat haze. Although the vehicles were in open leaguer none less than a hundred yards from the next, this one was well away on the outskirts of the leaguer and at least two hundred yards from his nearest neighbour.

"That's the bastard. Had three medics already. Don't give a shit for anyone." He gritted his teeth. "One day I'll get him."

Harry made a mental note of the corporal's threat. He might be new in the unit today but in a couple of months he'd be settled in. He let it pass.

"What happened to his other medics?"

The question amused the corporal and brought a fresh outburst of laughter.

"The first bloke was okay, got called up for the duration, thought he was in for an easy time in the medics but soon learned different. Got killed. Smithy, the second, had a piece of shrapnel go through his lung. Far as we know he's still in hospital in South Africa. Williams had a letter from him the other day. He likes it down there and wants to stay after the war. The last one lost both his feet when they ran over a mine. Tell you what, Jackson, sooner you than me. Williams is bloody suicidal. Hope you've made your will!"

Harry stopped to wipe the sweat from his neck and face and felt like kicking himself as he'd left his water bottle with the rest of his kit back at the orderly's office. He settled for a cigarette and as he took out his old battered tobacco tin, Sykes, without hesitation, took a dive at it. Harry gave him a sidelong look of disgust.

"Don't suppose you got a packet of these Woodies to spare? We don't get many decent smokes. All we get is bloody 'V' issues made of camel shit."

Harry shook his head. He had been warned back at the holding depot about those and so spent all his spare cash on supplies. Harry never considered himself a student of human nature, and rarely accepted a man at face value, but the more time he spent in Sykes' company the more he disliked him.

"I thought you only had twenty ambulances in this unit?" Harry pointed to a vehicle with the number 21 painted on its side.

"Oh that. The silly bastards are superstitious here. No one would take number 13 so they left it out," sneered the corporal as he squeezed a festering pimple on his chest and rubbed his hands down his shorts. "I hope you don't wear a watch," he went on, grinning. "Williams won't have anyone in his tub that wears a watch. Reckons they're bad luck."

So far they hadn't seen any sign of life apart from one man urinating at the side of his ambulance. He'd given them a cursory glance, shaken his penis a few times and then stepped briskly back into his ambulance.

"Where the hell is everyone?" Harry wanted to know.

"Kipping in the back of their ambulances. They're not supposed to but the old man turns a blind eye. Me, I'd put the bleeding lot on a fizzer!"

Harry stopped dead in his tracks. He stared hard at the ambulance a hundred yards in front of them, blinked several times thinking the sun was playing tricks with his eyes. Sykes followed his gaze then laughed, "Bleeding mess, ain't it?"

Harry swallowed hard and tried to lick his dry lips, his voice becoming a croak. "God, man, you can say that again."

He walked on slowly towards it, hoping that it was just a mirage, then touched the canvas sides to make certain it wasn't a bad dream. He walked around it several times and each time his heart sank a few inches. A hinge was missing from one of the back doors and had been replaced with a piece of twisted wire. Pieces of elastoplast, turning brown and peeling at the corners, covered a multitude of shrapnel holes in the canvas. The bulging convex metal that held the spare wheel behind the front cab was battered almost beyond recognition. He jumped into the cab and thought he was having a bout of vertigo. The cab roof was at a slant, held in position by an old broomstick on one side and what was left of the windscreen frame on the other. He jumped down shaking his head and walked round it several times more. He was beginning to wonder if he'd made a mistake in not taking that cushy number back in Cairo.

"Do you mean to tell me that this thing actually goes?"

Sykes laughed. "It's about the only thing I can say in William's favour. He keeps that engine going, purring like a kitten. I told you he went over a mine. Did you see those sand bags on the floor?"

Harry nodded. "I wondered what they were for."

"Well you can't say I didn't warn you, Jackson. He's a crazy bastard and bloody sex mad to boot. He's had more women than the average man's had hot dinners."

24

"What! Out here in this God forsaken hole? Where the hell is he going to get a woman out here?" Harry asked.

"Listen, Jackson. You have to learn that if there's a woman within fifty miles of his prick he'll find her. You wait till we hit town. I bet he has it away within a couple of hours. I tell you he's sex mad."

Harry was beginning to like the sound of his new driver.

"So where the hell is he?"

"He'll be playing cards with his cronies somewhere." He raised his hands to his mouth and bellowed, "Williams!"

It carried for miles across the open desert. A couple of men came to the back door of their vehicles, looked out at Sykes and then went back inside. Others had recognised the voice and didn't bother to investigate.

"Just take a look at that. They just don't give a toss around here. None of them should be kipping in their vans." He walked to the nearest ambulance, at least two hundred yards away, and banged on the back doors. A bleary eyed driver, dressed only in sweat stained shorts opened the door.

"Seen Williams about, Stan?"

Stanley shook his head and wiped the sweat from his neck and chest with a towel.

"Last heard he was off to Cairo after a gyppo bint," he muttered. "If his ambulance wasn't here I'd believe he was still with her." The driver looked around the leaguer and pointed to an ambulance about half a mile away. "His mate Chaplin is over there. They may have a brag school going."

A look of disgust spread across Sykes' acne-pocked face.

"Nip over and fetch him. I've got his new medic with me."

"Piss off, Sykes! I'm not running a fucking taxi service. You sit on your arse all day in the company office. Get a bit of exercise and let the sun get at those bloody pimples of yours! Trouble is, Skyes, you don't have it off the way Williams does and you play bell tents under the blankets all night. You'll go blind, you know," Stanley chuckled dirtily and slammed the doors on the ambulance.

"I'm ordering you, Stanley. You go over and get Williams or I'll have you on a fizzer in the morning."

"Bollocks," shouted Stanley from inside the ambulance. "You can send me back to Cairo for a spell in the glass house for all I care. Could do with a good rest."

Sykes walked back to the ambulance and found Williams sitting on the back step next to Jackson.

"Where the hell did you come from, Williams? I've been all over the sodding place looking for you."

"I was over in my slit trench, bit cooler below ground," he replied.

"Didn't you hear me yell for you?" snapped Sykes.

"You must be joking! Old Smith 425 must have heard you and that poor sod's been dead three months. What do you want, anyway?"

"Brought you a new medic. The old man said will you try and keep this one."

"Alright, Sykes, so you brought me another medic. Now, piss off!" Williams carried on stroking a small yellow dog which was curled up in his lap. The dog looked up at Sykes with pale yellow eyes that matched his coat, stared hard at him and then buried his head under Charlie's armpit.

"Spag can't stand you either, Sykes, so just piss off."

Sykes seemed immune to the insults. Instead he unhooked the brew can hanging from the back step of the ambulance, and cut down a petrol tin filled with blackened sand.

"What about a brew, Charlie?" Without waiting for an answer he filled the sand with petrol and the brew can with water. In minutes it boiled merrily away. Charlie threw in two handfuls of tea and tipped a tin of condensed milk in what had been, a few minutes before, a pot of clear bubbling water. Now it was golden brew. He scooped out two mugs and passed one to Harry.

"You'll find a mug without a handle under my seat, Sykes, but for Christ's sake don't let Spag see you drinking out of it. He don't like just anyone using his mug." Charlie lifted the small dog and held it at arms length. It wagged it's tail frantically and dribbled a few drops of urine.

"Who's my little beauty then?" crooned Charlie.

Sykes shook his head in disgust, wiped the sand from the handleless mug and scooped up the tea.

"Don't know why you keep the perishing little thing. Put bully down one end and shit comes out the other just where someone might step in it. Look at it pissing everywhere. You should have the filthy little bastard put down. It's quite useless."

"So are you, Sykes. I know half the unit would like to see you put down but we're not allowed to. You're not a lot of good at anything, yet they keep you here!" They sat down on the shady side of the ambulance, Charlie with his back against the wheel, the heat chiselled into the moist folds of his stomach and chest. "And I wish you wouldn't pick those pustulant spots of yours ... Christ, talk about poor little Spag!"

"Why the hell do you call him Spag, Charlie?" Harry wanted to know.

"Found him on an Itey gun site. All the crew had been killed. Little Spag here was shivering and whimpering by the side of one of them. I couldn't leave him there or he would have died of thirst, and I couldn't shoot him. So me and Tommy kind of kept him. Had him ever since. He took to us, we to him... Couldn't think of a name and Spaghetti was the only Italian I could think of."

A piece of dirty elastoplast covering one of the holes in the canvas chose this moment to give up, curled itself in a ball and dropped into Charlie's tea. He flicked it out muttering, "If it isn't the flies getting in your food, it's the bloody ambulance falling to bits." He patted the sides of the ambulance affectionately. "She's a grand old girl, take you round the word, this would, and never let you down." He threw the dregs of his mug into the sand, and a cloud of flies appeared from nowhere and descended on it before it was sucked down. "Jump in, Harry. Let's go get your kit. Sykes, you jump in the back."

Harry marvelled at the speed of the dilapidated ambulance. With Charlie negotiating the boulders better than any rally driver it responded to his slightest touch. The ambulance cab, although battered and very much askew, was very roomy. Besides the two seats for the driver and himself it carried six jerry cans of petrol and two jerry cans of fresh water. The eight cans were covered with blankets making a bed for Spag when they were on the move. It also served as a seat for two or three walking wounded when the back of the ambulance was full.

Sykes had been right about the engine. It ran as quiet as a Rolls Royce, covering the distance it had taken forty minutes to walk in about three minutes, and then Charlie pulled up sharply in from of the company office in a cloud of dust that enveloped the ambulance. Sykes jumped out, somewhat shaken and slightly bruised, muttering, "Dangerous bastard," under his breath and Charlie winked at Harry.

"Just sling your gear in the back, Harry. We'll sort it out when we get back." It was another way of saying 'let's get away from here as fast as possible.' Harry smiled to himself, a secure feeling spreading over him. He knew he was going to get along well with his driver. They both spoke the same language.

Charlie slammed the engine into gear but unfortunately he wasn't to get away that easily. The R.S.M. came charging from the lean-to.

"Hang on, Williams," he bellowed, the sound echoing across the camp. "I want a word in your dainty ear, Williams."

Charlie didn't switch the engine off but jumped from the cab, coming up to some sort of attention in front of the R.S.M. He

27

didn't look straight at him. His eyes focused over the R.S.M's shoulder and then they concentrated on the two soot stained Soya stoves outside the cookhouse.

"Now look here, Williams, you have a new medic, please look after this one. Lose any more and they'll start asking questions in the House of Commons." This was a favoured saying of his. "Jackson is a regular and he's seen plenty of active service. I'm just hoping a little of his discipline will rub off on you. One thing's certain I don't want him falling into your bad habits." The voice softened slightly, Harry detecting a kind of tolerance bordering on favouritism. "We return to the Blue tomorrow. You'll be attached to the Rifle Brigade, so don't get bloody stupid up there." He handed Charlie two chits. "Get your tub filled with petrol and pick up vehicle rations. I take it you have read standing orders about using petrol for brewing up?"

"Yes, sir. I'll get Jackson to chop down a couple of pine trees," said Charlie, but the R.S.M. chose to ignore the sarcastic remark.

Away from the office Charlie said, "He's always telling us not to use petrol. It's an offence but no one takes the slightest notice. Monty himself knows it goes on. When he took the job he wouldn't start without double petrol rations. Ever seen Monty, Harry?" Harry shook his head. "A real short arse. We saw him just before the push. Wears funny hats covered in cap badges and baggy shorts. Still, that little man got things moving here."

Over the next couple of hours, while drawing rations, Harry had a chance to study Charlie closer. Just an inch under six feet, thick set with a square face and short stubby blond hair his body was well tanned and muscled. He could be considered good looking with a slightly misshapen nose. He learned later that this had happened on Charlie's last leave in Cairo. The bottoms of his frayed shorts gripped his thighs. He hardly ever wore boots just plimsolls and both his big toes poked out. When he smiled he revealed a row of straight even white teeth and his handshake was firm and friendly.

"The ambulance is in a bit of a mess, Charlie. What the hell happened to it?"

Charlie gave a throaty laugh. "This your first time with an armoured division, Harry?"

Harry nodded. "Well, at times we're in amongst the big stuff. Casualties are high in this unit. Still it's not a bad number. Me, I just do my job and keep as far away from the company office as possible. That's one good thing about being on the ambulances, you're more or less your own boss. We get vehicle rations and a few comforts for the patients so we never go short. All we have to

do is get on with it till the bloody war is finished. Then I can get home to my little girl." "You married then?" enquired Harry.
The driver just shrugged his shoulders and grunted.
"S'pose so," he said, then lapsed into silence. Harry guessed he had touched a soft spot and immediately realised that Charlie's private life was a subject to be avoided.

He had heard of those 'Dear John' letters. He was convinced more than ever that he would never have a serious attachment while the war was on. He'd had plenty of chances but never allowed himself to get serious over any girl. He changed the subject.

"Won't they give you a new ambulance?"
Charlie looked surprised. "What for? There's sod all wrong with this one. Back's a bit battered, I admit, but just listen to that engine. No, Harry, I brought this one out from Blighty and if I have my way I'll be taking it back with me. I thought I lost it last time. Poor Tommy was a cool number - no feet and still conscious. He helped me put on a couple of tourniquets. That couple of miles felt more like twenty. The pratt kept saying 'drop me and I'll kick your balls in' ... I tell you, Harry, he was a bleeding hard nut."

He stopped the ambulance in its original spot. "We went on leave in Cairo just before the big push. The old man didn't want us to go together, but that bloody Tommy could talk his way out of a barrel of shite and come up smelling of roses. The old man eventually gave in with a stiff warning. First we were in a punch up in this sleazy night club called 'The Silver Slipper'. No booze for me normally, can't really say I like it, but you have to show willing when you're with the lads... Mind you, it's like gnat's piss in Cairo, but after a couple of pints and a couple of whiskies, I was well away. These Red Caps picked us up in this hotel with a couple of gyppo bints. There were four of us in this big bed. They said we had put these two bints on the game and we were a couple of pimps. I must admit I had fixed up some of the lads with a bint or two. Anyway, the bleeding Red Caps brought us back to the camp and dumped us outside the company office and handed the R.S.M. a list of crimes as long as your arm. They slung us in the back of the ambulance and the next morning the old man gave us a right bollocking. Funny thing, Harry, I went on leave with twenty gyppo pounds and when I emptied my pockets I had over thirty pounds. This R.S.M.'s not a bad bloke at all, Harry. He sticks up for his own."

Dusk quickly turned to night as a black veil was drawn across the sky, brilliant stars hanging from it like celestial ornaments.

29

The time must have been three am and Harry was still awake when a quarter moon sliced its way over the far horizon flooding the silent desert with its eerie silver glow. He lay back on his stretcher looking through the open doors and then he stubbed out his last cigarette, a feeling of contentment overtook him and, at last, lulled him into a deep sleep.

CHAPTER 4

Dawn was just breaking when he was aroused from his sleep by a loud banging on the side of the ambulance, and he could just make out a squat figure climbing through the rear door.

"Come on, you two pansies," a voice bellowed, "hands off your tools and stop playing the fool. You'll go blind, you know." He struck a match and lit the hurricane lamp hanging from the roof.

Harry blinked hard. The man could stand upright in the ambulance, so that made him about five feet six. He wore a balaclava helmet, well darned, that covered most of his face, and his overcoat looked about three sizes too big for him, the bottom scraping the ground and a well-worn enamel mug hanging from a button. His nose was badly battered and misshapen and there was an old scar under his left eye.

"Come on, you two," he yelled at them again, "abandon those flea pits and get some grub down you. I want you out of the compound by eight."

"What time is it, sarge?" Charlie never wore a watch and didn't expect Harry to wear one.

"What's it to you, Williams? Got a date, or something?" The sergeant pulled out an enormous silver pocket watch hanging on a thick silver chain from inside his greatcoat, the chain heavy with several silver medals. He flicked open the watch, gave it a few shakes and then held it against his ear. He squinted as he held it against the weak light given off by the hurricane lamp. "It's just after five," he noted. "Draw vehicle rations, petrol and water after breakfast, and trundle off down the divisional barrel track for a few miles and join the Rifle Brigade."

"Drew rations and petrol last night, sarge."

The sergeant nodded his head with approval. Then he turned his attention to Harry.

"You the new bloke, Jackson, are you?"

Harry nodded. He felt he could go back to sleep for several hours and regretted staying awake so long the night before.

"Well, watch this prat Williams, he's a randy bastard," the sergeant chuckled and winked at Charlie. There was a bond of respect between them, Harry soon discovered.

Throwing back his blankets, Charlie took his right foot and began to search the cold linoleum floor. The sergeant made a quick exit for he knew what was coming next. Now Harry was also to learn what to expect for the rest of the time he was with Charlie. He watched as Charlie slid from the blanket, stamped his right foot against the floor and farted loudly, the plywood walls of the ambulance reverberating with the sound. Harry covered his head as Charlie stood at the open doors and held his distended penis and urinated.

"Get your tape measure out, sarge, and see if that stream has made it over ten yards," he yelled. "I want to break my record."

"You're a disgusting bastard, Williams! One of these days you'll rip your arsehole from your ball bag to breakfast time."

"You don't know what you're missing, sarge," Charlie sang out and turned to Harry. "Get your head from under those blankets, Harry. Get your lungs full of much needed vitamins!"

A muffle from under the blankets answered, "No thanks, Charlie, I would rather smell my own stink under here."

Charlie slipped on his shorts and plimsolls, the toes poked through, and then his greatcoat and blew into his cupped hands.

"Fancy a brew, sarge?" Charlie unhooked his brew can and sand fire from behind the back step, poured petrol into the sand fire and dropped a match. Flames shot two feet into the air with a tremendous roar, and within minutes the water boiling madly, he threw in the tea and sugar and half a tin of condensed milk. The sergeant untied his mug from his coat button and scooped out a mugful of tea from the brew can.

From his cab Charlie took an old hub cap with a makeshift handle welded to it. He emptied a tin of bacon into the homemade frying pan, then a tin of tomatoes followed, and four hard tack biscuits.

"Fancy breakfast, Harry?" He asked. "I'm sure these biscuits are left over from the First War." They floated on top of the grease and tomato gravy as he poked at them with an old German bayonet. "Doesn't soften them much, but they taste better if you have a good imagination!"

As they sat eating and drinking their tea, Harry was bombarded with the usual questions. Was he a regular? How long has he been out? What were his qualifications? And the usual surprised look when Harry told him and, of course, the surprise when he said he wanted to get into the desert. 'You must be fucking mad,' was the standard reply.

It was daylight when they took off on the barrel track. Harry could do nothing but wonder at the performance of the engine and the way Charlie handled it. Once the back wheel became bogged down, but with no digging required from Charlie or himself, only careful negotiation and rocking of the ambulance, it was soon free and speeding away again.

The front became alive. Charlie reached for his steel helmet and Harry followed suit. A battery of twenty five pounders belted out a couple of miles ahead of them, and Charlie turned towards the guns. They were just off the track and he pulled in beside them. The gunners were stripped to their waists. Sweat ran down their glistening bodies as they stoked the shells into the guns as if there was no tomorrow. A sergeant, also stripped to the waist, a steel helmet perched on his head, bellowed orders in a voice that could be heard above the sound of the guns.

Brass shell cases piled up behind each gun into small pyramids. Charlie lit two cigarettes, passed one to Harry and then rested his elbows on the steering wheel.

"Fucking waste, wouldn't you say? I wonder what one of those shells cost - five, ten pounds? Let's say ten pounds. No doubt it could be double. Just look at those empty shell cases. There must be a couple of hundred! I bet my old man's not earned that much money in his whole working life. Probably hit sweet F.A. at the other end."

The shelling stopped with a suddenness that kept their ears ringing for minutes afterwards. The sergeant strode towards them.

"What do you two Linseed Lancers want? Get that bleeding blood tub out of here. You're making my men nervous."

"Seen anything of the Rifle Brigade, sarge?"

"What do you think this is? The AA Information Service?" He jerked his thumb over his shoulder. "Over there a piece. Now get out of here! Jerry might throw some shit over anytime and we don't want you to get hurt, do we?"

"I shouldn't worry too much, sarge. Those slit trenches of yours would take you, your guns and the bloody ambulance," Charlie replied. "Pretty deep, aren't they, sarge? You bleeding long range snipers do alright for yourselves." An officer appeared from behind a wall of sand bags and the battery phone started ringing. "Say, sarge, if that's my missus tell her I won't be home for Christmas - the fucking gunners have lost their braille books. They can't shoot straight," Charlie joked, a look of feigned disappointment on his face.

"Alright, funny fuckers, piss off out of here."

It didn't take them long to locate the Regiment. Men emerged from slit trenches in every kind of dress. Some had shorts and no shirts, others had long trousers and leather jerkins, most wore plimsolls. One man emerged from his slit trench wearing pyjamas tied round the middle with string, while quite a few carried gauze fly swats.

"No wonder they call them the Desert Rats," Harry chuckled. "Just look at the scruffy sods coming in and out of those slit trenches."

"Took a beating, Harry. I wonder how many of them'll be left behind in this God-forsaken hole," Charlie shuddered. "If I ever get it, Harry, get a forty gallon drum of petrol and cremate me. Then take me home in that old brew can at the back."

It was Harry's turn to shudder. "Don't talk like that, you prick. I can think of worse places to be buried. At least it's peaceful here. If you read the bible you'd know that all those old boys would go into the desert for months on end just to meditate and commune with God."

"I didn't know you were religious, Harry, reading the bible and all that."

"I'm not. I was brought up in a Quaker orphanage - and don't ask me how I got there, because I don't know. Anyway, they were nice people but very religious, and I couldn't take it anymore. If anything I'm a Buddhist. I believe in reincarnation. I don't think for one minute that there's a heaven and hell. If anything we're in some kind of hell during this war! And let's face it, you're born and from that minute you're dying... You may live your three score years and ten, but then as soon as you're old enough to think for yourself you realise that one day it'll all end. In my opinion, Charlie, your next life is governed by how you use this one, not by God's blessing or curse for no special reason. Anyway, why worry? If you're born rich you're worried that one day you may lose it. A famous model or film star? It's worse for them. The day they see their first wrinkle, or whatever, they panic and for the rest of their lives they're worried about losing their looks... If there is a God, and they say he's kind, and our lives aren't governed by reincarnational cause and effect, why are imbeciles born, cripples and spastics? No. We share our lives and our destinies with these people either pitying them or scorning them. It's a puzzling world. Like I said before, hell is all around us. Why does a man like Hitler come on the scene and turn his fellow countrymen against the Jews? Before this war is over he'll be responsible for the deaths of millions. To me Hitler, Mussolini and Stalin and all their cronies are the devil's disciples on this earth. If a man finds solace in religion and its prayers, good luck to him. Some of the Christians I've met are nice people. Others just think that because they go to church every sunday and put a few bob in the collecting box, their duty is done to God and mankind and they're assured of a place in a tedious psalm singing heaven. Just try to treat others like you want them to treat you and hope for the best, that's what I say, Charlie, and maybe your next life on this Buddhist wheel of cause and effect will be a fair cop."

"Bleeding hell! Wish I hadn't said anything now. I didn't expect a lecture on the meaning of life." Charlie raised his eyes skyward and paused to light up. "What about crumpet, Harry? How do you stand about that?"

"Don't get me wrong, Charlie, I just lead a natural life. Of course I like my crumpet. That's another thing... Some religions think sexual intercourse is just for the propagation of the species. That's a load of crap. It's there for humans to enjoy it. That's why the human animals are the only species that love facing each other."

"I don't know about that," laughed Charlie. "My missus always closed her eyes. I don't think she liked to see me enjoying myself!"

Harry tried to pump Charlie a bit more on the subject of his wife but he closed up like a disturbed oyster. Talking about Charlie's private life was like driving a vehicle over soft sand - treacherous. So Harry dropped the subject feeling sure that if ever Charlie did want to talk about it he'd be a good listener.

"Don't you ever get fed up with life, Harry? I mean, all this being shoved around?"

Harry laughed. "You must be kidding! Me, I live from day to day. If I do get depressed I think of all the good thing that's happened... Whenever I felt down back home in Blighty off we would go down to the N.A.A.F.I. I would play the piano and the boys would soon join in the singing. Then the beers would line up on top. Not that I'm a great drinker, mind you. A couple of beers and a sniff of the barmaid's apron and I'm away. There's more to life than just getting pissed. I don't have to dull my brain to enjoy myself."

"Like me. I'd sooner have a good woman than a pint of mild and bitter," Charlie agreed. "Don't know what the prats see in it myself. Up and down all night having a few slashes. The next day a head as thick as an elephant's arse! We have some right piss artist in out unit. You wait till you meet a few of them ... That's what I liked about Cairo. You should see the crumpet there."

"Not like London, Charlie," Harry replied. "I was doing this course at a large teaching hospital. They sent half a dozen of us on a crash course. There was this nurse, Victoria, a beautiful blue-eyed blonde, just about five feet tall and a figure like an hour-glass."

He shaped out her figure with his hands. "Her old man idolised her. He had her late in life. Before the war he had a practice in Harley Street and then retired to Devon. He let Victoria and her two mates have the flat in Chelsea and the parties we had there were unbelievable."

"Did she do a turn?" Charlie asked bluntly.

35

"You're kidding! I thought I knew all the answers but she taught me a thing or two. She took me home on leave to Devon once, but that's another story." Harry sighed, recalling happier moments.

"I can see you and me getting along just fine, Harry," chuckled Charlie.

They pulled up with a screech of brakes at the R.A.P., a three tonner with a canvas lean-to stretching down from one side, beside a small utility used by the M.O.

"We're home, Harry. The sergeant and M.O aren't bad blokes. The sergeant is all mouth but his bark is worse than his bite." Charlie waited for the cloud of fine sand to settle. Then he jumped from the cab, stretched himself a few times and unhooked the brew can from the back. "They'll be kipping in the lean-to. Have a shufti."

Harry parted the gauze net and waited for his eyes to grow accustomed to the gloom. A stretcher covered with a white rubber sheet stood on two trestles and at the far end were two deal tables scrubbed white. One held an assortment of surgical instruments laid out in white enamel trays, while the other table held several chromium drums of sterile dressings. Two stretchers mounted on empty ammo boxes lay along one wall, and both were covered with mosquito nets that hung from the canvas roof.

One of the nets parted and an unshaven face peered out, blinking a few times as he tried to get Harry into focus.

"Who the bloody hell are you?" bellowed the anonymous face.

"The new medic, sarge," said Harry, guessing at his rank as an officer's shirt hung over a chair by the other mosquito net. The sergeant slid his feet out of the netting and stood up. Like most of the men he was just wearing shorts and his body glistened with sweat. He took stock of Harry.

"Who's your driver?"

"Williams, sarge."

"Oh no! Not that scruffy oversexed bastard. God, I hope I'm still asleep and this is a nightmare," the sergeant muttered, scratching his armpits and crutch. Then he shook the hair on each side of his head. The top was completely bald and smothered with freckles. "Has he still got that sodding little dog with him?"

"Why hello, sarge," Charlie came in smiling, with two mugs of hot tea in his hands. "Mug of char, sarge? Sorry I haven't got any chocolate bikkies." He handed him a mug and put the other on the chair beside the officer's bed.

"You crawling bastard, Williams. Do you still have that bloody pooch with you?"

36

"Yes, and come off it, sarge, you know you love the little bastard."

"What's going on here?" The officer poked his head out. "Oh, it's you, Williams," he saw the mug of steaming tea. "There's a whisky bottle at the foot of the stretcher, hand it to me." He tipped a liberal dose in his mug and Harry was surprised to see how young he was - barely thirty, he guessed. He was as tall as Charlie but not so thick set. Ginger hair matched his two day growth of beard, and his accent was Liverpudlian with a faint touch of Northern Irish. "Any hot water out there, Williams?"

Charlie vanished outside and the officer glanced at Harry.

"What's your name?"

"Jackson, sir."

"Ah," he hesitated, "that's good. I can remember that. Just out from Cairo, Jackson?"

Harry nodded.

"What qualifications?"

Harry filled him in with the details and assured the M.O. he wasn't mad. "When the war is over I'll have to return to the hospitals and wards, sir, and frankly I could do with a rest from the sisters."

"I know what you mean, Jackson. I married one!"

Harry felt his toes tighten up with embarrassment and he tried to apologise but the M.O. put his hand up.

"Don't worry, Jackson, I was pissed at the time. Bloody party at Shepherds Hotel in Cairo. She isn't too bad really - not bad looking. Could have been worse... it could have been the matron! Six months up here and they all look beautiful in Cairo."

The sergeant used the side mirror to shave, using an open razor. Harry was fascinated. Then, without removing his shorts he poured a can of water over his head and shook himself like a terrier.

"No wonder you have all those freckles over your bonce, sarge, they must be redundant water blisters," joked Charlie who had returned.

The sergeant sat himself in the sun until he dried off.

"We were talking about you and this old ambulance of yours, Williams," he told Charlie. "We passed this Austin ambulance, knocked out it was but its windscreen was still intact. Although it looked a wreck it was in better condition than this old tub."

Charlie stopped cleaning out his brew can. "Where was this, sarge? How far back?"

"About five or six miles up by the R.H.A."

"Well, we just passed them, sarge, and we saw fuck all. I've been after a screen for months."

37

"It's a couple of miles the other side."

"Do you mind if we went back and had a shufti, sarge? It's bloody hell when the sand blows up. I can get that screen and frame unscrewed in minutes."

"Go on, piss off, but be back here in a couple of hours. The push starts in the morning. And, Williams, don't blow your fucking selves up," the sergeant burst out laughing.

Harry jumped in his seat. Spag was already under the blankets on the petrol cans and they left the R.A.P. in a cloud of dust with the sergeant and M.O. laughing their heads off.

"The crazy bastard will go in and get it, sarge. If he does blow himself up, you'll have to evacuate the wounded in the utility."

"He wouldn't dare. Not even Williams is that sodding crazy, and the medic looks as if he has his head screwed on alright."

CHAPTER 5

"Why, the lousy good for nothing cockney git!"

Charlie stared hard at the ambulance. It was tilted on one side some fifty yards from the track. "So that was why the lousy bastard was smiling when he told me about it." He nodded towards Harry and pointed at the white tapes strung along on flimsy poles with boards, spaced out warning them it was a minefield. "You just wait till we get back. I'll let that lousy sod have it!"

Harry was smiling, but not for long. The ambulance was well out of their reach, and Charlie was idly threading the white tape through his fingers while he studied the vehicle, perhaps less than fifty yards away.

"It would only be a ten minute job getting that windscreen and frame out, Harry," he said.

The tracks of the ambulance were still plainly visible in the sand, and he ran his hand round his chin, contemplating. Then he walked back to his ambulance and selected several tools. The whole frame and windscreen was held together by half a dozen screws, not a hard job by any standards.

"I'll show the bastard he can't make a prick out of me," Charlie fumed. "Hang on here. It won't take long." He held up the tape but Harry caught his arm.

"Don't be a fool, Charlie. You can't walk across a minefield."

But Charlie brushed Harry's restraining hand away.

"Sod it, Harry, I've had enough of driving that thing with no windscreen. If I follow the tracks it'll be safe as houses."

Harry could see the determined look on his driver's face, and knew there wasn't anything he could say that would stop him from getting that screen.

"No one is going to make a prick out of me." Charlie assured him with a wink. "If I put my foot on one of those mines see that I get a decent burial!"

"You must be kidding!" said Harry, taking some of the tools from Charlie. "I have to sit in the front of that ambulance, too. We'll have to get buried together." Then Harry smiled. Their friendship was cemented.

I must be mad, he thought, ducking under the tape behind Charlie, his heart thumping loudly as he took his first step into the ambulance tracks. The blood pounding against his temples, he felt slightly giddy as he took his second step and nearly lost his balance. He stopped and steadied himself, his throat dried out like old parchment, the sweat running in rivulets down his back and chest and saturating his shirt and shorts. He could hear his own heart pounding, counting every step that brought him nearer to the stricken ambulance, and, one false move from the tyre tracks - an inch either way - and they wouldn't be worrying about a new windscreen... Placing his own feet in Charlie's tracks, he gasped out, "I feel like that guy in the christmas carol, old Wenceslas." But his voice was just a croak. "The R.S.M. was right. When I joined these crazy bastards he told me I must be mad." Harry's mind was racing, trying to think about anything except the predicament they were in at this moment.

"Right now, I could be in a spotlessly clean hospital back in Cairo," he complained. "I could find myself a nice A.T.S. girl or a nice local, and I chose this ... Really, I must be mad!"

Charlie was picking his steps gingerly, and twice he bent down thrusting his bayonet sideways into the soft sand, Harry crouching behind him. He eased himself upwards to relax his cramped muscles, and the hammer slipped through his sweaty fingers. Then he held his breath as it rolled over and over and the shaft half buried itself in the sand. He reached down to pick it up, and a look of pure horror spread across his face, his eyes widening. The shaft was lying across a large round mine the size of a dinner plate, just a fine layer of sand covering it.

"Bleeding hell, Charlie," croaked Harry. But Charlie was striding towards the ambulance and didn't hear him. Then stopping at the back he glanced towards Harry bent over the track.

"What's up?"

"Me, nearly. I dropped the bloody hammer and the shaft's resting across a mine." He gently blew the sand away. The shaft was clear of the striking knob by less than half an inch. Then he flicked it away, just clear of the mine, the sweat running into his eyes and down his sand-grimed face. He wiped the sweat from his eyes with the back of his hand and, gasping with relief after what felt like an eternity, flopped down beside Charlie on the back step of the ambulance. His hand trembling, he searched his sweat-stained shirt for his cigarettes and realised he's left them behind. Charlie passed his half smoked one to Harry who dragged on it hungrily.

"I nearly shit myself when I dropped that hammer, Charlie. I must be some kind of nut following you across here."

Charlie started to laugh, Harry smiled and then burst out laughing with him. It released the tension.

"Just you wait till you have a shufti in the back of this ambulance, you'll have something to smile about then. Just listen ..." Charlie urged.

Placing his head flat against the canvas sides Harry heard a loud buzzing. Charlie slapped the back of the vehicle with the palm of his hand, and the buzzing increased to a loud constant hum, like the drone of an airplane. Then he took a sweat rag from his pocket and covered his mouth, mumbling for Harry to follow suit. He swung open the back doors and Harry could hardly believe his eyes. He'd seen flies many times in his life but never anything like this. The interior of the ambulance was filled with a blue black mass of them, some so fat they couldn't take off, although they buzzed their wings hysterically. They tumbled in a mass, turning golden like some huge live waterfall, from the back of the ambulance as the sun struck against their fan-like wings, and the walls and roof were also covered with them, interspersed with bloated maggots. Meanwhile in the centre of the ambulance one mass of maggots worked round and round in whirlpools.

The rank sweetish stench of death stung Charlie and Harry's nostrils and clung to the roofs of their mouths. Two bodies lay on the top stretchers, human breeding grounds for the flies. Maggots wove their way in and out of the eye sockets in perfectly straight lines with military precision. Harry followed Charlie. In seconds the exposed parts of their own bodies were a mass of flies, and, their feet grinding maggots and flies into a quagmire of slime made it nearly impossible to walk without stretching their arms and pressing against the sides of the ambulance's plywood body to avoid slipping.

"Jesus Christ," Harry muttered through the sweat rag tied around his mouth. "I never realised flies could make so much noise."

Charlie swung back the small door leading to the driver's cab, and he retched when he saw the driver slumped over the steering wheel. The front of his face was missing and both his legs just above the knees had now become a black stinking mess of decaying flesh alive with maggots. The medic wasn't in much better shape. His eye sockets were empty, the black holes staring into space and the lower jaw sagging. Half a dental plate lay sideways and his tongue hung split in two blackened strips, his upper lip creased in a perpetual snarl. Suddenly he sagged against the driver, pushing him sideways out of the cab, and as he hit the ground his stomach burst open, spewing forth the intestines in a slithering grey mass, the stench of its escaping gasses filling the cab and impregnating their clothes and sweat rags. Once more Charlie threw up, while Harry removed the medic's papers from his top pocket.

"They're Italian, Charlie." He thumbed through the man's pay book and papers and several photographs fluttered to the floor.

41

"It must have been one of our ambulances we left behind during one of the flaps." The sweat band around his mouth made it difficult to talk.

The flies hovering around in dense clouds, Charlie lifted a petrol can and splashed it about.

"For fuck's sake, don't smoke, Harry," he begged. Then he splashed the walls, roof and seats of the cab, not leaving an inch untouched. The flies that escaped became hysterical, most of them floundering in pools of petrol. Harry pushed the medic from the ambulance before he and Charlie turned their attention to the windscreen.

The screen was secured with half a dozen stout screws and the work could all be done from inside the cab. One or two flies tried to escape the fumes by climbing the glass, and Charlie pointed to them.

"They're pissed with the fumes," he remarked.

"Well, they're not the only ones," Harry grumbled. "Come on, let's get on with it and get away from here. The stink is making me feel sick." Harry was surprised and relieved to see how easily the frame came away. One screw with its head burred gave a bit of trouble, but the hacksaw soon made a clean job of it. Twice the frame slid from their grip and they held their breath as the metal corner struck the ground. Then with triumphant grins smeared across their faces they finally managed to drag the frame inside the cab, the slippery mass of squirming flies and maggots making is easier to get through the ambulance, a tidal mark of two inches deep on the glass, indicating how many maggots were sacrificed. Charlie and Harry whipped off their sweat rags as soon as they were outside the ambulance.

"See me back, Harry," said Charlie, "and watch I don't step outside those tracks. I can't see them very well. The sun keeps reflecting off the glass like a mirror." He tried to manoeuvre himself along the tracks several ways but it was no use, and he had to rely on Harry's instructions as he worked his head in circles and grabbed the other end of the screen.

"Holding my head up straight in there has given me a headache, and those fumes didn't help much either," he complained. The frame was much heavier than expected. The sweat ran down their faces and several times they stopped, Harry balancing the screen on his knee, steadying it with one hand and wiping the sweat away with the back of the other.

"If I go up on a mine now, Harry, for heaven's sake watch the glass. I wouldn't like all this trouble to be in vain!" Charlie panted.

"Bollocks," was all Harry could reply as he struggled with the heavy screen.

The way back to their own vehicle was more protracted than the outward journey, every step an effort with the weight of their hard won gains. Time eluded them. Harry couldn't talk. His mouth felt as if it had been sandpapered. A brooding silence enveloped them, their steps dominated by their heavy breathing and the thumping of their hearts. Harry didn't notice they had passed through the white tape for his mind was in a sombre trance. He bent down automatically as the driver lay his prized possession at the back step of their vehicle. Then Charlie lit two cigarettes and after passing one to his medic, flopped back in the sand, his eyes half closed. Harry's legs buckled beneath him as he lay down beside him, and as a shadow passed over them Harry opened one eye and closed it again quickly. The sun was directly overhead. Then he turned his head slightly and sat up fast. A Red Cap, his shorts creased to cutting edge and his webbing whitened to a brightness that glared harshly in the strong sunlight, a hat worn with the peak laid flat against his nose, forcing him to tilt his head right back above a pair of beady unblinking eyes, staring down at them. Harry nudged Charlie.

Reaching into his breast pocket the Red Cap extracted a small note book and pencil. He licked the end of the pencil and flipped open the book, never taking his eyes from the pair.

"Now tell me, what pair of idiots do we have here, who'll walk into a minefield to loot a bleeding ambulance?" He sneered and licked his pencil again, adding, "and an Itey one at that!"

"It's not an Itey one, corp. It's a British one they captured some time ago," responded Charlie.

"I know that, you bloody fool, but it's an Itey one now." The Red Cap grew irritable. He was sweating profusely and wet patches saturated his armpits, sweat running from under his hat and down his face. He would have loved to tilt his hat to the back of his head and wipe the sweat away, but couldn't do it in the presence of two lesser mortals. "What were you doing out there?" He jabbed the pencil towards them, then over his shoulders towards the wrecked ambulance.

"Well, it's like this, corp," said Charlie. "We were passing by when we spotted this ambulance. We though that maybe there was someone injured in there, so we went over and had a shufti. Well, when we got there, we saw the occupants were beyond help and the windscreen was still intact." He pointed towards their own. "As you can see, corp, we have no screen and it was obvious they had no further use for theirs, so we did the only sensible thing and brought it back with us."

A jeep was parked some fifty yards away and the corporal shouted to the driver at the wheel, "Corporal Harrington, would you come over here and lend an ear to Hans Christian Anderson here."

Unwinding his six foot from behind the steering wheel the second corporal threw away his half smoked cigarette and joined them, not in too good a mood at being disturbed. Charlie repeated the story adding some finer embellishments.

"Ain't that fucking noble, corporal," one said to the other. "To my knowledge that ambulance has been there four days. We understand it could have been there over two weeks, probably longer. Most of the Divvy must have passed it at some time or other. And then along come our heroes here. They calmly trip along over to see if anyone needs their assistance. Now that really is noble, the very stuff V.C.s are made of." He twisted his face into a sarcastic grin and sucked through his teeth, "Fucking liars!"

"No, corp, honest. We thought they'd just copped it. But if you say you saw it four days ago I'll have to take your word for it. That means it must have been here at least four weeks!"

The Red Cap glared at Charlie. "What do you mean, four weeks?"

"Well, it usually takes you two or three weeks after the shooting has stopped to get up this far," Charlie answered.

Harry tried to hid his smile.

"Oh, a fucking comedian as well," the Red Cap snarled. He placed his hands behind his back clenching and unclenching his fists. He had met Charlie's sort before - no respect for authority and always ready to bandy words. But he didn't want to take up the challenge in front of the other corporal, who was his junior, or make a fool of himself in front of Harry. He changed the subject.

He tapped his toe against the windscreen lying in the sand.

"And tell me, smart arse," he enquired, "what do we have here?"

"I told you already, corp. The crew was dead, and joy riding about in this thing with no windscreen in this God forsaken hole is no joke. It's no use to those poor buggers. They won't be worrying about a screen where they are." He blew his nose between his fingers and thumb to try and rid himself of the stench of death that clung to his nostril. "Anyway, my mate has got to burn the bloody thing. It's teeming with flies and maggots, some of them as big as sparrows." He pointed to the red blotches on his exposed skin.

Harry stared at him, his mouth open but nothing coming out. Surely he wasn't risking his life for the second time on a useless exercise? He was beginning to wonder what he had let himself in for. Perhaps everyone was right, he could be in a cushy number back in Cairo or Alex. He looked at the minefield again and a vision of the sisters in white passed before his eyes. No, come to think of it, he was better off here minefields and all. Perhaps Charlie was only bluffing.

The Red Cap turned on Harry. "Well, come on then, get on with it. We don't want those filthy flies polluting the nice clean desert air, do we?" His face was just a few inches from Harry's ear as he bellowed the words out, leaving his ears ringing.

"I'd better go with him, corp. It's a bit of a struggle getting those cans through the ambulance." Without thinking, Charlie had landed his medic in a real mess and the least he could do was lend him his support, not thinking for one minute that the Red Caps would allow them back on the minefield. It would be easier this time, for there were not only the tracks of the wheels to follow, but their own footprints so that there could be little danger.

He stepped over the white tape and stopped, tapping his top pocket. Charlie had noticed when the Red Cap took out his notebook that a brand new shiny lighter fell to the ground. He made quite a show of tapping all his pockets.

"I've run out of matches, corp," he muttered. Harry was about to search his pockets, but Charlie mumbled under his breath, "Take it easy, Harry."

The ruse worked and taking his lighter out of his pocket, the corporal tossed it to Charlie and said, "Here, use this."

The new lighter caught the bright sunlight as it sped through the air. Charlie made a half-hearted attempt to catch it, but it went sailing past, landing a few yards away in the unmarked minefield.

"Oh, silly me! Old butter fingers!" smirked Charlie.

"Fucking well go and get it then," snapped the Red Cap, red veins standing proud in his neck. The lighter lay on the unmarked side, well out of Charlie's reach.

"Piss off, corp. I don't mind going into a minefield when it's marked like the tyre tracks, but I ain't going to risk my life for a tuppenny-ha'penny lighter."

"Sod you, driver. My missus gave me that just before we left England. It was a bloody good Ronson - cost her twenty one shillings, that did."

Charlie muttered to Harry, "I don't believe those bastards have wives or mothers. I wonder how many clients she took on to earn twenty one shillings?" He started tapping his pockets again.

"Well, I'll be buggered, corp. I had another box of matches in my back pocket all the time!"

"Don't rile the bastards too much, Charlie. He could easily put his foot through the screen or confiscate it," Harry warned softly.

"Just let the bastard try, Harry. I'll blow their bleeding brains out," Charlie hissed back.

Then they gingerly picked their way back over to the stricken vehicle, and emptying the cab of half a dozen jerricans of petrol they splashed it all over the ambulance, dousing the plywood sides and canvas, not sparing the two bodies on the stretchers. Behind the jerricans they found half a dozen bottles of red wine, and they stuffed them into their shirts. Then with one jerrican they left a trail back to the white tape.

Harry dropped a match. The blue flame, almost invisible in the bright sunlight, ran along the trail of petrol at tremendous speed. The flames reached the saturated ambulance and at once it roared into a mass of flames, the plywood and canvas back flaring like dry tinder. There was a tremendous explosion as the petrol tank ignited. The chassis lifted and one of the scorched bodies fell clear and rolled in the sand. The chassis lifted clear and dropped, followed by another larger explosion. Charlie dropped flat to the ground, Harry and the Red Caps following. Pieces of blazing canvas and plywood sailed through the air. A large piece of canvas landed on one of the Red Cap's backs, and Harry brushed it away leaving a dark brown patch. The Red Cap jumped to his feet.

"That's made a bloody mess of your shirt, corp," Harry remarked.

The Red Cap, realising what a narrow escape he had had, brushed himself down frantically, not bothering to thank Harry for his quick actions. Without them the corporal could have been left with a severe burn. Instead, he was more concerned with the fate of his lighter.

"What about my fucking lighter?" he complained.

Charlie shrugged his shoulders. "You saw the ambulance, corp, resting on a mine. We had a narrow escape then. We've been in and out of that ambulance like a couple of randy rabbits. You wouldn't get me back on that minefield for all the tea in China." He took out two bottles of red wine and handed them to the Corporal. "Here's a consolation prize for you, corp. The Ginger Beers will get your lighter when they get here."

Harry and Charlie struggled through with the screen and laid it carefully on a pile of blankets, and as they were closing the back doors the Red Cap tapped Charlie's shoulder. "Don't think you're getting off that lightly. I want your name and number of your unit."

"Bloody hell, corp. What do you want - blood? If it wasn't for my mate here you'd have a nice burn on your back."

"And if it wasn't for you two, there wouldn't have been a piece of burning canvas there in the first place," he snapped back. "Right! Now let's have your pay books."

Harry was fumbling in the back of the ambulance for his pay book. Tapping him, Charlie winked and then handed the Red Cap two pay books. One he'd picked up from a former casualty and the other belonged to his former medic who was now on his way back to Blighty minus his feet. The Red Cap appeared satisfied and after taking down the details handed the books back. At this moment Spag chose to wake up, stirring under his blanket, and as the Red Cap lifted one corner a pair of doleful yellow eyes stared back at him.

"Does your unit know you keep this dog in this ambulance?"

Charlie lifted the dog in his arms and wagging his tail furiously, Spag dribbled down Charlie's shirt.

"Course they know, corp. He's the unit mascot," he lied.

The truth was that everyone from the C.O. downwards knew that Charlie kept Spag, but he was tolerated because Charlie was the best and most reliable driver in the unit. Shaking his head with disgust the Red Cap stood in direct line with the rear of the ambulance as they prepared to leave, his partner with him. Charlie had a good view of them in his mirror and they made no attempt to move.

"That's right, me mateys, just stand there a few more seconds and I'll cover the pair of you in shite," he muttered.

Hearing him, Harry ran into the back of the ambulance and glanced through the small rear window.

"Give them the full treatment, Charlie," he encouraged him.

A couple of seconds later both Red Caps were spluttering for air, covered in a cloud of fine sand. Harry struggled back into his seat as the ambulance made off at great speed, Charlie's foot pressing the accelerator hard to the floor.

Harry sat with his cigarette dangling from the corner of his mouth, blowing against it occasionally to keep the smoke from his eyes. He was dabbing the red blotches on his body with calamine lotion.

"What I wouldn't give just to lay back in the cool briny and soak," he reflected loudly. "Once I hit that coastline I'll have a dip that lasts all day." Then he sighed. "Don't you ever get the feeling that you stink, Charlie?"

47

"All the time. More so when I come in contact with a pair of toffed up poofs like those Red Caps. I felt right scruffy standing next to them."

"Well, let's face it, you are bloody scruffy, Charlie. But that's the idea. They get ponced up like that to give you an inferiority complex." Harry burst out laughing. "Forget the bastards, Charlie. At least we have a screen."

They pulled up with a screech of brakes and a cloud of dust outside the R.A.P. and the sergeant came out from the lean-to wiping his hands on a towel. His smile turned to a look of astonishment as they opened the back door to remove the screen.

"What's the matter, sarge?"

Charlie tried to sound indifferent as he started cleaning the screen.

Throwing the towel over his shoulder, the sergeant pointed to the screen, "Do you mean to say you actually took that from that wrecked ambulance?"

Charlie tried to feign a look of surprise, "Yes, sarge. Why?"

"You pair of pricks! It was sitting in the middle of a minefield. I was only kidding. I never thought you'd be stupid enough to cross it to get the fucking thing."

"Yes, sarge, but when you've seen the whole length of this desert without one, a little minefield wouldn't stop you from trying for a little comfort. It wasn't too far in. All we had to do was follow the old tracks. Christ, didn't it stink inside, though! There were four stiffs. They must have been dead for some time." He reached behind his seat and gave the sergeant a bottle of wine. "They won't be needing this anymore. We did have a narrow escape, though. When it went over the first mine it sat on another. We were lucky it didn't go up when we moved about. We set fire to it and the petrol tank exploded. Then it lifted in the air and landed on the other mine. Cor, you shoulda seen it go, sarge. Blood, snot and sand everywhere ... It looked like the sky was on fire." Then he told him about the two Red Caps.

"We heard the bang and saw the column of smoke from here. We wondered what it was," the sergeant said.

While Harry made the tea, Charlie cleaned the screen, first with petrol to get off the flies and muck, then with clear warm water until the glass shone like crystal. The M.O. came out to inspect his handiwork. Having seen the sergeant with the vino it was obviously just an excuse. If there was one thing the M.O. liked it was his tot or a bottle of wine. Charlie softened him up with one of the bottles and then stood back to admire his work.

"Nice work, eh, sir? Been looking for one of these for months. Usually when they go over a mine it's the first thing to go. That's what I can't understand. The cab must have caught the full blast. Both the crew were dead."

"It was rather foolish going over the minefield to get it, Williams," admonished the M.O.

Charlie shrugged his shoulders. "I don't know sir. I was getting sand-blasted to death in the front of this ambulance, so if I had gone up on a mine it would have been quick. We set fire to it, sir, so there wasn't any point leaving the wine in there."

"Thanks all the same, Williams," said the M.O. as he vanished into the lean-to, bottle in hand.

Just after noon, the shelling started screaming overhead. One or two landed near the R.A.P. Everyone dived head first into their slit trenches. It lasted twenty minutes or so, and at the first sign of it easing up, Charlie rushed from his trench to inspect his screen. He sighed with relief and patted it affectionately, like a child with a new toy. It took just a few minutes to secure it in place. "I don't think I'll worry about the windscreen wipers yet, Harry. I don't think it'll rain today, do you?"

Casualties started coming in. Two men slightly wounded walked in followed by several stretcher bearers weighed down with their loads. Harry pulled back the blanket to inspect the first. He was dead. He dressed the slightly wounded while the M.O. cleaned up the more serious cases.

"Better let the M.O. have a look at this one. There looks as if there may be a bit of metal still in there." Harry held up the man's arm.

"Do you think it could be a Blight?" There was a look of hope in the man's eyes.

The sergeant came over and lifted the loose dressing Harry had placed over the wound. Then he laughed. "Are you kidding? With a scratch like that you'll be lucky if you get as far back as the M.D.S." He dropped the dressing back into place.

"But I bled like a stuck pig, sarge."

"So what? The bleeding may have done it some good." The sergeant was a true believer in blood flowing freely, but he was also a kind man under his rough exterior, because he registered the dismay written all over the young soldier's face with sympathy. "Never mind, son, at least you can write and tell your girlfriend you've been wounded," he said. Then he prepared the dressing for the M.O. "I don't know what's wrong with you youngsters out here... Don't you like it, or something? Any excuse to get back home. I'll see that you get a few days rest back at the C.S.S. and that you get a wound stripe. So when you get back you can flash it round the neighbours. How's that?"

But what the sergeant said didn't impress the soldier one bit.

49

"Oh bollocks! I was hoping it was Blighty."
There were no further casualties that day and the night passed quietly with only sporadic shelling.

CHAPTER 6

Harry took to desert warfare like an old campaigner. In a few days, he wore the appearance of a man who had been in from the start. He was fortunate in a way. Unlike many men just out from Blighty, Harry had had the chance to become acclimatised during his service in the Sudan, retracing Gordon's and Kitchener's footsteps, if only from the opposite direction. The new men were thrown in at the deep end after a few days training in the Nile Delta. Since arriving, he had been attached to many regiments: Infantry, Tanks, Tank Recovery, Artillery, and now back with the Tanks again. The ambulance and his slit trench became his home, his relationship with his driver strengthening into a deeper friendship daily. Harry felt as if he had known him all his life.

Charlie hardly ever talked about his private life outside the army. During their conversation when he joined the unit, Harry asked him if he was married. There was an embarrassed silence. Charlie nodded and grunted an undecipherable answer. Harry didn't pursue the matter further - after all, it looked like they would be together for a very long time. Harry was a very patient man and there was plenty of time if Charlie wanted to tell him, the war might go on for some time yet.

They had a lot in common that helped to make a good relationship. Both drank very little but both smoked heavily. Harry wasn't averse to using bad language when the occasion arose and very often when it wasn't really necessary. However, Charlie could swear for ten minutes without repeating himself, in Arabic and English, and one or two other languages he had picked up during his travels. They shared the same sense of humour, an absolutely essential factor in their job, which daily meant handling men, half dead, badly mutilated or badly burned. Very often they were called out as part of a burial party, at times to find they were burying a friend they had recently played cards with.

Desert warfare wasn't so bad. At first light they would stand to, ready to bolt down their slit trenches when peace and calm was shattered by heavy gunfire. Then the other side would retaliate. Shells with their message of death would invariably sting the air above the dressing station with their banshee screams. Fortunately casualties were few from the morning charade.

Before arriving at the desert, Harry had assumed that desert warfare would be all sand dunes, shades of Beau Geste and isolated forts. This illusion had passed within twenty four hours, for nothing was further from the truth. However, the heavy artillery had surpassed themselves this morning, so heavy they

51

prepared themselves for a large scale attack. Shells screamed overhead in both directions. A couple of hundred yards ahead of the aid post, tanks lined up in formation ready to advance. It wasn't quite daybreak, a thin golden line edged the far horizon. The tanks like prehistoric monsters waiting for their prey, looked like black shadows against the golden ridge, their aerials and pennants swaying in the light early morning breeze. The shells landed all around. The ground was solid and the shells exploded on top, renting the air with jagged pieces of red hot metal, while the ground trembled like a sudden earthquake which rocked the morning air.

Harry raised his head above his shallow slit trench and hot shock waves slammed against his face, taking his breath away and forcing the hot blast into his lungs. Charlie raised his head from his slit trench not five yards away.

"What's up, Harry?"

Harry stared back in disbelief. "You kidding. The fucking Afrika Korps throwing every kind of shit at us and you have the nerve to ask 'what's up.' I just don't believe it."

"You better keep your head down, Harry," laughed Charlie, "that's our long range snipers firing back, that bleeding short sighted officer may be on duty." His head vanished down his trench.

Harry burst out laughing. "You are a stupid prick at times, Charlie," he shouted above the din of exploding shells. "The bastards are getting closer."

"Well, I warned you!" yelled Charlie.

It was times like these, when Charlie could joke about their predicament - making light of a bad situation - that made Harry feel confident he could face whatever the future had in store for them. The shelling continued, moving forward.

"There you are Harry, the gunners are really having a go at each other." There was a brief silence. "I often wonder what would happen if two shells collided in mid air."

"There would be a bloody great bang!" chuckled Harry. "I wouldn't like to be underneath them when it happened."

At this point, Charlie cleared his bowels of surplus wind. He was really in form this morning for in spite of the screaming shells, Harry could hear it five yards away.

"I think that's about the size of the bang, Charlie. I'm only thankful I'm not sharing that trench with you."

"Sod off, Harry. You know how to hurt a man's feelings!"

A rattling noise of metal against hard ground filled the air. The earth shook as the rattle became a continuous rumble. Harry raised his head and saw tanks moving forward, slowly at first, like

52

race horses going to the starting line, then as one, they leapt forward. The guns of the tanks swivelled round like elephant trunks swaying side to side. The aerials whipping back and forth like fishing rods with enormous bites their anglers could boast about for years. The stench of explosives, engine fumes and death filled the air. A tank faltered and spun around on one track, leaving the other trailing behind like some huge scaled serpent. He saw two of the crew half climb, half fall from the stricken tank as smoke poured from the turret and slits. Black smoke spiralled skywards and suddenly the monster was enveloped in a sheet of bright orange flame.

As the great steel monsters moved forward, almost hidden from view by the sand bellowing up from their tracks, the shelling moved up with them. The cries of stretcher bearers went up as the shells fell amongst the infantry supporting the tanks. Harry grabbed his medical satchel and rushed towards the stricken tank. There was very little he could do for them. One man, his back badly burned struggled to his feet and pleaded with his eyes, but all Harry could do was give him a pain killing injection and gently cover his back with a sheet of gauze to keep the flies and sand away. The other man was badly burned around the face and shoulders. Both showed signs of shock.

"The driver and the others are still in there," the tank commander said as Harry led him away. He kept turning around to look at the stricken tank and his dying comrades.

The aid post was already crowded. Several stretchers were laid outside and walking wounded sat around in small groups.

"Is the ambulance ready?" the medical sergeant enquired.

Harry nodded.

"Right, start packing them in as soon as their wounds are dressed."

When they returned to the aid post, it was overflowing with wounded. Harry stripped to the waist and donned a rubber apron.

"Nasty one here, Jackson."

The M.O. handed him the gauze mask and ethyl chloride. Harry placed the mask over the man's face.

"Count to ten," he instructed the casualty in a subdued voice.

The M.O. nodded with approval knowing he could get on with the job without worrying about the anaesthetic, his confidence in Harry grew.

"Right, sergeant. There's no chance of saving his legs, both femurs are shattered and what's left of his legs is just hanging by skin tissue. His scrotum is ripped open but fortunately there is no abdominal damage," the M.O. said after he inspected the casualty. With the speed of an old time surgeon who operated before anaesthetic was discovered, the M.O. tied off the arteries and cut the flesh and skin away and cleaned the stumps.

"That's his bleeding dancing days over, sir," the sergeant said.

"Artificial legs are pretty good these days and if they can save these stumps, he won't be so badly off," the M.O. replied.

Harry gave the man an injection of anti-tetanus. "We'll get him into the ambulance and back now, sir. If he wakes, I'll give him a jab of morphine. When he does wake, he'll think an elephant has kicked his balls in. I hope I won't be the one to tell him he's lost his pins."

The M.O. straightened up. The work load was beginning to tell; ashen face and dark shadows around his eyes.

"You did a good job, Jackson. Get back as fast as you can. Pack as many walking wounded in that ambulance."

Charlie had made a brew and was passing the hot sweet tea among the wounded. He passed a mug to Harry, but it was too hot. They could hear the tank battle raging up ahead, their own artillery had ceased shelling.

"Let's get loaded and away, Charlie. There's a bad bugger coming out. I'll sit with him, he's lost a lot of blood. Try and get as many up front with you as possible."

All fear left Harry, his main concern now was the welfare of his patients, no longer casualties as far as he was concerned, but his patients. This was what he was trained for and at the moment, nothing else mattered but to get them as far away from danger as possible, where they could be cared for. The heat and sand was as dangerous as shrapnel to a man's wounds. With four stretcher cases and six walking wounded the ambulance was well loaded.

Harry sat on the small seat by the side of the amputation case. He groaned several times as the ethyl chloride started to wear off and on two occasions opened his eyes and grinned at Harry like a Cheshire cat. Harry wiped the sweat away from the man's forehead.

By reducing his speed trying to avoid the large boulders, it took Charlie twenty minutes to do the three miles back to the aid station (ADS). As they came to their final stop, the back doors were flung open and the walking wounded helped out.

"Take it easy with this one, Tommo," Harry shouted to one of the men unloading the stretchers, "and get the M.O. to shufti him straight away."

Charlie lost no time getting back to the aid post, getting the absolute maximum out of the engine. Twice they hit large boulders sending Harry flying against the side of the ambulance. They hardly spoke to each other. The battle was still raging ahead and casualties still pouring in. He eased off as they neared the aid post.

"If this lot keeps up, Charlie, we won't be getting much grub today. My guts are rumbling worse than Vesuvius," Harry shouted.

"Yes, my bleeding guts think my throat's been cut," replied Charlie. He stopped suddenly and gasped, "Just take a look at this lot, Harry."

He nodded towards the aid post. Men sat around in twos and threes, several stretchers were laid in the shade of the lean-to. More bodies lay in the sand away from the aid post, completely covered with blankets.

"Looks more like Flo Nightingale's hospital at Scutari in the Crimea."

Several of the men had their casualty cards tied to their shirts, they had already been attended to.

Harry examined the tags. "Some of you chaps can walk back to the advanced dressing station, it's just a couple of miles away. There's plenty of mungie there and nice clean beds."

At the mention of food, some of the slightly wounded grew more enthusiastic and rose to their feet.

"Any bints back there, medic?"

Harry looked at the man and grinned.

"It's obvious that your balls haven't been shot away." He looked at his label, "bloody hell, with that scratch, you'll be lucky to get a sandwich." He watched them depart then shouted "We'll be passing you occasionally, if you feel you can't make it, just wave us down."

"We're back, sir," Harry poked his head through the opening of the lean-to, the stench of antiseptics and burnt flesh taking his breath away. "I've loaded and ready to go back. Is there anything you need, sir?"

"The only thing I need at the moment, Jackson, is a new back," groaned the M.O. as he straightened up. His body glistened with sweat, his rubber apron more like a butchers, covered with congealing blood. A white bucket beneath the makeshift operating table was full to the brim with dirty dressings, being attacked by a swarm of flies.

Harry retrieved the bucket and was attacked by the flies. "I'll just empty this before I go, sir."

The hole was already dug behind the lean-to. A hand and a foot fell into the hole from the bucket. He poured a strong undiluted disinfectant into the bucket before replacing it.

"I'll see if they can spare another ambulance, sir."

The M.O. just nodded.

55

There was no other ambulance available and it was left to Charlie and Harry to evacuate the wounded alone. In between trips, Harry helped dress the wounds. Occasionally he took a few sips of hot tea. By mid-afternoon the battle had quietened down sufficiently to allow them to stop for their first meal in twenty four hours. Harry flopped down on the sand beside the last two wounded men to be evacuated. The M.O. emerged with the sergeant from the lean-to and both breathed the fresh air in deep gulps. But the peace was soon shattered.

Hardly had they settled down to their first meal when a dispatch rider hurtled up and handed the M.O. a folded signal paper.

He took it and heaved a deep sigh, "Right, sergeant, get these last two evacuated, we have to move forward. The division has broken through and Jerry is flapping. Must have been a big job, they are thirty miles ahead, two Itey Divs and a Jerry Div are in the bag."

"What are our casualties, sir?" asked Harry.

"Negligible, they say here."

He handed the sergeant the signal.

"They wouldn't have said that if they had been here, sir," Charlie said.

The sergeant, a veteran of the First War smiled. "If you think this is tough, you should have seen the mess on the Somme in 1917. That was some battle. Casualties were so many it was impossible to count them. If you had one leg off, they expected you to hop back to the aid post under your own steam!"

"I'll believe you, sarge, thousands wouldn't. Some war that - at least the generals have more sense this time," Charlie said.

"Don't speak too soon, Williams. We have to get our feet back into Europe before this lot is over. That won't be a bloody picnic." The sergeant looked around the barren landscape. "This is the place for fighting a war. It's only us stupid prats that get hurt. You should have seen the poor people of France during the retreat to Dunkirk. Jerry mowed them down just like ninepins, soldier and civilian alike."

The desert was littered with burnt out and wrecked vehicles of every description. Waiting for burial, bodies lay in every grotesque position. A deathly pall hung over the macabre scene, the silence only disturbed by the faint rumble of guns in the far distance. Carrion birds hung on silent wings, circling the desolate situation. In the distance, columns of German and Italian prisoners walked silently towards the prison cages, well to the rear, the war finally over for them. Harry used Charlie's binoculars to study them.

56

"Looks like the whole German and Italian armies have jacked it in, Charlie."

"Don't kid yourself, there will always be plenty more where they came from," replied Charlie.

"Those Iteys look really dejected, Charlie. Looks like they haven't the guts for fighting. Anyway, they aren't a fighting nation. It was only Musso that kidded them along. They are far more interested in the arts, operas and love songs and all that crap, not forgetting screwing. Let's face it, who wants to fight when you can listen to some of the worlds finest music and screw some of the most glamorous girls."

"Bullshit, Harry. There is nothing better than a real English beauty, believe me, I've had the lot. Most of the Itey birds go to seed after thirty, fat and flabby. It's all that bleeding pasta they eat. And the kids, one year after year. I had this Itey bird in Cairo, she wasn't fat but when she stripped she had more wrinkles on her belly than a plate of tripe in a butchers window - good screw mind you!"

They travelled for nearly two hours before the M.O.'s utility pulled up. Charlie pulled alongside. Within minutes the lean-to was erected and the makeshift theatre prepared.

"There's three dead Jerries just over there, Jackson, get them buried. They'll stink to high heaven before morning."

The ground was soft. Harry searched the bodies and handed their papers to the padre before lowering them into the ground.

As he went to pick up a light machine gun that lay beside them, the sergeant yelled, "Don't touch it! It may be booby trapped or if you know sod all about it, it could go off accidentally. A burst from one of those could cut a man in half."

The sergeant dropped to his hands and knees to inspect the gun closely, then slipped on the safety catch before he carefully lifted it.

"Can't be too careful, Jackson, one of our lads picked one up once, it let off a blast and killed his mate - dead before he hit the ground."

"That's tough, sarge. What happened to him?"

"Sent him round the twist. As far as I know, he's still in the psychiatric ward back in Cairo."

Back at the aid post Charlie dished out the hot stew and a bottle of beer each, supplied by the M.O. The sun, a large golden ball, fell abruptly over the horizon, darkness following the dusk in rapid succession. A three-quarter moon cast elongated shadows along the ground and soon the whole desert was turned to a silver wonderland, helped by the brilliant stars hanging from invisible threads. Harry sighed, if it wasn't for the constant reminder of

57

war all around them, he could appreciate the beauty of the desert.

CHAPTER 7

They were still attached to the same regiment a few weeks later when action flared up again, although this time much smaller, but bloodier and more bitter. The first casualty was the RAP itself. A heavy high explosive shell landed nearby, and the blast blew the flimsy canvas lean-to across the sands. It took off like a balloon, taking with it bottles of lotions, medicines and antiseptics, smashing them into a thousand fragments. Drums of sterile dressings burst open, scattering the white gauze and lint pads across the ground like confetti.

The sergeant and M.O. by some fluke escaped any physical injury and picked themselves up from their makeshift beds without a mark. Harry gasped at the trembling apparitions.

"Christ, sarge! Another few inches and that shell would have sent you on a one way trip to Kingdom Come. We would have been scraping you off the sand for days, like horse-shit off the stable floor."

He gave the sergeant a knowing wink. For weeks, the sergeant had been preaching to them to sleep in slit trenches and not in the ambulance. The wink was sufficient. Charlie had already taught him to store these little tit-bits of information, as he liked to call them, to backfire on the so-called establishment.

Harry sat at the side of his ambulance waiting for the sergeant and M.O. to prepare a list of lost stores to take back and draw from their own unit's supply. Charlie was studying his features through his wing mirror. He wiped his hand around the three days growth. Fine sand mingled with the stubble and dust had hardened into the creases around his eyes, giving his face the appearance of a caricature. He wet the tips of his fingers with spit and traced them around his blonde eyebrows. "God, Charlie, you are handsome even with that shite around your face."

Harry tutted in disgust, pinched his nose between finger and thumb and cleared his nose of sand. He had lost count long ago of the times he heard Charlie praising himself. "You certainly fancy yourself, Charlie boy," he jibed.

"Yes," responded Charlie. "I'm starting to worry just in case this sand does permanent damage to my sylph like complexion."

The sergeant gave Harry the chit, his hand still shaking from his recent ordeal. "Jeldhi (hurry) lads, I think the shit will be flying again shortly."

Harry couldn't help but rub it in. He shouted to the sergeant as Charlie put the engine into gear, "Have you counted your balls yet, sarge?"

Handing the medical chit to the QM, they made their way over to the galley - always the galley in this unit - the cook sergeant was an ex-navy man. He looked them up and down as they each scooped out a mug full of tea from the soya stove.

"Bleeding hell, ain't you two pongos shaved yet? You look a bloody mess."

"You must be joking sarge, we had one of the closest shaves of the war yet. The sodding R.A.P. was shot away a couple of hours ago!"

Feeling a lot better after washing, shaving and a full stomach, they picked up the supplies and made their way back to the Regiment. Charlie stopped the ambulance a mile from the aid post, his attention drawn to a bank of sand rising like a thick London fog. At first, he thought it was a sandstorm blowing up, but occasionally he could see a tank emerging and then orange flashes. He took out his powerful binoculars and focussed them on to the area. "Just in time, Harry boy, a right shindig going on up there."

The tank received a direct hit and bowed out of the fog like an actor on the stage taking his final curtain call. It jerked to a stop, smoke pouring from the turret. Its crew scrambled to safety then it burst into a bright orange flame. Charlie whistled through his teeth, his hands dropped to his lap. He handed the binoculars to Harry but Harry shook his head.

"No thanks, Charlie. I've seen enough."

"Those poor bastards didn't stand a chance, Harry. I only saw two get out."

He focused on the scene again. A second tank received a direct hit, spinning it crazily on one track as the other snaked out behind him. Three more tanks broke from the cloud of dust.

Charlie's frown turned to a look of disbelief, "Ever see a Tiger tank close up, Harry?"

Harry shook his head and took the binoculars from Charlie, focussing them on the yellow painted steel giants. His mouth opened as he gasped and the stub end of his cigarette balancing on his bottom lip fell to the ground. The powerful binoculars bought the enemy so close he felt he could just reach out and touch them.

It looked like the enemy had underestimated the strength of the British tanks and were seeing a way out. The commander of the leading tank raised his head above the turret and looked around startled and realised his mistake as several British tanks surrounded them and pumped shells into them as fast as the gunners could load. In minutes, it was all over, leaving three blackened wrecks. The British tanks turned in the opposite direction to rejoin the battle.

Charlie slipped into gear and charged forward. Harry lost his grip and slid from his seat cursing loudly.

"Shit, Charlie. Don't tell me you're going to join them!"

Silently he wished then that he had applied for a hospital ship - at least the captain and crew wouldn't have a death wish. Charlie as usual gave his guttural laugh as he always did when heading towards a sticky situation.

"Don't worry. It's all over bar the shouting. There are a few tanks knocked out. Let's see if there is anything we can do. Those Jerries walked straight into it - they never knew what hit them."

They pulled up at the R.A.P. No casualties had arrived. They unloaded the medical supplies and, without waiting for further instructions, rushed over to the cloud of dust, now settling down to reveal a scene of carnage that could be mistaken for hell itself. All around German and British as well as a couple of Italian tanks lay smouldering, black smoke still spiralling from the blackened turrets. Survivors and dead bodies lay around like immobile statues. The miasma of death hung heavily on the air. The stench of fuel, burning rubber and explosives added to the stench of hell's slaughter house. Many of the bodies had been crushed beneath the heavy tank tracks of friend and foe alike. It was impossible to tell which was which.

Harry dropped beside a man hunched against his tank, nursing an injured knee. It had ballooned to twice its normal size.

"Does it hurt, mate?"

A stupid question under the circumstances.

"Of course it hurts, you prick."

"Alright, no need to get bolshie with me or you'll walk back to the aid post - or maybe hop."

Charlie came over and helped the man to the ambulance. Harry turned his attention to the other injured man. He was gasping as if every ounce of breath had been smashed from his body, his hands holding his chest tightly.

"Rushing to get out of that bloody tank I fell on a piece of protruding metal. I think I've done my ribs in."

Harry gently smoothed his hand over the mans chest. "You're right. It looks like one of your ribs has gone for a burton. If I help you, can you make your way over to the ambulance?"

The man nodded, but every step was torture.

When they arrived Charlie was in the throes of a heated argument with an uninjured member of the crew.

"What do you think this tub is, Carter Pattersons Removal Lorry?"

The man was protesting vigorously and trying to throw the crew's kit into the ambulance and Charlie was just as quickly slinging it out again.

"Our kit goes back with us to the aid post."

"Like fuck it does, we just take the wounded, and what's more, you aren't coming, so get walking."

Piles of kit and other gear formed a small pyramid at the rear of the ambulance. Harry thought his driver and the crewman would soon come to blows. He was astounded to see so much gear and wondered where the hell they stored it in the confines of the tank.

"Look mate, this stuff isn't coming back with us. My driver is in charge of the maintenance and the engine, my responsibility is in the back. I say it isn't going back and that's the end of it. Now look, we have more wounded to pick up, so piss off."

Harry helped the injured man into the ambulance. "Who's the tank commander anyway?"

"I am," the man with the damaged knee said. He was stripped to the waist and carried no insignia. He was in terrible pain and hissed through his clenched teeth, "I am Captain Woodruff, and I insist the gear goes back with us."

"Insist as much as you like, sir," replied Harry as he plunged a needle into the captain's arm and marked his forehead with a large M. "I wouldn't give a toss if you were Monty's twin brother, it stays here!"

"I will have you both on a charge when we get back."

Harry burst out laughing. "You do just that, sir." Then, patronisingly, he patted the officers bald head, "There, there sir, you have a nice bye, byes."

Outside the ambulance, he burst our laughing. "I don't believe it, Charlie! That prat talks about charges - here! Bodies and wounded everywhere, a bleeding great battle just over and the prick threatens us. He won't be in any state to make a charge when we get back. I just gave him a jab of morphine, now he's out cold."

They stopped at a German tank. Two bodies lay beside it. Harry rolled the first one on his back. Blood trickled from the corner of his mouth. Two large patches of blood stained the front of his shirt, his pulse just a faint beat. Harry shook his head, the man would be dead within minutes. He turned his attention to the other man. His arms were folded across his abdomen and he leaned against the tank. Harry lifted his arms away with some difficulty, the blood had congealed between his arms and his abdomen. Fear leapt from the German's eyes. He tried to shove Harry away but the loss of blood had weakened him.

"All right, Fritz, take it easy," soothed Harry in a soft sympathetic tone which couldn't be mistaken in any language. He wet a piece of lint and wiped it around the German's mouth. Charlie knelt down beside them and gave the German a friendly wink.

"How goes it, Harry, will he make it?"

He didn't answer for a few seconds, his attention was on the man's gaping abdominal wound. "Can't tell much, it's a jagged wound and covered in sand. The bloody flies are attacking it like squadrons of dive bombers. Now if he had been knocked down just outside the general hospital and got a wound like this, he might stand a fifty fifty chance but here, now, who knows."

He gave him an injection and painted the M on his forehead. They placed him on a stretcher and lifted him into the ambulance.

"You are a naughty boy, Fritz. You will go around fucking about in that tank of yours," Charlie patted his cheek after making him as comfortable as possible. "You shouldn't listen to old Hitler and his cronies. You won't win this war you know!"

They filled the ambulance with more wounded and returned to the aid post. The bearers and walking wounded had started to arrive. Several bodies covered with blankets were line up behind the lean-to. They lifted the wounded from the ambulance and Harry reported to the M.O.

"Just bought a few more in, sir."

"Thanks, Jackson, just what I need. Any bad ones amongst them?"

"A Jerry bad abdomen wound, sir. One damaged knee, one damaged chest. I think a rib has caved in. Doesn't seem much damage, must be bloody painful though. Another GSW in the leg, sir. I splinted that, looks like the tibia and fibula have gone. Two or three slight wounds we packed down the centre of the ambulance. Some have had morphine, I painted their foreheads with an M. That's about it, sir - although I doubt that the Jerry will make it."

"Alright, Jackson, I'll finish this one and then take a look. Now you take the ones that are labelled and get back here as fast as possible. Its quiet out there now, we should be finished before nightfall."

It was getting dusk when they made their last trip. While they were away, the cook had sent up a dixie of strong tea and a dixie of stew.

"Help yourself." The sergeant nodded towards the two dixies.

"What's all this crap floating on the top, sarge?" Charlie asked.

"The cook sergeant tried to make some dumplings. He soaked some hard tack biscuits in water for a week then mixed them with some marge."

"Is that what that yellow grease on top is. I thought he had melted down a chinaman."

"Talking of chinamen reminds me of when we were in Mombasa. We had this bloody foreign seaman in hospital. Our M.O. was treating him for three weeks for jaundice before they realised he was Chinese."

"God, Jackson, if I wasn't so bloody hungry I would fling this stew at you for a crack like that," the sergeant said, hiding a smile.

The canvas doorway parted and the padre entered, a bottle of whisky in his hand. He had been conducting a burial service behind the lean-to. He offered the bottle around. Both Harry and Charlie shook their heads.

"Not for me, sir, hardly touch the stuff."

Heavy blankets were hung around the flimsy canvas sides before the sergeant lit a couple of hurricane lamps. A head covered with a mop of ginger hair and a face with freckles from ear to ear appeared through the canvas. A wide cheeky grin spread his sand ingrained face almost in two.

"Just passing, thought you might like a couple of bods evacuating. Heard you had a bit of a do around here."

His sharp cockney accent was almost comical as his face. He looked at the bottle in the padre's hand and licked his lips and produced a badly chipped white enamel mug from behind his back. The padre poured a liberal measure into the mug.

"Very nice, sir. You must have read my mind!"

"Not exactly. I saw that filthy mug." He poured another measure into the mug. "Better give your driver a drink."

He took a couple of sips, "Well, must go, got a date with a couple of dishy blondes tonight."

"I've heard all about you, Dusty, you're a dirty bastard. You'll go blind you know."

Harry took hold of Dusty's hand and pretended to examine it under the pale light from the hurricane lamp and remove a couple of hairs.

"You'll go blind you know," he repeated. "You should sleep with your hands above the blankets."

Dusty feigned a look of surprise.

"Harry, I told you before, the minute I have to start wearing glasses, I'll stop. I went to see Captain Fellows the other day, before the war he was an eye surgeon. He tested my eyes, absolutely perfect, said with my sight I would make a brilliant night fighter in a Spitfire. I told him I had just volunteered as a parachutist in the Irish Submarine Service." He took another couple of sips of the whisky. "Well, I have to rush, can't keep the bints waiting. Lana Turner and Greta Garbo got up the pole the other night, wanted to make a threesome but that bloody Mary Smith came and ballsed it up!"

"Who the fucking hell is Mary Smith?" Charlie asked, well aware he would get some stupid answer, he knew Dusty of old.

"Buggered if I know, she just keeps interfering with my dreams. Came in my slit trench the other night, sod all on except a steel helmet."

While this conversation was going on, the sergeant, M.O. and padre looked on fascinated but speechless. After he had gone, the sergeant said, "Who the hell was that?"

"Dusty Miller, sarge," Harry answered. "Quite harmless, fantasises a lot. I think he's going crazy. Been away from Blighty for the last eight years. Went out to India in '34, then on to Palestine and later to Egypt. He was there when the war started. Full of bullshit but a good medic. The R.S.M. said he would get him posted back home. He refused, said all his friends are here. I don't think he has any family. He writes to his driver's sister, swears blind the first night they meet he'll put her in the family way."

"What does his driver say about that?" the padre asked, fascinated with the conversation.

"He just laughs, they've been together for three years now. He knows it's just talk."

The two lamps were giving off a black greasy haze, filling the lean-to with a nauseating stench. The others seemed immune to it but Harry found it sickening. He went outside for a breath of fresh air and looked at the star studded sky. The stars were so bright you could almost read a newspaper from them, and hanging so low it felt as if you could reach up and touch them. Occasionally, a flare would burst in the sky, flooding the desert with its silvery glow and for a moment the stars would vanish behind its brilliant light.

Harry sat down on a small hillock and lit a cigarette, consumed by the silence which seemed to crowd in on him. He thought of England and the great blitz, of the hospital in London where the army sent him for extensive training. He thought of Victoria and the matron of the orphanage and all those people he promised to write to. He still hadn't written those letters. Tomorrow, without fail, he promised himself again. It would be nice to receive some post instead of hearing other men's names called out. Charlie had received two a few days earlier. A lilac envelope he didn't bother to open, just tore into small pieces and let it scatter along the sand. The other, a brown official looking envelope which he opened, read the contents then folded and placed in the back of his shorts. For the next couple of days, he had hardly spoken a word - just sat in his driver's seat for three or four hours at a time, staring into space.

"Peaceful out here, isn't it, Jackson?"

Harry hadn't heard the padre come up behind him.

"Yes sir, hard to believe that happened a few hours ago," he paused and offered the padre a cigarette from an old battered tobacco tin. "Do you ever feel scared, padre?"

The padre laughed, "Of course. I'm well aware we all have to die at some time, but I would prefer to die at home with my family there. Why, do you get frightened?"

"Shit scared, sir," replied Harry, the glow of his cigarette lighting up his face as he took a deep drag. "It's strange, sir, when I'm up amongst it, I don't feel scared. It's just on my way up there, I shake like a jelly. I don't think it's so much dying, it's the thought of getting mutilated that scares me most. Being stuck in some home or institution. I would prefer to die."

"Surely, if that was the case, your family would look after you?"

Harry shrugged his shoulders. "I have no family. I was brought up in an orphanage, no girl friends either - well, no permanent girl friends. I swore blind I would never have a lasting relationship while this war was on."

They remained silent for a couple of minutes. The padre thought he had said too much already but he was the first to break the silence.

"You're lucky, Jackson. At least in your job you help to save lives. I know in war it's easy to say you have to kill or be killed, but believe me, it remains with you for the rest of your life."

Harry looked at the padre, his mind seemed to be on another planet. "You sound as if you're speaking from experience."

"I am, Jackson," confided the padre. "I wasn't always a padre. No, in the First War, I was a machine gunner. I was on the Somme. God, that was a war. The Germans were coming at us in droves, all I had to do was swivel my machine gun from side to side. I was like a child knocking down his lead soldiers. I felt sick, I lost count of the men I killed. One hundred, two hundred, there could have been more. Then suddenly, I felt this blast on my shoulder, and then another in my thigh. It was as if a horse had kicked me. When I woke up, I was in this large white tent in between crisp white sheets. You know, at first, I thought I was in heaven. I was returned to England but I couldn't get those men off my mind. I thought of their mothers and fathers, their brothers, sisters and sweethearts, and all the hatred and anguish I had caused them. Then I learned my two brothers had been killed. It jolted me back to my senses. My younger brother was just eighteen and been in France all of two days. My wound healed and I should have returned to my unit in France but someone informed the war office, about my two brothers' deaths. I think it was my mother although she denied it. I was posted to the training depot to train other boys to kill and get killed, it was sickening. The only place where I could find solace was in the garrison church. I spent hours in there. I realised then what my vocation was to be, and here I am."

"I think I understand, sir. It's very strange how fate deals her hands. It took a war with wholesale slaughter to determine your future and seek religion. Religion did quite the opposite for me and threw me into this conflict. I was an orphan and was brought up in a Quaker orphanage. Now, don't get me wrong, the people who ran it were kindness itself, but there were prayers for everything and I just could not fathom it all out. My brain kept on insisting there was more to life than the orphanage could offer. I suppose it was pure selfishness. They taught me to play the piano and the teacher was hoping I would take it up professionally. She said I would make a good concert pianist, but she kept pushing me, every spare minute she would have me at the piano. I just couldn't take it anymore. So, at fourteen, I ran away to London. Then one day, wet and hungry, I was looking in the window of the Army Recruiting Office. I went inside and looked through all the books. I was always well built for my age and saw that in man service I would get two shillings a day. Boy service was one shilling a day. Everyone knew a war was inevitable and they were eager for recruits. They never questioned me when I said I was eighteen."

"Any regrets, Jackson?" asked the padre quietly.

Harry shrugged his shoulders, "A few maybe - although I never regretted joining the army. There is no place in the world where you find mates like the services."

After a pause, Harry stood up to go. The padre caught his arm, a tear formed in his eye and ran down his cheek, glistening like a shining pearl caught in the strong starlight.

"Remember, Jackson, if you ever have to kill a man - and for God's sake alone, I hope you never have to - you will only find solace in the Lord, pray to him my son, pray hard and in earnest."

Harry turned, feeling somewhat embarrassed. The last thing he needed then was a sermon. He took a last look at the star studded sky. It was a peaceful night.

"Tomorrow, I'll write to Victoria and the matron."

CHAPTER 8

There was a strange fascination about the desert that appealed to Harry. During the lull in the fighting and after returning from a rest, he would wander away and find himself a small dune and sit there for hours on end. The time he liked best was the full moon, when he would stare at it until it vanished beyond the horizon and the silver fantasy land turned into a velvet black night that seemed to press down on him. Then the bright stars would break through the blackness.

Now the sun was shining brilliantly and they were alone in the empty desert. The only sign of life was the man-made sandstorm on the far horizon as the division with its thousands of vehicles moved up into new positions. Charlie had enough experience not to pull over and join them and get the full blast of fine sand smothering the ambulance. They would be stopping shortly, time to pull over and take up his post with the new regiment he'd been assigned to. The wheels struck a pot hole, throwing Harry forward, and steadying himself he braced his feet against the dashboard.

"How about a brew, Charlie?"

Never one to miss a chance, he pulled up sharply and while Harry prepared the brew Charlie cursed.

"It's a scorcher today, Harry," he said finally. He wrung the sweat from the rag around his neck, then wiped the sweat from his crutch cursing again. "That bloody sand gets everywhere. I'm red raw."

They sat on the shady side of the ambulance sipping the hot tea while the sweat oozed from every pore, and Charlie smacked his lips. "God, Harry, I needed that."

Charlie studied the wall of sand. "They should be stopping shortly and as soon as we've had a drink we can start pulling into that direction."

He poured Spag a tinful of water, who drank it and then immediately cocked his leg against the rear wheel. Charlie ruffled Spag's ears and muttered fondly, "That's a waste, you little Itey bastard." Wagging his tail furiously, Spag dribbled more along the sand.

The division had stopped and the sand was beginning to settle when they finally pulled over beside the aid post, where the sergeant looked sternly at them.

"Where the hell have you two been?" he barked.

"Had a hell of a job finding you, sarge," Charlie answered. "Been up and down the column for a couple of hours."

68

"Bullshit, Williams! Been all the same if we had to evacuate anyone."

"It's worse than driving in a London fog behind this lot, sarge," Charlie defended himself.

"All right, Williams, cut the crap and get your mate to help with the aid post," the sergeant ordered. "The regiment is moving up tonight. The heavy stuff is moving up behind them. Shouldn't get undressed if I were you tonight, Charlie, we may have to move back in a hurry. It looks like Jerry broke through and we've been sent up to fill the gap. They reckon he's thrown everything in on this attack. We're getting into Musso's backyard. And, if this goes to plan, we should be crossing the Libyan border in a few weeks time. Then the next big town will be Tripoli."

Charlie had heard about Tripoli, the jewel in Musso's North African empire. Next to Cairo and Alex, it was North Africa's largest city. His face lit up, civilisation at last!

A lecherous grin spread across his face as he thought aloud, "Month after month we've been across this desert and now civilisation, at last. You aren't kidding are you, sarge? Do you mean we could actually be in Tripoli within weeks? It's too good to be true. It seems like years since we left the delta."

Carefully eying Charlie up and down the sergeant said, "Christ, Williams, you should see your face! I know what civilisation means to you. Crumpet. You're just hoping that all those Itey birds will be there greeting you with open arms."

"No, sarge, you can keep the sentimental crap. I would sooner be welcomed with open legs," Charlie chuckled.

Shaking his head in despair the sergeant said, "Alright, Williams, get on with it and let's get organised here."

The barrage started just before light, heavy shells screaming overhead and just ahead of them the small twenty-five pounders opened up. The distant horizon became a blaze of colour as shells exploded and columns of sand spiralled skywards. Spag shivered under his blankets. Harry sat in his trench, his head just above the ground. It was the heaviest concentration of guns he'd ever seen in action. The guns flashed all around him, orange balls of flame spitting out of the shells, and the guns became enveloped in their own black smoke which wafted back over the aid post.

"Christ, Harry, I wouldn't like to be on the receiving end of that lot!" Charlie shouted across to him. The stars paled in the softening light, a zephyr of early morning wind wafting across the sand and bringing with it the scorching scent of explosives. Charlie gripped the shivering dog in his arms.

"The tanks will have to move out shortly, Harry," he said. "With this sun behind them they'll stand out like a pair of dog's balls."

69

As he spoke a salvo of enemy shells dropped all around them, followed by a continuous barrage. Spag buried his nose in the crook of Charlie's arm and, stroking the dog's head gently as the barrage crept nearer, they both settled down further into their slit trench. A vary light arched into the sky leaving a trail of green smoke to mark its progress. Then, as one, the whole brigade of tanks moved forward, their thin aerials flaying the air. Another series of vary lights arched against the sky, trailing coloured smoke. Like banshees, men rose from their slit trenches and moved forward, their steel helmets set at rakish angles, and their rifles and bayonets held high across their chests, determined looks on their faces.

"Have a shufti at this lot, Harry. There's a sight you'll be able to tell your grandchildren about - if you live long enough," Charlie called to him.

Harry was about to answer but Charlie held up his hand and strained his ears. From their right, the faint but heartening sound of bagpipes came across the still air, just audible above the sounds of battle.

"I bloody well thought so. It's the bloody Jocks with their doodle saxes. That's all we need!"

It was one of Charlie's favourite pastimes, having a go at the Scots. Harry never took any notice. He knew deep down Charlie was a deep admirer. Their own division often supported the Highland Division and a friendly rivalry had developed between them. Once a town was taken they were always sure of an argument as to who had arrived first. This often led to a friendly punch up. Someone would paint their divisional sign, like an animal marking its territory by urinating, then a member of the other division would over paint their sign and the fireworks would start.

A platoon passed close to their aid post. The shelling eased up and Charlie stamped his feet to get the circulation going. He was wearing his greatcoat and balaclava but the cold morning air penetrated the thick clothing.

"Christ, Harry, I feel sorry for those poor sods wearing just shorts and a bush shirt," he muttered.

Harry suggested a brew up but Charlie wasn't interested. This was a battle that would bring them nearer Tripoli. He slid to the bottom of his slit trench and covered himself with blankets, his mind exploring Tripoli's red light district.

"Keep the brew, Harry," he dismissed it. "I'd rather be enjoying a piece of Itey or French crumpet." He cleared his nose then raising his voice, shouted across, "I bet it's our luck to take Tripoli with the Jocks."

70

"So what's wrong with that?"

"Well, with the Jocks, they'll spend the first twenty-four hours drinking the place dry, then the next twenty four hours fighting and screwing every bird in sight." He paused as he thought over past incidents. "I suppose you know why they don't wear kilts on active service now?"

"I thought they were abolished after the last war because they bred lice!" Harry yelled back.

Charlie answered with a guttural laugh, "Don't be a prat, Harry, they were getting too much in the French brothels. Their tools hung below their knees. Most of them spent half the war in French nicks for indecent exposure." Charlie was in a boisterous mood, and Harry didn't answer or bother to laugh. Whatever he said, Charlie would answer with another wisecrack.

He settled back in his trench and lit a cigarette. It wasn't long before the cry for stretcher bearers could be heard above the shelling, and the vibrating sounds of small arms fire echoed back. Machine guns opened up with quick bursts. Heavy shells dropped amongst the advancing infantry, and Harry watched helplessly as the lines of advancing men began to thin out. A platoon became the sole target of a machine gunner. Each man fell in turn, some raised their arms falling backwards, and one man spun round and round until his knees buckled, hitting the sand in a distorted heap. Another fell to his knees, tried to crawl along and was again hit by a string of bullets. He pitched forward onto his face, lifted his head then rolled onto his back. His hands gripped the air then dropped, and he didn't move again.

It was an hypnotic spectacle - a stupendous symphony played with men's misery. No living man could have staged this slaughter. It must surely be the work of the devil himself. There was no rhythm to the sound. Shells would burst and then a machine gun would clatter. No German could have survived that barrage. Nothing could possibly have survived that storm of red hot metal. And yet the Germans put up a protective defence, while the sun, just fresh over the horizon, glistened on the advancing men's bayonets. They weren't walking now. They were trotting and soon they would break into a run, their bayonets pointing forwards. Mortar bombs turned somersaults in the air dropping amongst the survivors, and then there were the lighter explosions of hand grenades. Surely there could be no survivors left to force home the attack ... But there were. They were in amongst the enemy and it was bayonet against bayonet, man to man. Harry felt that he could no longer be spectator to this carnage. His eyes misted over. He grabbed his medical satchel and ran forward towards the pitiful cries of the wounded as fast as his legs could carry him.

71

He heard the whine of a shell and plunged forward, forcing his body as close to the ground as possible. A large stone embedded itself in his crutch, the pain excruciating ... The shell landed only a few yards away. The ground trembled, and jagged slivers of red hot metal whizzed across his head and body. His medical satchel had landed on his back as he'd plunged forward, and a small piece of shrapnel now forced it away. He stood up dazed but miraculously unhurt, the stench of explosives stinging his nostrils. He could feel his body shaking and a hot lump rose in his throat. He ran a few more steps, stumbling over a boulder as two more shells dropped to either side of him. His head seemed to explode but nothing touched his body. He crouched now as he ran towards a wounded man. The man's arm had been torn away above the elbow and he was bleeding profusely, Harry tied off the arm with a tourniquet.

"Do you think that you can make your own way back, mate?" Harry asked as he dressed the stump. The man nodded and tried to stand up, but then fell backwards. "You stay here then. I'll have a shufti round and I'll come back to you. The stretcher bearers are around here somewhere."

Harry dressed several more wounds before he felt that he could rest and wait for Charlie to bring up the ambulance. The shelling was easing off, and bearers were already picking up the more severely wounded. A stray shell screamed over and landed squarely amongst them, a bearer sprawled forward, the casualty on his stretcher rolling over and over. The other bearer ran to help his mate but as he turned him over his intestines gushed out from the open wound. Harry walked over but there was nothing that he could do. He picked up the casualty who had been thrown from the stretcher. He was unconscious and had severely wounded legs and as there were no other bearers about, Harry bent over and picked the man up, throwing him over his shoulder. The only thing left was for Harry to run the five hundred yards back to the aid post.

"Pleased to see you back, Harry," Charlie welcomed him. "I thought you'd had it amongst all that shit. What's all that blood running down your shirt?"

"Didn't you see me struggling back with that man? I thought I saw you watching."

"I was but I had to load this lot into the ambulance. We're ready to go now."

"Christ, that was some shit flying around out there," Harry said, as Charlie wove in and out of the uneven ground. "Do you know, I was flat on the ground when a shell dropped so close that I felt myself lift off the ground by a good couple of inches."

They spent most of the day evacuating the wounded. Then tragedy struck. Just as they reached the aid post the front wheel hit a boulder so hard that it broke the front offside spring.

"That's fucked it!" swore Charlie amongst a stream of other expletives.

Fortunately they kept a spare spring along with the other bits behind Charlie's seat, and with the help of a mechanic Charlie set about changing it.

"I think I'll go and give the bearers a hand while you're pissing about with that. There isn't a lot I can do in the aid post at the minute. They've got all the help they need," Harry said, and grabbing his satchel ran forward towards the wounded.

A corporal lay face down, his arms and legs spread-eagled. Harry turned him over, but a quick glance showed that he was beyond help. Another man lay nearby, possibly hit by the same shell. Harry placed his hand under his head and carefully lifted it. The man opened his eyes and a faint smile flickered across his face. He gasped and opened his mouth trying to say something. Harry lowered his head and put his ear close to the man's lips,

"Don't bother with me, mate, I've had my chips," he hissed out in a soft whisper.

Harry lifted the man a little higher until his shoulders rested on his knee and hot sticky bloody ran down Harry's bare leg. He cut the small pack from the man's back so that he might be a bit more comfortable, and then lowered him back to the ground. Harry had to make one of those decisions that were beginning to haunt him, and would be with him for the rest of his life. This man was dying, and there was absolutely nothing that could be done to help him, apart from sitting with him until the life finally flickered out, a time when a man needed company most. But all around them men were groaning, lying crumpled in agony. They needed Harry's attention, and yet he could hardly tear himself away. The man, a boy, could hardly have been twenty. After wetting his head with a damp towel Harry covered his forehead.

"I'm sorry, mate, but I've got to go ..." A lump the size of a golf ball filled his throat as he turned away towards the next casualty.

He returned to the aid post with his arm around a man's shoulder and helped him inside. They were still evacuating the wounded when darkness fell, but fortunately there was a full moon. The main dressing station was well overcrowded, but there was no chance of another ambulance helping out.

The next morning it was the turn of the tanks to go into action. The aid post was moved forward but even before it was set up the casualties were starting to come in. By midday they had evacuated at least forty.

73

Harry sat down in the shade of the ambulance and someone handed him a mug of tea. He took a few sips and dozed off, the mug still in his hand. The sergeant gently took it from him.

"I think your mate's knackered," a corporal told Charlie.

"He isn't the only one!" Charlie replied sharply.

They prepared to move forward again as the tanks broke through once more. they sat around waiting for the order to move as Harry asked, "Have we got to bury those blokes out back, sarge?"

This was a job that Harry was not looking forward to. The ground was as hard as granite. The sergeant shook his head. "Not this time. We've got a couple of three tonners coming up. They'll take the bodies back."

As he said it, two lorries pulled up beside the ambulance. The driver of the first, a freckled faced young man of about twenty, poked his head out of the side and shouted to Charlie, "Have you got a few blokes that's to go back to the rear?"

"Dunno, mate." Charlie jerked his thumb towards the lean-to, "Sergeant's in there." Charlie raised his voice, "You got some blokes to go back, sarge? Couple of drivers here doing a sightseeing tourist run."

The canvas side of the lean-to eventually parted and the sergeant emerged wiping his short cropped hair with a towel. Like the ambulance crew, it was his first respite in over twenty-four hours - and he wasn't in a very pleasant mood.

"They're round the back, lad," he growled.

"Send 'em out then, sarge, I want to get back before the light goes. I'm not used to this desert yet and I'm still 'aving a bit of trouble finding my way around."

It suddenly struck the sergeant that these men hadn't the foggiest idea what their cargo was. He realised that they hadn't seen much action, never mind handled dead bodies. The sergeant had a macabre sense of humour.

"I'd like to, son," he said mildly, "but I don't think that they'll be able to walk around - bit off colour, you might say."

Harry looked at his mate, a faint smile on his lips. Charlie winked, and while the lorries were making a wide arc towards the rear of the lean-to, they both dashed around to the other side. The young driver got down from his cab still grumbling.

"Don't know what kind of a bloody army this is - no discipline, wants wet nursing, the bastards." His Welsh accent became more distinctly sing-song as his temper rose. "Blokes these days won't walk a yard if they can 'elp it." He looked around for the group of men but all he could see was the rows of dead bodies all wrapped

74

up in army blankets. Then the truth struck home and his face became a mask of fear.

The other driver joined him and stammered, "God, they're all dead, Taffy." But Taffy stood transfixed with shock. Then he suddenly pulled himself together and charged to the front of the aid post, where the sergeant and the M.O. were sitting drinking tea. Harry slipped back between the lorry and the lean-to, not wanting to miss a thing.

"Eh, sarge, they're all dead back there," the Welshman's voice had a kind of helpless quiver in it. "Don't tell me we 'ave to cart all those dead bodies back?"

"Why? You don't expect those poor buggers to walk do you?" snapped the sergeant.

Both drivers were trembling and Harry wondered if either of them had ever seen a dead body before, never mind handled a couple of lorry loads.

"Well, get on with it, lad, it'll be dark soon."

If this was meant to hurry them on it had the opposite effect. Taffy's legs were shaking visibly and his throat must have dried up for when he spoke, it came out more like a croak.

"But we can't 'andle them on our own," he pleaded.

The sergeant wasn't showing any signs of sympathy and was starting to loose patience.

"You have your mate to help you."

But if anything his mate was in far worse shape. Getting to his feet the sergeant knocked his pipe against the back of the lorry, then he blew down the stem to clear it. He nodded to the drivers.

"Come on, I'll come with you."

The drivers took a long time letting down the tail gates, and the Welshman was in a terrible state, his knees shaking so much Harry expected to see them give way under the weight of his body. But he'd watched them suffer enough and with their backs turned to the rows of bodies, Harry tapped the Welshman on the shoulder. Harry boasted later that he must have jumped six feet high, but Taffy had in reality turned sharply and stared transfixedly at the bodies with renewed horror.

"What's the matter, mate, this the first lot of bodies you've ever seen?" Harry asked.

Taffy didn't answer, but just shook his head and a shower of spittle came out instead of words. "They can't hurt you, mate," Harry said, as he and Charlie lifted one on the lorry. "You get up there and we'll pass them to you. I know they're dead, but treat them with a little respect."

"I served out in India with this one," the sergeant said as he slapped the bare feet of a corpse protruding from the ends of the blanket. "Been out here donkey's years. Should have been shipped home but wanted to stay with his mates." He gave the feet another almost affectionate slap.

"Well, he's certainly staying with his mates. Of the fifty that came out from India with me, there's only ten of us left now. Some were wounded but most of them have been killed. He'll have plenty of company."

"You'd better keep your fucking head down then, sarge," Charlie said with a grin.

"Don't you worry about me, Williams, everyone here has a covenant with death. I'm very philosophical about these things. There's sod all you can do about it when your number's up. I think Jackson here will confirm what I say. I've seen men rant and scream when they knew they were dying. I've seen them lie calm and placid and greet death as if it was a long lost friend. I've watched them die with a smile on their faces and I've seen brawny six footers with tears running down their faces calling for their mothers. Scream and kick or smile or cry, they go just the same."

They finished the gruesome task of loading the bodies. Then the sergeant squatted down behind the first lorry and took his soot encrusted pipe from his pocket, scraped inside the bowl with a pen knife and blew down the stem a few times before filling it with sweet smelling tobacco.

"Anyway," he continued, "what's wrong with snuffing it out here?" He sucked at the pipe and blew out clouds of blue smoke. He spoke quietly and sincerely, almost as if he had a death wish to join his mates. "This is just as good as anywhere. When I was a kid in Yorkshire there was this cemetery in our town. I shudder when I think of it now. It was like something out of Dickens. All the grass was overgrown and the bramble was like the headstones, black with several generations of soot and chemicals from the factories. My aunt was buried there and when my mum visited it, it gave me the creeps." He swept his hand around the barren landscape. "It's nice and peaceful here."

"Don't be fucking morbid, sarge," Charlie rubbed his hands up and down his arms a few times to get rid of the goose pimples.

"Is anyone coming back with us, sarge?" the Welshman asked.

"What the hell for?"

"To take the bodies back. To tell you the truth I'm shit scared, sarge."

"No you're not. That takes guts to admit," the sergeant told him gently. "Pull yourself together, lad. They won't harm you. Remember, it's not the dead you have to worry about, it's the living. The other lorry will be behind you." He turned his attention to the other driver who so far had been silent. "Shit, he looks more scared then you do. Now, come on the pair of you, cut along and get these lads a decent burial."

They gathered around in a group to watch the two lorries depart in a cloud of dust.

"God, you're a hard bastard, sarge. They could have shacked up here for the night. It'll be dark in a few minutes," Charlie said.

The sergeant shrugged his shoulders, took a drag at his filthy pipe and then spat out the brown spittle.

"They'll have to learn, Williams, just like you had to." Hands clasped behind his back, he walked towards the lean-to.

CHAPTER 9

The division was withdrawn to the rear for a well earned rest, as the battle had been severe with men and vehicles taking heavy punishment. The vehicles were easy to repair or replace, but reinforcements were much harder to come by.

They were so far back that their only contact with the enemy was a slight distant rumble from the far off guns and an enemy spotter plane which made frequent sorties overhead. The pilot seemed to bear a charmed life, appearing at frequent intervals through concentrated anti-aircraft fire that filled the cloudless sky with black powder puff balls. It was hard to imagine any aircraft surviving such a concentrated effort to shoot it down, but the slow lumbering plane remained miraculously intact. It appeared as if the pilot hadn't a care in the world, even going to the extremes of cheekily dipping the wings of his plane in salute as he banked towards his home base.

The ambulance unit was further back than the main body of the division. They had lost two ambulances with one driver killed and two men wounded, one seriously. In open leaguer - no vehicle less then two hundred yards from the next - their ambulance was parked on the furthest perimeter, a position well chosen by Charlie. Slit trenches were dug beside the vehicles for emergency only, and by nightfall the far away guns gave off bright flashes, lighting the distant horizon in a kaleidoscope of colour.

Sheer exhaustion forced them into a deep sleep, broken only by the forces of nature. On the third day Harry lay awake, his head resting on one hand, staring at the blue skies through the open rear doors. He was smoking cigarette after cigarette and his eyes were sunken and rimmed with dark shadows. Five days' sand matted beard clung to his chin, the ambulance was filled with the stench of stale tobacco smoke and sweating unwashed bodies, and the floor was covered with cigarette butts. Harry hadn't the slightest idea what the time was - for that matter he didn't know exactly what day it was either... Not that it mattered much. One day was very much like the next.

Charlie lay still, fast asleep on the opposite stretcher, his chest a misshapen lump with Spag lying across it. But Harry was in torment, his bladder stretched to its utmost limit. He could hold back no longer and threw back the blankets and rushed for the back door. There he let out a gasp of relief and satisfaction as he watched the yellow stream of urine arch over and soak the hot sand, drying out immediately and leaving a faint white rim. He covered his eyes against the strong sunlight and was about to step back inside when he heard Charlie rouse himself. Throwing the blankets back his right foot searched for the floor, he stamped three times, and then standing completely nude in the middle of the ambulance, Spag cradled in his arms, he let out a long surplus flow of wind accompanied by an explosion that rocked the ambulance. Poised at the back door he warned Harry to 'Stand aside and let a real man have a slash!' He let go of a long stream of urine. He passed Spag to Harry, who in turn placed the dog under the ambulance against the back wheel, where he immediately cocked his leg against the wheel and let go a steady stream, Harry was fascinated. It seemed to go on and on.

"Bloody hell, Charlie, where the hell does he store it all? A few more minutes and the old tub will be floating away."

Charlie didn't answer, but suggesting that as Harry was up and about he could cook the breakfast, he collected Spag and returned to his bed. A little later, as they settled down to a hearty breakfast of greasy tinned bacon, soya links and hot tea the silence of the leaguer remained undisturbed. Not a soul was in sight. An almost deathly silence hung over the whole area as if they were all expecting a catastrophe to happen. Someone dropped a brew can against metal and it resounded like a church bell. The heat was oppressive.

"Monotonous, ain't it, Harry?" Charlie said through a mouthful of food. "There has to be something wrong with me. I miss the noise of the front when we're away."

Harry almost choked.

"There's something wrong with you all right! Have you got a death wish or something?"

Charlie grinned as he stuffed a spoonful of bacon and sausage in his mouth.

"You wait. In a few days the bull really starts. They'll have you scrubbing out the ambulance, then there's parades and inspections. Believe me, when it comes to bull, the Brigade of Guards have nothing on the Medics. Anyway, the sooner we get back up there the sooner this lot'll be over and we get to Tripoli. I just hope we get there before the Jocks and the Aussies. Those bastards drink the place dry and then wreck the joint. That gives G.H.Q. an excuse to put the place out of bounds, especially the brothels."

"That's all you think about, Charlie, bints and brothels. I thought you were a married man?" This gave Harry a chance to delve into his background without making it too obvious and it appeared to work.

Charlie laughed. He was in a good mood, the long rest having worked miracles. "Put that in the past tense, Harry. I was married, but I think I hold the army record as the first man to receive a 'Dear John' letter." His attention was drawn to two flies indulging in a bit of sex play. He watched them for a few minutes, grew tired of their game and then swatted both of them with one clean swipe. "Now that's the way I want to go Harry, when I'm on the job. It's my ambition to screw through the alphabet starting with Anne, Betty and so on. I only need an F, X and Z now. Some twat told me there were plenty of girls in Greece with names starting with X and Z. I was at the holding depot on the Nile Delta at the time and heard the Paras and Commandos often did a raid or two on the Greek islands. I volunteered, but they said I was no good as I'm colour blind. What the hell that has to do with it I don't know... Still, it turned out to be a load of bull anyway. The blokes were stitching me up." He was lying full length on the sand, his head cradled in his hands, staring up at the pale blue sky.

"What wouldn't I give for a nice brown eyed, raven haired bint now."

It wasn't a question, more of a statement directed to the sky above. "I feel like a novice priest that's taken his vows of celibacy. It's been so long now, Harry, I don't know if I could rise to the occasion if some glamorous film star stood naked in front of me."

Harry coughed out a laugh. "I bet. Do you really mean to tell me you've been through the alphabet? What about U? That must have been difficult."

"No. I had this Welsh bit in Pembroke Dock. Lovely girl. Name of Eunice."

"You prat, Charlie, that starts with an E," Harry laughed even more.

"I know it does," Charlie grinned, "but it sounds like a U."

Their conversation was brought to an abrupt halt by someone smacking the flat of his hand against the side of the ambulance. They hadn't heard him approach, his footsteps muffled in the soft sand. Now a red, pimply face appeared out from the far side of the ambulance grinning like a Cheshire cat.

"Hello, you randy pair," Sykes shouted as he sat down by Harry's side helping himself to a mug of tea at the same time, the inevitable clipboard in his hand. He wrinkled his nose. "This ambulance pongs to high heaven."

"That's very strange. We didn't notice anything until you arrived," replied Harry.

Sykes grinned. Insults fell off his shoulders like water off a sailor's oilskin. "Had a good kip, Williams?"

"Smashing... Had this fantastic dream."

Sykes moved in closer. Charlie was always good for a sexy yarn, and being a specialist in fantasy he elaborated on the smallest detail.

"Yes," recalled Charlie, lingering as he drew the word out, and gaping as Sykes moistened his lips. Sykes's mouth dropped open.

"I dreamt there was this little desert flower. Very pretty it was lying all on its own way out in the desert. Now me, I was a great hairy camel and I was bursting for a slash, and spotting this little lonesome flower I go over and slash all over it. Then I shit on it. The pretty flower fights its way through the morass and pokes its pretty little head through. And low and behold, Sykes, that little flower's face turns into your ugly mug! But the shit must have done you some good because there wasn't a single pustular spot on your obnoxious face. It was clear as a bell, although your eyes were full of shite, just like they are now."

"Still pulling those old potatoes out of the oven, Williams?" laughed Sykes.

Harry jumped inside his ambulance and folded his blankets. It had been a terribly cold night and he'd needed four blankets.

"Come on, Charlie," he called to him. "Let's give the old tub a good clean up."

"You better had," said Sykes looking down at the clipboard. "You have to report to the company office straightaway. I should get yourselves cleaned up. The old man wants to see the pair of you a bit sharpish, and I warn you, he's in a foul mood." After he'd failed to scrounge a cigarette, Sykes took a sweat stained stub from behind one ear and using three matches finally managed to light it. "All the ambulances are in now. Your mate Solly came in a couple of days ago. He's parked well over there." Sykes jerked his thumb over his shoulder, and watched Charlie running around in the nude, his one and only pair of shorts soaking in a can of petrol. Charlie jumped into the back of the ambulance his huge penis almost bouncing off Sykes's shoulder.

"Bloody hell, Williams, what a tool! Where the hell do you garage that? Down your gaiter tops?" Sykes gasped.

"Ah, I see you do appreciate the finer things in life, Sykes. One of these days, when you grow up, you too might have a tool like mine!"

"Don't want one, thanks," Sykes scoffed. "With the size of that thing it's no wonder your missus did a runner..."

Sykes shouldn't have said that. Charlie's arm struck out like a snake striking at its prey. It caught Sykes round the neck in a death-like grip. The smile froze on Sykes's face as Charlie's expression changed from a smiling boastful one to a determined deathly glare, his grip tightened. Sykes gasped for air, his face brilliant red, accentuating the bulging whites of his eyes, his arms thrashing like the sails of a windmill.

"Why, you pimply faced little bastard, don't you ever mention my private life again. Mention her once more and I swear I'll kill you," Charlie snarled. He towered almost a foot over the diminutive weed of a corporal and weighed twice as much. Sykes was on the point of collapse when Harry intervened. He leapt on Charlie's back and tried to pry his stranglehold away.

"Take it easy, Charlie, you'll put his bloody lights out altogether."

Sykes stumbled back as Charlie loosened his grip. Then he lashed out with his foot which came into contact with Sykes's rear sending him sprawling across the sand. On his hands and knees Sykes gasped for air, and it was ten minutes before he spoke.

"I'll get you for this, Williams," he threatened, his voice just a hoarse whisper. Then he pointed a shaking finger at Harry.

"You saw him, Jackson. You're my witness. He tried to murder me."

Sykes voice rose to an hysterical whisper. "This means a court martial, Williams."

"Nearly murdered you? Why, you little red faced fart, the next time I'll finish you off! Then I'll take your miserable little body out into the desert and bury it where no one will find it ... Better still, I'll leave it on top for the wild dogs and shite hawks to feed on. It would be a treat for them. They wallow in shit. Just you keep that snotty nose of yours out of my affairs, see?"

"Don't worry, this time you've had your chips, Williams. Jackson witnessed it. I nearly died. I saw all those lights flashing before my eyes and I blacked out. Jackson's my witness." Two red blotches appeared on his cheeks and neck. "You saw him throttle me, Jackson."

Harry shrugged his shoulders an innocent, almost pious look spread across his face. "I saw bugger all except you trying to bum a packet of fags. Then you lost your rag when you were refused. Now bugger off, you short-arsed bastard, before I finish off what Charlie started."

Sykes picked up his discarded clipboard and slunk away croaking to himself, "I'll get you two bastards one of these days," as he rubbed his throat. "My time will come. Don't forget the old man wants you at the office."

Charlie took his shorts from the can of petrol and flicked them at Sykes covering him in petrol. "For goodness sake, Sykes, don't smoke," he sneered, before he lay the shorts out to dry across the sand. In a few minutes they were not only dry but almost bleached white as well.

"Bloody hell, Charlie, I thought you'd finished him off. You should go a bit easy. He's in the Orderly Room and could do us a bit of harm," Harry reproached Charlie, but he was well aware of his driver's temper and should have held his tongue for a while.

Charlie turned on him. "Well, if you don't like it go and see the old man and get a change of ambulance. Or perhaps you'd be better off here in the Main Dressing Station."

"Come off it, Charlie, there's no need for that," Harry replied softly. "You know I can't stand the snidey little sod at the best of times. He grates on my nerves just as much as he does yours. Thump him if you like, I'll always stand by you, but don't kill him. Try to control that temper."

A silence that could be cut with a knife settled between them. It was akin to that between a married couple of many years standing, and it wasn't until they were on their way to the Orderly Room that Charlie spoke sheepishly, "Sorry I lost my temper, Harry, but that git really gets up my nose." He grinned. "Did you see his lights go out? Tell you the truth, Harry, it scared the shit out of me."

Charlie's attitude often puzzled Harry. He knew he was capable of violent moods but that could change in seconds. He'd seen him receive three lots of letters since joining the unit, and each time he'd wander away from the ambulance and stare at them for a while. Each time there would be just two letters, one in a blue envelope and one in an official buff envelope. The lilac one, with neat writing, he would tear into small pieces without opening, the buff one he would read then neatly fold it into the back pocket of his shorts. This, at the first opportunity, he would answer.

The company office was a lean-to canvas on the side of a three tonner situated on the far side of the leaguer. It was meticulously laid out with two tables scrubbed white, an ancient Olivetti typewriter and two makeshift beds. The room was sub-divided by a canvas sheet. It was the nerve centre of the unit.

As they entered, Sykes, sitting at one of the tables, croaked, "Williams and Jackson are here, sir."

He shifted uncomfortably on his chair and tried to concentrate on the paper in his typewriter, knowing that both pairs of eyes were concentrated on his back. A faint rustling came from behind the canvas partition. It parted down the centre and the R.S.M. stepped out. He sat on the corner of the unoccupied table not speaking for a moment or two, but wrapped a spent broken match stick around his index finger, a habit of his when something was on his mind. Broken and flexible, it wrapped right round, and he held his arm out to admire his handiwork. Then turning his attention to them he ran a critical eye over them and sniffed at Charlie's shorts. "Bloody hell! You been doing your washing in petrol again, Williams?"

Charlie couldn't deny the evidence of the unique reek. Sykes smothered his croaking laugh, but the R.S.M. turned on him.

"What's the matter with you, Sykes? Bloody laryngitis or something?"

"Don't know, sir, could be."

"Well, better go sick and let the M.O. have a shufti."

"I'll be okay, sir. It isn't too bad, sir. Just my voice gone," Sykes croaked on.

Harry and Charlie began to laugh, but the R.S.M. threw them a glance. "What's so bloody funny?"

"Not much, sir," Charlie snorted, "just thought if his voice is on the blink you should be in for a quiet time."

The R.S.M. ignored the remark and got down to the business in hand. "I suppose you two are wondering why I sent for you?" He allowed them to digest the words.

"We guessed you hadn't called us over to invite us to a party, sir," Charlie answered.

"Well, that's exactly what I want to do - invite you to a party," the R.S.M. replied. "Only for this party I need two volunteers, or to be more precise, an ambulance crew."

At the mention of volunteers Charlie shrank back and Harry didn't seem over-enthusiastic either. After his initial training at the depot he'd been warned not to volunteer for anything but they would keep an open mind until they heard more. The R.S.M. folded his arms studying their every action and expression. It was a waiting game. He wanted them badly for the job in hand and they didn't want to volunteer until they were more enlightened. After a long silence it was the R.S.M. who was the first to speak.

"The Hussars and R.E.s are throwing this party. It's rather a big stunt and holds a certain amount of danger. The officer in charge wanted a medical officer but the higher up said no. However, they could have an ambulance with a medical orderly that knew his job and a driver capable of keeping the engine running."

Charlie wasn't sure if he was trying to butter them up. He didn't think so, as it was well known throughout the unit that they were the most reliable crew. "I've heard some good reports from the various units you've been attached to," he said. He also knew that if they didn't return, he would be losing his most valuable team.

"Where's the party being held, sir?" Harry asked.

"That I don't know. Obviously it's behind enemy lines. But where - your guess is as good as mine. It's very hush hush ... You, Williams, have been on a similar stunt I understand, but I think this will be more dangerous. I'm not pulling any punches. Go away and think about it and let me have your answer in one hour. I'll understand if you refuse. Then I'll throw it open to the rest of the unit."

They stepped into the bright sunlight and talked it over, then Charlie winked at Harry and they stepped back inside. The R.S.M. knew his men. He hadn't moved from the corner of the table.

"Right, we'll go, sir," Charlie said.

"Good lads." The R.S.M. stood up. He was two inches taller than Charlie. "Let your mate Solly take care of that dog of yours. Bring your ambulance over here. They're sending a captured Italian ambulance over. Draw plenty of petrol, and you, Jackson, draw medical equipment." He gave them a chit. "Take this to the N.A.A.F.I. truck and draw your fag and chocolate rations. They'll be Italian, but I understand you get used to them after a while." Charlie read the chit outside. "Crafty sod. He knew we'd go. Our names were already on this."

Harry returned to the office. The R.S.M. was inspecting Sykes's throat.

"You did say Thursday didn't you, sir? What day is it today?" Each day was the same as the next, so they were never sure exactly which day it was. The R.S.M. looked at Sykes whose job it was to tick the calendar.

"Tuesday, sir," he croaked.

"Right," answered the R.S.M. "That gives you a full day. You have to report to the Regiment by noon on Thursday. By the way, can you drive, Jackson?"

"More or less, sir, Williams is teaching me."

They stepped outside and the R.S.M. called Charlie over. "This is an Italian machine. I want you to spend some time getting used to it and teaching Jackson how to use it. Anyway, how's he coming along?"

"Fine, sir, by the time I'm finished with him he'll be ready for Brooklands."

"Sod Brooklands! I want him to cross the desert blindfold if he has to. Or should I say, I want him to be as proficient as any of my best drivers." He wouldn't commit himself to saying that Charlie was without doubt his best driver.

They inspected the Fiat ambulance Charlie running a critical eye over every part, but his attention taken mostly by the engine itself. He stripped the engine right down and reassembled it.

Then he tuned it until, as he said, it sang like a canary, and, for the next two hours he put both Harry and the ambulance through their paces. Finally he reported to the R.S.M.

"All ready, Williams?" enquired the R.S.M.

"Jackson is ready to take that ambulance to hell and back," responded Charlie. Little did he know when he made that remark, that that was almost exactly what they would be doing. Harry gave a demonstration of his capabilities, with the whole of the unit watching, crashing the gears only once.

"Any idea how long we'll be away, sir?"

The R.S.M. shrugged his shoulders.

"Your guess is as good as mine, Williams. A week, ten days, who knows? Good luck!"

CHAPTER 10

So much for the secrecy of the operation. Within hours the buzz was around the unit. One half speculated on their ultimate destination, and the other half were envious they hadn't been selected. But everyone greeted them with the comforting words, "You want your fucking heads seen to!"

By darkness, Harry fully realised what he had let himself in for. Walking away from the ambulance he settled down, making himself comfortable on a small sand dune, as he always did when he wanted to think. Then wrapping his greatcoat around his shoulders, he stared up at the star-riddled heavens, and his mind became as clear as the skies above. Was it really six months since he's left the Sudan? So much had happened. If someone had said then that he would be penetrating behind enemy lines, he would have laughed. Yet, here he was, getting all tensed up with the forthcoming venture, and within days he could either be in the bag serving out the war in some Italian or German P.O.W. camp or, worse still, be dead and buried out in the lonely desert. The latter made him shudder. But at least there was one spark of comfort, Charlie would be beside him. In the months he's been with the unit so much had happened...

He was closer to Charlie than any other person he had known in his life, and yet he hardly knew him at all, with his personal life remaining a complete secret. All he could say for certain was that Charlie was married, parted from his wife and that he had a young daughter who was in a children's home. At times Harry looked at Charlie and saw him staring into space, not speaking for hours, his thoughts miles away. Harry would speak and Charlie would react as if he had woken from a deep trance. Then he would smile at Harry and ask him to repeat the question. But most of the time Charlie would act as if he hadn't a care in the world, which was just as frightening. For it was in these moods that he would take unnecessary risks, although his skill as a driver over some of the worst terrain in the world was never questioned and, with the greatest patience, he'd taught Harry the skill of driving. Today alone he'd had Harry behind the wheel for six hours non stop, until he was sure Harry could drive the new ambulance should anything happen to himself.

Harry had finally settled down and written those letters - six in all. Two to Victoria, who would be over the moon to receive two in quick succession. One to the matron of the orphanage and one to his old music teacher. Both would be relieved to know he was still alive. He also wrote a letter to a girl he'd met in Durban when the ship had docked there. Her family had been so decent to him, taking him all over Natal by car. And the last letter was to another girl whom he'd met in Suffolk before he'd embarked. He laughed to himself. He really had been on form, writing so many letters at once. Tomorrow he would sit down and write again to Victoria, and she would be tickled pink to get three letters in a couple of months! With any luck he would receive replies in about six or eight weeks.

It was midnight when he returned to his ambulance, but was stopped in his tracks as he reached the leaguer.

"Halt! Who goes there?"

Harry recognised the voice, and a man appeared from the shadows wrapped in a greatcoat, his face almost completely covered by a balaclava helmet. He stepped from the shadows of an ambulance, his rifle and bayonet at the high port, then he quickly lowered it until the tip of the bayonet pointed a couple of inches from Harry's throat.

"Password!" he demanded.

"Don't be a prick, Langbridge. How the hell should I know what the password is?"

Langbridge relaxed and placing the rifle between his legs, retrieved his lighted cigarette from the cab of the ambulance.

"Well, you should know, I could have had your ring piece at the end of this bayonet by now."

"It would have had a long way to travel, mate," Harry replied with a chuckle, "it was pointed at my throat."

Next morning Charlie pulled alongside Solly's ambulance, but only after warning Harry not to believe half of what Solly said.

"He's not a liar exactly," said Charlie, "but he's full of bullshit."

Charlie shouted out from the cab of his ambulance, "Solly, you old circumcised Yid, how are you?"

There was a shuffle from inside the neighbouring ambulance and a small wiry man appeared at the back, shielding his eyes from the bright sunlight. A shade darker than most men in the unit, with a shock of dark curly hair, he could easily be mistaken for an Arab. He brightened up as he recognised his old friend.

"Charlie, you old piss hole." He threw his arms about Charlie's neck. "Man, it's good to see you. I've lost count of the months since we caught up with each other. You know, Charlie, if you were kosher I'd let you sleep with me tonight. Ever thought of becoming a Jew, Charlie boy?"

"What?" Charlie feigned a look of horror. "And have three inches lobbed off the end of my chopper? No thanks, Solly, I'll stay an atheist."

"Charlie," Solly teased him, "you wouldn't miss three inches, or six, off that tools of yours. I remember the first time I ever saw it

88

at the training depot. You'd just stepped from the shower and I thought, my God, his feet are still dry. It was like watching a horror movie. I had nightmares for weeks afterwards!"

Solly had enlisted the same day as Charlie. They had passed through basic training and been posted to the unit together, and though they were bosom pals they were as different as chalk and cheese. A devout Jew, Solly would wear both his small skull cap and shawl during his devotions. This had caused some ragging by the other troops, who would have made his life a misery without the protection of Charlie, for Solly was small and wiry and Charlie towered head and shoulders above him. Charlie was a confirmed atheist but respected other people's beliefs.

He introduced him to Harry. Solly's grip was firm and strong. He looked Harry directly in the eye, and Harry stared back in disbelief at the size of Solly's nose, large even by Jewish standards. Then he was brought back to reality when another man stepped from the ambulance. He must have been all of six feet two with a thin wiry body that clung to his ribs and legs without a trace of fat. All he wore was a pair of baggy shorts which stretched to his knees, and a pair of plimsolls. Harry reckoned he must be in his mid-thirties, the spare hairs on his chest turning grey, as was the hair at his temples. He was tanned brown - but not as dark as his driver. Solly saw Harry weighing up his medic.

"Take no notice, Harry," he said. "He never speaks. Hardly spoken a couple of words a day since we came together three years ago."

"I don't suppose he gets a chance to get a word in edge ways with you around. You say enough for the pair of you," Charlie replied with a grin.

"You're right, Charlie," Solly agreed with him, "old Yorkie is a bloody good listener. Mind you, he did say a long sentence once." Solly stroked the side of his huge nose with his finger as he tried to recall the words. "It went something like... 'man is quite intelligent until he opens his mouth and then he's a bloody fool...' I'm still trying to figure out whether he was having a go at me or not."

Before the war Solly had worked the markets in the east end of London, and his stories had kept Charlie and many other men amused for hours, his main line having been imitation jewellry and cheap perfumes, like most of his family.

The exception was one elder brother who had become a ladies' hair dresser, working his way up from a back street shop in Whitechapel, through the West End, and finally to the Savoy, or so Solly had said. It didn't matter if it wasn't true, everyone enjoyed the stories. For Harry's benefit, Charlie tried to start him off on a story. There was only one way to get him going, just mention his brother. It wasn't as though he was envious. After all, he sent him regular cartons of the best cigarettes. Envy just added spice to the stories.

"How's that brother of yours, Solly?"

Solly stopped dead in his tracks. He turned to Charlie and slapped the palm of his hand against his forehead. Then rocked to and fro shaking his head slowly as if he was hurt.

"Charlie boy, I wish you hadn't asked. My poor Jewish heart bleeds for that boy. I had his latest letter only the other day. That man is suffering, Charlie, I mean suffering. Because of the air raids, they have moved his salon to the basement. He says the heat is terrific down there and he can only work in shorts and a cotton overall. Can you imagine it, Charlie? Poor lad, he really is having a bad time. Mind you he still charges his punters five guineas a time and only uses soapy water. He says the real thing is hard to get, and he still expects a tip! He has five girls he ponces for. He calls it an escort agency. He introduces them to rich guys. They think he's doing them a favour. They tip him and then he gets a cut from the girls... He's richer than some of the guys that pay him! Nice little flat in the King's Road, Chelsea and up till the war started he drove a nice little sports car. That sod could fall into a barrel of shit and come up smelling of roses. I shouldn't go on about him, really, Charlie, he sends me two cartons of fags every week. Knowing my brother, he probably gets them for fixing some man up with a bint."

Solly pulled out a round tin of fifty of the best cigarettes and handed them around. "I promise you, Charlie, and you, Harry, if we ever get back to the big smoke, I'll get us fixed up with three of the most beautiful girls you ever set your peepers on."

Solly reached for the cupboard above his head and took out a pack of greasy playing cards. "I keep asking him to send me a few packs but he says they're like gold dust. He's trying hard. I suppose one day they'll turn up."

At the very mention of cards, Yorkie stepped back into the ambulance and brought out two empty jerricans, creating a makeshift table by spreading a blanket over them. Solly placed two empty baked bean tins in the centre. One was the kitty and one was to be used as an ashtray.

"Three card brag, Charlie, and no I.O.U.s," Solly said.

"Come off it, Solly! I never welshed on a bet yet," Charlie replied.

"Who's talking of welshing, Charlie?" Solly picked up his three cards and fanned them out, covering his mouth.

"This trip of yours won't be any picnic. We would like all bets settled. That right, Yorkie?"

Yorkie took out a large briar pipe, blackened with age, and proceeded to fill the large bowl. Then he answered his driver with a nod of the head.

"Thanks for the vote of confidence! How the hell did you know what and where it is? If you do, it's far more than we do. It's supposed to be top secret," Charlie said.

Solly laughed. "Don't be a prick, Charlie. Knight is running a book on you. Everyone is speculating about the trip. They're even taking bets on whether you get back or not. At the moment it's evens you won't. I have a week's pay riding on it. Everyone is saying it's a demolition job, and at the moment the odds on that are 10 to 3 on." He readjusted his cards. "And when you leave that pooch don't forget his drinking bowl. And if the scruffy little bastard thinks he's kipping on my bed, he's got another think coming."

"Thanks, Sol, I won't forget you for this. Do you mind if I leave a few personal things behind?" Charlie asked. "There's an unopened letter for my little girl. Will you see that she gets it if we don't make it? Take it back home with you and see that she - and no-one else - gets it, won't you, Sol? Anything left of my personal gear is yours."

"What do you mean? That old bush shirt and those rotten old socks? Don't worry, mate, you'll be back," Solly assured him.

"When a ship sinks the shit always rises to the surface."

"We might get put in the bag." Charlie tried to take the melodrama out of the conversation.

"Alright, Charlie, if it makes you happy, I'll see her personally," Solly promised, "and I'll give your missus the bad news and let her know what's happened to you."

"Fuck the missus! That's the greatest regret of my life. Should I get it, she'll get a bloody good widow's pension. That's what most of the letter is about. When she gets older and can understand, I want my girl to know exactly what a shite hawk her mother is."

Harry detected the hatred in Charlie's voice. It was the most he'd ever heard him say about his family. But Charlie's mouth was clamped tight. Now Charlie changed the subject and an argument arose about who had fought shy of the kitty.

"Hello, what do we have here, a gambling joint?" A deep Glaswegian voice boomed around the interior of the flimsy plywood walls. "Any room for a braw Scottie and his wee Sassenach friend?"

Harry noticed a smaller man standing behind the Scotsman. He hadn't seen them before. Both stripped to their waists, the

Scotsman was of average height with a well-formed body, dark skin and a prominent scar ran across his forehead. The smaller man stood about five feet six, his sinewy body knotted with muscles that jerked the slightest movement of his body. His face resembled that of a weatherbeaten gargoyle and the work of a drunken plastic surgeon. The nose itself had taken a lot of punishment, broken so frequently there was a permanent red ridge across the bridge, and the tip was a swollen blob and sickly waxy colour. His right eye was half closed and showed a deep scar just above the eyebrow. Another scar ran from the corner of his mouth to an inch below the left eye and looked like it had been stitched with an oxy-acetylene welder. It was rumoured that he'd threatened someone in a Cairo bar with a broken bottle. However, the tables were reversed and instead of giving, he had been on the receiving end and his own driver had stitched the wound. Looking closely at the scar Harry could well believe the story. The face looked like a national disaster.

"Right, count me in," Jock said, throwing in a packet of ten issue 'V' cigarettes, rumoured to be made from dried camel shit and uncured tobacco. The smell of stale whisky on his breath filled the ambulance.

"Sod off, Jock, and take these with you." Charlie threw the packet of fags into the sand.

"Don't be like that, Charlie." Jock took out a round tin of fifty Woodbines.

"Sod off," Charlie repeated, and folded the cards across his nose and mouth. "Hell, Jock, your breath is foul. I don't know where the hell you get that gut rot from out in this God forsaken hole."

"Knowing the right people, Charlie," Jock winked.

"Ain't we good enough to play with then?" the little medical orderly asked, his deep Brummie accent so thick you could cut it with a knife.

"No, Brummie, every time you pair of shite hawks play it ends in a punch up," Solly said, trying to recover from the fumes of Jock's breath, of which he was getting the full blast.

"Look, Solly, scout's honour." Brummie wet two fingers, and wiped them across his throat. Then he raised them in a boy scout salute.

"Scout's honour?" laughed Solly and even Yorkie's mouth quirked in a slight grin.

"You two wouldn't know the meaning of the word honour. Let's get on with the game. Right, Brummie, you sit between Harry and Yorkie. You, Jock, sit this side between me and Charlie," Solly said sharply. "No cheating, and if you start anything, God help you. You're both lousy losers. I'm not sure which is worse, you Jock, or this Brummie Frankenstein."

Yorkie removed his pipe from his mouth. Then he opened his mouth as if to say something, but closed it again and replaced his pipe.

"Christ," gasped Jock, "I thought he was going to say something then."

"Don't worry, Jock, if there is one thing Yorkie looks forward to, it's his game of cards. He doesn't say a lot but should you bugger this game up, you know what to expect. He'll knock ten kinds of shite out of you," Charlie answered.

A sardonic grin spread across Jock's face. He didn't answer. Instead he took a flat half jack of whisky from the back pocket of his shorts and emptied half in one swig. Then he burped loudly and Harry caught the full blast of his foul breath in the face. Charlie shook his head in disgust.

"Hell, can't you leave that kidney rot alone for a couple of hours?" Solly spat the words out.

"Shut up and get dealing, you long nosed prick," Jock snarled. He'd lost several hands in quick succession and he was as bad a loser as a drinker. From inside his shirt he pulled out two packets of 'V' cigarettes and placed them on the table. Solly threw them outside.

"I told you already, we don't play for that crap. They're only fit for drunken Scotsmen and pissy-arsed Brummies," he insisted.

Jock finished off the bottle of whisky and threw the bottle outside. Then he looked around the table at the men and saw no one was in the mood for a good argument, and the half bottle of whisky he'd drunk wasn't sufficient to rouse his Dutch courage. His luck continued to fail for the next two hours during which time he had sent Brummie to his own ambulance twice for cigarettes and once for another half bottle of whisky.

With the five of them puffing madly on their cigarettes and Yorkie with his pipe, plus the stench of Jock's foul breath, the inside of the ambulance became almost unbearable. The cards, already greasy from months of use, became wet with sweat. Sweat trickled down the men's naked chests, settling in the folds of their skin, and tempers were stretched to the limit - with the exception of Yorkie's. He retained an air of patience and calm, sucking away contentedly on his pipe.

"Haven't you got another pack of cards?"

"No, I haven't. If you've had enough, jack the game in," Solly answered.

"You'd like that, wouldn't you? You long nosed Jewish bastard!"

93

The Scotsman stood up and swayed unsteadily on his feet, his heavy eyelids hanging like badly fitted curtains. Then he moved his head from side to side as he tried to focus his eyes on Solly.

"The cards are marked, you crafty bastard. You know every card by heart. Just like the rest of that bloody tribe of yours, you just can't play fair."

Solly was one of Charlie's oldest friends in the unit and he would never stand by and watch him being insulted by an uncouth drunken Jock. Now, never taking his eyes from his cards, he hissed through clenched teeth, "Shut up, Jock."

"Who the hell are you telling me to shut up?"

Jock lurched forward and shoved against Charlie's shoulder. This was a signal to Yorkie. Harry had been watching him most of the time, and he'd never spoken or shown any sign of emotion, yet Harry could detect he was waiting for something to happen.

Yorkie calmly removed his pipe and placed it out of harm's way. He moved the makeshift table in a wide sweep of his arm and in one stride he grabbed Jock by the back of his neck, just as Jock lunged at Solly. Then he pulled Jock's head down, at the same time bringing his knee up and making contact with the Scotsman's chin. He sank to his knees, and Yorkie held both his hands together making one huge fist as he brought them down heavily on top of his head. Jock's jaw connected with the metal stretcher runners. His eyes crossed as he sank down and he sprawled headlong along the floor. But Yorkie wasn't finished. His muscles rippled and knotted as he picked the heavy Scot up bodily and threw him in a heap outside the ambulance.

At this point, Brummie joined in the fight. Harry was the nearest so Brummie took a swipe at him, but Harry saw it coming and ducked. He heard the fist hiss through the air and finish up crashing through the flimsy plywood wall. Harry took advantage, seeing Brummie's hand inside the splintered wood and noting the effect of Yorkie's double handed punch on Jock, thought he would try it on Brummie. It worked. The effect was devastating. Brummie's legs turned to jelly and buckled beneath him, but not before Harry got another punch in. It opened up the scar above Brummie's eye. Blood spurted everywhere. Then Yorkie picked him up and threw him alongside his Scottish partner.

A moment later Harry wondered if his eyes had been deceiving him. Perhaps it was all a dream. Here was Yorkie, that quiet unassuming man, calmly refilling his pipe and sitting in the corner as if nothing had happened. Harry was sure that Yorkie had actually enjoyed the punch up, despite the fact that throughout the fight, although it lasted only a few minutes, the man hadn't uttered a word.

94

Leaving the two bodies where they had landed, Solly and Charlie moved their ambulances to the far side of the leaguer.

"What about those two?" Harry asked.

Charlie just shrugged his shoulders and laughed.

"Sod 'em, they'll come round later. They don't look a very pleasant sight, do they? Brummie wasn't a bad lad when he first joined the unit. Then he was teamed up with Jock. Jock's from the Gorbels in Glasgow, and it's the survival of the fittest there... Well, soon Brummie was almost as bad as his mate. They're a right pair and have been in more punch ups than they've had hot dinners."

The next morning Charlie handed Spag over to Solly. But Spag sensed they were parting, and wagging his tail with excitement let out a squeak that almost resembled a bark. Charlie rubbed his ears but didn't speak. It was the first time they would be apart since he'd picked Spag up from the Italian gun site.

"You behave yourself, you little bastard," he muttered as he gave Solly the dog. Then, turning he walked sharply away.

CHAPTER 11

It was noon when they joined the regiment, and they had very little trouble locating the column forming up for the raid. It was well away from the main body with plenty of activity around. There were two large Italian armoured cars at the head and a couple of Italian lorries, the rest of the column comprising British and Italian scout cars and utilities well intermingled. They were going to probe inside enemy territory and it was not unusual for either side to use captured vehicles.

Charlie whistled through his teeth. This wasn't his first raid, but he had never seen such a large column before. He counted six armoured cars and six scout cars. Six utilities, all, with the exception of one, had their canvas covers removed and bren guns were mounted on the cross bars, but all were fully loaded with equipment.

A stocky sergeant walked briskly over with short sharp steps. His chest was puffed out and chin pulled in. His face was as red as a beetroot, arms swinging shoulder high in regimental manner, as if he was on the parade ground back home. He waved them down.

"Taken your time getting here," he barked. "Tag on the column. The captain wants to see you. Leave your ambulance here and follow me."

Charlie didn't answer. He'd met the sergeant's type many times before. They were to be together for a long time and there was no point in making life difficult. They were taken to the leading armoured car, the large Italian job, with two officers and a warrant officer sitting on the shaded side. They stood to attention as Captain Bellamy ran a critical eye over them.

"Which one is the medic?" he enquired. Harry stepped forward and gave the officer his name.

"Well, Jackson, I'll be frank with you. I wanted a medical officer but the powers that be denied me that honour - said the job was much too dangerous and M.O.s too valuable. However, they said I could have a fully qualified orderly. I asked for the best and they've sent you. I only hope you live up to my expectations should we run into a spot of bother. Do you feel confident enough? It's going to be a very big stunt. We expect no trouble on the outward journey, but all hell will be let loose on the return. Can you cope with it?"

Harry listed his qualifications and the campaigns he had already served in, together with his desert experience. The officers all appeared to approve.

Captain Bellamy turned to Charlie. "We've met before, and I know you're a good driver. Do you think you can cope with that Italian ambulance and keep it running? Should you break down you'll stay exactly where you are. We have no room for passengers, and we'll only pick you up on our return. Is that absolutely clear?"

Charlie nodded.

"We'll be pulling out at dusk," Captain Bellamy went on. "Now, see that small utility with the almost white cover? At all times you must be right behind that and the small dingo scout car behind you. And don't, whatever you do, stray from that utility. Is that absolutely clear? That applies on both the outward and return trips."

"Yes, sir," Charlie remained at attention. There weren't very many officers he could stand the sight of but there was something different about this one - perhaps it was the glint of humour in his penetrating blue eyes. He stood up. He was three or four inches taller than Charlie, thick set and with just a shade of grey at his sideburns. Charlie put his age at somewhere in his late twenties or early thirties.

He held the inevitable fly swat in his hand and his dress was immaculate. Above thick crepe-soled 'brothel creeper' shoes, he wore perfectly fitting shorts and neat woollen socks that turned down a couple of inches just below the knees. His well pressed shirt was open at the neck, and his face and arms were tanned to a walnut brown. He looked as if he was preparing for a day in the sports field instead of organising a column to penetrate behind enemy lines. He dismissed Charlie and Harry with a wave of his fly swat.

"Right, men, go and get a good meal down you. It may be days before we can prepare another hot meal. I take it you provisioned your vehicle before you left your unit?"

Charlie nodded, then he and Harry saluted smartly and turned on their heels.

"Bloody hell, Harry, did you see those shorts and shirt?" Charlie said afterwards. "Bellamy must have a good wardrobe or a bleeding good batman. I can just see some doting mother sitting down and knitting those socks. Did you notice? Not one word about where we're going."

They had just settled down to their meal when another officer approached. Much shorter than both of them and wiry in structure, he looked scruffy wearing a South African military issue sun helmet, a bush shirt two sizes too large and shorts that reached his knees. He carried a leather jerkin over his arm and a fly swat in the other. He too wore brothel creepers, and his army issue revolver hung from his belt like some western six shooter. Harry thought he was wearing two wrist watches but one of them turned out to be a wrist compass. His public school accent, Harry observed, was toned down with a hint of humour.

"You two lads settling in alright? Been sent to look after our well-being, I believe," the officer said. His face broke into a boyish grin, and he could have been no older than Harry. Then the grin changed into a deep throated guffaw as he swatted two flies on his forearm. "Damn flies," he muttered, and lashed out again sending the fly swat skimming past Charlie's ear as he dodged to avoid it.

"Glad to have a medic along. Never know what will happen when we get behind those damn Jerries." He broke into another long laugh, treating the forthcoming action as if it were some kind of game. "Might meet a bit of bother, don't you know." He touched his hat with the fly swat in some resemblance of a salute, then strode away.

"Hell, Harry, did you hear that accent? Must have swallowed a five pound note. I bet he went to Eton."

Charlie hadn't realised how sound travelled as the officer turned with that boyish grin of his and said, "No, old boy, not Eton, Winchester actually."

A sergeant on the next vehicle laughed. "He's from the Engineers, been on a couple of stunts with him. What he doesn't know about explosives isn't worth knowing. He speaks Arabic and Italian fluently. You'll find most of the men in this column specialise in one thing or another, and most of them either speak Italian or German. We all went on a crash course to get a knowledge of the lingo. And don't be deceived by their looks," he pointed to a scruffy looking individual urinating against the back wheel of a scout car. "Doesn't look much, does he? He speaks fluent Arabic... They say he speaks it in several dialects... Apparently the further you go down the Delta so the dialect changes, like ours at home, I suppose. But Stewart understands it no matter where he is. He's also the battalion crack shot. Shot at Bisley. Those two sitting on the tailboard of that utility are both experts at demolition ... The bloke with the thick glasses, like the bottoms of jam jars, they call him Guy Fawkes. He's always boasting he intends to blow up Parliament when the war is over. He hates all politicians, especially socialists. That sergeant astride that motor bike? He's the photographer... What else do you two do apart from the ambulance and medics?"

"Screwing," Harry answered.

The sergeant shook his head in disgust.

"That's about all we need, a couple of sex maniacs."

98

The unit sprang into life with everyone shouting orders. The column formed up, and Charlie took up his position behind the utility and in front of the scout car. They moved off, slowly at first, with a twenty yard gap between the vehicles. Two motor bikes took up positions ahead of the column and two more were well to the rear, with two dispatch riders weaving in and out of the long column like sheep dogs keeping the flock in order. Small knots of men stood around watching the column, some envious and others silently condemning them as reckless bastards.

A tingling sensation ran up the insides of Harry's legs, making knots inside his intestines. It gripped the linings, pressing against his bladder. He felt he wanted to urinate and tried to relax. He knew when they were away from the regiment it would pass. Then he ran his fingers over his face and smooth chin and was surprised to see the fingers wet with sweat. But he felt far from sweaty - more cold and clammy. For nothing better to say, he said, "Here we go, Charlie, no turning back now."

They moved slowly in the gathering dusk, travelling due south. As the speed increased, Charlie nodded at the screen of sand in front.

"It's going to be a dirty ride, Harry," he predicted. The fine penetrating sand had started to work its way inside the cab through the cracks of the ill-fitting doors. Within minutes the screen was covered in a fine film, forcing Charlie to keep his face pressed hard against the glass. Harry tried to hang out the side window to clear it away, but he couldn't reach far enough to clear Charlie's side.

They continued to travel south stopping only for brief moments to enable the C.O. to take his bearings. This gave Charlie time to slip out of the cab and clear away the sand with a damp cloth, with Harry following with a dry cloth, the operation took less than two minutes. There was no moon yet, but the light given off from the clusters of bright stars was sufficient to let them see their way.

"Bloody hell, what I wouldn't give for a rest, pee and a fag," grumbled Charlie.

"Forget it. No smoking during darkness," Harry said, his nerves calming down. Like the rest of the men in the column, once they started and were well and truly on their way a strange calmness settled over them. At times the column reached twenty miles an hour, good progress for vehicles travelling in unknown desert territory, they slid down into a deep wadi where they were forced to reduce their speed, the starlight casting deep shadows from the high walls. It was midnight when they stopped for their first real rest. The sharp desert night air penetrated their clothing and the men lucky enough to own one put on their greatcoats and leather jerkins. The C.O. clambered up the side of the wadi to take his bearings. He scanned the desert with his powerful binoculars, while Charlie stood at the rear wheel of the ambulance and let out a deep sigh of relief as he released a stream of urine. He tried to suppress his wind, but had held on too long. He drew in tight and the wind came out in and elongated squeak, like a set of deflating bagpipes.

"Sign here, Jock," someone in the dark called out in a hoarse whisper, and a series of giggles ran along the column.

"Quiet!" An N.C.O. called out in a loud whisper, trying to put authority in his voice. Silence reigned once more as the officer slid down the side of the wadi on his backside.

"Why don't you get your head down in the back, Harry? Not much sense both of us sitting up here."

"It's all right, Charlie, apart from a sore arse I don't feel tired," Harry replied. He readjusted the folded blanket covering his seat, for although he no longer felt nervous he still retained his excitement and knew he would never be able to sleep. Apart from one or two rumours running along the column, they still hadn't learned their final destination or what they were about to do. Harry just couldn't understand why, if it was so important, they hadn't used the Long Range Desert Group. They all had the experience being experts at working behind enemy lines.

"Turn your money over, Harry," Charlie suggested. This was yet another of Charlie's superstitions coming to the force, as Charlie stared up at the starlit sky, where a thin slice of moon had broken through.

"What for?" Harry answered. "And what bloody money?"

"It's supposed to be lucky, and by the size of this column, we need all the luck in the world." Charlie always carried an English half-crown, tucked away. He turned it three times and kissed it for luck.

"You know, Harry, this column has been well thought up. We have this little moon going out. Every night it gets that little bigger. It's not too bright just now, just enough light with the stars to let us creep along. By the time we get back we'll be able to belt hell for leather."

Deep down Charlie admired the planning of the raid. The rumour was getting stronger by the hour that the operation was to blow a large ammo and supply dump. What puzzled him was why the R.A.F. didn't do it with a mass bombing raid. It was obvious that they knew of its location. There must be more to it than destroying the dump.

At dawn they pulled into the towering side of the wadi where the overhang almost covered them. The officers and senior

N.C.O.s came along the column checking every vehicle, making sure they were well covered. Everyone was called together for a briefing, to where Captain Bellamy stood on an ammo box, a towering impressive figure, his eyes darting everywhere making sure everyone paid attention.

"All of you are seasoned desert men and must know that all night we have been travelling due south. Another few hours driving tonight and we turn west, still following this wadi. By dawn tomorrow we will be well and truly behind enemy lines. We are staying here till nightfall. As you see, we are well covered here from the air, but," he looked around the men, making sure every one was still paying attention, "should a shufti plane make an appearance, wherever you are and whatever you're doing, just freeze. Don't move a muscle or blink an eyelid. Stand still just as if you'd been struck by lightning but whatever you do don't look up at the plane. If I or any of my officers see any man move an inch, he has my permission to shoot that man on the spot. Remember, we are a close-knit column, every man's life depends on the next man. We started as a team and I want it to stay that way. Don't dig any slit trenches tonight. Don't smoke in the open or leave any butts, bully or food tins or litter of any kind. If you want a crap dig a hole and when you fill it in make sure it's covered with fresh sand. Before we leave tonight I want a few men going around with old blankets to try and cover the tracks. I know it will be impossible to obliterate the lot, but if Jerry sees anything, it will be hard for him to estimate how strong the column is. Remember, the Jerries are not morons. No fires - sorry, lads - and no brewing tonight."

A party of six men and two bren guns were posted a mile behind the column and the same a mile ahead. Two men were concealed above the wadi, and Captain Bellamy never seemed to sleep. Whenever Harry looked around the C.O. was either sitting at the side of the wadi or walking around the vehicles. At times he would be reading a paperback or studying his maps. According to the speedo on the ambulance they had covered almost a hundred miles. Harry was sleeping when Charlie shook him.

"Eh, Harry, we covered a hundred miles last night give or take a mile."

Harry sat up rubbing his eyes. "Don't be a twat, that's kilometres, not miles."

"What's the difference?" laughed Charlie.

"Bloody hell! Divide your hundred by eight, then multiply by five. The answer is a lemon so go and suck it and see. For heaven's sake, let's get some shut eye."

But Charlie wasn't having any, and he shook Harry again. "I make that in the region of sixty miles taking into consideration the twisting and turning and doubling back. I should say we must be about fifty five miles south. At this bleeding rate we'll finish up in Timbuctoo."

For four more days they took advantage of the wadi, falling into a monotonous routine of driving by the increasing moonlight and by day hugging the walls of the wadi. Then, before their departure on the fourth day, they were called together for another briefing. Lookouts were posted while the gathered men sweated in the ferocious heat. Harry's shirt, drenched with sweat, clung to his body like a wet chamois leather, and most of the men felt it would be better to take a chance at the top in the open desert.

But none dare voice their opinion, for without exception every man had faith in their C.O. So far they had travelled four days and nights without detection, but if Jerry came to know of their whereabouts the stunt would have to be aborted.

"Our problem," the C.O. said, "is now we are so far behind enemy lines our own planes could mistake us for the enemy. Should we make contact with any of the enemy, we will have to try and bluff it out and let them think we are an Itey column. Don't start shooting. The job we have in hand is far more important than killing a few of the enemy. What I want is to go in, do the job then get out so fast you'll think your balls have burst into flames. It's more or less certain we'll be spotted on our way back so leave the fighting till then." He stuck out with his fly swat. "Any questions?"

Every man appeared to be waiting for this moment, and several hands shot up. "Yes, sir, where are we going and what are we doing?"

The C.O. smiled. "Don't kid me. You've all been making wild guesses and you all have a good idea. I wouldn't be in the least surprised if all the gyppo bints from Cairo to Tobruk knew all about this stunt. However, it's all rumours, let it stay that way. Should it fail and we get put in the bag before we get there, what you don't know you can't tell. All I can say at this moment is the job's very important and you will get all the excitement you crave. You have your special jobs, do them well. I know you won't let me down. In years to come you'll be able to tell your grandchildren what you did."

Harry could sense the confidence of the C.O. rubbing off on to the men. He was the type of officer who could lead his men to hell and back and everyone would enthusiastically follow him.

"Tomorrow we will be leaving this wadi," he said. "No doubt most of you will be relieved to hear that. We'll be crossing over open ground. Then we can all brew up. You will be wearing Italian caps and this will be an Italian convoy. Now try and get some rest."

They settled in the shade for the day. The heat became more oppressive by the hour. At noon the sun was high above them, stripping back what little shade there was. Harry suddenly sprang up into a sitting position. He and Charlie were stripped to the waist.

"Christ sake, Charlie, don't move ..." He swung his arm across Charlie's chest and sent a large scorpion flying against the wadi wall. Then he jumped up and looked around. "Look at these bastards, Charlie." He ground several scorpions into the sand, and Charlie, still half asleep, sat up.

"What's up, Harry?"

"Sodding scorpions, mate. We must be on a nest of them. I felt this large sod walking across my face, it's tail upright and wagging like a boy scouts flagpole." Harry loosened his shorts and shook them to make certain none were hiding in the creases. "Get one of those sting your balls you'll never know what hit you," he warned Charlie. A dark shadow passed over them and a shite hawk glided gracefully over their heads, its wing tips moving slightly as it lifted on the hot air rising from the wadi. Normally it would have been a perfect target for Charlie. But Charlie was preoccupied with the scorpions.

He hated scorpions and spiders and a great deal more, but he would never kill one of the latter. He said to kill a spider was unlucky. He had no such compunction about killing scorpions and it took three cigarettes to calm him down. The heat was becoming more intense - the ground shimmering. A terrible silence stalked the ground. They felt they were intruding, as if it hadn't been disturbed for a million years.

It was impossible to sleep, so they strolled towards the next vehicle, a small armoured car, its crew, also unable to sleep, sitting in the shade.

"How goes it?" asked Harry.

A corporal answered, "Not bad."

Like the rest of the crew he was stripped to the waist, continually wiping the sweat from his back and chest with a towel. Every inch of the corporal's chest was covered in tattoos, as well as his arms and shoulders. Reaching down to his wrists, hardly a square inch of skin had escaped the tattoo artist's needle, and a few done recently still retained their glorious colours. Now a battle started between the corporal and a large fly. It would land

103

on his forearm to be lost in the array of colours. Then the corporal would take a swipe, but the fly beat him every time. Undaunted, he took out a large pipe, lit it, and blew the smoke over the fly. Enraged, the fly took off and landed on the next man.

"What's the matter with you?" Harry turned to another man as he limped past.

"Nothing, just twisted my leg. Must have slept badly," he muttered.

Harry knew cramp when he saw it and this wasn't it. "Better let me take a look," he insisted. Harry walked towards his ambulance but the man turned and limped off in the opposite direction. This made Harry even more suspicious and he persisted, but the man was obstinate.

The corporal became suspicious as well. "Get over to that agony wagon, Tyler," he ordered, "and let the medic have a shufti at that leg. Come to think of it, I noticed you limping the other day."

Quickly Harry lifted the leg of the man's shorts and gasped, silently whistling through his teeth. "How long have you had this sore?" he asked, concern in his voice. "Lay on that stretcher and let me clean it off. You silly prick, you must have been in the desert long enough to know not to let a desert sore go unattended. That's asking for trouble. What with the flies and sand you could get gangrene in no time."

He couldn't light a fire, so he boiled some water using one of his concentrated meth blocks to sterilise a spoon. This done, he scraped away the festering puss. The sore was almost an inch deep and gave off a nauseating odour. He cleaned the wound and sprinkled it with sulphanilide powder.

"How long have you had this?" he wanted to know.

"Just a couple of days," the man answered.

"Bollocks! This sore is over a week old, maybe two. I suppose you wouldn't report it in case you missed this trip. Well, you stupid bastard, you may have damaged that leg permanently. I'll have to report it to Bellamy."

Harry had hit the panic button. The man sat up straight, his voice raised. "What for?" He sounded more scared of the C.O. than the damage to his leg. Captain Bellamy had insisted that only the fit were wanted on this stunt. "There's no need for that, medic."

"Yes? And what will happen if you contract gangrene? Let me give it to you straight," Harry snapped at him. "That wound is in a very dangerous condition. I don't intend to stick my neck out for a stupid bastard like you." He dressed the wound, told the man to report back every two hours while they rested and took the man's temperature. It was just above normal but he put that down to the extreme heat. Then he turned to Charlie who had been watching the operation with the keenest interest. "Better use a couple of meth blocks and make him a brew. We can have a bit of breakfast, too. Do it in the back of the ambulance."

It took far longer to boil the water on the meth blocks than on an open petrol fire, but soon the wadi was filled with the fragrant aroma of frying bacon and soya sausages. The tattooed corporal moved in nearer, breathing in deeply, and soon a small crowd gathered around.

"My mouth feels like the inside of a miner's clog," the corporal said, smacking his lips as he watched the bacon curling up in the makeshift frying pan. Harry closed his eyes and also smacked his lips as he took a noisy sip. It was their first tea since they'd set out. He winked and nodded his head at the tattooed corporal.

"Twenty fags for a mug of tea," the corporal's voice was almost pleading. Harry shook his head and took another tantalising sip, slurping loudly.

"Fifty fags. I'll give you an unopened tin of fifty Players."

Harry shook his head and wished the Q.M. had given him a few more boxes of meth blocks. He could make a fortune here. The smell of frying bacon hung on the still air and filled the wadi with its mouthwatering aroma. Soon more men gathered around and then the bartering started with promises of untold wealth in the form of cigarettes. But Harry just shook his head. This raid was an unknown quantity and the meth blocks must be saved for emergencies only.

Captain Bellamy strolled over to see what was going on. He looked over the men's shoulders and drew in a deep breath. A faint smile crossed his lips. "Good show, lads," he said and turning, slapped the fly swat against his legs.

The day wore on with increasing monotony. The walls of the wadi pressing down on them with claustrophobic severity. The heat was overpowering and the men shuffled around like zombies in some horror movie. Charlie referred to them as the living dead. Fortunately every vehicle carried far more water than they expected to use so they were able to replace lost fluid. Charlie had also managed to scrounge half a dozen bottles of beer. These he had wrapped in wet blankets and placed under the seat. Sand drifted along the wadi floor, and it took a few seconds before they realised it was the evening breeze that greeted the dusk. The men stood facing it, their chests bared, breathing deeply at the cool air. Charlie opened a bottle of beer, drank half of it and then passed it to Harry. Now the tattooed corporal really thought he was seeing things - drinking tea had been a minor miracle, but there they were, the two of them, sharing a bottle of beer ... What's more it looked cool.

The corporal turned to his mates. "See that pair over there? Sodding medic and his mate drinking beer? Anyone would think they were on their firm's outing." He shouted across to Harry, "Are you sure you haven't got a cocktail bar in the back of the wagon?"

The red faced sergeant came striding along the column, cane under one arm and the other swinging in his usual barrack square manner. He threw a glance at Charlie who was still clutching the empty beer bottle, and giving way briefly to military discipline he ran his tongue along his lips. Then he pulled himself together and snapped, "Bury that bottle, driver. Don't leave any tell tale signs around."

"Having a kit inspection before we go, sarge?" Charlie joked.

"Don't be funny, son, leave that to ENSA. You heard what the captain said, don't leave any visiting cards."

Charlie smiled and muttered to Harry from the corner of his mouth, "Who ever said ENSA was funny?"

Dusk fell abruptly and the column moved off sharply, the moon a bit stronger now, giving off sufficient light to allow them to increase their speed. They travelled through the night without incident, without stopping, and as dawn crept over the horizon, much to everyone's surprise, they just carried on. Then they speeded up with Captain Bellamy taking the lead in the large Italian armoured car. At full speed, they took a steep gradient and emerged from the wadi onto open desert and fanned out. They knew what dangers they faced now, both from the enemy and the R.A.F. but everyone was completely relieved to have left the wadi. It was better to face the enemy than be roasted alive. They were just happy to be on the final lap and no longer driving in a fog of sand.

The sun was high above their heads when they made their first stop. Harry and Charlie rushed along each side of the ambulance, both heaving a sigh of relief as they urinated against the back wheels. Then right across the column came the sound of brew cans being untied from the vehicles, the men almost hysterical with the prospect of their first hot tea since leaving the regiment. Acting like dipsomaniacs they sipped mug after mug of hot tea, impervious to the heat.

A motor bike roared round the vehicles with the red faced sergeant bellowing out orders. "Just act naturally. Any enemy planes swanning around, should they come down to investigate, just wave to them. If the R.A.F. come snooping, spread out, with you, Williams, tagging right behind that small utility."

Harry shrugged his shoulders, a frown on his face. That was the second time they had been told to stay with the utility.

CHAPTER 12

The run down the wadi had been tedious, uncomfortable and claustrophobic, with its towering sides trapping the heat and turning it into something akin to a baker's oven. And, although the vehicles were well spread out, the fine sand created a fog-like atmosphere which penetrated every nook and cranny. It was almost as bad in the cab of the ambulance as outside the wadi which made life extremely uncomfortable. The men's eyes and noses became clogged with fine sand.

Harry heaved a sigh of relief as the column raced to the top of the wadi and stretched in open leaguer across the desert. He no longer felt the tingling sensation that run up the insides of his legs, stretching into his guts and clenching it tight like two enormous hands. In the open desert there were three options left. He could soon be standing before his maker, or he would be starting to spend the rest of the war behind barbed wire in some P.O.W. cage, or they could all be on their way home after a successful operation. He, like the rest of the men, was banking on the last option. After all, Captain Bellamy had brought them this far without a hitch - a miracle in itself - and surely they couldn't be very far from their final destination.

Just before dusk they stopped for a meal and also to rest up for the night. Harry prepared two stretchers outside the ambulance feeling far more confident. Sleep came easy that night. Charlie, too, did not find it hard to sleep.

Long before first light the column was standing to, waiting for dawn to creep over the horizon and, as the first rays of the sun stretched out across the sand, brew cans came out and a hurried breakfast was prepared. They were soon on their way with orders to fan out across the desert. On the far horizon and well to the left of them small black blobs filled the sky, until soon they spotted three darker specs hurtling towards them - the shapes unmistakable.

"Christ! Those are hurricanes and they're heading straight towards us. Be bloody ironic, Charlie, if we were finished off with a bullet made in Brum."

The three planes circled high above them, and came down with a roar to get a closer look, the roar of their Rolls Royce engines drowning the punitive sound of the ambulance engine. Charlie took evasive action, swerving first one way then pulling hard on the steering wheel until the ambulance tilted on its outside wheels, righted itself, and immediately banked on the opposite side trying all his strength as he fought to control it. He hit a boulder and the ambulance shook. How he wished he could have their own ambulance, he could turn a somersault if he wanted to do so. The planes' engines roared again and came into a steep dive, this time with all guns blazing.

The column, swanning around like fairground dodgem cars, was in more danger of colliding with each other than being hit by the planes' bullets. Then, just as suddenly as they appeared, it was all over and the planes roared off into the distance without leaving casualties.

"Lousy shots," Harry said as he nervously fingered his unlit cigarette.

"Don't be bloody stupid, Harry. That was for the enemy's benefit. You forget we are well inside enemy territory. Perhaps there's an enemy unit up ahead. They may have spotted them and we were attacked to make the gunners look good."

The sun was high above their heads when they made their first stop.

"Must be noon," Charlie said as he tilted his head. Charlie never wore a watch and forbade Harry to wear one.

They'd just settled down to a tin of meat and veg when Charlie spotted sand rising on the horizon. He focused his powerful binoculars on it, but it was ten minutes before he recognised several vehicles emerging from the heat haze.

"Looks like we have company, Harry."

Charlie already knew about Captain Bellamy's warning with regard to panicking. He casually walked over to where he was sitting with two other officers in the shade of the large Italian armoured car.

"Enemy column approaching, sir. I think they're Jerries," Charlie informed him bluntly and handed the captain the powerful binoculars.

"Right, men, there's a German column approaching. Act natural. Get the brew cans going. Use coffee this time. Some of you start shaving. Gunners and drivers, keep near your vehicles just in case. The remainder of you keep your rifles at the ready."

The German column was small. It was just three armoured cars and a half track. Captain Bellamy was relying on the animosity of the enemy. The Italians hated the Germans and the Germans despised the Italians. He was hoping they wouldn't come too close to investigate, although the column was strong enough to wipe out the Germans with little trouble. It was the last thing he wanted and his hunch paid off. The German column stopped three hundred yards away.

The tingling sensation rose up the insides of Harry's legs again. In three years of war this was the first time he'd come face to face with the enemy. He'd seen many POWs and attended many enemy wounded, but this was his first contact with the enemy where he could see their features and hear their voices.

Charlie had a much better view. He lay full length under the ambulance and studied their ugly mugs through his binoculars. He smiled to himself when one man took a shovel. Then, when he thought he was out of anyone's sight dropped his shorts and went about his business.

"God, Harry, one of them is having a crap," Charlie chuckled. "What a beautiful target he is from here. One word from Bellamy and I could have a bullet right up his ring piece!"

The German commander went into conversation with his second in command and repeatedly laughed and pointed towards the column with an attitude of utter contempt for their allies.

Captain Bellamy called Corporal Waring over. He was fluent in both Italian and German, having worked in both countries for several years. Waring, stripped to the waist, was wearing Italian plimsolls and an Italian forage cap.

"Go and see what our square headed allies want, Waring, that's a good chap. Try and wheedle a bit of information out of them."

Waring slouched over to the German column both hands in his shorts pockets and threw up as sloppy a salute as any Italian would. Then he became immersed in a deep conversation with the German officer, gesticulating and throwing his arms about in true Italian fashion. He and the German talked for a full five minutes before he strolled back to report.

"He wanted to know where we came from and our destination," Waring disclosed the contents of their little chat. I told him I was a captain and it was none of his business. He got a bit bolshie and complained the Germans were doing all the fighting while we, the Italians, are doing nothing put sing and play with our puds. I told him we were returning with a couple of British prisoners, and he said that he'd spotted us earlier and wanted to know if the British planes had done any damage. I told him they'd hit a couple of our vehicles and wounded a man, but nothing serious. We chatted on and I told him we have to get back to Tripoli and hand over our prisoners to H.Q. then get fuelled up. He said there was a large fuel depot less than thirty miles from here and wished me luck!"

"Are you sure he fell for your story, Waring?" Captain Bellamy wanted to know and Waring nodded emphatically.

Once more the German officer stared at the column through his binoculars waved and turned soon to be obscured in the heat haze that floated on the distant sand.

"They fell for it, Harry," Charlie whooped. "The bloody bastards fell for it! I told you that bloody air raid was a phoney. I

110

was certain the bastards would come to investigate. That Bellamy sure is a cool customer."

It was well past midday when they moved off. They followed the German tracks for a couple of miles and then turned sharply south, travelling several more miles before coming to a halt. The half moon lit up the sandy wastes with a fluorescent glow and they were called together for a final briefing.

"Right, men, we're almost at our final destination. So far luck has been on our side. You saw Jerry come to investigate after we were strafed. We were lucky they didn't come in too close - put that down to the love between our enemies... They could have radioed their base, although that's improbable or they would have wiped us out by now. Our chaps twiddled around on our radios but they didn't hear any messages being flashed around. Now, I've reccied this place several times from the old shufti plane and I have a good idea of its layout. From here we have about ten miles to go and our target is probably one of the largest ammo and petrol dumps in North Africa. We're going to destroy it completely." Captain Bellamy gave them a few minutes to allow the enormity of the drill to sink in.

"Why didn't the R.A.F. bomb it, sir? Why such a large raiding party?"

"Good question, Spencer, and one I was hoping someone would ask."

He looked at the sea of expectant faces staring back at him waiting for an answer they would all like to know.

"Well, this dump serves most of the Italian army and some of the Jerries. What we want is the records as well as destroying the dump itself."

He hesitated and spread out a large map on the canvas side of a utility. There was sufficient light by the moon without using the torch he held in his hand and he pointed to a large shaded square. "Now this is the dump. About a mile off it's circled by anti-aircraft guns. Don't worry about them. The road we use passes right through them. It's used by columns all day long, though very rarely at night and when it is used for nocturnal activity there's not much cause for concern ... These records are important," he emphasised, "and what plans are being made to move the dump as the allies approach. After we finish with it tomorrow that should be the least of their worries."

He passed several aerial photographs around for the men to study.

"As you can see the dump has two large barbed wire fences right around its perimeter. They're a hundred feet apart. The dump is staffed by low category men. We don't know the exact strength of the staff - it's twenty-five maybe. When we approach, the outer guard opens the first gate. I will take the first large Italian armoured car. The second one must follow me and our own little scout car will be the third. Now Jenkins will be behind the turret of the second armoured car with a pickaxe handle in his hand, but I don't want any shooting or we'll have those ack ack boys round us like flies round a pile of dog shit. As the sentry opens the inner gate, Jenkins will slide out of the car and, as quietly as possible, put the inner sentry out of action with the pickaxe handle. At the same time Renshaw will be behind the turret on the scout car, and he will do likewise to the sentry on the outer perimeter. Hudson and Willis will immediately take over the Italian sentry's job.

Now this operation is very important, and will have to be done with as little noise as possible. Once this part is over, the rest of you put on your own British steel helmets, if you do have to finish anyone off, you must use your bayonets. I don't want you, in the confusion, to start stabbing one another up the arses. You're all seasoned desert men, and you know how sound carries. I don't want any of those long range snipers from the A.A. guns to come snooping around. Now, you radio wallahs, the wireless hut is right behind the guard room just inside the dump, and as soon as you hear us inside the guardroom and the orderly room, you get into that radio hut and take over the radio, where you must monitor any incoming calls. I know you're both good at Italian, but take Waring with you - he's fluent." He paused to allow his orders to sink in and give them time to study the aerial photographs.

"Now, good luck to all of you. By the way, this is a dump. There may be some decent stuff laying about. Take care not to grab too much though. The last job like this the men loaded their vehicles with all kinds of goodies and they could hardly move." A ripple of laughter went through the assembled crowd.

"Right," Captain Bellamy restored order. "You form up the column in line, twenty yards apart. We'll be hitting some kind of road shortly that leads straight to the dump."

They stopped once more to form up on the road and a dispatch rider came alongside and gave them their final instructions.

"The dump is just over this incline," he said. "I'll be behind Captain Bellamy. We've just passed the A.A. gunners and it was all very quiet. I bet the stupid bastards were still asleep." He pointed forward. "We go over a wooden bridge, over a wadi in a few minutes. Then, we'll be dropping a couple of sappers off, so for fuck's sake don't run over them."

Ten minutes later they passed over the shaky wooden bridge, its planking long since dried our sounding like muted drums as they bounced up and down under the ambulance wheels. Two ghostly figures, dragging haversacks behind them, slid from a utility and as silent as snakes slithered under the bridge.

The large dump loomed up ahead resembling more a P.O.W. cage under the eerie silver glow of the moon. Harry felt that queer sensation riding up the insides of his legs again, and his feet trembled until he pressed them hard to the floor of the ambulance to stop their involuntary shakes. Before the gate swung open there was a brief conversation between the sentry and Captain Bellamy. The Captain spoke harshly to him and he threw up a sloppy salute. Then the first three vehicles entered and there was a pause before the second gate swung back on its rusty hinges.

Then it all happened so quickly it was over before Harry realised what had happened. Jenkins and Renshaw slid from the backs of the armoured cars, swinging the pickaxe handles so hard that Harry heard the crack as they made contact with the Italians' skull above the noise of the ambulance engine. Both sentries slumped forward. Two men jumped from the back of a utility and helped Jenkins and Renshaw drag the sentries into the shadows before picking up their rifles and taking their place. Not a moment too soon - for the curtains of the guardroom parted and an Italian officer looked out. Then addressing himself to him, Captain Bellamy saluted and waved, but the Italian officer didn't appear to be too pleased at being disturbed at night. He dropped the curtains and they waited for him to come to the door. Obviously he was quite satisfied the sentries had done their job properly and so far the operation had gone entirely to plan like a stage play run by a top director.

The ambulance was soon inside and stopped right outside the administration office. A thin sliver of light showed under both doors. A gramophone was scratching out an old Neapolitan tune on an equally old gramophone record. Harry felt himself humming and tapping his toes to the rhythm of the music, his underlip trembling. From the other office came the tinny sound of an ancient piano, while another man was doing his best to outshine the great Caruso himself and failing miserably.

Captain Bellamy, his heavy service revolver in his hand, stood at the guardroom door with his sergeant beside him. At the other door another officer prepared himself with a revolver, a corporal with a sten gun beside him and then at a given signal they simultaneously kicked both doors open.

Six men sat at the table playing cards, the table was littered with wine bottles and the room filled with tobacco smoke. The table went flying as the men stood up, hands held high above their heads staring at the large apparition at the door who stood grinning, his British steel helmet set at a rakish angle on his head. They stared unbelievingly at the revolver.

The piano player slowed down his playing and the singer wound down like a church organ running out of wind. As his voice faded, his hands came together in supplication and he whispered several 'Hail Marys'. The scene developed into one fitting for a comic opera, as the singer sprang up and his shorts - he must have had the two top buttons undone - fell to his knees. The men were now ordered to stand in front of the table and they walked towards it like puppets pulled along on strings. Then Captain Bellamy began to bark out orders in fluent Italian. Men were sent to the sleeping quarters and half asleep the Italians were herded into the guardroom. Two more were dragged from their cots in the outer room.

"Why you dirty little Itey, playing with your pudding, you will go blind you know."

Trooper Masters led a small Italian prisoner into the guardroom holding his ear. The man must have been about the lowest medical grade possible. He tried to hold his spectacles on with one hand, the lenses were so thick they resembled the bottoms of jam jars.

"There - I told you so... You are going blind." Masters took the glasses and held them up to the dim light bulb then whistled before handing them back. "Come on. Let me see if you have any hairs in the palm of your hand," he jeered and unclenched the man's fist.

"Don't piss about, Masters. Keep your eyes on this shower." Bellamy read standing orders. "Should be twenty-seven men. How many have we rounded up?"

"One man missing, sir," the sergeant replied.

Captain Bellamy briefed the Italian C.O. He appeared to be in a trance from which he seemed to hope he might emerge any minute to find the appearance of the British had all been just a bad dream. The men that understood Italian burst out laughing. The missing man was sitting on the lavatory afraid to come out.

"Shall I go and get him, sir?" Masters asked, fingering his rifle and bayonet.

"Don't be a shit, Masters. Let the man finish in peace. If there's one thing I hate it's being disturbed when I'm communing with nature. You just stand outside till he comes out and I've no

114

doubt he'll crap himself again when he sees your ugly face looming at him."

Only minutes before the Italians were going about their normal duties without a care in the world. For three years they'd been safe and snug with a deep concrete bunker right outside the guardroom back doors. A bunker that could have stood up to the largest bomb ever invented. Between the dump and the allied front guarding them from any intrusion from the enemy stood the German and Italian armies. They were also heavily fortified by a ring of anti-aircraft guns. Now they stood in various modes of undress before a guard of British Tommies. Two men, in the process of packing to go on leave the following morning, stood shivering with fright. They were unaware of what the future held. Captain Bellamy became involved in a conversation with the Italian C.O. Then he turned and called Harry over.

"Right Jackson, it's time you earned your keep. It seems they've no medical staff here. Their M.O. calls once a week from Tripoli. They've lifted their two injured men into their beds so you go and have a shufti and see if there is anything you can do for them."

Harry examined the first man. "Looks like this man has had his chips, sir." He raised the man's head gently and his hand came in contact with a jellied mass. "I doubt if he'll be long for this world." But after he'd examined the second man he told Captain Bellamy, "Not too bad, sir. He seemed to take the blow on the side. He'll be out for a few hours though. I think he may have a fractured skull. So long as he isn't moved he should be alright. Mind you, I'd fancy his chances a lot more if he could go into hospital straight off."

"Too bad, Jackson. Get the man patched up. He must come along with us. We can't leave him here."

"But it'll kill him, sir. I wouldn't call that ambulance very stable, sir. It'll rock the guts out of him when we go over that rough ground."

Captain Bellamy shrugged his shoulders. "Sorry, Jackson, we can't leave him. Should he come round after we've left he could tell everything. Best to take him - sorry and all that... Besides, when we leave, what will happen when this place goes up? He'll go with it."

Masters returned prodding a small uncooperative Italian ahead of him with the tip of his bayonet. The Italian was stripped to the waist, one hand held high and the other holding his shorts in position. Just a few minutes earlier he had been concentrating on the call of nature and dreaming of his mama's spaghetti and special bolognaise sauce back home in Italia. He'd been so sure of his safely this far from the front line. Undoubtedly he'd prayed to the Holy Mother every morning and night and attended mass at every possible opportunity. Also, to be on the safe side, he'd prayed for the Pope and Holy Mother Church itself, and he'd vowed, perhaps, that should he survive this war he would consider taking Holy Orders. So devout - or superstitious - was he that he wore several saint charms and carried not one but three rosaries. Yet the Holy Mother, all the saints, the Pope and dear Jesus himself had failed him completely, it seemed - for here he was trembling and staring death right in the face as he peered down several black revolver barrels. His lower lip shook and he blinked rapidly, his dark complexion greyish with fright, and he looked to all the world as if he might burst into tears at any moment.

"The little sod heard all the commotion going on in here and locked himself in the karzy," Masters said as he bent down to remove his plimsoll. "Hurt my bloody toe kicking the door down." The big toe was already turning a darkish blue. Masters clipped the small Italian's ear. "You are a naughty, sodding little Itey, mate, that's what you are." He tapped him on the elbow with the tip of his bayonet. "Come on, raise your arms."

His whole body shaking with fright, the Italian's glance jerked around each of the grinning faces and slowly he raised one arm, his other hand clutching tightly at his shorts.

"Come on, raise the other." Masters tapped the other elbow and indicated what he wanted.

The Italian looked stupefied. One of the others of his race spoke to him. He clenched his knees together and slowly raised the other arm, but the shorts like most of the Italian uniforms were far too large and the tops buckled over and his shorts fell down.

Masters gulped and stared at the man. "Christ sir," he spluttered to Captain Bellamy, "just look at the size of that little sod's tool. Almost down to his knees, it is... For a man so small he's not only got his share but someone else's piece too. Bloody hell," Masters whistled enviously, "he must have been in the front rank when tools were issued!"

"Don't be bloody disgusting, Masters," Captain Bellamy reprimanded him, shaking his head. "Let the wretched man pull up his shorts... Just who the hell wants to stare at that gross damn thing, anyway? More likely to frighten a woman than attract her, I would think."

But the officer failed to control the twitching hint of a smile which played around the corners of his mouth.

CHAPTER 13

With the plans of the dump set out on the table before then, the officers and senior N.C.O.s went into a deep conference.

"It's much large down here than it looks from the air." Captain Bellamy remarked. He turned to the engineer officer.

"How are we getting on with the charges?"

"About another two hours, sir." He pointed to the chart.

"We started here and are working out way downwards. I have ordered the screw tops of the petrol drums to be opened, but I won't pour the petrol out until the last minute. One of the men may get careless smoking and I want to be a least five miles away when it goes up."

"Sergeants Heslop and Waring, you go and get all the records. I was just going to take what was needed but we can use a couple of Itey trucks and take all the filing cabinets. What time are the fuses set for, Mr Nightingale?" the captain asked.

"Six thirty, sir. If we leave at five that will give us plenty of time to put a fair distance between us and the dump."

Orders were given to find out who was the cook amongst the prisoners and get him making breakfast.

"See if they have any Italian food around - I fancy a plate of pasta," the captain ordered. A corporal returned with two prisoners. He spoke to them in Italian but the taller of the two answered in perfect English with a strong cockney accent. Captain Bellamy looked up from the plans of the dump.

"Good God man, your English is perfect - if you can call cockney dialect English."

"It should be sir, I was brought up in Hackney for fifteen years, ever since I was six years old."

"Right lad, we'll have a long chat later. What have you in that larder of yours? Prepare my men some food and some for your mates down below in the shelter. If you have any pasta, make some - it will be a change from bully beef and hard tack."

"Plenty of food here, sir. When they come in for stores, we usually feed the drivers. We have tinned bacon and soya sausages, we nicked them from your own dumps when we overrun them. We also have eggs and tomatoes and German sausages, and there's plenty of cold cooked chicken, sir."

All eyes shot up at the mention of chicken. There was much licking of lips to prevent saliva running down their chins.

"And bread, sir. It's a bit dark but we get fresh bread sent up every morning. It comes up with the P.O.W. working party."

"What do you mean, P.O.W. working party? What time do they get here?"

"Seven thirty, sir, give five minutes either way."

"Right lad, get into your kitchen with your mate here and cook up breakfast. Sausages, eggs, bacon, fried bread and tomatoes. If you have any tea make tea for the boys and coffee, if you have any, not the Jerry ersatz crap. The cold chicken you can cut into portions with plenty of bread and butter, put the lot in a container and we'll take it with us."

Captain Bellamy turned to the assembled officers and winked, "Nothing like a nice desert picnic on the way home. Put some bottles of vino aboard, too. I suppose you have plenty of vino?"

"Yes, sir," grinned the Italian.

After the two Italians departed, Captain Bellamy thumped the table, "That's buggered it. Two lorry loads of prisoners come through those gates at seven thirty, just as the bloody dump goes up. I wanted to be near that wadi by the time this place went up, or at least well on may way to it."

He turned to the Engineer Officer. "Mr Nightingale, call your men and alter those fuses. Better make it eight thirty and let's hope no one comes in before that, seeing a dead sentry and no one around, they'll know something is wrong."

He felt he could kick the table over. Harry had never seen him in this state since he joined the column.

"When we've eaten, get that man in again and see what happens when they arrive. Send me the wireless operator."

Charlie was sent down with the cooks to keep an eye on them. He sat on the corner of a table watching every movement, the smell of bacon and eggs frying bringing hunger pangs. The Italian gave him a mug of tea.

"How come you're out here with this shower? You a bloody fascist or something? Waited for Dunkirk and old Musso to stab us in the back then couldn't get back to Italy fast enough to help bite the hand that fed you for fifteen years."

"You have to be kidding." It sounded like he had picked up plenty of Americanism - watching too many Hollywood movies, no doubt.

"I had applied for British citizenship just before the war. I went home to visit my mother in the August of thirty-nine, she's a widow with just me and my sister. She lives in a small village just south of Naples."

"On my last night with my mama, we were sitting down to a meal when the front door was kicked down and four military police rushed in. The local fascist leader informed on me, said I was an Italian and a deserter. I'd dodged my military service. It seems this bloody fascist was after my sister and she said she wouldn't marry the fat pig. The bastard took it out on me. Next

118

thing I know, I was running round some army barrack square in northern Italy. If I had stayed in London, I would be wearing that uniform now. Bloody ironic, isn't it? To rub salt in the wound, a few days after I was in the Italian army my uncle in England sent me a letter saying my application for citizenship was more or less accepted. I had a smashing job, too. I worked at the Savoy in London."

Charlie almost choked on his cigarette. Recovering slightly, he said, "You did say the Savoy?"

The Italian nodded.

"How long were you there?"

"Seven years - I went there straight from school. Only job I had. I wanted to be a chef, and I would have been. A bloody good one, too. I loved the job, and my girlfriend, she worked there, too. Fucking war, fucking Mussolini and fucking fascists."

Charlie laughed.

"Never mind your girl or Musso or the fascist pigs, you certainly swear like a trooper. Did you know a Leboff that worked there? Supposed to be a hairdresser."

"What do you mean, supposed to be? Abe Leboff was a hairdresser - the best." His dark brown face spread into a wide grin showing a row of perfect white teeth.

"God, man, Abe was one of my best friends and I tell you what, mate, it was an honour to have him amongst my friends. What a man! He had every racket under the sun going. The women loved him. Apart from his nose, he was a good looking guy."

Charlie laughed.

"That's him. If he has a nose like his brother, it must be Abe."

"Why, do you know his brother?" A look of astonishment spread over his face.

"You joking, Solly is in our unit. We enlisted together - been together since the war started."

The little Italian became excited. "Do you mean that Solly is here with your men? Here in this dump?"

"No, he's back at our own unit. This is just a raiding column, we've come to blow the joint up."

The Italian whistled through his teeth. "God, man, this is one of the biggest dumps in North Africa and we're only a few miles from Tripoli."

"Well," remarked Charlie, "it will soon be the flattest!"

"What about the prisoners?"

"We'll stop for them. How many are there?"

"About forty, British and Australians. Between nine and ten in the morning the men from the ack ack guns come over to see if they can scrounge some grub. We won't get many columns in

119

tomorrow, it's Sunday and the prisoners only come to clean up. All the Aussies do is come here to see what they can nick. They caught one of them pouring sugar into the drums of petrol. He's very lucky, they wanted to shoot him, but the general said no, he would go to prison for life. He's no fool that general, he knows this war is lost."

They lifted trays into the guardroom and office, piled high with crispy bacon and eggs with sausages and tomatoes and plenty of tea and coffee. Charlie told the captain exactly what the Italian had told him.

"Thanks, Williams, I'll give him a going over shortly."

It was the first bread most of the men had tasted for months. They ate slowly, savouring every mouthful, and the Italian cook had made the tinned sausages and bacon taste as if they had been cooked in the kitchens of the Savoy itself.

The two Italian trucks carrying the prisoners were lightly guarded. The driver and officer in charge in the leading truck and two sentries in the back. The second truck had a sergeant and driver in the front and two at the back.

"Are you certain about the time they arrive?"

"Yes sir. All the time I have been here, I have only known them be late once, and that was when one of the lorries broke down. I know the Italians are sloppy and unpunctual but the officer in charge of the prisoners is a real fascist and tries to throw his weight around."

Two Italian speaking sentries were posted at the gates. The hours ticked slowly by, the men continually looking at their watches. A deathly silence fell over the party as if every man dare not speak. Someone broke wind. A ripple of laughter went through the group.

"Was that you, Harris? Sounded like a pansy's love call."

Another ripple of laughter.

"Alright, Harris, cut it out laddie," the Scots sergeant said in a hushed tone. They should have been preparing to leave when a golden line painted the distant horizon, the stars above them faded as the sun flashed its rays across the barren sands, converting the sands into a series of fascinating colours. No one could help but admire the changing scenery.

"The Bedouins say if you spend forty days and forty nights in the desert you always want to return," the captain said to Lieutenant Nightingale.

"That's ballsed me up then," Jenkins said as he overheard the comment. "I've been out here for four bloody years!"

Captain Bellamy consulted his watch again and calculated they were already twenty minutes behind schedule. He called the cockney Italian in again.

"Now, when these two lorries come in, tell me exactly what happens from the minute they arrive."

"Well, sir, the front gate is opened, the sentry doesn't bother closing it again, then the second gate is opened - that stays open, too. The prisoners get out and stand by the guardroom. The officer goes direct to the officer and hands in the chit. Two men are detailed to each lorry to help load at the ammunition pits. The remainder of the P.O.W.s are detailed for various jobs around the dump but they get up to all sorts of tricks. I think they only volunteer for the job to see what they can scrounge. That's about it, sir."

"You say they leave both gates open once they are in?" Captain Bellamy smiled. "That will suit our purpose. They won't be suspicious when we leave with the gates wide open, what about the sentries?"

"They don't always stay there, sir, once the fascist officer goes. They are all shit scared of him - even the officer in charge here, although he's senior rank. He's as bad as any SS officer, him and another corporal who comes with him. A right pair, I can tell you."

"Right, Waring. Get in that bunker and tell those Iteys not to smoke or try and light any cigarettes. Sergeant, tell the men here to do the same. Make sure all those cookhouse fires are out. Mr Nightingale, take a few men and stick a few pickaxes through those petrol drums. You're sure to find a few picks in the stores. Make sure you open the drums in every pit, when they light up the heat will cause all the other drums to explode all over the place. Unscrew a few of the tops and throw in a few belts of ammunition into each pit, just to make sure."

Another party was detailed to load up several land mines in the utilities.

"When we get down that wadi, we can lay a few behind us, it will slow them down."

All eyes were on the road leading to the dump. Tension was mounting. If the cockney Italian was right, there was just fifteen minutes to go. The men were back into their Italian hats, some standing by their vehicles making out they were servicing them. Waring was talking to a sentry, three or more stood near the gates trying to look inconspicuous. They saw two columns of sand above the slight rise in the road then they heard the engines. The two men acting as sentries picked up their rifles. The front gate

121

opened when they were first spotted, the lorries passed through and stopped while the inner gate opened.

The fascist officer turned on Waring and shouted about the sloppy attitude of the sentries and opening up before they arrived. "We could have been British for all you cared!" he shouted as he walked straight into the office, first dusting off his shiny boots before entering.

Captain Bellamy was sitting at the table in his Italian uniform. The Italian was berrating him for the sloppy turn out when the words faded as he failed to recognise the officer. He looked at Harry who was bent over the sick Italian. A puzzled look spread across the officer's face, no one had informed him there had been a change of personnel. Captain Bellamy casually took his service revolver from its holster and lay it on the table, without speaking. Harry couldn't believe what was happening. The two officers just stared at one another.

"Jackson, just go over and take that Beretta from the Italian officer's holster."

Harry walked over. The officer never spoke, he just stood there like some wax work statue. He lay it on the table in front of the captain. It was a full five minutes before the silence was broken. The Italian opened his mouth several times but no sound came out. He stuttered and stammered. Bellamy put his elbows on the table and held his clenched fists in front of his mouth, waiting for the Italian to recover from the shock

"Give the officer a chair, Jackson."

Harry pushed a chair behind the officer. He sat down sharply, still staring unbelievably at the captain.

"Would you care for a brandy," the captain asked him.

The Italian nodded, obviously he spoke English. The captain ordered Harry to get a bottle of brandy from the cupboard. The Italian gulped down a glassful.

"I suppose this has come as a bit of a shock to you but you see we have just captured this place and in a few minutes it will be blown to hell."

The Italian looked around terrified and finally regained his voice. "But you can't, you're supposed to be more than a hundred miles from here, I saw the maps yesterday."

"No, you're wrong. Most of our army is fighting their way up here and they must be at least two hundred miles away, but we are here and you, sir, are now a prisoner."

While this was going on in the office, another charade was happening at the gates. The Italian sergeant was off to the toilet as usual, followed by his own corporal. Jenkins was waiting outside with his sten gun pointing at them as they were leaving.

Slowly they raised their hands. Jenkins led them towards the bunker. Waring went to the rear of the first lorry.

"Right, you guys get out of the lorry after you've disarmed these two prats at the back."

No one moved, they all looked at one another.

"What the hell's the matter with you pricks? Do you want to spend the rest of the war as prisoners?"

"Jesus," a man said and slowly rose to his feet. The two Italians froze in their seats. Suddenly there was a mad rush as the prisoners leapt from the lorry.

"The bleeding Poms are here!" an Australian voice shouted.

"Bloody hell, it's taken you long enough to get here. Is the cowing war over or something?"

"No such bleeding luck, mate," Harris said. "We've just come to get you shower out of it. Resting on your arses in some P.O.W. cage well out of the way."

A tall Australian looked around him. He was without a doubt the tallest man Harry had ever seen, looked around him.

"Where has that Italian corporal vanished to?"

There was hatred in his voice. He adjusted his well worn and soiled diggers bush hat and snatched a sten gun from one of the men. A sergeant stood in his way.

"Lay off, Digger. Don't shoot the bastard, we don't want to wake those gunners up. What's he been up to, this Italian corporal?"

"Been up to?" he glared at the sergeant. "That dago swine only killed my mate, kicked him to death, the dirty rotten swine. You might think the German SS are animals but they're nothing compared to this fascist swine. He loved to show off when the Jerries were around, at least to prove he was as good as they were. He would kick out at any P.O.W. especially the small blokes, and always aimed for their balls."

The Australian went in search of the Italian corporal who was outside the toilet with his hands in the air staring down at Jenkins' sten. If he was scared, it was nothing compared to when he spotted the Australian striding towards him. He sank to his knees begging for mercy before he was within ten yards. The Aussie grabbed his hair and hoisted him to his feet, then brought his knees up with a thundering crash between the Italians legs. He screamed with pain and writhed along the ground like a wounded animal. The Aussie lifted his feet and brought his size ten army issue boots down on his face with all the strength he could muster. Harry came rushing over and placed himself between the Aussie and the Italian.

123

"Pack it in mate! I have enough to do now. I have two sick Iteys inside now, I don't want another."

He pushed Harry away and sent him flying, landing on his back a few yards away.

"Don't worry, mate, you won't have this one to look after! I'm going to kill him, just like the swine killed my mate."

Lieutenant Nightingale and the sergeant came rushing over.

"Stop this at once! This man is a prisoner and has every right under the Geneva convention."

"So had my mate. It didn't stop this bastard from killing him! Now piss off and let me get on with it. Sod you and your Geneva convention."

"This man will come back as a prisoner and be tried in the proper manner. If he is found guilty, he will be shot."

"Save your bullets, mate. I swore I would kill him and that's what I mean to do." He bought his foot back and kicked the Italian in the jaw, his head snapped back, blood trickled from the mouth and ears.

Harry bent over the Italian and felt for the man's pulse. "He's dead, sir. The neck is broken."

The floor of the guard room was littered with butts when Harry entered to examine the two Italians.

"This one is dead, sir."

"How about the other man?"

"In a bad way, sir. He needs hospital treatment - shouldn't be moved yet."

"Sorry, Jackson, but we're preparing to move off now, better put him in the ambulance."

"He'll die, sir. He should be kept still and quiet."

"Well, Jackson, if he's left here he will surely die. I want to be at least ten miles clear of this place when she blows"

Captain Bellamy walked from the hut as smartly as walking across the parade ground back at Tidworth. One of the ex-prisoners, forgetting his military discipline, ran across and shook Captain Bellamy by the hand, pumping it up and down like an old farm house water pump.

"Sir, it's so good to see you again." Tears ran down the man's sunburned face. "Captain Bellamy, sir."

"Why, it's Corporal Lane. It's good to see you, too. We'll talk later." He called the N.C.O.s together.

"Are the ex-prisoners fed?"

They nodded.

"Alright. Bring the Italians up and get them back in their trucks." He smiled to himself as he ordered several of the British ex-prisoners to drive and guard them. The remainder of the ex-prisoners were distributed amongst the small utilities.

"What happened to him, sergeant?" He pointed to the dead Italian in front of the toilets.

"He had an accident, sir. Sunstroke."

Captain Bellamy looked up at the cloudless sky. It was hot, but not enough to give anyone sunstroke. He asked no further questions.

"Right, get him standing over one of the ammo pits. There's another dead Italian inside, stand him over another pit, prop them up with something. The place won't look deserted with those two hanging around."

The Italians were herded into the two large lorries.

"One word from you as we near those guns and you'll all get a burst from this gun." Waring menacingly swung the gun around.

"Keep quiet and no one will get hurt."

They passed the nearest gun site without incident. Several gunners waved and the raiders waved back. They kept to the rough road for several miles before turning towards the wadi and home.

CHAPTER 14

It wasn't a case of every man for himself but resembled something of a race as they made all speed for what little protection the wadi would give. When that ammo dump blew, all hell would be let loose.

The ambulance swayed and bumped over the uneven ground. The small vehicle, unlike their own back with the unit, had no communicating door from the front to the rear, only a tiny windowless panel. Harry kept a continual watch on the unconscious Italian in the back. Fortunately he had had the foresight to strap him into the stretcher.

"You don't think Bellamy has any intention of shooting the prisoners, do you, Charlie?"

Charlie laughed. "I shouldn't think so, Harry. Mind you that Aussie let that Itey have it. Did you see the poor sod's face?"

"Yes, I did. He shouldn't have done that," Harry replied.

"It's all very well for us to sit back and say what he should or should not have done. When you get a real Fascist Itey they can be worse than their S.S. counterparts. He had every reason to do what he did if what he says is true."

"Perhaps so. But handing out justice like that makes us no better than the worse Fascist or S.S. man. Far better to take him back and try him by court material."

Charlie wasn't interested in the rights and wrongs of warfare. He had seen enough injustices so far. At the moment he was much more interested in dodging the boulders and bumps over the uneven ground.

The column stopped near where they had been attacked by their own planes. Captain Bellamy dropped from his armoured car and called Sergeant Legge over. Sergeant Legge was from the Army Cinematographic Unit and an expert photographer. They walked to the top of a rise, where it was possible to get a view of the dump and they studied it for a few minutes through their powerful binoculars. The dump remained deserted, the two dead Italians still propped up by the ammo pits.

"Right, Sergeant Legge, what do you think? Can we get a decent picture from this far off?"

"I can only do my best, sir. I have some very powerful lenses. The air is clear." The sergeant smiled. "It will be like taking a family picture back home." He attached a long lens to his camera and focused on the dump.

"Right, Sergeant Legge, you have your motor bike. As soon as the dump goes up get the pictures and get out of here as fast as possible. We are well behind now. Waiting for those prisoners costs us time. Follow our tracks to the wadi. We will leave a D.R. there and a jerrican of petrol. We intend to keep in the wadi as long as possible. There are so many wadis about they won't know which one we are in and I don't want you going up the wrong one. Good luck, sergeant."

The column moved out. Harry threw a glance at the lonely figure, legs wide apart and head resting on his arms, his camera and binoculars beside him. Charlie picked up the tracks of another vehicle but kept his distance. He didn't want his windscreen obliterated by the dust. He had his foot pressed down to the floorboards and the ambulance groaned in protest at the punishment it was taking. Both Harry and Charlie were wishing that they had their own one. Harry jammed himself tightly into his seat with his feet pressed hard on the dashboard.

"The poor bastard in the back won't make it if we keep this up, Charlie."

"I am sorry, mate. It's either him or us and, frankly, I would rather it be him. The sooner we get to that wadi the better. It may not give us a lot of protection, but it's better than out in the open."

The column came to a brief halt. Harry ran to the rear and swung the doors open. He made a quick examination of the Italian and bathed his forehead with cold water.

A dull drone filled the still air and the azure sky clouded with powder puff balls of smoke. A squadron of heavy bombers escorted by fighters battled their way through.

"Jesus, Harry, I just remembered them. They were supposed to come when we blew the dump. How the hell did they know we were two hours late? They will be in for a surprise when they find it still intact."

"Oh no they won't. Look!"

Charlie pointed towards the direction of the dump. A cloud, mushroom in shape, blotted out the sky and a few seconds later they heard a low rumble and felt a warm blast of air. Brilliant flashes slashed through the dense smoke. Tons of debris and sand blotted out the light as if a deep fog had settled on the horizon. From this distance everything looked as if it were happening in slow motion, and further mushrooms of smoke sprouted skywards, centres illuminated with brilliant flashings. Every man was hypnotised by the scene unfolding before his eyes.

Charlie stood fascinated, the cigarette in his hand still unlit.

"Christ," he exploded, "that must have been the biggest bang of the war. I was dubious when this trip started, but watching that was worth every minute of it. It's absolutely incredible."

"Right, lads, we have seen the fun. Let's get to that wadi," an N.C.O. shouted. The message was passed from vehicle to vehicle.

Harry took another look at the Italian and, again, bathed his head with cold water. The man's breathing was shallow and dark circles appeared around his eyes.

"He won't make it, Charlie," Harry muttered. "The poor sod is burning up."

"We won't make it if you don't jeldhi (hurry)," Charlie snapped back. "The others are almost out of sight, so let's get cracking, Harry."

Charlie's dexterity with the wheel soon made up the distance between themselves and the column. They caught up just in time to see a small utility's front wheel hit a boulder. The vehicle skidded along the ground spinning crazily, its driver tugging at the steering wheel in a frantic effort to regain control of it. It hit another boulder. This proved too much for the small overloaded vehicle. The front off-side wheel buckled, sending it skidding along the ground and digging a deep furrow with the stub of its axle. Charlie swung over to see if the occupants needed assistance, but another utility had seen their plight and raced to their assistance. One man limped from the vehicle and willing hands helped him and the driver into the rescuing utility.

With sighs of relief the members of the convoy reached what protection the wadi could offer, but they knew they couldn't be certain of that once the enemy knew their whereabouts.

Once more the high walls of the wadi closed in on them, and the heat became oppressive. The sun cast dark shadows along one wall, the column hugging them closely. A small scout car was ordered half a mile forward, while another was detailed to bring up the rear. Both were to warn of any attack from the enemy inside the wadi.

"Just take a shufti at that stupid bastard showing off," Harry pointed to a D.R. standing on the pedals of his bike rough riding along the perimeter of the wadi. Harry became absorbed in the D.R's performance. He would ride the perimeter for a while, study the desert with his binoculars then ride down again. Whenever he spotted an opportunity to get to the top he would roar up at tremendous speed like a circus performer on the wall of death.

"One of these times there will be a bloody great square head at the top holding a bloody great machine gun, and he will blow his sodding head off."

"I hope not, Harry. If we get caught down here we will be like sitting ducks. Let the prick show off if he enjoys it. I suppose he's been detailed to do the job."

128

Charlie adjusted the red sweat rag around his neck, then wiped the sweat from his forehand with the back of his hand. Harry lit two cigarettes and passed one to his driver.

"Just think," he said, "we were so near to Tripoli with all those lovely dark eyed Itey bints. While the boys were laying those charges and pissing about at the dump we could have borrowed a motor bike and roared down there, found a couple of bints and stayed in Tripoli till the Division caught up with us. What wouldn't I give to run my hands through a senorita's silky dark hair, get this dirty water off my chest and get my feet under someone's table while being served a real civilised meal, cooked to perfection, and washed down with chilled white wine. Then I'd loll around afterwards sipping black coffee and brandy, and to round it off I'd carry some raven haired beauty off to bed."

"You mean, dine them, wine them then screw them."

"That's right, Harry," Charlie slammed his hand down on the steering wheel. "You have just described it in a nut shell."

Harry laughed and shook his head. "Stop living in a fool's paradise. Whenever did you take a girl out for a meal and have wine with it?"

"Never, but the thought was there. After all you can't blame me for having dreams. I did see it at the cinema once or twice."

"Yes, and your dream ends there." Harry stifled a yawn and tried to make himself comfortable. They had been without sleep for almost thirty six hours. He folded up in his seat and dropped into a comatose sleep, only to be rudely awakened by the roar of a plane engine as it swooped low over the wadi. The sky darkening towards evening, the roar of the plane's engines savagely assaulted his own and Charlie's ear drums.

A couple of scout cars managed to get in a few bursts of their bren guns.

"Sodding Jerry shufti plane!" Charlie cursed it. "Now we'll be in for it when he gets back and lets his mates know where we are."

Slowly the plane's engines faded into the distance.

Stringing out made them less vulnerable. Many of the men would have preferred taking their chances up top where they could open out across the desert. However, the entire column was divided on the issue. The ambulance crew were determined to take a chance on top convinced that having been spotted, a clear getaway might be more likely. The wadi had been their salvation on the way to the dump but the situation had been different as the enemy had been unaware of their presence. Now an enemy column skillfully directed could pick them off like flies in a jam jar. Their one and only consolation was that every mile they made was just that mile nearer home. But everyone, at this point, was resigned to the reality that they could expect the worst at any time.

With the help of the almost full moon, brighter than on the outward trip, they were able to keep up a steady pace throughout the night, even though the men were exhausted and the overloaded vehicles taking a lot of punishment.

The sun had hardly crept over the horizon when they received their first visit from the German Air Force. Three stukas flew majestically overhead. They couldn't help but spot their target below with telltale clouds of dust spiralling skywards. The planes banked, then screamed down, levelling up and screaming away as if they were just selecting their targets. They reached skywards, with a nerve shattering roar, as if to gain height, so they could swoop screaming terrifyingly towards their targets. One after the other they banked and then, with a hysterical scream that sounded as if the wings of the planes were tearing themselves from the fuselage, they dived at their selected targets. One after the other the bombs rained down while the planes levelled off. The wadi reverberated in explosions. One bomb embedded itself in the wadi walls before exploding and bringing down tons of sand. A small scout car ran into the avalanche, shook itself like a terrier, and emerged in a cloud of fine sand, unscathed. The remainder of the column was able to skirt around the fallen wall.

The attack seemed to last hours when in fact it was only a few minutes before the last stuka came in for a dive. Harry could plainly see the rivets on the underside of the plane. The roar of its engine filled the wadi as the egg shaped bomb plummeted earthwards, screaming like a demented banshee. The bombs narrowly missed the ambulance, shaking it violently. Red hot shrapnel tore through the air, embedding itself harmlessly into the walls of the wadi. The machine gunners were ready for the last plane and as it dropped its bombs, it flew along the column and a row of bullets ripped through its fuselage. More bullets raked the wings. A thin column of white smoke trailed from its rear getting wider as it soared away. A huge black ball of smoke belched out from its engine, and it coughed like an asthmatic old man. The plane tried to gain height, the wings flapping erratically while the pilot struggled with its controls. Then as if it had hit an invisible wall it stopped in mid air, pancaked, lifted its nose in a kind of curtsy, flattened out again and roared into an uncontrollable dive hitting the sand with a great flash and bang. It was all over so quickly that the pilot had neither gained any height nor had a chance to bale out.

The two remaining planes circled above their heads. The gunners, confident of their first success, pumped bullets into them. One plummeted down, guns blazing, skimming along the wadi and filling it with the acrid stench of explosive as it released its last bomb.

The D.R. came roaring towards the ambulance.

"Utility had a direct hit, and one of those lorries carrying the Itey prisoners was strafed."

Harry set up an aid post in a small recess in the walls of the wadi covering the top with tarpaulin. It was big enough to take the ambulance and two utilities. Captain Bellamy came over to see what it was all about.

"The two men from the ute are dead, sir," Harry explained. "Two Italians dead and five wounded, one very badly. I doubt if he will make it. And one of our ex-prisoners wounded. I will have to put a splint on his leg. The femur is broken and it looks as if a bullet is jammed in it, but he should be alright."

"Right, Jackson," Captain Bellamy replied, "we will have to push on. I am leaving these four sappers with you and we are dropping the prisoners off here. Jerry knows where we are and it's overcrowded in those lorries, what with the filing cabinets and the Iteys as well as a few of our own men. Luckily when he shot up the lorry he did very little damage to it. Get those Iteys burying the dead. We have left the prisoners plenty of water and food and with luck they will be picked up in a day or two. Is that Itey in the ambulance still alive?"

"Just about, sir. I will get this leg case in the back and strap him down well. I have plenty of morphine. The other wounded can travel in the backs of the utes."

"Right, Jackson. I will leave them in your capable hands. You can catch up with us when you have finished. We will get out of the wadi as soon as possible. When I find a way out for all the vehicles I will leave someone there to show you. Look after yourselves."

Harry worked on the wounded for almost an hour, the Italians' officers watching every move. The four sappers had their stens trained on them, although they didn't offer any resistance as they were glad to be shut of the back of the three tonner. The four graves were dug, the Italian officer, a devout Catholic, said a few words over them while the Italian prisoners kept crossing themselves, thankful to have survived the ordeal.

The Italian cockney cook succeeded in persuading Captain Bellamy to take him along. With the breakfast he had served, it took very little persuasion on his part. The following weeks he would be working in the officers' cook house. They also took the senior Italian officer.

131

Harry made the wounded as comfortable as possible under the makeshift awning. He left them a few medical supplies including morphine. One of the sappers speaking Italian explained to the officer how to use the drug.

"They will be picked up in a day or two," Harry said. "They have enough water and food to last a week."

They rejoined the convoy two hours later. One of the utilities stopped several times to lay mines. Should they be chased up the wadi, the mines would slow the enemy down. Soon after they rejoined, the column came to a halt. Captain Bellamy called the men together, with the exception of the gunners who remained alert in case of further trouble from the air.

"Right, men." Captain Bellamy never raised his voice, speaking calmly and to the point. " We got away with few casualties then but next time we may not be so lucky. We must get out of this wadi as soon as possible now they know we are here. In the meantime the D.R. up above is keeping his eyes open. Well, we gave that Jerry pilot what for but don't let it go to your heads. The Germans are not morons, they know what to expect and won't take any more chances next time. I don't want a repetition of wasted ammo. We are still well behind enemy lines and may need every bit we have. Just wait till you see the whites of their eyes, or at least the rivets on the fuselage. Sergeant Legge will be with us soon."

His speech was interrupted by the roar of a motor bike engine reverberating against the sides of the wadi. Sergeant Legge skidded to a halt beside them. Legge lifted the celluloid sand shields from around his eyes, leaving a white mark, the remainder of his face was encrusted with sweat stained sand baked hard, and his mouth cracked open into a wide grin.

"Perfect, sir, just bloody perfect, I have some of the most magnificent pictures you are every likely to set your eyes on."

A few of the crowd hung around to hear any more information and Jenkins burst out laughing. "I hope you didn't forget to put the film in your camera, sarge."

Sergeant Legge cast a withering look at Jenkins.

"Don't say such stupid things, Jenkins, not even if its meant to be funny." He cautiously turned the camera, making sure the film was inside, although he had repeated the operation several times, checking it thoroughly.

"I thought the game was up when two more lorries approached. They hesitated when they got inside the gates and two men climbed out and went over to the dead sentries. They just pushed them over and walked around completely bewildered, but one of them must have spotted a charge because suddenly you couldn't see their arses for dust. The lorries swung round almost on two wheels. But two more lorries were just coming up and they collided at the gates. They jumped out and started running in all directions. The lorry at the back tried to reverse. He went haywire and backed into the outer barbed wire fence knocking one of the gates off its hinges. It lay across the lorry and he couldn't move. Burning drums of petrol went flying through the air and it was just like watching those naval destroyers launching their depth charges. The offices and guard room were the first to go up, just like tinder boxes. It looked like a lorry from the gun site came along to see what was going on. The driver stopped on that wooden bridge, then all of a sudden there was this mighty bang and the lorry actually sailed through the air like some kid's model car."

"How many men were in the dump when it went up?"

"Hard to say, sir. At that distance, twenty, maybe."

"But the best, sir, was when the R.A.F. came over all the gunners on the ack posts. They were more interested in the dump and they hardly fired a shot. I bet the R.A.F. got some very good aerial pictures, sir."

"Right, Sergeant Legge, keep those films in a safe place - an old ammo box - I don't want them destroyed. Guard them with your life. Now let's get away from here. We have had one visit from the Luftwaffe and managed to get one of them."

"Yes, I know, sir, and I took some photographs. The pilot was still inside the cockpit."

The leading D.R. came back and, without cutting his engine, saluted.

"The scout car has found a way up, sir, and it looks like enemy activity about. I saw several columns of sand on the horizon."

"Which side?" The Captain asked.

"Both sides, sir, although there is more on the left. There is a way up on the right, sir."

"Right. That's the way up then. Get mounted men."

Real action was imminent. Captain Bellamy changed his Italian cap for an Arab head dress which had been given to him when he was seconded to an Egyptian regiment before the war. He treasured it and always wore it when action was about to happen. It was some sort of lucky omen. Just as some of the fighter pilots carried a rabbit's foot or some other lucky charm. Now, with his deep tan, he sat on the turret of his armoured car like some Arab desert fighter.

Charlie nudged his mate.

"Thinks he's bloody Lawrence of Arabia."

Sergeant Legge overheard the remark.

133

"Less of that, Williams. Bellamy is alright. Remember he brought us all this way with little harm. We could have been away from that dump a couple of hours earlier, but he took a chance and waited for those prisoners. He comes from a very wealthy family and with their influence he could have settled for a cushy number back home. His family have had connections with this regiment for generations, so keep it closed, Williams."

"No harm meant, sarge. Me, I like the bloke, sooner have him than some of the officers I've met."

CHAPTER 15

It was almost daylight, the sky dulled by a false dawn that gave way to a deep blue sky. The stars paled and finally disappeared as golden fingers of sunlight probed the desolate wastes, giving the sands and scrub a fascinating collection of colour that had hypnotised conquerors, travellers and Arab nomads for centuries.

The column roared on, spread across the desert in a wide arc, each vehicle only distinguishable by the columns of sand shooting out from the rear. Although the ground was still firm there were deeper sand drifts that added to their discomfort.

"What the hell is that, Charlie?" Harry pointed to what, at first sight, looked like a small outcrop of rock.

"Let's take a shufti."

Charlie swung the wheel over and within minutes pulled alongside the remains of a soldier in khaki uniform, completely skeletonised. He, or what was left of him, lay spread eagled, the bleached white bones gleaming in the bright sunlight. The skull with its permanent grin and sightless eyes stared up at the cloudless sky. The wristwatch strap, like some devilish torture instrument, hung on his wrist. A regiment of ants had taken up residence in the tattered uniform.

"It's a Jerry, Charlie. How the hell did he get here?"

"By the look of that hole on the top of his skull he must have been stonked by a plane."

"But why the hell didn't his mates bury him. Look around you, there are no vehicle tracks and certainly no signs of footmarks, not even his own. Just a bit of a mess where the shitehawks came down for a feed. I mean he hasn't been dead all that long or his body would have been covered with drifting sands."

He studied the skeleton and the area directly around it, a puzzled look on his face. He searched the pockets for any means of identification but all he found was a packet of dried up cigarettes.

"It's bloody strange, Charlie. Did you ever read Robinson Crusoe? Well, one day after he had been marooned on his island, he was walking along the beach and came to one solitary footstep, nothing else, just one footprint. Although it was half way up the shore, there were no prints leading to it." He picked up the man's forage cap; inside was his name, rank and number.

"I will take this back and make a report, perhaps the Red Cross will trace his family."

"You're not taking his watch then?"

"No bloody fear." Harry was like the remainder of the men in his unit and was surprised Charlie asked. They were superstitious about carrying loot taken from a dead person. Convinced it was a sure way of courting disaster, they knew of only one man in the unit who defied that rule.

"Chalkie White would have had it. His ambulance is like Aladdin's cave. He reckons he intends to finish this war a rich man. His poor driver shits himself every time they join a regiment."

"I won't go along with that, Charlie. Robbing the dead isn't my way. Poor bastards. Let's cover what's left of him with boulders. We can't hang around here too long. I don't suppose anyone will find him."

"Well they do say, rest in peace." He looked around the miles and miles of sandy wastes. "There can't be anything more peaceful than this anywhere in the world."

"You know, Charlie, that D.R. that was supposed to wait for Sergeant Legge and never showed up. Looking at this skeleton here has made me think of him. I wonder if he came off his motor bike somewhere and is laying down pinned underneath it, rotting away, all alone." He gave an involuntary shudder.

"Gives you the creeps, don't it."

Harry made his casualty comfortable in the back of the ambulance. The joyride over the bumpy ground hadn't affected him too much. He gave him a drink of water. The delay cost them another two hours before they caught up with the rest of the column.

Suddenly, and without warning, the screams of three planes deafened them. Flying low in V formation, they suddenly peeled off as if they were giving a flying display, then skimmed across the vehicles. The sky was cloudless and the planes turned and came in at them with the sun directly behind them. Rows of bullets ripped up the earth with their tell-tale fountains of sand. A small utility vanished in a cloud of smoke and bright flame. The pilots were no novices, they were making the best use of the sun as a backdrop blinding the gunners - who were seasoned desert fighters and realised the tactics. At the third swoop the gunners on the armoured cars had their backs to the sun and waited till they were over the column, then they poured bullets into the leading plane. The rescued prisoners fired the captured Italian rifles at the plane, which zoomed for the sky.

The wheels of a second utility buckled under and it reeled over onto its side, ploughing a deep furrow along the ground for several yards. Two men staggered from the back and ran for safety behind a large outcrop of rock.

Two planes converged on the column from different angles, trying another tactic, realising the troops below them were no amateurs but seasoned desert troops. One plane directed his fire towards one of the large captured Italian lorries. The troops inside had removed the canvas top and saw it coming and baled out, except for the Australian sergeant and a sapper from the Engineers who stayed with their two bren guns mounted on the cross bars, pumping several magazines of ammo at the oncoming plane. The lorry jerked to a stop as the driver and his mate dived for cover. By some miracle, neither the ex-prisoners nor the driver and his mate were hit.

Charlie wove the small ambulance in and out, criss crossing the deep furrows made by other vehicles, sending the ambulance into a crazy roll like some small ship in a rough sea. He almost collided with a small scout car as it flashed in front of him, spitting death at the planes. Charlie braked and the ambulance skidded round, facing the same direction it came from. He made a wide arc and found himself directly behind the C.O.'s armoured car. He waved to them as if he was enjoying the trip.

"Try and take it a bit easy, Charlie. We have a wounded man in the back."

"Yes, and if I don't try and avoid the planes we will have two dead in front and one dead in the back."

A series of bombs fell among the column. One landed less than twenty yards away from them, rocking the ambulance badly and filling the air with its stench of explosives. All around them the men were firing as fast as they could load their rifles and brens. The ex-prisoners were enjoying every minute, some had waited years just to get their hand in again. The planes soared up high, waving their wings frantically in a defiant gesture, then all but one made towards home. He made his fatal mistake, banked, then soared down to take one long blast with his guns, perhaps like his mates, to finish off his ammo.

He may just as well have sent them a postcard of his intentions. Every gun in the column was waiting just for the opportune moment. As it dived then levelled off everyone fired, pumping the deadly bullets into the fuselage of the plane. Every man appeared to be having the time of his life as each one tried to outshoot his neighbour. It was too much. The plane's engine coughed, a black ball of smoke puffed out of its engine leaving a trail behind as the pilot frantically tried to regain height to make use of his parachute. It wobbled crazily as the pilot lost control. They could see him struggle to slide back the cockpit. The tip of the wing touched the ground and the plane crumpled like a piece of silver pager from a cigarette packet and exploded with a brilliant flash.

"Bloody hell, Harry, they hit it! They brought the sod down! Just take a shufti at those flames."

The two remaining planes circled above their heads, obviously out of ammo and unable to come to their comrades aid. They roared away in the distance. To bring down a plane with small arms was rather unusual but to bring down two in a few days was nothing short of a miracle.

They counted the cost of the air raid. Two men killed, including one ex-prisoner, three wounded, and one man injured his knee getting from his armoured car. Two small utilities and a scout car written off.

Harry attended to the wounded. The ambulance would only take two stretcher cases. He spread blankets on the floor between the stretchers; he could now take three men including the one he already had. The man with the bad knee and the other wounded man were made comfortable in a utility. A burial party was detailed to bury the two dead men. It was impossible to remove the pilot's body from the burning plane and he was left on his own funeral pyre.

The men were stretched to the limits of their endurance - almost asleep standing up - as the C.O. called a conference. The order was given to brew up. One man from each vehicle was detailed to stay behind while the remainder gathered around the C.O. The D.R.s were posted out on the flanks.

"Well, men, we have done it once again. According to the training manual it said that concentrated small arms fire can be very effective against low flying aircraft. But don't let's get too excited, no doubt they've returned to let their comrades know they're not dealing with amateurs. We are on the home stretch but still in a very dangerous position. We can expect air cover from the R.A.F. in a couple of days. Keep a good look out."

"How will they know who we are sir - the R.A.F. I mean?" enquired Jenkins.

Captain Bellamy smiled. "Well I suppose it will be alright to tell you. Williams and Jackson in their ambulance told them on that phoney raid."

All eyes turned towards the ambulance crew who looked astounded. Charlie shrugged his shoulders as Captain Bellamy continued.

"The red cross on top of his ambulance has one fluke missing, or rather one of the flukes has been covered in oil and sand. Also, did anyone else notice what happened when those utilities were knocked out?"

Everyone looked at their neighbour, puzzled looks on their faces.

"We took the canvas canopy off one, sir, and changed it with one of the others," someone answered.

"Nothing strange about that?" the C.O. enquired. The question was met with stony silence. Everyone taking it for granted that the crew that changed it over thought it was better than their own. Not an unusual incident in desert warfare, when a driver took something better from a vehicle to replace a worn out or damaged part of his own vehicle.

"Well that canvas cover was almost white and it always stayed close to the ambulance. Now to the business in hand. When we came out of the wadi, a column was spotted on both sides. We caught a glimpse of the sand throwing up from their tails, but they have vanished. Whether they are in wait for reinforcements before attacking, I just don't know, so keep your eyes peeled. Also watch for that dispatch rider. He missed Sergeant Legge and I am sure he must have taken the wrong wadi."

"What about the bombing raid on the dump, sir?" Sinclair asked. "By rights they should have bombed it while we were there?"

"Yes, that was touch and go. There was a chance of the enemy intercepting the message. Every half hour we sent out one word. That was from the minute we took the dump, just to let them know we were still there. Obviously, luckily for us, they must have picked the message up. When we were about to leave, the code word was changed."

It was a chance for Harry to see to his casualties. He redressed their wounds and injected them with pain killers, making certain they were securely tied down. It was mid morning when they moved off again. Harry and Charlie looked at one another. They looked like two wrecks with three days' growth and sand encrusting their faces. From the corners of Harry's mouth the matted beard and sand had formed a dark line as if it was extending his mouth like a clown's makeup. His eyes were just dark hollows and his left eye bloodshot. He yawned incessantly.

"When I get back I will hit those blankets and if anyone comes near me for the next three days I'll personally shoot him."

"That goes for me, too. I won't even get up for a piss. I'll take two empty beer bottles to bed with me."

They were running short of petrol. Charlie pulled up and emptied a Jerrican of petrol into his tank. Harry stood on an outcrop of rock and scanned the desert with Charlie's binoculars.

"Eh, Charlie, trouble ahead." He spotted several columns of sand on the horizon.

Charlie took the glasses while Harry tended to the casualties.

"You're right, Harry, here comes the D.R."

"Just sighted an enemy column up ahead. The old man thinks it may be a German raiding party, similar to our long range desert group, on their way to get behind our lines. With the sand they are throwing from their tracks they won't be seeing us. Watch the fireworks shortly, Charlie. Half a dozen armoured cars will shoot them right up their rectums before they realise we are there. You should see Bellamy, he's like a cock with two arse holes." He wiped the sand from his goggles.

"Lieutenant Nightingale said you are to move in closer."

Three armoured cars closed in on the cloud of dust behind the enemy while the other three cars went round to the flanks. All six vehicles opened up simultaneously. Two German armoured vehicles vanished in an eruption of smoke and flames. The remainder of the scout cars moved up to engage the enemy. Captain Bellamy's large Italian armoured car sped right into the midst of the battle, its guns blazing. A German half track skidded round. Several troops dashed out of the back, only to be mowed down by the guns of a small scout car. A German recce armoured car burst into flames. A man jumped from the turret and grabbed a spandau machine gun from beside a dead German and sprayed it around indiscriminately. A tyre burst from a scout car, and Captain Bellamy moved in to protect the crew as the car settled into the sand.

The surprise attack had its effect. In minutes it was almost over. A German half track skidded sideways as it shed one of its tracks. It clanged against the side of another half track, sounding like some gigantic cathedral bell as metal met metal. Both vehicles shuddered, the German occupants running in all directions. Some, realising it was already a lost cause, held their arms up high. Others fell in twisted contorted heaps. Two more half tracks and an armoured car tried to make a dash for it, but several armoured cars closed in like a pack of hunting hounds. One half track pulled up suddenly, the small German armoured car following crashed into it, almost turning over on its side. It quickly recovered - too late, it was just those vital precious seconds. A hail of bullets crashed into the German armoured car from several scout cars. It stopped and the crew baled out, their hands high above their heads. It was the same with the men in the half tracks. Hands held high above their heads they jumped to the ground. The ex-prisoners acting as infantry men moved in quickly.

For such a small engagement casualties were high. Three men of the column killed and eighteen Germans. Ten Germans wounded and four men from the column, including another of the released ex-prisoners. Harry remained undaunted. As the casualties were brought in he set his aid post. The Germans had been carrying two medical orderlies, both were killed in the battle.

"Can you cope, Jackson?" the C.O. enquired. He watched for a few minutes to see the confident way Harry went about his job. It left him in very little doubt.

"It will be a very difficult job evacuating them, sir. There is no more room in the ambulance," Harry reported.

Three of the German half tracks and a small vehicle similar to our own utilities were still serviceable. Besides the casualties they now had another ten prisoners they had to take back with them. If they left them there they could set fire to a pile of tyres and black smoke would be seen for miles. Someone would come over to see what was going on before they realised it half the German army would be on their tails.

"Get the casualties into the vehicles first and distribute the German prisoners amongst the vehicles. We have enough men to guard them as well. You make the casualties as comfortable as possible, there are plenty of blankets around. I understand you have sufficient pain killers, Jackson?"

"Yes sir. Strange, out of all the casualties only one is seriously wounded. A couple should have splints on. I'll take a shufti round the column to see if there's anything I can use."

"Right Jackson, do your stuff but jeldhi (hurry)," said the C.O.

"A cloud of dust on the horizon behind us, sir!" shouted a lookout stationed on the flanks in his armoured car. He had his glasses focused towards the distant heat haze.

"Looks like a solitary vehicle, sir, and heading this way. Do you reckon it could be a Jerry come over for a shufti, sir?"

The C.O. jumped on the armoured car and took the binoculars, shouting at the same time.

"Don't waste anymore time, sergeant, get the column moved up."

The cloud of dust settled as the solitary vehicle stopped.

"It can't be," gasped the C.O. He wiped the lenses of his glasses to make sure his eyes hadn't deceived him.

"Well I'll be buggered, it is."

Charlie was intrigued. He jumped on another armoured car and focused his glances on the solitary figure distorted in the heat haze astride a motor bike. Captain Bellamy waved his arms; the bike remained stationary.

"Come on, you stupid bastard," he muttered under his breath. Everyone's eyes were riveted by the solitary figure.

"You're not going to believe this, Harry. That stupid D.R. has just turned up. He's sitting out there and won't come closer. I bet his thinks we are Jerries so he's taking no chances."

The C.O. overheard Charlie.

"You are right, driver. He's being very cautious - not that I blame the poor sod, stuck out there all alone for days on end, I suppose he heard the gunfire and is staying there trying to work out who won."

"I bet he's crapping himself, sir. I would like to suggest we get the casualties out of the ambulance and I will go to him. My mate has his work cut out at the moment looking after the wounded. It wouldn't be much use sending a D.R. or armoured car, he would be away quicker than a rat up a sewer."

Captain Bellamy smiled, but admitted it was the best idea that anyone had come up with. An armoured car or a D.R. approaching would scare the life out of him, especially in his exhausted state.

The D.R. was standing off a couple of miles. Charlie didn't hurry but approached slowly. The man never moved but kept his motorbike engine ticking over. They started to play a cat and mouse game. As Charlie moved forward the D.R. retreated. Charlie stopped and stood outside the ambulance waving but the man took no notice.

Stopping once more, Charlie pondered over the situation. It was no good going further. He had a pencil and tore the plain leaf from inside the paper back book he had been reading and scribbled a note. Taking off his steel helmet he walked a few yards and placed the note in the helmet, then retreated in his ambulance a hundred yards. Through his powerful binoculars Charlie watched the man cautiously approach the helmet and pick up the note. His sand encrusted face broke into a broad smile. He waved to the ambulance then slumped across the handlebars of his bike. Charlie drove over stopping a few yards from the D.R.

The D.R's eyes were deep sunk sockets and his cheeks were hollow. His eyebrows and the stubble on his face were caked with sand, and his lips matted with pus and inflamed sores. His body was racked with pain where he had sat on the wide saddle of his bike for days. He lifted his head and croaked an imitation of a laugh. His bloodshot eyes stared wildly at Charlie. As his face split into a wide grin his mouth revealed discoloured teeth. His service revolver was in his hand. His arm fell to his side and the revolver dropped to the ground. Tears left white streaks down each side of his face. His steel helmet fell to the ground; he made no effort to pick either gun or helmet up, but began laughing hysterically.

Charlie stood helpless, looking at the men. They couldn't stay here forever. The column must be on the move shortly and Harry still had the casualties to attend to. There was only one thing he could do. He gave the man a hefty slap across the face.

"Jack that fucking lark in, sonny boy, we have to get back! While you've been swanning around this bloody desert we've been having a go at Jerry!"

The sharp words and the hefty slap seemed to bring the man to his senses. He made a grab for the water bottle Charlie was carrying, but Charlie held it away from him. The man was dehydrated and Harry had taught him that it was dangerous to give a man too much water in that condition. Instead he took a piece if lint from the ambulance and soaked it. The man nearly went mad when he saw the surplus water falling onto the sand. He tried to get off his motorbike but staggered, then got to his feet and came towards Charlie, feet wide apart and shuffling along like some drunken cowboy. Charlie was powerfully built and it took no effort to control the man. He sat him down and moistened his lips; he sucked hungrily at the wet lint. Charlie gave him the lint to suck, then helped him into the cab of the ambulance.

They must have been observed by the C.O. all the time, for on the way back they passed a D.R. on his motorbike with a pillion passenger, obviously another man going to fetch the motorcycle in.

All the casualties had been attended to. Harry took the man in hand. As he cleaned the man's lips with glycerine, the skin broke away leaving red blotches. There was a deep sore between his matted moustache and another stretched under one eye where the man's eye shields had been. He allowed the man to suck at a piece of wet lint.

"How long have I been away?" he croaked. He tried to rub the inflamed red patches on the inside of his thighs, rubbed raw by his saddle.

"Four or five days," replied Harry, although the truth was he just didn't know how long. Like most of the men they had lost all sense of time.

They prepared to leave. The wounded were distributed amongst the utilities and lorries. The prisoners, or most of them, were placed in the German half-tracks with ex-prisoners guarding them. The dead were buried in three rows of seven graves. The C.O. said a few words over the graves, German and British lying alongside each other. With the wrecked vehicles dotting the area there was every chance the graves would be located and the bodies moved to a central war cemetery. The C.O. had also marked the appropriate position of the graves on his map.

It was ten hours before they stopped, but the progress had been very slow. They had spotted several columns of sand on the distant horizon and cut down their speed to a bare minimum to keep the dust down. Then one of the half-tracks broke down and it was hours before they could fix it, but everyone was on the alert, watching the distant column of sand, none daring to light a fire for a brew up.

Dusk descended on them. The prisoners were given an ultimatum. They could have their hands and feet tied, or they could give their word no one would try and escape. If they did they would be shot. Although this ultimatum was unnecessary, the desert was their prison. Trying to escape from this situation without proper food and plenty of water would be courting death. However, their word was given and an officer with them spelt it out in very plain language.

Harry talked to the D.R. He gave him a drink of water laced with a little brandy.

He told Harry, "I waited for Sergeant Legge, I don't know what happened but when I went to the top of a rise to see if he was coming and sat there on my bike the sand gave way and I slid down the other side. The bike crushed my leg, it seemed like hours before I could free myself and another half hour before I could get some life back into my leg. Luckily it didn't break. When I got back the Jerrican of petrol was empty. It looked like Legge had filled his tank and then thrown the rest on the ground. I don't know how I kept my cool. I followed some tracks, I thought it strange as Bellamy said he was going down the wadi, this was on the surface. Then I realised they were heading north. I almost bumped into another regiment on the move and realised at last I had been tailing an Itey column. I turned, luck shadowed me, I was getting short of petrol, then I found an abandoned Italian lorry. I drained the petrol tank. In the back I found a Jerrican of water and a couple of bottles of red wine, real crap. Next day I was driving along and felt for my water bottle. It was gone. Must have bumped off during the night. I saw several columns of sand in the distance and almost gave myself up, but I had plenty of petrol and decided to try and find that bloody wadi again. Once more my guardian angel took over. I saw this lorry in the distance. It was burnt out, but the petrol tank was alright. I managed to fill my tank and I found half a bottle of water. I spotted another column in the distance, I honestly thought I had caught up with you lot and was in amongst them when I realised it was an Itey column. I thought I was going out of my mind. Two Itey D.R.s gave chase. I think they were Itey military police. I shot one of them and out rode the other. Christ, it was a bloody close shave. I was almost out of water again. I still had nearly a full bottle of wine, but drank it sparingly, booze on an empty stomach doesn't do a lot for the brain box and I wanted to keep a clear head. I went back for the water bottle of the dead Itey but they had removed the bottle and the body."

He paused while Harry gave him more water laced with a little brandy. He also mashed some corned beef with a little Italian bread, quite stale by now but palatable in soaked water. He spoon fed the D.R. who collected a few spectators as he recalled his ordeal.

"Then I heard this loud explosion and went to investigate. I looked inside the wadi and there was this Itey lorry. It must have gone over a heavy mine, there were bodies everywhere. Other men sat around nursing their wounds. I don't know what mine it was but it must have been a hell of a big one, half the bloody walls on both sides of the wadi had caved in."

One of the men listening laughed.

"That must have been one of the mines we planted after Legge joined us. Bloody good job you didn't follow him down that wadi. We connected a couple of mines together and also put one in each side of the wadi. They all went off together."

"Anyway," the D.R. continued, "it was almost dark so I slid down the wadi and wandered amongst them till I found a water bottle. You know I don't speak their lingo so I just grunted and tapped one man on the head when he asked me something. I reckon they were all suffering from shock. I soon scarpered, I couldn't find any grub. It was or must have been at least three days before I caught up with you lot. I couldn't make out if you were Jerry or Itey. It was a bloody relief when I saw that ambulance."

CHAPTER 16

Knowing they were on the last leg of a very successful operation, the men were filled with pride accomplishing a foray right into enemy territory and blowing up the largest ammo and supply dump in North Africa. Both the ambulance crews reviewed the end with mixed feelings. First the excitement, then leaving the friends they had made, for there is nothing better than sharing dangers to make real friends. But like every man in the column, it was a memory that would last them the rest of their lives.

Like the vehicles they were driving, they were completely exhausted for during the raid they had had only one complete night of unbroken sleep. For once the rumble of heavy guns in the distance was welcomed for it heralded their return.

There was no welcoming committee. Small groups of men stood around staring at the scruffy, unkempt group with their clapped out vehicles and two, thirteen hundred weight utilities being towed in by two German half-tracks. Harry made straight for the aid post with his casualties, the utilities carrying more casualties following suit. Harry filled out his report, pleased with himself that since collecting the wounded he had lost only one man who had suffered a haemorrhage on the previous day. The wounded were laid out on stretchers and the M.O. carried out his inspection.

"Well done, Jackson. Rejoin your unit and get some sleep. Don't worry about this lot. Captain Bellamy radioed in this morning, ambulances are on their way from your unit."

Completely exhausted, Harry fell into his seat in the cab of the ambulance. Charlie was already asleep, his head resting on his forearms across the steering wheel. Harry woke him and gave him a lighted cigarette.

"Home, James. Let's get our heads down for a few hours."

They located their own unit with very little difficulty and pulled up outside the company office - the canvas lean-to against a three tonner. The R.S.M., not one to show his feelings at any time, took one look at their dishevelled appearance: dirty, hollow eyed and sunken cheeks hidden under several days growth of matted beard - Harry's eye still bloodshot.

"Right, you pair." He eased himself up from the corner of the table he was sitting on. "Get down to the cookhouse and let the cook sergeant make you a decent meal. Shave and clean yourselves up, then pick up your own ambulance and leave that one in its place. The regiment will send someone over to pick it up. Take your ambulance as far away from the rest of the unit as possible, and I don't want to see your faces for the next two days."

146

Almost pushing them from the lean-to, he gave them a cursory dismissal and quickly turned his back on them. He knew he had strained them to their limits and once again proved they were one of the best ambulance crews in the unit.

Charlie burst out laughing when they were in the open again.

"See the way he got rid of us? Do you think we smell or something?" Harry lifted his arm to smell under the armpit and grinned.

"Could be right, Charlie!"

After a good meal of meat and vegetables, followed by tinned rice, they picked up their own ambulance and Charlie drove to the outer limits of the leaguer. They didn't bother to wash but both fell exhausted onto the stretchers. Back in their own ambulance they felt they were home at last. The back doors hanging on their makeshift hinges, the jagged holes and the fly droppings on the shabby plywood interior, all contributed to the welcome home, making them feel as if they had just returned from a disastrous holiday.

They only rose from their beds to allow nature to take its course. On the second day, when Harry woke, there was a letter by his bedside. He stared at the envelope for a full five minutes then lifted it and held it to his nose. There was still a faint trace of perfume although, according to the state of the envelope and several addresses on it, it was obvious it had followed him around. The handwriting was small and neat with each word ending with a flourishing artistic scroll. He smiled. Only Victoria could write so beautifully.

It was the usual humorous gossip from the hospital in London where he had done his crash course. God, what a sense of humour she had, he thought. There were five pages of small neat handwriting with a laugh in almost every sentence.

"I nearly volunteered to become an army nursing sister," she wrote, "but then I thought there was no sense in two silly prats trying to get themselves killed." She was now a theatre sister. Not once did she mention the blitz or anything about how London and great cities were suffering. Neither did she mention that she was working at times up to sixteen hours a day patching up blitz victims, mostly children, women, and old people. She spared him the gory details, well aware that he had his own troubles. To read the letter one could be excused for thinking there was no war going on back home.

There were also the usual two letters for Charlie - one buff official looking envelope and one lilac envelope with neat writing.

Harry searched for his cigarettes and not finding any he took one from Charlie's battered tobacco tin. He cradled his head in his hands and stared up at the roof of the ambulance, his cigarette dangling from his mouth. The roof was pitted with fly droppings and two flies were busily mounted amongst it. Charlie snored, how he snored. The flimsy plywood interior shuddered with every dull note. Harry looked at the misshapen lump under the blankets and wondered if Charlie ever worried about anything, and for all the while they had been together he knew very little about Charlie's private life outside of the army. The misshapen lump stirred and Charlie raised himself up on one elbow and stared round unaware for a few seconds just where he was.

"I must have slept heavy. I have got a man size hangover." He ran the palm of his hand across his forehead, then pressed the balls of his hands into his eye sockets. "Any chance of a brew, Harry?"

Then he noticed the two envelopes. He picked them up and immediately tore the lilac one into tiny shreds. Harry was out of his bed like a shot as he watched a naked leg appear from under the blanket, the foot searching for the cold lino floor. He knew exactly what to expect, he had seen the exercise repeated every morning since he arrived at the unit. Harry fell from the ambulance, as Charlie stood up completely naked, stamped his right foot three times on the floor, then let out a long loud stream of wind.

"I needed that, Harry." He stood at the open doors of the ambulance and let go a fountain of urine, the hot sand mopping it up like a sponge.

"A couple of aspirins and a nice hot mug of tea and I should be as right as rain."

The rot had set in for them. Harry had aching muscles where he never knew they existed.

"Rumour's going round we are moving down to the coast, Charlie."

He could hardly straighten up from the petrol fire. The brew can was boiling merrily and, still bent over, he returned to the ambulance for the tea, milk and sugar.

"Bloody hell, Harry, you look like Quasimodo!"

Harry swung his arms down to his sides like an ape and distorted his features.

"It's the bells, Charlie, the bells."

"That's not the bells, you prick, that's the bloody guns up ahead."

"Whatever you do, Charlie, don't bend over. I didn't realise I had so many muscles. I ache all over. I did hear the Div is moving

148

to the coast. What wouldn't I give for a long soak in the Med. I would just float and soak for hours."

Just one movement sent stabs of pain racing through his body as he painfully climbed back into the ambulance. The two flies were still at it.

"Lucky sods, ain't they, Harry." The flies broke and buzzed around frantically. One landed on Charlie's forearm. He slapped his hand on it and it turned into a black mess.

"That's the way to go, Harry. Just as you have finished on the job. I bet it died happy."

They each drank two full mugs of steaming tea. The sun was high above them and they both sweated. Charlie, still naked, walked to the front of the ambulance and adjusted his wing mirror so he could see himself. He gave a mock scream, recoiled in horror and ran his hand round his chin. His legs felt weak as he steadied himself against the side of the cab. Harry was right, he was experiencing aches and pains throughout his body. He collected hot water from the brew can, lathered and shaved three times before he was satisfied his face was clear.

"You are right. A nice long soak in the old briny would do me the world of good. Better still, some nice bint giving me a massage. They say out in the far east these tiny Asian birds walk up and down your spine. Fancy that, Harry?"

At the mere suggestion of anyone touching his back, Harry's face became distorted with pain.

"You have to be kidding. If a fly landed on my back at this moment I would double up with pain."

"Good God, man! Walking around like that in the nude. Make yourself decent, Charlie." There was something effeminate in the sound of the voice. Charlie rushed for his shorts.

"Bloody hell! Mundy, you old poof! I never heard your ambulance come up."

Harry turned to see a tall slim figure standing against the ambulance, one hand on his hip and the other resting against the side of the ambulance. His hairless tanned legs were accentuated by the very skimpy tight shorts and his fine blonde hair was carefully groomed and parted on one side. He lowered his arm from the side of the ambulance and inspected his manicured nails, removing the one or two isolated grains of sand that had escaped his previous manicure, with a long thin nail file.

"Less of the old poof, Charles."

"Hell, Mundy, it must have been at least three months since I saw you last."

It was nothing unusual in the unit. Each of the twenty ambulances in the unit were posted to various regiments.

"Actually Charlie, it's been over six months." He glanced at Harry.

"Is this your new medic? Let's hope he survives longer than your previous ones."

Charlie just laughed. He liked Mundy, he was an old member of the unit, although they were different as chalk and cheese. Charlie was totally heterosexual and his great love, apart from his daughter, was cars and engines. Mundy, on the other hand, hated the filthy things. Prior to the war he had served as a male nurse in one of the country's leading criminal asylums and his knowledge of medicine outshone some of the younger medical officers. Apart from one or two bird brains in the unit, he was accepted by the majority as an efficient medical orderly.

"I have brought your small dog round for you, Charlie. I gave the scruffy little devil a good bath."

"Hell, Mundy, how did you manage that? I can never get him in the water."

"Terrible dog, Charles. When he saw me taking him to the water he went mad. Played me up no end, and worse, he dribbled down my front. I gave him a few whiffs of ether, that soon put him out."

Charlie and Harry burst out laughing, and Charlie said, "I never thought of that."

But his smile was soon torn from his face.

"Where's Solly then?"

Mundy, knowing that Solly was one of Charlie's best friends, hesitated.

"Sorry, Charles, Solly was killed two days ago."

Charlie's jaw dropped as he fought back his tears. The news had shattered him. He had so much to tell Solly about the little Italian friend and how the raid went. He had found several new packs of cards for him at the dump. He sat down on the back step of the ambulance trying to take control of his emotions.

"What happened?"

"He shouldn't have been there really, with the Div out of action. He was having a good rest. It seems like a field ambulance from another div was getting it heavy and asked for help. They sent three ambulances. Solly was amongst them."

"What happened?"

"A German gun site had been knocked out. There were two men badly wounded but still alive. One of them was an officer. Solly bent over him to see to his wound and the German had a luger in his hand and shot him. He was an S.S. Officer, and let's face it, Charles, Solly looked every inch a Jew. You know what those stupid Nazi fanatics are. Poor Solly, he was dead before he

150

hit the ground. Yorkie went mad. He rushed over but the German put a bullet in his guts. You know how strong that Yorkie is. He kicked the luger away from the German, then picked it up and emptied the magazine into him. He just went crazy. Yorkie is on his way back home now. He hardly talked before this happened. Poor sod won't say a word now, just stares into space."

"Where have they buried Solly?" Mundy jerked his thumb over his shoulder, towards the C.O.'s lean-to.

"Just behind the lean-to. Chalkie White is buried there too."

"Blimey, don't tell me he caught a packet too."

"Well they certainly didn't bury him alive."

Spag must have woken up, hearing the familiar voices. He jumped from the ambulance and ran around in small circles gradually working his way towards Charlie leaving circles of wet patches, dribbling and crunched up, with his tail between his legs. Then suddenly he ran forward and jumped into Charlie's outstretched arms.

"Sodding hell, Spag, you smell nice and sweet. What did that naughty Mundy do to you?"

"I used my best shampoo. Well, Charles, I must take my leave. Cherrio. You too, Harry. Watch the blighter, Harry." He nodded towards Charlie.

After he departed in a cloud of dust, Harry laughed. He could see Charlie was still depressed about the news of his best friend and tried to cheer him up. There was only one thing that would do that, get on the subject of women.

He said, "I didn't know that was your scene, Charlie."

It brought a smile to Charlie's lips.

"You must be kidding. What a man does with his sex life is his own business. My mutton dagger is used for the thing it was meant for. I have one ambition, that is to go straight through the alphabet. I only have F, X and Z. Did you know once I volunteered for the paras? They said they are always dropping over Greece, and the blokes were always telling me that was the place to go for girls with those stupid names beginning with X and Z."

"Yes, yes, Charlie. You have told me a dozen time, but do go on, it all helps to pass the time."

They visited the two graves. Someone had put a cross above their graves.

"Stupid prats! Fancy putting a cross on Solly's grave, he must be turning over down there."

He stood silent for a few minutes. He adjusted the steel helmet hanging on the crossbar.

"No, I don't think Solly will be turning in his grave, very likely laughing his bloody head off."

Solly's ambulance was outside the company office. Charlie went inside and returned a few minutes later with the plywood table they had used for the card game. He took it to the company workshop and marked out the Star of David. It was a long laborious job cutting it out. All he could find was a steel hacksaw. The sweat rolled off him. After a bit of an argument with the workshop staff, as to how many points there were on the Star of David, he settled for six. He had no sandpaper and made do with some coarse emery cloth to sand down the edges. Then, with black paint, he carefully painted on Solly's name, number and regiment. He stood back to admire his handiwork.

"Strange, you know, Solly was rather proud of the old corps. I will write to his brother and get Denzy to take a photograph. He's the only bloke in the unit with a camera. His brother would like a picture of the grave. Pity he didn't hear about that Itey prisoner." He nailed the Star over the cross then hung Solly's helmet on the top of it.

They went to the R.S.M. Harry handed him his report.

"Thanks, Jackson." He glanced at the three pages of writing, swiftly taking in the more important points.

"This confirms the official report the C.O. - Captain Bellamy, wasn't it - sent to div H.Q." He placed the report on the table.

"I will read it thoroughly later. You appear to have coped alright Jackson. You will have quite a story to tell your grandchildren in a few years time."

He turned to Charlie.

"Right, Williams, get filled with petrol and see you have plenty of water and rations. The Div moves up tomorrow and you will be going to one of the infantry regiments. Make sure you have plenty of supplies, Jackson. We will be going nearer the coast and with a bit of luck we should be in Tripoli in two or three weeks time."

So far the news had been depressing for Charlie, what with Solly's untimely death, but the mention of Tripoli helped to cheer him up.

"If I had known you were coming so soon, sir, we would have stayed behind and welcomed you."

But they were never posted to an infantry regiment. They were held back at the M.D.S. (main dressing station) to evacuate wounded further back. The news didn't go down well with Charlie. Harry was quite indifferent but Charlie wanted to be well up front. If Tripoli was to be the next stop he wanted to be well in there first.

His request was turned down flat by the R.S.M.

"You are a bloody glutton for punishment, Williams. Take it easy for a few days, let someone else have a go."

The continuous throb of the heavy guns led them back into the direction of the war. As the sand track led over a crest they got their first sight for many months of the blue Mediterranean. Harry gasped. The sight of the water sent his back into spasms of anticipated luxury. From the distance, and it must have been three miles at least with the haze dancing on the far horizon, it looked cool and inviting.

The unit stopped less than two hundred yards from the wavelets lapping smoothly at the shore.

Harry drooled, "Just let me get at that water. When I was at the orphanage I didn't see the sea till I was almost twelve. Then one day it was arranged for a trip to the seaside. We were all given a small spade and a couple of buckets between us, and two new pennies for ice cream. Charlie, you could have called the king my uncle. We were all so excited, two of the little girls pissed their draws and my mate pissed the bed the night before. That sea is just having the same effect on me."

"Well don't you piss yourself in the ambulance tonight. Did the kids enjoy themselves?"

"I don't know, Charlie, it pissed down with rain the minute we arrived."

"It won't piss down here, that's for sure, but you won't get on that beach that's certain."

He pointed to a notice,

"Keep clear, this shoreline may still be mined, keep away from the water."

They moved inland for five hundred yards and set up the dressing station, ready for business the next day when the division was to plunge once more into action. But there was very little sleep for them that night.

At midnight the heavy tanks loaded on transporters rumbled to a stop not less than a hundred yards away. Steel clattered against steel as the monsters were unloaded. Then the tanks' engines revved up as they jockeyed into some semblance of order. No sooner had these mighty steel dinosaurs settled down, waiting for orders to move in, than heavy lorries started to roll up and stopped near them disgorging platoon after platoon of infantry, all wearing greatcoats and balaclava helmets, swinging their arms and stamping their feet trying to keep the cold at bay. It was one of the largest concentration of troops they had seen for quite a while.

It was a moonless night, but there was sufficient light from the stars to help the troops to sort themselves out. A battery of

153

twenty-five pounders were digging in well up ahead of them, and they knew they had the heavier guns behind them. When they opened up it would sound like hell had suddenly opened its gates. Neither Charlie or Harry could sleep. Harry tried to relax on his stretcher but it was no good. In ten minutes he was back on his feet again, smoking incessantly.

"Let's dig a couple of slit trenches Harry. When this lot opens up they will throw every kind of shit at us."

They sat besides the slit trenches, their legs dangling inside.

"You know, Harry, with Tripoli almost in view, I bet Tunis won't be all that long. Then you watch, the real fighting will start. No Dunkirk for Jerry and the Iteys. The navy has the grip on the Med round here," said Charlie, but his main topic was reaching Tripoli. Since he had heard the news officially from the R.S.M.'s own lips, no longer a rumour but reality. It was supposed to be the Italians' largest city in North Africa, much on a par with Cairo and Alex. Some said it was far more modern.

"Can you think of any Italian girls' names beginning with an X or a Z, Harry?"

"Bloody hell, here we go again! Doesn't your mind ever rise above your belly button, Charlie?"

But Charlie wasn't listening. He was away in Tripoli, picturing all those glamorous Italian beauties. In spite of the continuing warning from all around that once the place was taken the division would speed through and the brothels and every other place of enjoyment would be placed out of bounds. More to himself than anyone, he said softly, "They wouldn't dare." Then louder so Harry could hear, "I would like to see anyone try do me out of my crumpet after coming this far. Once in that fair city, Harry boy, if there is any spare around you can be assured that Uncle Charlie will sort it out."

Which in a way was exactly true. Charlie had his reputation to think about, but the top of his efforts would be to sort out any female with their name starting with an F, X or Z. He was halfway there, the cockney Italian they had captured had given him several addresses in Tripoli, although he had shaken his head when Charlie asked him about Italian girls with the elusive initials.

The infantry lolled around in groups talking and laughing as if they were preparing for a picnic the next morning.

"Just listen to them. In the morning I bet quite a few of them will be laying out there in the sand."

"What do you expect them to do? Hold a bloody Irish wake? Ask anyone of them now what they expect and look forward to the most. The answer will be: entering Tripoli! Death happens to the other bloke, Harry."

The men were talking in hushed tones. Someone started playing a mouth organ and 'Lili Marlene' came wafting across the sands. The talking stopped and some men, not knowing most of the words, started humming. Harry liked the tune, he'd heard it several times since he arrived in the desert. The mouth organ player switched to a medley of cockney songs. It was a London regiment that would lead the attack and most of the men were cockneys. Harry's imagination stretched to someone doing the Lambeth Walk out there in the shadows. Then he froze; the musician was playing 'Roses of Picardy'. It sent a cold shudder through him, he didn't know why. The tune held no sentimental memories for him and he had heard it thousands of times. He had played it many times on the piano, yet here, out in the cold night air of the desert it seemed to have a sobering effect on his senses. It was the First World War song and shouldn't have disturbed him - this war was a replay with its own songs and music. Then suddenly the player stopped but the tune lingered on in Harry's mind. He knew somehow, somewhere, that tune would play an important part in his life. He dropped into a fitful sleep.

They were rudely awakened from their sleep. Above their slit trenches, and heavily wrapped in blankets, the night air bit into their exposed faces.

"Come on my little beauties, rise and shine, let's be having you."

Harry sat up startled.

"What's up, sarge?"

"Fuck all my son." The stocky little Scots sergeant stood at his feet, his greatcoat trailing in the sand and a balaclava helmet covering most of his face, just the flat mishapen nose showing. His voice strained through the thick woollen scarf covering his mouth.

"In a few minutes all hell will be let loose and I don't want you and your mate shitting the blankets when it starts. Come on, on your feet."

He had seen Charlie emerge from his blankets on many occasions, completely nude, but he was taken aback when he saw him this time, right in the battle area.

"Bloody hell, Williams, if Jerry had attacked last night and saw you they would have thought we had some new secret weapon. God, man, just look at the size of it."

This brought a smile to Charlie's face, he was proud of his build.

"I have promised myself, sarge, that when we hit Tripoli and there happens to be a tattoo artist there, I am having all my mates who have copped it tattooed there. I'll call it my roll of honour."

"With the size of that malformed prober you could call it a roll of lino. My God, I pity the poor girls."

"Never had any complaints, sarge." He smiled as he slipped on his shorts and worn out plimsolls.

The division moved in for its penultimate attack towards Tripoli.

CHAPTER 17

It became a static battle with neither side gaining much ground, before it receded into the pages of history. From various sections of the front the city was quite visible, and the division poised for the final thrust, but everyone appeared to be in a jovial mood and wanting to get it over and done with.

Charlie and Harry sat on the back step of the ambulance watching the infantry form up. A group near them, greatcoats on and the collars turned up around their ears took advantage of the lull and lit their cigarettes. A man broke wind. The small knot of men broke up.

"There he goes again, sarge," someone shouted.

"Do I have to follow him, sarge? He stinks terrible - I think he's shitting himself."

A ripple of laughter spread round the platoon as Jones tried to defend his actions.

"It's nervous tension, sarge. I lose control. I can't help it. I always get the wind when my nerves are keyed up. It was the same on my wedding day. We were in the church and as we knelt I let one go. Christ, you should have heard it! It was at that critical moment when the church was absolutely silent - except for the wife's old lady, she was sobbing her heart out. Then I started sniggering, shortly the whole congregation was in an uproar. Even the old vicar was covering his face with the Bible. His cassock was bobbing up and down, he could hardly continue with the service. I thought the wife was going to faint. My bleeding wedding night was a disaster, the wife wouldn't even speak to me, never mind getting my end away. She sat up for three nights and kept saying all the girls from the factory were there, and she couldn't go back and show her face."

"Alright, laddy, take control of yourself," the sergeant said. "And all of you remove your greatcoats and fix bayonets, then form up, we will be moving up in a few minutes."

"That bloke sounds like you, Charlie."

"Not me, Harry. You know me, I'm a one fart arse hole. One good blast every morning usually clears me for the day unless of course I have eaten anything that detrimental to my wind machine, like baked beans or a good curry."

"Well thank heavens there's no curry out here."

The guns blasted out their version of a Wagner symphony. Heavy shells from behind screamed overhead. Spag ran around in small circles leaving damp round patches in the sand. The ambulance shook violently. Harry felt he was in the centre of an earthquake as the earth trembled. A vary light arched high in the

157

sky dazzling the earth with its brilliance, suspended there for a few minutes, spluttered then drifted slowly earthwards. The whole front erupted into action. Twenty-five pounders cracked incessantly. Shells from the heavier guns screamed overhead sounding like an express train emerging from a long dark tunnel. At times the ghostly forms of infantrymen in the half light showed up against the brilliant gun flashes moving forward. It looked like the whole of the Eighth army was taking part on the final assault on Tripoli. It was half an hour before the last man went through. Hardly a man spoke, just the sound of their shuffling feet was heard in between the noise of the guns.

The short medical sergeant reappeared and spoke to Charlie.

"Alright, Williams, follow that three tonner." He pointed to the medical lorry.

"We will be setting up the aid post. They are figuring on heavy casualties. We have the 21st S.S. in front, you know what fanatical bastards they are. Bear in mind this is the largest city between Cairo and Tunis. When this place goes they will be fighting every inch of the way back to Tunis so you can expect some real stick."

He vanished without waiting for an answer still muttering to himself and his greatcoat trailing in the sand.

As expected the casualties started to roll in. Soon they were making their way to the main dressing station with their first full load. Several other ambulances were waiting to unload, rows of stretchers lay outside reception, most of the men waiting for surgery. Another row of stretchers, with the bodies completely covered with blankets, lay behind the operating theatre. Sykes came out to greet them, the usual clipboard in hand and pencil poised,

"How many, Jackson?"

"Four stretchers and five walkers."

"Bloody hell! I am pissed off with this and we've only just started."

He turned to Charlie. "By the way, Williams, your mate has caught it. Mundy and his driver. Direct hit. Fuck all left of his ambulance."

Charlie stopped dead in his tracks.

"What do you mean? He's dead?"

"I should think so. They are getting ready to bury the both of them."

The news was a shattering blow, they had been friends since joining the unit. Everyone called him a bum boy, but Charlie knew him for what he really was, a good efficient medical orderly.

Another ambulance pulled up beside Charlie, empty of casualties. The driver shouted, "Heard the news, Charlie? Old Mundy caught it, him and his driver."

Charlie nodded.

"Old prick face here just told me. Hard lines, nice bloke."

"Come off it, Charlie, he was a bloody pansy. Gave me the creeps. They reckon there are a dozen blokes over by the graves, some of his boyfriends, eh Charlie? ..."

Anger choked the words in Charlie's throat. He looked at the other driver.

"Let the poor bastard rest. He was a bloody good medic. Pity there aren't a few more as efficient in the unit."

"Oh dear, seemed to have touched on a raw spot. I didn't think you were like that, Charlie."

Charlie took a step towards the other driver who, realising he had gone too far, quickly started his engine and threw the ambulance into gear.

"Bye, bye, dearies." He threw Charlie a kiss, followed by an effeminate wave. "Bye, deary," he repeated as the ambulance vanished in a cloud of dust.

"Good job that bastard took off." He turned to Harry who was trying to hide a smile. "And you can wipe that silly grin off your face."

By midday the aid post had handled over two hundred casualties. The sergeant wasn't kidding when he had said the casualties would be heavy. The shelling never ceased, the heavy rumblings shook the earth. A few houses on the outskirts of the city were shattered, columns of smoke rose skywards. A high chimney stack rose from the sand and mist of war, a clear indication they were near civilisation. Charlie's spirits soared and he took a bet with Harry as to how long the chimney would remain standing.

A loud crash set their eardrums ringing. Harry slammed the palms of his hands against his eardrums, the ambulance swayed to one side as Charlie struggled with the steering wheel. The hot blast wafted across Harry's face and he felt a slight sting below his left leg. His hand shot down, red sticky blood trickled through his fingers.

"Bloody hell, Charlie! I've been hit in the leg!"

He bent to examine it, as he did so another shell landed a few yards away and a large piece of shrapnel tore through the side of the ambulance where he sat. He looked up sharply.

"Bloody hell! If I hadn't bent down that would have taken my bleeding head off."

159

Charlie stopped the ambulance and rushed round to examine Harry's wound. It was about an inch long and brushed past the skin, blood oozed from it. Harry cleaned it away, the wound wasn't serious. The small piece of shrapnel had carried on and smacked into a Jerrycan of water and started to flood the cab.

"Just take a shufti at that hole in the side of the wagon, Harry! God, man, if that had hit you, you wouldn't be here now. It must have gone straight over your head and through the open side. I never heard it. By the way, how's the leg?"

"Bit painful. I'll get the M.O. to stitch it when we get back."

"I'll stitch it, Harry."

"No thanks, after the bloody mess Jock made of Brummie's face, it can wait."

Once again they were in the thick of it, enemy shells dropped all around. Shells from their own heavy guns behind them screamed overhead. Tanks all around them moved forward. Casualties were rolling in. They pulled up behind a battery of twenty-five pounders to get their bearings. Gunners, stripped to the waist, fed the hungry guns as if there were no tomorrows. Charlie was feeling a little apprehensive about the gunners. He winked at Harry and walked over to the first gun. A sergeant glared at him.

"Careful with the guns, sarge. You're shelling the brothel area."

He snapped round at Charlie, "Piss off and get that bloody tub out of the way."

But the ambulance crew were certain as they moved off the elevation of the guns moved slightly.

Several armoured cars came rushing from the front. The leading car skidded to a halt, black smoke rising from its tyres as it skidded along the hard packed sand. The commander, breathless, jumped from the car and ran towards the colonel's car. Suddenly the enemy guns stopped, followed quickly by their own heavy guns at the rear, one sharp crack from a twenty-five pounder, then all was silence, a shattering silence like the guns themselves.

Harry jumped from the ambulance, all around the men gathered in groups talking in hushed tones as if scared to speak. A dispatch rider spun round beside them.

"Alright, it's over bar the shouting. It looks like they've jacked it in. The Div's getting ready to move in." He sped away as fast as he arrived.

It was a spectacular sight as the regimental armoured cars formed up in three columns. Charlie took up his position behind the M.O.'s utility at the end of the middle column. The homes on the outskirts were deserted, makeshift white flags hung limply

160

from the open windows. What little breeze there was moved the tatty net curtains slightly. A fitting tribute to the ignominious end to Mussolini's African Empire.

The road widened into a dual carriageway. The regiment split into three separate columns. The ambulance was still tagged behind the centre column when it broke away and made its way towards the dock area. Infantrymen went from house to house. Columns of smoke spiralled skywards from several houses. Occasionally there was an explosion, as either escaping gas or a hand grenade was thrown - for in spite of the defeat there was still one or two fanatics reluctant to surrender.

The modern part of the city was well planned and virtually untouched. The streets were laid out in neat rectangles intersecting the main dual carriageway. The men in the vehicles were still a little jumpy, turning their guns at times to an open, darkened window that could hold a potential sniper. After a while their confidence grew and tension eased when it was more than apparent there was no enemy remaining.

"God, it's more like a ghost town," Charlie said as he pulled nervously on his cigarette.

The column closed up as the colonel's car came to a halt. Two high ranking German officers stepped from a large building holding a white flag. Besides them strutted a fat nervous looking Italian officer, well decorated. A brief exchange of words then the colonel pointed towards the M.O.'s truck.

Charlie leaned across the steering wheel and casually looked up, his cigarette fell from his mouth as his lower jaw dropped.

"Jesus Christ!"

He let the words out in a quiet long draw, his eyes widened. Harry followed his gaze to an upper window and nearly choked on the smoke of his cigarette. A young girl, probably about eighteen and well acquainted with the ways of the world, waved frantically at them. She was well endowed and wore a low cut white blouse, each movement of her hand sent the breasts moving madly. Her jet black hair hung in thick folds. She folded her arms and rested her breast on her forearms, forcing her breasts to thrust out till her blouse tightened round the two bulging masses. She waved frantically to the men down below. The infantry men were hypnotised with the sight, they walked in small circles unable to take their eyes away. One man walked backwards into a doorway and fell over the doorstep sending his sten gun flying. Charlie's hands flopped to his side, he leaned back and hung his head.

"For heavens sake, Harry, I just can't take any more." He covered his hands over his eyes. "Has she gone yet?"

Harry's voice was dry and raspy. He moistened his lips with the tip of his tongue. She was without doubt the most beautiful thing he had seen in months.

"Are you kidding? If she moves another couple of inches further out of that window her Bristols will shoot out. My God, she's beautiful."

He nudged Charlie. "Just take a shufti."

"I dare not, Harry. I just dare not." He sighed but bent forward and took a look under his lowered eyelids.

"Right, Williams, move that ambulance forward towards that large warehouse." The medical sergeant pointed towards a large building. More German soldiers were coming from the warehouse holding their hands above their heads.

"WILLIAMS!" The sergeant shouted at the top of his voice.

The ambulance shuddered, Charlie shook himself from his wild dreams, coming back to earth with a crash. He switched on the engine and slammed the ambulance into gear; it shot forward and stalled.

"Come on, Williams, pull yourself together man. Haven't you seen a pair of tits before?"

Still in a trance he softly murmured, "Not for a decent while, sarge, and never hanging from a window like that."

The odour of decaying flesh hung thickly on the air of the warehouse as they stepped inside. Rows and rows of stretchers spread over the concrete floor with hardly room to walk between; casualties prepared to be shipped across the Med to Italy - not only Italian and German but British, Australian, South African, New Zealand and a few Polish, every representative of the Allied forces.

The two high ranking German officers, the M.O. and colonel walked between the rows of stretchers sorting out the Allied troops, most of them in the recent fighting and relieved to be back in friendly hands once more. More ambulances were called in and the Allied wounded evacuated. The Italians and Germans had their own medical officers and staff. With the Allied wounded evacuated there was room left to convert the warehouse into a hospital. The enemy had left plenty of medical supplies behind.

Gradually, the civilian population came out of hiding from their cellars and bomb shelters, taking to the streets and surrounding the vehicles. The extra ambulances evacuated the remainder of the wounded to a British general hospital near the Italian airfield.

They sat wearily on the back step of the ambulance. If only for twenty-four hours they were free of the war. A sense of relief flowed through their bodies, but inwardly they knew it would soon start all over again, this was just the first major part. The next part of the campaign would be the toughest but at this moment it was time to relax. Two Arab urchins came up to them, hands outstretched, pleading.

"Bukshees, Tommee. You give me cigarette Tommee," their dark eyes peering first at Harry and then at Charlie.

"You give me cigarette." A smile lifted the dimples on one of the boy's cheeks.

Charlie shook his head and laughed.

"Bloody marvellous, isn't it? Haven't been here a day yet and the little sods are scrounging in English." He turned to the two urchins

"Bugger off, you are too young to smoke." He patted their heads and smiled. Both boys grinned, as if they knew what Charlie was saying. He reached behind him for two packets of hard tack biscuits and threw them to the boys. With a flick of the wrist each lad caught one, saluted smartly, then walked away.

"You're a soft bastard, Charlie." Harry grinned, he knew Charlie loved kids.

"They aren't much older than my own kid."

They made their way towards the large hospital near Castle Bento airport. Charlie decided to take the side streets. The town was alive. Military police directed traffic at every intersection and as predicted H.Q. had taken over most of the largest buildings. Civilians flooded the streets now they were confident the troops weren't bent on looting and pillaging. Already a few shops opened selling what goods they held, most of it of inferior quality: postcards and cheap albums, sticky sweets and a watery ice cream with little flavour - just cold and wet.

Charlie turned down a deserted side street, not yet discovered by the troops. He swept past a small wine shop, then skidded to a halt with a squeal of brakes. A young lady, half hidden, stood in the darkened doorway of a wine shop. He just had time to see her give him a charming smile. It was a narrow street with no footpath, not made for motorised vehicles.

"See me back, Harry?"

There was about twelve inches to spare each side. Harry hadn't the slightest idea why he wanted to reverse but slowly they moved backwards. She was still standing there when they came level with the doorway. Charlie's head was just about three feet from the girl's face. He gave her that fascinating smile and winked.

She stepped back into the wine shop. Charlie jumped out and followed her and beckoned to Harry. He strained his eyes in the dim interior taking a few seconds before his eyes became accustomed to the gloom. Several tables were dotted around the red flagstone floor. In one corner there was a small bar with several shelves behind it all filled with bottles of wine. To the side of the shelves was a small doorway covered with a beaded curtain.

Four Arabs sat at one corner table hardly giving them a second glance after they entered. After all they were just another bunch of foreign soldiers and the Arabs took their presence for granted, certain they were here to stay and occupy the country.

Harry nodded towards the four Arabs.

"Nice friendly lot, ain't they, Charlie? Do you reckon they are pleased to see us?"

"Balls to them."

He poked a cigarette in the corner of his mouth and as the match rubbed the surface of the box, four pairs of eyes became riveted on the cigarette. Harry placed the round tin of fifty on the marble topped table. The Arabs eyes followed his every move, then settled on the tin of fifty. Charlie threw a packet of issue "V" cigarettes to their table. Four pairs of hands made a grab for it and soon a terrible argument ensued. The girl came rushing out and grabbed the packet, then shared them out equally.

The girl had a tight fitting blouse that bought a gasp from Charlie, she looked gorgeous in the semi darkness. Charlie gulped and went to speak to Harry but the words were dry and inaudible. He rubbed his hand across his mouth and croaked, "Christ, Harry, just take a shufti at those Bristols. After seeing you stripped for months, she looks deformed."

Her dark brown hair looked black, a silky black, in this semi darkness, but her eyes looked as if they were on fire as they caught the sun filtering through the one and only tiny window high above them. Charlie caught his breath, the sweat oozed from his forehead and neck.

She walked, or rather she swayed across the room, causing his heart to miss several beats. His mouth dry, he sipped at a glass of wine she held out to him. She placed a slender bottle of wine on the table and gave Harry an empty glass, then picked up the bottle and started to fill the glass from Charlie's side, reaching across the table. Her buttocks pressed against Charlie. She went to refill Charlie's glass and their fingertips touched, sending a shiver right through his body. Their fingers locked together, she peered down at him and smiled, revealing two rows of almost transparent white teeth. Charlie grasped her hand and she made no move to remove it.

Charlie took a quick sip of wine, he knew he couldn't talk with a dry mouth, he spluttered, "Ye Gods, I'm in, mate, I'm in."

Did she speak English? Hardly. Charlie, as usual, was using his charm. This was the first time Harry had seen him in action with a woman. He was soon to learn that it didn't matter much whether they spoke English or not, they soon fell for his charm. Within minutes Charlie's hand was gently stroking her buttocks. She moved and sat on his knee, pushing the table forward. That tickling sensation reached the pit of Charlie's stomach, he could feel his body trembling.

It was Harry what broke the silence. He took a great sip of wine, more than was usual for him, he was beginning to feel heady.

"Nice wine, Charlie."

"Sod the wine." He drew the girl to him, she sat on his lap as his hand explored the well shaped body.

"Do me a favour, Harry, just pinch me. This has to be a dream. Any minute now I am going to wake and find myself in some slit trench out in the desert."

Standing up she smoothed her hands round her well shaped body, her dress clung to every contour. She picked up the tin of cigarettes and made towards the door.

"There goes your fags."

The girl stood framed in the doorway, with the bright sun shining through the thin dress it left nothing to the imagination. She walked towards the table occupied by the four Arabs and gave them each five of the cigarettes from the tin, then jerked her thumb over her shoulder towards the door. The Arabs grinned and hurried away without a glance toward Harry and Charlie. She bolted the door behind them. As she walked across the stone floor the bead curtain behind the bar parted and a small blonde entered and smiled at Harry, just as he thought he was about to be the wallflower. She was much prettier then the dark haired girl and a lot smaller. She had green eyes and was shaped in the right place. Harry gulped and couldn't take his eyes away from her.

"Wow, Charlie, do you reckon they are on the game?"

"Don't know, what's more I don't care. All I know is back there, out in the desert, the bloody camels were starting to look attractive. If I wake up before this dream finishes, Harry, don't ever speak to me again." Charlie was living up to his reputation, a reputation not only amongst the men in his own unit but amongst the whole division. It was said that if there is a bint within twenty miles Charlie will sniff it out.

"Blondie here has got her hand on my knee, Charlie." Then as an afterthought he said, "Do you think she's a real blonde?"

"Well here's your chance to find out."

The dark haired girl had him by the hand and was pulling him towards the bead curtains, not as if he needed a great lot of pulling. He was like the proverbial lamb being led to the slaughter. Harry and the blonde followed.

The bedroom was big, and the large bed almost filled it. Apart from the bed was a wardrobe and a side table with a china jug and wash basin. She slammed the door and rammed home two large iron bolts. Charlie, always cautious, opened the wardrobe door and peered inside. It was known for a pimp in these foreign parts to hide, then when a client was settled down, have a knife through his back. But apart from a couple of flimsy dresses the wardrobe was empty.

He filled the basin with cold water, then washed the sand and dust from his short cropped hair and chest. The dark girl washed his back, the cold water revived him. There was no soap but he felt fresher and much better for the wash. He slipped off his shorts and jumped into bed. She followed him, slipping out of her flimsy dress.

Harry realised he had drunk too much wine. He felt in a trance as she led him through the door and on to the bed. He lay with his legs dangling over the side; she removed his shorts, then stepped out of her dress. He giggled to himself realising she was a real blonde. He stared at the ceiling thinking 'a couple of days ago she could have been sharing the bed with some German or Italian.' He pulled her on top of him.

He woke up during the night with a splitting headache and looked around at his strange surroundings. A wisp of hair fell across his mouth. She looked at him with her green eyes and smiled. But he was uncomfortable. The wine had done its duty and was waiting to be evacuated. He looked round for the toilet. The blonde scrambled from the bed and took a chamber pot from beneath, then sat down and urinated, smiling up at Harry. By this time the sound of running water had put him in agony. She finished and he grabbed the chamber pot and sighed with ecstasy.

"If it's the only way," he gasped as relief gushed right through his whole system.

The sun was well up when they finally woke. Harry stared at the open window, the memory of the night came flooding back and he slipped out of bed and stared underneath. The full chamber pot was still there, so he hadn't been dreaming.

Feeling fully relieved and a lot fitter they walked downstairs. Charlie flopped into a chair in the kitchen, while Harry went to his ambulance, surprised to see it still there with its wheels and contents still intact. He removed their ration box and took it

166

inside. The fair haired girl prepared a meal of tinned bacon and sausages, and - holy of holies - she produced eggs, tomatoes and a small loaf of brown, almost black, bread. Harry made a large pot of tea. Both he and Charlie tried to avoid looking directly at each other. Harry realised if they did they would burst out laughing. After a good meal in the desert Charlie was inclined to belch loudly, but self control took over and he lit a cigarette. It was time to go but the girls were reluctant to let go and the dark haired one tried to drag Charlie back up the stairs. He shook his head and made his way towards the door. They left the box of rations and several hundred "V" issue cigarettes, that would keep them going.

"That was a bloody strange night, Harry," Charlie said as they got into the ambulance.

"Do you realise that we were with them for over eight hours and they never spoke one word to us. I wonder if they were Italians or Arabs?"

Harry shrugged his shoulder, "Who cares, I had to laugh when she started pissing in that pot. I couldn't believe my eyes, she didn't care one bit, just looked at me and smiled."

"That happened to me, too. I was going to piss through the window, then she took out this piss pot and had a go herself. Try and get out again tonight, Harry, bring some more mungie (food) and fags."

The streets were quiet, apart from a few Red Caps on duty and sentries posted at the large buildings. Charlie stopped the ambulance and asked a Red Cap the time and was surprised to learn it was just after six.

"Right. Where the hell have you two bastards been all night?" The sergeant rushed out to greet them, shaving lather all over his chin and his shaving brush still in his hand.

"It doesn't take all night to return from the hospital to here."

"It does, sarge, if you break a bloody axle spring." He sorted under his seat and brought out a broken leaf of an axle and held it up triumphantly.

"Ask up the hospital if you like. The corporal in the guard room sent out a couple of janker wallahs to give us a hand."

"You lying bastard, Williams. Where have you been?"

Charlie was in a jovial mood, after all he had just spent the best night for many months. He smiled at the sergeant.

"I see you don't believe me, sarge, so I had better come out with the truth. We met these two birds in a wine shop, a little blonde and a dark haired beauty and that was it, sarge. They insisted we spend the night with them. I can tell you, sarge, we didn't have much kip."

Harry swung round to see what the sergeant's reaction would be when they told him the truth. As Charlie predicted, he didn't believe one word.

"You are both a pair of liars, I wish we had time to check the story of the broken spring. Unfortunately we move out in a couple of hours." He turned and stormed away.

Charlie shouted after him, "By the way, sarge, some bastard nicked our box of rations, can we get more from the Q.M?"

Without turning the sergeant roared back so half the regiment could hear.

"Starve, you pair of bastards! Starve!"

"Do you think he believed us, Charlie - about the broken spring I mean? I often wondered why you kept that broken spring in the cab."

Charlie laughed and took a notebook from the cab, sucked the tip of his pencil and made a few hurried notes.

"Couldn't care less, Harry. It's always a good excuse and so far I have always got away with it. I have just made a note, I don't want to use that excuse again with this regiment."

As predicted by all the old hands in the div, they wouldn't linger once the city fell. By midday Tripoli was miles behind them and they were on the way to the Tunisian border. Charlie had proved his point to Harry. If you pick up a bint, tell the truth, no one will believe you.

CHAPTER 18

When they reached their new posting the regiment was out of the line. The men had been called together for a pep talk by the medical officer. He was standing on an upturned ammunition box with several large illustrated posters pinned to the canvas lean-to, and was giving a heart to heart talk to the men on the perils of associating with loose women.

"Now men, this is very serious. For just one half hour of enjoyment you can ruin your lives. Blindness, gonorrhoid arthritis, paralysis, insanity - they are just a few of the things resulting from V.D. so before you associate with these women think twice, and if you can't control yourselves at least take a precaution. Use a rubber preventative. But leaving sex alone is the best advice." The lecture went on for another ten minutes with the M.O. heaping on the hidden dangers then he said, "Any questions?"

From the back of the crowd one arm shot up and a small man kept leaping to his feet in an attempt to attract the M.O's attention.

The sergeant at the M.O's side said, "What is it, Newman?"

"How do you make it last half an hour, sir?"

There was a roar of laughter from the assembled men and Newman was marched off to the C.O.'s office.

"Bloody right shower, this lot, Charlie," Harry said. They waited for the crowd to disperse then reported to the aid post.

With the regiment resting the next three days were pretty boring. Harry gave the interior of the ambulance a thorough going over and replenished his medical supplies. Charlie serviced his ambulance engine, correcting the timing till he got a perfect balance.

"You know, we could take this tub round Brooklands and give the rest a good run for their money," he commented. Then he switched it on and the engine purred like a contented kitten.

On the third day they were on the move again. They stopped at a small dilapidated house boasting a pool of fresh water surrounded by palm trees and a smallholding of crops. It was not more than two or three acres, just sufficient to keep the farmer and his family from starvation, but within the hour the men were lolling round the pool, stripped naked, as if they were on the beach back home on a hot summer day.

Charlie and Harry sat on the back of the ambulance chatting.

"You know, Charlie, less than six years ago I was playing in the sand pit back at the home. I loved that sand pit. It seemed the only place at the home that the staff kept clear of. Little did I know then that within six years I would be playing in the largest bloody sand pit in the world."

But Charlie was in a pensive mood, and he had hardly spoken for the last two hours.

"That home, Harry. Were you every lonely? Did you miss your parents? Were they good to you - the staff, I mean?"

Harry realised immediately what was wrong with his driver. A few days ago the mail had arrived and he'd received the usual two letters. The one, lightly perfumed, he'd torn to shreds without opening it. The other, in the usual buff coloured envelope, he had read over and over again.

"It was alright," Harry lied. "I can't say I missed my parents. My father I never knew and my mother died of T.B. when I was six months. They were pretty good at the home. There was never any chance to get lonely, too many kids around for that. Mind you, it wasn't the usual run of the mill orphanage. It was run by Quakers. The benefactor made one stipulation. He was a music freak - Mozart and Chopin - and every child had to learn a musical instrument. That home had a very good name for the musicians it turned out. They taught me the piano. When I ran away and joined the army the matron and my tutor did their nuts. As you know, the Quakers are pacifists and the matron was a true Quaker, when she spoke it was all thee's and thou's. It was the religion that got me down. The music teacher wasn't so bad but she hit the roof when she knew I was in the army. She said in time I would have made a good concert pianist."

"Didn't they let you out? Let you mix with the other kids outside, I mean?"

"Oh yes, we went to the local village school. Then there was this farmer and his wife. Crafty pair of bastards, they were. They would invite us over for the day, then they would get us cleaning out the cow sheds. Me and another kid, once we had to whitewash the cow sheds. He said he would teach us how to milk the cows and he did that alright - that became our regular job. Sometimes he would invite all his cronies around and me and my mate, he played the violin, would play for them. When the visitors had gone the crafty sods couldn't get rid of us quick enough."

"Do you think my little girl will forget me, Harry?"

"Don't be a prick, Charlie, she's in good hands. At least they write to you regularly and keep in touch. I bet at this moment she is boasting to all her mates about her dad fighting the Germans in Africa."

Spag sidled up to Harry and rubbed himself against his leg.

"Bloody hell, Spag! You stink to high heaven."

170

"Stop victimising him, Harry." Charlie bent down and fondled the dog's ears, and its watery eyes gazed up at Charlie as if they understood every word and were pleading with him to take no notice of what Harry was saying.

"But you're right, Harry, the little sod does pong, so I'll give him a bath after we've had some grub. I'll use the old brew can."

"Over my dead body, you dirty bastard. There's an old Jerry dump back there. Go find a Jerry helmet. I would say throw the dirty sod in the pool but the men out there might lynch you."

When Charlie called out to Spag and tapped his knees with the flat of his hands, Spag looked up at him.

"Come on, Spag. Let Daddy go and find you a nice little bath tub," he called to the animal. Then Charlie watched Harry's face as he knew it irritated him when he spoke to the dog in this way.

"And after din dins you can have a nice tin of bully, all to yourself, and we won't let that nasty Harry have one slice. We won't even let him sniff at the tin, and after, you can have a tin of rice pudding. You like ricey wicey, don't you? Now, let's go and find a tablet of Q.M.s carbolic, 'cos Daddy thinks you might have a little fleasy weasy... In fact, Daddy was scratching his balls all last night."

Harry tutted and shook his head in disgust. Spag was backing away from Charlie towards himself and gently placing his foot under Spag's rear end he lifted him, with equal gentleness, upwards into Charlie's arms.

They soon found the dump where rifles, ammunition, leather straps, hand grenades and helmets were piled high.

"There you are, Spag," Charlie exulted. "One of those helmets will make a nice bath for you." But he had only taken a couple of steps forward when he froze.

Just below the sand he saw a round object the size of a large dinner plate and kneeling down he blew the layer of fine sand from off it and gasped, "Bloody hell, mines."

He put Spag on the ground and immediately realised his mistake as Spag shot away a few yards and turned towards him yelping. "Heel, Spag. Heel," he commanded. Unfortunately Spag couldn't or wouldn't heel. He didn't have the remotest idea what heel meant. Spag was good for three things only - eating, sleeping and urinating. Harry swore blind he had something wrong with his waterworks. There was only one thing in the dog's favour. He could warn them of an approaching air raid.

Charlie yelled at the top of his voice for Harry. He was almost hoarse by the time he answered.

"What the hell do you want?"

171

"I think I've walked onto a minefield, Harry. When I get on my knees I can see several with pieces of wire sticking up. I think they are A.P. mines. But this one near me is a bloody large one." He remained rooted to the spot. "Shout a warning to the lads and get an officer. Then fetch me my bayonet."

Fortunately there was a squadron of sappers nearby who had just completed clearing a minefield. Charlie was prodding the ground with the tip of his bayonet, and had already uncovered a large mine and was about to lift it when the sapper sergeant shouted, "Don't touch it!

With his mine detector he made his way towards where Charlie was kneeling. "Don't touch the damn thing!" he rapped at him. "It could be booby trapped to several others. Nice trick of Jerry to make a mine obvious. You lift it and, bang, before you realise it you can be kissing your arse all the way into the hereafter, and also several other sappers who could be sweeping the area would go with you."

The sergeant bent down besides Charlie and scraped away a tunnel under the mine, then he nodded his head towards Charlie.

"Alright, piss off and follow that white tape."

A crowd of sappers descended on the mine field making several sweeps and recovering thirty or more mines. While the ambulance crew sat on the back step of the ambulance watching.

"That's a bloody near one, Harry," Charlie said, holding out his shaking hands. Harry made a brew and gave each one of the sappers a mugful after he'd laced it with brandy from his medical pannier.

The sapper sergeant grinned. "Is this the way you ambulance crews live? Lashings of tea laced with brandy? If you find any more mines give us a call." He made an imaginary search of his pockets. "Sorry, but I've run out of business cards."

"Don't let that brandy fool you, sarge. One of the tank officers gave it to us. His tank had been knocked out and he was wounded. He said we could have it. Can't stand the stuff myself, but it comes in handy when someone is badly hurt," Charlie said as he poured out a liberal portion for the sergeant.

The sergeant tipped the drink back. "Right, Taff, one more sweep to be in the clear. Stupid place to bivvy up here, anyway." He spotted Spag. "And it's about time you gave that bleeding dog a scrub."

One of the sappers dropped a German steel helmet at Charlie's feet.

"Here's your helmet, boyo, and thanks for the brandy."

It was almost dusk when another ambulance pulled alongside them. The medic stood up his blonde hair falling round his eyes, which had become narrow slits from his being in the desert and Sudan so long that they always looked half closed. His shirt was wide open revealing a mass of fine blonde hairs on his chest and his frayed shorts looked much the worse for wear. A round tin of fifty cigarettes bulged from the top of his shirt pocket, and a soggy half-smoked cigarette hung over his bottom lip as if it was glued into position.

"Hello you pair of sex maniacs. Hear you had it away with two Itey bints in Tripoli. That right, Charlie?"

"Bloody hell, it soon gets around."

"Well, Charlie, knowing you and hearing you had the night away, I could only put two and two together." As he spoke the red glow on the tip of his cigarette went up and down like a semaphore signal.

Harry smiled, obviously pleased to see Jordan. He was always good for a laugh with his dry Yorkshire humour. Also if there were any rumours around the divvy, he was always one of the first to know. Like Harry he too was a regular, fully qualified. He had worked in a general hospital in Cairo after coming up from the Sudan, but he'd insulted a sister and like a true biblical character he'd been banished into the desert. Not as though he minded - far from it. The wide open spaces and being amongst the action suited him.

"How's Eddie, your driver?" asked Charlie. Just as he spoke Jordan's driver swung himself from his seat in the ambulance and out onto the desert sand. Then, directing himself towards a front wheel, he started to relieve his bladder against it in large circular movements as if he were washing the sand away. The others watched, fascinated.

"He's always doing that. Likes making patterns. Lost his girlfriend over that back home."

"How come?" Harry asked.

"It was snowing one day when he took his girlfriend home, and outside her door he started pissing and writing his name in the snow. The girl's old lady saw it the next morning and told the father. He said, 'So what? We all did that as kids.' But the old lady complained that it was in her daughter's handwriting."

"You lousy bastard, Jordan. If you expect me to believe that one you must think I'll believe anything."

"No. Actually I heard it on an E.N.S.A. concert. The best joke of the night. Thought it might come in handy."

They spent an hour chasing Spag for his bath. Jordan wanted to do a Mundy on the dog by giving him a whiff of ether and would have done, except Charlie stopped him before he could. By the time they had washed the animal it was quite dark. Jordan took out a new pack of cards.

"Right," he declared. "Five card brag."

They lit two hurricane lamps and closed the ambulance doors. But it was too hot to play cards so they sat outside smoking and talking over old times. It was a beautiful night, the sky ablaze with stars. In the distance they could just hear the faint sounds of gunfire and occasionally the bright flashes of guns would light up the distant horizon. As far as they were concerned, the war could have been on another continent.

Nearby, Eddie, the pattern making driver, hauled the shovel from his ambulance and informed them, "When you got to go - you got to go!"

"Careful, Eddie. They just cleared some mines down there. I don't want to frighten you, but one of the sappers was wearing an enormous hearing aid," Charlie teased him and they all laughed.

Unperturbed, Eddie strolled a few yards back and saw the pile of defused mines the sappers had left behind. He did his business, buried it and then on his walk back picked up a defused mine with the end of his shovel.

"Eh, Charlie," he enquired innocently, "when I dug that hole I picked up this round thing. You think they missed it?"

The other three jumped up and ran as fast as they could from the two ambulances.

"For fuck's sake, Eddie, what are you trying to do? Blow us all sky high?" Harry yelled back at him.

But Eddie threw the mine down and rolled up in a ball off laughter.

"Christ, man, I never seen three men move so fast! Just like cats with a pack of drooling dogs after them. Couldn't see your arses for dust."

"You're a stupid prat, Eddie. Defused, or not, I wouldn't touch one of those things for a million pounds."

All over the leaguer, men sat around their vehicles in small groups, their voices a slight rumble carrying across the still air of the desert. There was hardly a ripple of air and it became cool, but not unpleasantly cold. The heads of the palm trees were black silhouettes against the moonlit and cloudless sky, the bright starlight intermingled amongst the broad palm leaves. Peace had descended on the area.

A few yards from the ambulance someone started to play the mouth organ. Everyone stopped talking. A sweet, sentimental First World War song wafted across the sands. It was 'Roses of Picardy.' A few men started to hum it. Harry fell silent, his arm dropping to his sides. There was something about that tune that

174

touched an unknown spot and it was the second time that this had happened. He shuddered. Why should that song affect him now? He'd heard it scores of times and played it more often than he cared to remember on the piano at the home. He squatted down on the sand and folded his arms. Another man was accompanying the mouth organ with a violin. Together they played that haunting melody through once more, but it played on his mind long after the two men had started on several other requests. These came in from all sides. Then a thick Glaswegian accent boomed across the sands, "What about 'I Belong to Glasgow?'"

"Yes, what about it?" came a chorus of voices.

Although the song could rightly be described as the Glaswegian anthem, there wasn't a soldier in the British Army - Scot, English, Irish or Welsh - that didn't know it, and now they all sang in pseudo-Scottish accents. Whether these could be understood in the Glasgow Gorbels was another thing, however. The happy singing went on well past midnight.

Darkness fell with sudden ferocity when the moon dropped over the horizon leaving just the starlit night. Faces that has once been recognisable now became plain blobs under the pale stars. But it was easy to recognise that dark silhouette with the sparks flying from a freshly lit pipe, and the long greatcoat trailing in the sand, his small legs moving back and forth like irate pistons.

"Come on, lads, get mounted. We're moving up."

The order took them completely by surprise. They had expected to be a few more days out of the action.

"What's the idea, sarge? I thought we were supposed to be resting?"

The sergeant grinned.

"You're a regular, Jackson. You should know what the army gets up to."

They took their leave of the other ambulance crew. Eddie, wrapped in several blankets, snored loudly and grunted some kind of answer. Within minutes the battalion was spread across the leaguer.

As they neared the front line the flashes from the heavy guns became brilliant. In front of the heavy guns they twenty five pounders opened up with short cracks which sounded like doors being slammed in an empty house and echoing throughout the building. A star shell burst in the sky, bathing the desert in its eerie glow. A heavy machine gun opened up and the tracer bullets arched across the sands stabbing the velvet blackness. Another flare burst above their heads and its bright, fluorescent glow illuminated the advancing battalion. The light spluttered for

175

a few seconds, then fizzled out leaving them temporarily blinded until their eyes became accustomed to the darkness. Then they came to a halt.

"That bloody machine gun sounded near, Harry. Can't be all that far from the front."

Harry didn't answer. He was listening to the deadly rumble of mortars as they rolled over and over, giving a deathly moan that rose and fell as the bombs tumbled their way to their targets.

"I hate those bastard mortars. That gives me the bloody creeps," muttered Harry.

He dropped from the cab, and in spite of being covered with his heavy greatcoat and balaclava helmet the cold night air bit into the exposed parts of his body. He could feel his legs and face turning blue with the extreme cold. He walked over to the M.O.'s utility, then returned a few minutes later.

"Looks like we'll be here for a while. Jerry has made a counter attack and the battalion may have to go in at first light. Looks a bit dodgy up front."

At first light the regiment moved in and shells started to drop all around the aid post. Harry dropped flat as hot shrapnel screamed through the air. The earth trembled. A large shell dropped less than twenty feet away lifting their bodies from the ground, and a jagged piece of metal six inches long tore into the ground beside Harry's head. He felt a tingle and a cold clammy sweat oozed from his body. A trickle of blood filled his mouth as he bit hard into his bottom lip. The shelling eased off and, sitting up, Harry wiped his hand across his mouth. It left two streaks of blood on the back of his hand. He pulled the shrapnel from the ground. It was shaped like the blade of a sheath knife. He tossed it to Charlie. It was still warm, but before Charlie could comment the sergeant rushed over.

"Right, lads. Let's pull back. It's getting a bit hot round here."

"What's the matter then, sarge? Another balls up?" Charlie grumbled as he rose from the ground and tossed the piece of metal away.

Hardly had they set up the aid post when the casualties started rolling in, some carried by stretcher bearers, others brought in on bren gun carriers, but quite a few walking wounded. They were just on the edge of the German shelling range, the casualties running the gauntlet towards the aid post. A man with his arm in a sling and a field dressing round his head came walking towards them. Suddenly a large shell dropped and after the smoke and the sand had cleared, all that was left of the man was a boot with half a leg still in it.

Charlie shook his head and muttered to Harry, "It just wasn't his day, Harry."

They loaded the ambulance and made their way back towards the advanced dressing station. It was a hive of activity already crowded with casualties from other regiments. Men were at hand to unload the ambulance and they were soon on their way back. The battle was reaching fever pitch. Harry helped to dress the wounds before they loaded the ambulance. This routine was kept up until midday.

With the incessant clatter of the guns from both sides, the eerie sounds of the mortars and the chatter of machine guns, the casualties at the dressing station and a row of dead behind the canvas lean-to, the station resembled a scene from hell itself. Occasionally the M.O. would emerge from his makeshift theatre to gulp in fresh air, his rubber apron splattered with congealing blood and his unshaven face and uncombed hair making his look like the devil himself.

Late in the afternoon a soldier with a serious head wound was brought in. They were ordered to take him directly to the C.C.S and, as the C.C.S lay some ten miles to the rear, it was as real break. Another ambulance was ordered in to take their place.

"And make sure you get a good feed and a couple of hours rest while you're there," was the parting shot from the M.O.

The C.C.S. was in a quiet zone with just a faint rumble of guns from the front line. It was laid out in the usual manner. There were large marquees on three sides, two flag poles in the centre of the rectangle and the paths were lined with whitewashed boulders. On one of these a man was busy wielding a paint brush and Charlie shot him a look of disgust.

"Surely a man can be put to better use than that."

But Harry had seen it all before. "That's the medics alright, Charlie. I suppose there is a method in their madness. It's easier for the ambulances to see their way in at nightfall."

"Sure, Harry, but there must be plenty of prisoners around capable of doing jobs like that."

Four men were waiting at the reception. A sister came out her well starched apron crackling as she entered the ambulance to inspect the man. She felt his pulse in a most professional manner.

"Alright, men, take it easy with him, he's in a very bad way." She threw a critical glance over Charlie and Harry. "You two look as if a good meal wouldn't hurt you. When did you last sleep?"

"Three days ago," Charlie lied. He didn't mind a bit of sympathy.

"Well, you must take it easy, men. Get some food down you and return to your unit."

The cook sergeant filled Harry's mess tin with meat and vegetable stew and Charlie's mess tin with hot tinned steam pudding and a thick gooey mixture that resembled a custard which had stood for several days and had then been warmed up. They drained the tea from two large china mugs and retreated to their ambulance with the full mess tins.

"I can't stand this bullshit," Charlie muttered. "Let's find a spot on the way back to the regiment."

Harry grinned, only too ready to agree.

Halfway back to their unit they pulled up from the track. Harry lit a petrol fire and soon warmed up the stew and pudding and then made more tea. They ate until they felt they would burst, despite the fact that the custard was watery and tasted faintly of chlorine. Replete, they dozed off on the shady side of the ambulance.

It seemed they had only been asleep a few minutes when someone kicked the bottom of their feet. Charlie opened one eye and closed it immediately as the sun reflected off some brightly polished buttons and white webbing. A boot tapped his foot a little harder and Charlie squinted and look up at a Red Cap. His face was half hidden under the peak of his cap which was pulled flush on top of his nose.

"A nice pair of sleeping beauties we have here, corporal," one of the Red Caps said to the other.

Charlie sat up and looked into his mug still half filled with cold tea in which two flies were struggling through a swimming lesson. Using his forefinger and thumb he flicked them out and then straining the cold tea between his teeth, he casually studied the two Red Caps from under his eyebrows without making a move to get up. They were as immaculate as ever in their well pressed shirt, shorts and polished brassware.

"Where the hell did you two come from?" Charlie growled as he refilled his mug with cold tea from the brew can.

With his eyes peering down the inside peak of his cap, the Red Cap regarded Charlie in the way he might a bad smell.

"Come on, lad, get to your feet and stand to attention when an N.C.O. speaks to you."

For the past twenty four hours the ambulance crew had hardly had more than two hours sleep, and Charlie was in no mood for such bullshit. Harry was about to scramble to his feet when Charlie put a restraining arm across him. Slowly Charlie rose to his feet and turned his back on the Red Cap. Then he threw the dregs of his tea into the sand. The Red Cap screamed at him,

"Stand to attention, you bloody scruff."

With a look of contempt, Charlie answered, "Balls."

The Red Cap stuttered. What could be seen of his piercing eyes bored right through Charlie, the bottom half of his face turning crimson.

"If you don't stand to attention I'll place both of you under arrest," he blustered.

"Bollocks," Charlie said with slow deliberation and continued to rinse out his mug.

The Red Cap was rooted to the spot. When he spoke the words issued forth in an unintelligible jumble as excitement overpowered his speech. At any moment now Harry expected the Red Cap to lash out at Charlie. The situation was saved from becoming a rough house when a utility pulled up beside them and their own R.S.M. stepped out. He took in the situation straight away. He wasn't too fond of Red Caps himself and he knew Charlie hated them. So did the R.S.M.'s driver, who was rubbing his hands together and grinning from ear to ear as he stepped from the utility to watch the fun, but he was in for a disappointment.

The R.S.M. ignoring the Red Caps turned to Charlie and enquired, "Have you two had any sleep and food yet?"

"We had food, sir, and just made a brew and was having a doze when these Red Caps kissed us awake."

Harry joined in the conversation straight away. He didn't want Charlie putting his foot in it. Calmly he explained the situation. The R.S.M. listened then turned on the Red Caps who came up to attention smartly.

"These men have been at it solidly for the last twenty-four hours. They have just returned with a badly injured man and were given orders to get some sleep."

"That's all very well, sir. We just came over to see what was going on when they became insubordinate. Especially this one here." He jerked his thumb in Charlie's direction. "Swore at me, sir."

"I think I would too, if you had just woke me from a deep sleep."

The R.S.M. looked at Charlie and jerked his head towards the ambulance.

"Leave this to me, corporal. I know the situation and will deal with this the moment they rejoin the unit."

Reluctantly the Red Cap returned his note book to his pocket and glared at Charlie as much to say, "There will be another day, you scruffy looking bastard."

Charlie couldn't help but give the Red Caps his usual parting gift, skidding the tyres of his ambulance and covering them from head to foot in sand. The R.S.M. expecting it, beat a hasty retreat.

He sat in his utility and muttered to himself, "Williams, you're a bastard..."

It was the last Harry and Charlie heard of the incident.

CHAPTER 19

The division passed over the Tunisian border leaving Tripoli as just a memory for Harry and Charlie. The enemy was making every effort to stem the advance of the allies, throwing everything at them. Field guns went on non-stop and land mines were laid everywhere. A combined force of allied troops, American and British, were attacking from the west after a seaborne landing, so dividing the axis powers, who like the proverbial rats in a trap with nowhere to go were fighting back desperately.

Every bridge, small or large, over every dry wadi had been destroyed. The Royal Engineers, often under heavy shell fire, made every effort to repair them and in so doing suffered heavy casualties.

The regiment entered a small colonial desert town where the entire civilian population turned out to meet them in front of the one and only large building in the town square. A temporary platform had been set up. The small crowd cheered and a short rotund man stood on the podium waving a large bottle of champagne. He wore a tricolour sash around his chest.

"Must be the Lord Mayor," Harry remarked, trying not to laugh too loudly. The man looked completely out of place wearing a black tailed suit and top hat while throwing kisses to the troops. Makeshift union jacks were hung from every window with smaller flags and garlands strung across the streets.

The C.O. stopped his car in front of the podium and was invited to join the fat man. The mayor immediately threw his arms around the C.O's neck and planted a wet, slobby kiss on each cheek. This was met with a series of cat calls from the rank and file. The C.O. looked round sharply and glared into the mass of innocent faces, unsmiling and staring back at him.

"Sergeant Major, the next man to make a crude remark, get his name and put him on a fizzer. I'll have him running round this desert in full pack till his balls drop off."

Someone cloaked in the anonymity of an enclosed scout car shouted through the driver's slits, "Bollocks, you old pansy ..."

A young girl pushed through the crowd and threw a bunch of flowers into the cab of the ambulance. Harry gasped as she pulled herself up into the cab using his thigh as a lever. She looked straight across the cab directly into Charlie's eyes. He gave her a slight peck on her cheek and gently slapped her bottom.

"Hop it, miss, and come back in two or three years time," he said gently. She smiled at his words and jumped from the cab as if she had understood every one of them.

Harry dozed off during the long boring speech given by the Frenchman in his own language, but was woken by a commotion from outside. Everyone was shouting and cheering as four Free French Military Police struggled with the fat mayor and bundled him into the back of a lorry.

"Bet that bastard was a Jerry collaborator, Charlie," Harry muttered grimly.

"Yes, guess so. I noticed the C.O. kept the bloody champagne."

Everyone was barking out orders. All of them trying to impress the local population with their superiority. The regiment tried to move, but every vehicle was hemmed in by the crowd, and the men were reluctant to move since all the female population were kissing and cuddling them freely. They, in turn, were unashamedly groping them. Unfortunately within the hour all the men were back in the desert again.

By late afternoon the regiment turned north and was running on a straight metal road parallel to the sea. It was almost dark when they pulled up for the night. A dispatch rider from their own unit pulled up beside the ambulance and handed Harry a bundle of letters. Much to his surprise there were four for him. The first was from his old matron who had just about forgiven him for enlisting, and the second from his old music teacher who was still insisting that no matter where he was, Harry must carry on his piano training. The next one, which was from Victoria, Harry decided to read last. She was always good for a laugh. Then there was also a letter from a girl he had met in Scotland. He had almost forgotten her. In fact he couldn't put a face to the letter which still bore traces of perfume, although it had been chasing him from one unit to another and taken eighteen months to catch up with him.

He handed Charlie his usual two letters and although, this time, the envelope was white, the familiar neat handwriting revealed the writer. Charlie carried out his usual routine. He gave the white envelope a cursory glance and then tore it into tiny bits before letting it filter away between his fingers. The long buff envelope he folded neatly and placed in the back pocket of his shorts.

After the evening meal of a tin of vegetables and meat stew with a tin of bully cut into squares and all boiled together, Harry borrowed a hurricane lamp and walked across the sands to be alone with his letters and his thoughts. As expected the matron and his music teacher had the same old story, Matron - 'You are a silly boy for joining the army,' and his music teacher hoped he was still practising his piano. Harry laughed at that, but both gave him a strict warning to be careful. Victoria's letter was all about the hospital, plus scandal, laced with some humour. The little Scottish lass, try as he might, he just couldn't remember. Tomorrow he would answer all the letters and ask the girl if she had a photograph of herself. It was refreshing to receive mail from home. He had no family and England, every mile of it, was home.

Charlie was fast asleep on a stretcher by the side of the ambulance. He had prepared a stretcher for Harry. Sleep didn't come easy that night. He lay with his head cupped in his hands staring up at the stars with Victoria on his mind. He must have dropped off, for the next thing he knew someone was tugging at his blankets and shouting, "Rise and shine, my beauties, rise and shine. Stand to. Hands off your plonkers. Stand to. Stand to."

Charlie in the nude, as usual, sat up and stared at the medical sergeant with bleary eyes and scratched his armpits.

"What the hell do you want us to stand up for, sarge?"

"Don't argue, Williams. This is what it's all about. What you get paid for, you might say."

With the departure of the sergeant, Charlie lit a cigarette and threw his blankets to one side grumbling, "Better get up and placate the old bastard." He was still completely nude, Spag cradled in the crook of his arm. "Some bleeding pay," he grumbled, climbing into his shorts and shirt and shivering as the cold morning air bit into his naked flesh.

The sky brightening, the stars paled and the regiment came to life with the familiar sounds of brew cans being unhooked from their vehicles echoing across the sands like a chorus of church bells. One by one the drivers tested their vehicle engines. The ambulance crew drank several mugs of hot tea and Charlie tuned the engine for the hundredth time. Harry answered the letters in order of importance, leaving Victoria's to the last, and once more savouring the humorous passages. But try as hard as he possibly could, he just couldn't put a face to the Scottish girl. He wasn't above laying on a sob story, and he asked her for a photograph to remind him of their good times together.

Much to all the men's surprise they spent the whole day in idleness and managed to soak themselves in the briny.

"Not a lot happening, sarge. When are we pushing off?"

"Ask me another. You know as much as I do, but I promise you when we move we won't go without you."

True to his word the sergeant tugged the blankets from them without ceremony the next morning. It was still dark. They dressed quickly, complete with greatcoat, Harry's teeth chattering in protest.

"I was having a terrific dream, Charlie," Harry told him, his voice muffled as he struggled to put his balaclava helmet over his face.

The regiment was moving fast across the open desert to take up their allotted positions, but they had hardly travelled more than ten miles when the first shells were dropped indiscriminately amongst the racing vehicles. The ambulance shook as a large shell dropped within yards of them. The steering wheel spun violently and Charlie lost control. Hot jagged metal rent the air with its eerie whine. The regiment slowed down and then came to an abrupt halt.

A dispatch rider skidded to a halt beside them and Harry was busy digging the slit trenches while Charlie made a closer examination of his beloved ambulance to ensure it hadn't suffered in the bombardment.

"Better get up front. Some of the vehicles are in the shite," the D.R. said. Charlie revved up his engine and pushed his foot down hard on the floor. The ambulance roared forward. A small scout car was burning up. A man was scrambling from the turret his shirt smouldering. Harry knew the drill and grabbing a blanket from Spag's bed, he was out of the ambulance and smothering the man's back before the ambulance came to a stop. Carefully he lifted the blanket. The man's shirt had welded to his skin and his shirt and flesh had become one black gooey mess. The man moaned, his face distorted with pain, and pointed a trembling finger.

"My mate's still in there."

"Sorry, mate, it's too late," Charlie replied, helping to lift the man on his stretcher into the ambulance.

In spite of his pain, tears flowed from the man's eyes.

"We've been together for two years," he sobbed. Harry gave him a jab of morphine and painted a bright M on his forehead using iodine.

They scouted around and found four more men injured. Three of them had bad burns and the other had a large piece of shrapnel lodged in the fleshy part of his thigh. The ambulance, now filled with casualties, roared to the rear and kept the same routine going throughout the entire day. In between runs, Harry helped out at the makeshift operating theatre. It didn't take long for the aid post to take on its familiar face. Rows of stretchers filled up with the wounded. More stretchers at the rear of the aid post filled with the dead. The familiar smell of burnt flesh, antiseptics, anaesthetics, eusol and chlorine and, above all, the nauseating stench of death dominated. It was a foul and hellish stink which Harry believed would never leave him. To add to the

184

overall discomfort, a slight breeze sprang up bringing with it the odour of explosives, burnt rubber and diesel fumes.

A shell landed near the lean-to. The explosion blew the flimsy canvas sides in like the sails of a ship weathering a storm. A large piece of red hot shrapnel tore through the canvas and embedded itself in the rear tyre of the three tonner, but only after ripping away the handle of the stretcher the M.O. was using as a makeshift operating table so neatly, that it appeared to have been cut through with a circular saw.

The infantry was brought up in three ton lorries. The battle grew more fierce. The M.O. decided to be prudent and pulled the aid post back a few hundred yards. Then the heavy tanks came up and moved into position. Tiger tanks sprang forward to meet them and soon the gap between the Sherman and Tiger tanks grew narrower, each holding their fire until the crucial moment. From Harry's position, as he studied them through Charlie's binoculars, it looked as if they would clash head on. At last the leading tanks on both sides, a German Tiger and a British Sherman, swerved and fired their guns simultaneously. The Tiger tank burst into flames. The commander of the Sherman tank raised his head above the turret just as a shell blasted against the steel sides and, a moment later, the remaining lower half of the commander slid back inside the tank.

Harry jumped onto the tank. Inside a man was crouching in a corner staring at a jellied mass of intestines and gore. Harry dropped inside the tank and skidded on the jellied mass. The man in the corner wouldn't move. His eyes were wide open in terror and another man was attempting to coax him from his shocked hypnotic trance. It was hopeless. The man was no longer in charge of his wits. Harry took the situation in immediately. He'd seen this sort of reaction on several occasions.

"I can't do anything, and I've got my work cut out on top. Better get him back to the aid post and see the medical sergeant. Poor bastard. It's not often you see a man cut in half a couple of feet away from you," Harry instructed the crazed man's companion and cover the remains of the body in a blanket. But the unfortunate mental casualty darted forward and grabbed the blanket. He yanked it off the body and then retreated, cowering and staring, to his former spot in the corner.

Outside again, Harry assessed the Tiger tank. Two Germans beside it were badly burned. Two stretcher bearers passing helped him to load the burned men's stretchers onto the ambulance, and then Harry went back and peered through the driver's slits on the tank. A man's face was pressed hard against the grill, teeth bared in a perpetual snarl.

185

"Poor bastard, he must have roasted alive," Harry sighed to Charlie beside him now.

"Can you do anything for this bloke?" Two more stretcher bearers stopped by the ambulance.

"He's bleeding heavy," the other said looking hopelessly at Harry.

Harry lifted the man's covering to reveal a wound which, at first, made him shudder. The wounded man's left arm was hanging loosely by a thin piece of flesh and skin no more than an inch thick and blood oozed from the stump.

"Why didn't you arrest the blood, you stupid prat? The poor sod could have bled to death," Harry muttered and pressed the man's arm to staunch the flow of blood. Then he cut the arm off. It dropped into the sand and one of the bearers fainted.

"What the hell's the matter with him?" Harry fumed as he quickly applied a tourniquet.

"He's new to the game, same as me. We've only been in the desert a couple of weeks. Didn't expect this fucking lot."

"What the hell did you expect to see - blokes bashing one another over the head with balloons on sticks? Don't worry, you will see much worse before this war is over."

They placed the stretcher in the ambulance and Charlie gave each of the stretcher bearers a good dose of brandy, for although the voyage had taken a tedious six weeks in an overcrowded troopship they looked whiter than the day they had left Glasgow.

By midday the casualties were down to a thin trickle and Harry and Charlie scanned the deserted battlefield. Dead lay everywhere. Tanks and armoured cars belched forth black fumes creating a thin screen of smoke a few feet from the ground.

"What a bloody sight," Harry fretted. "I'm pleased I chose the medics. I would hate to think I was responsible for helping in this carnage." He poured water over his hands. "What was it Pontius Pilate said? 'I wash my hands of this whole affair.'" Harry shook the water form his hands in a defiant gesture.

The fighting died down to a sporadic duel between the big guns throughout the long night, and as daylight edged its way in a golden glow over the horizon the stars faded into the deep blue sky. While flimsy clouds pursued the night and vanished in the distance, heavy tanks reformed for the assault. Infantrymen stood around in small groups amused to see Charlie rise from the stretcher on the ground by the side of the ambulance stark naked, with Spag cradled in the crook of his arm. Before dressing, he placed Spag on the ground and the dog immediately went into its normal morning routine. First it ran around in small circles, tail at half mast, and then it scrambled under the ambulance and cocked a leg against the inside of the rear wheel.

It wasn't long before the peaceful dawn turned once more into a nightmare. Shells landed all round them. The infantrymen dived for cover. Then there was the mournful drone of mortars as they somersaulted through the air. Under cover of darkness the enemy had brought up several of them. Heavy machine gun fire rent the air.

A Sherman tank revved, then moved up, first at a leisurely pace, its nose rising like a hunted deer sniffing the air. Suddenly it shot forth guns blazing away at the mortar positions and the infantry moved forward.

"Anyone lost a foot?" someone shouted as he held up a boot with a man's lower half leg still inside.

"Crude bastard," Harry muttered striding off to search for the wounded man. He found him, but his leg wasn't the only thing he'd lost. When Harry turned the man's body over his sightless eyes stared, unblinking, at the sun. Harry found four more wounded and another dead. He filled the ambulance with the injured and it was driven back to the forward aid post, but this hadn't been set up, so the casualties were taken further to the rear to an advanced dressing station.

Charlie, more mature in desert warfare, reckoned it would all be over by midday, but noon came and went without respite. The enemy withdrew with the sky turning a dull grey before nightfall descended upon them, and the infantry moved up to consolidate the half mile of ground they had taken at a very heavy price.

"Well, so much for it being over by midday, Charlie. Any other good stories to tell? I once knew a chap in a unit I was attached to would bet on anything. He would have made a fortune out of you," said Harry.

But Charlie was far too exhausted to argue. He dropped alongside the ambulance and Spag, as if understanding and wishing to sympathise, snuggled down beside him licking his face. Harry threw a couple of blankets over Charlie and his dog before settling down himself.

The next morning the heavy tanks moved up again, but they remained static. Suddenly the guns stopped and an eerie silence fell over the battleground. It resembled the ritual practised back home when, at 11.00 am on November 11th, everything came to a halt. The traffic drew to a standstill and the factories stopped their machinery while the last generation paid homage to the men of the earlier conflict. When Harry was a small boy it had always brought tears to his eyes.

187

"This silence gives you the bloody creeps, don't it, Charlie?" he whispered and Charlie nodded sagely, no doubt thinking the same.

Immediately after their first meal the regiment was on the move again. Then, after a few miles, they turned north and were soon travelling along the straight metal road running parallel with the sea once again. The sun bounced off a million wavelets resembling the countless stars that shone at night. The water lapped gently against the shore and, at times, the sea was less than fifty yards from the road.

Harry couldn't take his eyes from the sea. It looked so cool and inviting.

"You would think they'd pull off the road and let us have a good soaking, Charlie," he complained.

"Just to lay on the shore and let the water lap over my goolies would be paradise to me," replied the other grinning from ear to ear.

As if in answer to their silent prayer, the convoy suddenly stopped. From where the ambulance came to a halt the sea was less than thirty yards away, and they could all hear the waves lapping the shore as if daring them to come over and splash around.

A deserted farm house flanked the convoy on the far side of the road, and it was surrounded by several acres of neglected indian corn, the heavy husks sagging with weight. The ground looked desolate and barren. Sand had blown into and filled the irrigation ditches, and nature was doing its damndest to seize the land and return it to the desert. A wind pump droned high above the men's heads - useless.

One man, obviously a farmer in civilian life, assessed the situation. The farm, which couldn't have been more than five acres all in, was quite modern compared with most of those they had seen in North Africa. Beside the house the pump that relied entirely on the wind for its energy also had a small petrol pump to draw the water from underground.

The man cranked the engine a few times but nothing happened. He filled it with petrol and cranked it a few turns more, the engine coughed and spluttered and emitted a large cloud of black smoke before settling down to a steady rhythm. After a couple of minutes water shot out in small spurts and emptied into the irrigation ditches. In a frenzy of delight the man ran round the ditches with his spade unclogging the dams.

"Just take a shufti at that prick, Harry, running around happy as a cock bird with two arseholes. I bet if the silly sod was detailed to dig a karzy he would play up like hell. He's a farmer.

Farmers are as secretive as a Freemason's Lodge and stick together in the same way. No farmer worth his salt would see ground and crops go to waste. They're dedicated to the land. Have you ever noticed that whenever we pass a farmhouse there are never any signs of livestock, sheep, goats or chickens? They look like vegetarian farmers. They eat goats out here and drink plenty of goat's milk. I suppose you can understand that. When civilians piss off they take their livestock with them. They heard the Aussies were on their way and them sods would soon have the chicks in the pot. Bloody shower of Ned Kellys, that lot. The poor farmer will be lucky if he has any corn left when they get their thieving hand on those cobs. Ever had any boiled, dripping with hot melting butter?"

"No, but I mean to in a sec," Harry promised, and jumped from the ambulance returning some minutes later his steel helmet filled with juicy corn on the cob.

The sergeant came along. "Looks like we're here awhile, lads. The Jocks and Aussies are coming through and the armour is being held in reserve. The sappers have scanned the foreshore. Looks like they're clear of mines. If you feel like it you can have a dip after your conner (food), but don't go too far, we're on standby and have to be ready for off in a few minutes." For some reason known only to himself the sergeant was speaking in a hushed whisper, as if he were divulging some deadly secret.

Without waiting for food, everyone made a mad dash for the water. Charlie lay, Spag on his chest, his lower half under the waves letting them gently lap over him. Harry, a strong swimmer, lashed out from the shore for a half mile. Having done so he slowly rolled over on his back and let the tide carry him back to dry land, so confident of himself that he almost dozed off. His head touched the beach sand. He rose and grinned at Charlie. Then he dived back into the sea, making a belly flop in the shallow water and struck out again. This time, however, he went much further until his head became a faint blob breaking through the surface of the water. He rolled over and gently repeated his first performance. The war, the guns, the casualties, became a distant memory and Harry felt he could remain there, out in the cool wet depths of the sea for the remainder of the night.

Hitting the shore again he didn't wipe himself down with a towel, but just sat staring at the stars reflected in the still water. He wished there was a moon. The thought of that silver lane across the sea would bring back memories of England, and that period during the so-called phoney war. Victoria had taken him down to her home in Devon just after Dunkirk, July 1940. It has been warm and sultry but they had sat under the promenade shelter and watched the moon on the water. It had been a full moon casually throwing its long reflection across the sea.

They walked back to the ambulance. It had been quite light with a strong sun when they had left. Now it was dark and rather chilly. Charlie was in a jubilant mood.

"Makes you feel good, that water, Harry."

"And bloody hungry. I've got some meths blocks. Let's make a brew in the back of the ambulance."

The water took longer to boil using meths blocks, but it made the inside of the ambulance warmer.

"That beach and those sands reminded me of Madagascar, Charlie," Harry reminisced. "Long sandy beaches, except out there in Madagascar they were almost white with coral, but warm waters. It was like swimming in a warm bath. What an island that was. I would sit on that seashore for hours. The only trouble was the insects. They were monsters. Beetles two inches long flew through the sky at a tremendous speed. There were also enormous centipedes... One night I was sitting alone in my tent trying to write a letter when my interest turned to a centipede - blood red it was and at least six inches long. The tent flap was open at the time and, while I was eyeing the centipede one of these beetle things whizzed past my ears like a bloody aerial torpedo and hit the hurricane lamp. It smashed the glass! I thought it was some silly bastard shooting at me. Scorpions. Man, was they a size! Bodies two inches long they had and tails that stood up like flag masts... The boys would catch a large one and an extra large centipede and place them in a metal bowl and watch them fight it out."

Harry paused and shook his head in grim reflection. "We had this corporal, a right snidey little bastard, he was. You think Sykes is a crawler. Well, he'd nothing on this bastard. He was trying to make sergeant, but he never would. The R.S.M. hated his guts and didn't want him in the Sergeants' Mess. Most nights the pig would return to camp pissed to the eyeballs. At the time we were sleeping in a bloody great marquee, about thirty of us. They waited for him to come in pissed one night and after he flopped in his kip they put a couple of bloody great scorpions in his boots. Next morning he was out of bed and sat on the edge of his bed nursing the biggest hangover you ever saw with all of us waiting, heads under our covers, for the miserable sod to put his boots on. You could have heard a bloody pin drop. Suddenly there was this almighty scream, and he was leaping about like his balls were on fire."

"Christ... Did it kill him?" Charlie queried, sniggering. He was wondering if he could do the same to Sykes.

"No, but he was as sick as a dog and in pain for days. At times I felt sorry for him. It cured the swine. Ever since the landing, there he was, the one that was always lecturing us about safety and taking precautions. He'd been out east for some time and should have known better. He always said the first thing to do before dressing was to make sure no 'airy fairies' were in your clothes and boots. After that incident whenever anyone passed him they would either limp or hop ... Shortly after he volunteered for the army prison service. Me, I felt sorry for the poor bastard under him."

"Any birds out there, Harry?"

"Feathered, or two legged?" Harry enquired with a grin spread across his face. He knew what Charlie meant.

"If I told you about them, Charlie, you would never sleep," Harry boasted. Charlie was a good listener and Harry had told this story a dozen times during the long desert nights when they were tucked under their respective blankets but Charlie never tired of hearing about it. Harry had served in so many different countries, while Charlie had spent most of his service on the desert apart from a short break when the troopship called in at Durban.

"This Madagascar doesn't sound such a bad place, Harry. What say after the war we settle out there and start a stud farm? Build ourselves a couple of thatched huts and get ourselves a few bints?"

"No thanks, Charlie. After the war I want to find myself a nice English rose. I don't give a damn if she's a plain Jane. I've had enough of this carnage and I don't want to settle in any place that reminds me of it. I will stay in the army, though. It's not such a bad life. Although I'll train as a chiropodist. I never ever want to look at a dead body again. I've seen quite enough of them to last me a lifetime."

On the front line someone played the mouth organ and the overall mood became melancholy, while Charlie drifted into a sort of daydream wondering what he had missed on that tropical isle of Madagascar. He conjured up all sorts of weird and wonderful reveries until his thoughts turned to the letters he would write the following day if the men didn't move up.

Then the mouth organist began to play 'Roses of Picardy' and Harry felt a shudder pass through his body. "Someone must have passed over my grave," he muttered to himself. Restless he turned in, but the melody persisted in his consciousness until he fell into a deep sleep.

191

The tank regiment pulled back to lick their wounds, but there was no rest for Charlie and Harry. They had hardly settled down when the regimental medical sergeant came cover.

"Sorry, lads," he apologised, "but you have to return to your own unit. It seems that one of your ambulances serving with the infantry has been hit. The driver has been killed and the medic badly wounded. Looks like they got in the way of a German Spandau. Sorry to lose you, lads." Abruptly the sergeant turned and walked away without another word.

Being swapped around from one regiment to another was no surprise to the ambulance crew, who would get used to the medical team and then suddenly find themselves being moved. So Charlie shook his shoulders in resignation and within minutes the ambulance was on its way back to its parent unit. Hardly had they entered the leaguer when Sykes came running towards them the inevitable clipboard in the crook of his arm.

"Here comes that pimply faced marvel with his clipboard," Charlie snorted. "If he ever gets one I'll shove that board up his arse before they bury him," he promised grimly, shaking his head in disgust.

"Right, you two, get over to the Infantry Battalion," Sykes ordered, handing each of them a slip of paper. "Andrews has caught it and Webster is in a bad way. They're expecting you."

When they arrived the regimental medical sergeant was waiting for them.

"Took your bloody time getting here," he complained, and glaring into the ambulance he saw the driver. "Oh, it's you, Williams." The sergeant took a heavy silver watch, suspended on a heavier silver chain from his breast pocket and studied it. "Now get ready to move. The regiment is going to mosey up to the front for a shoot out."

Charlie slumped against the steering wheel.

"Oh, my God! The stupid old sod has been reading one of those cowboy books again."

The sergeant was a good laugh throughout the regiment. Whenever he read a cowboy novel - and there weren't many he hadn't read - he would take on the part of one of the wild west characters, living it out for real.

The sergeant replaced the heavy silver watch in his breast pocket and took out a tobacco pouch and cigarette papers.

"Just a minute, lads," he called out in a friendly tone, "I have the makings here. Want a roll?"

Charlie shook his head.

"No thanks, sarge, can't manage them. Like mine tailor made." He watched the sergeant trying to roll the cigarette. The tobacco was powdery and the effort was failing miserably. He twisted the paper at both ends and when he lit it, it went up in a small ball of flames.

"One of these days, sarge," Charlie warned him with a chuckle, "you'll burn your bloody nose off."

The sergeant gave a hack performance of a cowboy as he walked away with a slow blow legged gait.

"I'm sure that poor bastard is going sand happy, Harry," Charlie grumbled, "just look at the prat. He thinks he's at the O.K. Corral."

They were preparing to move off, the M.O. taking the lead in the small utility, followed by the three tonner. Charlie should have tagged on the end but he had two light casualties to take back, as well as Andrews' body.

"He was one of the old boys in the unit who came out with us," Charlie explained to Harry, pulling back the blankets. Harry saw Andrews' face which was a waxen grey, a line of bullet holes stretching across his chest and stomach, the intestines protruding like small blisters.

"Caught that alright, Harry. Well, at least he didn't feel a thing," Charlie sighed.

"Quiet bloke, Andrews. Never had a lot to say. Used to be a dustman before the war. When he was in a talking mood he could keep you laughing describing what he found in the dustbins. He reckoned he could tell the fortunes of the family by what they threw in the bins."

"Wagons roll!" the medical sergeant shouted at the utility and the three tonner moved off.

"Lives in a dream world doesn't he, Harry? Bloody good job he isn't into Frankenstein or Count Dracula." To Charlie's exasperation the two slightly wounded infantry men didn't like the idea of sharing the ambulance with a dead body.

"It's not the bleeding dead you have to worry about, mate. He can't do you any harm," Charlie assured them and slapped Andrews' bare foot protruding from the blankets.

"It's the bleeding living. Don't worry, he can't harm you."

"Can we leave the back doors open?" One of the men asked.

"Please yourself and don't worry about Andrews, his troubles are over. Those small scratches you two have will soon be looked after and you'll be on your way back to your unit, which is when your worries will start again."

They buried Andrews with several others at the M.D.S. Then, within the hour, they were on their way back to the new unit. The

193

aid post was already set up, a sterilising pan bubbling furiously away on a side table. Sterile dressings and antiseptics, together with an assortment of bright surgical instruments lay neatly on a well scrubbed table.

"Expecting trouble, sarge?" Harry enquired, and almost burst out laughing when he saw the sergeant in an old Australian bush hat shaped like a cowboy's stetson.

"Sure." He rolled spittle around his mouth, fluted his lips and let go a thin stream of spittle outside the lean-to in true cowboy fashion. "Expecting Jerry to break through tonight or at first light. Bags of movement up front from the Jerry lines. The regiment is moving up to reinforce the Jocks and the Aussies to the left of us and there'll be plenty of shit flying."

Half way through the conversation the sergeant took on a soft American west drawl then lapsed back unthinkingly into a broad Yorkshire accent.

"Better get your slit trenches ready. We're a bit close up. I think the doc is after his M.C."

For the first few hours the war seemed far away and their section of the front remained quiet and stable. From their left there was the steady thump, thump, as the guns cracked out their message of death, and Spag raised his head from under the blanket in front of the ambulance and cocked an ear towards the gunfire. Then he jumped from the cab and ran under the ambulance, crouching against the back wheel. Charlie nodded towards the dog.

"He's restless, Harry. There's something afoot. I'm sure the little bastard is aware of it."

The last few words trailed away as a heavy shell screamed directly above them. It hit the hard ground some fifty yards behind them with a loud bang, shrapnel skimmed across the sands, and they dropped to the ground amidst the sand, choking on the stench of explosives.

"Smells like they're using camel shit in their shells these days, Harry," Charlie said as he coughed and spluttered. "I felt the hot blast from that sod."

A few more shells screamed over but none landed anywhere as near as the first one. Quickly the men dug their slit trenches. It was tough going with the ground being as hard as granite, and for almost an hour it remained deathly quiet. They hardly heard the next shell. It landed close, sending a large slice of shrapnel through the ambulance, and then hit a solid piece of metal with a distinct ping - loud enough for Charlie to hear.

"Christ, I hope that didn't hit my engine," he gasped, his mouth full of soft sand.

Harry sat up sharply in his trench.

"Bleeding hell, I thought I was going to be buried then. The side of my slit trench caved in. Fucking close, Charlie."

Once more the shelling stopped and inspecting his beloved ambulance, Charlie discovered that shrapnel had hit and smashed a stretcher runner. He wrenched the metal away and muttered, "Don't fancy getting that up my jacksie, Harry."

Harry cleaned the sand from out of the trench and took it down another foot, which was just as well as the shelling continued for several hours. The enemy would fire half a dozen shells, stop for half an hour, or sometimes a full hour and then start again.

With the coming of darkness the same routine was maintained. To everyone it seemed as if the enemy was running out of ammo and was keeping up this sporadic firing to let them feel their presence. For each time the enemy would change their position, first hitting round the aid post, and then shells would fall to their left, and the next lot would fall far to their right. Surprisingly, casualties were few. They only made two trips to the rear, and both times the ambulance wasn't full.

About 4am the ground erupted in one continuous roar as the enemy lay down a blanket barrage with shells dropping all around them. Then the whole front erupted into one mass explosion. The ambulance rocked as blast after blast hit it. Spag became frantic and huddled himself close against Charlie's chest. A star shell burst directly above them and the brilliant glow coming off the ground made it look as if it were on fire.

A soldier came in carrying a colleague over his shoulder and place him near the aid post. Harry pulled himself from the safety of his slit trench.

"How far you carried him, mate?" he enquired.

"About half a mile. It felt more like ten miles," he answered.

"Well you've wasted your time, he's dead," Harry said.

"He can't be, I spoke to him a few minutes ago and he answered," the soldier replied.

"Well, you won't speak to him again. Sorry, mate." Harry covered the dead man with a blanket and returned to his trench.

Shrapnel shells burst above them, raining down deadly steel fragments. Then they heard the rolling crump crump as mortars landed.

"Hear that, Charlie?" Harry muttered in his ear. "Bloody mortars."

Then the symphony was peppered with the staccato cracks of a machine gun, and raising his head Charlie saw a steam of tracer bullets arch across the ground. Then there was the occasional crack of a single rifle shot.

"Pissing hell, that's small arms," Charlie hissed. "Have the Jerries broken through?"

As if in answer to his question a dispatch rider roared up.

"Where's the doc?" he shouted urgently. Charlie pointed toward the lean-to.

"His slit trench is over there."

The dispatch rider ran over and the medical sergeant came to meet him.

"Get out quick, sarge," he advised. "Jerry has broken through and the regiment is flapping back. Don't bother to pack up, just get away as fast as you can. Leave everything." He pointed in the direction of the small arms fire. "I reckon you have ten, maybe fifteen minutes at the most, unless you want to spend the rest of the war in the bag." The dispatch rider didn't wait for an answer, he just jumped on his bike and roared away.

They only had one casualty, and after making him comfortable they slammed the doors closed. The medical sergeant didn't bother to pack his medical supplies away. He simply started the engine of the three tonner and pulled away leaving the canvas lean-to trailing behind in shreds and the instruments all laid out on the tables. The M.O's small utility followed in hot pursuit of the three tonner.

Charlie's engine purred beautifully. But instead of moving forward with the three tonner and the utility he reversed onto the wrecked aid post, and much to Harry's dismay he stopped.

"Get out quick, Harry," he ordered, "and get those medical panniers aboard. I think there's a bottle of brandy in one of them and there must be other gear we can swap for something useful. I don't intend leaving it to those square headed bastards."

With a concerted effort they quickly dragged one of the basket panniers free and loaded it. The second one, Charlie had to cut the canvas away with his jack knife. All the time they could hear small arms fire getting nearer. The second pannier was much heavier. They sweated and tugged before they finally loaded it.

"Come on, Charlie, that rifle fire is almost on top of us. I can see the flashes," Harry urged.

"Don't worry," Charlie replied, "they're our own."

"What? With the bloody flashes pointing towards us!" Harry was in a cold sweat. A bullet passed between them and buried itself in the sand, so close the sand covered their boots. Another bullet buried itself in the canvas lean-to.

"If they can see us they're pretty bad shots or are trying to frighten us," Charlie said.

"Well as far as I'm concerned they're succeeding," Harry answered with an anxious edge to his voice.

A machine gun chattered, much nearer this time.

"Reminds me of my school days, Harry. There was this set of iron railing round this big house. As kids we used to run along with a piece of wood clicking away and the old lady would go bloody mad."

"Yes, as mad as those bloody Jerries. Let's get moving." Harry wasn't at all interested in Charlie's reminiscences at this particular moment.

"It's hardly the time or place to bring that up now," he said.

They both jumped into the ambulance and Charlie slammed it into gear, it lurched forward and stalled.

"Shit," he shouted. As he started the engine the ambulance moved into a recently made shell crater.

Luckily the ground was hard and the crater shallow, and Charlie made easy work of rocking it to and fro until gradually it eased forward and freed itself.

Harry let out a sigh of relief. The machine gun spat out again, Harry watched in fearful fascination as the tracer bullets arched over the ground he could feel his heart thumping against his chest as his pulse raced through his body, his temples feeling as if they would burst at any moment.

Again the engine stalled and Charlie pulled on the choke placing his ear as near as possible to the engine. It started, coughed and spluttered and the odious stench of petrol filled the cab. "Fuck it," he exclaimed, "I've flooded the engine."

Harry stood up in the cab, peering into the darkness behind them. At the best of times the desert was a lonely place at night, for in spite of having Charlie alongside him, he had never felt lonelier in his life or more frightened. It was the first time, since he'd met up with Charlie, that the engine had decided to play up. And this was with the enemy approaching from three sides ... Were they about to be put in the bag? Were they going to spend the rest of the war in some P.O.W. cage? Or would some scared young Jerry with an itchy trigger finger come up and shoot the pair of them?

No, if the worst came to the worst they would abandon the ambulance and make a dash for it. But he knew he could never do that with the casualty in the back of the ambulance.

Charlie was unperturbed by the situation. Calmly he raised the lid of the engine and in the darkness felt around for the carb, an exercise he could do with his eyes shut. Then he removed its cover, wiped it dry and calmly replaced it. The engine started first time. Common sense prevailed. He moved slowly forward, the wheels gripping the hard ground. He pressed down on the accelerator and the engine back fired.

"That should liven the place up a bit, Harry," Charlie laughed. But Harry shook his head in dismay for nothing ever seemed to worry Charlie.

"One day that bastard will get us both killed," he muttered to himself.

"Next time, Charlie, balls to the whisky and brandy, let it stay put," he said aloud. "I don't know why you worry about the bloody stuff. Neither of us drink it and when we do have a sip of that gut rot we never enjoy it. You can give me a mug of hot tea any day."

A large shell exploded within yards of them, the blast knocking the ambulance sideways. Charlie struggled with the wheel and shrapnel cleaved a hot trail through the air. Nearby a bren gun team felt the effect, men crying out in agony and the ambulance screamed to a stop.

Harry rushed forward. One man rolled around clutching his arm. Another man slumped over the bren, his head cut clean away from his body, blood saturating the ground all around him. Harry helped the wounded man into the ambulance. Two uninjured men moved the headless corpse and took over the bren gun.

Their own artillery opened up to stop the flow of enemy troops. Shells screamed overhead and landed with a crump not too far in the distance behind them. Harry dressed the soldier's wound while the ambulance was still moving, although it was a little cramped in the back with one man already on a stretcher and those two blasted panniers in the centre.

"Bloody panniers in the back, you want your head seeing to," Harry shouted.

"Barter, Harry. Barter. When we get to Tunis that will open a lot of doors for us. Did you have a shufti in those baskets while you were in the back, Harry?"

"Sod them, nearly kicked the bloody things out! It was bloody murder out there, Charlie, bullets flying everywhere. I really thought we'd had our chips. I'm sure I heard Jerry ramming a bullet up the spout of his rifle." Charlie laughed, nothing seemed to worry him.

"That was the medical sergeant's false teeth rattling, Harry. They always do that when he gets nervous."

"Well, I nearly shit myself. If I survive this war, and I very much doubt it with you around, I'll tell my grandchildren about this episode, though they'll never believe me."

Well, thank heavens for the black velvety night, Harry thought, although it was turning into a man made daylight hell with the continuous flashes from the guns and burning vehicles. Flares would burst suddenly in the sky. Infantrymen retreated on foot. Twice Charlie swerved to avoid hitting a retreating figure, and ahead of them the skyline lit up with brilliant flashes.

The moon appeared over the distant horizon and soon the whole desert was lit with its silvery glow. The barren landscape stretched flat, broken only by small outcrops of scrub. A man lay in the shadow of a small hillock. The ambulance pulled over and, with the engine still running, Harry jumped down to investigate. A crimson patch spread over the man's shirt. Harry felt his pulse and shook his head.

"He's dead," he shouted. Harry lifted the man's rifle, the bayonet already fixed. He plunged it into the ground above the man's head. It swayed on the flimsy bayonet for a few seconds, and then it was still, as still as the man on the ground.

"It's almost like daylight now. That's a full moon," Harry called out.

"That's why Jerry put this attack in. I suppose the nearer we get to Tunis the more desperate they become."

Charlie laughed, he didn't know why. They were still in a desperate situation but he shrugged and blew his nose to clear it of sand.

"This lot caught us with out pants down, Harry," Charlie remarked bitterly. Then they headed towards the German barrage. "This is where we have to run the gauntlet," he said. "Hold on to your goolies, mate."

"After that last episode with those damn panniers this will seem like a picnic," Harry flung back.

"I tell you, Charlie, if we had finished up in the bag your life would have been made a misery while we remained in some P.O.W. camp. I hate being shut in at the best of times."

A three ton lorry up ahead burst into flames with a direct hit from a shell and went careering across the sands like some wild bronco, before hitting a boulder and coming to a stop, and then the vehicle exploded into a bright orange flame. Two men dropped from the tailboard, one with his clothes still blazing rolled over and over. A moment later two more men dropped from the cab.

"Right, as fast as you can," shouted Harry.

There was no need to give the order. The picture had unfolded before their eyes. Charlie's foot hit the floorboards and the ambulance turned towards the stricken vehicle, careering on two wheels. Charlie brought it back under control as it swerved erratically and he raced towards the stricken vehicle coaxing every ounce out of his beloved engine.

Harry spilled out, grabbing a blanket from his seat and threw it over the smouldering figure writhing on the ground. The stench of burning flesh penetrated Harry's lungs. He had come to hate that stench more than anything else, and he retched his empty stomach regurgitating and spilling green bile down his chin. Then he wiped the back of his hand.

"Jesus Christ," he whistled through clenched teeth as he looked at the man's face or rather, all that was left of it. He would have retched again but now had full control of his feelings.

He pulled the blanket away. The skin and flesh together with the man's shirt and greatcoat had welded into one black mass and exposed parts of his rib cage that glistened in the bright moonlight. The injured man turned his head and grabbed Harry by the wrist. Harry was surprised at the strength left in the man. His fingernails dug into Harry so hard that he couldn't stand the pain any longer and tried to loosen the grip. Blood trickled from his wrist as the man tried to pull Harry toward him.

"Don't move me..." The words gargled on the spittle in the man's throat. "My stomach is wide open..." Every word was barely audible and took a great effort on his part. He pulled Harry closer until his head was a few inches away from the man's mouth. Harry gasped with horror and forced the man's hand away and stood up.

"I can't do that, mate. Bloody hell! I can't do that ..." he babbled.

"What does he want?" asked a sergeant sitting near them nursing a wound in his arm.

"He wants me to shoot him." There was terror in Harry's voice.

The sergeant dragged himself towards the badly injured man. He went to place his uninjured hand on the man's forehead, but shrank away when he saw the extent of his injuries. Then he bent down and whispered in the man's ear, and placed his own ear by the man's head to hear the answer.

"Alright, mate."

He turned to Harry. "Surely there is something you can do for him?"

"Do you think I would be standing here useless if I could?" Harry's voice trembled. "I can't even turn him round to inspect his back. His stomach is wide open. Half his face is missing and what's left is almost burnt away." He stared at the man for a few seconds, then said to Charlie, "Let's get the others aboard."

"For Christ sake, medic," the sergeant pleaded, "you just can't leave him here like this."

"Look, sarge, you can see the wounds. It doesn't take an expert to tell you he hasn't very long to live."

"Then shoot the poor bastard," begged the sergeant. "You can't let him lie there in agony. Jerry will be here soon. They'll stick a bayonet in him if he's lucky."

The sergeant scrambled to his feet and took his revolver from its holster. He threw it to Harry. It lay at his feet almost covered in sand, the menacing barrel staring up at Harry like some one eyed black monster, the black steel standing out against the silver background of sand. Harry shivered, the sweat on his body now cold and clammy, and horrified he kicked the gun away.

"I am here to save lives not destroy them," he told the sergeant.

"You are also here to relieve the pain and suffering. You know he's dying and shortly Jerry will be here. So do your job and put the poor sod out of his misery. I know this man and he certainly wouldn't want to live his life out with a face like that should he live. Look at that face now. Can you imagine what it would be like when the tissue dries up, should a miracle happen and he were to survive? His right eye is hanging out."

He made a grab for the revolver but Harry kicked it away from the sergeant's reach.

The sergeant said, "If you haven't the guts to do the job, let me do it for you."

"Bollocks," Harry replied.

There was little to say that could possibly justify any action he took, but taking a man's life - there was no answer to that.

With Charlie's help they managed to get the survivors into the ambulance, and then they closed the doors and their eyes met. Charlie could feel what Harry was going through and felt the utmost sympathy with him. The man was dying. Harry knew his job too well to make any kind of mistake like that, and to place him in the ambulance and run the gauntlet of falling shells would add to the man's misery. Yet to leave him here to the mercy of the advancing enemy was the only other alternative. He may live for a few hours, and should the enemy be beaten back he could lay exposed to the merciless sun at daybreak.

Harry knelt beside the man. He hadn't cried since he had left the orphanage, but now the tears flowed freely, while he searched for the man's pulse. It was weak and his breathing was shallow.

"Can I ease you over a little, mate?" he whispered.

The man shook his head and gabbled weakly, "Shoot me... shoot me..."

"What will you do, Harry?" Charlie's voice was soft and compassionate, and for once he was pleased that he was the driver and not the medic. Charlie realised that this must be one of the rawest deals the war had ever presented to Harry.

Harry looked first at the revolver with the barrel, stark and threatening, jutting from the sand. Then his eyes fell upon the man, writhing in pain, his groans driving inside Harry's brain.

"You had better leave me, Charlie. This is one decision I have to make alone. Take the casualties back. I see I have two choices - stay with the man till the Jerries catch up or..." He paused, his gaze falling on the revolver.

Charlie's hand rested upon Harry's shoulder. "Take it easy, mate. I'll wait for you the other side of the barrage."

The ambulance pulled slowly away. Harry dropped to his knees beside the wounded man. Oblivious to the shells screaming overhead and the nearness of the small arms fire, Harry bowed his head and his arm fell to his side and came into contact with the cold steel of the revolver. It shot through him like a high voltage electric shock, and he couldn't take his hand away. His fingers curled round the grip of the gun.

Harry lifted his head to the sky in silent prayer, and his religious teaching at the Quaker home rushed through his brain. "Life is a precious gift from God, no man has the right to take it away." This is what the Quakers had taught him, but none of them had ever been in a position such as this.

He rose to his feet, the hand holding the gun slid to his side, and he felt his finger sliding the safety catch off. Slowly his hand moved till the muzzle was pointing towards the man's head. He felt he was sliding into a trance, but he wasn't shaking anymore. His finger closed round the trigger. He squeezed gently. There was a loud explosion and a brilliant flash. It was unexpected. He didn't realise it would go off so quickly and so effortlessly and stared at the smouldering barrel in disbelief. He looked down at the man whose body arched upwards monetarily and then fell flat, a gaping wound in his temple.

Harry dropped to his knees beside the man shaking uncontrollably. Tears ran freely down his cheeks, and he remained there for several minutes. Shells were still exploding all around him, so close that at times the hot blasts folded around him. Then, as if woken from a trance, the enormity of his actions rammed home to him. Blood from the man's head had splashed down Harry's leg. He picked up a handful of sand and scoured his leg, wishing he could somehow clear away the awful memory of this scene forever. But he knew it would remain with him for the rest of his life.

"The only shot I fired in this damn war and it had to be for one of our own," he muttered, and found no consolation in the thought that the man would have died within the hour. Still, to convince himself he examined the man's wounds. A large piece of shrapnel had opened his abdomen and his intestines protruded like grey ping pong balls.

He didn't remove the man's identity discs. He wanted his identity to remain anonymous, he threw a greatcoat over the still body and picked up the revolver. He could still smell the discharged cartridge. With all the effort he could muster he threw the revolver away from himself, and it landed in the back of the still blazing lorry.

Slowly he turned and walked towards his own line, slowly first, his steps quickening with each step until at last he was sprinting across the sands. He was not afraid, he just wanted to put as far as possible behind him the shocking action he had just carried out.

Finally he reached his own lines and fell to his knees. Reserve battalions had been called in and the enemy halted. A gunner handed him a mug of cold water and he gulped it down. Nothing seemed to matter anymore, and it was midday before he found his unit. Charlie was sitting on the back step of the ambulance with Spag in his arms. They didn't speak. But Charlie made him a fresh mug of tea and Harry sipped it slowly.

"It's a lousy fucking war, Charlie," he sighed deeply. "I wonder if any of us will feel the same after it's finished. I always thought after this war I would get posted to some large military hospital. But seeing all this carnage and how cheap life is has changed my mind. I think I'd be wasting my bloody time." He stared out brooding into the desert.

"That goes for me too," Charlie replied. "I doubt if I will ever be the same." He sighed and took out the bottle of brandy from the pannier. Then he poured Harry half a mugful. But for a second Harry didn't realise what it was and drank it down in one large gulp, and the fiery liquid coursed down his throat painfully after biting into his tongue and chapped lips. Eagerly he held the mug out again and Charlie stared in disbelief, because he knew Harry hated spirits. Then he shrugged his shoulders and poured another half mug. On an empty stomach and unused to alcohol the fiery liquid had the desired effect. Harry staggered to his feet and flopped down on a stretcher in the ambulance, loud sobs racking his whole body. Charlie lifted Harry's inert legs onto the stretcher and covered him with a blanket. If only in a drunken stupor, he would be out of the war for a few hours, Charlie reckoned.

The incident was never mentioned again by either of them while they remained together.

CHAPTER 21

A few days passed and the division retreated or, to put it officially, had withdrawn to strategic positions. The fifty-first Highland Division and an Australian Infantry Brigade, together with the Armoured Division, regained the lost ground.

Charlie took a short cut across the unmarked sands and soon found himself all alone and bogged down to his back axle in soft sand.

"That's all we need," he grumbled. "Us right at the back of the mob and no one around to pull us out." He jumped out and inspected the ambulance. "We'll never get out of this lot, Harry, not without a tow. It's getting dark, make a brew and let's settle down for the night. We'll have to wait till morning when we may spot a recovery vehicle or a tank."

"There was a phone box two hundred miles back. Shall I go and give the R.A.C. a call?" Harry asked, trying hard to keep a straight face. Being bogged down for the night suited him. They'd hardly had any rest for a few nights.

All alone, the last vehicle having vanished before sunset, the silence descended on them like a ghostly apparition. The loneliness fascinated Harry and it was at times like these that Charlie opened up about his own life, usually with questions to Harry about his time at the orphanage.

The cold bit into their flimsy khaki drill shorts and shirts. They put on their greatcoats and sat down, each with a coarse blanket wrapped round him, looking like two Indian squaws.

"I wonder what'll happen when this lot is over, Harry. Do you reckon we will go back to Blighty?"

"Who cares?" Harry shrugged. "One place to me is just as good as another." He pulled up his knees and rested his elbows on them. Then cupping his chin in his hand he stared across the desert. So far his life had been divided into two sections - the orphanage and the army. "You could say my life has been completely institutionalised," he mused.

"Wouldn't you like to go back to Blighty, Harry?" Charlie wanted to know.

"I wouldn't mind, but I might miss this lot," Harry replied.

Charlie burst out laughing and almost choked on his cigarette.

"Don't tell me you're going bloody sand happy. You want your head examined. Who would miss this lot?"

It was Harry's turn to laugh. "Don't be a prick, Charlie. What I'm trying to say is that there's something fascinating about the desert - its vast open spaces, the beautiful sunsets and sunrises, the hot days and the cold nights. Just take the sunsets. You see the desert change from a dull yellow to a variety of colours. Then there's the early dawns when the sky changes to lush gold as the sun comes over the horizon. Then there's those powder puff clouds speckled with gold, scurrying across the sky as if to dodge the hot sun that follows. I can understand why those old holy men took to the desert for days, sometimes months on end, just to meditate. Look at old Moses. He would spend forty days and nights on end, all alone."

"Poor old sod. Must have had a wife and mother-in-law like mine. I never took you for a romantic, Harry." Charlie snorted cynically. He lit another cigarette and pulled the blankets closer round his shoulders. "You could go back and see one of those nurses where you did your training in London. Don't forget, you promised to take me to the Smoke and arrange a date for me."

"Oh, I'll go there alright. I told you about Victoria, I went home to Devon with her. Her old man was a major in our mob in the last war. Great bloke, no snobbery with him. Victoria is the apple of his eye. He's loaded, runs a rest home in Devon for old folk. He also has a practice, mostly well-to-do patients. Bought a flat in the King's Road in Chelsea." Harry paused.

"He said it was for when him and his wife came up to London to see the shows, but really it was for his daughter. I stayed there a few nights. He wanted Victoria to be a doctor but she felt she couldn't stand all that training so to satisfy the old man she took up nursing. Strange thing is, she's a bloody good nurse. I got on marvellous with her mother. She's a lot younger than the Major, as he liked to be called. When we went down to her home in Devon, me and her old lady played the piano together for hours. The Major would do anything for his daughter. Thought the sun shone out of her arse. I liked both her parents."

"Not like my wife's old lady. She's a rotten cow. God, Harry, if that bitch could charge for haunting a house she could make a fortune. And her daughter, what a bitch ... I can tell you, between the two of them they wrecked my life."

Charlie was in a talkative mood. This was the longest conversation about his private life that Harry had ever heard, and he remained silent, listening.

"As soon as I joined up, Harry," Charlie went on. "that cow placed my daughter in a home. Now what kind of mother do you call that? My daughter wasn't a year old. I will never forgive her for that Harry, although all the blame can't be placed on her shoulders. Her old lady is as much to blame. Her mother was only sixteen when my wife was born, and she only just made it, just two months after the wedding. And like her mother my wife wasn't sixteen when I put her in the family way. Her old lady

205

really done her nut. She wasn't thirty-two and was about to become a granny. After she calmed down she realised it wasn't such a bad thing. She would get her daughter off her back. She threatened if I didn't marry her on her sixteenth birthday she would tell the police. I was shit scared, Harry, I can tell you. So we trips down to the registrar, her with her with her belly sticking right out. That old sod behind the desk gave me some dirty looks, I can tell you. I had a decent job, hardly enough to keep a family, but at weekends I did a bit of window cleaning and chimney sweeping. My old man was still alive and he let us have the top half of the house rent free."

Charlie laughed as he recalled his chimney sweeping episode. "I was cleaning the chimneys up at a big house when the bloody brush got stuck. The more I tried to wrench it free the worse it became, so I unscrewed the brush and left it there."

"What happened?"Harry asked.

"I already had a large sack of soot and I told the boy I'd finished," Charlie chuckled. "He was as pleased as punch, gave me a shilling tip. So I pissed off as fast as my bike would carry me. I often wondered what happened when the poor old sod tried to light the fire. I did the job in August. I was in the army the next month, long before the winter sets in. Poor old sod, my conscience pricked me and I nearly sent the shilling tip back."

Charlie rambled on. To date his life had been a closed book, opened occasionally to flick over a page. This was the longest conversation so far, and it seemed as if he could trust Harry.

"The trouble with that bitch of a wife of mine," he grumbled, "was that she was too beautiful. It was alright for the first couple of months after the baby was born, then she realised she was attractive to other men. Heads would turn when she pushed that pram and men would whistle after her. She revelled in it and would roll her arse deliberately. Her mother was a good looker too. She went to seed a little after the baby was born, but she soon perked up. I think it was the thought of her being a grandmother so young. Out together they looked like sisters. Then the war started and that got them going. I was away and there were plenty of uniforms about around our town. They would leave that little girl with anyone who would have her for a couple of bob. The next thing I knew, they had put my daughter in a home. I went home for a weekend and the house was empty. A neighbour soon put me in the picture. I went berserk and I was three days adrift. I found my daughter, but there was sod all I could do about it. Still the C.O. was good about it. When he heard the story he gave me a bollocking and said I should have phoned. We sailed three weeks later."

Charlie was quiet for a few minutes.

"I guess my guardian angel was watching over me because if I could have found my wife I would have been up for murder, double murder, for believe me her old lady would have been the first to go. I could have understood it if she wanted to get rid of me, but the girl... I'll never forgive her for that. I've had time to cool down, though, and I don't suppose I'll do her in. The army is seeing I get a divorce but the padre tells me it takes at least three years. The only thing that grieves me is if I get killed that bitch gets a war pension. If she does I will haunt the cow day and night. She won't get a minute of peace."

At least, thought Harry, he's got it of his chest. He was getting to understand Charlie better.

"She'll be alright now, Charlie," Harry soothed him. "Being in a home has its good points. I was in that kind of home myself. She's better off than I was. I was there for keeps. At least she comes back to you when this war is finished. It isn't going to last forever."

Harry guessed this would be a time when Charlie would like to be by himself. So, he picked up his blankets and walked a couple of hundred yards into the desert. Then he selected a small dune, wrapped himself in his blanket, and stared across the desert. It was dawn when he walked back to the ambulance.

A heavy tank transporter thundered by some two hundred yards away. They waved it down and within minutes they were towed to firmer ground.

While he was busy making breakfast and brewing tea, Harry heard loud shouts and jeers from a passing lorry full of troops. He walked round the other side of the ambulance and saw Charlie standing there, stripped naked shaving in front of the wing mirror, just in time to hear Charlie's answer. Flapping his penis up and down Charlie shouted. "You wouldn't like this in your eye for a wart, would you?"

"Put it away, Charlie, and come and get your breakfast." Harry suggested, placing a large plate of beans and greasy bacon on the back step of the ambulance.

"That's the trouble with you, Harry, you don't appreciate the finer things of life," Charlie complained, grinning broadly. He looked at the plate of beans swimming on the lake of grease, two hard tack biscuits floating on top like a pair of deserted rafts from a sinking ship.

Charlie was about to say something and glanced at Harry. He could see he was in no mood for criticism.

The truth was, during his sojourn in the lonely desert during the night, Harry's mind had been crowded with doubts. The

207

incident with the man from the blazing lorry kept haunting him till he felt his head would burst. He would never shake it from his mind. Why did it have to happen with the campaign nearing its end? Then he wondered if, after the campaign, the division would be split up. Hardly likely. It was a crack division. But so far, it had only been tested in desert warfare. If they did split up and his unit disbanded he would miss Charlie. What they had endured made them closer than ever. Would he get sent to a general hospital? After three years in active service units that would be purgatory.

It was well past midday when they caught up with the regiment. He tried to sneak in but the medical sergeant had seen the column of dust from miles away.

"Where the hell have you two mavericks been moseying around?"

"Oh, Christ," Charlie muttered under his breath. "Is he still reading that sodding cowboy book?"

He tried to tell the sergeant what had happened, but the sergeant tool off his Australian bush hat cum ten gallon stetson, wiped around the inside rim and took a John Wayne stance, trying to roll a homemade cigarette with one hand and failing miserably.

"Right," drawled the sergeant, "get off this corral. There are a couple of wounded. Mosey back to M.D.S. and get back here pronto."

"Can you believe it, Harry? Did you hear that Yankee accent? Thick old sod," Charlie scoffed, shaking his head in disbelief. "One of these days we'll be taking him back branded on the cheek of his arse with a piece of red hot shrapnel. Daft sod lives in a child's dream world."

They arrived at their own unit in record time and as they had two casualties unloaded, Sykes came running towards them.

"Here he comes, Harry, the bearer of good news," Charlie growled and stuck his head out from the side of the ambulance. "What's the matter my pimply friend?"

"Jackson, you report to the R.S.M. Williams, back up to reception and unload your wounded, there's another man to take straight to the C.C.S."

Harry unshaven and unwashed, stood to attention in front of the R.S.M. The sergeant major looked him up and down for a minute or two, but he made no remark about his appearance.

"Jackson, there is a very sick man who had to go back to the C.C.S. He needs constant attention. Tell Williams to take it easy, if he makes the C.C.S. the man should survive. The road is about three miles north of here. It's the long way round to the clearing station but it'll be a lot smoother."

When he returned to the ambulance the casualty was already loaded and a drip feed secured to the side of the stretcher. Harry examined it and gave Charlie the R.S.M.'s instructions. They had no trouble finding the clearing station, for the road was filled with traffic running in both directions.

It was impossible to miss the station. There were three large marquees formed into a rectangle. Inside the three-sided square stood three large flagpoles, the union flag in the centre was flanked on each side with the corps flag, a cherry red, royal blue and gold tricolour, on the other side a white flag with a red cross. White washed boulders, so white it was impossible to look at them in bright sunlight, lined the square marking out a one way system for the ambulances, and while Harry groaned Charlie stared with disbelief at the well laid frontage. He shook his head from side to side. "I can see it, Harry, but I just can't believe it."

"Don't park there, driver! Move that damn ambulance!"

Charlie glanced about to see where the voice was coming from.

From the darkened doorway of the centre marquee the voice boomed out again, and Charlie couldn't make out if the voice was male or female as it reached fever pitch, almost hysterical.

"Don't just sit there like a stuffed dummy. Get that cigarette out of your mouth and get that ambulance to reception."

Two orderlies in spotless white gowns came running forward. One held a stretcher and the other directed Charlie as he backed into the reception, the two orderlies looking continually over there shoulders. Then one asked, "What you got, mate?" He talked from the side of his mouth like some old lag.

"Bad G.S.W. in chest and neck. In a proper state. Ordered to bring him straight here, no stopping. He's had morphine and is on a drip." Harry handed him the waterproof envelope with the mans records. "He's in a bad way."

"Where from?" The man was whispering, almost afraid to talk out loud.

"Up the blue, attached to an infantry regiment," Harry answered.

"What's it like up there?"

The orderly kept looking at Harry's unkempt appearance, envying him, and by the look of the bullshit around them, Harry could well understand.

"Bit quiet at the moment, but there's been a lot of shit flying around. More shit than in a Birmingham sewer," Harry said.

More orderlies came running out to help unload the seriously injured man, all looking envious of Harry's ragged appearance.

Charlie lit a fresh cigarette and he followed Harry and the orderlies inside the enormous tent. It took a few seconds to become accustomed to the gloomy interior. It was enormous and hygienically clean. Rows of beds lined the tent on each side, and above each bed hung a meticulously rolled mosquito net. Charlie nudged Harry.

"I bet the flies are too scared to shit on those nets, Harry."

Harry felt uncomfortable in such hygienic surroundings. He looked down his open shirt and saw the fine chest hairs covered with sand, the shirt itself black with sweat. His shorts, with half the fly buttons missing and the bottoms frayed, could have done with a good wash some days ago. The tops of his canvas plimsolls were threadbare and the big toe on each foot was struggling to break through. His appearance was in striking contrast to the orderlies going about their business in a truly professional way. They threw a glance at him from time to time as if he were some alien from outer space, doubting very much if Harry belonged to the same corps as themselves.

A nursing sister, small in stature but with a voice that would have done justice to a drill sergeant, glided down the ward between the beds. She looked down her stubby, rather porcine little nose at both of them, then shouted at Charlie, "Put that cigarette out! How dare you smoke in my ward!"

Charlie, a grin still on his face, made a quick exit. Harry waited for his chit. Everything had a chit to be signed for, whether it was toilet paper or a corpse. The sister turned on him.

"I suppose you are the medical orderly. You should have told him he wasn't allowed to smoke in here."

Harry stared blankly at her. A medical orderly slipped him a chit, and Harry turned his back on the sister without answering. Then breathed in deeply, inhaling the clean fresh air. But the sister wasn't letting them off that easily. She followed them, dogged as a pugnacious bulldog pup, barking, "How dare you turn your back on me while I am speaking!"

Harry leant against the side of the ambulance picking his nose, and Charlie gazed down on the pair of them from his driver's seat, Spag snarling softly in his lap. The sister glared at Harry and then at Charlie. They looked a lot worse in the bright sunshine.

"My God," she fumed, "you two are filthy. Don't tell me you handle casualties in that filthy condition!"

Charlie was grinning from ear to ear. He knew the medics were renowned for discipline, but this performance was ridiculous.

"No, you silly cow," he snapped at her. "We spot a casualty then we send a message to Jerry to stop shelling while we scrub up and attend to the wounds."

From the gape-mouthed expression on her face it was evident that the little sister couldn't believe her ears. Five years as a military nursing sister and no orderly had ever dared to speak to her like this. Her breast swelled until she resembled a pouted pigeon so top heavy it looked fit to overbalance. Her colour changed to a deep red, like a chameleon crossing the Russian flag, and the veins stood out from her temples in unattractive deep mauve bands as she stammered and stuttered, "How dare you... " Her eyes narrowing and her lips drawing back into a snarl.

Harry looked her over with contempt, and turning swung into his seat. Already tired, hot and miserable, the sight of the C.C.S. had done nothing to help his mental state. "Get stuffed, you stupid bitch," he exclaimed, blowing his words out on a sigh.

"Sergeant Major!" she bawled, tears in her eyes.

She turned on the two orderlies standing behind her and took her wrath out on them. They'd just stood there since the start of the rumpus and having heard nothing like it since they joined the unit, it had taken all their self control to stop bursting out laughing. Now they snapped to attention.

"Get back to your duties," she yelled at them, "and don't stand there like two idiots! I'll deal with you two later. Go and find the R.S.M.!"

One of the orderlies must have been inspired by the ambulance crew's bravery. "That's two orders, sister: back to duty and fetch the R.S.M. Which one first, sister?"

"Are you being as stupid as these two, Earnshaw?" She pointed a finger at Charlie and Harry. "Go and get the R.S.M." She turned on Charlie. "Get that cigarette out of your mouth and stand to attention."

"Bollocks," he replied, rolling the word around carefully in his mouth before spitting it out. Then folded his arms and stared down defiantly at her from his commanding height. "Why don't you fuck off back to that tent and play Florence Nightingale, like you're supposed to do, you boot faced bag," he suggested with an acid snigger.

If she had been a candidate for a burst blood vessel when Harry had back-chatted her, she was about to have a stroke now, or in Florence Nightingale's hackneyed Victorian terms, a full blown apoplexy. She stared at Charlie, eyes bulging unattractively, unable to absorb the fact that he had sworn at her. She was speechless. It seemed that her tongue had become glued to the roof of her mouth.

211

A tiny man, about the size of the sister, strutted from the far tent with Earnshaw behind him. It was the first time in Earnshaw's medical career that he'd witnessed any man speak to a sister in that tone of voice, and he certainly didn't intend missing a thing.

The R.S.M.'s back was straight as a ramrod, his silver knobbed cane gripped under one arm and held in place with his hand, the other arm swinging back and forth like a well greased piston rod, in unison with his strides. His uniform was starched with the creases in his shorts razor sharp. His Sam Brownes and brasses shone in the bright sunshine. And although his boots were covered in a fine film of sand they bore the marks of well polished leather. His cap was pulled down over his eyes causing his head to be thrown back and his eyes to look down his nose.

He marched directly to the sister, brought his right knee waist high and then slammed it down hard on the sand. He saluted in strict regimental fashion.

"Sister!" he bellowed, as if she were a hundred yards away.

"I want these two men charged with insubordination and using obscene language. And just take a look at their filthy appearance. They are not fit to handle casualties."

The R.S.M. studied Harry in disbelief. He walked round him then, with his cane, lifted his shirt tails.

"Tuck that shirt in and do those trouser buttons up," he ordered.

Harry reluctantly drew up to attention. "No buttons, sir," he said.

"Have you no boots either?" The R.S.M. poked the end of his cane into one of Harry's big toes, and looking down at his feet Harry wriggled his toes, a smile spreading across his face.

"I did have a pair once, in Cairo, just before I joined the unit."

Was this man taking the mickey out of him? The W.O. peered right into his face, a sudden flicker of recognition in his eyes.

More faces appeared behind the gauze covered windows, or stood in darkened doorways. The news had soon spread that two men, one a medic and the other a driver, had actually had the audacity to stand up to a sister and that short arsed tyrant of a sergeant major. The R.S.M. was anxious not to have his authority dashed away and undermined, and Harry was doing it very subtly.

The R.S.M. bellowed to Harry, "If you are trying to be funny, my lad, I'll soon have you smiling on the other side of your face."

From his driver's seat in the ambulance, Charlie thought it was time he took a hand in the argument. He had an audience, and Charlie loved playing to the gallery. He settled Spag in his makeshift bed, then taking a firm grip on the steering wheel he lifted his left buttock and let rip the most enormous fart. It shook the ambulance. The two medics standing behind the sister almost collapsed in fits of laughter, although one tried in vain to convert it into a fit of coughing.

The sergeant major took two strides towards the ambulance, and tilting his head back till he was looking straight down his nose, he glared at Charlie.

"Get off that ambulance at once and go and stand next to that other man!" he ordered.

Charlie stood there scratching his crotch in the most undignified manner, his audience enjoying every minute. Crowds gathered at the windows, each pushing for a better view, and as the windows were just squares cut in the canvas and covered with gauze, they could hear every word.

The sergeant major directed his attention towards Harry. He smoothed one hand round his chin and then he studied him. His interest was renewed and this was his second mistake. He moved closer, till his face was just a few inches from Harry's.

"I know you." He stepped back and casually stroked his chin. "Yes, I know you alright."

Suddenly his eyes widened in recognition. Then for the first time he realised the mistake he had made, or rather, serious blunder.

Before the war he had been in the hospital where Harry did his training. Harry had been a raw recruit and the sergeant major a lance corporal then. He had been a despicable character, hated by one and all. The war had been a godsend to him. He had clawed his way to the top within the first twelve months of the outbreak, and he knew Harry was no fool. But he couldn't retreat, and the sergeant major knew he had to go through with it.

"You were on wards at the Royal Victoria Hospital at Netley."

"Yes, that's right."

Harry's face broke into a broad grin, and he held out his hand in a friendly manner, but the sergeant major completely ignored it.

"Yes, I remember," Harry said. "You were a shit house wallah at the time. You used to walk around the hospital all day with another short arsed bloke." Harry scratched his head trying to remember the man's name. "What was his bloody name now?" He put a hand over his eyes and shook his head. "Don't tell me. It will come to me in a minute or two."

Without realising what he was saying the sergeant major blurted out, "Fletcher." Then he realised he had really put his foot in it.

Harry was in quick, like a snake striking at it a helpless prey. If he kept the baiting up he knew the R.S.M. wouldn't be able to get rid of them quick enough, and remembering the two comic figures around that great hospital he was quick to capitalise on it. "You shouldn't have told me. I have remembered it, the way you two blokes would strut around that hospital like two midgets. Surely your name was Bradley?"

Nervously the R.S.M. turned around, hoping no one had overheard the conversation and silently wishing the ground would open up and swallow him. The two medics behind the sister were almost in a state of collapse trying to suppress their laughter, and taking out a handkerchief one blew his nose, tears of silent laughter trickling down his cheeks. Seeing this, the R.S.M. took his wrath out on them.

"Get back to your duties at once! Report to me at nine in the morning. You're both on a charge!"

Quickly the two men made a dash for the middle tent and burst out laughing. They had heard enough gossip to keep the unit happy for months to come.

After they'd disappeared the R.S.M. turned to Harry.

"You'll regret those remarks. I was a fully qualified sanitary assistant, First Class."

"Still a shithouse wallah in my books, sir." He emphasised the word 'sir' with contempt.

"I'll be making a report to your C.O. In fact, I'm in two minds whether or not to call in the military police now."

Charlie sucked in his breath. "I wouldn't, sir. Our C.O. can't stand base wallahs and we are very short staffed. We lost a couple of ambulances within the last week. We'll have to give some explanation for this delay."

"Quiet, man," the W.O. bellowed. He was back to his old form and he knew Charlie was having a go at him, trying to make him look small in front of the staff and patients. He took a notebook from his top pocket and licked the point of his pencil. "I want both your names."

Harry knew he was on safe territory. If the R.S.M. hadn't remembered his name so far, it was pretty certain he had completely forgotten it, and it was obvious the R.S.M. didn't want to make himself look more of an idiot. He had dropped several clangers by crossing swords with the ambulance crew, and admitting to recognising Harry.

"I am Lawrence, sir," Harry lied. "Don't you remember, sir, they used to call me Lawrence of Arabia?"

The R.S.M couldn't make up his mind whether he was telling the truth or not, but the farce had gone on long enough. With great reluctance he answered. "That's right, I remember." Then he pointed his pencil at Charlie, not saying a word.

"Peters, sir. Driver Peters of the R.A.S.C." Charlie gave them some fictitious unit and hoped that the R.S.M. hadn't noticed the divisional sign on the mudguard, although there was very little chance of that. Like the large red cross on the side of the ambulance it was covered in a film of sand.

"Right! Now the pair of you clear out of here. When we reach Tunis you will hear more of the escapade. You, Lawrence, are a disgrace to the corps."

Throughout, the sister had remained speechless, and hadn't moved an inch. It was as if her feet were glued to the ground, her face remaining a deep crimson, her expression one of bulldog aggression.

Charlie glanced through his wing mirror. The R.S.M. and the sister hadn't moved. They remained talking to one another in the middle of the sand path, and it was time for Charlie's party piece.

The engine roared into life. There was just a couple of inches of loose sand, sufficient to put on a good show. He adjusted his mirror to get a better view, and Harry, anticipating the move, rushed into the back of the ambulance to obtain a better view. He peered out of the small back windows, and wished he had cleaned them as they were covered in a film of sand. Luckily he could just see enough.

"Alright, Charlie," he encouraged his mate, "let the bastards have it. Let's see them do a soft shoe sand shuffle."

Charlie pressed his foot down hard on the accelerator and also on the foot brake. The engine roared as he let the brake off slowly, just sufficient to spin the back wheels round. A thick cloud of sand spewed out from the rear wheels, and then blanketed itself over the R.S.M. and the sister who had caused the furore.

Losing all self control and covered from head to foot in sand, the R.S.M. rushed towards the reception, changed his mind halfway there and, charged after the ambulance like a demented baboon cursing them in typical military language. As for the sister, she stood transfixed with rage, her still scarlet face somewhat toned down in colour by the shower of sand.

Out in the open desert Harry and Charlie were still laughing their heads off.

"I don't know how you managed it, Charlie, but that was spectacular. Serves the stupid bastards right. Snotty little cow, that sister. But let's hope the R.S.M. doesn't remember your name later, Harry," Charlie chuckled.

"I shouldn't think so. It was a bloody large hospital with a thousand staff. Mind you, I thought he might remember me. I was in trouble with one of the sisters there. It was all over the bloody hospital. I was in the limelight, you might say. For a minute I thought he may have connected me with the incident."

"What happened, Harry? They catch you getting the old leg over with one of the sisters?"

"Not bloody likely! She was a sour faced bitch bar none. She said I swore at her." He laughed again. "That did me a power of good, seeing those two covered in shit. And that R.S.M. - how he's changed. Bloody creep was always bumming fags from patients and staff. Not many people liked him. He knew my face alright. I'll be surprised if he wants to take it any further."

Harry and Charlie again chuckled long and hard.

CHAPTER 22

Charlie was doing his usual thing, shaving in front of his mottled wing mirror and admiring himself.

"My mouth feels like a ruptured Zulu's jockstrap." He stuck out his tongue.

Harry caught a glimpse of it. It had a thick yellow coating.

"It looks like one of those adverts you see in the newspaper for woollen blankets, folded to exaggerate the thickness of its woolly texture."

Harry gave him a couple of number nine. "Take these, and be careful where you point your arse."

The division was preparing to move up again. All the vehicles had been serviced at divisional workshops, tanks and armoured vehicles replaced and reinforcements brought up.

"Right, you two, let's be having you. Stand to and get ready to move up."

It wasn't quite light yet. A few stars splattered the dawn sky and the far horizon was still tinged with a purple fringe, while the opposite horizon glowed with a golden tint as the sun struggled to top the distant ridges, casting long deformed shadows across the irregular sands.

"Christ, sarge, we haven't been out of line more than two days. I'm still shagged out."

"So what? Write to your bleeding M.P."

It was a rough ride to their forward positions with Charlie swerving constantly to avoid the boulders and the heat becoming more oppressive by the hour. The twenty-five pounders were already in action when the R.A.P. vehicles pulled up with a protesting squeal of brakes. The agonising screech of shells filled the air as they arched through the sky towards the unseen enemy, the gunners feeding the guns as fast as feeding strawberries to a donkey.

Immediately Charlie started digging two slit trenches while Harry helped to set out the aid post ready for its first casualties. Spag crawled forward on his belly, his head to one side. He became agitated as he nuzzled his head against Charlie's leg. Then, when he knew he had Charlie's attention, he ran around in circles, his tail between his legs, and leaving a trail of urine.

"I am sure this little bugger is trying to tell us something. Just take a shufti, he's like a bitch on heat." Charlie stopped shovelling and watched Spag's antics.

Harry didn't poo poo the idea. When he first met Charlie and the dog, Charlie had told him about the dog's sixth sense. Harry was skeptical but now he was more inclined to go along with

Charlie, and he wasn't wrong this time. Spag crouched safely behind the back wheel of the ambulance as heavy shells screamed overhead and crashed down all around them. Fountains of sand reached for the sky and shrapnel pierced the air. A loathsome stench of explosives fell across the aid post and the smell of death filled their nostrils. The earth trembled and the soft walls of the trenches caved in. The shelling lasted fifteen minutes.

Cautiously they lifted their heads above the shallow trenches. Harry peered round like some small prairie dog and sniffed the air. Then they gradually pulled themselves from the slit trenches. Charlie's eyes fell upon the dying petrol fire, the bottom of the brew can had burned away.

"Bloody square headed bastards," he shouted, in the direction of the enemy guns. He kicked at the dying petrol fire. It came to life with renewed energy for a few seconds, then died down instantly. Next to his treasured ambulance and Spag, that brew can was his pride and joy. He had made it himself from an old jam tin and carried it through some of the toughest action in the desert campaign. He lifted it and looked through the bottom of the tin.

"Bloody shame after all this time." He threw it into the sand.

Charlie was examining his beloved ambulance for any sign of damage. Miraculously it was intact. Suddenly there was a deafening screech as a salvo of shells dropped all around them. They had time to drop flat and crawl snake like across to their trenches. Harry was thrown the last few feet and landed on his back on the rim of his slit trench, his life's breath knocked out of him. He rolled over into his trench and lay there gasping for air and fighting for breath. Without realising what he was doing, he sat up and tried to get to his feet, only to be knocked down again by the blast from an exploding shell a few yards away.

Charlie, seeing Harry stagger along, thought he had been hit. Regardless of his own safety, he slid along on his belly and peered over the trench.

"You all right, Harry?"

Harry couldn't answer, air vacuums jammed his throat. Instead he nodded his head towards the aid post. Charlie turned and saw the padre staggering around. He lurched towards the canvas lean-to and grabbed it with one hand. His other hand clutched at his chest as bright red blood oozed between his fingers. He stared at it in disbelief. Charlie ran towards the padre, indifferent to the shells exploding and the shrapnel flying around. He put his arm round him and called for the medical sergeant. Together they led him to the aid post and placed him on the makeshift operating table.

218

"Take it easy, sir," Charlie said.

"Don't worry, son, I'm finished," he whispered. A trickle of blood ran from the corner of his mouth. Bright red blood stained his shirt front. The sergeant ripped open the shirt; blood spurted out. The M.O. entered the lean-to, looked at the padre and shook his head. Death was already etching its permanent scars on the padre's face. Gasping, he made a supreme effort to say something, but the words were inaudible. The M.O. stroked his hand across the padre's face as he took a final breath; his head dropped to one side.

"Get out of here," the M.O. shouted. "Let's get back to our trenches. There's nothing we can do here apart from getting ourselves killed."

For two days the aid post worked continually. Eight men lay dead behind the canvas lean-to, there was no telling how many lay out on the battlefield.

There were sighs of relief all round when the last casualty was evacuated. The crews of the ambulance and aid post sat down in the shade. Charlie fell asleep with his arms across the steering wheel and his head resting on them. Harry shook him awake some two hours later with a steaming hot mug of tea in his hand.

"Get this down you."

"Thanks, Harry. Just what the doctor ordered." He sipped noisily at the tea. "When I get this down I intend to take the shovel for a walk. Since you gave me those tablets I have been afraid to fart in case I shit myself!"

Daylight next day; there had been no shelling for twenty-four hours, and they emerged from the back of the ambulance, with empty stomachs. A calmness lay over the desert. German and Italian prisoners came streaming through. A party of them was detailed to dig several graves for the bodies which were already bloating after a couple of days under the intense heat.

After burying the dead they moved forward again, the menacing sound of the heavy guns getting closer with every turn of the wheels. They stopped and set up the aid post just out of range of the heavy shells. Casualties started arriving. In the distance Charlie spotted two stretcher bearers struggling with a casualty. He pointed it out to Harry and they raced forward.

The man was laying face down on the stretcher. There was a gaping wound, covered with a field dressing, in the man's back. Every time the man breathed, the dressing was sucked towards the wound. Harry threw the dressing away and replaced it with a large shell dressing. He held it in place while the bearers lifted the stretcher into the ambulance. Harry placed his ear near the man's chest and heard the ominous sound of air being sucked in

219

through the wound every time the man breathed in. His face told the rest of the story, with its sallow complexion, ashy grey lips, and forehead clammy to the touch.

"It looks like a sucking wound, sir," Harry said, as the M.O. stepped into the ambulance.

"Better get him straight back, Jackson. There are another couple of wounded in the lean-to, get them loaded. I don't know where the M.D.S. is, it can't be too far behind."

The engine of the ambulance ticked over like a well serviced watch, as Charlie waited for the rest of the wounded to be loaded.

"Right, driver, take them straight back and report to your R.S.M. Tell him I want another ambulance here. You two get a bit of rest."

The right hand sector must have been taking the brunt of the action, for when they arrived the M.D.S. was crowded with casualties.

"I can't deal with them here, I'll patch this man up, but he's in need of urgent attention. Take him straight back to the C.C.S. He's lost a lot of blood. The C.C.S. is only a couple of miles down the road."

Harry's heart nearly missed a beat at the mention of the C.C.S. He looked at Charlie and a smile froze on his face as he tried to wriggle out of it.

"We are supposed to hand over here, sir, and take a rest period."

The M.O. laughed. "Me too, Jackson, so would all the men here. I haven't been out of that theatre for forty-eight hours, and most of the men are asleep on their feet. Come on lad, get cracking."

Quite resigned to their fate, they drove on to the smooth coast road where Charlie put his foot down. They reached the C.C.S. in less then fifteen minutes, and much to their relief, they were greeted by a different corporal clerk. A pleasant, petite sister entered the ambulance and smiled. Harry was immediately on the alert, his love for sisters vanished long ago and a smiling sister looked even more suspicious. This sister proved to be a real professional. She examined the casualty carefully, then called over the bearers.

"Get this man into intensive care immediately. Tell Major Reid he is wanted urgently." Then she turned her attention towards Harry and Charlie, but she didn't criticise their appearance; she took a sympathetic tone. Harry shifted, uncomfortable under her steady gaze.

"You two don't look in the very best condition yourselves. It looks as if you both could do with a good bath and a rest." She turned sharply on her heels and followed the stretcher into the gloomy interior of the large tent.

Harry's jaw sagged as his gaze followed the sister.

"I must be dreaming, a civilised sister."

Charlie's mind was on a different track.

"How old do you reckon she is, Harry?"

"Dunno," Harry answered, with a shrug of his shoulders.

"Thirty-five, forty maybe. I wasn't taking much notice, I was subdued by her civility. There are two kinds of sister, Charlie, good and bad. If they are good they're amongst the best. If they are bad they can be bastards, there's no in between."

"To me she looked about eighteen." Charlie laughed and shook his head.

"The sooner we get to Tunis and civilisation again, the better for all of us. I couldn't take my eyes off her then. I almost had her stripped and lying in the sand. It's just not natural, Harry."

Above the noise of the comings and goings of the M.D.S. they heard their R.S.M. shouting to them. They tried to ignore it, but Sykes was walking towards them and pointing towards the R.S.M. There was no way they could get out of it. They stood to attention in front of the R.S.M. He walked round them a couple of times making both of them feel a little uncomfortable.

"Tell me, have you two any boots?" The question was plain, direct and to the point.

Harry smiled. "No, sir."

"You have no other clothes either, I suppose."

Again Harry shook his head.

The R.S.M. walked round them again, scratching his head in disbelief.

"You two are the scruffiest pair of bastards in the unit. Jackson, when you joined this unit I thought you, being a regular, would instil some kind of discipline into Williams here, but no, instead he has turned you into a scruff like himself." His voice softened, scruffy they may be but he knew they were the most efficient ambulance crew in the unit.

"When did you have your last full night's sleep?"

"Undisturbed, about three weeks ago," Harry answered.

"Right then," the R.S.M. folded his arms and stroked his chin with his finger.

"Take this ambulance as far away from the orderly room as possible and get a good night's kip. I will send Corporal Sykes round in the morning. First report to the galley and get some connor (food) down you. In the morning I want you to take a

221

chitty to the Q.M. and get kitted out. In two days time the old man wants to see you; report properly dressed. Now shove off and keep out of my sight for the next couple of days."

"Rise and shine, you couple of pimps. You have to be at the C.O.'s tent in a couple of hours, get out of those flea pits." Corporal Sykes flung open the back doors of the ambulance. The doors slammed back against the side of the ambulance making it shudder. The strong sunlight flooded in. With an effort, Charlie opened his eyes. He didn't bother to sit up, he could recognise that whining voice anywhere.

"Piss off, you pimply faced bastard. We'll let you know when we're up. S.M.'s orders, we can stay a kip for a couple of days without being disturbed."

"Well how long do you think you two have been laying there stinking? Pair of lazy sods." There was a sarcastic grin on Sykes' face.

"You have to collect your kit from the Q.M. and parade outside the C.O.'s tent." He threw the chit on Charlie's bed.

Clean shaven and freshly clothed they reported to the R.S.M. He gave them a look of approval.

"A decent haircut and you might resemble soldiers." He took a couple of steps back and sat on the corner of the table used as a desk.

"Right, a couple of weeks ago you took a casualty to a C.C.S. While you were there you gave a sister and the R.S.M. a bit of lip." He didn't look directly at them, but concentrated on wrapping a spent match around his finger; a habit of his when he concentrated.

Feigning a look of hurt expression, Charlie pointed a finger at himself.

"Who me, sir?"

"Yes you, and don't get giving me that crap, Williams. He described the pair of you down to your last shoe lace - scruffy. When he said that my ears pricked up. Worn out plimsolls, dirty appearance, unkempt unwashed and unshaven. Frayed shorts and no button on your shirts. To put the lid on it, you had the scruffiest ambulance and a scrappy little yellow dog. In the whole of the eighth army there is only one ambulance that bears that description." His gaze fell on Harry first, who for a change looked like a regular soldier.

"Christ, haven't you two any sense at all. You both gave him false names, didn't you, Private Lawrence?" He threw a quick glance at Harry, although his main complaint was concentrated against Charlie.

"But I knew who he was talking about the minute he mentioned the word scruffy. Then to make matters worse, you, Williams, with that old trick of yours, covered the pair of them from head to foot in shit and sand."

Harry thought he noticed a flicker of a smile in the corner of the R.S.M.'s mouth, but he dare not look at the R.S.M. too long or cast a glance in Charlie's direction for he feared he would burst out laughing.

"You, Jackson, being a regular soldier, should know better. The R.S.M. said he had been stationed at the same hospital as you before the war."

Harry nearly put his foot in it and nodded in the affirmative. Fortunately, at that moment the R.S.M. was concentrating on the final piece of wrapping the match round his finger. He must remember not to fall into that trap again.

"If I had the time I would personally take you back there myself and make you apologise personally to the both of them. However, we have more important jobs in hand. Stand at ease." He took a sheet of foolscap paper from behind and studied it carefully.

"The C.O. wanted to see you himself but was called back to H.Q. In future try not to rub these people up the wrong way. I know what these base wallahs can be like." He turned his head and shouted "CORPORAL!" although there was no need to shout, Sykes had his head against the flimsy canvas wall to catch every word. He almost fell into the room before the R.S.M. had recovered from shouting.

"I understand Richardson has broken a spring, corporal. Is that right?"

Sykes nodded, and the sergeant major continued.

"That bastard always manages to break something when there is a bit of action around. I will be sending these two up in his place. Now don't forget you two, use a little decorum in future. You will be going back to the infantry."

Charlie, anxious as ever to put as much distance as possible between the ambulance and the M.D.S., sprang to life, and when the sergeant major suggested sending Richardson as soon as he was out of workshops, Charlie protested.

"It's alright sir, we've had a good rest and clean up, we can stay with them."

The medical sergeant greeted them with a nod of the head. He put his book down and studied them over the top of his steel rimmed spectacles.

"What's all this then, new uniforms? What did you do, drop the Q.M. a few fags?"

Four wounded Germans were brought in, two with serious wounds. The M.O. inspected them.

"No more than boys, they should still be at school, not out here." He finished amputating an arm and leg from one young German.

"Just a boy. He's still a man with a rifle in his hands, or slamming shells into an 88 sir."

"I suppose you're right, sergeant. Take him away."

They were ordered back with an ambulance full of casualties. When they returned, much to their surprise, the regiment had attacked and moved forward. They inquired at a nearby battery of twenty-five pounders.

"Oh yes, the whole division moved up a few hours ago. Seems like someone pressed the panic button up at Jerry H.Q. The buzz is going round that they've taken another town and your infantry mob is going in to do the mopping up."

A bringer of good news, he sauntered back to the ambulance and put Harry in the picture.

"Should we wait for first light?"

"No." Harry couldn't be more positive with his answer.

"We've had one bollocking from the sergeant major, better not push our luck. Don't want to upset the old bastard."

It was dark as they picked their way across the debris strewn battlefield. The stench of death hung on the night air. Although they had become accustomed to the smell, it still sent a shudder through Harry's body. He wasn't frightened of death, he had seen it so many times and in so many different guises. Walking hand in hand with it like a constant companion, it held neither pain nor terror.

A faint breeze sprang up spreading a layer of sand across the tyre tracks they were following. Then the ground became firmer and progress faster, and as dawn broke the distant horizon blazed with a copper glow. Charlie pulled up and taking his binoculars scanned the open desert from horizon to horizon. The sand had covered all the vehicle tracks. They were alone in an ocean of sand.

"That's buggered it, Harry. There's not a bloody thing to be seen, not even a burnt out vehicle."

Harry dropped beside him and took the glasses. While Charlie had driven through the night, Harry had managed to get some sleep sitting up in his seat with several blankets round him. After that drive Charlie's eyes could be playing tricks. The sun hadn't been up long enough to create a heat haze. Harry scanned the horizon.

"You're right. Hope you haven't been travelling south, we might end up in Timbuktu." He took the compass and pointed westward. "Keep the sun on our back for a while, we're sure to catch up with someone."

They had been travelling for a little over half an hour when, from out of the blue, a German plane roared over them. Charlie pulled up as the plane made a second swoop. It swerved upwards, rolled over on its back making several turns like a ballet dancer, before zooming low over them again. Spag ran around in small circles, his tail hitched up between his rear legs.

"Stupid bastard is showing off." Charlie's eyes never left the plane. It swept round and gained height, then came careering towards them.

"Fuck's sake, Harry, run for it! The bastard is going to use us for target practice!"

They both ran for cover behind an outcrop of rocks, the only outcrop for miles in any direction. A zig zag of bullets stitched up the sand.

"Bastard must be colour blind if he can't see those red crosses," shouted Charlie as he fell flat behind the rocks.

The pilot made three more runs and on his last trip dropped two small bombs. They fell harmlessly away from the ambulance. Charlie stood up and dusted himself down.

"That's a bloody turn up for the book. That's never happened to me before." They inspected the ambulance. Apart from a couple of bullet holes in the back door and a dent in the step, it was undamaged.

"Bloody lousy shot, too," Charlie muttered.

It was noon when Charlie pulled up again. He pointed to a distorted blob dancing on the heat haze on the far horizon. He focused his glasses on the object and with a puzzled frown handed the glasses to Harry.

"What do you make of that?"

Harry studied it for a few minutes. "Don't know, looks like tents of sorts."

Ten minutes later Harry's guess was confirmed, it was a small tented hospital. They approached it with care. There was no sign of life. Much nearer, Harry studied it through the binoculars.

"It's a bloody Jerry hospital, Charlie. I reckon you have skirted the town and we are behind Jerry lines."

"Don't be a prick, we would have heard gunfire or something. Anyway there isn't any sign of life there. Looks like the Marie Celeste of the western desert."

Charlie put the ambulance into low gear and handed his rifle to Harry.

"Shove one up the spout just in case and hang on like hell if I make a sudden U turn."

They closed on the hospital slowly. It was eerie, there wasn't a sound or sign of life. Harry handed Charlie the rifle, jumped down and cautiously approached the first large tent and lifted the opening flap. The silence from the gloomy interior pressed on his ear drums. His heart throbbed and his mouth dried up. He held his hand against one of the tent's timber uprights, while his eyes became accustomed to the gloom. The inside of the tent was some sixty feet long. A row of beds ran right round the tent with another two rows head to head down the centre. Above most of the beds hung a neatly rolled mosquito net.

A few minutes later Charlie entered, his rifle still in his hands. As he lifted the flap the smell hit him like a gigantic sledge hammer, throwing his head back.

"Bloody hell, what a stench! Smells like someone has snuffed it."

The beds were in perfectly straight lines befitting with Teutonic thoroughness, some of them with the bedclothes thrown to one side as if the occupants had left in a hurry. At the foot of one of the beds lay a German infantryman's pack with a bayonet sticking out from the top. Harry pulled it from its scabbard and slashed at the canvas sides of the tent. Sunlight and fresh air rushed in. Slowly, Harry walked between the rows of beds where swarms of blue black flies fed on the blood stained sheets.

Above the untiring buzz of the flies something made him pull up at the foot of a bed, its mosquito net tucked into the bottom of the bed. It could have been a faint murmur or just a slight movement. He fought the urge to turn and run. His flesh tingled and he could feel the hairs rising on the back of his neck. He took a firmer grip on the bayonet still in his hands and whipped the net away. A pale waxen face lay deep in the pillow, its eyes wide open and mouth stretched to a tight slit across the unshaven skin making it look like a caricature from a cartoon film.

"Charlie," Harry's voice echoed down the silent tent. "There's a bloke still alive down here." He pulled back the sheet covering him and reeled back. The man's left arm and shoulder was covered with a soiled dressing. Green pus and blood soaked through the dressing, turning it into a greenish brown solidified mess.

Charlie, a piece of gauze covering his nose and mouth, looked over Harry's shoulder.

"Bloody hell, he looks worse than my granny did, and she had been dead a fortnight when they found her. Stinks, don't it, Harry?"

226

Harry threw the sheet back over the man.

"He's covered in shit from arsehole to breakfast time. Must have been here a few days." He placed his hand on the man's forehead; it was hot and clammy.

"Get me plenty of hot water and keep it coming. Make a brew at the same time, it might settle my stomach."

"You don't intend to clean him up, Harry? The man is dying and that shit must be like granite."

"You don't think I intend to leave him here in that condition do you? Look he has survived that long, let's give the man a chance, or at least let him die with some dignity. So sod off and get me some water."

"You make me laugh. A couple of hours ago some colour blind German pilot tries to shoot up the ambulance and use us for target practice, and now you're trying to save some Jerry's life."

"Well, I am fucking sure this poor bastard wasn't the pilot. Get the hot water, Charlie."

Harry picked up a white coat lying near and smiled as he fingered the wings and swastika on the pocket. There was also a pair of stethoscopes. He listened to the man's chest and was surprised at the condition of the heart and lungs. He found a face mask and sprinkled it with disinfectant hoping to minimise the smell. He cleaned around the man's lips, then forced them apart and gently rubbed the inside with glycerine. Charlie returned with a white bucket of hot water. Gently Harry saturated the dirty dressing; it was like stiff cardboard. The clear water in the bucket turned a dark brown before Charlie returned with a second bucket. Gradually the dirty dressing eased away. There were two bullet holes in the man's shoulder, another in his chest and still another in his upper arm.

"Christ, mate, someone had it in for you alright." Harry gently prodded round the wound; pus oozed out. He spent an hour cleaning the wound, then sprinkled it with sulphanilamide powder and redressed it.

He then started cleaning the man's lower regions. As he eased him over, the man's arm lay by his side clutching a luger pistol with its safety catch off.

"I think he intended to shoot us, Charlie. Poor sod, in his state he couldn't knock the skin off a rice pudding."

Charlie was searching through the man's locker.

"Just as I thought Harry, the sod belongs to the S.S." He sorted through the man's papers and medals. The medals and luger he put in his pocket.

"The base wallahs will give anything for those."

"There's a big silver pocket watch here."

Charlie stopped dead in his tracks. "I don't want that bloody thing in my ambulance. Don't ever bring a watch on the ambulance, they're bad luck." Superstition was rife with front line soldiers, just as it was with fighter pilots, but without a doubt Charlie was worse and Harry abided by his wishes. He dropped the watch back on the man's locker.

Charlie was all for leaving the man behind but Harry wouldn't hear of it.

"Sod off, Charlie. Go and have a shufti around. The bloke's got bed sores as well. I should be finished in ten minutes or so."

With the luger in his hand, Charlie went from bed to bed. There were two dead men further down the ward. He placed the bed sheets over them. He returned to Harry.

"What do you want, the good news or the bad first?"

"As you wish. Nothing can be as bad as this bloke."

"Don't you believe it, there are three more down there. The good news is two are dead, but the other one... Just prepare yourself for a shock."

There was nothing else he could do for the wounded man. He followed Charlie to the other bed. As he approached the bed the smell became unbearable. He renewed his face mask and soaked it in disinfectant, then threw back the man's bed covers and recoiled in horror. He thought he had seen it all before, he was mistaken. How could anyone leave a fellow human being in such a condition. The man's legs had been amputated just above his knees, but he had been left unattended for so long the stumps and dressing were a seething mass of yellow bloated maggots. The remaining portions of his legs, testicles and the lower abdomen were swollen into a series of large round hard balls with a deadly poison spreading across them, interlaced with intricate red veins reaching to his chest. The tea Charlie had just brought for Harry filled his mouth with bitter tasting bile. He tried to control himself but another gush of the foul tasting liquid rushed into his mouth and poured through his nose as he vomited all over the floor.

He felt the man's pulse; it was just a faint throb. The man was unconscious, if he lasted two hours he would be lucky.

"Nothing we can do here. Let's get that other man loaded into the ambulance."

"Will he have a chance, Harry?"

"Who knows? I'm a medical orderly not a doctor. His pulse has a kick like a mule. I should think he stands a good chance. Not like this poor sod, he's dying fast."

Charlie had nothing but admiration for his medic. How many other men would have cleaned a man up like Harry had, and a

228

German at that. Not a couple of hours previously one had been trying to kill him, contrary to the Geneva convention.

"Do you know, Harry, if ever I get one I hope to God that you're near."

He passed if off lightly, coming from Charlie that was a compliment.

"Shut up, you prick. Let's go and have a shufti round the other tents, who knows we may make the trip worthwhile."

The second tent wasn't so large, perhaps thirty feet. This, too, was sectioned off with a canvas screen a third of the way down that served as an operating theatre. The remainder of the tent was taken up with three rows of beds. All the beds were empty, but Charlie was taking no chances, he held the luger in his hand with the safety catch off.

A section of the canvas screen had an opening covered with gauze; Harry walked through. Two operating tables stood in the centre and heavy lamps hung from the ridge pole. Tables covered with dressing and instruments lined the walls. In one corner was a large box made of polished oak. It was three foot long, two foot deep and two foot wide. The lid was secured by a large brass padlock. On the top was a brass plate with the owners name engraved in old German style writing.

"What do you reckon's inside, Harry?"

"Buggered if I know. The way it's secured it could be a surgeon's private booze box." Finding nothing to force the lock with, Charlie brushed Harry aside and pointed his luger at the padlock. There was an almighty explosion as the bullet ricocheted off the padlock and passed between Harry's legs. He fell backwards.

"You stupid bastard, you very nearly blew my balls off."

Completely ignoring Harry's plight, Charlie scratched his head.

"That's bloody funny. I saw this cowboy picture once, the bandits held up this stage coach. The driver threw down this steel cash box. The bandit took one shot at it and the lid flew open."

"Sod the cowboy films. You very nearly castrated me."

"You're all right, Harry. If I had hit you, you'd be speaking with a high pitched voice now." He pointed at the box again with his luger.

Harry took the hint and sprinted to the far end of the tent as three shots rang out.

"It's open," Charlie shouted.

Harry was just as interested in seeing the inside of the box but he wasn't prepared for the magnitude of his find. As Charlie wrenched the remainder of the padlock away, the front fell down revealing five drawers. The dovetailed joints so fine they would have done justice to Mr Chippendale. Each drawer contained surgical instruments. The exact shape of each instrument was carved in the bottom drawers and covered in a velvet material to hold it in place undamaged. Harry whistled through his teeth.

"God, Charlie, I have never seen anything so beautiful before. Whoever left them must have been in a terrific hurry."

"Everything for the home surgeon, eh Charlie?" He picked up a scalpel and examined it closely. It was made of the finest steel.

"It looks like we struck gold. To the right person these must be worth a fortune."

"Shall we take them with us?"

"You don't think I was going to leave them here for some stupid infantryman to get his mucky hands on and use the scalpels for opening his bully tins."

"Any chance of getting them home? We could open up an abortion clinic and go in for illegal operations. We could make a fortune. The girls would flock there in their thousands after the Yanks leave their small deposits behind." He rubbed his hands together enthusiastically. Harry wasn't taking a lot of notice, he had seen Charlie's imagination running riot many times.

"Would we have enough instruments there?"

"Charlie, there are enough instruments there to remove a man's brain and stuff it up his arse."

"Sod that! We've enough N.C.O.s and officers now."

"The only place to hide it is in the cab. Move those petrol and water cans, put the box in their place and rearrange the tins. Old Spag will be a couple of feet higher but he'll soon get used to that. When we get back, I will have a chat to Captain Carlton, he's one of the lads. His old man was a miner and scrimped and save to send him to medical school. Thinks the world of his old man. We'll try him when we get back to the unit. Said he hopes to be a top surgeon one day."

"Well, after this bloody lot he won't need a lot of training," Charlie answered.

Harry took a last look at the dying man. He was fading fast, his breathing had become shallow and there was hardly any pulse.

"He'll be gone in a few minutes. Shall we hang on?"

"Come on, Harry, we are in for a bollocking when we get back and there isn't a lot we can do for him now."

Reluctantly Harry had to agree with him. They loaded the other German, and Charlie was quite pleased with the way the box was hidden. Harry made one mad dash to the dying man. A faint noise came from the man's throat.

"Sorry, mate," Harry muttered under his breath.

CHAPTER 23

For several days the front remained static and without the steady rumble of heavy gunfire. It was far too quiet for Charlie's peace of mind and to convince him that things were far from normal, Spag, his small dog, 'was acting strange' as Charlie was fond of saying.

"It's Spag doing his pre-action war dance," Harry would chuckle. He tried to doze. Normally sleep came to him quite easily for, after months on continual active service, he had learned to sleep in some very awkward positions, usually sitting up in the front seat of the ambulance wrapped in blankets. But now Harry had a premonition that something was about to happen.

"Strange, Charlie. There is sod all between us and the enemy and yet everything seems so strangely quiet. Not even the sound of distant gunfire. Do you think this could be the lull before the storm?"

The feeling was endemic to the whole leaguer for everyone remained alert. The regiment was spread out across the open desert with all eyes strained towards the enemy positions, while the oppressive heat turned the armoured cars into ovens fit to bake bread. Spag made for the rear wheel of the ambulance, taking advantage of the shade, and Charlie and Harry reached for their steel helmets not a moment too soon. They had just secured them when the enemy shells screamed overhead with an agonising screech and dropped amongst the vehicles.

A small patch of dry scrub burst into flame and a Jerboa hopped across the burning sand to another patch of scrub nearby. A small piece of hot metal ricocheted off a boulder and thudded into the ground a couple of feet from the front wheel of the ambulance. A small scout car received a direct hit and burst into flames. The car, devoid of its front wheel, settled onto its front axle like a wounded animal. The crew jumped to safety unhurt, but the burning vehicle filled the still hot air with the revolting stench of burnt rubber.

With no slit trenches prepared Harry ran behind a small out crop of rock. Charlie was quick to follow. They threw themselves flat against the ground and the bombardment continued for over an hour. An armoured car and two three ton lorries went up in flames. There were no casualties.

An armoured car sped forward to reconnoitre and immediately became a sought after target for the guns as it zig-zagged towards them. Another two cars detached themselves from the regiment and went to the aid of the single car. Within minutes the three of them became deformed blobs dancing on the heat haze. The regiment moved forward very slowly, and Charlie handed Harry his binoculars.

"Have a shufti, Harry. It looks like they found the guns." As he spoke bright orange flashes spat out from the haze.

Three more cars sped forward in an effort to take the sting from the first three. The column stopped and taking the binoculars from Harry, Charlie watched the scene of the guns and armoured cars. These were swanning around like a pack of hunt hounds sniffing out their prey.

"Looks as if they're playing Russian roulette with the guns. They're all over the place."

All six cars were speeding towards the enemy, small guns blazing away, from all directions. Charlie counted four guns. They had found a good spot on uneven ground surrounded by rocks and scrub.

Suddenly without twisting and turning the commander's car turned and raced at top speed towards the first gun. The other five cars converged from every direction in a pincer movement. The commander sat upright in the turret of his car urging the other cars on, and the strategy paid off because the enemy became so confused that they didn't know which car to target first. Machine gun fire erupted from the gun pits, but the cars were so fast that when a German officer stood on top of his sandbag wall and started firing at the oncoming cars with his luger pistol, he only lasted a moment before he threw up his arms and fell back into the gunpit. Defiant to the end, his final shot fired wildly into the air.

Then, suddenly, the leading armoured car, less than twenty yards away, received a direct hit against the turret. It rocked and wove round a few seconds as the driver fought to regain control and finally headed towards the low wall of sandbags. Two enemy machine gunners behind the wall jumped to their feet but too late. The car hit the wall, and also the machine at top speed sending the top layer of sandbags flying and burying the two men beneath the wheels. The commander of the car was slumped over the turret blood pouring from his wounds and onto the hot metal in a cloud of dust and it was all over in minutes. The surviving gun crews came out with their hands well above their heads.

"We're in business, Charlie. The commander is slumped over the turret. It looks like he's had it."

The ambulance shot forward and it seemed like hours before it reached the gun site. In fact it was less than two minutes.

"Blimey, Charlie, it's Captain Bellamy. Remember he took us on that stunt?"

232

Two men were lifting the officer from the armoured car and Harry turned abruptly away after seeing into his face.

Shrapnel had taken away one arm above the elbow and on its upward journey the piece of shrapnel had also taken part of his lower jaw bone. His right eye hung from its socket and bright crimson blood spurted from the artery of the upper arm. Taking fast action Harry applied a tourniquet, and seeing that Captain Bellamy's tongue was blocking his windpipe and that he was struggling for breath Harry commanded, "Quick, Charlie, get that Jerry instrument box down."

Two men helped Charlie as he tried to free the box hemmed in by the petrol and water cans throwing them quickly to one side. Charlie dropped the box, already open, beside Harry. He took out a long pair of forceps and pulled the tongue back, but the windpipe remained blocked.

"Quick, anyone got a piece of rubber tubing or a thick fountain pen?" Harry shouted removing a scalpel from the box and making a small hole in the officer's windpipe. Then he held it open with forceps to allow the air a free passage and one man offered him a large piece of rubber tubing.

"Don't be a prat. I want to open his wind pipe not put out a fire," Harry muttered.

Instead he selected a large fountain pen from amongst a dozen offered to him and having done this, gave the man who had offered him the pen a surgical saw from the box. "Now," Harry instructed, "cut about four inches." The man did exactly as he was told and Harry inserted the pen into the small hole, afterwards securing it with a surgical sticking plaster. Captain Bellamy seemed to relax. Then Harry applied a large surgical shell dressing to the officer's face.

A German medical orderly was standing nearby and Harry gave him his medical satchel. "This officer is very ill. I have to take him to the rear immediately. Look after the rest. They don't seem too bad. I'll return as fast as possible. Do you speak English?"

The German spoke excellent English. He stood to attention and clicked his heels. "It would be an honour to work with you," he announced.

Turning sharply, Harry took his seat in the back of the ambulance where Charlie with the help of a couple of men, had already manhandled the surgical chest back into its place.

Back at the aid station the M.O. took one look at the officer, removed the temporary tube from his throat and inserted the correct one. Having done this he redressed the other wounds.

233

"Good work, Jackson," he complimented Harry, "you saved this man's life."

Harry looked at the damaged face and the socket where the man's eye had been, now swelling to the size of a balloon.

"I doubt very much if he will thank me for that, sir, when he wakes up." Harry replied and the M.O. answered by shaking his head, for Captain Bellamy was the epitome of the true, blue English officer. Tall, broad shouldered and blue eyed. The sort of hero written about in 'Boys Own' or 'Magnet' magazines. He had been popular with his men as he had been with the officers in his own unit, and it wouldn't be long, Harry felt sure, until Captain Bellamy cursed the day he had saved his life.

Within minutes the ambulance was racing down the straight metal coast road towards a small unit that specialised in repairing facial wounds. But it was well over an hour before they found the unit. Harry rushed inside and two orderlies in snow white gowns helped them remove the stretcher. They placed it on two metal frames. A major came out to inspect Captain Bellamy and closely examined his face as an art connoisseur would examine a work of art. He touched parts of the officer's face with the tip of his small finger and when another officer came in, the major turned to him and said, "God, Clarence, if I had this face for a few months you would hardly know he'd been injured. But all we can do now is patch the poor sod up and send him on his way."

The major then sat down on a chair beside the stretcher, his head resting on his hand, rebuilding the face in his own mind as he spoke aloud. "A little cut here... A little cut there... Take a slice of his tit and rebuild his cheek. Wire this small bone here... Pity about that eye, wish we could have saved it."

He turned to Harry. "Alright, orderly, you front line wallahs have done a good job. He's in good hands now and you can piss off back to your unit. Good luck, son." He dismissed him. Then the surgeon smiled at his opposite number. "Right, Clarence, Nelson touch here. One eye, one arm... "

Returning to the gun site, Charlie and Harry discovered they had been away much longer than anticipated, and they expected to see another ambulance there. The German medic had treated four of his own men and another from the regiment. Six Germans and one man from an armoured car lay dead. A scout car was towing the wrecked armoured car away from the sandbagged wall, and two more Germans lay crushed beneath the wheels. Harry pulled one away and the head fell forward throwing a mouthful of congealing blood down the front of his shirt.

"Right, you shower, get this place cleared away. Those dead, I want them buried. You, medic, piss off back with the wounded."

"Want any help with the wounded, sarge?" Harry asked without much enthusiasm.

Much to his relief the sergeant answered, "No, piss off. We have a few Jerries around. They can dig the graves and bury their own. They started the fight. Let the bastards bury their own dead."

Charlie was strolling around the gun site. The German officer who had been killed standing on the sandbag wall was laid out on the ground. A large silver pocket watch hung from his tunic pocket. Charlie picked it up to examine it, flipped open the cover and much to his surprise discovered that it was a stop watch. Inside the lid words were engraved in High German script and the only ones he could decipher read, 'Adolph Hitler.' He took the watch to the German medic for a full translation.

"This officer," the German medic told Charlie, "was a great German runner. He was in the 1936 Olympics and ran against the great American negro, Jessie Owen. You will recall the incident. Hitler refused to shake the man's hand because he was black. After the Games were over Hitler presented the officer with this watch."

He took it from Charlie and turned it around to show him that what he actually thought to be the back was the front. Then the German flipped the watch open and this side of the cover, also, was engraved on the inside listing the grand achievements of the late, great Aryan sportsman.

"This watch will become very valuable in the future," the German gravely assured Charlie.

But Charlie's superstition was overriding the value of the watch. It was one thing he would never keep in his ambulance believing it to be bad luck. While Harry supervised the loading of the remaining wounded, Charlie hawked the watch around the armoured car crews and managed to exchange it for a hundred Players cigarettes.

"That was a very nice job you did with the officer. Where did you learn such surgery?" the German medic enquired of Harry.

Harry raised an eyebrow and assessed the German. By the absence of a tan on the man's face and arms he didn't think that he could have been in the desert long.

"How long have you been out here, mate?"

"Two months," the German answered with hardly a trace of accent. "I was a medical student."

"Well, if you had still been on active service instead of being in the bag, you could have considered yourself a fully experienced surgeon in a year. I take it this is your first taste of action?"

"Yes, and with this carnage," he glanced around at the devastated gun positions, "I am pleased it is my last. I am no soldier, you understand. I should not be here."

"Yes. I'm sure that's what all you Jerries say once we've got you in the bag."

"Well this time it is true. Can you believe it? After two years of being a medical student I was drafted straight away to be a driver. Obviously drivers are more important than a medical man in the German Army. Eventually I was posted to this regiment. The C.O. seemed to have more brains than the drafting authorities. He made me medical orderly straight away. As you see, I wear the artillery insignia and not that of the medical corps."

Harry laughed. "That sounds like our army."

Charlie butted into the conversation at this point.

"One of our ambulance drivers was a captain's mate on a large fishing trawler before the war. Quite capable, he was, of taking over a captain's job when he was on sick leave."

From the way the German medic carried himself anyone could see he was no soldier. Charlie offered him a cigarette. "Your English is good."

"Yes, my grandmother was English. My grandfather was in the mounted police in South Africa and served in the South African War. They returned to Germany after his service was finished. My grandmother would never learn to speak German although she lived there for over thirty years. So, there was only one thing left - we would all have to learn English. She could just about say 'good evening' or 'good morning' just to be sociable, but after the first war started she even cut out those friendly greetings. She was a most stubborn old lady. But, of course, that is a British trait or you would have given up the fight at Dunkirk."

"Yes. That's where you Germans and other foreigners get it wrong. We lose many battles but rarely lose a war," replied Charlie with true patriotism.

The German glanced nervously around, making certain none of his comrades were within earshot and lowered his voice. "My grandmother told me that when Hitler came to power he would be the ruination of Germany, and she said that Britain would lose many battles but not the war when Britain declared war in 1939. After that September day in 1939 she never left the house again and she became a recluse, then she lost her will to live after Dunkirk. When she lay dying she grasped my wrist and warned all of us that Britain would have the final victory. My grandfather died a few months after."

Both the German medic and Harry sat in the back of the ambulance with the casualties. They unloaded casualties at the aid post, then Harry took the German to one side.

"Is it true about your concentration camps? Rumours are flying around that the occupied countries are full of them and that the S.S. are gassing the Jews by the thousands."

Removing his steel helmet the German gazed directly into Harry's eyes, his blonde hair falling over his broad forehead, his steel blue eyes seemed to bore right through Harry, and he didn't reply as he took his time working out an answer.

"Well," he said at last in a level tone, "I do know that before the war the Jews were being persecuted, and that gradually at my university the Jewish professors were vanishing, one by one. It was a terrible shame, really," he emphasised with a certain, characteristically German earnestness and paused before he went on.

"Some of them were great people. Our family doctor was too, a Jew, and my father would let no one but this man touch his parents. Then someone had the bright idea that my mother was an English Jew because, just before the war, she refused to give the authorities any information. Finally my father was forced to go to England and trace her family. They live in Kent and he had to furnish proof to the German authorities that she was not Jewish and, even then, it was difficult, very dangerous... There was still much anti-British feeling. But when I was called up for military service no one bothered me. After all, with my blue eyes and blonde hair there could be no mistake about my race."

"Yes, but what about the concentration camps, mate? Do they exist? We have plenty of Jews in our army and most of them great blokes. When they get to Germany there'll be hell to pay and no mistake," Harry insisted.

"If anyone should know about concentration camps," he replied, "you British should. It was you who invented them in the South African war."

The conversation was brought to an abrupt halt when several three ton lorries pulled up beside them and all prisoners were ordered aboard. The German medic shook hands with Charlie and Harry, and Charlie thrust a carton of 'V's inside the medic's tunic. "They're a load of crap, mate, but they may come in handy when you get to the cages. All the best of luck and I hope when this lot is over you get back to your medical school."

As the last German prisoner was about to board the last lorry he turned, clicked his heels together and gave the Nazi salute. A man standing nearby sipping hot tea from a chipped enamel mug, with a quick flip of his wrist, threw the tea straight into the German's face.

"Get on that lorry, you square headed bastard and fuck Hitler, and fuck you." He lashed out with his foot to help the German on his way.

"Wonder how poor Bellamy is getting on?" Charlie ruminated as they watched the lorries carrying the German prisoners fade into the distance.

With a slight shrug of his shoulders, Harry answered, "Who the hell knows? His face looked an awful mess, but it's surprising what the doctors can do these days. After all they've had plenty of practise on the boys from the Battle of Britain. They're evacuating them by hospital ship from Tripoli now. He could be home in a couple of weeks. Then the big boys will take a shufti at him. I heard his family is loaded, so money's no object and he'll get the best treatment."

Before the sentence was out Charlie realised he had touched on a tender subject.

"I wouldn't like to go back to face that... "

The last word faded, for it wasn't long before that Harry had been forced to make a choice: a choice that was now affecting his daily life, and not a day passed without his thinking of the incident. At night he would wake up trembling and in a cold sweat that menacing revolver rising from the sand like a one-eyed black monster. Charlie immediately changed the subject.

Once more the division was on the move and negotiating some of the roughest terrain of the campaign. The vehicles were alternatively stuck in the soft sand or climbing over what could only be called perpendicular hills. They had lost count of how many times they were forced to dig the ambulance from the soft unyielding sand.

Sweat poured from every pore of Charlie's skin as he alternatively cursed and coaxed the engine up one of the steepest inclines they had encountered. A large Daimler armoured car sped past the commander laughing at Charlie's efforts.

"Want a tow, medic?"

Charlie was in no mood for jesting. These armoured car wallahs thought they knew everything. He shouted back, "Up yours," and gave the car a two fingered salute.

"Think we'll make it, Charlie?" Harry enquired.

Charlie pointed to a small Humber armoured car riding the crest of the hill. "See that little bastard there, Harry? If he can make it I'm certain we can."

Revving his engine to its highest pitch Charlie released his foot brake, and the ambulance shot forward throwing Harry hard back against his seat. The ambulance roared forward at breakneck speed and it was a quarter of the way up the steep incline before he changed gear. Then cautiously zig-zagging and avoiding the largest of boulders he jerked the wheels inch by inch but not too hard, for he knew the wrong move at this crucial point would send the ambulance sliding backwards. The plywood back creaked and groaned like a wooden ship in rough sea.

"Hold tight, Harry," Charlie yelled at him and down to his lowest gear, the engine stalled and the ambulance slid down a couple of feet before he regained control. He gave the front wheels full lock. The engine started again and they crept forward inch by inch. Charlie could almost sense the water cooling system boiling over. Steam filled the cab. Charlie stopped the ambulance and holding the radiator cap in an old oil soaked cloth he unscrewed the cap. It exploded in his hand covering both him and Harry in dirty water and Charlie tried to make a joke of it.

"Fancy a brew, Harry?"

They allowed the engine to cool. Several vehicles hadn't made it. The column looked like a herd of wild animals exhausted after a long run and the two men smoked three cigarettes each before Charlie decided the engine was cool enough. He then topped the radiator up and after several more agonising minutes they reached the top where Harry glanced back. "Quite a few will have to be given a tow there, Charlie."

"Sod them. Just take a shufti at this. Now there's a sight for sore eyes."

Ahead, at the foot of the hill, lay a long plain devoid of all plant life. Beyond it lay more hills but nothing like the ones they had just traversed. Already vehicles were spread out across this desolate landscape.

"God, Harry. What the hell are we fighting over a place like this for? Have you ever seen anything so depressing in your life? I bet the heat down there will be well into the hundreds."

He didn't start the engine, but the ambulance rolled down the incline and gravity did the rest. He used only the foot brake to keep control. He asked Harry to walk down as it may be a little dangerous, but Harry only laughed and told him, "Get stuffed, Charlie," and then remained in his seat, eyes closed, praying silently.

Safely down at last, like most of the crews they started brewing and waiting for the regiment to reform.

Hardly had they finished their meal when there was a warning shout, and looking up the hill they saw a small scout car hurtling towards them completely out of control. Charlie took the situation in at once. He jumped into the cab and moved the ambulance from the scout car's path. But Harry stood his ground, mesmerised by the car, and flung himself to one side as it hurtled past between him and the ambulance taking the beloved brew can with it. The ambulance came to a rest fifty yards away.

"I just couldn't hold the bastard," the driver said when he had emerged from the car sweating and shaking while Charlie retrieved the can. "The bloody engine just cut out. I couldn't hold it. I think the brakes are kaput."

Charlie inspected his brew can carefully. Apart from a large dent that could easily be knocked out it was none the worse for the unexpected ride beneath the scout car.

"You would have been kaput if you'd fucked up this brew can, mate," he grumbled.

They all bedded down for a couple of days and it was two more before they hit more hospitable territory and were making their way towards a small French colonial town.

CHAPTER 24

To Harry it was always a miracle how one victory led to another with the utter confusion that reigned, and the last few weeks proved to be no exception. For less than a month they had been attached to three different regiments and the entire regiment was in the same predicament. First, the division would be fighting their way towards Tunis on one flank. Then, suddenly, they would race across often hostile country to another. Fortunately casualties were at a bare minimum and usually the results of a lone sniper, or a pocket of resistance left behind to try to slow down the Allied advance, thus allowing the key personnel to try and make their escape.

These delaying tactics made it difficult for the ambulance crew. Although the casualties were few, the line of evacuation for the casualties stretched further back, and the ambulance was covering two and three times the normal distances.

"You got a cigaretta for me, pliz, Tommy?"

A shadow was cast over Charlie as he bent across the petrol fire, brewing up. He rose slowly to his feet and his jaw dropped, his eyes opening wide as they followed the Italian's body upwards. Charlie was no small size. He was six feet tall and broadly built, but the height of this colossus made Charlie feel like a midget. He was the tallest man Charlie had ever seen. He must have been at least six feet ten.

Charlie gasped, "How the hell did our chaps miss you? A bloody short sighted sniper couldn't have missed a hulk like you!"

The Italian's walnut brown face split into a wide grin revealing two rows of brilliant white teeth. The smile was infectious. Charlie couldn't help but smile back and whether it was at the sight of the Italian's naively friendly face or his phenomenal size, he couldn't make up his mind. Without answering he handed the Italian a packet of 'V's. He took one out and then offered the packet back, but Charlie pushed it to one side.

"You have them, mate. If our lads missed you they may rot your lungs instead," he joked.

The Italian sat on his haunches staring at the blazing fire. Throughout the campaign he had been brainwashed into believing the allies were short of fuel, Charlie gleaned from the incredulous expression on his face, and yet here he was sitting in front of a blazing petrol fire. He puffed hungrily on his cigarette obviously his first in a number of days.

"You speak English, mate?" Charlie asked as he passed the Italian a mug of steaming hot tea. The amiable giant tossed his head to one side and replied in very broken English, "Leet-ul ... " and grinned happily.

Charlie's knowledge of Italian was no better so their conversation was very stunted and only Spag seemed to enjoy it. For every time the Italian spoke, Spag would become hysterically excited and run towards him whimpering, yapping and leaping at him. His enormous ham of a hand scooped the animal up and fondled its small head, while he whispered in its ear. Spag appeared to understand every word he said and wagged his dusty stump of a tail furiously.

Harry joined them and sat on the back step of the ambulance.

"Where the hell did that bloody giant spring up from, Charlie? God, he must be seven feet tall, and I always thought Iteys were two foot by seven inch hip wonders." Harry was also surprised at how quietly the man spoke in his mixture of almost unintelligible English and native Italian. They were usually such noisy bastards.

"So how about the brothels, mate?" Charlie wanted to know.

The Italian stared vacantly at Charlie, not comprehending the rapidly spoken English. But after a few unmistakable gestures and a lot of bellowing in English and bad Italian, Charlie finally got through to him. Harry clutched his stomach which ached from laughing at Charlie's lewd grimaces, gestures and coarse expostulations, and soon the Italian was guffawing too, his laughter resembling a series of rifle cracks on a firing range - ragged but loud. His enormous shoulders shook and his chest heaved up and down in the ponderous rhythm of a huge man.

"Over." He jerked his thumb in a direction north of the city where the houses were shrouded in a lake of thick fog and only the larger tops of buildings were barely visible.

"Look at those stupid bastards, Harry." Charlie nodded towards a battery of twenty five pounders firing in the direction of the houses of ill repute. "Trust those hairy-arsed gunners. I'm sure they like destroying things just for the love of it... Nip over and let them know the girls are in a line of fire not quite to their taste or beneficial to their health. If those long range snipers have buggered it up for us I will personally bugger that battery sergeant with a twenty five pounder shell up his rectum."

"Oh, ow," howled Harry, tears of mirth streaming down his face. "With or without vaseline?" Then he began to cough, almost choking with hilarity at the mental image of a large shell vanishing up someone's arse.

The Italian stood up slowly - perhaps unravelled would be a more appropriate description - and Harry gaped up at him.

"Bloody hell, Charlie ," he muttered, "I wouldn't like to handle that Goliath on a stretcher... "

The man gravely shook hands with both of them and Harry shoved a packet of hard tack biscuits into one of his ham like hands. Charlie gave him two more packets of 'coffin nail' cigarettes, and the Italian wrote down several addresses of brothels for Charlie.

After the man had gone, Charlie walked towards the battery as if he were in a trance. Harry scratched his head in disbelief as Charlie got into a heated argument with the battery sergeant major and kept pointing at the distant houses and, as he watched him, Harry shook his head slowly.

"There are times when I think that bastard is serious," he muttered to himself, but like the previous time Charlie had approached the gunners, Harry felt sure the guns deviated slightly from their target after their debate with the sergeant.

When they arrived at the aid post, Harry and Charlie were surprised to see Wilkins waiting for them in an obviously distressed state. Tears had left two white streaks furrowing his cheeks and his eyes were red and puffy. Concerned, Charlie placed a reassuring arm around his shoulders.

"Christ, Wilky, what the hell is the matter with you?" He enquired and frowned in bewildered consternation as Wilkins' body racked with several more gut ripping sobs.

Since the episode with the knocked out tanks a couple of months previously, and those times when they were attached to the regiment, he would always be the first to greet them. He would sit for hours on the back step of the ambulance fondling Spag's ears. Wilkins wasn't much of a conversationalist, but Charlie and Harry would listen to him when he had something to say, for Wilkins was a loner with few friends in the regiment. Now he looked a forlorn figure, bawling like a distraught child.

Harry and Charlie both knew something serious had happened and realised Wilkins was in shock. Charlie searched for the bottle of brandy and he poured out a good dose then he made Wilkins drink it.

The medical sergeant standing by the lean-to nodded at Charlie to come over and whispered confidentially in his ear, "His brother was killed last night. Six of them on patrol walked straight into a German ambush. The whole six were killed outright. They've just brought their bodies in." He nodded his head towards the back of the lean-to.

"Fucking hell," Charlie gasped. Right at the end of the battle too." He threw his cap down in anger.

"Oh, shit, Wilkins, I am sorry," Harry muttered when Charlie passed him the news. He gripped Wilkins shoulder. "There's nothing I can say that seems adequate. Look, we have a couple of casualties on. Do you want a trip back with us? They are really in the shit at the rear. Nobody seems to know where anything is." He winked at Charlie. "Charlie'll take his time finding the rear medical unit."

Wilkins shook his head. He'd regained a little composure.

"No thanks all the same... "

He sat down on the back step and Spag ran towards him as Harry poured out another brandy. Wilkins swigged it down and it fired a little courage in him. "They have Joe round the back with the other blokes. I'll sit with him awhile. He was younger than me. I was supposed to keep my eye on him. Our old Dutch will do her nut when she gets the news."

His cockney accent thickened in his grief and with the effects of the liquor. "He was her favourite, you know. I didn't mind that, he was a smashing bloke, always piss-arsing around. Pity you never met him."

Charlie was speechless. At heart he was a softy. He knew if he spoke now, like Wilkins, he would break down.

"Never mind, Wilky, your old Dutch can't blame you for that. It was no fault of yours. Why the hell don't you have a run back with us? A few days rest will do you good. I'm sure the M.O. wouldn't mind," Harry insisted, casting a glance towards the medical sergeant.

In truth the medical team had been trying to rid themselves of Wilkins for months. They would have no objection to losing him now. He was pretty useless. When they returned from the rear with the empty ambulance Wilkins had completely recovered. The tragedy appeared to bring out the man in him and he declined a further trip to the rear.

"No thanks, Harry, I haven't many friends in the regiment but I'll stick it out. I feel I must take Joe's place. The Div may go home after this. I know every bastard here thinks I'm bomb happy - but I'll show 'em."

"That's what I like to hear, son."

The medical sergeant had come up softly behind them his footsteps muffled in the fine layer of sand. "Don't you worry, lad," he added, "we'll see you through alright."

Resentment showed clearly on Wilkins' face as he pushed the sergeant's hand from his shoulder. "Come off it, sarge, you've always despised me. Stick your bleedin' aid post up your arse. I am asking - no, not asking - I am telling you that I am returning to my old platoon."

No one had seen this side of Wilkins before and Harry was puzzled. He had seen people react in different ways to the war, Harry couldn't make up his mind whether it was dormant courage brought to the surface or the thought of facing his mother without his younger brother.

Wilkins was the eldest of a large family. His father was a costermonger and a booze artist and his mother not much better. As the eldest son he'd been left to do all the fetching and carrying. His daily routine had started with a trip to Covent Garden on a ramshackle horse and cart, out in all weathers. When the old man was drunk it had been left to him to do the buying, and heaven help him if he bought anything wrong! It meant a real back hander from his mother. Call up to the army had been a relief to him - until he heard the first shells fall when his nerve had failed him...

Joe, his younger brother, had been called to military service the same day. He'd not only been favourite with his family but his ready cockney wit had made him favourite with everyone with whom he came into contact. The final words from their mother to Wilkins when the train pulled out of Waterloo station on its way to Winchester had been, "If anything 'appens to our Joe, don't you bother comin' back home."

"Will you two do me a favour?" Wilkins asked them. Harry nodded. "Will you two help me bury our Joe decent like? You've both been pretty good to me."

"Well, Wilkins," Charlie hated burial parties and hesitated as he looked at the medical sergeant who nodded his head. "Oh, sure, Wilky..."

At the rear of the lean-to the graves were already prepared. The bodies wrapped in blankets were at the side of each grave. Wilkins wouldn't allow anyone other than Harry or Charlie to touch his brother. They'd been close when they had grown up together running wild in the dirty and narrow streets of Lambeth. They'd earned a few shillings together, carrying cases for travellers at Waterloo, and they'd both been smacked across the ears by the porters for doing them out of their tips. Together the boys had attended the same dingy school and the great double bed with their two brothers, sinking deep into the great feather mattress. Their hand-me-down clothes had passed from one elder brother to the next. But in the empty future they would no longer laugh together and chase girls down the side streets of London. Joe was now just a shape under a dirty grey blanket - dead as a lump of cold mutton.

The padre nodded and Charlie jumped into the grave. Harry and Wilkins lifted the body, Charlie took the head and Harry jumped into the grave too. Gently they lowered Wilkins' younger brother to his last resting place. The padre read a short lesson and a volley of shots rang out. Alone the bugler sounded the Last

245

Post and the mournful tune wafted across the lonely wastes. A poignant moment, it was made worse when Wilkins started singing The Battle Hymn of the Republic. The sergeant and several men joined in. Harry shuffled uncomfortably on his feet and Charlie, overcome with embarrassment, pinched his nose between his finger and thumb. He didn't know the words but was familiar with the tune and hummed it softly. What in the past had become an every day occurrence and meant very little suddenly became an emotional and tender scene. Wilkins, with his two closest friends near him, had forsaken his tears.

"It was Joe's favourite tune, you know. He knew every word. When the Sally Army played down our street on Sundays, he would ask them to play that hymn. He would give them a penny," Wilkins laughed. "He always nicked a penny from our old Dutch's purse to give the Sally Army after she came home from the pub pissed. We never had pocket money."

Charlie filled in the shallow grave. Wilkins refused the assistance of the men who were detailed for the job.

Just before Wilkins returned to his platoon he gave Charlie a letter.

"Look, Charlie, this is a letter to my mum. If I get killed will you please hand it to her? Tell her, personal like, I was sorry about our Joe ... "

"Don't worry, I'll return this to you on the troopship on the way home," Charlie insisted in a tone of forced optimism wondering if he would make it there himself.

The last time they saw Wilkins he was walking toward his own platoon. Two days later he was killed and they buried him besides his younger brother.

The regiment came under heavy small arms fire accompanied by sporadic shelling throughout the long night following the younger brother's death. Tracers from the machine guns etched a brilliant pattern in the sky. The call for stretcher bearers echoed across the desert. Walking wounded dodged the bullets and flying fragments of hot steel. The ambulance made several trips to the advanced aid station, but it was daylight before the full realisation of the casualties came to light. Many wounded had remained in their slit trenches, while others had been killed in the struggle to reach the regimental aid post. It seemed the enemy was putting forward everything they had to delay the advance into Tunis. It was Harry who brought Wilkins' body in. Looking for casualties he'd seen Wilkins, face down, and recognised him. He'd picked him up and swung him over his shoulder.

"Looks as if you're a postman, after all," Harry sighed beside him, his voice thick.

"I suppose that's what you would call a death wish," Harry said.

The grave had been prepared and gently they lowered the dead Wilkins into it. But this time they did not sing his brother's favourite hymn. Instead they stood and paid silent tribute to their lost comrade.

Houses loomed up in front of them. Surely this must be Tunis. German and Italian prisoners were streaming past in platoons, companies and battalions as well as stragglers. Exhausted, hollow-eyed, unwashed, bedraggled, they shuffled past the regimental aid post. For the survivors of Dunkirk in the battalion it was the brightest aspect of the whole campaign. Some had waited two years for this glorious moment. The tables were completely reversed. The enemy were not strutting conquerors now, drunk with power, but a defeated rag bag of an army, that's all - except for a company of Hitler's elite corps. They marched past the crowds of allied troops heads held high and in perfect formation. Charlie was standing with Harry at the side of the road leaning against his ambulance and sipping tea.

"Arrogant, goose-stepping bastards, ain't they Harry?"

Harry stared at the Germans then at the two Red Caps guarding them.

"Who do you mean, Charlie? The Jerries or the Red Caps?"

They laughed harshly and without humour. They loathed both groups.

A corporal returning from the front walked up to Harry. His right ear was covered with a large shell dressing. Blood had soaked through it and caked hard on the outside.

"Sit down on the back step and let's have a shufti," Harry said and gently eased the old dressing away after he'd soaked it in a solution of water and antiseptic. "Bloody hell, mate, you've had a narrow squeak here. Another inch or so and it would have taken half your skull away and your brains with it. As it is you'll have this burn mark all your life. It looks like you've been branded with a red hot poker, and half your ear is missing."

Harry cleaned the wound up and applied a fresh dressing. "Apart from the lobe that's gone and that burn you're alright, though. Sorry you won't be able to wear matching earrings now."

Charlie's voice took on a mincing tone. "Oh, deary me, darling, your sergeant major will be so distressed at the next mess dance, dear."

But the corporal was not in a humorous frame of mind and muttered, "That sniper was a lousy shot, anyway." He then assumed a sullen and haughty manner and later rejoined his mates in the column.

247

"It makes me laugh, Charlie," Harry said. "If that had happened a week or so ago that bastard would have been out of the line and back to the aid post quicker than a rat up a sewer. Just because we're almost in Tunis he didn't bother going sick. It's not a bad wound. Those ear gashes always bleed a lot, but with this heat and sand the slightest wound turns septic."

Cautiously the regiment entered Tunis with the ambulance behind the first squadron of armoured cars. Some of the houses at the side of the road hadn't escaped the shelling. Riflemen were going from house to house searching for any enemy in hiding. One rifleman came out of a house, a German walking before him with his hand in a sling, and Charlie stopped to attend to his wound and discovered that two of his fingers were missing. With gestures and sign language he directed the casualty towards the main dressing station.

A sergeant stopped the ambulance and pointed to a house. The walls were pitted with rifle bullets. Paint was peeling from the walls and its' front window shutter hung on a solitary hinge.

"One of our blokes in there, medic, shot up badly," he muttered. He led Harry into the dimmed room and it took him several minutes for his eyes to grow accustomed to the gloom. "I don't know how the bearers missed him. His leg is shattered and he's in terrible pain."

The man was lying on a couple of old blankets groaning. It was still a bit dim in the house. Harry gave the man a jab of morphine, and with the help of a Red Cap, who'd come inside to investigate, and Charlie, they each took a corner of the blanket and gently lifted the man towards the open window.

"Are you sure he's British, sarge?" Charlie enquired curiously.

"Yes, he's one of ours. What made you ask that?"

"Well this wound must be at least three days old and we only took the place this morning. How the hell did he get here?"

"Must have been on patrol. Got hit and his mates nicked a couple of blankets and poked him in that dark corner hoping Jerry wouldn't find him. Looks like they succeeded. He's bloody lucky. A couple of hours ago this place was crawling with Jerries and Iteys. It's a wonder they didn't hear him."

The wound was a femur broken by a bullet. It really called for a Thomas Splint, but Harry had used the one he usually carried a few days previously. As he made up a temporary splint, with the help of the military policeman and the sergeant, he carefully stowed him aboard the ambulance, but not before Charlie got a dig in at the Red Cap.

"What time is it, corporal?"

The corporal studied his watch for a few seconds. "Ten thirty-two," he said finally then looked at Charlie strangely. "Why - what the hell's the matter? Got a date with some Gyppo bint in Tunis, or something?" He laughed at his own supposed joke.

"No," Charlie answered. "It puzzles me you standing there, clothes clean and neatly pressed. God, man, it doesn't take long for you bloody base wallahs to get in and spread the bullshit."

It took Charlie over an hour before he could find an established aid station and Harry sat with the man. Finally he regained consciousness and opened his eyes. Although drowsy with the effects of the jab Harry managed to get a bit of sense from him. "How long have you been like this, mate?" he asked quietly.

"Fucked if I know. Three days maybe. I kept waking up then everything spun round and I would flop out. We were on this patrol and when we got into Tunis we just kept going. Then a sniper had a go at us and we beat a hasty retreat but the bastard hit my leg. My mate lifted me over his shoulder, but they couldn't take me all the way, so they dumped me in that house. They found some blankets upstairs in a big house, and made me as comfortable as they could. It's a wonder Jerry didn't spot me. They actually came right into the room a couple of times. I nearly shit myself. Sorry about the mess though ... I couldn't hold my piss a couple of times."

"Forget it, mate," Harry answered. "We're used to that. You'll be alright as soon as they can splint that leg. You have a real blighty there."

"Will I lose my leg?"

"Doubt it. Bags of blood, but the bullet went straight through. Pity it hit the femur," replied Harry, but he may just as well have been speaking to someone deaf for he had slipped into a coma-like sleep.

As soon as they disposed of the casualty the ambulance raced back to the column. It had hardly moved, and it was late afternoon before it penetrated further into the city.

CHAPTER 25

Suddenly, without warning or ceremony, it was all over. No waving of flags or tumultuous welcome from a grateful populous, no blaring of bugles or welcoming brass bands. Just a confused silence, with men who had been up and down the desert with monotonous regularity, walking around as if in a dream, hardly believing or daring to believe that at long last it was all over. There were very few of the original members of the division left. Was it possible that they had traversed that inhospitable desert for the last time and conquered an unconquerable army leaving them in complete disarray?

By no means were they the first vehicle into Tunis, but they were certainly the first ambulance, or at least they thought so. Small groups of Arabs stood around, indifferent to the new conquerors, while the small groups of French colonial settlers stared at the ambulance as a sign of victory. To them the war was over and won. France lay on the other side of the Mediterranean, still occupied, but as far as they were concerned that was their problem. To the colonials the main worry was how they would handle the Tunisians they had mastered for years, garrisoned by the French Foreign Legion. But that regiment hardly existed now, and Tunisia's future was already in the balance.

What was left of the enemy forces, those who had failed to make their escape, were being marshalled together in the docks area to await their march to the P.O.W. cage far to the rear. The infantrymen detailed to guard them weren't in too good a frame of mind. Having won the war so far, they wanted to enjoy the spoils.

Charlie swung into a side road and pulled up. He hadn't the slightest idea where he was or where he had to report to. He relaxed, leaning on the back of his driving seat, and lit a cigarette, puffing slowly as he tried to evaluate the situation.

"Christ, Harry, this is a turn up for the book. I anticipated being greeted by thousands of mademoiselles all wanting to whisk me away to their bedrooms. Just take a shufti at the joint, it's more like Aberdeen on a flag day."

"I can see that, you prick. Maybe it's because we came in the back way. Perhaps those that came in along the coast road got a better reception. Best thing we can do is find the regiment or try and find our own unit. We'll push off down to the docks area, there's always excitement by the docks."

They had taken the right path, for as they drew nearer the dock area more and more people stood around the streets, and they could also hear the distant sounds of a bagpipe band. Charlie shook his head.

"Just as I thought, the bloody Highland division with their bloody doodle saxes; that will put the shits up the local populous. Now the Jocks will be painting their division signs all over the place and boasting they were the first to enter. Let's piss off down there and find a nice spot, a real conspicuous spot, where we can see them and make sure they can see us." He laughed. "I wish we could find a couple of French bints and have them sitting on our knees as they pass."

As if in answer to his silent prayers he spotted two French beauties, teenagers with passable figures. They were hurrying towards the sound of the bagpipes. Charlie whistled and beckoned them to come over.

The two girls stood by the cab of the ambulance giggling. Charlie tried to talk to them in very bad French, but foreign languages weren't his strong point. After ten minutes of shouting and gesticulating he finally convinced them it was safe to get into the cab. He moved the ambulance forward, making sure the men on parade wouldn't miss him.

"Christ, Harry, this will give the Jocks something to think about. You mark my words, Harry, tonight they will find all the vino shops, drink them dry, and then go on the rampage. Then everywhere gets placed out of bounds. Let's just wave the sods in, then go and have a shufti round the town while everything is disorganised." He tapped his shirt pocket to make sure the addresses the Italian had given him were still there and winked at Harry.

One thing Harry had learnt since joining the ambulance, you don't argue with Charlie. Making sure they had the right spot where they had to be seen, Charlie pulled a girl on his knee. The other girl jumped on to Harry's lap. The pipe major cast a sidelong glance at them, and the first line of pipers could hardly believe their eyes. One man's mouthpiece sagged from his lips with a dying drone. The first company faltered in their stride as the men nudged each other. Charlie grinned from ear to ear and stuck his two fingers up behind the girls back. After the Jocks came the armoured cars. Men almost fell from the turrets as they stared at the ambulance. A driver tried to throw a sidelong glance and almost lost control pulling up sharply to avoid another car. The car behind hit him up the back with a sound of grinding metal. Charlie was really enjoying this.

"Just look at the sex starved bastards." He recognised a sergeant in one of the scout cars and waved. "Right, Harry, now

251

we've disorganised that parade let's shove off. I can see our own unit further down the parade."

They helped the two girls to the ground. They sulked at first so Charlie said, "Come back in a couple of years time."

They couldn't understand a word he said but both of them started giggling again. One girl ran back and kissed Harry firmly on his lips then ran away, turning every few minutes and smiling.

"Bloody pity, Charlie. A couple of years older and they would have been O.K. While she was sitting on my knee she kept pressing her tits against me."

"Never mind, Harry, it looks like the whole of the population has turned out to see the conquering heroes, let them bathe in their glory. In a few minutes the citizens here will be pleased to see the back of them." He backed the ambulance out and roared away.

A dispatch rider caught up with them; he was a military policeman.

"Where the hell are you two going?"

"Separated from our unit, corporal. Trying to find it. Any ideas?"

"Forget your unit, I have orders to round up as many ambulances as possible. Just follow me."

Charlie made a U turn and followed on the heels of the motor bike as he roared towards the dock area. Two military policemen at the dock gates held the traffic up to allow them to enter. They pulled up outside a large warehouse. There were several ambulances already there loading stretcher cases. Charlie jumped down.

"What the hell's going on?" he asked the driver.

"Oh it's you, Charlie," the man answered in a thick Scottish accent.

"Hiya Jock, what's the gen?" he nodded towards the large building.

"Looks like they were ready for evacuation on one of their hospital ships; we beat them to it. It's crowded in there, some of our own lads, too. The Jerries are going to their own P.O.W. hospital just out of town. Our own hospital ship is due in a couple of hours time so our own boys can be evacuated."

"That's understandable, same situation in Tripoli as you remember. Any idea how long we will be here? We were just about to recce the town to see if we could find a couple of bints."

"Who knows, Charlie? My mate said the place is crowded, but I don't think it will be all that long. They have some Jerry and Itey medics with their ambulances and it looks like they are finding as many of our ambulances as possible. Apparently we are still in

252

bombing distance from the Itey mainland and they want the docks area cleared fast." He reached behind his seat and took out a bottle of red wine which he drunk greedily, then burped loudly.

"Then you haven't had your end away yet, Charlie?"

"Give us a bloody chance, Jock. We did have a couple of girls in the front of the wagon but they were too young."

"If they are big enough, they are old enough," said Jock, belching for the second time.

"Not me" Charlie answered. "I like them mature. These two kept giggling, that's enough for me, puts me right off."

"Right, lads, get these lads loaded, I want them away from the docks area," shouted a senior medical officer.

"First our lads, then take them as they come, Aussies, Kiwis, South Africans, Indians and British. If the Jerries want to come and bomb it, that's up to them, I don't want our lads in there."

Fully loaded they made their way back to the main hospital on the edge of town. There seemed to be a never ending line of ambulances. The wounded were left on their stretchers, for as soon as the hospital ship arrived they were to be evacuated back to Britain. Charlie went on the scrounge at the hospital and managed to get food and tea for themselves.

"Well, Harry, that's taken care of the inner man, let's go and find that house."

They sped through the city streets back from the dock area. Charlie collared a small street urchin and showed him the paper the big Italian prisoner had given him. The urchin held it upside down, staring at the writing with a blank look on his face. Charlie realised the boy couldn't read and gave him a couple of "V" cigarettes and sent him on his way. A few minutes later he returned with another boy, a lot older than himself. The urchin pointed to the breast pocket where Charlie had put the paper.

"Come on, Charlie, use your loaf," said Harry. He reached over and took the folded paper from Charlie's pocket.

"He's brought his mate to read it for you."

They handed the boy the sweat stained piece of paper; it was hardly legible. After studying it for a few minutes the boy's face lit up with a grin, as if he had unlocked a secret of his grown ups.

"Don't be bloody stupid, son. Where the hell is this place?" Charlie asked impatiently.

The boy went into a long conversation with the smaller boy but they made no move except to keep looking at Harry and Charlie. Suddenly it dawned on Charlie to offer them cigarettes. He handed the larger boy a packet of disgusting issue "V"s. The boy pushed Harry's knee to one side and scrambled aboard. He jumped as he sat on the petrol cans and Spag shot out from under his blanket. The boy started to laugh and picked Spag up, stroking his head and ears.

"Better watch out, Charlie, he might take the dog home for the family dinner!" said Harry, his face breaking into a wide grin.

The boy directed them through a labyrinth of narrow side streets in what was obviously the seedier side of the city. They drove on till they reached the suburbs and a more refined residential area which was plainly a more prosperous part of the city. The boy pointed to a large house on an intersection with roads running in all directions. The boy grinned and held out his hand for more cigarettes. Charlie didn't mind, he'd been preparing for this event for months and was stacked out with the filthy "V" things. No self respecting soldier would smoke them unless they were desperate. He gave the lad another pack and he jumped from the ambulance bowing as he walked backwards. Suddenly he turned and ran, his long sheet-like gown dragging along the road.

The smell of the closed-in back streets of the poorer quarter gave way to the luscious perfumes of the tropical vegetation that lined both sides of the wide street. The gardens of the houses were overflowing with tropical flowers giving off a rich perfume. The faint breeze of the falling night rustled the wide leaves of the overhanging palms.

"This is it, Harry. God, just take a breath of that fresh air," said Charlie as his chest swelled with a deep intake of breath.

They pulled the ambulance into a side road by the large house. The light was fading fast and already the stars were showing, speckling the sky with their twinkling light. Making sure the ambulance was tucked away out of sight of the main road, they made their way to the house. Charlie hesitated at the wrought iron gate, peering through the metal trellis work. The house was in darkness apart from a light in the passage. At the door hung a large metal handle and each side of the door was patterned with coloured glass, sectioned into a neat arabesque design. Charlie peered through the glass but could make out nothing of the inside as the shaded light was too dim. He pulled at the heavy chain and a bell sounded, so loud that Charlie looked round to see if he had disturbed the neighbours.

A few minutes passed before there was any response. He was about to pull it again when the door opened slightly and a soft yellow light splashed onto the verandah and concrete path. A large woman stood at the open door, her enormous breasts bulging out from the top of her tight fitting black blouse. She beamed at them as she opened the door wide and beckoned them in, no doubt anticipating that they were her first Allied customers since the Allies arrived. Not so very long ago they had been German and Italian customers, before that French. She shrugged her shoulders in resignation. Charlie took the fat podgy hand she offered, lifted it to his lips and kissed it gently. He turned his head slightly towards Harry and winked. Inside, Harry was almost choking with suppressed laughter. However the madam seemed to like it as Harry did likewise. She placed her arm round them and led them to a large richly furnished sitting room.

It was comfortably furnished with overstuffed armchairs and settees, all covered with the same patterned material which also graced the windows. The curtains hung from the ceiling to the floor. Potted palms in abundance were scattered around the room. All had been tended with great care and patience. A glass chandelier hung from the centre of the room. It had been specially imported from Paris before the war, and lovingly washed regularly, making the glass droplets sparkle like huge cut and polished diamonds. The floor was covered with a rich red, heavy pile carpet which stretched from wall to wall. Lewd photographs hung right round the walls. Charlie studied one.

"Bloody hell, Harry, you would have to be a bloody contortionist to have it away in that position."

Harry left it to Charlie to bargain with the madam while he made detailed study of the pictures around the walls. Madam pulled on another silken rope and a large pair of velvet curtains at one end of the room parted to reveal a large bar. It was stacked with Scotch whisky, Beefeater gin, Jamaican run, Russian vodka - in fact, there wasn't a spirit from the greatest distilleries of the world that was missing, as well as a stock of Italian, French and Spanish wines.

She pressed a bell at the side of the bar and a few minutes later girls entered the room and draped themselves on the settees. All wore flimsy dressing gowns that left very little to the imagination. As if they were well drilled like a row of chorus girls, each one crossed her legs to allow the dressing gown to fall apart and reveal a bare leg that reached up to their thighs. Charlie gasped, he had met girls from all over the world, but without a doubt these were the most professional and the best.

"Better make the best of it. In a few days this will be taken over by the officers and be out of bounds to the likes of you and me."

He pointed to a petite redhead sitting alone sipping a small gin. "Fancy that one, Harry?"

As if brought out of a dream, Harry answered, "Anyone will suit me, Charlie."

For there was certainly a choice, brunettes, two blondes, a redhead, and a shapely negress with the features of a Sudanese.

255

Her skin glistened in the light from the glass chandelier, her breasts pointed forward and her back as erect as a flag pole. There were several Italian girls and a small Arab who looked the youngest. Her hair like black silk fell around her shoulders like a waterfall. A price was settled, fifty Players for the girl and the same for the madam.

"You two Poms are being overcharged and you'll make it bad for everyone. One thing these girls have taken a fancy to is English cigarettes, they ran out months ago." The voice came from behind the bar. They looked up sharply. A few seconds later a head and shoulders appeared, the face like a tanned walnut and white cloth around his head. If it wasn't for his Australian accent he would easily have been taken for an Arab. He grinned at them and came out from behind the bar, his hand fully extended.

"Boy, am I glad to see you. I hope you brought the rest of the eighth army with you." They remained speechless and just nodded.

"I heard those bloody bagpipes but dare not show my face just in case there were Jerries still around."

Harry was the first to react. He gripped the man's outstretched hand.

"Where the hell did you come from? I thought we were the first in the city."

Charlie took the man's hand. There was no doubt he was Australian.

"What the hell are you doing here?"

The girls crowded round the three men, smiling at the Australian, obviously very fond of the man, each jostling for the most advantageous position.

"Look, lads, you are in a filthy condition, this place was reserved for the top brass. Madam is only letting you stay because you are the first Allied troops she has seen. She is French and has hardly stopped crying since France jacked it in. You two take a good bath, I'll send a girl with each of you. When you return smelling a bit better we can sit down and I will tell you all about it." He patted them both on the back and then called two girls over, speaking to them in fluent French. Charlie chose the redhead while Harry settled for a blonde.

The Australian's white robe swept across the floor as he led them to the bathrooms. The robe made him look taller then he really was. Strands of hair hung below his turban and curled over his white gown. They looked very dark; later they were to learn his hair was very blonde.

It was surprising what a good hot bath with real toilet soap and bath perfume made to them. It was Charlie's first real bath for nearly two years and Harry's for twelve months. The filth of the desert just fell away from them. Harry's blonde rubbed shampoo into his hair, then massaged his back; every few minutes she would top up the bath with hot water.

A maid had taken their clothes away and left a pair of baggy silk trousers and a dressing gown in their place. They returned to the lounge. The Australian was sitting in one of the overstuffed chairs next to the madam, her fat podgy hand over his. All the girls sat round sipping their drinks.

"Right, cobbers, find yourself a seat and I'll let you in on it." He sipped a large whisky laced with ice. "Take a drink, mate."

After a lot of persuasion they settled for a brandy each. They could see he was a hard drinking man and wouldn't take no for an answer. One of the girls set a small wine table before them and served the brandy.

"Thank God I can speak to someone in my own lingo, even if it's only Poms. I tell you, you're a sight for sore eyes."

Still bewildered by the vision sitting before them and in the company of some of the most beautiful women either Harry or Charlie had seen since arriving in North Africa, as if in a trance Harry asked, "How the hell did you get here?"

The Aussie burst out laughing.

"I was put in the bag at Tobruk, I'd only been in the desert a few weeks. We were taken to a camp this side of Tripoli. A week later we were sent to Tunis to be shipped back to Italy or Germany. The camp was just outside Tunis. One day we were marched to the docks. We kicked up hell, the docks were at least twenty miles. I'm pleased we didn't get transport. We were coming along this road when there was this terrific air raid and some of the prisoners were killed. The Itey guards ran away shit scared. It was the best chance I ever had, although I hadn't the slightest idea how I would get back to our own lines. I jumped over this garden wall. As you saw when you walked in, the garden is thick with tropical vegetation. That's to cover the front windows, more privacy like. The madam saw me and indicated to me to go round the back. She opened the cellar door and I slipped down. Seems like madam's two brothers are serving with the Free French. Madam has been looking after me ever since. The girls dyed my hair black and rubbed this stuff all over me to darken my skin. I doubt if I will ever get the bloody stuff off. After they dyed my hair they made me a turban and dressed me in this bloody nightgown. I hardly knew myself when I looked in the mirror."

"This place turned out to be a high class brothel used exclusively by high ranking Italian and German officers. There's twenty rooms in this house. They gave me a crash course in Arabic; I already knew a bit of schoolboy French. After a while I had to serve in the bar and take the drinks. It hurt my guts having to bow and scrape to them but I got my own back in little ways like gobbing in the cocktails. Then I kept a bottle of piss under the bar and if I got chance I would lace the whisky. One bit fat Itey got used to it and would ask for one of my specials, stupid bastard."

"What about the girls, weren't you afraid they would split on you?"

"You're kidding. I don't know who they hate more, the Jerries or the Iteys. One Itey got rough with that little Arab girl, bruised and bit her all over. Madam fixed him alright. She arranged to have him knifed one night as he returned to his quarters. The only fly in the ointment is Madam. She's jealous as arsehole, can't move, poor old sod is getting on a bit and a touch on the plump side, so she regards me as her private property. Still, I have a go while she's away. She owns an orange grove about seventy miles away and sometimes she arranges transport with one of the Itey officers so she's away for a few days. Then I'm like a bull who's been let loose in a field of cows!"

Feeling in a receptive mood and cleaner, Charlie sipped casually at his brandy, never taking his eyes from the bevy of beauties sitting round the room, whilst nonchalantly casting an envious eye at the Australian.

"How many girls here?" he asked.

"Ten full time and about the same amount part time. We have this one that comes every Tuesday and Friday, I tell you lads, she would put a film star to shame. Skin like olive and a figure you would have to see to appreciate. Her old man is a gendarme. He brings her to work then collects her in the mornings. I tell you mates, it's a strange old world here. She says she does it for the money but I don't believe a word of it. That girl's a raving nympho. She caught me down the cellar one day, when Madam shouted for more drinks, I thoughts I'd had my chips. Madam told me if ever she caught me with one of the girls she would hand me to the Jerries, jealous old bastard."

Harry and Charlie remained speechless as the Aussie's story unfolded. For months, ever since Harry had teamed up with him Charlie had been bragging about opening a brothel and having to do the stocktaking every week, and here he was, actually talking to a man who was doing that very thing.

"I bet you felt sick when you heard those bloody bagpipes, and the thought of liberation."

"You have to be kidding. When you go in the morning I will be coming with you and hand myself over to the Aussie military police. If you had seen some of the narrow escapes I've had you'd never believe me. I have learnt quite a bit of Arab lingo, but not enough to fool anyone fluent in it. One night we had this party here for some big wigs, Italian and Germans. I was being run off my goolies when this big fat Itey caught hold of me. His Arabic was fluent. He had been boasting to everyone that not only was his Arabic fluent but he could tell exactly where an Arab came from by his dialect. Madam came over and told me what was happening. She tried to tell me to stutter like I had a speech impediment and to look scared. She took over the conversation told me to fetch him a drink. She had some specials, not my special. These drinks she kept just for troublesome customers. That bastard went out like a light in a few minutes. I carried him up to bed and went through his pockets. He had a heavy silver cigarette case and a wallet full of Itey and Jerry money. Poor bastard was out for almost two days. Madam sent for the Itey military police; haven't seen the stupid bastard since."

"Still got the cigarette case and money?" asked Charlie.

Winking his eye he answered, "Stashed away with the rest of my gear. I don't intend to finish this war poor. When they get drunk here I always help myself to money and nick nacks. When I get back to Queensland I want to set myself up in a decent sized pineapple farm, after suffering all this time here."

Thinking he was hearing things Charlie slammed the flat of his hand against his ear. Suffering, this man is actually talking about suffering. Been locked up with a harem of beautiful women and complaining he was suffering.

"You took a chance robbing customers like that."

Walking to the bar, the Aussie searched around beneath it for a few minutes, then returned with a handful of signed photographs of high ranking German and Italian officers. As Charlie and Harry went through the photographs they could hardly believe their eyes. Most of the officers held such high ranks that they were frequently seen in most newspapers. Harry was the first to speak.

"These will be worth a fortune later on. How did you get them signed?"

"When these blokes are half pissed and get with the women you can get then to eat out of your hand," answered the Aussie.

More beautiful girls entered the room, all hoping the Allied troops had sorted the brothels out. These were the part-timers and disappointment showed on their faces when they saw there

259

was just Harry and Charlie. As the girls came over they shook Madam's hand and patted, then kissed the Australian face.

Charlie fell back into his chair and gasped, "Have you ever seen anything like it in you whole life, Harry? Just look at them." He turned to the Aussie. "You must be mad to give this lot up."

But it was Harry who was filled with his own bizarre thoughts. Surely this wasn't really happening, any minute he would wake up and find it's all a dream. Or perhaps he was dead, killed by a stray shell as they closed in on Tunis. So this is paradise after all. The sweet smell of expensive perfume, soft carpets to walk upon, not white flowing gowns but silk dressing gowns. Angels of all colours and sizes. Plates of sandwiches thinly sliced and flavoured with eastern spices. Any minute they would wake up, for surely if this was heaven every man in the Eighth Army would be queuing up to get here. No, something shook him. Although the room was filled with the voices of twenty or more girls, the faint melodious tunes of 'Roses of Picardy' came from one corner of the room where the small Arab girl was attending to an ancient windup gramophone.

Suddenly the room went quiet. A tallish girl entered, her back straight and neat breasts thrust out. She wore a long flowing red dress that accentuated her height. Her hair hung down over her shoulders like thick brown curtains framing a beautiful photograph. Her eyes were almond shaped with long eyelashes that fluttered up and down like a painter's brush. She smiled revealing a row of shining white teeth. Her face had no need of makeup. The Aussie nudged Charlie, this must be the French girl he had spoken about.

It had been a long and tedious day. Harry had drunk two brandies and they weren't short measures. He could hardly keep his eyes open. The Aussie rose to his feet.

"I can see you two are whacked out. Take the two girls you picked and if you survive the night I'll see you both in the morning. If you have any spare medical kit in that ambulance of yours, Madam would be grateful if you could leave some aspirin, iodine, antiseptic and bandages, anything like that."

"Plenty, mate, she can have the lot. This is one night of the war I shall never forget." Almost asleep, Harry was helped up the wide, winding staircase by the girl. He flopped on to the wide bed wishing he hadn't drunk that last brandy. The sheets were satin and smelt of perfume. After months in the desert this was payment in full.

After bathing in hot water, the next morning they were enjoying breakfast, consisting mainly of tropical fruits, when the Aussie came in. He was dressed in his uniform, his bush hat looking the worse for wear, but all his clothes washed and pressed.

"Can't get this bloody dye off my skin, the lads will think I have gone Abbo."

Several of the girls followed him in, all crying and sobbing into their handkerchiefs. Two of them had their arms around the Australian; he stroked their heads. He looked like some Greek god surrounded by a bevy of nymphets.

"Look at that, Harry," Charlie remarked, a look of envy on his face. "Just think, my missus couldn't shove me out of the house quick enough."

"Madam won't come down, she sends her farewells, she is too upset at the thought of me going. I only have my small haversack, she's saving my loot. I don't want some shitty arsed Red Caps poking their noses into my business."

Clinging to the Aussie tightly, the girls grew more hysterical as they neared the door. Two of them tried to bar his way. Harry tried to hide a smile.

"Hell. I just can't imagine this happening to me, that Aussie must have something special. He has to be built like a donkey. Looks like he's modelled on your lines, Charlie."

All the girls lined up in the hall leading to the doorway. The Aussie hugged each one in turn and they splattered his face with kisses, then they were out in the open. Bathed, well fed and their uniforms cleaned and pressed, Harry felt the world belonged to him. All the girls were standing outside in the garden when the ambulance pulled up. Harry filled his medical haversack with all the aspirins and every other piece of medical equipment and tablets he could find then threw it at the girls. The redhead caught it with one hand and tried to force a smile through her tears. The curtains parted in Madam's room just above the front door. She gave a feeble wave and bravely wiped her tears away with a snow white handkerchief.

After Charlie got over the shock of seeing so many girls grieving over the parting of just one man, he turned to the Aussie and with a grin said, "You lucky bastard, I bet when I tell them about this back at our unit, no sod will believe me. I don't suppose you would mind coming back with us and substantiating our story, would you?"

The Australian laughed as he usually did before answering the question.

"You must be kidding. Get me back to some Aussie unit and with a bit of luck they may send me back home after the way I suffered the last year or so. God, man, times are very hard."

Fifteen minutes later they pulled up besides two Australian Red Caps. The Aussie jumped out and reported to them, then turned and waved.

"Cheers chaps, if ever you are up Queensland way look me up. Everyone knows me up at Cairns. I'll shout you a beer."

It was some months later they learned the story he told the military authorities. In his last action he had been posted missing, believed killed. He told the story he had been living rough near Tunis, raided the city for food, and had been befriended by some French woman. He was awarded the military medal for his fortitude and suffering.

They found their own unit by midday and were greeted by the R.S.M.

"I guess you two bastards wouldn't be here like the rest of the men. Last night I laid bets on in the mess, that you would be shacked up with a couple of bints." Charlie opened his mouth to protest and make some kind of excuse, but the R.S.M. held his hand up.

"I don't want to hear any of your bullshit, Williams. I just hope you were careful and took precautions, and didn't make fools of yourselves."

Harry nodded, afraid to speak, and he dare not look at Charlie in case he burst out laughing. He certainly couldn't tell the truth, it was too fantastic, but a faint smile did flicker across his face. It didn't go unnoticed, the R.S.M. was too smart for that.

"Did I say something to amuse you, Jackson?"

"Not really, sir."

"I am pleased about that because I have something really funny to tell you. Tomorrow the division is pulling back. I was keeping you two for the main party, but seeing as how you have been enjoying yourselves you can go on the advance party. To make sure you will not be sneaking our for another naughty tonight you are both on guard duty. After all, you have a long drive ahead of you and I don't want you wearing yourselves out."

Pleased he had turned the tables on them the R.S.M. turned and strode away grinning, sure he had won his bet.

CHAPTER 26

Most of the ambulances had returned to the main unit which, like the rest of the division, was camped on the outskirts of Tunis. And with the whole of the Eighth Army, and a good many regiments of the First Army, it was a predicament that couldn't last for long. The city was overcrowded with allied troops so it came as a relief to know the unit, with the division, would be moving back. The order to prepare was given a few days later. It was done by splitting the unit into two parties to avoid congestion on the road, their destination being a small town seventy miles east of Tripoli.

They were mustered outside the orderly room tent for briefing, Charlie being singled out for attention. The R.S.M., with a list in his hand, called out the names, starting with Charlie.

"You will be on the first section out, the convoy consisting of ten ambulances, two utilities and three three tonners, all under Captain Conway. He will be leading in his ute, Williams next in his ambulance followed by Sergeant Hawkins who has strict orders to keep his eyes on you. There are plenty of refugees making their way back to Tripoli and there is sure to be a piece of crumpet amongst them. If there is, Williams is sure to find it."

There was a ripple of laughter amongst the crowd.

"Those on the list draw three days' vehicle rations, I want you away by first light."

Next morning saw the convoy travelling along the coast road at a steady thirty miles an hour. The traffic was far lighter than they expected and most of what there was travelled towards Tunis, with very little going in the same direction as themselves. It was noon, with the sun high above their heads before they stopped. While the R.S.M. was wrong about the traffic, he was partly right about the refugees, they had passed quite a few. Twice Charlie had slowed down when he thought what he called a prospect was worth giving a lift, only to be reminded by two long blasts from the sergeant's ute hooter that he was right behind him. Charlie cursed under his breath.

The convoy stopped at noon. While Harry prepared a meal Charlie filled his petrol tanks and checked the water and oil.

"There you are. She's ready for another thousand miles." He sat down beside Harry and filled Spag's plate with bully beef and tea; Spag loved his tea. Charlie stroked the dog's head.

"If we go back home, Spag, they won't let you back, old son."

"I wonder if we will go back home, Charlie. After listening to all those rumours flying around the camp back at Tunis I wouldn't be surprised if we landed somewhere in outer Mongolia, that and the South Pole were the only two places not mentioned so it wouldn't surprise me if we did land up in one or the other."

Charlie wasn't interested, at the moment he was more distressed about passing so many good prospects.

"Did you see those two birds in that small village we passed, I could have done that slim one a bloody good turn. Poor sod was carrying that large bundle, I wonder if she was going back to Tripoli?"

"It's no good. With Sergeant Hawkins almost up our exhaust pipes, one false move and he's got you."

Sergeant Hawkins squatted besides them.

"Next stop just after dark. Captain Nichols wants to be in Tripoli by tomorrow evening."

"What's the hurry, sarge?" Charlie had a plan working through his mind. Those two girls from the small wine bar lived this side of Tripoli. With a bit of luck they may get a chance to sneak away.

"He's knocking about with a sister from a general hospital, they're at the airport, Castillo Benito or something," the sergeant informed them.

Charlie winked his eye at Harry.

"I know that place, sarge. There's one or two hospitals there, we took those casualties from that warehouse near the docks. Any chance of any of the boys getting into town for a couple of hours?"

"Not a chance, Williams. Certainly not for you. I have strict instructions to keep my eye on you both. A couple of hours means all night to you. No, Williams, you are staying close to me."

It was dark when they pulled off the road again. There was a full moon so Harry took full advantage of it. He stripped and dived into the sea, swam out till he was almost invisible from the land, then gradually floated on his back and allowed the tide to draw him to the shore. Several other men followed suit. Harry didn't bother drying himself with a towel but ran up and down the sandy beach till he dried out. His stubbly hair became encrusted with silver salt specks. Charlie offered him a mug of hot tea.

"I will have to do something about tomorrow night, Harry. Any knockout tablets in your medical kit?"

"Don't be a prick. You'll have to control your emotions," answered Harry.

But it was just after lunch the next day that their luck changed. Harry was half asleep when the ambulance started chugging along, stopping and starting for a few minutes, then the engine cut out completely. Harry woke and looked around startled.

"What's up?"

"That rickety bridge we just passed over, there were two bints down in the wadi. If no one else in the convoy spotted them we could be in luck."

Charlie, with a slight of hand that would have done justice to a member of the magic circle, whipped off the distributor cap and removed the rotor arm, then just as fast replaced the cap. The sergeant came running up quite out of breath.

"What's up, Williams? What the hell you stopped for?"

"Dunno, sarge. Just conked out, coughed and spluttered a bit, then the engine cut out completely."

"Right, get out of that seat and let's have a go."

But what Sergeant Hawkins knew about engines wouldn't get a bald man a haircut. He was very much like Harry, if it had four wheels and an engine it must be alright. He tried the engine a few times; a small whirring sound, nothing. He wiped round the plugs with a dirty rag, then tried the engine again, nothing. Despair in his face he tried and tried again, nothing.

"Jack it in, sarge, you will piss the battery up. She's had it."

"Williams, if you're pissing me about I'll roast your goolies over an open petrol fire. Get this thing moving, we have to be outside Tripoli before it gets dark."

It was obvious the sergeant hadn't seen the two girls or he would have suspected something amiss straight away. Charlie felt confident he could work something out now. He winked at Harry who tried to ease the situation.

"Do you think she's starved of petrol. Remember that time just outside Sfax, something like this happened."

The idea cheered the sergeant slightly, like a drowning man he started clutching at straws.

"Yes that could be it Williams, starved of petrol."

"Don't think so, sarge, just smell the petrol, it's getting through alright. I'll have to strip it down."

A look of suspicion flashed across the sergeant's face. He knew Charlie of old. If there was something wrong with the engine he would know.

"Williams I'm warning you, if you have one of your bright ideas up your sleeve, forget it."

"Come off it, sarge." He patted the side of the ambulance affectionately.

"The old girl is tired, sarge. Remember where the hell she's been and some of the rough ground she's covered. The old girl must be ready to give up."

"Shut up, Williams. You will make me cry in a minute. Strip the bastard down if you have to, but get back on the road as soon as you're ready." He went to his utility and returned with a map. He pointed a grubby finger at a spot just outside Tripoli.

"I want you there tonight." The sergeant stamped away and slammed the door of his ute behind him, then glared at Williams, still unsure as to whether he'd pulled a fast one.

"And bollocks to you, sarge," said Charlie when the ute was out of earshot.

It seemed that the goddess of love and randy sex starved soldiers was looking down on them. For no sooner had the sergeant disappeared in a cloud of dust, exhaust smoke and petrol fumes when Charlie spotted the two girls walking down the road struggling with a large bundle each. At first he thought he would do the manly thing, replace the rotor arm and go and help them.

"They must be a couple of miles away. I was about to go and help them because there is a chance some other sex starved bastard will pick them up, but I decided to take a chance. When they get here they'll be knackered. A nice mug of coffee and a meal of bully beef and beans and I reckon we'll be away." He turned as he heard a motor bike roar up.

"What the hell does Farraday want? Get rid of him as fast as possible, I don't want him sodding things up."

Farraday, like all motor cycle fanatics, skidded to a stop beside them.

"Captain Carlton wants to know how long you are going to be."

"Better tell him it's going to take longer than I expected." The D.R. removed his steel helmet to reveal the smoothest bald head Harry had seen for quite a while.

"Heaven's sake, Farraday, put that helmet back on. I got a welders flash when the sun bounced off it."

"Ho, ho, ho, the same old corny jokes. Think up something original Charlie. Anyway, what the hell's the hold up?"

Charlie didn't answer but replaced the rotor arm and started the engine.

"Nothing, Farraday. Just spotted a couple of bints and waiting for them to pass. Fancy a mug of coffee while you're waiting, then piss off and not a word to anyone."

"Come off it, Charlie, you know me. Would I say anything?" The D.R. sounded insulted.

Farraday sipped slowly at his coffee. Harry could hardly take his eyes off the D.R.'s bald head. It was the first time he had seen him without his helmet or his South African issue sun helmet. Farraday noticed him staring.

"Wasn't always bald you know, lost the hair last year, remember, Charlie? All my hair came out overnight. I had gone

266

up to a tank regiment to give the ambulance crew the mail. They were loading this knocked out tank on a recovery vehicle. Halfway up the slope the fucking chain broke and the tank came tumbling back down. Some tanky standing there pushed me out of the way. For his trouble one of the tank's tracks crushed his foot. Next day the shock caused all my hair to fall out; fucking stuff came out in handfuls. Every bastard in the unit was creased up laughing. It was no laughing matter for me, I can tell you. When I left home I had this head of wavy blonde hair. It was my girlfriend's pride and joy. We used to sit in her old lady's front room combing each other's hair." He shook his head. It was too much for Harry, he went behind the ambulance trying not to laugh out loud, but Farraday kept on with the story to Charlie, in spite of the fact he had heard it a dozen times.

"Everyone seems to think it's one big joke. That prick Riley saw a dead horse just outside Merza, and cut the tails off and gave it to me for a wig. Even that prat Sykes in the company office indented for two large wet mops to make a couple of wigs."

Harry was creased up with laughter behind the ambulance, but Charlie tried to be sympathetic in a coarse way.

"Just look on the bright side, Farraday, no more haircuts, no shaving, all your pubes have gone so you wont get crabs, and if your bird loves you do you think she will worry if you have no hair on your body." He paused and looked at the D.R.

"I suppose the hairs have gone from your balls, haven't they?"

"You know fucking well they have, Charlie."

"Well, look on the bright side, you could always go on the stage as a female impersonator and make a bloody fortune. With a completely bald head you'd have no trouble getting a good female wig. Mind, it would help if you were a bit of a pansy."

Charlie looked at Farraday as if he was looking at a new kind of man.

"I don't suppose you are a pansy, are you?"

"No, I'm bloody well not. And if that is all the advice you can give I will piss off."

He replaced his steel helmet, kicked the engine into life and, like all motorcycle fanatics, soared away in a cloud of sand and black smoke. None too soon as it happened, for the two women were almost at the ambulance.

Charlie kicked the petrol fire; fresh flames roared up. He threw a handful of coffee into the fire after dragging it closer to the road. Both he and Harry stood at the fire sipping coffee from their mugs, exaggerating the slurp as the girls came level with the fire. The strong aroma of coffee made them pause. Charlie winked and held the mug out to them. They paused, then the elder one of the two took it, while the other girl moistened her lips. Harry offered her his mug. She almost threw it down her mouth. In a mixture of broken French, Italian and Arabic, shouting and gesticulating in typical Italian fashion, Charlie asked them if they were going to Tripoli. Much to his surprise, the elder one answered him in flawless English.

"Yes, we live there."

"You speak English." Charlie was taken aback.

"Yes, and German and Arabic. I was a teacher in a school in Tripoli, then when the Germans came I was forced to work for them as soon as they knew I spoke German. When they moved out we were forced to go with them. My friend here only speaks Italian and Arabic."

"Would you like to ride with us to Tripoli? We are going straight through." Charlie was using all his charms. The girl was in her late twenties or early thirties. She had a slim figure and short but neatly trimmed dark hair. When she smiled her face and nose wrinkled into a series of minute folds and her dark eyes sparkled.

"But you will get into trouble with the military authorities. We are not supposed to accept rides."

She turned and spoke to the other girl, she in turn looked at Harry, then both the girls started laughing. Then she spoke to Charlie again. "My name is Francesca and my friend is Sophia."

Charlie took her slender hand and shook it gently.

"My name is Charlie, this is Harry. He is the medical man, I am the driver."

"Are you both English?" asked Francesca.

Charlie nodded.

"And you two are Italians?" asked Charlie.

"Yes, Charlie. I am from Napoli, or Naples as you English say. My friend is from a little coastal town called Amalfi. You know it?"

Charlie shook his head and asked the girls if they were hungry. Francesca politely said no, but both Harry and Charlie could see they were refusing out of politeness. Harry threw more petrol on the fire. The small explosion made the girls jump. They made a meal of tinned stew. They moved back behind the ambulance away from the view of prying eyes from passing vehicles and also from the rude remarks and gestures.

"You are married?" Charlie spotted the plain ring around her finger.

"I was, Charlie, but my husband is deaded. He was missing in Abyssinia but it's two years since I last heard from him or the authorities. He must be deaded."

This was the first time she had slipped up on her English. Charlie wanted to tell her, but it sounded so funny and at this moment he was in a joyful mood. Sophia had moved closer towards Harry. Unlike Francesca, Sophia was a little plump, not fat exactly, but a little rounded. At a guess Harry thought she would be about his age but with more spaghetti and olive oil down her she would soon be going to seed like most Italian women in their thirties. She had a pleasant round face and deep brown, almost black, eyes. Her skin was flawless and her breasts well proportioned as was her backside. In fact she was quite rounded in the right parts, but best of all was her infectious laugh.

The girls were drinking coffee like it was going out of fashion, savouring every sip.

"It's good, Charlie. It's real coffee."

"Of course it's real, what did you think it was?" He put the petrol fire out. "We must get going."

"Just wait, Charlie." Francesca went into deep conversation with Sophia.

"We won't be a minute, Charlie." The girls left their pathetic bundles by the ambulance and ran behind a clump of sparse vegetation.

Charlie was in the best mood Harry had ever seen him, jumping around the ambulance like a two year old.

"I would never believe it. Here I have been searching around the world for an F and right here in this God forsaken hole, one, Francesca, walks straight towards me. I just can't believe it. That just leaves X and Z. I hope we get sent to Greece or one of those out of the way islands. There's sure to be a girl's name beginning with an X or a Z."

"You're a prat, Charlie. How do you know you are getting an F yet? They have only agreed to a lift back as far as Tripoli, don't count your chickens. Mind you that Sophia could be a bit of hot stuff. Her hand fell on my knee twice while we were having that meal."

"There, what did I tell you? I can just feel it in my bones."

Sophia pouted when she was told she would have to ride in the back of the ambulance alone. Francesca was wearing Harry's greatcoat so she wouldn't easily be spotted by any passing vehicles. She held Spag in her arms and spoke softly to him in Italian. But Sophia was still kicking up a fuss as they pulled back on the road. Francesca told Harry to sit with her while she took his seat. Then she did the most unexpected thing. She leaned across the cab and kissed Charlie on his cheek. It was the wrong thing to do at that moment. A lorry filled with troops saw them. With her short hair and his army greatcoat she was mistaken for the medic and the passing troops tried to outdo each other with crude remarks, one loud mouth shouting, "Don't get sand in your vaseline!"

Of course Francesca hadn't the slightest idea what he meant and asked Charlie all about it. He just laughed it off.

"I will tell you when I know you better."

Two hours later they stopped beside a derelict house. It must have been vacated by the owners when the axis troops pulled out.

"Shall we stay here, Francesca?" Charlie didn't want to go nearer to Tripoli in case the convoy had pulled up near the road and would see them pass. Harry almost fell from the back of the ambulance, his face flushed and his shorts unbuttoned.

"We are staying here for the night, Harry!"

"Why? We have another three hours of daylight left, we could be in Tripoli by then."

Francesca and Sophia went to the rear of the house. Charlie looked at Harry.

"You seem to be alright. Had it away?"

"You kidding. We had it on your stretcher, my stretcher, standing, on the floor, the only place we didn't try was the bloody roof. She went at me like a bloody wild animal. What's the idea of stopping here anyway?"

"If we get too near Tripoli we might pass the convoy. That bleeding sergeant has got eyes like a cowing shite hawk."

There was a loud scream from the back of the house and the two girls, on the point of hysteria, came running out.

"Charlie, we can't stay here. There is a dead soldier with his leg sticking up from the ground. It's terrible Charlie. I think it's a Tommy soldier. There's a cross."

Harry and Charlie went to the back of the house and saw the bone of the man's leg with an army issue boot still on, sticking out of the ground. There was a white cross at an angle with the man's name, rank and number, crudely painted on.

"Looks like the dogs have been at it."

Harry straightened the cross, while Charlie looked around for large stones. Then they pressed the leg down and shovelled more sand over it, then placed the heavy boulders on the top. When they returned to the ambulance Francesca was sobbing. She ran to Charlie's arms and he soothingly patted her back.

"I can't stay here tonight, Charlie. Come to my house, it's not far from here, you stay."

This wasn't the time to ask if they would be sleeping together. She was genuinely upset.

"We will have to wait till dark Francesca. My unit will be camped somewhere near this road just before we get to Tripoli. If they see us, we will have to report."

"That's alright, Charlie, we stay here till it's dark but we can move a little. I didn't like that grave and that poor man's leg sticking out." She shuddered.

Sophia made the sign of the cross and started to read her rosary, but they wouldn't move from the ambulance and kept staring at the rear of the house as if expecting the young soldier to come marching round.

Before setting off, Harry and Charlie went to the side of the house to relieve themselves.

Out of earshot Harry said, "Let me drive Charlie, you get in the back with Sophia."

Charlie laughed. "Not on your Nellie mate, I've waited years for an F to turn up, and when and if I get it, I want it in bloody comfort, not in the back of that blood tub."

"You've had it there before. This ambulance was called the Mobile Brothel long before I joined you."

"Yes, but the circumstances were different then. Anyway, Francesca is a lovely girl, a bit older than me but she's quite pretty. And I don't know what you're moaning about, Sophia isn't bad looking and you have to admit there's plenty to catch hold of."

"That's all well and good, Charlie, but she's insatiable."

"You lucky bastard. Come on, let's go or the girls might get the wrong idea about us." Charlie was still laughing when they arrived back at the ambulance.

It was quite dark when they started off down the road towards Tripoli. Both the girls were sent in the back just in case they were spotted passing their own convoy. But nothing happened and Harry opened the small door leading to the rear of the ambulance to allow Francesca to guide them towards her own house. She led them through the narrow winding streets of the Arab quarter. Somehow the streets looked familiar. Harry nudged his driver as they passed the small wine shop crowded with allied soldiers. Soon they were in the better part of the city. Francesca became more excited as she neared her own house.

"Next turning, Charlie."

They travelled for another mile before she told them to slow down.

"Turn here, Charlie, this is my house." There were tears in her eyes when she jumped from the ambulance and walked towards the front door. It wasn't locked.

The door swung back on its rusty hinges. Charlie was right behind her. He shone his torch.

"Why didn't you lock the door before you left, Francesca?"

"There was no point. If your soldiers wanted to get in they would break the door down and do damage. To be honest, Charlie, I never expected to be back."

They tried the electric switches. There was no response. Harry brought in the hurricane lamp from the ambulance. The whole place was covered in a film of dust. There were rats tracks through the sand. Charlie shuddered. Two things he hated most were rats and snakes. He stamped his feet to make a noise and heard what sounded like a dozen of tiny feet. He shone his torch in a corner. Two large rats scrambled to get out of the beam, but Francesca, who obviously wasn't afraid of rats as much as Charlie, lashed out with her feet. The rats squealed and one rolled over. She stamped on it.

"They will soon go when they know we are here," she said.

Francesca took the lamp from Harry and went into the kitchen, returning a few minutes later with two large paraffin pump type lamps. The room became flooded with a brilliant light. They were in the sitting room. It was sparsely furnished with two large armchairs, a bamboo settee, a sideboard and a bookcase full of books. In one corner stood a large ornate grandfather clock. The sideboard was covered in framed photographs of her family. Charlie picked one up. It was of an officer in the Italian army, with one foot on a chair and a thumb stuck in his shiny leather belt, his chin thrust out in true Mussolini style.

"Your husband, Francesca?"

"Yes, I think he is deaded. He was in Abyssinia, but he was - what you call it, Charlie?" She threw her chest out and strutted up and down, looking down her nose.

"Pompous."

"Yes, that's it, pompous. He was also a Fascists. Mussolini was his hero. My mother would always say that Mussolini would ruin my beautiful Italy."

Francesca stared up at a large picture of the bay of Naples with Vesuvius in the background. She placed a small finger below Vesuvius.

"That's where I live, Charlie. My mother is still there."

Francesca's conversation didn't centre around her husband at all, and by her attitude Harry could tell it hadn't been a very happy marriage. When he tried to turn the conversation round to Abyssinia she would try to avoid the subject as if she wanted to cleanse her husband not only from her life, but also from her mind. She picked up each framed photograph in turn and gave

272

them a run down on her family back in Naples. She opened the back door and they all set to cleaning the house. Water was drawn by a pump over the kitchen sink. At first it came out like mud, then gradually it cleared. There was an old door leaning against the back of the house. Harry smashed it up and soon had the kitchen stove roaring away.

They brought out the ration box. Francesca found a bottle of olive oil and a bottle of red wine. She sliced the tinned potatoes and made chips with the oil. She also made corned beef fritters and heated some tins of peas. Finally they settled down to a decent meal.

Sophia said very little. The only words of English she appeared to know were yes and no, and occasionally, please. But the look in her eyes assured Harry he was in for a good night. They had washed and shaved before they sat down to their meal. Francesca had taken their uniforms and soaked them in hot water. She had given them each a moth-eaten dressing gown that had previously belonged to her husband. They also looked as if the rats had been making a meal of the lower edges. Francesca made up for Sophia's silence. Whether it was to try out her English or because she had company, they never knew. She didn't seem to want to stop.

It had been a long day for Harry and Charlie and when they sank into the armchairs it wasn't long before their eyes told the story. This was a signal for Sophia to drag Harry towards the bedroom. Charlie was more patient. One thing Charlie always did was treat women with respect and certainly not rush things.

"Yes, Harry", he was to tell his friend later, "we talked till what must have been at least one. She was asking me all sorts of questions, like was I married? I had to go through my whole life history. It was no good trying to kid her. I could hardly stand when she dragged me to my feet and led me to the bedroom. What a night, Harry. No wonder the Italians don't like fighting. If all the Itey women make love like Francesca, who the hell wants to go to war and get themselves killed?"

Next morning it was a sad farewell when they parted. They left what food they could for the women. Sophia was reluctant to let Harry go. As he walked to the door she fell to the floor and clung to his knees. He dragged her to the ambulance. Francesca wrote her name and address on a piece of paper, together with her parents' name and address in Naples. She held Charlie tightly, one arm round his waist and one round his neck.

"Goodbye, Charlie. Write to me after the war. I suppose we will have to return to Italy, they won't want us here." She held him close and kissed him.

273

"You are a lovely man, Charlie. Send me a photograph of you and your little girl."

She fondled Spag's ears and waved a tearful farewell as the ambulance pulled away.

Chapter 27

"What next, Charlie?" Harry enquired and slumped back in his seat, exhaustion clouding his usually cheerful expression. "What other devious excuses has that distorted mind of yours conjured up?

"Well, first let's get back to the spot where we were supposed to rendezvous with the rest of the convoy or at least make a start from that direction."

It appeared that their guardian angel must still be keeping an eye on them. Just as they arrived at the rendezvous, the convoy, led by Captain Carlton, was just preparing to pull onto the road. The sergeant almost fell from his vehicle in his eagerness to approach them.

"So where the hell have you two bastards been? It 'asn't taken you all night to get that blood tub repaired. Come on and I don't want any bullshit... Where the hell have you been?"

"I told you it was going to be a long job."

Charlie attempted to sound innocent of all accusations about to be slung in his direction. "It was dark when we finished and we were both shagged out so we kipped for the night. Didn't sleep very well either. We knew you wanted us back with the convoy." He tried to suppress a make-believe yawn.

"Yes, and coming from the direction of Tripoli, that's where you should becoming from." The sergeant pointed in the opposite direction. "We've had the D.R. up and down this sodding road like a yo-yo, 'e 'asn't cast a sight of you... Is that right, Farraday?"

Farraday was sitting astride his beloved motor bike and shifted uneasily on its seat.

"Well, there was a lot traffic about. I could easily have missed them."

"Don't you make excuses for them! You know where they left the road. You was the last bastard to see them." The sergeant's mood was anything but friendly. Now he turned from Farraday towards Charlie. "I want to 'ear what bullshit 'e 'as to spout to save 'is skin. Why are you coming from Tripoli?" The sergeant moved towards Harry. "You've been with a couple of bints, you two 'ave. I can smell cheap perfume on you."

Harry's quick thinking helped save the day. "That's not women's perfume. That's cheap after-shave... it's Italian... bought it when I was in Addis Ababa."

He took a half filled bottle of after-shave from under Charlie's seat and almost cursed Sophia aloud for drowning both of them in her whorey perfume. Francesca had said it was a joke on silly bitch Sophia's part.

275

"Bullshit! Bullshit! Bull-shit!" screamed the sergeant, his face blue and a vein pulsating dangerously in his left temple with frustration. "I know you two shits have pulled a fasty on me. You must 'ave passed by us during the night, as we wasn't far from the road... What time you reckon you passed this spot?"

"Between three and four. Can't be certain. You know I never carry a watch. It was certainly no later than four and we guessed you would be pulling out at first light. So, we took a chance on you being still here..."

"What a load of crap, Williams!" The sergeant's voice had become shrill with rage. "A man with a white stick and guide dog couldn't 'ave missed us. At that time of mornin' there was a bright moon and not a cloud in the sky." The sergeant glanced at his guard roster. "Carter!" he shouted harshly at another man nearby. "Carter! You were on between three and four. Did you see these two shit headed bastards go past?" Receiving no answer he went on nastily, "Or was you asleep on the job?"

"No, neither," Carter stuttered back. "But I could've been having a slash when they passed or having a crap, even. I have got the shits a bit."

"You lying bastard, Carter," the sergeant blustered. "You're as bad as them. Right, Williams," he fumed on, "and you Jackson, get on that agony wagon and don't disappear from my sight for a minute. If you break down again, you'll get out and tow the damn thing every mile of the way."

Carter winked at Charlie and Charlie stuck his thumbs up in such a way that the sergeant couldn't see them. Then, as they passed by Farraday, he asked him in a hushed whisper, "Have it away, Charlie lad?"

Charlie winked and smiled.

"What do you think?"

They took their place behind Captain Carlton, while the sergeant still fumed because he knew that Charlie had put one over him, they kept within a couple of yards of the ambulance. Harry fell back in his seat sighing with relief.

"That was a bloody close shave."

But Charlie just smiled.

"You don't think for a moment that they were waiting for us do you, Harry? Don't be a prat. I bet old Carlton didn't get in so long ago. He's been on the nest with that bloody nursing sister, lucky bastard."

"You had your end away," Harry retorted. "Don't see what you've got to grumble about. Anyway, him being late saved our bacon. I bet we would have had some thinking to do to get out of

276

that one! I notice the good captain didn't get out of his wagon to bollock us - hadn't the strength, no doubt."

They passed through the city of Tripoli and made their way to their final destination keeping to the straight military road which ran parallel with the sea. It had been built by Mussolini before the war, no doubt inspired by his idea of conquering more of North Africa - but it did have its uses. Motor racing was held along it with some of the world's top drivers. However, during the war the bridges over the dry wadis had been destroyed and most of them were still being repaired, causing some very serious delays.

When they stopped for a midday meal and a rest, a crowd soon gathered around Charlie and Harry. Led by Farraday they started to pump the two men with questions, for everyone knew or thought they knew what had happened and Charlie didn't disappoint them embellishing every word of his night-time activity. Charlie couldn't quite be called a liar, but he did like to play up to an audience, calling upon Harry from time to time to corroborate his story. Listening, the men sat open mouthed with the occasional interjection thrown in such as, "Lucky bastards."

One man asked, "Aren't you scared of the clap, Charlie? Do you ever use Frenchies?"

Charlie guffawed and shook his head. "I'll take my chances... Do you ever go swimming with your greatcoat on, Carter? I only use them if I actually do suspect a bint may give me a dose - and because sometimes I get fired up by the smell of burning rubber."

Harry left his driver talking bull while he took a swim in the cool waters of the ocean. As usual he swam right out and turned on his back to float shorewards again. 'We should have time to do some writing now it's over,' he thought, never imagining that the next couple of months would be taken up on hard training for the following offensive. But he was going to shake Victoria. He would write to her almost every day telling her all about the desert, though certainly not the incidents in Tripoli and Tunis.

Their hearts sank when they reached their final destination for it was a very small town, although it boasted a pokey cinema of sorts. Their hearts sank even faster when they reached the camp site. It was on the foreshore with miles and miles of desolate beach stretching in either direction, while behind the camp site was a rather substantial building which had already been taken over by the division as a club house. In it the men were already preparing for newcomers, so Charlie and Harry were informed, and they strolled over to it. Here local brewed beer was on sale. It was almost dishwasher weak, but cold and refreshing, and the building itself was thankfully cool. It also contained a small theatre.

"Looks good, Harry," Charlie expressed his opinion with an approving nod.

Harry didn't answer. He was eyeing the piano in the corner of the stage. He went over and tried to open it but it was locked. Hearing him muttering over the instrument, a slightly built corporal came out from behind the stage curtains.

With a click of his tongue and an admonishing wag of a forefinger, the corporal tittered in a high pitched lisp, "Don't play about with that thing, dearie."

Like most men of his inclination his clothes were immaculate and his soft, feminine features so rosily spick, span and doll pretty you could be forgiven for believing he might be wearing make-up. The corporal could see the look of disappointment on Harry's face.

"Do you play, dearie?" he enquired in a tone of sugary sympathy.

Harry nodded and the corporal took a key from his shorts pocket and thrust it delicately towards Harry who noticed that the corporal's hands were beautifully manicured.

As he returned behind the curtain Charlie said, "Reminds you of poor old Mundy, doesn't it, Harry? It amazes me how those pansies can keep so immaculate in this bloody desert."

They had a little trouble unlocking the piano, but once they'd succeeded Harry entwined his fingers and pushed the palms forward until his knuckles cracked before he ran the back of his hand along the keys.

"Don't sound too bad, Charlie," he enthused and started of with all the latest tunes he'd heard before leaving Scotland on the troopship, then afterwards, he played a few pre-war tunes. Gershwin being Harry's favourite he played his numbers over and over. Soon the staff of the club crowed around the doors, some bringing in chairs and making themselves comfortable, the men from Harry and Charlie's unit came into the theatre too, all of them requesting favourite tunes that brought back memories of home.

Suddenly a voice much louder than the others called out 'Roses of Picardy' and Harry shuddered. He couldn't explain why but since he'd sat down he been waiting for someone to request that tune. He glanced around but, the men simply stared back at him. He felt a lump rise in his throat and a strange sensation that he couldn't account for crept through his body. He played the first few bars and stopped, feeling as if someone was standing beside him. Now he played it more slowly, every note echoing round the small theatre. At long last, to his relief, he finished playing the disturbing song and as he stood up everyone clapped.

"That was great, dear boy," the effeminate corporal gushed at him and coming over to him, pressed his fingers into Harry's shoulder. "You can come and play the piano whenever you please."

Harry wasn't listening. He had this very strange feeling - not of depression nor exactly of elation, but a strong sensation that someone was trying to tell him some thing. He'd never experienced the likes of it before, he didn't speak to Charlie all the way back to camp.

The next morning one of the three tonners made a straight line across the camp, every three yards throwing out a small bivouac. A long rope, not unlike a housewife's clothes line, was stretched along the ground, and the sergeant walked along it pushing a wooden peg into it at regular intervals.

"Right, you men, it's time you started working for a living. One bivvi at each of the pegs and they had better be in a perfect line - in fact - three perfect lines. You don't know how lucky you people are having a decent beach with cool water just a few feet away, a nice club house and what's more a cinema. What more could you ask?"

"How about a brothel? We could do with a brothel."

"There you go, Carter, your mind don't travel much above your navel. If you want crumpet keep your eye on Williams. If there's any about he'll find it. Better still, keep an eye on his ambulance. No doubt it'll live up to its name Mobile Brothel." As an afterthought he added grimly, "I'm still not satisfied with 'is 'alf-arsed story at Tunis."

The sergeant knew his words were falling on deaf ears. Like everyone in the unit he knew Charlie wallowed in his reputation as the unit's ram. He was also aware that Charlie, in his own way, was one of the best men. He knew his case history: about the wife that walked out on him and his small daughter.

"Some day, Williams, you'll meet someone what's good and true," he sermonised, "and when you do you'll be ashamed of your past. You'll regret all this shitty screwin' around, you mark my words... There are some decent women about, you know."

"When I find one," Charlie chuckled cynically, "I'll invite you to the wedding. That's if they let you out of the Chelsea pensioner's hospital. You can be best man... Ah, balls to the women," he waved dismissively. "I respect them when I'm with them, but I never want to make a meal of it again. No, keep marriage. I'll be content to screw my way through the alphabet."

279

"So what's it now, Williams, an X, Z and an F?" wisecracked the sergeant.

Without thinking, Charlie replied, "No, I had an F the other night..." The words trailed to a full stop and Charlie put his hand over his mouth.

"So, you bastard - so you did 'ave a couple of bints in Tripoli again! It's lucky for you lot that Captain Carlton was late, else you would've been singing soprano while your mate 'ere tickles the ivories. You, Charlie, would not 'ave had any balls!"

Charlie wasn't too worried. The sergeant had his moment of glory. He wasn't a vindictive N.C.O. and Charlie knew he could consider the matter closed, but he also knew that in future he mustn't get carried away.

A couple of days later the remainder of the unit drove into camp. The men that had been used to the comforts of sleeping in their ambulances looked at the rows of tents in dismay.

"What's happening, Charlie?" Garrety a small Irishman, shouted from the back of the ambulance as it jolted to a halt.

If there was one thing Charlie loved it was baiting the small Irishman. Garrety was always boasting about Ireland and forever singing the praises of the Emerald Isle. The only trouble was that Garrety had been in London since he was four and only returned to Ireland once for a few days! If anything, his accent was far more East End than Irish.

Charlie would ask, "If Ireland is such a wonderful place, why the hell do you Irish all want to come and live in England? And what the hell are you doing in the British army if you've been treated so badly?"

"Well, Charlie," Garrety would reply and try to adopt an Irish accent, which, mixed with his broad cockney, sounded more like geordie. "It's like this, Charlie. We love to fight the English but when someone joins in we just can't stand by and let 'em win. We have to come in and help you."

Charlie snorted with disdain. "What with - a crate of booze bottles? Hey," he hurried on before Garrety could interrupt, "have you heard the news since you've been away?"

Garrety shook his head.

"Well," Charlie continued, grinning broadly, "they towed Ireland into the middle of the Atlantic and sunk it... What's more, it's a load of shit about no snakes in Ireland, because as it was sinking loads of snakes rose to the surface with the rest of the crap. Half the Atlantic is a no-go area now that it stinks to high heaven of dead Irish bullshitters... By the way, Garrety, they're putting on a show at the theatre, Snow White and The Seven

Dwarfs, and I've put your name down as one of the dwarfs. They're asking for volunteers."

"Piss off, Charlie, you long streak of shit. I hope you get a hefty dose of crabs from the next bird you kip with," the cockney-irishman shouted at him.

Over the next few days the unit was drilled daily and men detailed to clean the camp and do the usual kitchen fatigues, but most of the day was spent resting and swimming. At night they would saunter over to the divisional club and Harry was pressed into service at the piano. He didn't mind, he'd been getting a bit stale and at last he had something to tell his old music teacher in his letters home.

Then one morning, a three ton lorry drew alongside the ambulance and the crews were called to stand beside them. The lorry was at the end of the line and each crew was ordered inside to empty their vehicles of anything they'd stowed aboard.

"Shit, Harry, that box of instruments..."

Charlie dropped to the ground and rolled under the ambulance, digging furiously with his hands. Then quite satisfied the hole was large enough, Harry and the crew from the next ambulance tore at the box and slid it under the vehicle and into the hole. Charlie shovelled the soft sand in with his forearm. Harry spread top sand from outside the ambulance and Charlie managed to stand beside it when the three tonner was only a couple of ambulances away.

"That was bleeding close," Charlie whispered and wiped the sweat from his brow.

There was little left inside the ambulance other than a Jerry helmet and an Italian helmet Harry was saving for the boys back at the orphanage. The matron wouldn't be pleased with the spoils of war, but she had no worries, the helmets were confiscated and thrown into the back of the three tonner.

"Where the hell do you keep all that crap, Harry?" Charlie remarked, astounded at the amount of gear taken from the ambulances.

The following day each vehicle was issued with four gallons of green and four gallons of brown paint, and orders were issued that the vehicles were to be painted and camouflaged. This gave rise to speculation and an abundance of rumours. Tommy came past, his face thunderous.

"This is it. That's jungle green or my dick's a bloater! Just look at it, Charlie, dark brown and dark green... I tell you we'll be carrying fucking stretchers through the jungle, mark my words. No ambulance like this will get through that jungle."

"Well, what the hell are we painting them for if we can't use them?" Charlie was smiling to himself as he answered. For Tommy, although a great friend, was a pessimistic bastard.

"You tell me. What does the army do right at the best of times? Tell me why that bale of dressings we opened a few months ago happened to be ladies' what-nots instead of dressings? I tell you, Charlie, I am thoroughly pissed off. They won't get me on that troopship if it's going in the opposite direction."

But Charlie was studying Carter's piece of handiwork. In dark brown he'd painted the outline of a naked woman her breasts as large as barrage balloons.

"God, Carter, if she turned round quick and hit you with one of those she'd brain you!"

Carter moved back and stood next to Charlie to admire his handiwork.

"What a way to go, Charlie," he enthused, smacking his lips. "Imagine... smothered in tits..."

They didn't hear the R.S.M. come up behind them.

"Get that disgusting thing off there, Carter," he bellowed. Then as an afterthought he said, "she'd never survive with tits like that. The weight pulling down on her throat would choke her. Get it off!"

"It's a work of art, sir," Carter protested.

"Get it off, Carter!" the R.S.M. roared.

In the vehicle's new livery, speculation about their intended final destination grew and rumours flew around the unit faster than tennis balls on the centre court at Wimbledon. Both Harry and Charlie would sit in the back of their ambulance and make up some story. Then they would relax and watch it do the rounds until, a couple of days later, it returned to them blown up out of all proportion.

The best one being that when they sent the two most docile men in the unit to report to the Q.M.'s stores to be issued with a large umbrella each, as the unit was about to take up equatorial duties. They were sent back by the Q.M. with a flea in their ears and later, a bollocking for Harry and Charlie with an extra night of guard duty. For months they had dreamed of lazing on a sandy beach for hours on end. Now it had become a monumental bore. If anything, the inactivity was leading them to do things they would never normally dream of doing.

"Right, Williams, and you, Jackson. You report to Sergeant Frazer. The old man wants the camp cleaned up." Sergeant Walters, a fatigue list in his hand read of the names. "Also get Farraday and Carter S."

"Bloody hell, Sergeant Frazer's a lunatic. He was out in India for years. He don't know what he is half the time."

"Alright, Williams, less of that. We all know Frazer should have gone home years ago, but I don't want any more lip."

Sergeant Frazer stood on the far side of the camp, six men already with him. In spite of the heat the sergeant was wearing a leather jerkin.

"Bloody hot one today," Charlie greeted the Scot. He knew what the answer would be. In fact all the men knew word for word the reply would be.

"Hot! You bastards don't know what the word means! In Doolahli in '37 - that was the year... You could have fried eggs on the ground there. And, we had to march - march, I mean, not all this mincing about like the hairy fairies today... I was with a Light Infantry mob, twice as fast as this shower." As he was talking every man was mouthing the words silently behind the sergeant's back.

"Did you have full packs?" Charlie tried to ask, without smiling.

All the men's mouths started to work again.

"Full packs, you say? Full packs? If you were caught in a sudden inspection and there wasn't the right gear in your pack, heaven help you. They filled your packs with sand and, by Christ, you, and not only you but the whole regiment went back to the start line. Those officers knew how to get discipline and you knew how to work. So - we will do the same here. Pick up a sand bag each and get into a nice neat row and we will go straight through the camp... You, Williams," he snapped at him. "Take your mate and get the crap from the cook house. We'll all meet at the disused well further down the beach."

No one knew the depth of the disused well. The men could shout abuse at the N.C.O.s as they passed and would be away before the echo reached the surface.

Harry tipped several sandbags of bully tins and other greasy refuse. The men took turns in emptying their respective bags. There were several forty gallon oil drums filled with dirty oil and petrol and they tipped them in, too, first emptying them then flinging the empty drums on top.

"Is that okay now?" several of the men asked. They wanted to get back to their lazing on the beach. The sergeant looked up and down the beach and then glanced into the deep well.

"Fucking hell, that petrol stinks," he complained and promptly threw his lighted cigarette down the well. Nothing happened for a few minutes but then from the bowels of the earth there came a slow, low rumble that gradually turned into a roar. Next a tongue of flame thirty feet high accompanied by a large explosion roared

283

through the camp, and a tube of black smoke emitting smoke rings at regular intervals reached for the sky. The roar continued for at least five minutes, and rooted to the spot the men stared at it, mesmerised.

"For fuck sake, run!" shouted Charlie.

He knew what went up would have to come down and when that rubbish reached its pinnacle it would come hurtling towards them in flames, and spread over a very wide area. Most of the men ran towards the sea. Harry in the lead dived in head first and quickly swam away from the shore until he was just at the depth when his toes touched the bottom.

It was an unbelievable spectacle. The smoke and rubbish mushroomed outwards high in the sky. Then, as if in slow motion, it all started to fall earthwards... Burning bully beef cans filled with petrol hung suspended in the air before plummeting down. Cardboard and wooden boxes, several old rubber tyres and filthy clothing all became deadly torches. Panic stricken men ran from the camp gathering what possessions they could, while others who where less fussy ran towards the sea. A three tonner burst in a ball of fire when an old bully tin half filled with petrol landed on its canvas roof. Several of the small tents became a blackened mess, resembling umbrellas caught in a gust of wind and turned inside out. The well itself continually belched black smoke rings like a dyspeptic old man.

"I bet none of the bastards in that Light Infantry mob of yours moved as fast as this shower. They say the olympic flame spurs the sportsmen on at the games. These flames certainly spurred these blokes on. Farraday - did you see him move? He ran faster than when he rides his motor bike!" Charlie chuckled.

The camp was in a far worse state than when they started. Tins filled with petrol were still blazing and men were pouring sand over them. Officers turned out of their mess gazing in incredulity at the destruction. The R.S.M. twitched nervously, no doubt wishing he had got rid of Frazer months ago. The man had been out in the sun too long and he was quite mad.

Luckily no one was burned or injured, but Sergeant Frazer wandered about aimlessly a dazed expression on his grim face. A bully beef tin, still blazing, must have retained a pocket of air for, as Sergeant Fraser passed by it, flames sputtered from it and at him. He kicked it. This was his second mistake. The tin landed in the back of an ambulance that had its back doors open and in seconds, the flimsy plywood interior took fire while the sergeant just stood and gaped at it.

"Just take a shufti at that and I've just painted the bleeding thing," the driver gasped, hardly daring to believe his eyes.

Two weeks later Sergeant Frazer was transferred to a base unit in Egypt for shipment to Blighty. Charlie suggested to the R.S.M. that the divisional sign on the unit's vehicles be changed to a Phoenix rising the ashes.

"Another bright idea like that, Williams, and you'll be out like Sergeant Frazer - and I don't mean Blighty bound. It'll be more likely a trip to the glass house in the Delta."

Spag followed Charlie and Harry everywhere as if he understood that their relationship was coming to an end. For even if Charlie could smuggle him to their next campaign, there was no telling where it would be and how long the dog would have to stay alone - probably in the bowels of the ship. But Spag became a favourite at the divvy club and Charlie offered him to one of the pansies who worked there.

"No, dear boy," he declined the offer. "Dogs and I don't get on very well and, you forget that when you lot go - I go. We are in the same division, you know." Oblivious to his rejection Spag wagged his tail. He loved this man. He loved everyone and in particular, here, the small cinema, so that whenever he wasn't with Charlie or Harry he could be found in its centre aisle gazing up at the screen.

"Right, lads, pay attention," R.S.M. addressed the whole unit. "In the morning - at first light - I want you all on parade at the water's edge. Draw a full day's ration and parade in full battle order and water bottles filled, with water, Spencer, not that bloody gut rot red wine you've been pissed on for the last few weeks."

"Why at the water's edge, sir? Are we going to swim home?"

"Alright, Carter, who said anything about swimming and who said anything about home? Anyone late, and they're for it. Right dismissed!"

But the next morning proved disappointing. It was just a whim of the officers to see who could and who could not swim, and those that could - whether they were capable of swimming in full battle order or not.

"There are times, Harry, when I despair of this man's army," Charlie grumbled. "We're not going on an invasion. This exercise is just to confound everyone. You think we two start rumours? It's sod all compared with the rumours the R.S.M. tries to get going."

But even Charlie, one of the biggest rumour-mongers of the unit was wrong. For the next day and for very many more they practised landing from a small assault landing craft. Life went on: swimming, a few fatigues - not enough to occupy every one in the unit. Charlie sold the box of surgical instruments to one of the officers for a tiny fraction of their true worth. He was superstitious and so far he'd had two narrow escapes with them. He was only too glad to get them off his hands.

CHAPTER 28

"Right, you shower! On parade outside the company office in five minutes!" the orderly sergeant shouted.

Charlie jolted up from his comfortable position, laying flat on his back with his feet just in the sea, the small wavelets massaging his feet and ankles. Harry was about two hundred yards from the shore, floating on his back.

Most of the unit was stretched along the beach, either swimming or just lazing, and no one seemed to be intimidated by the sergeant's bellowing. But soon he was down amongst them, his voice like rough sandpaper rubbing down an uneven surface.

"The trouble with you shower, you have been having it too easy since we arrived here. Come on, the company office," he studied his wrist watch, "in four minutes now."

The sergeant's shadow fell across Charlie's face. He opened one eye and looked up,

"What's up, sarge? Bleeding fire?"

"Will be, Williams, if you don't get your back off that sand, your arse will be on fire. Now get moving and bring that mate of yours with you."

He ticked their names off the list he held in his hand.

Harry came out of the sea and stood completely naked and let the hot sun dry him off. They were joined by Chappie and his driver. Both squatted down beside Charlie.

"What's going on Chappie?"

Chappie just shrugged his shoulders.

"Buggered if I know. Some bullshit they have cooked up, I suppose."

Life hadn't been too bad since they arrived. What training could be given to men who had just finished a two year campaign? After cleaning and servicing the vehicles there was very little to do; a little drill now and again, but no one's heart was in it. But as hard as Harry and Charlie tried they couldn't convince the R.S.M. to let them have a couple of days leave in Tripoli. Francesca and Sophia were only seventy miles away, just a couple of hours drive. It would have been better had they been a thousand miles away, it would have been easier to handle.

The sergeant returned and squatted beside Charlie and Harry. He lit his foul smelling pipe, allowing several clouds of blue smoke to bellow out before saying with a sadistic look on his face.

"There's an E.N.S.A. party up at the Div club tonight."

A deep throated groan rose simultaneously from the four throats. They stared at the sergeant with the incredibility of four innocent men that had been sentenced to a long term of imprisonment. Charlie was the first to express his disgust.

"Oh no, sarge, do we have to go?"

"Yes, we fucking well do, it's the old man's orders. As he said, these people have come a long way to entertain us, the least we can do is show our gratitude."

The sergeant directed a stream of brown spittle and scored a direct hit on a fly resting on an old cigarette packet.

"Bet the old man won't be going himself. Some of these E.N.S.A. wallahs know they have a captive audience, they just come out here to inflict punishment on us."

"Hopefully," Harry added, but without much conviction. "Is Vera Lynne there, sarge?"

"Some bloody hopes."

The sergeant consulted his programme and read out several names and his face lit up with masochistic glee.

"Here's one that should interest you lot of culture vultures, Madam Sinclair, late of Covent Garden Opera House."

The sergeant chuckled as he studied the faces.

It didn't take long for the word to spread and most of the men vanished like phantoms in the night. Just before seven the unlucky ones reported back at the company office and marched across the sand to the small theatre. The hall was crowded by protesting men from other units throughout the division, growing uneasy and restless on the hard bench seats. Many of the faces were familiar, the ambulance had been attached to the various regiments.

'Heaven help those poor artists,' Harry thought to himself, for most of the crowd had already been sampling the raw, but strong, local red wine and were the worse for drink. Red Caps were stationed at all exits to make sure no one escaped.

The lights dimmed and an uneasy silence fell on the audience. A dreary groan rose from behind the closed curtains, and as the curtain parted a string quartet came into view. A bald headed man of somewhat miniature stature sawed away at a violin, and three elderly women played various stringed instruments. After a few minutes the music came to an abrupt stop, the men clapped politely, but Harry knew they wouldn't tolerate this much longer. The women bowed to each other with fixed grins on their faces.

The balding man put down his violin and to prove his versatility sat at the piano, starting with Elgar's 'Pomp and Circumstance', several more patriotic songs followed. But when he started to play 'There'll always be an England', a drunken Scot shouted, "Awa with England. Whit abit Scutland?"

By the tone of his voice he was from the back streets of Glasgow. This caused more reaction from the Scots, joining in the

288

banter with massive support from the English amongst them all shouting for the glorification of Scotland and the fact that not many English were not well acquainted with the Scottish national anthem, 'I belong to Glasgow'. The piano player was now reduced to a nervous wreck and gazed round the hall, a plastic smile on his face, this was his first army audience.

"What about Ireland?"

A small wiry man danced up and down on a table at the side of the hall. From the centre of the dimmed room came a single shout, soon echoed by many more.

"Fuck Ireland! Tow it into the middle of the Atlantic and pull the plug out."

"Who said that?"

The Irishman shaded his eyes and gazed round the hall, and a hush fell over the crowd at the prospect of an international punch up. There was an air of defiance from the Irishman till he saw a six foot trooper from the Hussars unroll himself from his seat, and look squarely at the small Irishman.

"I did, wanna make summit out on it mate."

He vaulted over the chairs and grabbed the Irishman by his shirt front and lifted him bodily from the table, the Irishman's legs pedalled frantically in thin air.

Two Red Caps stepped in quickly and parted them before it got out of hand.

"Well lads, it looks as though it won't be such a bad night after all," Charlie said.

With a grinding sound and a shower of dust the curtains closed on the string quartet and the pianist heaved a sigh of relief. The hall became flooded with light. Miss Sinclair, the soprano parted the curtains slightly, her hands shaking so badly she brought down another cloud of dust from the curtains, she coughed and spluttered and held her small handkerchief to her nose. Seeing those toughened and bronzed veterans of the desert fighting made her wish she had never volunteered for this lot and wished she had stayed in her neat Surrey home. She looked with some trepidation at the unruly mob and nudged the comedian standing next to her. He was a small balding man with a bulbous red nose that looked as if it had been painted on. A flat half bottle of whisky protruded from his back pocket.

"Go out first, Mr Percival and get them warmed up. Tell them a few of your funny jokes it may quieten them down."

She smiled hoping it would sweeten him although, as a comedian, she had little faith in him, but she certainly wasn't game to take the stage first. They both squinted through the slight gap in the curtains. The men not already drunk, sucked at oranges and over ripe mangoes. Poor man, it had sounded patriotic volunteering to entertain the troops. Now he faced the grim reality of it all staring in front of him, like Madam Sinclair, he was no doubt wishing himself back in dear old England and the comparative safety of the London blitzes.

"Good heavens, Madam Sinclair."

She always insisted on her full title amongst the concert party.

"They look like a pack of wild animals, are you sure you won't go out first and soothe them with that melodious voice?"

She smiled at him, rather a sweet compliment from the drunken slob she despised.

With a trembling hand he put on his white bowler and adjusted his enormous blue velvet bow tie, then took a large swig of whisky and stepped through the curtains. Unfortunately there was a tear in the curtains, held together with a piece of wire, one end of the wire protruded out a few inches, it caught in his bow tie jerking him back with such force he was catapulted flat on his back.

The unexpected action caused instant appreciation from the audience, they fell around laughing, it was the best reaction he had ever received for an entrance. Stroking his neck and adjusting the bow tie, there and then, he decided to keep the entrance in any future performances. Unfortunately the real part of the act spoiled it, with his jokes as old as N.A.A.F.I. buns. Each joke finished with the punch line being yelled out by a member of the audience.

The curtains parted and Madam Sinclair took up her position at the side of the piano. She remained silent for a few minutes waiting for the audience to simmer down. They did the minute she walked to the centre of the stage and took a bow, for her tight velvet dress clung to her ample figure as if she had been poured into it. Her breasts stood out like two enormous twin mountain peaks, separated by a wide cleavage in the material.

She tapped her hand with a large white ostrich feather a couple of times, this was a signal to the pianist. The men gasped and fell silent holding breath as her breasts rose, trying to break free from their velvet imprisonment at the same time as her voice reached its limit. Bottles of drink, oranges and mangoes finished half way to the men's mouths. The powerful vibrating voice rattled round the hall, no one was listening, every mans eyes were on those enormous breasts and the dancing nipples.

The pianist, although he had accompanied her on many shows, couldn't take his eyes from her breasts and trembling nipples, accidentally, he turned two pages of his sheet music and caused a bit of a furore. She bent over the piano to consult him and gave her audience a better view of the cleavage. There were gasps all round as her tits defied the laws of gravity. The men sitting at the sides of the hall ran to the centre aisle to get a better view.

The first song ended amidst a deafening silence, one or two men clapped, more out of politeness than appreciation. The remainder of the men joined in, hoping, in spite of the dancing tits, it would be the last song. Unfortunately she got the wrong message, the clapping had the opposite effect. She had no intention of giving in so easily, she had a captive audience and intended to make the best of it in her fading years. Having seen the men run into the centre aisle she took it as a compliment, not realising the sad fact that she was singing to a hall of sex starved depraved and battle weary men, who would have made a date with a camel if such an opportunity rose.

Ignoring the groans from the audience she took her stand against the piano and opened her mouth, but the novelty of the rising breasts and shivering nipples had gently faded and no one was in the mood for Madam Butterfly or the Merry Widow. The audience grew restless. Chappie, sitting next to Charlie, noticed the never ending queue at the toilets although it wound half way round the hall. No man was leaving the toilets and there was just one conclusion to draw from this, the men must have had a way of escape.

Chappie was no idiot or appreciative of the classics. He grabbed Harry's arm, "Come on, they are escaping through the shit house window."

In two strides the three of them tagged on the end of the long queue, but this, unfortunately, had attracted the attention of the Red Caps standing at the rightful exits. One went to investigate, dragged the last man, who was half way through the small opening, by the seat of his trousers and pulled him back inside. Then the Red Cap took his stance at the outlet to freedom, his evil eyes staring at the quickly dispersing queue as if they were fugitives escaping from prison. Charlie took his seat a couple of yards from the Red Cap at the toilet door and shattered the silence with a masterpiece of escaping foul air, the Red Cap looked at him with disgust while a ripple of laughter went round the hall.

Madam Sinclair was just finishing her fifth song when peace returned to the hall. Enough was enough. The men demanded to know when the dance girls were due on. Regrettably, it wasn't that kind of concert party as they had already learned, much to their regret. The men started throwing snide remarks and suggesting Madam Sinclair should do a strip dance or belly dance, at which suggestion the audience cheered and stamped their feet. Unfortunately the clapping and shouting coincided with the end of her last song, she smiled benevolently and bowed very low, hand stopped in mid air and every man held his breath as the huge breast flopped down, still defying the laws of gravity, once more there was a mad stampede to the centre aisle, but the velvet dress took the strain and stretched out to its utmost limit.

She smiled once more and no doubt, would have loved to continue, but her throat had taken too much. She managed a nice curtsy and gracefully made for the wings of the stage.

The back doors of the hall swung open and the escapees were herded back into their seats by a platoon of Red Caps and Regimental police. Most of them were completely out of their minds with the local weak brew strengthened by the local potent liquor, which also had the reputation of causing premature blindness.

While waiting for the next turn, one man had taken out his mouth organ, and Harry, seeing the piano stool empty jumped on to the stage. Soon there was a great thumping of the floorboards which made the whole hall tremble and the foundations shake, as Harry and the mouth organ player played request after request. Like true troupers, the concert party returned and led the whole hall into community singing. Harry, above all, was enjoying it the most, he seemed to know every song off by heart.

Then rather a strange thing happened, as he finished his last number a silence fell over the hall and he found himself playing 'Roses of Picardy'. No one had requested the tune and it certainly wasn't a favourite of his, he liked the tune well enough but to say why he played it, he just hadn't the slightest idea. Madam Sinclair, her throat revived with a glass of gin, accompanied him through the second time, and half way through the song the audience sang softly, and as the last notes died away he felt an involuntary shudder pass right through his body. He stood up and took a bow, then jumped from the stage.

Madam Sinclair proved that she was anything but a snob. Now the ice was broken and she realised her type of audience, she let her hair down, dancing a knees up with several men on the stage. The comedian, having demolished the remainder of the whisky in the bottle, his nose now two shades deeper red and his eyes glazed over, started on with the real deep blue jokes, the men went wild and stood up while he took a bow to a standing ovation. He had learned two main points that night, that fighting men loved a comedian who could ridicule himself, and he certainly did that with his entrance, and the troops loved blue jokes, the bluer the better. His next performance would be a sell out.

From the hall, much happier then when they went in, they made their way back to their bivvies. Charlie knew he would suffer the next morning, for unintentionally he had soaked back half a bottle of local red wine, which he hated, and two small bottles of the weak local beer. That in itself would have been sufficient for him, not being a drinker, but the inaction over the past weeks was starting to get him down. For the past couple of years death and destruction had been his constant companion - without them, he was finding it difficult to adjust.

Harry and Charlie sat outside their bivvi and gazed across the sea at the full moon which reflected across the slight wavelets in a million fragmented silver lights. The waves rippled back shorewards to lap lazily against the sand smoothing the foreshore out till it glowed like a silver mirror. They both stripped naked, and while Charlie, with Spag across his chest lay on the sand and let the sea gently massage his feet, Harry swam out till the shore looked like a faint line in the distance, then he turned on his back and gently floated shorewards.

It was well past midnight when they returned to the bivvi. Harry rolled himself into his blankets and would have swiftly dropped off to sleep but he thought Charlie was in a talkative mood.

"This sodding war."

Charlie's head was resting in his hands and he stared at the ridge of the tent and the light from the moon filtering through the flimsy canvas.

"If it hadn't been for this war I might have been happily divorced or strung up for doing in that bitch I married."

But that was the last of the conversation, for Charlie started snoring. It was a pity really, for Harry knew very little of his driver's past, just fragments he had picked up from time to time and pieced together. He had hoped the small amount of booze had loosened Charlie's tongue.

It was still dark when they were jolted from a deep sleep by someone shouting at the top of his voice and ordering them to parade outside the company office in full battle order.

At first they thought it was someone playing a practical joke, no one moved, then the senior N.C.O.s moved amongst them shouting inside the bivvies, "On parade!"

Charlie sat up straight with his head feeling twice its normal size and a pain in the back of his eyes that sent brilliant light flashes spurting through his brain, he cradled his head in his hands and cursed Chappie under his breath for passing him the bottle of red wine while he was engrossed in the comedian's blue jokes.

293

"God, Harry, there's a fireworks display going on behind my eyes."

He crawled through the open end of the bivvi, the cold air slammed him between his eyes, the huge moon was suspended over the horizon, hesitated, then took its final plunge from sight. Charlie, with Harry close behind, staggered to his feet, his legs like jelly, wobbled towards the sea. Several men were lined up along the edge, urinating and the rhythmic sound of water against water was like a fast running brook broken only by bursts of pent up wind. Charlie excelled himself, the other men groaned and without looking round to see the culprit, in unison, greeted him with, "Morning, Charlie." He didn't answer but the local brew had worked wonders, he gave them an encore.

If someone in the unit had bothered to read daily orders the previous day the chaos of the next ten minutes could have been avoided. They hurriedly packed their small packs, not as regulation standing orders stated, but hurriedly with anything that came to hand, hoping and praying that there would be no kit inspection. Charlie couldn't find his shorts, and wasn't likely to - in his hurry he had stuffed them into his small pack. Seeing another pair on the guy ropes of the bivvi next door, he struggled into them, and struggle he did, for the owner was at least six inches shorter than him. The air became blue with the rantings and ravings of the owner of the shorts, throwing everything from his bivvi cursing and swearing.

"Just listen to that filthy language first thing in the morning."

Charlie held his hands over Spag's ears.

"Don't swear in front of my dog, Groves."

"Fuck you, Williams and fuck the dog, some thieving bastard has nicked my shorts."

Charlie tutted.

"Nothing is sacred any more, Grovesy."

And Harry could hardly keep a straight face. More problems were heaped on Charlie's shoulders. He couldn't find his water bottle and although Groves water bottle was at hand just outside his bivvi, they dare not nick it, not with the state Groves was in, running around with his shirt tail flapping in the early morning breeze and his skinny legs going back and forth like a pair of piston rods.

"I will kill the bastard that has nicked my shorts," he kept shouting.

They tried to placate him.

Harry said with his face all innocent. "I bet it's those thieving Arabs from the village, they are always hanging around the camp."

Then Charlie asked, "I don't suppose you have a spare water bottle do you, Grovesy?"

"Get bleeding stuffed, Williams."

Groves grabbed his water bottle from outside his tent and put it where he could keep his eye on it.

"I was only thinking, Groves, you can't go on parade like that with your bare arse pointing windwards, so let's borrow your bottle."

"Shut your bloody cake hole, Williams."

Groves emptied his bivvi to no avail.

A voice from out of the semi darkness shouted, "For Christ sake, Groves, get these on and let's have some peace and quiet."

He slung a pair of shorts over, they landed round Groves's neck. Just in time for him to get on parade.

It was worked out that Chappie and his driver on one side of him and Harry on the other side, they would unbuckle Chappie's water bottle as soon as he had been inspected then pass the water bottle to Charlie, standing directly behind Harry. This worked out perfectly.

So in a disorderly array, it was impossible to keep in step, they were marched along the beach and then down to the foreshore, where several large ships, looking like stranded whales, were drawn up on the beach. Not unlike small frigates with a ramp down each side they proved to be Landing Ships Infantry or as the Navy, like every other branch of the services enjoyed shortening titles, they were called L.S.I. This puzzled the men, why Infantry landing ships? Perhaps after all, the rumour suggesting the division was going to be disbanded and turned into an Infantry division, perhaps even an Infantry assault division, bore some truth.

The unit was split into two with the first half sharing the ships with two companies of infantry and a squadron of engineers. Heavy hob nailed boots clattered along the steel deck, wet with early morning dew and sea spray making every step treacherous, the men slid and skidded all over the deck, cursing and swearing and clinging to anything that was fixed down.

Directed below by grinning sailors they took their seats in the hold, laid out with large chairs, not unlike arm chairs and quite comfortable. A Mae West life preserver lay on the back of each chair and it didn't take long for the unit comics to make use of them. The hold had no portholes and within minutes the heat was unbearable. The steel walls of the ship became soaked with condensation running down the sides. No one was aware of what was about to happen and questioning the crew bought no results, they lived up to their reputation of the silent service. The truth was, they were just as much in the dark as the Army, and it turned out the Navy were worse rumour mongers than the Army.

The heat in the hold became oppressive, and they could hear the crew above on the steel decks going about their duty. They sat there for over an hour, when they felt the ship rock slightly and the shingle under the hull crunching as the ships engines went into reverse, pulling away from the shore with the help of the two anchors dropped astern a couple of hundred yards before the ship hit the beach. The two anchors were hoisted aboard, and the steady rhythm of the engines and gently swaying of the ships told them they were in deep water.

"Silence!" a voice bellowed in the dimly lit hold.

A senior N.C.O. of marines stood in front of them, he waited for the murmuring to die down. He took his short cane from under his arm.

"Right men."

His back as straight as a flag pole, with his cane he pointed to three lights above his head, not unlike traffic lights.

"When the red light comes on you stand up and get into your battle order kit, keep your Mae Wests on, half inflated. Amber light." He tapped the centre light. "Turn inwards to the middle aisle and wait for the green light I want you to start moving off, not in one mad rush, but in orderly rows. I will walk down the passage and give you the order of disembarkation. Now the leader of the following rows make sure the last man in the row before you is clear. Don't, and I emphasise DON'T, come out of your order or it will be a real cock up."

He walked up the passage giving the man at the end of the row a number.

"The book says this hold should be clear in four minutes, I say I can do it in three minutes. No stalling on the steps up from the hold, across the decks and down the ramps."

Legs astride he glared at them daring any man to challenge him when he asked, "Any questions?"

To himself he couldn't have made his instructions any clearer, to the men in the seats they were as clear as mud.

"Yes, sir." A voice came from the rear of the hold.

"What is it?" the marine sergeant asked impatiently.

"The lights, sarge, I am colour blind."

The sergeant chased down the passage like a bull on heat, and stood before the culprit who just about came up to the sergeant's shoulders. The sergeant's face was two inches from the man's.

"Are you taking the piss, sonny?"

It was obvious the man was the unit's joker and was certainly the smallest man aboard, he never flinched as the huge red face almost smacked into his own. The men around trying to stifle their laughs, a silence fell over the crowd.

"No, sarge, and do you mind." The small man turned his head to one side. "Your fucking breath stinks."

Harry had never seen the man before and could hardly stop himself from laughing out loud. Turning several shades of purple the sergeant glared at the little soldier, he was speechless for a few minutes trying to regain his composure, then hissed, "Get up to the front row you short arsed little bastard, you will be the first off the ship and any slip ups and you will find the toe of my ammo boot right up your ring piece. UNDERSTAND?"

If the sergeant thought he would intimidate the soldier with his shouting, he had made a mistake. The little man stared back at him with complete indifference and collected his kit.

"I don't like funny fuckers on my ship. This is no laughing matter, when you hit the beach, it doesn't matter how many ships there are or how many men, you will be the loneliest man in the world and as far as you are concerned every shell that whistles over or every bullet that hits the sea and sand around you, you will think you are the only target on that beach, and every shell and every bullet has your name on it. It's my job to prepare you for that initial landing, so I want you, every man jack of you, off the ship as fast as possible."

"To hear the prick talk you would think this is our first time in action. I doubt if the prick has ever heard a shell fire in anger," Harry said quietly.

A silence fell over the ship's hold, broken only by someone dropping their rifle, as the red light appeared above the marine sergeant's head. The men fitted their battle order webbing and turned inwards as the amber light and the ship's keel scraped the shore simultaneously as the green light flickered on. Contrary to the sergeant's instructions, orders started flying all over the hold, what had once been rows of orderly men waiting patiently for orders, now turned into a disorganised rabble, falling over one another as they struggled up the companionway - the navy never referred to them as stairways - heavy boots clattered along the steel decks and down the ramp.

Charlie missed his footing.

"Bloody hell!" he shouted as he slid down the ramp.

Coming into contact with the men in front, he fell and pushed the man in front of him. It was like a car pile up on a busy road as the rank folded up into one gigantic heap and tumbled into the water, fortunately it was just three feet deep. The clear blue water turned into a thick dark yellow mud pit as the men struggled to sort themselves out. The ships crew hung over the rails doubled up with laughter. They had witnessed the same scene so many time they looked forward to it with eager anticipation as men going to the theatre to see a good musical. It was the main item for breaking the monotony of ship life.

Wet and bedraggled they formed up in lines again waiting to board. The formidable figure of the instructor was waiting to greet them.

"What a bloody shambles."

He struck the sides of his leg with his short cane.

"You bloody pongoes. A real cock up and make no mistake. Jerry would have had a picnic if that had been the real thing. I doubt if any of you would have made ten yards up the beach, he would have picked you off like flies feasting on dog shit. Even his shit house wallahs would have made mince meat of the lot of you."

He swiped the metal post supporting the deck above with his cane. It rang out sharp and clear like a church bell.

"Follow my instructions and it's as easy as falling off a log. Red light, packs on, amber turn inwards."

He smashed his cane against the steel post once more.

"Green light, start filing out in the order I gave you."

He rushed down the centre aisle glaring defiance at the N.C.O.s. sitting on the end of each row.

"We have one captain on this ship, I don't go on the bridge and tell him how to run the ship, he doesn't come down here and tell me how to get you shower off this ship in under four minutes."

He pointed belligerently at each N.C.O. in turn.

"I don't want you fucking pongoes giving me orders when those lights go on. Now this time we will get it right and with no interference from you N.C.O.s."

He addressed the rest of the men.

"Now remember - off as fast as possible. Just imagine the beach is full of hairy arsed Jerries waiting for you, get straight off and find some sort of cover."

"That's ballsed it, sir. If they imagine that, you won't get them off this tub in a month of Sundays."

It was the small Infantry man again. The marine chose to ignore him, he was still fuming over the way the short arsed sod had made a fool of him a few minutes ago.

Harry nudged Charlie as he felt the ship making a fast turn towards the beach, the steel hull vibrating as it gathered speed, the red light came on and the ship ground ashore throwing some of the men forward. They eventually grew more reliant on that sound than watching the lights and after several more runs into shore managed to get the disembarkation down below ten minutes, with the instructor disgusted at the attempts.

They assembled on the beach, wet through, tired and fed up to the teeth. If they thought the ordeal was over they were soon to be disillusioned. The marine N.C.O. came down the ramp. The men were drawn up in three ranks.

"Alright you shower, note the number of the ship, I will have the pleasure of your company at first light in the morning till such times as I get the disembarkation down to four minutes."

And every morning for the next five days they assembled under the watchful eye of the marine instructors till eventually they reached the acquired time. It wasn't due to them becoming more experienced, far from it, before the week was out the men discovered cubby holes to hide in and at least a quarter of the men managed to miss a turn. Two seats efficiently hid one man, at least four could conceal themselves in a lifebelt locker with sufficient light to play cards, while others lay on the top of the partition that concealed the toilets.

"Right men, back to camp," their own sergeant shouted as they landed for only the second time that morning. He scratched his head as he looked at the sadly depleted assembly, for it had been the unit's turn to lay concealed aboard the ship. As if paying homage to the dead, the remainder of the unit stood motionless as they watched the landing ship pull away, the gap between the ship and the shore growing rapidly. The ship was a good five hundred yards away when the panic stricken stowaways lined the aft end of the ship waving frantically at their mates ashore who were singing 'We'll Meet Again'. Two of the better swimmers dived over and struck out for the land.

"How many do you think are still aboard, Harry?"

He could hardly speak for laughing as the full realisation of the situation hit Charlie.

Harry looked at the three ranks, "About twenty of our own unit I reckon, altogether there has to be at least forty still aboard, and just as many on the other ships. With their bleeding luck they could be back on their way to Blighty."

"Not a hope in hell. They are on their way to Tripoli. There will be hell to play when they get there. I bet those bloody marines knew half the sods are still aboard."

But Charlie couldn't stop laughing and counting his luck, for next time it was their turn to miss the run in.

CHAPTER 29

Rumours were rife throughout the division that it was about to be reformed with a brigade taken from the Scottish 51st Highland Division and two Yankee divisions. The invasion was to be through the underside of Europe travelling into Spain and then France. It had started simply because the unit rumour-monger overhead the tail end of a conversation when Charlie said he wouldn't mind if they were sent to Spain as he fancied a nice dark haired senorita!

"Well, Charlie, we've only to go to Australia and South America and the div will have travelled all round the world," Harry said, lowering his voice as he mentioned the last two countries.

At that moment Chappie came along and slapped Charlie on his bare back between his shoulder blades. It was apparent Chappie was in a good mood.

"Well, lads, it's certain to be Greece. I have the 'gen' on good authority," he said, but got no further.

Charlie stared at him hard for a few seconds and then he and Harry jumped on Chappie forcing him to the sand where the three of them grappled together before Corporal Sykes came along and parted them. He held the inevitable clip board and pencil in his hand.

"Williams, Jackson. The old man wants you in the company office straight away. Go on - jeldhi the pair of you!"

"That's good." Charlie had a serious look on his face. "I want to see the old man for compassionate leave. I never told you did I, Sykes? I have an aunt that lives in Tripoli. She married an Itey just before the war and I must try and find out where she lives."

"Bullshit, Williams. What you really want is a couple of days with those two bints of yours, you pair of dirty bastards." Sykes' lips curled in a contemptuous sneer. "Go on - Get up to that office straight away."

"That reminds me, Harry," Chappie's face took on a puzzled expression. "How's that tool of yours? Bloody hell, you took a chance with that sexy Italian piece. From what you told me she probably accommodated half the Italian and German armies."

There was a look of relief as Harry answered, "It's alright, Chappie. But to be truthful I did have the wind up for a few days. I know I went at it like a bull in a china shop. Still it was worth it."

"You should have seen him, Chappie. Every morning he'd rush out of the bivvie and down to the sea and crouch over inspecting it, trying to make believe he was having a piss. He was just like a dirty old man playing with himself," Charlie chuckled as he recalled the daily routine that had lasted a fortnight.

With Sykes tagging behind them they crossed the hot sand and stood before the canvas lean-to. The R.S.M. called them in. He was sitting on the corner of a well scrubbed table and didn't bother to look up for a few minutes.

"I have a job for you two. You have to go to the British General Hospital at Castell Benito Airfield and pick up a Captain Smithers who's joining the unit."

There was a quick flash of excitement on Charlie's face that quickly turned to stone, but it hadn't gone unnoticed by the R.S.M.

"That's alright, Williams. I know you have a couple of bints stashed away. You can leave at seven in the morning and you should be at the hospital by noon. Then, given a couple of hours at the hospital and five hours to get back you should be here by seven at the latest. Is that understood?"

"Yes, sir," Charlie answered.

He knew the R.S.M. had been generous with his timing for the R.S.M. was no fool. It was a straight road to Tripoli and it was common knowledge that Charlie was not the best but fastest driver in the Division. Five hours he could cut in half as most of the diversions over the damaged bridges and across the dry wadis were repaired, so easing up the long delays.

Harry guessed what was going through Charlie's mind. Three hours at the most to Tripoli, four or five hours with the girls, an hour at the most at the hospital and then return. And it appeared that the R.S.M. also guessed what was going through their heads.

"Now look here, you two, I don't want you wandering off to see those two Itey bints," he warned. That order was falling on dead ears and he knew it. "I want you back here by seven - or else ..." He dismissed them with a nod towards the canvas flap that served as a door.

Charlie was elated on the way back to the bivvie.

"I feel like jumping in the air and shouting, Harry," he chuckled.

With a large empty ammo box they went to every vehicle collecting unwanted tins of food and cigarettes, and that evening they visited the divisional club and went round the tables scooping up packets of issue 'V' cigarettes, of which there were enough to fill another ammunitions box. Well prepared, they left camp well before seven. The R.S.M. was standing behind the flap of his lean-to and smiling to himself, Charlie noticed, glancing in his rear view mirror as they speeded out of the camp.

Charlie raced along that straight road as if he were doing trials for a racing circuit, slowing down only at the diversions. Then half way to Tripoli they were stopped by a military patrol utility.

"What's the hurry? Bloody fire or something?"

Harry foresaw what was happening and hastily crept into the back where he lay on a stretcher and covered himself with a blanket. The M.P's cap was pulled down over his eyes, his mouth the straight line that Charlie was used to seeing in Red Caps.

"Very sick man aboard, corp. Have to make the hospital in a hurry."

"What's the matter with him?" asked the Red Cap.

Charlie didn't want the Red Cap snooping in the back. He didn't know how far Harry had got with the sham, and of course there was those two ammo boxes in the centre of the ambulance which would occasion some difficult questions if opened.

"Don't know, corp, some infectious disease. That's why they didn't send a medic. It's highly contagious. You wouldn't get me in the back for a pension."

This seemed to satisfy the Red Cap who stood on the back step and peered through the rear window.

"Right, driver, get on your way, but try and take it a bit easy. There are one or two dangerous diversions this side of Tripoli."

There was a faint patch of grey sky as they entered the outskirts of the city and they weren't exactly sure where the Italian women's house was situated, so they cruised around in its general direction and found it a half hour later. As they pulled up it was if the girls were expecting them.

Francesca was a little doubtful at first when she saw the ambulance stopping in its new livery, but she became reassured when Charlie jumped down from the cab and she ran out and threw her arms around his neck, although she was still in her nightdress. Sophia jumped into the cab and as she threw her arms around Harry's neck she was crying and laughing at the same time, her tears leaving a wet stain on Harry's bush shirt. Charlie steered the ambulance to the rear of the house and Spag hearing the familiar voices of the two women lifted his head from his blanket, jumped down and wagged his tail furiously.

Then Francesca, her eyes red with tears asked, "How long you here for, Charlie?"

They wouldn't be expecting him at the hospital until midday and he placed his arm around Francesca's shoulders. "Two or three hours. Then we must report to the hospital. I'll try and work something out. We'll try and get back."

When they entered the house, Spag trailing awkwardly between their legs, Harry and Sophia were already closeted behind bolted doors in the bedroom.

Charlie looked around the room. It was spotless, unlike the first time they had entered it when it had been covered in a film of fine sand. The old kitchen wood fired stove shone line the burnished buttons on a professional soldier's uniform and Charlie was about to sit down in an arm chair, but Francesca caught him by the hand and led him straight into the bedroom.

Charlie could see that Harry had stood up well to the ordeal when they all emerged from their bedrooms at midday. The two men hurried to the ambulance and returned with the two ammo boxes. When they emptied the contents on the table the girls whooped with joy.

They were reluctant at first to accept, thinking that Charlie and Harry would be short, but the men reassured the girls that neither of them would touch the 'V' issue cigarettes at any price. They also assured them that the food was surplus to requirements, although it was a matter of pot luck what they contained, as none of the tins were labelled. The girls didn't smoke, but cigarettes were almost legal tender so with luck they would have enough to live on until things returned to normal.

It was a tearful farewell. Sophia became hysterical and Francesca dabbed her eyes with a small lace handkerchief when Charlie took her in his arms for a farewell kiss.

"I think I have a cold coming, Charlie," she sniffed, thrusting a piece of violet paper into Charlie's bush shirt pocket. "This is my address in Napoli. My momma lives there... Write to me, Charlie." A mischievous smile spread across her face. "If I have a little bambino, Charlie, I will call it Charlie," she teased then seeing Charlie freeze, his face blanching, she laughed gently. "Don'ta worry, Charlie. I can't have the bambinos."

Charlie reached over and tousled her hair. "I'll do my best to write, Francesca, as soon as I can. Only I think the war will be much harder from now on."

It was almost a straight road to the hospital and the last they saw of Francesca and Sophia was the two of them standing in the middle of the road, Sophia crying hysterically and Francesca waving her small white handkerchief.

Charlie and Harry reached the hospital in fifteen minutes and turning in at the gates they pulled up alongside a long low building with a wide verandah. On it stood a solitary figure resplendent in well-laundered and neatly creased shorts and shirt, snow white belt and gaiters, his brassware polished and gleaming like lead crystal glassware, while beside him a brass shell case hung from a rafter.

It was quite the largest one Charlie and Harry had ever seen and it was polished like a mirror, the piece of flat metal dangling beside it serving both as a fire alarm and air raid warning. Harry in his sweat stained shorts and shirt, felt uncomfortable beside the sentry.

"Called for a Captain Smithers. Any idea where we can find him, mate?"

"He can only be in two places, the operating theatre or the officers' mess. If he's in the mess he'll be pissed to his eyeballs. If he's in the theatre for God's sake don't disturb him or he's likely to carry out an unofficial castration on you."

Charlie brightened, his fertile imagination working overtime. He must at all costs get back to the girls as this would be the last chance for him and Harry getting their ends away. And who knew what lay around the corner? He discussed this proposition with Harry who was in complete agreement. The sentry was trying to get rid of them.

"That's the officers' mess over there," he pointed a forefinger. "The first large hut with a veranda. Do you mind getting a move on? About this time there's a smashing Itey nurse passes here with the biggest pair of tits in the country, and I have to rush inside to watch her pass. With these shorts on if she sees me she will know exactly what I'm thinking... So, piss off, mate."

"Man's a pervert, Harry," Charlie laughed.

But a few minutes later they passed a petite, dark Italian nurse, chest thrust forward and backside thrust back.

"Look at those bristols, Charlie," Harry whistled under his breath. "See what the man means now."

Charlie strode across the wide verandah. It was littered with bamboo chairs and tables, the tables covered with half empty glasses.

"Here we go, Harry. If that bastard is pissed we may work something out."

A vaporous smell of stale booze filled the air. He tapped on the door and placed his ear flat against it, listening for any sign of movement. There was none and his heart sank. The place must be empty. Harry stood beside him and he nudged him.

"That's shagged it, Harry. He must be in the theatre," Charlie whispered.

Cautiously opening the door they peered inside and their hopes rose, then Charlie gasped, "Bloody hell!"

Mess was the right name for it. It was a complete shambles and it looked as if a wild party had been going on for days. Home made garlands were strung around the room, some of them in shreds. French letters, all blown up, were serving as balloons, gaily decorated by someone with an artistic flair and a wilder imagination, and the place was also buzzing unpleasantly with pot-bellied blue bottles gorging themselves on the unfinished sandwiches.

The best sight for Charlie and Harry was seeing a man fast asleep, mouth open, sitting upright at an ancient piano, the keys brown with age and mottled with cigarette burns. They also noted another man, small and wiry, his ginger hair thinning at the top wit a wisp of hair above his upper lip, his bush shirt wide open, his face covered in orange stubble, clutching an empty whisky bottle. Another officer, extremely fat, was sprawled across an easy chair, his blubbery, accordion pleated chin resting on his chest, while another shabby officer lay curled around his feet like a great Irish wolf hound.

"Some party," Charlie sniggered. "It looks like a bomb's hit the joint."

"Just look at all those half eaten sandwiches, Charlie," Harry muttered. "Bloody hell, we haven't seen bread in months... Ah, shit," he sighed, "come on and let them die in peace. I wouldn't want their heads when they wake up."

They made their way to the rear of the building and finding the cook house, they pulled back the gauze and inner door at the same time. It took a few seconds for their eyes to become accustomed to the gloom, but the cook, dressed in white and with a large chef's hat, hardly noticed them at first. He stood over a solid fuel stove stirring unconcernedly at a large dixie of soup with sweat running down his face and neck. His attitude was that of someone who doesn't give a damn about anything. A fag end with an inch of ash hung precariously from the corner of his mouth and he gave them a sidelong glance.

"Worra youse two want?"

The ash on the fag end couldn't taken the sudden movement of his lips, bent, wavered and then fell in the soup. The chef stirred vigorously for a few seconds and then carried on as if nothing had happened.

"Could you tell us where we could find Captain Smithers, chef?"

Charlie never once took his eyes from the chef's back as he talked and edged towards the long table in the centre of the kitchen. A large platter of succulent beef steaks, freshly cut, lay under a muslin cover. He winked at Harry and nodded towards the tempting steaks. Harry got the message. He buttoned his shorts half way and tucked the shirt tails inside his shorts. The chef, a trusting soul, never once glancing at the two thieves behind him just nodded towards the door leading into the mess.

"In there. Captain Smithers is that balding, ginger haired bloke taking his rest on the easy chair. He won't be out of his drunken coma till this afternoon." Never once did the chef take his eyes from the cauldron of soup, concentrating on the vortex of scalding liquid. "They were all pissed to the eyeballs last night."

With the speed of lightning Charlie's hand went under the muslin cover, grabbed two steaks and flicked them towards Harry. He caught them deftly with one hand and tucked them inside his shirt. Then he casually took his leave and him them in the ambulance.

The chef stirred at the soup and gave Harry a sidelong glance as he re-entered the cook house.

"Smithers is not a bad bloke. Bloody good surgeon. Don't know how he does it. He gets pissed regularly yet the operating boys in the theatre say his hands are as steady as a rock. We'll be sorry to see the back of him. Can't take that fat bastard who's pissed to the eyeballs though, fat bloody pig!"

Although Charlie was only slightly interested in what the cook was saying he was trying, without being too obvious, to draw Harry's attention to the patch of blood from the stolen steaks which was soaking through his shirt. Charlie's surreptitious thumb jerks and shifty sidelong glances finally got the message across and Harry slid his shirt from his shorts and folded it back.

Charlie peered into the inner sanctum, shrine of Bacchus and rendezvous for the unholy rave-ups. The captain was still stretched out along the settee, a persistent grin smeared across his face. Charlie had a much better view of him now. The hair had completely retreated from the front of his head and his bare skull was covered in freckles, as was the bridge of his nose. His features had taken on a boyish look in unconscious repose, and you had to look closer to note the flimsy ginger hair above his top lip. He'd tried to hid the bald patch by allowing a strand of his receding hair to grow long, so that with a flourish he could sweep it over his exposed scalp. However, it now hung limply to one side of his face, plastered with sweat.

"Not a pretty sight, is it, driver?" The chef wiped his hands down the front of his apron.

Charlie just shook his head. His mind was on any alternative to his advantage other than waking the officer and taking him back to camp straight away. Charlie wiped his hand across his damp lips.

"How long he been in that state, chef?"

"Well, it started just after midnight, the officers filling those Italian F.L's with wine and water and throwing them at each other."

The chef returned to his soup, stirring it vigorously as if trying to rid himself of his pent up feelings.

Now Charlie stared at the steaks as if seeing them for the first time.

"Bloody hell, chef. They do themselves proud, don't they?" He lifted the corner of the muslin and Charlie, in his most patronising voice enquired, "Haven't got a couple to spare have you, chef? It's been years since I saw a steak like these."

The cook's face clouded. "You have to be kidding, mate. Every slice is well and truly accounted for. The officers all chipped in and bought this stuff on the black market. I haven't the foggiest how they managed it, but I bet the unit's fag ration will be in short supply at the next issue." The cook tucked the corner of the muslin cover back under the plate. "I have to cook it for dinner tonight. The cook sergeant himself came and cut it. I have to recut every slice into three portions. That sergeant is a crafty bastard. I cook it, then if anything goes wrong I get a bollocking. I bet he nicked a slice for himself and his bit of Italian crumpet."

Charlie gulped and stared at Harry and he could hardly stop himself smiling. Three portions from each slice... They had just nicked six officer's dinners.

He shrugged his shoulders and muttered to himself, "C'est la Guerre," and sympathised with the cook.

"I go along with you there, chef. These sergeants are all of the same calibre. They leave you to do the grafting and then if anything goes wrong you carry the can back, and they give you a bollocking in front of the officers. But if you make a decent job of things, what happens? He gets you off duty or away from the cook house, while the lousy sod gets into his whites and takes the credit. Believe me we have our share of crawlers in our unit."

The cook's ruddy face shone with pleasure. At last he'd found a soul mate, someone who really understood.

"You have it in a bloody nutshell, driver. At the moment he's out screwing some little Itey nurse. You should see the rations he takes her then hopes I can make it up, and it's no good telling the R.S.M., he's screwing the Itey nurse's sister."

The mention of an Itey female set Charlie's brain whirring and put his hormones on red alert. He had the steaks, now if he could just work it out they could have a good meal and spend the night with their own girl friends, but first they must get more food - and a couple of loaves of white bread.

"Couldn't spare a few eggs could you, chef?" Charlie casually handed one of his best cigarettes to the cook.

"Help yourself, driver. That's one thing we're never short of."

Chancing his luck and without mentioning the bread, he asked the cook if he could help himself to sandwiches left over in the officers' mess.

"You don't want that crap. The flies have been shitting and fornicating over them of the past twelve hours."

He opened the large cupboards. It was overflowing with loaves of freshly baked bread. "Help yourselves to a couple of these. The pigs won't miss them."

With boyish grins, Harry and Charlie fingered the bread and breathed in hard until they felt their lungs would burst from the mouth watering, fresh baked smell of it. Now if they could only work things out to their advantage... Charlie winked at Harry and he immediately guessed that his perverted mind was working something out. All Harry would have to do was agree occasionally, and often only a nod of assent was necessary.

The chef was saying to Harry, "That Captain Smithers is something of a piss artist."

Charlie tittered and said, "The old man won't like that."

But this statement was a bit over the top for everyone knew the old man could knock it back with the best of them. However Harry nodded in agreement.

"Oh, yes," he murmured. "That's true."

Unseen by them a huge man was framed in the doorway. He grunted and they swung around. The man was wearing khaki shorts and a bush shirt freshly washed and creased, and his Sam Browne leather was polished to the point that when he moved and the sun caught it, the leather flashed like a high powered torch. A large florid face propped on top of a treble chin poked out from under a peaked cap pulled well over his eyes. Still Harry and Charlie could see them glaring at their persons in bloodshot suspicion as he ducked under the flimsy gauze-fronted door. Both men sprang to attention. At this point Charlie didn't intend to blot his copy book. It was one of those rare occasions that called for a bit of crawling. The officer stroked an enormous moustache and with the other hand held on tightly to a leather covered cane, a silver mount at one end.

"And what won't your old man like?" His voice boomed around the spotless kitchen. Harry stared speechless at the R.S.M. and the R.S.M. repeated, "Out with it, son. What won't your old man like?"

Harry was still at a loss to know exactly what Charlie was up to, but he stepped in smartly now. He hated the N.C.O.s and warrant officers, and even more so the loud mouthed type, but he was determined he would stay the night. If there was anything the loud mouths enjoyed the most it was bullshit. They could really identify with that. Charlie clicked his heels.

"Sorry, sir. I didn't realise you were there, sir."

The R.S.M.'s cheeks puffed in florid self-importance. Then slowly he expelled the air in his cheeks.

"Right, lad, let's have it. What is it your old man won't like? And, I take it by old man you mean your C.O."

"Yes, sir. It's Captain Smithers, sir. We have to collect him and all due respects, sir, he's in no fit state to travel."

Charlie didn't relax, but remained rigidly to attention, and Harry could hardly believe his ears. For the whole time he'd known Charlie it was the first time he'd openly shown any servility to a superior, and this surely must pay off. Charlie always boasted he could make any woman eat out of his hand, and after watching him now Harry could well believe that Charlie would soon have the R.S.M. dancing to his tune too.

"If we return to the unit with the captain in this condition, sir, our C.O. would be most upset. He's a Seventh Day Adventist, sir, and as you know, sir, they are rigid T.T."

Harry doubted very much if Charlie knew anything at all about Seventh Day Adventists, but he also felt confident the R.S.M. wouldn't have any knowledge of their activities as he looked perplexed and suitably vague at the mention of the religious sect.

The game was starting to play off. The R.S.M was making excuses for the captain and although Captain Smithers lacked all sense of military discipline the R.S.M. appeared to have a soft spot for the officer.

"He'll be alright," he insisted loudly. "Good chap, Smithers. Had a few drinks. Be right as rain in the morning."

His words were clipped and spoken at a volume sufficient to waken the dead if not a man dead drunk.

"We'll... We'll dose the chap up with black coffee and dry him out," he hee-hawed on.

This was turning out to be too good to be true and it was taking all Charlie's self-discipline to contain his feelings. Harry listening to him knew he was hearing a master shit sprayer at work. It wasn't only what Charlie was saying but how he was putting it over. He dared not look at Charlie, and instead concentrated on watching a fly trapped in a cobweb in the corner of the ceiling. He struggled to control a smile as he equated the fly with the vast and pompous R.S.M. As the fly was trapped in the web so was the grotesque upper crust fart choking on Charlie's verbal crap.

"It's taking a chance, sir," Charlie continued. "But he's to report to the C.O. the moment he hits camp. I think it would be best, sir, if he was kept off the booze and remained here for the night, sir. Bags of black coffee and a good cold shower, plus a good night's sleep, that should do the trick. It'll also allow him time to get rid of the smell of booze, sir."

"Right! Driver, put your ambulance in the motor pool and report to the guard room. The cook here will fix you with food. Report to me at nine in the morning and I'll give you a chitty explaining the delay. Right!"

Ignoring the intended dismissal, Charlie couldn't resist adding a little trimmings to his tale. But listening to him Harry still concentrated on the spider's meal.

"Our C.O. is a regular like yourself, sir," Charlie expanded his line, "and a strict disciplinarian." He noticed the row of ribbons on the R.S.M's chest. "One of the old school, sir."

"Don't overdo it, Charlie," Harry almost prayed to himself. That cynical look and that inverted 'V' over the eyebrow of the R.S.M. unnerved him. "Take it easy, mate..." But Charlie had pulled it off and, arms swinging, the R.S.M. strode out of the cook house a smug smile on his overfed, over-superior face.

"Report to me at the guard room at nine, driver," he finally dismissed Charlie.

"You bastard, Charlie, you pulled it off," Harry chuckled with glee as the two of them gathered the eggs and bread, shouting as they departed, "Thanks a lot, chef."

Driving to the girls' house again Harry asked his mate, "What's all this crap about Seventh Day Adventists, Charlie? What the hell are they?"

"Fucked if I know. When I was called up we had to do church parade at the depot. This one sod dodged it every time. He said he was a Seventh Day Adventist. It just came to my mind then."

They had no difficulty finding the house this time and both girls were almost delirious to see them again in such a short time. After they had both showered in cold water they fell on a meal of fresh steak. It was their first fresh meat for many months. Tinned potatoes in olive oil after a slight argument as they shook several unlabelled tins before deciding they had found potatoes. Tinned peas. Followed by tinned rice spiced with nutmeg found in Francesca's pantry. All this was washed down with a couple of bottles of white wine and before they retired Harry played several tunes on an old treadle organ found in an empty room.

It was well past eight when they woke. They breakfasted on a hurried cup of coffee and a sandwich each. Fortunately they had very little time for a long drawn out farewell, but Francesca must

310

have sensed that this would be their final farewell for now she couldn't hide her feelings and tears welled in her eyes and flowed down her cheeks while Sophia, as usual, became hysterical.

Captain Smithers was standing on the verandah of the guardroom when the ambulance sped through the hospital gates and skidded to a halt.

"Sorry we're a bit late, sir, had difficulty finding the place," Charlie apologised.

"Lying bastards, you've been down at the brothels getting you leg over," he snorted and grinned. They both smiled. This was their kind of man.

"Chance would be a fine thing sir," Harry replied as he helped the officer's batman to stow the gear in the back of the ambulance. Little did the officer realise how near the mark he'd been, except the girls' house was nothing like a brothel.

"Don't rush it, driver, my orderly has more gear to bring over."

Taking a chance they went back to the officers' mess kitchen and sat at the table.

"Any char going, chef?" Charlie was at it again.

"Christ, chef, don't you ever sleep?"

The cook had his back to them stirring a large steaming hot dixie of porridge.

"Help yourselves. Boiling water there. Take one of those small teapots. Fancy a dish of porridge?"

"No thanks, chef." Harry stared at a large tray of crispy bacon on the stove. "Wouldn't say no to a bacon sandwich, chef."

"Help yourself."

The chef sat on the bench at the opposite side of the table and filled a large bowl of porridge, then he scooped the cream from the top of a bucket of milk.

"Some fucking ructions here last night," he sighed gloomily. "There was a riot in the bloody mess. Some bastard son of a bitch stole a couple of slices of steak. The officers wanted to commit murder because they could only have a slice not much bigger than a postage stamp. They accused me and the cook sergeant of nicking it. The sergeant had a go at me and I accused him of taking it to his Itey piece. Him, he threatened to put me in the fizzer and I said that was alright by me, then I could tell the C.O. where most of the rations go." The cook slurped at the creamy bowl of porridge. "Don't suppose you saw anything suspicious did you?"

"I noticed that fat, buffalo toothed old R.S.M. couldn't keep his beady eyeballs off them when he was here," Harry replied, his face a mask of innocence. But he and Charlie hurriedly finished off their tea and bacon sandwiches and beat a hurried retreat.

Captain Smithers was waiting for them, shaking hands and saying goodbye to the R.S.M.

"Goodbye, R.S.M. and thanks for everything. Perhaps we'll meet again someday."

"I do hope so, sir," he lied.

Charlie suppressed a cynical sniff. Captain Smithers was going to a front line unit and the doughty R.S.M. was jolly happy, what, back at base General Hospital making life hell for the other ranks and quite content with his well fed, more likely for survival situation.

The trip back was uneventful. Charlie had his foot pressed down to the floor. At times the ambulance took the beds on two wheels and the officer sitting in Harry's seat was gripping it for dear life. Harry sat on the petrol tins, Spag firmly on his lap. Charlie knew it was N.A.A.F.I. cigarette and chocolate issue day and he sure as hell had no intention of missing out.

Harry instructed the officer to press his feet hard against the dash board to prevent himself from falling from the seat. Charlie was taking the corners like a demented rally driver. The captain's face took on an ashen aspect, fear clenching his mouth tight in a perpetual grin. It was impossible to smoke. In record time they reached the camp and Harry and the driver jumped to the ground with Captain Smithers looking as if he hardly dared to believe he'd survived the trip.

They dropped the officer's kit outside the office and Captain Smithers remained silent as he crawled out of the cab. He hadn't spoken once since they'd hit the main coast road. Now he stared at both of them hard, as his hand went to his breast pocket where he extracted a small note book and pencil.

"What's your name?" he asked Harry. "I take it you're the medic?"

"Yes, sir, Jackson, sir." The officer nodded towards Charlie. "Your name?"

"Williams, sir."

Harry gave Charlie a puzzled look. They had thought this officer wasn't too bad, not it looked as if they were really in for the high jump.

"You... You're not going to report us are you, sir?"

Smithers gave them a long withering look and slowly walked around them, and assessed each of them up and down as if making sure they were still in one piece.

"No, driver, I am not going to report you," he said slowly and in the grimmest of tones. "I am just making a note that I never, and I mean never, intend to ride that fucking ambulance with you two mad bastards ever again."

CHAPTER 30

There was very little doubt about it. The Italians themselves were fed up with the war.

The invincible German army had suffered an ignominious defeat at Stalingrad and the British had pushed them out of North Africa. Now a quivering Italian leadership realised that in the war they had been so happy to join when Britain stood alone, they were no longer the prancing victors, so when the rumour went around that the division was to take part in a landing on the mainland of Italy everyone was prepared to believe it.

The unit was now at full strength for the first time in many months and most of them would congregate at the divisional club most nights to drink the weak local beer and the strong local wine, the latter leaving everyone who imbibed with a sore thick head the next morning. But to Harry the attraction at the club was to rattle the stained ivories on the tinny piano.

It was the highlight of his life and he would play for two and three hours every night. For some reason that he could not fathom out, he would always start with 'Roses of Picardy.' It seemed as if some unknown hand was guiding his fingers over the keys, he played it so frequently that it became known as his signature tune. As soon as he stopped playing the tune the requests would start flowing in, each one reminding some man of an incident at home. But he always finished with the same tune he started with. He just couldn't understand why that tune. Sometimes in the bivvi he would hear the tune pulsating through his brain.

One night he was sleepless, it must have been at least three in the morning when he went to the water's edge to relieve himself. Sitting down he stared at the far horizon, a sliver of moon crouched over casting a million reflections across the wavelets. He was thinking of nothing important when that tune started to ram itself into his brain. He could think of nothing else, so much so that when he returned to his bivvi it was another three hours before he felt the calmness of sleep. That night at the club he played it over and over again till he heard a chorus of "Give it a rest, Harry," so he settled down to a series of Gershwin tunes, his favourites.

They were laying in their bivvi that night when he told Charlie, "I just don't know what comes over me, Charlie, that 'Roses of Picardy' just pushes itself into my brain, it's as if someone is trying to give me a message. It's strange really, when I am playing the tune I feel so much at ease. Some nights I just can't sleep thinking of it."

"Might be a message. Who knows - you might just finish up there."

He laughed it off as a joke. But a cold shiver ran down Harry's spine and for once he didn't join in Charlie's joke. For two days Harry remained in a melancholy mood, a mood that wasn't a stranger to many desert veterans.

Two days later they had just finished their routine jobs and were laying outside their bivvi when Corporal Sykes came striding over shouting at the top of his screeching voice,

"On parade everyone, no exceptions, every man and officer on parade."

A group of officers and N.C.O.s were already gathered outside the orderly room tent.

"Wonder what's up Harry, must be bloody important to get the officers out of their flea pits."

The C.O. emerged from his tent on one of those rare occasions to address the parade. That job was usually left to the R.S.M. The C.O. was a little unsteady on his legs, bleary eyed and looking the worse for wear.

"I thought you said the C.O. was a Seventh Day Adventist, Charlie?" Harry spoke from the corner of his mouth.

"No, Harry, you got me wrong. I said he was advocating seven days opening. That R.S.M. must have misunderstood me."

His holiness mounted two upturned ammo boxes that had been prepared for him, the R.S.M. steadying his elbow as he stepped up.

The Sergeant shouted, "Silence in the ranks," and glared at Charlie who was in deep conversation with Harry.

"Right men," the C.O. shouted with a slight slur in his voice. "You all know there has been some activity in the division, it must be obvious to everyone, even the most stupid, that there is something afoot. There have been plenty of rumours flying around. I would like to squash these rumours, but that would be as impossible as stopping a tiger tank with a rotten egg. All I can tell you is, be prepared to embark at any time. We are on a twenty-four hour standby but I don't know the destination."

He waited for the rippling of soft talk to die down.

"Some of you have been in the desert for two years, some of the regulars have been in perhaps longer, and I know it's at least six years since some of you were in England. I would like to say we will be on our way home. Alas, I can't, we still have another job ahead of us. All I can say in truth is, you will be saying goodbye to the desert forever. I know most of you have cursed it. Some of you lads are just in your late teens or early twenties. In years to come you will look on this exciting period with nostalgia."

314

There were stifled laughs amongst the crowd, the C.O. held his hand up for silence.

"I know you may laugh now, but mark my words, in years to come you will consider this amongst the highlights of your life. After the war when you are all back to your peacetime jobs, farmers, miners, dustmen, bus drivers, and those that work on the railways, going to work at a set time, reading the national papers in the mornings and then the local rag at night, pictures once or twice weekly. You will miss the comradeship and changes of scenery."

A ripple of laughter went through the assembled parade. His mood changed to a more serious nature. They had lost many good men and officers, there were new faces on the parade.

"Unfortunately we have left many comrades behind, we must never forget them. Some of the bodies have been brought back to a large military cemetery a few miles from here. Tomorrow I have been given permission for the unit to visit it; we will hold a parade and a few minutes silence. Other than that, if anyone leaves the unit and expects to be more than an hour away, let them know at company office. When we do embark it will not be as a unit, the ambulances will be attached to various units as usual. Now for heavens sake, from now on read daily orders. Good luck to everyone of you."

Two days later Harry returned to his bivvi after reading daily orders and didn't look too happy. Charlie, as usual, was stretched out on the sand beside his bivvi, Spag laying full length across Charlie's chest. Dog and man had been together almost since the big push started and long before Harry joined the unit. Apart from his little girl back home, Spag was the only thing Charlie loved. Now Harry was trying to figure out the easiest way to break the bad news to him and was so absorbed in his thoughts he didn't hear Sykes approaching, a triumphant grin across his face.

"Read daily orders, Charlie?" Sykes quizzed, still grinning.

Charlie squinted up at Sykes through half closed eyes to avoid the devastating rays from the sun. The look on Sykes face told him he wasn't the bearer of good news.

Sykes repeated himself. "Read daily orders, Williams?"

His wide grin revealing his tobacco stained teeth. Sykes had been waiting to pay Charlie back ever since that incident when Charlie almost choked him, so bad news for Charlie meant exactly the opposite for Sykes, he revelled in the suspense. Charlie closed his eyes again.

"Right spotty chops, let's have it."

315

"Piss off, Williams, you're supposed to read daily orders, go and find out for yourself."

Harry brought his elbow back smartly, making contact with Sykes ribs causing him to bend over with pain.

"Alright, Sykes, don't stand there gloating, and I won't give you the pleasure of breaking the news, piss off and do a bit of crawling round the R.S.M. before I put my foot up your jacksie."

Charlie realised it was something serious; he sat up sharply. Sykes was still bent forward recovering from the dig in the ribs he'd received from Harry. Charlie's head caught under the corporal's chin throwing him backwards.

"You bastard, Williams, you did that on purpose." He wiped his hand across his mouth looking for traces of blood. But Sykes remained seated, he wasn't going to miss telling Charlie the bad news.

Harry squatted down beside Charlie and stroked Spag's head. That dog was everything in the world to him out here.

"Sorry, mate, but the news is grim." He lit two cigarettes and gave one to Charlie.

"It's Spag, mate."

Harry drew his breath in sharply, it was almost a sigh and he could feel a lump rising in his throat.

"It's not just Spag but anyone who has a pet, you know - dogs, chickens, you all have to get rid of them."

Charlie didn't answer, he just stared out to sea and brought Spag closer towards him, stroking his head. Spag licked his fingers. All along he knew the day would come when they would have to part. It was certain, never mind what the circumstances, that he would never take Spag back to England.

"What will they do with them?" Charlie's throat was dry and his voice echoed the dryness.

"Don't really know, Charlie. Shoot them I suppose. You couldn't set him loose in the desert, he'd starve to death after you've mollycoddled him so all this time. Apart from that, if those wild desert dogs got hold of him they'd tear the poor little sod apart. After all, Charlie, you've done everything for him apart from wiping his arse after he's had a crap. It would be criminal to turn him loose."

"When do we take them?"

"Tomorrow, a lorry will take them out into the desert and Harvey will shoot them."

"No bastard is going to shoot Spag." Tears welled up in his eyes. He cradled the small dog in his arms and it buried its head into Charlie's armpits, its favourite position.

316

Charlie racked his brains for a solution. He should have left him with Francesca the last time he was there, she liked Spag and would have taken care of him. There was no possible chance he could go that far away from camp. The unit was on one hour's standby and the military police were patrolling the roads. Corporal Reynolds had tried that a few days ago. He'd borrowed the D.R.'s motorbike to try and see his Italian girlfriend in Tripoli. The Red Caps caught up with him after just five miles; he was now Private Reynolds.

Corporal Sykes kept his distance, a satisfied smirk on his face. At last he had one over on Williams and Sykes hated that bloody little dog. He moved quickly when he saw Charlie take his rifle from his cab and insert a clip of five cartridges. Charlie threw Spag's old blanket over his shoulder. Harry joined him and they walked right along the beach till they reached a deserted spot. Spag ran between their legs waiting for Charlie to throw a ball.

"You know it's the best thing to do, Charlie." Harry was just as upset as his mate.

Charlie never answered but quickened his pace as if he wanted to get the job over with as quickly as possible.

Charlie remained silent and Harry knew how a condemned man must feel. They stopped between two sand dunes that created a hollow, it looked like a small valley. Charlie bent over and fondled Spag's ears. He wagged his tail furiously and ran around in small circles dribbling. With tear stained eyes Charlie rammed a cartridge up the spout. Everything became blurred as the tears filled his eyes and his shoulders shook. Spag pressed close to Charlie's leg. A tear fell and splashed on his back, he turned to lick it away, his pale watery eyes met Charlie's.

It was too much for Harry, he turned away, his throat dry, and he felt a lump swelling, he choked as he forced back a tear. He had seen men torn to pieces, burnt to death, maimed beyond description and crippled for life, blinded and driven out of their minds, yet he had only felt like this on one other occasion. The night he picked up that 45 and put another war casualty out of his misery, an action he would never forget. Yet he felt so bad over a small dog. Perhaps it was seeing Charlie suffer so much. They had become such firm friends and he looked upon Charlie as the brother he never had.

Charlie took a rubber ball from his pocket, the same one that Spag always played with, now half eaten away by Spag's sharp teeth. He played about with it for a few minutes, then showed it to Spag. He wagged his tail furiously, waiting for Charlie to throw it. Then, with one mighty heave, Charlie let go the ball. It arched up into the air curving down and burying itself in the fine soft sand between the two dunes. Spag excitedly chased after the ball rolling over and over. Normally Harry and Charlie would be laughing themselves sick at the dog's antics.

With a triumphant jump, Spag tossed the ball in the air with his mouth. He was about to run back towards them when Charlie sighted him through the rifle sights. Spag was a perfect target; Charlie squeezed the trigger gently, the explosion rent the air. Charlie shuddered and Harry held his breath till he felt his lungs would burst. He had heard a similar shot and that still gave him nightmares. Charlie sank to his knees and buried his head in his hands. The rifle, blue smoke curling from the barrel, dropped from his hands into the sand.

Harry picked up the blanket and wrapped it round the small warm body. The shot had found its target, half Spag's head was blown away, the lower jaw sagging into a half grin, the teeth shattered into an irregular row.

Harry placed his hand on Charlie's shoulder.

"Come on, mate, let's bury him."

Harry scraped out a deep hole with his hands, but Charlie shook his head.

"Let's take him to that military cemetery. Old Solly and Mundy are buried there. We'll tell the old man we want to pay a last visit to their graves."

When they arrived at the cemetery, men were still bringing in bodies from the surrounding desert, pathetic bundles wrapped in blankets, some of them reduced to mere skeletons. The cemetery was laid out on the same lines as all Commonwealth war graves. Local Arabs were building a wall three feet high around the perimeter. Rows of temporary crosses stood in perfectly straight lines. New rows of graves recently dug waited open for fresh bodies. Two officers, both of them padres, and a Pioneer officer, stood in a small group talking while Pioneer N.C.O.s supervised local Arabs at work.

Snapping to attention Charlie saluted, with Spag wrapped in his blanket under his arm.

"Could I bury my small dog here, sir? Perhaps over in the far corner?"

"It's a military cemetery, lad, we can't bury him here." The padre in charge was a small man who would have looked more at home living in some small village tucked away in the English countryside. He sported two rows of medals on his bush shirt, most of them from the first war. The colourful display glared out sharply from the drab khaki shirt. He looked sympathetically at Charlie's tear stained face, then at the other two officers and shrugged his shoulders.

318

"How long did you have the dog, driver?"

"Over a year, sir, almost two, it went everywhere with me."

"Yes, I remember you, driver. Weren't you with the Hussars when we crossed into Tunisia? Always had this small yellow dog snapping at your heels?"

"Yes, sir, that was Spag." Charlie lifted the pathetic bundle, half choked he said, "I had to shoot him, sir."

"I am sorry to hear that, driver. This sort of thing will happen again and again for the next few days till the division embarks. Well, I have no objections if Captain Martin doesn't."

Captain Martin didn't object, he just shrugged his shoulders in complete indifference. He had been an infantry officer in the first war and after demob had joined his father's undertaker's business. When he volunteered for the second world war he was far too old for active service. However his invaluable experience in the disposal of the dead earned him a commission in the Pioneer Corps. It could be said that his life had been devoted to the dead, and another body, human or animal, meant nothing to him.

"Drop him in one of the graves before we fill it."

Charlie shook his head.

"I would rather not, sir, if you don't mind, can I bury him in the far corner?"

"Please yourself." He turned his back on Charlie and continued his conversation with the two padres.

Alone that night, they sat at a table in the corner of the club room. Charlie stared into the empty beer glasses. Usually at this time Harry would be playing the piano, but an air of gloom hung over the pair of them. Harry sat there silent, making patterns on the table with the bottom of his damp glass. Harry nodded his head towards Sykes who was walking towards them.

"Here comes old shit face, Charlie."

Sykes took one of the vacant chairs and sat down with them.

"Twelve dogs to get rid of tomorrow, Charlie. Heard you shot that little bastard of yours today, couldn't get rid of him quick enough, eh Charlie?"

As the fury built up inside him, Charlie remained silent. If he answered he wouldn't be responsible for his actions, and with the crowd around Sykes knew he was safe. Sykes pressed the issue.

"I would have done it for you, Charlie, if you'd asked me nicely. It would be doing the unit a favour."

Charlie slammed down the glass. It shattered into a hundred fragments flying around like shrapnel.

"Sykes, I would willingly put a bullet through that ugly head of yours and believe me I would be doing the whole Eighth Army a favour. Now why don't you piss off, no one invited you to sit here, you bloody arsehole crawler."

Sykes jumped up sharply sending his chair flying backwards and sliding along the smooth red tiles.

"Miserable bastard. I was only wanting to do you a favour," he shouted, as he retreated towards the bar in double quick time.

Alone, they slipped back into their melancholy mood.

Tight lipped, Charlie said, "One of these days I will swing for that bastard. When I think of the decent blokes lost in this unit and that dead beat is still around it makes you wonder if there is any justice in this world."

At the continued insistence of the crowd, Harry reluctantly took his place at the piano and played a couple of tunes. When he looked up and saw that Charlie had left the club, he jumped from the stage amidst a load of booing and ran after his mate. Out side it was almost a full moon. Charlie was strolling along the seashore, his hands thrust deep in his pockets, a solitary figure. He stopped and gazed out to sea. Harry decided to leave him alone and return to his bivvi.

The camp was a hive of activity. Men were shouting at each other, striking tents and packing their gear.

"What's going on, Chappie?" queried Harry.

"We are moving out at midnight. They have just gone up to the club to call the men back to their units. My driver has gone to Tripoli to see his bird."

"How the bloody hell did he manage that with all those bloody Red Caps on the road?"

"Well you know Toddy, he's almost as bad as Charlie where women are concerned. It seems he knew one of the Red Caps; went to school with him. Fixed him and his mate up with a couple of bints. Now when they are on road patrol they let him through. There's worse to come. He's borrowed Early's motorbike so they'll both be in the crap. The unit has to assemble on the main road at twelve."

Charlie returned just as Harry was packing the bivvi away into the ambulance. Everything was happening so quickly, soon it would all be a memory. Would the colonel be proved right, would this become part of their lives they would never forget, would it become just a nostalgic memory? The unit, although small, was made up of men from all parts of the British Isles, all with their own dialects and local slang. Now all the dialects had become linked, together with the occasional word of Arabic, German, Italian and any other language they had picked up on their travels, creating a dialect of their own. Would they ever remember the bad things? The sand that penetrated everything and everywhere, the flies, and a scratch that would rapidly turn into a foul smelling suppurating desert sore? The dry heat that knew no bounds making every vehicle feel like a blast furnace causing the sweat to ooze from the body in small rivulets? The equally cold nights? But worst of all, the shortage of water, most of it with a saline tang or tasting of chlorine, reminiscent of the days Harry had spent at the local swimming baths back home? Yet Harry had to admit it had had its compensations. He would wander away from his ambulance and sit alone in the sand wondering at the millions of stars hanging above his head as if they were attached to invisible silken threads. Then there had been times when the full moon had turned the sands into a silvery wonder land. These lonely sessions had given him time to think, out there his head was clear, with only the distant guns to remind him what he was out here for. Maybe the colonel was right. In times to come it would stir up distant memories.

Harry turned round when he heard what he thought was a voice from the distance.

"Bloody hell, I spoke to you three times and you didn't answer. Got sand bunged up in your lug holes?"

"Sorry, Charlie, my mind was miles away. What did you say?"

"Never mind. I only asked you if you'd tied the brew cans on the back. I've done the job myself now."

Chapter 31

The unit was drawn up on the main road well before sun up. Most of the men walked about with their great coat collars turned up, stamping their feet and rubbing their hands. For those still abed, the small Scots sergeant, his great coat dragging along the road, slammed the palm of his hand against the vehicle.

"Rise and shine, rise and shine, hands off your cocks and on with your socks," he yelled.

Knowing Charlie and Harry would leave things till the last minute, he opened the back doors of the ambulance, but they were both wide awake sitting up smoking.

"Out of the flea pit, Williams, you lazy Sassenach," the scotsman bellowed.

The unit was now wide awake with a urgency and knowledge that something different was about to happen. Brew cans rattled along the column, beacon-like flames bringing them to boil. But this morning was different for Charlie as they no longer had to let Spag out for walkies. Charlie's bare leg searched for the cold linoleum, he sucked in his breath and the remainder of his body tore itself away from the comforting warm blankets. Completely nude he made his way to the back doors. Harry stared blankly at his bare back and then with one swift movement, taking the blankets with him, pushed Charlie to one side and jumped to the ground - and only just in time. Charlie strained at the leash and let go a blast of wind that would have done justice to a constipated elephant after feeding on wet grass for a week.

Harry went on parade with his mug still in his hand. Corporal Sykes ticked off their names. Someone held a hurricane lamp above Sykes and the festering pimples stood out sharply against the dull yellow flame.

"Right, Williams, and you, Jackson, stand over there with the rest."

He jabbed his pencil to the right. His great coat was wide open and the bulge of his shorts too much of a temptation for Charlie who flicked the tip of the bulge with his fingers.

"Been playing with yourself I see, Sykes."

Sykes winced and doubled up with pain and Charlie passed without faltering looking the picture of innocence.

"Don't be bloody funny, Williams," Sykes hissed through his teeth.

"Right, men," the R.S.M. came up behind the corporal, giving him a look of contempt, "What's the matter with you, Sykes? Been abusing yourself again?"

The R.S.M. turned to the men. "Ambulance crews report to your regiments," he ordered and gave each crew a slip of paper.

It was like a raffle except this could seal their fate, depending on which regiment they picked.

"You report as soon as possible at first light, so for those that haven't eaten, do so immediately. The division will be embarking later this morning."

This caused a murmur amongst the assembled crowd. So that night had definitely been the final night in North Africa.

They could hardly believe their ears nor could they contain the excitement welling up inside them. The destination didn't matter, just a change of scenery would suffice.

The R.S.M. continued. "I understand the convoy will leave at midday, but knowing the services I wouldn't bank on it."

This caused gusts of laughter.

"However, we do have to be at the assembly point by noon. For the ambulance crews leaving the unit, I wish to say good luck and also that I hope we shall all be together again as a working unit."

"Any ideas where we're going, sir?"

"Griffiths." His rich Cornish accent was unmistakable in the darkness. He was the only Cornishman in the unit. "You should know better than to ask a question like that. No doubt as soon as your aboard."

But Griffiths, like some of the men, still clung to the hope they would be homeward bound in spite of all indications to the contrary. A new campaign was a certainty; freshly painted camouflage on the vehicles, extra fuel and rations for all of them and above all the unit brought up to battle strength.

Both Harry and Charlie were overjoyed to be posted to a tank regiment - one which they had been attached to on many occasions so that most of the faces would be familiar. They just had time to make their acquaintance with the medical sergeant and M.O. when orders were given to move off. The embarkation point was twenty miles from Tripoli and the marshalling area clearly marked with the divisional sign. The area itself was made up of heavy steel mesh laid on the beach right to the water edge and it covered many acres. Red Caps directed them to their posts out on the mesh exactly the same positions they would have had in the hold of the landing craft. In the same way the other units were laid in front of the steel leviathans pulled up on the beach, the great doors wide open at the front as if waiting to swallow them up.

Lighter vehicles, lorries, scout cars and utilities were already aboard, hoisted to the top deck by a gigantic lift in the centre of the landing craft, not unlike the lift used in aircraft carries to hoist the planes to the flight deck.

Now it was their turn to be swallowed by the monster. Engines revved and tanks discharged clouds of black smoke. Harry experienced that familiar feeling. A tingling sensation rose up the insides of his legs and then reached for the pit of his stomach, making his hands tremble. He would be alright. Once he was inside a calmness would settle over him. The ambulance moved up a couple of yards.

The heavy treads of the tyres gripped the steel mesh, hesitated a couple of seconds and then, as Charlie accelerated, the ambulance shot forward right into the path of a large Sherman tank. It hit the back of the ambulance and in seconds reduced it to a useless pile of wood and canvas. They both jumped clear just in time but the tank continued at speed as if nothing had happened, taking with it one of the ambulances back wheels, which was trapped between its tracks.

Regaining their feet, Harry and Charlie stared at the heap of rubbish which had been the ambulance that had taken them through the roughest part of the North African campaign, and all they could salvage from the wreck was Charlie's beloved brew can.

He picked it up and stared at the tank. "If he had squashed that, Harry, I would have gone and pissed down his turret," he muttered and made a two fingered 'v' sign towards the tank.

A Red Cap came bounding over.

"Who the hell is responsible for this lot?" he blustered.

"Don't ask me, corp," Harry answered. "We were just going to board when this bloody great tank loomed up from nowhere and hit us up the arse."

"Like all bloody accidents, corp, never a cop around when you want one," Charlie butted in.

"Cut that crap out," the Red Cap snarled at Charlie.

"It's the truth, corp. Someone should have been directing the traffic." Charlie was still vexed at losing his ambulance. "Been with me since the start."

"What do you expect? Someone to hold your bloody hand? We're supposed to get a whole division and some extras aboard these craft by noon. The convoy is pulling out at any time now."

"Well you had better piss off and do your job then, hadn't you?"

Charlie was just getting into his stride. He loved having a go at authority and he knew he was on a safe wicket here. The Red Cap couldn't place him under arrest.

But before the argument escalated the unit transport officer came rushing up. He could hardly believe his eyes as a bulldozer arrived and started pushing the heap of rubbish towards the sea.

"Bloody hell, Williams, trust you to make a balls up."

"It wasn't my fault. Bloody Red Caps should have been directing the vehicles aboard," Charlie defended himself.

At this the Red Cap's face turned a bright purple and he was about to make more of the situation when one of the unit D.R.s passed by and the officer waved him down.

"Take Williams to a reserve vehicle compound," he instructed, scribbled a requisition chit and handed it to Charlie. "Get yourself a bloody ambulance, and this time try and take care of it."

On his return, Harry was waiting beside the ship and Charlie was ordered to reverse straight aboard, all the tanks and armoured vehicles already having done so. Then as the great steel doors shut after them, encasing them in the gloomy interior, Charlie gasped, "Hell, Harry, I know how Jonah must have felt in the belly of that damn whale."

"That's sod all, Charlie. Do you realise that when those bloody doors open again we will be right in front and we'll be the first ones out?"

Two crew members secured the ambulance to the deck with steel clamps. The ship's engines revved up and they could feel the keel dragging along the sandy bottom into deep water. The stern rose up and down as the ship's propellers churned up the bottom.

"Alright, you pongoes," the sailor shouted above the din of the ship and he pointed to a small door, "that's your mess deck."

They didn't hesitate for stench of the hold was thick with fumes from the vehicles, the ship's engines and navy blue paint. They grabbed their haversacks, steel helmets and gas masks, but stopped dead at the door. The smell of the mess decks was worse than the hold for they had the added discomfort of sweaty bodies, cigarette smoke and men who were lying on the steel mesh cots in the throes of violently fetid sea sickness, and this with the ship hardly having reached deep water.

"Reminds me, Charlie, coming from that stink in the hold into this stink, of that old saying, if you pissed in the Severn at Worcester they'd be drinking it at Bristol," Harry tried to joke.

The mess deck, for want of a better word, was like the double skin of the ship's hull, the inside wall separated them from the hold and the outer wall and the ship's hull too. The walls were about six feet apart. Each wall had three steel mesh beds on top of each other that folded flat against the wall during the day, and

325

when lowered at night they were left with about two feet to pass through.

"Now I know how those poor sods felt in those convict ships to Aussie in the old days, Charlie," Harry remarked.

They picked up their life preservers laying on the bunks and made their way towards the top deck, available only by a straight steel ladder. Not only did you need to be a contortionist to use it but also have a good head for heights. Both Harry and Charlie had travelled extensively by sea during the war and knew the drill. Harry also took the added precaution of carrying a flat half bottle of brandy in his back pocket. In this respect he had been fortunate, one of the Arabs had managed to get the local brandy and sold it to him for five hundred cigarettes.

"That stuff will make you go blind, Harry. They use it here to strip paint off the walls," Charlie had warned him.

"If it's that potent, Charlie, it's just what I want. If I have to get in the sea I don't want to die of hypothermia."

As in the hold, the upper deck was crammed with vehicles. At times they were forced to turn sideways to pass the vehicles, stepping over the shackles securing them. In one corner they saw a three tonner with a red cross and Charlie brightened up.

"We were told to report to you, sarge, as soon as we boarded the ship."

A small butt dangled from the corner of the sergeant's mouth. The smoke lazily curled upwards forcing the sergeant to close one eye.

Without removing the butt he said, "You're a lying bastard, Williams. You know and I know that you haven't been in contact with the C.O. since our pep talks yesterday. We were just watching that debacle with that blood tub of yours and that tank a few minutes ago. Call yourself a driver?"

Normally this would have been the start of an argument for Charlie, but there was a chance of a bed on deck here.

"Hard luck about the wagon, sarge. I was attached to that ambulance. But the old man was up at the motor pool and gave me my instructions."

"Cut the bullshit, Williams, the old man boarded the other landing ship an hour ago. What you mean is it stinks to high heaven down in the mess deck. My lorry is sitting up here in the healthy atmosphere and your brain ticked over in its usual twisted way. Sorry, Williams, I am full up."

But he was still a little cautious, after all there was a possibility he could have bumped into the C.O. and the sight of those powerful binoculars hanging around Charlie's neck clinched the deal. They may come in handy during the voyage. "Alright

Williams, there's a pile of stretchers and blankets in the lorry. You and your mate help yourselves - under the lorry if you don't mind. I've had the doubtful pleasure of hearing that morning serenade of yours."

"Thanks, sarge, I won't forget your generosity in a hurry." Charlie turned to Harry. "Go and get the gear from the bunks," he told him.

Sleeping under the lorry turned out to be much better than inside it, and shielded on each side by bren carriers, and with unlimited blankets it became quite pleasant.

In three columns the landing craft headed out to sea under the protection of heavy ships, and they in turn were screened by swift moving destroyers and corvettes and M.T.Bs. Three large aircraft carriers took up position at the end of the landing craft.

Charlie carried out a detailed inspection of the ships through his binoculars. "God, Harry, you should see the guns on those bloody battleships. They're as big as sewer pipes." He handed binoculars to Harry and then to the sergeant.

"I'm bloody pleased to see we're in the centre of it," Charlie said to the sergeant.

It was mid-afternoon when they ate their first meal of boiled potatoes still in their jackets, corned beef and afterwards boiled rice with a blob of black treacle slapped in the middle. It tasted good for they'd been so absorbed in the excitement of the preparation that they hadn't eaten for over eight hours. By the size of the galley on the landing craft it was a miracle they managed to warm the meal at all. It was so small that a good efficient housewife would have refused to work in it.

Hardly had they settled down to their meal, when the ships tannoy system crackled out in a distorted voice that sounded like a man shouting on a gut tanked up with whisky. Silence fell along the deck as every man strained to catch the words.

"As you can see the convoy is now well out to sea. At all times every man amongst you must carry his life preserver. Those amongst you who cannot swim would be advised to keep it half inflated. Half filled they will keep you afloat should it be necessary. Perhaps in the water one of your mates who's a good swimmer will fully inflate it for you."

"Some bleeding hopes," Charlie chuckled. "If a torpedo hits this sardine can it will sink faster than a lead filled balloon, and those that can swim will be off like a rocket... That's of course, if he don't get killed in the explosion."

The tannoy crackled on. "Should we have to abandon ship leap as far away from the ship as possible, grabbing with one hand the Mae West, pulling it down when you hit the water. Although it's only rubber it can come up and give you a nasty blow under the chin. With the other hand grab your family jewels, hang on to them tight. From the height of the deck to the water is higher than you think and if your balls hit that water it could be bloody painful. During the passage do not, and I must emphasise it, do not throw any gash into the water - that means cigarette packets, old letters, newspapers... In fact, nothing... Use gash bins scattered around the deck. Those papers floating about could tell an experienced U boat commander a convoy had just passed. He would radio his mates ahead, and we would have a reception committee waiting for us. Then, before you realise it you'll all be up to your balls in water."

He waited for the laughter to clear after his corny joke, for at the moment the men were so elated they would laugh at anything.

"Now we come to the most important item, smoking. After dark there is to be no smoking on the top deck, and you men sleeping on top deck no crafty drags. Any man caught smoking on deck will be immediately thrown in the chokey on the arse end of the ship, right over the propellers. It's a nasty uncomfortable place, no blankets and just the steel floor. Oh, and don't worry it's not cold. In fact it gets like a furnace. Moreover, all you will get down there is bread and water, and after you land you will be court marshalled and receive six months in what you pongoes call the glass house. In my book that's too lenient. If I had my way you would be shot on the spot. For not only do you risk your own life and the men of this ship, but you jeopardise the whole convoy and even the landings. A cigarette's glow can be seen for miles out at sea."

"Fucking hell, it's the reincarnation of Captain Bligh," someone said.

The tannoy continued, "You will get a warning of a series of short blasts to abandon ship. Should this happen, get as far away from the ship as possible, for as you can see it's just a hollow carcass and, should it go down it will make a dreadful suction and take anything nearby down with it."

"That's me for the chop," someone remarked. "I can't swim a bloody stroke."

"As yet I am unable to tell you your final destination. All I can say is the passage will take three days so make yourselves as comfortable as possible. The weather bods inform us the weather will stay fresh and the sea calm, so make the best of the passage and look upon it as one of Thomas Cook's Med cruises."

"I bet Thomas Cook didn't make them sleep under any sodding lorry," Charlie grumbled.

"Some of you bastards are never satisfied," the sergeant said, hardly stirring from his sitting position on the tail end of the tonner. He'd changed from cigarettes in favour of his old pipe and puffed away contentedly.

Harry watched the great red ball of sun sink lower on the horizon and then with a final flourish it dropped leaving the sea and the sky a kaleidoscope of colour flashing on the undersides of the few clouds left scurrying across the sky. Darkness shrouded the ship. Charlie joined Harry at the ship's rails and they watched silently as the blunt ship's bows ploughed through the blue fluorescent sea.

The grey hulk of a corvette came alongside like some ghostly apparition and ran parallel to the landing ship for a few minutes almost colliding at times. A message was shouted from bridge to bridge, coherent as the words floated away on the breeze, but just as quickly as the small boat had appeared it vanished into the darkness once more.

Charlie and Harry vanished below deck for a few puffs of their cigarettes before settling down for the night. It was deathly quiet, each man hardly daring to speak for noise could be heard for quite a distance. They spent the night fitfully sleeping.

Most of the day was spent playing cards. They would sit on their vehicles while the ship's crew hosed down the decks.

"You do realise, Charlie, that when we hit that beach our ambulance will be the first off, and if there is much shit flying we'd be on the receiving end."

"So what?" Charlie's attitude was completely indifferent. "First off or last off - what's the difference? If your name is on the list what the hell does it matter? I once knew a chap that went through hell and to be on the safe side he dug his slit trench deep - too bloody deep. There was no shelling and what happened? The bloody sides of the trench caved in and buried the poor sod alive!"

Fresh water was in short supply, which made it rather tough for the ambulance crew. They had plenty on the ambulance but weren't allowed back into the hold. Shaving in salt water was horrendous. They were issued with special soap as they could only shave and wash in sea water.

After a couple of attempts Charlie threw his soap away in disgust and allowed his stubble to grow. "I feel as if my jaws been savaged by a blunt lawn mower."

Harry assured him it looked like it had.

At lunch time on the third day the convoy altered course, although it had been zig-zagging since leaving the North African coast. There was a definite turn towards the east.

Harry sprang to his feet and rushing to the ship rail he pointed to the far horizon and shouted, "Land!"

Charlie focused his powerful binoculars in the direction Harry was pointing.

"Ships, Harry, and bloody big ones at that."

He focused his glasses on their own convoy. The flagship had made no move to alter course so he assumed, correctly, they weren't enemy ships, and as they tore through the seas to join them he made out the American flag at the stern of the one in the lead. "Yanks, Harry. It certainly looks as if this is going to be a big show."

It turned out to be a combined American and British fleet from Gibraltar.

"Better get our lifebelts on," some wag from the crowd gathering round Charlie said, and everyone laughed, false laughter, which eased the tension, in the way releasing a tightly wound up spring might.

The combined fleet took up their positions without reducing speed. A few signal flags were hoisted, but to the troops they meant very little and everyone felt a little safer in the bosoms of the growing fleet. Lamps blinked and flickered tapping out messages and a Yankee torpedo boat sped through the lines of landing craft, everyone cheering as it passed.

As they pressed deeper into Mussolini's private lake more ships joined them from other North African ports. The tension mounted, for everyone knew that this night would be their final one aboard the ship and while some were relieved, others were a bit apprehensive.

It felt as if they had just dozed off into a stunted sleep when the ship was rocked by a terrific explosion.

Harry lifted his head smartly and caught his forehead on the underside of the lorry. Lights spun in front of his eyes and he gasped, "Christ, we haven't landed yet and I've been wounded."

He took his hand away from his head but couldn't tell if it was blood or grease in the dim light. They scrambled from their beds and rolled into the open, grabbing their Mae Wests. The wet decks saturated their trousers but they didn't notice the discomfort, as they were under the impression the ship had been torpedoed. Men ran about the deck and others who had braved the stench on the mess decks came up the ladders.

Several explosions soon followed and great water spouts rose from the tranquil sea, shells screamed overhead as the enemy opened fire only to be answered by the giant guns from the capitol ships. The shoreline could just be made out in the early morning mist, and as the large shells landed the shoreline became an inferno, the shells heading landwards so fast it looked as if every ship was trying to outclass his neighbour. Field guns never sounded so high pitched as these shells. Harry held his hands over his ears as they passed under a giant British warship and felt as if his eardrums would burst. In half an hour it would be daylight and they could already make out the infantry landing craft heading towards the shore completely shrouded in smoke and haze.

A shell landed between them and the next landing craft, the ship rocked and steel splinters tore into the hold through the flimsy hull.

"Prepare for landing," came the distorted voice over the tannoy. The ship's crew ran to their posts, unshackling the vehicles. N.C.O.s shouted orders, men prepared their small battle order haversacks, shells tore faster towards them, most dropping harmlessly into the sea, but a couple of landing craft had received direct hits and were making it as fast as their engines could take them towards the shore, smoke bellowing from the holds.

They clambered down the steep ladder and through the mess decks and into the hold. Already tanks were revving up. The air was thick and Charlie wet the scarf he always wore around his neck and covered his nose and face. This helped a little and Harry followed suit. A large Sherman tank was behind them. Charlie started his engine. He didn't want that monster pushing him into the drink. The engine faltered once, but the second time it started. Then cut off as soon as soon as it had warmed up.

There was little light in the ship's hold. Charlie and Harry felt the ship turn towards the shore and Harry felt that old sensation run up the inside of his thighs and settle in the pit of his stomach. He held his hand in front of him and found that it shook slightly. Two sailors unshackled the ambulance, and, while other crew members ran towards the large steel doors Harry tapped one of the sailors on his helmet.

"So, where are we mate?" he wanted to know.

"Salerno, Italy. Lucky bastards, all those birds waiting for you." The sailor eyed the ambulance and the large doors. "Your mob must be fucking desperate sending in the ambulance first. Good luck to you, mate. That bloody beach is like hell out there."

"Thanks, mate, for that vote of confidence."

Harry had to smile to himself, for at this moment the ship itself was in the most imminent danger, a prime target for enemy guns. A shell dropped alongside it causing it to roll violently and more shrapnel tore through the flimsy ship's plates, bounced off a tank and hit the upper deck. Harry held tight onto the sides of his seat. Charlie gripped the steering wheel till his knuckles turned white and more shrapnel tore into the ship's side as the enemy shells landed.

"Ever get the feeling you're not wanted, Harry?" Charlie said as he watched thin rays of sunlight streaming through the holes left by the shrapnel.

Harry smiled to himself in spite of the feeling which tore at his guts. A smoke would have come in handy. A petty officer came along inspecting the shackles and making sure the ratings had carried out their work efficiently, as he wanted no obstructions when vehicles left.

"Just watch the lights come on as you did in your training," he shouted into the cab.

"What bloody training? The only training we had was in Infantry landing craft."

If Charlie thought this would raise sympathy with the petty officer he was wrong. He just laughed and exclaimed, "That's the bloody army alright!"

An army major came up next.

"At the moment I don't know what's going on," he shouted at the top of his voice. "We should be ashore shortly. Who placed you here?"

Charlie explained the mishap at the embarkation point and the officer thought it all rather stupid for an ambulance to head the landing.

"We can return to North Africa and reload, sir, if you like. I don't think we're very welcome here."

The major gave Charlie a filthy look. "Just start the engine and keep your eyes on those lights above the doors," he snapped, pointing to the traffic light lookalike. "Have you tried that engine yet?"

Charlie nodded.

"Good. We don't want any cock ups. If your engine stalls get ready to jump for it. That tank behind won't wait. He'll be off like a rocket and take your ambulance with it."

The first crack of light appeared above the massive steel doors and the cool air rushed in like a miniature tornado. Harry could feel the hairs of his neck raising. This was it. His first grip on European soil after all these years. They both adjusted their steel helmets. It wasn't much protection, but it gave them some semblance of safety. Charlie shivered and shrugged his shoulders.

"What's the matter, Charlie? Someone walked over your grave?" Harry's voice sounded strained through the tightening of his throat muscles.

It was the worst thing he could say to Charlie, for in spite of his denials at times he was very superstitious.

"For fuck's sake, Harry, don't you say things like that - not even in a joke."

Charlie fell into a gloomy mood which was a bad start for the landing and Harry regretted his words, the tense atmosphere only being broken when they felt the ship grind along the sea bottom.

Immediately the great steel doors began slowly to part, creaking in defiance in spite of the great blobs of grease on the hinges. They struggled to release themselves and then, suddenly, they opened with a mighty crash, the ramp falling into position and shovelling the shingle forward a few feet at the same time.

For three days they had been part of a mighty organisation with their fate in the hands of a naval officer not much older than Charlie. Now, once more, they were on their own - a tiny fragment in a great wheel of destruction and instead it was their job to clear up the mess. A job just as important as that of an infantryman or a gunner, for they took a few weeks to train whereas Harry trained for three years. No longer did the army send inexperienced camp followers and untrained medical staff, most of the medics were highly trained.

The ambulance engine ran smoothly, ticking over, inaudible with all the noise around them, but the vibrations felt good and they moved forward with great confidence. Tension rose. Harry could feel his heart thumping against the walls of his chest. The landing area was centred in thick haze. Shell craters littered the beach and the clatter of heavy machine guns rattled their greeting with the unmistakable scream of mortar bombs tumbling through the air. Sweat ran down the insides of their steel helmets. Harry rubbed the sweat away from his eyes. Directly in front of them a party of infantrymen ran up the beach and a shell landed amongst them scattering flesh and bone fragments through the air. Then more infantrymen ran from their landing craft for the safety cover of the gorse bushes. The green light came on and the beachmaster, oblivious to the death surrounding him, waved the ambulance forward.

Charlie accelerated and hit the wire mesh already laid by the engineers and pioneers, it gripped the mesh, the back wheel spun on the sand that came through the steel lattice and he took his foot from the accelerator. The ambulance settled, he pressed his foot down hard on the accelerator and the vehicle lurched forward on the mesh through a barrage of gorse bushes and onto firmer ground. Shells dropped either side of them. The dead lay in grotesque patterns amidst the debris of war. These were a burnt out bren carrier and two scout cars burnt out. The commander of one who'd nearly made it hung by one ankle trapped in the turret. There was a large gash in his back and the sides of the scout car were crimson with the dead man's blood. The wounded cried for help and one man, still a boy in his teens, called for his mother. There was a dead German with a bayonet sticking out from between his ribs and his mouth gaped open, his face distorted with horror. Yet through all this carnage men struggled up the beach.

While Charlie followed the bulk of the traffic, Harry jumped from the cab his medical satchel hanging from his side. He reached the boy still crying for his mother, but it was hopeless. He could not be saved. A large piece of metal was embedded his chest. The young boy clutched Harry's wrist sobbing, "I don't want to die. I don't want to die."

Harry gave him a large dose of morphine.

"Cut the bullshit, mate," he tried to soothe him. "You ain't going to snuff it. In a few days you'll be sent back to your unit on light duties."

These words were all a lie and he compressed his lips as he covered the boy with a piece of torn blanket. "Take it easy, pal," he murmured on. "Anyway," he tried to sound brisk, "what do you want your mum for? Still being titty fed are you?" He made the boy as comfortable as he could. "Be back with the agony wagon soon, mate," he assured him.

He swallowed the gall in his throat. He hated to leave the youngster to die alone and he would be dead within minutes, but there were salvageable casualties lying around.

An infantryman lay a few yards away. He was still clutching his rifle with one hand and his foot inside his ammo boot with his other hand. His eyes were fixed vacantly at the foot and the stump of his leg lay in a mixture of congealing blood and sand. Harry applied a tourniquet to the stump and took the man's water bottle and washed the sand away. Then he applied a large shell dressing, and took the foot from the man's clutching fist.

"It's no damn use to you now, mate," he told him in a no-nonsense tone and digging a hole with the heel of his boot into the soft sand, he threw the foot in it. This done he gave the man an injection. "The stretcher bearers should be along shortly, mate," Harry told the man, but he'd sunk into shock. As for Harry, the nervous tension he'd built up before the landing was gone.

Infantry and armour were pouring ashore and gradually the bridgehead widened. Stretcher bearers worked hard without any let up to clear the beach head, helped on by the cajoling of officers. The sight of so many dead and wounded was bad for the morale of fresh troops landing, and so the wounded were carried

334

to small landing craft which ferried them out to hospital ships
anchored behind the battleships.

CHAPTER 32

Still under the protection of the big guns of the combined British and American fleets, the landing area expanded - although the bridgehead was still under fire from the enemy with small arms and artillery. The rattle of a machine gun close at hand still warned them the danger wasn't over. Wounded were being evacuated from the beach to hospital ships by the small assault craft. At night there was no let up, flares burst above their heads turning the night into day.

"Right, Charlie, let's get rid of these four stretcher cases and get away from this lot."

Two shells landed yards away in the sea spraying both of them with stinging salt water. They had left the ambulance on the road. As they turned towards it, Harry started to run and almost tripped over a man groaning on the sand, clutching his shoulder. Harry bent over him as a flare burst above their heads.

"I think I have been hit in the legs as well, medic."

There was little time for ceremony; a small assault boat was filling up with wounded.

"Sorry mate," said Harry as he lifted the man over his shoulder. The man groaned with pain. Harry ran the few yards to the landing craft and shouted to the two medics.

"I haven't had a chance to dress the wounds, looks like he's been hit in the legs and shoulder."

One of the medics shone a torch on the man.

"Pity, you've wasted your time, mate, he's dead."

Nothing surprised Harry. After four years of war he'd seen it all, a few minutes earlier he'd spoken to the man who'd answered in a firm voice, his pulse strong and steady. Harry shrugged his shoulders.

"Well you can't win them all."

He jumped in the ambulance beside Charlie and they raced back to the R.A.P. set up alongside a bombed out building where another full load of casualties awaited them. As they turned a machine gun opened up, so close they could hear the bullets whine through the air and thud harmlessly against a wall.

Charlie gasped, "Do you know, Harry, I could just close my eyes and sleep for a fortnight."

"I hope you are speaking for both of us," he answered and took a long drink from his water bottle.

Charlie, his foot down hard, urged the ambulance forward, taking the deep ruts left on the ground by the heavy armour as gently as possible. They had given up going to the shoreline to unload the ambulance a long time ago. Instead, although it meant hard work, they carried the stretchers down from the road.

It was on their fifth trip when the skies were just turning grey and they had finished unloading, when a shell whined over, so close they ducked instinctively. The shell landed amongst a group of men just disembarking. Harry grabbed his medical satchel, sprinted across the wet sand and tripped over a headless corpse. A man sat upright, rocking to and fro groaning, clutching the stump of his leg. Another staggered, grabbing his crutch.

"I've been hit in the bollocks. Jesus Christ! They've hit me in the bollocks!"

Charlie ran to try and grab him but the man, although just about six inches shorter than Charlie, threw him to one side, then gradually sank to his knee grabbing his crutch, his life's blood oozing between his fingers. He keeled to one side and lay lifeless.

Another soldier, kneeling, held his hands over his eyes. Harry took his hand from his face.

"I've been blinded mate. Look, mate, I have a wife and three kids back home, don't let me go back like this. Where's the shells landing now?"

The man's shoulders shook with deep sobs. "I would sooner be dead than go home like this."

Harry covered the soldier's eyes with a field dressing and led him to the landing craft. They returned a few minutes later with a stretcher for the other man.

"Christ, man, my bleeding foot is cold, feels like the toes are dropping off."

He tried to reach for the leg but his badly adjusted equipment held his arm back. Harry held his hand in front of the man's face. He didn't move a muscle and Harry realised that this man too had been blinded, yet his face was unmarked. He was too far in shock to realise what had happened to him and his platoon.

On their return they found the R.A.P. full with wounded waiting to be evacuated.

"They would be safer here, sir," Harry told the M.O.

"That beach is still under heavy fire. It looks like one of the hospital ships has sailed and the landing craft are running the gauntlet. You think it's bad here, sir, you should see the beach. They say the Hampshires have really been hit, sir."

"Alright, Jackson, I will take your advice." He looked at Harry, unwashed, face drawn and haggard with four days' growth.

"There's tea out back, get some and a bit of food, then get your head down, if only for a couple of hours."

It was five hours before the M.O. decided to risk sending more wounded to be evacuated, and only then after he received a

337

report from the unit D.R. The sight that greeted Harry was one he would never forget. The dead lay about, spread out in distorted forms. Assault boats floundered against the beach, moving only with the rise and fall of the slight waves. A large tank landing ship lay on its side. By some miracle a few vehicles had made it to the beach. The rest lay in piles against the ship's side in the hold. Deck cargo vehicles hung from the guard rails like decorations on a christmas tree. A member of the ship's crew was crushed between two bren carriers. Piles of vehicles from the ship's top deck lay in great heaps in the water.

"I wouldn't like to sort that lot out."

They couldn't linger too long, there were more casualties to be evacuated, but on their return they were told by the M.O, "The Hampshires have broken through, our armour is going in now so hurry up with those casualties, we will be moving up shortly."

It had been a costly landing, with the Hampshires taking heavy casualties, as the rows and rows of fresh graves testified. Steel helmets hung limply from the cross bars of the white crosses. Other men sat in small groups watching the heavy armour pour through. The convoy paused and two men sitting by a ditch made a gesture towards Harry with two fingers, asking for a smoke. Harry threw them a packet. They took out two cigarettes and went to throw the packet back but he told them to keep it and threw them a box of matches. The two men lay on their backs taking deep drags; it must have been their first fag in days.

Harry still in his own seat, dropped into a deep sleep and woke with a startled shock as the convoy pulled up when the M.O.'s truck and lorry pulled into a vineyard.

"Right you shower, we make our R.A.P. here. Come on Williams and Jackson, lend a bloody hand, it isn't a picnic you know," yelled the stocky sergeant.

From here the armour would take over the infantry. The tanks moved forward, their wide steel tracks biting into the soft ground taking with them the olive trees and vines. All that was left for the grower was deep ruts and mangled vines.

A lone German plane swooped down low, leap frogging the hedges. The nose of the heavy tanks moving forward muffled its engines and the plane was on them before they realised what was happening. A few small arms retaliated and a mobile bofors managed to burst off a couple of magazines before it zoomed upwards and back to the safety of its own lines.

"Wait till the bugger gets back home, Harry, he will send all the shit over."

But they didn't have to wait for his return, for Harry had just completed his slit trench when the air was rent with screaming

338

shells. Olive trees uprooted, went sailing through the air, a water tower alongside a farmhouse topped to one side, a shell bounced off the turret of a Sherman and failed to explode, burying itself in the soft soil. Harry lay full length in his slit trench where the earth felt rich and damp, a far cry from the dry hot sands. How different this battle seemed to be. Trees were all around them, mostly orange and lemon groves with trees in straight lines like soldiers on parade. Hedgerows and houses were dotted all over the place. And the smell, so different; the pungent sharp scent of the citrus groves mixed with the odour of cattle. The mountain range was visible in the distance. Not a clear blue sky like the desert and what they had hoped would welcome them to sunny Italy, but low thunderous clouds that bode ill for the future.

Nearby a farmhouse stood gutted, its windows devoid of all their glass, the chimney stack rocking at a crazy angle. A cow wandered aimlessly around the farmyard, its udders almost dragging along the ground. A large, overfed rat floundered near a small pond, so fat it could hardly move. Two dead ducks floated on the water, one with its entrails floating behind, both being attacked by thousands of small fish, no longer than an inch, so frantic that the water churned around the two bodies stirring the water till it looked as if it was boiling. Charlie hit the rat with his shovel, neatly beheading it, then kicked it into the water where it was immediately attacked by the small fish.

Two German Tiger tanks crashed through the undergrowth. It was impossible to tell where they came from. The Sherman tank crews were on the ground brewing up and before they realised what was happening the German tanks had knocked out two Shermans. Other crews scrambled aboard their tanks. One Sherman drove between the two tigers separating them. Then, quickly more Shermans joined in the battle. It was a brave but foolhardy attempt for the two German crews; in minutes both the tanks were blazing infernos. One German managed to dive from his tank, his black uniform still smouldering.

The C.O. quickly realised his mistake. The ground should have been reccied before they'd settled down. Orders were shouted for the tanks to swan around, making sure none of the Germans had left their mates around, and there were no anti tank guns concealed in the area. There was plenty of cover for them.

"Bring the bastard over to me," shouted the C.O. to the two men guarding the prisoner.

"Get ready to move."

The order rang through the regiment. The men scrambled aboard their tanks. As the tanks moved forward the infantry came up behind them, walking in sections each side of the road. Harry walked round the farmyard. A body hung over an open gate, a sickly stench already rising from it. Word was passed along.

"Keep away from the orange grove, they're alive with anti personnel bombs."

"God, Harry, shufti that." Charlie pointed to half a human body hanging from a branch of an orange tree, its intestines shiny and already blackening.

"Get that down, Jackson."

The medical sergeant pointed to the half torso hanging from the orange tree. But just then a fresh salvo of shells sent them running for the safety of their slit trenches. A shell did the gruesome job for Harry, sending the body crashing to the ground, as two other anti personnel bombs, exploding as they fell, sent hundreds of ball-bearing-like shots scattering through the grove.

"Hubert's been hit, sarge."

"Is he dead?" the sergeant shouted back.

"It would be a fucking miracle if he was alive, half his head is shot away."

"Alright, Walters, cut that out. Report to me after this show is over," ordered the sergeant.

Nothing the campaign was turning out to be was left to the imagination. Most of the men were already wishing they were back in the desert with a war they could understand. A few minutes previously there had been a well-arranged orange grove, with trees in straight lines like a regiment of guards on parade standing on a green carpet of grass. Now the trees were down or half down and the green grass carpeted with great clumps of dark soil. What had taken generations to achieve was almost laid to waste inside an hour.

With the smell of fresh brown earth still filling his nostrils, Harry clambered from his slit trench, his limbs aching. He looked around him, at least he wouldn't have the unenviable task of taking down that torso. Treading warily into the grove, he made sure he kept away from the trees, one shake could have sent an anti personnel bomb down riddling him with shot.

The enemy had certainly chosen their target well, for the area lay thick with casualties, many dead. Walking wounded were already returning to the aid station. The ambulance itself hadn't been touched but a large piece of metal was embedded in the ground beside its back wheel. Harry picked it up, it was almost a foot long and still warm.

"Fancy that up your jacksie, Charlie?"

"No thanks."

Charlie was preparing his ambulance. He had already tuned the engine till it purred like a kitten. He backed on to the aid

340

post where several casualties were waiting to be evacuated. Walking wounded were returning and stretcher bearers were already out. It took two hours, three medical teams and three ambulances to clear the mess.

Harry spotted a casualty he thought the bearers had missed. He dropped down beside him and turned the man over. He was still clutching his rifle and bayonet, and his steel helmet fell over his face. Cautiously Harry turned him. The man's chest was wide open, his lungs, heart and parts of his stomach fell out in one bloody gory mess. Harry choked back on his own vomit, four years of this carnage and he still couldn't get used to the idea of seeing men torn apart.

Two days later the division started moving inland, cautiously coasting along a narrow road with several roads criss crossing it, each intersection a potential danger spot. It was only when the convoy stopped that they realised they had been climbing steadily, and the battleground below looked like some giant panorama; an active model built by a fanatic. Warships stood out to sea, great puffs of smoke belching from their massive guns still pounding the enemy further inland. Small assault boats ferried fresh troops ashore and wounded back to the white hospital ships.

A derelict farmhouse loomed into view, a large white sheet hanging from one of its open windows. The ideal place for an aid post. One room had escaped the shelling so the M.O. commandeered this for an operating theatre.

Squadrons of armoured cars and heavy tanks concealed themselves amongst the citrus groves, their guns pointing menacingly towards the enemy positions. Cautiously Harry and Charlie went up the stairs in the farmhouse. Charlie looked through the window. The infantry was dug in along the road, using the drainage ditches for cover. A man was cleaning down his bren gun with an oily rag while his mate lay back on the grass dragging on his cigarette seemingly without a care in the world.

"I don't like the look of this one little bit, Harry. Look around you, I bet we must be right up the front line."

"Well, there is only the beach behind us, so you must be right." Harry was sitting on the floor, resting his back against the wall. Any minute now he felt he would close his eyes and fall fast asleep. His steel helmet clattered to the floor. A picture of an old lady hung on the wall, her staring eyes fixed on him, as if questioning his right to invade the privacy of her house and bedroom.

They returned to their slit trenches. Harry found two sheets of corrugated iron, which he laid over the top, leaving just enough room to dive down.

341

"That's it, Charlie. They can throw what the hell they like at us now." The words had hardly left his mouth when shells started screaming over. They dived headfirst into their trenches. Charlie had a mouthful of brown soil.

"Why the hell don't you keep that big mouth of yours shut, Harry?" he gasped.

Without let up the bombardment continued throughout the night, denuding the trees of their branches and exposing the sap saturated white wood. Red hot metal splinters criss-crossed the trenches, bedding themselves into the stucco walls of the farmhouse. Sheets of plaster fell away and one wall of the farmhouse collapsed covering their slit trenches. One side of Harry's trench tumbled inwards. It hadn't been such a brilliant idea digging the trenches so close to the building.

Dawn was just breaking when they emerged from their trenches. Charlie grinned, his mouth a narrow slit across his muddy brown face, his eyes just two white smudges. Harry grinned back at him, his face in much the same state.

"Some shelling that, Charlie. Did you hear that small arms fire? I nearly shit myself, I thought the enemy was counter attacking."

"Could have been some trigger happy infantryman just out from Blighty."

They reported to the aid post and were surprised to see only two casualties from the night's shelling, and those two weren't seriously injured. Later they found one man killed.

Several scout cars revved up and shot forward, followed quickly by the heavy tanks. More tanks in the distance formed up ready to move off. Charlie took his binoculars upstairs in the house again. A mountain range stood out in the distance, slate grey in the early morning light. Pinpoints of flame stabbed the dull mist and shells screamed towards the landing area, too far for Charlie to make out exactly where they were landing.

Without warning a shell raced through the window of the next room with an ear splitting bang. The interior walls collapsed and shrouded Charlie in brick dust. Blindly he felt for the narrow staircase. It had vanished and flames were already leaping up the stairwell.

More shells surrounded the house. Charlie had to get out quick as he felt he was the enemy's prime target. He hung from the window, hot blasts from the shells brushed his trousers. It was eight feet to the ground. The tips of his fingers went numb, he let go. The earth was soft. He ran for his trench but it had filled with brick rubble. His pulse thumped at his temples, his lungs felt as if they would burst. He flung himself between a pile of rubble and what was left of the wall of the house.

"I think the bastards have got it in for me," he shouted across to Harry's slit trench. Then there was a roar that echoed from trench to trench.

"Stand to, stand to, come on you shower, out of those bolt holes."

Harry was the first at the aid post.

"You and your mate alright, Jackson?" queried the M.O.

"Yes, sir, bit of a show last night and this morning, sir."

"Should be alright now, Jackson. Word's come through, the tanks have broken through. Better start evacuating shortly, they certainly threw some shit over. Did you hear that small arms during the night? Our lads shot up a Jerry patrol. Killed the six of them. Cheeky buggers!"

On their trip back to the beach they passed columns of infantry on each side of the road, making their way to the front line. Then they passed a company of American rangers. It looked like the breakthrough was going to be a combined effort. It was the first time the division had fought alongside their American counterparts. To their amazement, when they returned to the aid post it was under heavy shell fire again with heavier shells than usual falling around what was left of the house. The wall of what was once their operating theatre was missing. The medical sergeant was sitting in a corner, his eyes staring into space, a thin trickle of dried blood oozing from the corner of his mouth, and a gaping hole torn through his chest.

The continual shelling lasted the whole morning, then a strange silence fell over the dismal scene.

"Looks like the old sergeant has had it, Charlie."

"Bleeding shame, he wasn't such a bad bloke."

Then they realised they were both whispering. They looked at one another with an embarrassing smile.

"What the hell are we whispering for?" Charlie asked.

"Buggered if I know. I was whispering because you was," answered Harry.

They lifted the sergeant's body out into the yard. Then searched through what remained of the house.

"Wonder what happened to the doc and the sky pilot? The place is deserted."

"Looks like the Marie Celeste."

"Who the hell is this Mary, some bint up at Aldershot?"

For the second time in twenty-four hours the ambulance had received only very slight damage.

"It bears a charmed life. We would be better off sleeping in it."

Everything was so quiet, all they could hear of the war was the distant shelling from the warships. The roads were deserted with

343

no signs of any troops. Harry walked towards the spot where he had last seen the two bren gunners. All that remained was a pile of empty cartridge cases.

"Lets bury the old sergeant, then get some food."

They sat with their back against the damaged wall of the farmhouse nibbling on hard tack biscuits and scooping out spoonfuls of bully from a can and sipping hot tea.

"Bloody hell, what's that?"

Charlie held his hand up for silence. Harry strained his ears.

"Can't hear a bloody thing."

"There it goes again."

Charlie placed his mug of tea on the ground and walked into the house; Harry followed. Then they both heard a thump, thump, very faint as if someone was slapping a flat hand against a brick wall.

"Yes, I heard it that time."

Charlie rushed out side and grabbed his rifle, ramming a cartridge up the spout.

"Could be the rest of the aid post," said Harry.

"Well, I ain't taking any chances."

They moved away half a ton of rubble. The lime from the cement in the mortar burnt into their fingers. Harry tore his nails till they bled. The more rubble they moved the louder the thumping. They came to a carpet and as they pulled it aside a wooden trapdoor lifted. Charlie grabbed his rifle, his finger on the trigger. A small wrinkled face appeared and when he saw the rifle pointing at him he squealed and fell back down the steps.

Harry lifted the trapdoor and shouted, "Come up out of there with your hands above your head."

There was no movement.

"Perhaps they don't understand English."

Harry peered down the hole. Six frightened faces looked up at him. Gesturing with his hands on his head, he motioned to them to come up slowly and stand against the wall. The old man was the first up. The man, his face like a wrinkled walnut, stared about the house. His eyes widened and he burst into tears, wringing his hands and shouting to the old lady following him. She put her hand to her mouth and burst into tears like the old man. Then up came two young girls in their late teens, followed by two boys, identical twins, about fifteen years old. They wandered aimlessly about what was left of the house screaming and gesticulating. They kept looking at Charlie and Harry.

"They think we did it, Harry."

"Well, there you are, Charlie - your first two senorinas."

344

At the mention of the word senorinas, the whole family looked at the two girls and crowded round them for protection. Harry laughed and waved his hand.

"I think they think we are going to rape them."

Charlie burst out laughing.

"They must be kidding, look at the nose on that, looks like Pinocchio's mother. No, Harry, my girls have to be willing parties."

They heard the roar of a motorcycle and went outside to investigate. Having crossed the road they waved him down, only to be greeted with, "Where the hell have you two been with that ambulance? The old man is going spare! Casualties are piling up like a slaughter house."

"You have to be kidding. We came up here from the beach and found the sergeant dead and every sod vanished. We found these civilians hiding in the cellar," answered Harry.

"There's a big breakthrough, your mob is at least fifteen miles further on, better follow me."

They left the Italian farmer and his family screaming hysterically and chased after the D.R. How different this warfare was turning out to be. The roads became closed in, a nightmare for any tank regiment where a thousand anti tank guns could confidently hide.

On their arrival, they were immediately pressed into service, no questions asked. The padre was carrying out the medical sergeant's duties and was pleased to hand over the job to Harry. A man was called from the regiment to work on the ambulance. This would make a welcome break for Harry. The walking wounded were already making their way back to the beaches for so far no C.C.S. had been set up. There were several civilian casualties.

"What will happen to them, sir, after we treat their wounds?"

The M.O. shrugged his shoulders.

"Don't ask me. We certainly can't evacuate them to the hospital ships, and as far as I can see there are no civilian hospitals in the area. I suppose they will have to wait until we capture a small town with a hospital. Keep them here until we move."

The stretchers bearers ran in with a casualty, his face covered with a shell dressing. Harry removed the dressing and felt the bully beef and biscuits he had just eaten rise in his throat. He checked himself and spat raw bile into the dirty dressing bucket.

"It's Murdoch, sir," one of the bearers told the M.O. "Got it right in the face."

345

Where the man's eyes had been was just a congealed mess with blood baked on his face. Harry gently washed it away. A bullet had skimmed across the man's face taking both eyes and the bridge of his nose, leaving a mass of splintered bone and fleshy pulp. He grabbed Harry's wrist thinking Harry was the M.O.

"Am I blind, sir?"

Harry forced back a sob. He looked at the M.O. who nodded in the affirmative. Harry placed a comforting hand on the man's shoulder.

"Yes, I'm afraid so."

Yes. What else could he say. This wasn't the time to tell the man of the progress science had made to help the blind, or the functions of a guide dog. Soon the seriousness of his injuries would hit him with the force of a sledgehammer. For days, weeks, or even months he wouldn't talk to anyone, but inside himself he would be saying, "Why me? Why me?"

He led the man towards the aid post where the M.O. carried out a more thorough inspection. He slowly shook his head. One of the man's eyelids hung like an ill fitting curtain over an empty window while the other eye was just a mass of jelly substance. He gave the man a strong sedative and ordered Harry to evacuate him with his next load.

No longer to the beach itself this time, a Main Dressing Station was set up three miles along the road. Everything was gradually sorting itself out. It was also learned that the Yanks had come up against stiff opposition and sustained heavy casualties.

From their vantage point they could look down on the landing area below. The huge naval guns elevated higher and higher, which meant the enemy were being driven back. Another hospital ship had joined the fleet bringing the strength of the hospital ships back to two. Their coats of white paint gleamed in the faint sunlight against a background of azure blue sea.

"They look like cruise ships from here. Just think, I could have worked a job on one of those. Do you know, they actually sail with all their lights on during the night?"

"You forget one thing, Harry boy, they have sisters on those ships."

Harry looked at him with disgust.

"That's right, you mean bastard, go and spoil my daydreams."

There were times when they were visited by the enemy air force, occasionally dive bombed by Stukas or strafed by fighter planes, but they were outnumbered by the combined squadrons of American and British planes from the aircraft carriers.

Before the end of September the rains came. At first they treated it as if they had never seen rain before.

"Come on, Harry, get that soap out."

Charlie rushed to the ambulance and stripped naked. Standing under the torrential warm rain he lathered himself from head to foot, the warm water foaming soapy puddles around his feet. He could feel the dirt, accumulated over the past months, rapidly clearing away. He stood there for almost half an hour with the rain lashing his naked body.

Harry joined him and they both fell around laughing.

"Bloody great, Harry, it's been a long time since I felt as good as this."

He soon realised it was a stupid thing to say, for within twenty-four hours he was to curse the rain. The fields became quagmires of liquid mud which spilled onto the roads making every trip to the rear a nightmare.

Returning from one trip the ambulance was bogged down for almost two hours, sandwiched between a large tank transporter and an American six wheeled lorry; several vehicles lay bogged down in the mud. A half track ambulance was taking them to the fields, the red crosses on its side splattered with mud but making easy work as its broad tracks bit into the ground. Harry waved him down.

"Give us a tow, mate, we've been here a couple of hours."

"Right, mate."

He jumped from the half track and sank to his knees in the mud.

"Looks like the soup our cooks dish up."

He placed a chain on the ambulance and towed them back to the aid post. It took very little effort on the half track's part. In wet clothes and after making tea, they settled down for the night. It was impossible to dig a trench for as fast as they dug the trenches they filled with liquid mud. So for the first time since landing in Italy, Charlie stripped off and turned in. Harry made do with just stripping to his underpants and saying, "We might just as well get shot up here as lay in those trenches and drown, Charlie."

The next morning the division moved up and further inland. The first phase of the landings was finally over.

CHAPTER 33

A dog barked in the distance. Harry lay awake on his stretcher; he stirred restlessly, then raised himself on one elbow listening to the muted sounds around him. The rain pounded the sides of the ambulance. Outside the storm turned the ground into a quagmire of dark brown liquid mud. Thunder echoed down through the mountains and shook the ambulance on its heavy springs till they groaned in protest. Lightning flashed, its fluorescent brilliance shining through the small squares of light which served as windows just above his head, and filling the dim interior with its iridescent light. A cock crowed; he smiled to himself wondering how the creature had escaped the attention of the regiment and how many, since arriving in Italy, had found their way into a cooking pot. 'Better keep quiet my son or you may find yourself in the same predicament,' he thought to himself.

A strong gust of wind beat down bringing with it a torrent of rain, followed quickly by a long rumble of thunder and a sharp flash of lightning. The ambulance rolled; Charlie pulled his blankets up to his chin, but nature called and he knew he would have to escape from the warm coarse blankets. Reluctantly he put one bare leg out, the ice cold lino sent a shiver through him. Gathering courage he stood naked at the back doors and urinated, followed by a loud burst of wind. He gasped with relief. Harry was sleeping on the opposite stretcher and awake at the first movement. He murmured, "Dirty bastard," and covered his head with the blankets.

Charlie poked his head out. The rain splashed his face and he shuddered. The regiment's vehicles were scattered over a wide area of the olive grove, but there was no one in sight. After the long battle the men were content to stay in their vehicles as long as possible.

The large farmhouse had remained untouched by the war, and, by its condition, untouched by a much needed paintbrush for a great number of years. Great slabs of plaster were missing, and the continual rain and sun had blackened the bare patches of brickwork.

Deserted by its owners when the first shot of the invasion was fired, it was taken over as an officers' mess. Charlie as usual made friends with the officers' cook who was now drying out some of his uniform. His first duty when joining a regiment was always make friends with the chef, never call them cooks, and if possible always make it the officers' chef. His second duty was make friends with a clerk in the company office. As he always said, "look after your stomach, then always try and get to know what's going on behind the scenes."

"In for a penny, in for a pound," he shouted to Harry as he swung open the door and stepped out into the pelting rain. He always slept in the nude, he couldn't sleep any other way. He was surprised that once he got used to the rain it was quite warm. Dripping wet he rubbed himself down with a coarse towel till his skin burnt, bright red.

"God, Harry, that was great. Get out and have a shower, it'll do you the world of good."

Rubbing the sleep from his eyes, he stepped on the floor and sucked his breath sharply.

"You bastard, Charlie! You've soaked the bloody floor again."

But Charlie was in a playful mood. He lifted Harry and threw him out into the rain then closed the door.

"Charlie, you bastard."

He smacked hard against the door, then realising that the rain had a refreshing effect, he stripped off.

"There you are, Harry, don't you feel better for that." Charlie picked up the mess tins. "I will slip over the mess for tea, Harry, and some water. I think I might shave today."

Harry was still smarting from his rub down with the towel and didn't answer.

Cautiously pushing open the cookhouse door he peered inside. A large pan of eggs was bubbling away on the red hot stove. It was an open, log burning stove with flames that sent a warm glow over the kitchen. The oven door was open revealing two blackened trays laid out with rashers of crispy bacon. Another tray was filled with rich brown sausages, their skins bursting at the seams. Charlie smacked his lips; he could feel the juice running down his chin. He drooled over the sight for a few minutes, his empty stomach protesting. He called out for the chef, not too loud; there was no answer.

To the far side there was another door leading to the room used for a mess. He pushed it open slightly, only the mess orderly was there preparing the tables. He hadn't seen Charlie. Gently, Charlie closed the door again.

He peered through the window, the camp was still deserted. A few yards from the house was a box like structure, not unlike the old sentry boxes. There was a gap about a foot wide at the bottom of the door. A pair of boots was visible with trousers drooped over them. He stroked his chin, had he got time to help himself? Then he saw a piece of timber lying by the side of the hut. It was about six feet long and pretty stout, at least four by two inches. It could only be the cook in there. He rubbed his hands together.

Walking quietly, his feet cushioned by the muddy path, he quickly jammed the timber against the door, securing it under the latch. The man inside was now a prisoner. He was hoping and praying it was the cook and not an officer.

This was confirmed when a frightened voice shouted, "Whose there?" in a deep Brummy accent.

"What the fucking hell's going on? Who's there?" the man repeated, thumping on the door. In his struggle to stand up and pull his trousers up in such a confined space, he fell against the door and cursed again.

"What the bleeding hell?!" His terrified voice was muffled by the sound of heavy rain beating against the tin roof.

The hut was shaking so violently, Charlie thought it might topple over any minute. Keeping his eyes on the sand, he filled his mess tins with bacon and half a dozen hard boiled eggs, then scooped up two mugs of boiling tea and, sheltering them under his groundsheet cape, ran for his ambulance. Passing the hut he gave it a gentle kick with the toe of his boot.

"What the bleeding hell is going on out there? I'll kill you you bastard! Is that you, Lovelace, you bastard?" the prisoner cried out.

Charlie sighed with relief, at least he hadn't seen through any cracks in the wooden structure. Satisfied that he hadn't been observed and the door was holding securely, he took his time; he didn't want to spill the tea. He would have preferred his eggs fried with great gold eyes staring up at him, but beggars can't be choosers, or in his case, spontaneous thieves can't be choosers.

He held a mess tin under Harry's nose. The smell of the sausages and bacon filled the ambulance. Harry grabbed his mess tin and stared at them in disbelief.

"Bloody hell, don't tell me you've nicked this lot from the kitchen, Charlie?"

Charlie nodded and grinned.

"I thought that chef was a mate of yours?"

"So he is, Harry, but let's face it, all's fair in love and war, and as my grandpappy would say, an empty stomach and a standing prick have no conscience."

"Your grandpappy knew what he was talking about," he said as he picked up a sausage and bit off the end.

Laying back with full stomachs watching the smoke from their cigarettes drift idly towards the roof, they listened to the rain beating down. A satisfied smirk on his face Harry said, "Christ, Charlie, I haven't tasted sausages like that since before the war. I wonder where they got them from?"

"I don't give a damn, I know where they went!" replied Charlie.

350

It had been a lucky day for Harry, the day he joined the unit and being assigned to Charlie's ambulance. Since then he'd become a proficient driver capable of taking over the ambulance from Charlie under any conditions. They had been through a few tight spots together, but then they had also had some good times. Charlie was popular with everyone and it was amazing how often they got surprises like the good breakfast they'd just finished. When cigarettes were in short supply they were never without. It was the same with food and water, and the occasional bottle of beer. Charlie lay opposite him picking his teeth with a sharpened matchstick. Strange how his private life never came into the conversation. He had managed to piece parts of it together but it still remained a mystery. Perhaps one day he might open up, but Harry never pushed him.

Picking up the tell-tale egg shells, he pushed them into his mess tin.

"Better get back and see if the poor bastard is still locked in the karzy."

"What karzy?" He stared at him his eyes widening.

"The cook, of course, I couldn't resist it, he was there sitting all alone having a crap." He filled him in with the rest of the story.

"I'll sling these eggshells under Lovelace's lorry."

Lovelace wasn't a very popular man, an aggressive type who had crossed Charlie a few times in the past.

Banging on the cookhouse door, he didn't wait for an invitation, just barged in. The cook was sitting in front of the fire toasting bread on a homemade toasting fork; two pieces of stout wire intertwined and finishing up as two prongs.

"What the bleeding hell do you want?" snarled the cook. From his tone he hadn't recovered fully from his recent ordeal, which Charlie thought was quite understandable under the circumstances. But he played him along, under no circumstances did he want any suspicion thrown his way.

"Christ, chef, you have a real shitty on this morning. What's up, the lousy weather getting you down?"

"What's up?"

He swung round on his seat to face Charlie. His face was bright red and Charlie couldn't tell if it was caused by rage or just the heat from the fire. The cook threw the toast on the pile in the centre of the table. Charlie froze. Had the chef rumbled him? Reynolds, the cook, was heavyweight champion of the regiment and he had been in line for the army championships when the war broke out and interrupted his boxing career. Charlie was quite capable of looking after himself, but he realised with Reynolds he was outclassed, there was no way he wanted to tangle with him.

He relaxed as he watched him put another slice of bread on the fork.

"You need ask what's up? I don't suppose by any chance you were around here a bit earlier?"

Charlie's face was a picture of complete innocence.

"You're kidding, chef. It took me all my time to tear myself away from the warm flea pit and come and scrounge some water. Why, what happened?"

"Some lousy bastard came in here while I was having a crap and helped himself. They locked me in the karzy, jammed a piece of wood against it, then helped themselves."

It was only the chef's size and his boxing ability that prevented Charlie from bursting out laughing.

"I was in there for a good half hour. I tell you, Charlie, if I ever catch the bastard I'll kill him."

To emphasise the fact he clenched his fist and brought it down on the table. The pile of toast jumped and Charlie shuddered. The fist and bare forearm were more like a large leg of lamb. One clout from that could disfigure him for life. He feigned a look of disgust and clicked his tongue.

"The rotten bastard, nothing is safe these days, Reynolds." He shook his head in sympathy with the cook.

"The rotten bastard, he's rotten alright. He nicked at least twenty rashers of bacon and as many sausages. Then there was the bread. When I left the bread was piled up there ready for me to toast." He held his hand a couple of feet above the table top.

"Then, when I got back it was down here," he indicated, his hand almost level with the table top.

"The old man will do his nut. They bought the bacon from the mess funds - well, that's what they said. What they did do was club together and gave that old farmer down the road cigarettes for a couple of pounds."

Charlie was hardly listening, he was puzzled, he had only taken enough for two. He could only assume that other men on the same errand for hot water or possibly a mug of tea, had seen the cookhouse empty and having noticed the predicament the cook was in, took full advantage of it. War had at least taught them the art of survival.

He rested his elbows on the table.

"Any idea who it could have been, chef?"

He wanted to get back for a shave, but lending a sympathetic ear to the chef's troubles could pay dividends later. Reynolds slid a mug of hot tea towards him.

"Who let you out of the karzy then?" asked Charlie.

"One of the officers." He wiped his neck with a sweat stained piece of cloth.

"And of course it had to be that shitbag, Fielding. I shouldn't have been there, it's for officers only. He gave me a right bollocking. Anyone would have thought I had infected the seat with crabs. No self-respecting crab would want to make its home there, it stinks to high heaven. God man, being locked in there turned my guts. I only used the bleeding thing because it was pissing down with rain. Give me a shovel any day and a nice clean hole to crap in. A nice secluded spot in a corner of some field with newspaper, nothing like it."

The cook turned and spat in the fire. It bounced off the red hot top and just missed the dixie of tea. Charlie was a good listener and kept nodding his head in agreement.

"Have you ever been in that karzy?"

Charlie shook his head.

"All it is is a deep hole, must be at least twenty feet deep, with a wooden thunder box on top. You know you can say a dozen Hail Mary's before your turd hits the bottom. It must be fermenting down there. Stink! I reckon half the German army and most of the Itey army had used it before we got here. It turned my guts."

"Why didn't you knock the door down. The size of you I thought it would have been a piece of cake?"

"You're kidding, Charlie. It's so small in there I couldn't get my shoulder behind it. That thunder box might have moved and I would really have been in the shit. It's just big enough to take the thunder box and one man standing up. You have to be seated with your knees up before you can bolt the door."

"Did Fielding put you on a fizzer then?" asked Charlie, trying to show a bit of concern.

"No, just a bollocking and a warning not to use it again."

"Me, I wouldn't use one of those karzies if you paid me, not after that incident just outside Tripoli. Me, I would rather use the shovel outside. It could be pissing down for all I'd care."

"Why, what happened outside Tripoli?"

"Surely you bloody heard?"

The cook shook his head. Charlie smiled as he told the story.

"There was this house with one of these karzies outside, almost double the size of that." He pointed to the sentry like structure.

"Some bleeding Jerry sapper with a crude sense of humour planted a booby trap down there. It only had a light charge of course. The officers spotted it and immediately put it out of bounds to the rank and file. 'Reserved For Officers' was plastered all over it. The first day this major came striding over. A big bastard, nobody could stand him. Swaggered about as if he was on general staff, a right cocky arsed sod. He drops his cacks and sits on the old thunder box. As soon as his turd hits the bottom there was an explosion, up it goes. The bloody shit comes rushing up and covers the sod. He must have been sitting there with his head between his knees, watching it disappear. He comes rushing out, his face and shoulders covered and clutching his balls. To make matters worse, the whole regiment was on parade and saw it happen. The place was in uproar; the men were falling about. Of course from then on everyone calls him old shit head, but only behind his back. They say he has never used a karzy since. The M.O. was telling my mate he will have to have psychiatric treatment when he gets back so he can use one in comfort again. Every time he passes a karzy now he shivers."

The story cheered the chef up. He hated officers only second to the Germans and he only hated them because they had put the final touches to his boxing career.

The door leading into the mess swung open. A mess orderly came in with a tin tray held high.

"Sausages, bacon and tomatoes with a lightly boiled egg for Captain Fielding. He said he would like his egg done for two and a half minutes."

Plunging a large bread knife into the middle of the table top, the chef stared at him.

"Sod Fielding and sod you! He might be high and mighty back home with his valets and butlers, but now there is a bloody war on. The eggs have been boiling for over an hour, the toast is burnt and the bacon's crispy. If he don't like it he can come and kiss my arse. I'm cheesed off with this lousy job anyway and would rather be back on the tanks. Fielding, like all the other pigs in there, gets what's given them."

He tossed a slice of bacon on a plate, scooped up a ladle of tomatoes and juice, and tossed in a sausage. The sausage floated on the gravy, then wedged itself between two egg shaped tomatoes; the bacon floated by. Charlie looked at the sausage and two tomatoes and smiled. He could almost have modelled for it. The smile was wiped from the waiter's face and turned to a look of disgust.

"Christ, Reynolds, I can't take it in like that, it looks revolting, and that sausage wedged there is absolutely disgusting, just like a phallic symbol."

"So what, it's better than the troops are getting. Greasy tinned bacon for them. Any hanky panky from that shower in there and I'll throw the bleeding towel in."

354

Reynolds was hardly a man you could argue with. Reluctantly the waiter put two boiled eggs and toast on another small plate, deciding he would rather face the wrath of that bastard Fielding than the unhealthy temper of the cook. He had heard the saga of the shit house and vanished quickly into the mess.

Charlie thought it was time to make himself scarce, and remembered what he had come for.

"Any hot water, chef?"

Reynolds nodded towards an old dixie bubbling away on the stove and grunted, "Help yourself."

"Christ, Harry, don't go near that cookhouse, the chef's in a filthy mood. The fireworks are about to fly at any minute." He placed the mess tin of hot water in the ambulance.

"Some rotten bastard has just locked the chef in the karzy and nicked the officers' breakfasts." He shook his head in disgust as if he was still sympathising with Reynolds.

"There's some right pricks about, it amazes me what lengths some blokes will go to to fill their guts."

He had been through this routine with Charlie a few times so he just nodded his head in agreement.

"I know what you mean, Charlie."

After carrying out routine servicing on their vehicles, the regiment moved out. The rain came down with renewed energy. He took up his position behind a large loaded tank transporter, a move he was to regret before the day was out.

The road to the foothills of the mountain was straight, well laid and narrow, with the division well stretched out and travelling at full speed. But their troubles started as soon as they reached the first incline. After the flat countryside it looked like a vertical wall. The engines of the transporters groaned under the strain and black smoke belched from the exhausts. The thunder clapped with tremendous roar, echoing against the sheer mountainside with a continuous rumble. Hardly had one roar vanished when a new, and louder one, shook the convoy. Shafts of bright lightning penetrated the walls of rain which was so heavy now that the mechanical wipers became useless. Charlie stuck his head from the side of the cab.

"Christ, Harry, it's like driving through a goldfish bowl!"

The fog-like diesel fumes filled the cab with a deadly stench. Charlie dropped back a few yards, only to be warned by the D.R. who was shepherding his section of the convoy, to pull in closer. The worse was yet to come. The windscreen had become impossible to clear. He completely removed the side canvas screen and hung halfway out of his cab, his eyes narrow slits, his greatcoat heavy with rain. He shivered and through clenched teeth shouted,

"What price the desert now?"

But Harry, with his knees covered with two blankets and another round his shoulders, was half asleep and didn't answer.

Every half kilometre or so the tank transporter would stop to negotiate a stiff hairpin bend, the tank crew and spare driver jumping down into the road all shouting instructions and advice to guide the monster round, the driver sliding it back and forth with only inches to spare from a sheer drop hundreds of feet into the chasm below. The higher they reached the more the tempers became frayed. Harry shook himself awake and stared round blankly. His mouth felt dry and his nose blocked with diesel fumes.

"Bloody turn up for the books this lot, Charlie. Why the hell did you get behind that big bastard? I can see a punch up brewing shortly with all these silly sods shouting out advice."

Charlie shrugged his shoulders. He was wet through, cold and hungry. Every time he placed a cigarette between his lips it became wet through after the first puff. He was in no mood to argue with Harry.

"This transporter, the next - what the hell's the difference? We have to be behind someone. It should be dark in three or so hours' time and then the fun will really start."

The transporter was negotiating a very bad bend. The tank crew were out with picks and shovels breaking away a wall or rock.

"If I get a chance I'll try and overtake him if the road widens. There's only a small scout car in front of him." He cut the engine.

Harry could see they would be some time. He looked back, the transporter behind them was still on the other bend. He had the road to himself. The rain had eased off, not that it worried him, he was wet through and couldn't get any wetter. He wedged his steel helmet on and covered his shoulders with a greatcoat. Then he walked back a few paces and sat on a low stone wall dividing the road from a sheer drop, and let his feet dangle over, the rain bouncing off his steel helmet. It was one of those times when he enjoyed his own company, to be alone with his own thoughts. He found the mountains fascinating with the thunder and lightning flashing and reverberating around him. He picked up a large loose stone from the wall and let it drop between his legs. He whistled through his teeth and gasped, he never heard it hit the bottom of the mist shrouded valley.

"Yes, you're right there, son, it really is fascinating."

356

He spun round startled. He hadn't heard anyone approach and thought he was still alone. The regimental padre was sitting astride a huge 500cc Triumph motorbike. He smiled.

"A wonderful sight isn't it, pity it's raining so hard, you should see it on a bright sunny day. Do you know, this trip we are making is considered one of the finest sights in the world? Certainly one of the most beautiful. Tourists pay hundreds of pounds just to come and look at this." He paused and swept his arms around in a wide arc, taking in a deep breath.

"Just smell those orange and lemon groves. Isn't it all so fresh?"

He pointed to the distant mountain.

"Over there is Amalfi. That's where St Andrew, the patron saint of Scotland, is buried."

Harry nodded. At this moment he wasn't interested, he just wanted to be on his own for a few minutes before the convoy started. He breathed in deeply trying to rid his lungs of the heavy diesel fumes.

He never made a point of being rude so to make polite conversation he said, "You seem to know a bit about this place, sir. Have you been here before?"

"Yes, I was at theological college before the war, not far from here. It's all so beautiful in the summer, even now it's very fascinating. Just listen to that thunder and lightning rolling through the mountains."

"That's just what I have been listening to, sir. It makes one of our artillery barrages sound a bit puny, doesn't it?" The padre laughed. How unfortunate such a young man should have only an artillery barrage to compare it with.

"Yes, son, it does. If I were you I would make the very best of it, I don't suppose you will ever have the opportunity of ever seeing it again."

He would have loved to have told him to "piss off," but unlike Charlie, he did have a little respect for the cloth. No doubt he would have been making enquiries about the love stakes in a roundabout way, but how could you discuss it with a Catholic priest.

"Goodbye, son."

He patted Harry's back. Harry turned round.

"Excuse me, padre."

"What is it son?"

He hesitated. "Well."

"I went to a Quaker school - well, an orphanage really - and wasn't up much on my geography. Could you tell me where Picardy is, sir?"

He smiled.

"Well, son, I thought every schoolboy would know that. Haven't you ever heard that old song from the last war, 'Roses of Picardy'? All the troops sang it then."

"That's just it, sir. That song keeps going through my head. Where is Picardy? Northern Italy, isn't it?"

He laughed.

"No, son. It's in northern France, between Normandy and Flanders, takes in the Somme and parts of the Pas de Calais. I should think every front line soldier of the First War must have sung that at some time or other. Goodbye, son."

He waved again and rolled his bike down the hill. So that's why he never heard him approach. He took one more look at the mountains with the mist curling in and out on gossamer wings. Perhaps the padre was right, it was beautiful but he would have appreciated it more without the rain.

The torrential rain had become a bit of a shock after all the sand and sun of the desert. After all, Italy was well known for its sunshine and dark skinned senorinas.

The transporter behind him had finally negotiated the hairpin bend, but the one in front was making hard work of it. Charlie was slumped over the steering wheel, his head resting on his arms. At last the transporter made its way round the hairpin bend. It had been the most difficult since negotiating the mountains. Pulling away with a fresh burst from its engine, it filled the cab with diesel fumes.

Charlie, coughing and spluttering, eased off a few yards. In between coughs he shouted, "If that sodding D.R. tells me to pull in closer I will ram that sodding motorbike up his rectum."

A few minutes later they came to another bend. His luck was in. There was just sufficient space for him to squeeze his ambulance through. Pressing down hard on the accelerator, he shot forward, and with inches to spare, raced through slightly scraping the stone wall sending stones crashing into the chasm. Harry clung to his seat and felt sick as he looked over the sheer drop, sweat mingling with the rain on his forehead.

"Crazy bastard," shouted the tank crew from the transporter. Their words were carried away on a fresh burst of wind and rain.

Charlie was angry. His voice was angry, and harsh, too.

"Those bloody fumes, Harry, another couple of hours of that and I would have had my chips."

They settled in behind a small scout car as the convoy wound its way over the mountains, climbing and dipping steadily throughout the night. Harry felt confident now as he took the wheel for a few hours while Charlie tried to catch up on some sleep in the back. Dawn was just breaking when Charlie, his eyes swollen with sleep, stuck his head in the cab.

"Fancy a kip, Harry?"

He took over.

Hardly had he closed his eyes when Charlie shook him by the shoulder, a steaming mug of hot tea in his hands.

"We're only stopping for a few minutes, Harry, better get that down you."

The valley below was still shrouded in mist. The rain belted down, but the thunder and lightning eased off. Villages clung precariously to the sheer sides of the mountains. They passed through deserted villages and were occasionally greeted by one or two old men standing in the doorways of their squalid houses. The villages were always dominated by a large church. Sometimes an old woman, shoulders hunched, would give them a toothless grin, her mouth burying itself into a wide slit across her weather beaten face, and always dressed in black. The convoy never stopped; they were pushing the vehicles to the point of exhaustion.

"So much for the beautiful senorinas, Harry. I haven't seen one that I really fancy yet."

Harry was still half asleep. He had tried to sleep in the back after his mug of tea but the road was bad and he could hardly keep his place on the stretcher. His clothes were heavy with rain and the rough serge chaffed his skin where it came into contact. For the past three years he had been wearing smooth tropical clothes. Now the rough serge of the battle dress was really having an affect, rubbing with every movement till the skin became red raw.

They came upon two women, possibly in their late thirties or maybe younger, but like all the peasant women, dressed in dreary black. That, together with the hard life, and diet of pasta and olive oil, did nothing to enhance their figures and general appearance. They knelt in front of a statue of the Virgin Mary which was resting inside a large cavity cut in the side of the mountain. Lighted candles, shielded from the wind in jam jars, stood at the Virgin's feet. Fresh flowers in vases decorated the statue. The women's backs were bent in prayer. The ambulance stopped. They cast a nervous glance towards the driver, then, pulling their shawls round their shoulders, they scurried away.

Harry laughed for the first time since they started to negotiate the mountains.

"There you are, Charlie! Your reputation has preceded you. As soon as those poor devils saw this ambulance they scurried away like two rabbits with ferrets up their arseholes."

"They had no worries. I ain't that bloody hard up," retorted Charlie in disgust.

Water cascaded down the mountain sides, levelling out to two or three inches on the road, before continuing down the other side. Everywhere a piece of flat land could be cultivated, the farmers worked on it with loving care, carefully conserving every bit of soil. Now, without care, the rain was washing it away. Oranges, lemons, grapes, olives, or any other crops filled every small space; nothing was wasted. Harry nodded towards a small patch where a few withered olive trees tried to break through the harsh earth.

"Who would think the poor bastards could scratch a living out of that."

"You're right there, no wonder the poor sods want to emigrate to America and England. I think I'd want to get away from this place." Harry felt a pang of sympathy towards the villagers.

They were descending, but it wasn't the way out of the mountains yet. Another, far steeper mountain road lay right in front. The roads improved slightly, but not for long. As soon as they hit the next mountain the hairpin bends started once more.

Pulling to a halt for dinner on a wider stretch of the road that boasted grass verges, a D.R. pulled alongside of them. Harry offered him a mug of tea. Lowering the wet dirty scarf from his face, they handed him a towel.

"A tank transporter has just gone over the edge. Fucking hell, you should have seen it go. I never thought it would hit the bottom."

"What happened then?" asked Charlie. "Anyone hurt?"

"The driver was negotiating this bend, hanging from the side of the truck with his door wide open. Everyone was shouting advice and the back wheel went over the edge. The weight of the tank pulled it over and whoosh." He made an exaggerated arc with his hand.

"Over it went taking the driver with it."

"Was he killed?" Before he finished speaking Harry realised what a foolish question he'd just asked. The D.R. stared at him with disbelief.

"What the bleeding hell do you think - with a bloody great transporter and a thirty or forty ton tank smashing you against the jagged side of a mountain? He must have been dead before he hit the bottom. It's a bloody good job the tank crew and the spare driver weren't aboard or they would have had their chips too. That was the bloody trouble, they were all alongside shouting instructions, the poor bugger didn't know whether he was coming or going."

360

Waiting for the other transporters to catch up they had at least forty minutes to spare. The D.R. handed round his tin of cigarettes while Charlie poured a liberal dose of brandy into his mug. The D.R. elaborated on the story of the lost transporter. He sipped the brandy slowly.

"Just what I needed, I'm chilled to the marrow."

He emptied the mug, then lay back on a stretcher while the glow of the brandy tore through his stomach, the warmth circulating his body. He closed his eyes. Bright lights flashed beneath his eyelids as sensation crept back into his extremities.

"Your own medical unit is right behind these transporters. I have just had a pow wow with one of your D.R.s, a scouser. Thick set bloke, swarthy with dark curly hair. Has a tuft hanging in front of his helmet over his forehead, name of Earley?"

Charlie was interested. Earley was one of the originals from the unit.

"Didn't say his name, but it must have been him, he fits your description alright. I told him you were up here, he sends his regards. Said he will try and pop up here when it gets dark and we pull in for the night."

Charlie clicked his tongue and laughed.

"I haven't seen that bastard for months. Just before we went through Tripoli was the last time. When we were resting up at Homs he was sent back for a course. I don't suppose he will remember our last meeting, he was pissed to his eyeballs. What a lad though, bloody handsome and couldn't he pull the birds. They say he was knocking off one of the sisters from a general hospital in Cairo. There was a hell of a stink over it. When the unit was at Alamein he would piss off on that motorbike of his and spend the weekend with her. Bloody officers were jealous, you know how they think. All sisters are sent out just for them, but not this sister, she was no snob, thought the world of Earley. Old Earley didn't give an arse for anybody, but you know how it is, word soon got round and he never went on leave again."

"What about that motorbike of his, Charlie? He could do anything with that," said Harry.

The D.R. got ready to leave, buttoning up his wet greatcoat and adjusting his leather jerkin.

"Thanks for the brandy, I'll make a point of catching up with that mate of yours." He swung open the back doors.

"Shit! Just take a gander at that rain."

CHAPTER 34

It was two days before they met Earley. The division was forced to come to a halt on the tortuous winding mountain road. It had been a feat of endurance. This alone, in normal times and under peace time conditions, would be a tremendous effort for the armoured division, but in the torrential rain that had hit them since they begun the uphill climb, it was a superhuman effort for every man in the division. Fortunately the weather had grounded all enemy aircraft. The light was fading when they pulled to the side of the road and both Charlie and Harry flopped down in the back of the ambulance, wet through and exhausted, onto the stretchers, almost too tired to remove their soaked clothing.

"Harry," Charlie groaned, "know what I could do with? A nice hot mug of tea."

"Well, piss off out and make it. I'm knackered," Harry grunted.

"Come on, get a move on, Harry, you've done sod all but sleep all day long."

Reluctantly Harry rose from his stretcher. It was still pouring with rain when he lit the petrol fire and standing near it he was soon enveloped in clouds of steam. They still had half a loaf of bread left that they'd taken from the officers' kitchen. It was stale but edible and he made two bacon sandwiches.

They were just settling down for the night when they were awakened by someone thumping the side of the ambulance. Charlie sat up with a jerk as the back doors opened letting in a blast of wind and rain.

"I don't know who the hell you are," he bawled out, "but if you don't close that sodding door I'll come out and throw you over the mountainside."

"It's me, Charlie, you old sex pot. Can you do with a lodger for the night?" a voice called back.

"Oh, it's you, Earley, you old scouse git. Get on one of those stretchers underneath. Don't disturb, Harry. He's shagged out. He's been sleeping in his seat all day."

"Lying bastard," Harry answered. "Who the hell can sleep with you driving?"

"I just don't give an arse where I sleep, Charlie. I'm knackered. I've been driving that bloody motor bike up and down this sodding convoy for days," Earley replied and pulled a half bottle of whisky from his back pocket and took a long drink.

Then he handed it to Charlie and Harry, but they both refused.

"Got some mail for you two ponces in my saddle bag. Give it to you in the morning. You'll hurt your eyes in the light from this

362

hurricane lamp if you try to read it now. Christ, Harry, when did you last clean the bloody thing? It stinks to high heaven."

"By the way, Charlie," he went on, "did you hear we passed a bloody brothel a couple of miles back? A high class joint. Seems in this area it's all large houses. Before the war all the film stars lived here. Apparently this was the place to live, and you had to be a millionaire to live here. When the Jerries came they took the houses over for the high ranking officers. This house was for officers. A kind of club where they recuperated, or some would say shagged themselves to death."

It was as if Charlie had come to life. He sat up sharply, all thoughts of sleep completely out of his mind.

"How far back, Fuzzy?" He asked, referring to Earley by his nick name.

"A couple of miles."

"Shall we go and have a shufti?"

"Sod off, Charlie, I'm just thawing through. I feel I could sleep for a fortnight and who the bloody hell wants to chase crumpet half way through the night?"

"I do," Charlie answered and was out of bed and climbing back into his wet clothes. "Can I borrow your motor bike?"

"Sure. Go back a couple of miles. You'll see two Red Caps guarding the front of the house. About five hundred yards past them you come to a path. Go up and follow a low stone wall till you get to the back of the house. It's a nasty climb. You'll have to leave the bike somewhere. When you're level with the house you'll see a faint red light. Careful how you go down the hill, it's all grass and mud and very slippery, and if you get caught don't drag me into it. You'll have to say you borrowed the bike."

"Come on, Harry, let's go."

Charlie donned the D.R's leather jerkin and strapped Earley's revolver to his hip.

"Piss off, Charlie. You don't want me to come, do you?" Harry was reluctant to get out of the warm blankets, but if Charlie was going to get himself caught he would have to be there with him. Anyway he knew they didn't have a chance in hell. If the men knew there was a brothel in the area the news would have swept through the division like a bush fire.

Charlie was just as expert with a motor cycle as he was with the ambulance. The rain and wind blew in his face as he raced past the convoy, almost deserted apart from a few sentries crouched against the sides of the vehicles sheltering from the blast of rain. Harry was crouched behind Charlie, clinging to the leather jerkin. They passed the two Red Caps, who hardly gave the bike a second glance.

363

There was no mistaking the path leading to the hill. A stream of yellow mud six feet wide ran like a volcanic lava from it across the road and down over the other side in a yellow waterfall. Charlie made a quick turn, skidding around on the mud and was a hundred yards up the side of the mountain before the engine gave up and the wheel skidded round and round.

"Have to walk from here, Harry."

It was a tortuous journey. The mud accumulated on their boots and several times they were forced to rest on the low stone wall.

"After all this effort, Charlie, I won't have the strength to do a bloody thing," Harry gasped.

Through the straight lines of orange trees they finally spotted the pale red lamp. They sat on the wall to get their breath back and while they did, took in the situation.

"It's a bloody long way down, Charlie, and that ground looks treacherous," Harry said.

But Charlie was already over the wall. He crouched down hanging onto the trees for support and as he swung from each one, a shower of rain came down on top of them. Harry followed him, and then they let go with Harry clinging to Charlie. His foot slipped and they both slithered down the hill, trees flashing by like telegraph poles passing a train window, until at last they came to a halt as Charlie's feet hit the middle of a man's back.

"You clumsy bastard, what the hell do you think you're up to?" He shouted and from behind a dozen or more trees men were calling out in furious whispers for silence.

"Bloody hell, Harry," Charlie muttered, "half the bleeding division is here."

The man Charlie had knocked down was still breathless as he told them, "It's the Rifle Brigade. They've got things organised. What happens is that when you see the door half a dozen men come out and another half dozen takes their places. These are blokes in the Rifle Brigade and when you get to the last tree you give the blokes a packet of fags then he lets you pass. It's very well organised."

"What do you mean you give this bloke a packet of fags? What is he a bleeding pimp, or something?" Charlie wanted to know.

"No, it's a bloke from the Rifle Brigade, and if I was you I wouldn't argue. He's built like an outside brick shithouse and his two cronies make him look like a dwarf." The man eased his back with a groan. He was still suffering from the accidental boot Charlie had put in his kidneys.

Charlie didn't like the idea of giving his cigarettes to some unknown racketeer.

"Bloody marvellous, i'nit? Here we are in the middle of the Mafiosa country and these bastards, no doubt from the east end of London, come here, in the country just a few days, and are already taking over. Stuff them, they're not taking me for a ride."

He straightened up his leather jerkin and his hand coming in contact with Earley's revolver strapped to his side a sudden inspiration came to him He tapped Harry's shoulder and nodded towards the top of the hill.

"Come on, Harry, I've a bright idea."

They scrambled to the top again slipping and sliding, the air heavy with cursing. Then drenched with rain and sweat they sat on the low brick wall Charlie fighting for breath.

He gasped, "How long did it take to get up here, Harry?"

Harry appeared to be in much the same condition and replied, "Twenty minutes at least. Every step I took forward I must have slipped back two."

Charlie forced a laugh.

"That just my point. Now I have an idea. If we can get this shower running to the top and at the same time get rid of those two Red Caps we could slide down to the bottom in two minutes."

"And pray, how the hell are we to get rid of them? Besides there's no way I'm going to slide down that death trap. There's still two inches of mud clinging to my arse."

"You don't have to slide down on your arse, Harry."

He lifted a flat box about three feet long and two feet wide from a large pile of boxes by the wall. Boxes the farmer used for gathering the citrus fruit.

"When I was a kid we used to play on the corporation tip and slide down the hill on sheets of corrugated iron. I became quite an expert. You see, Harry, you sit in the box and let yourself go and if you want to stop you push your body forward. The box collects the mud in front and comes to a halt. Then you ease back if you want to start again. Tell you, Harry, it's bloody great."

"Piss off, Charlie. How about those trees? Hit one of them and it's kiss your arse goodbye time. When you reach the bottom you'd be doing fifty miles an hour. And anyway, you haven't solved a way of getting rid of that shower waiting to get in."

"Oh, yes I have. Wait till there's a lull in the thunder and rain. Then while I'm preparing the sledges you go along the top for a couple of hundred yards."

Charlie gave Harry the D.R's revolver. "You fire that in the air. Remember only a few days ago this area was crawling with Jerries. They'll think a pocket has been left behind and I tell you Harry, old mate, you won't see their arses for dust. None of them are armed except the two Red Caps, so no one will hang around."

"When it comes to women you're a devious bastard, Charlie. I don't know," Harry was weakening, "I don't like the idea of the boxes, even if the shots work which I very much doubt."

"Look, Harry, the boxes are as safe as houses. On this wet grass it'll be like a helter skelter." He sat in a box to illustrate.

Reluctantly Harry took the revolver.

"I'll save one shot, Charlie, and if it doesn't work I'll blow your bleeding brains out," he joked. Then bending forward against the wind and rain he set off along the top road. It was twenty minutes before there was a lull in the wind and rain. A series of flashes and shots rent the air and then echoed round the mountains like a miniature thunder storm.

There was silence for a few minutes before the citrus grove seemed to come alive. Men scrambled from behind every tree slipping and sliding in their panic to reach the top. It seemed as if half the div was there. Twenty more minutes elapsed before the first man reached the top, his hands on the low wall, wheezing and coughing and when he arrived he found Charlie sitting there, smoking a cigarette.

"What the bleeding hell is up?" The man gasped out, fighting for breath. "Were those fucking shots I heard?"

"Yes," Charlie answered. "Looks like a pocket of Jerries has been left behind to kick up a rumpus. Some men have gone up there armed to the teeth to sort them out. I should get out of here if I was you, there's bleeding Red Caps all over the place." His tone was one of complete innocence as he continued, "What the hell is going on down there?"

"Brothel," said the man, "but you can have my share..." And he was away down the slippery path as fast as his legs would carry him.

As every man reached the top exhausted they sat down on the wall to regain their breath and asked Charlie the identical question, each time getting and identical answer. He could see a couple of flashing lights from torches. It could only be the Red Caps about to investigate.

At last Harry came striding down and handed Charlie the heavy revolver, which he replaced in his holster, a satisfied grin splitting open his face.

"Didn't I tell you it would work? Let's wait for it to clear before we put the second part of the operation into gear."

Those men that had been near the bottom and wouldn't rush out of the gate because of the Red Caps reached the top of the hill in a state of complete exhaustion. Then as neither Charlie or Harry wore a watch, they could only guess that an hour must have passed before it was completely quiet, with only the flashes of the Red Caps' torches between the trees.

Charlie selected two rows of orange trees with the widest gap between them.

"There you are, Harry, it's just one straight row to the house. We're almost in line with that red light. Don't forget forward to stop, lean back to move."

Harry sat in the box adjusting his steel helmet, Charlie gave him a gentle push and he moved off. Unfortunately the wet grass was angled forward flattened by the rain and Harry wasn't picking up the mud. Charlie jumped in his box to follow, just in time to see Harry hit the large white stones surrounding the house catapulting him in a somersault. He hit the gravel path flat on his back. Charlie immediately realised the trouble and being well versed in the tactic threw himself off the box a few yards from the stones, and rolled forward lightly bumping one of the larger ones. Hurriedly he picked up his helmet and went to investigate.

Harry was out cold and Charlie put his hand inside his tunic to check his heartbeat, breathing deeply with relief when he found it strong and steady. He lifted him over his shoulder and staggered towards the house, gently kicking the glass panelled door with his toe.

A raven haired girl came to the door dressed only in a silk dressing gown, the top parted in a 'v' which left very little to the imagination. She took one look at Charlie and let out a low scream tempered by her fist clenched in her mouth. Then she tried to slam the door in Charlie's face but he jammed his foot in the opening and she was forced to open it and let him in. Now the girl flew back against the passage wall, her fist still remained in her mouth. Two more girls stood at the far end of the passage and they gasped in horror at the two mud covered apparitions.

Charlie gently lay Harry on the carpet. More girls ran down the stairs and from the rooms, keeping their distance under the impression he was a casualty from the recent shooting.

Charlie's jaw dropped. "And to think they are all mine," he muttered aloud and laughed, his mouth splitting open to reveal two rows of even white teeth accentuated by his mud splattered face. Now he brought his few Italian words into play, surveying all the while his luxurious surrounding.

A large ornate gold framed mirror faced the door and he examined himself with Harry just coming round.

"Hell, look at us. No wonder the poor girls screamed Harry," he chuckled.

But as Harry sat up and he gazed round his eyes glazed.

"What the hell's happened, Charlie?"

He rubbed his head and felt a lump the size of a duck's egg, the throbbing beat in it an insistent hammering on his brain. One of the girls took in the situation and kneeling beside him gave him a sip of brandy.

Charlie couldn't take his eyes away from the bevy of women.

"When I get to the bathroom I'll show one of you my worldly charms," he proclaimed in English and looking the girls up and down studied their faces.

He was in a quandary which one he should pick, but not for long. One girl stood out from the rest. She had dark almond eyes, jet black hair that fell to her shoulders in neat waves and the loose fitting dressing gown couldn't quite conceal her rich voluptuous body. He winked at her and indicated he wanted a wash. Harry seemed to be in good hands, but Charlie knelt beside him and smacked his face until he opened his eyes.

"Just going to have a bath, Harry boy. Pull yourself together, mate." He studied the pretty girl tending Harry. "You're in good hands, mate."

The girl Charlie fancied led him to the bathroom door and he gasped. This was luxury in its fullest sense, for, although it was over decorated in the usual Italian fashion, it was a sumptuous joy after the army. Pink tinted glass mirrors were laced with gold and one huge mirror covered the entire wall above the bath and the ceiling. The opposite wall was covered in relief sea motifs, prancing dolphins, starfish, shells and twin golden cherubs and mermaids. The bath itself was pink marble with gold plated taps in the form of dolphins. Neptune stood astride the taps grinning down at the bathers and the bath could easily accommodate four persons. Hot and cold water gushed from the dolphin's mouth and soon the girl had filled the bath.

Charlie wasted no time getting in and lying back in the hot water, and he decided to call the girl Sunshine for every time he spoke to her all she did was beam radiantly at him. Greedily he watched as she leaned over the bath to wash him, her smooth breasts falling from her loose fitting dressing gown while he admired them, and thoroughly aroused, Charlie's hand caressed the smooth silk draped over her bottom. Sunshine really warmed him up, that was for sure.

His skimpy knowledge of Italian mixed with a smattering of German, Arabic and French got him nowhere, and like all true Brits he believed that the louder he shouted the sooner she would understand. He tried to glean from her how often the military police visited the place, but she just shook her head and beamed hugely.

368

Then after several minutes of seemingly futile hard work in trying to communicate with her, she at last said in the most drastic English, "They nota nev-air ina thees 'owsa." Then she began to negotiate the terms of Charlie's stay.

He smiled and slid down to his neck in the great bath and winced as the water soaked into the cuts and scratches suffered in his downhill ride. Closing his eyes he leaned back completely relaxed. Sunshine slid open a small cupboard under the bath. It was filled with sweet smelling bath lotion and she tipped a few drops in the water just as he opened his eyes again. He sprang forward to take the bottle from her, accidentally knocked it into the water and on hands and knees groped frantically for it. Then having found it, he discovered the contents were completely dissolved.

He held the bottle to the light and gasped, "Bloody hell," he exploded but Sunshine burst out laughing and closing his eyes again he fell into a kind of relaxed stupor.

As if from a far distance, he heard knocking on the door.

"Is that you in there, Charlie?"

Harry was back on his feet again after having been revived by two ministering angels. He knocked again. "That you, Charlie?"

"Yes, Harry, and at the moment I'm having this wonderful dream. I think I must have been killed on that slide down the hill and I've arrived in heaven. This really can't be happening. But just in case it is a dream and you've disturbed me before I finish it I will bloody well kill you, mate."

"Alright to come in and have a wash, Charlie?" Harry's voice was still a little shaky.

Sunshine was about to step in the bath with him and looked somewhat disappointed when Charlie told her to open the door. She did so completely naked and Harry's jaw sagged as he stepped inside. He could hardly take his eyes from the shapely figure. Then he wrinkled his nose and gasped for breath as he smelt the strongly perfumed water.

"Bloody hell, Charlie, you are lording it up a bit, aren't you? Hurry up and get it over and let's get the hell away from here before those Red Caps return."

Charlie looked at Harry as though he'd lost his wits and committed some form of sacrilege, and he poked the water from his ears to make sure he was hearing correctly.

"Did you damage that brain of yours when you fell out of that box, Harry?" he enquired.

He handed the girl, who was now in the bath with him, an oversized sponge and she gently massaged his back.

"We have it made here, Harry. A deserted brothel filled with lovely girls, and, I might add, the first chance we've had since we arrived in this God forsaken country for a bloody hot bath and a real bed with clean sheets. What more do you want?"

Gloomily Harry rubbed the top of his head and grumbled, "I've got a lump like an ostrich egg and my head feels as if it's about to burst."

"Forget it, Harry, and go find a nice girl. You have a hot bath and get to bed. That is just what the doctor would order."

Sunshine drained the water from the bath. It left a filthy ridge round the top. She cleaned the bath thoroughly then refilled it, ordering Charlie to get in again.

"How many fags have you got, Harry?" Charlie asked, delighted with the turn of events.

"Two tins," he replied.

"I have three. That should do. We can stay the night. She says no Red Caps come inside the house."

Sunshine turned to thunder, scowled, and clicking her tongue angrily interrupted him shaking her black hair vigorously as she spat out, "No fockinga Reda Cap ..."

"See what I mean, Harry? She speaks perfect English." Charlie flashed her an admiring glance. "We can stay till first light. If the convoy moves out, Earley will drive. The speed that convoy travels it won't take long to catch up. I'll get Sunshine here to fix you up with a good girl. They want three tins of fifty for the night, she tells me. I think I can work if for two and a half tins each. You can have half of one of my tins."

"It's pressing our luck, Charlie, staying the night."

"So was sliding down the bloody hill, but we made it alright."

"Only just." Harry's face was distorted with pain as he massaged the lump.

"Stop pissing moaning, Harry. You might be bloody dead next week. I can't see our luck lasting much longer. Get in the bath and you'll feel as good as gold in the morning."

Charlie winked at Sunshine, then nodded towards Harry and the door. She took Harry's hand and led him out and then shouted along the passage. A well endowed red head appeared and took him in charge. As for Sunshine she was anxious to get back to Charlie and the hot bath.

In the morning Harry hurried to join Charlie whom he found staring through the window at the end of the passage. The convoy hadn't moved and black smoke from dozens of petrol fires curled upwards for the first brew of the day. There were two Red Caps stationed at their posts at the gate some hundred yards or more from the house.

"There the bastards go, Harry," Charlie muttered. He was naked, a blanket draped around him. Harry was wearing one of the girl's housecoats.

"Go and have a shufti round the rooms, Harry. Look through the windows and see if any Red Caps are patrolling the grounds."

He returned a few minutes later, his face split by a wide grin.

"Know what, Charlie? That bastard hypocrite Major Reid whose always lecturing us on not going with prossies and foreign women is laying on top of a bed starkers with this brown skinned bird beside him. Wish I had a bloody camera I'd blackmail the bastard! Earley told me he'd been missing all day yesterday. No wonder!"

After a breakfast of omelettes, made with fresh eggs and cooked in olive oil and seasoning, and lots of strong black coffee the two men prepared to leave. Two girls came in with their uniforms cleaned and neatly pressed and their shirts and socks washed.

"Let's go upstairs and nick old Reid's greatcoat, Harry. That will put the sod in a spot. I could wear it and we could both go past those Red Caps and I could say in my pound note accent that we have been inspecting the place. They won't quiz us much. After all he's got a medic's cap badge and it would sound feasible. Reid is just about my size."

"Don't be a bloody rat bag, Charlie. If that greatcoat and cap goes missing these girls will get the blame, and they looked after us last night."

Charlie grinned, "Yeah, you're right, Harry, we'll just have to think of something else." He was concentrating on the window. "Here, Harry, have a shufti. See that path leading through this grove on this side? All we have to do is bypass those Red Caps, get across that gravel path and dash through the grove. It'll bring us out level with the bike. There's no need to climb the hill. Pity about the mud, though, I feel nice and clean for the first time since we landed at Salerno."

He called Sunshine over and after a while instructed her to take the Red Caps cups of hot coffee. Then while the Red Caps' interest was concentrated on the half-dressed women they decided they would sneak out.

Smiling as usual Sunshine took her time and walked down the path. The Red Caps' attention was riveted on her luscious figure as she walked towards them the gravel crunching under foot. She held the cups towards them turning round so all the Red Caps' backs were towards Charlie and Harry as they made a dash for the trees. She was no fool, for she did the job well. In the safety of the trees Harry and Charlie turned and waved to the other girls who were giggling at the window.

Charlie had taken the precaution of covering the bike with some of the farmer's boxes. It was still covered in that sickening filthy mud. He kicked it into life and the roar of the engine echoed around the grove and surrounding mountains.

"God, Charlie, that noise is enough to waken the dead," he muttered.

The two Red Caps waved them down.

"Christ, Harry, the sods must have seen us slipping out of the side of the house," Charlie muttered. He knew he could have made a dash for it, but he might drop Earley in the crap. Instead he slowed the bike.

"Where's your helmet, soldier?" a Red Cap rapped.

Harry hadn't recovered it when he crashed down the hill.

"Lost it a couple of days ago, corp. Reported it to the Q.M. but he can't issue another while we're on the move."

Charlie nodded towards the house. "What was all that shooting last night, corp? Bit of a punch up was there?"

"No, it seems there was couple of Jerries left behind. They decided to fight their way out. Where the hell they were going to God only knows. We sorted them out."

He turned to his mate and pulling himself up to his full height threw out his chest. "That right, Ern?"

"Sure."

"Did you shoot the bastards, corp?" Charlie asked hardly keeping a straight face.

"We thought we heard some groans. We're just waiting for daylight and more men so that we can make a thorough search."

Ten minutes later Harry and Charlie pulled up at their ambulance. Earley was fast asleep on his stretcher. They woke him with a hot mug of tea and after smelling it Earley directed his nose at Charlie and wrinkled it in distaste.

"Bloody hell, Charlie, you smell like a Cairo brothel."

"Believe me, Earley, you would never see a brothel like that one in Cairo," Charlie told him and then went into minute details of the events of the past evening.

"You're a jammy bastard, Charlie," Earley sighed enviously.

Charlie threw Earley his revolver.

"I tell you, Earley, it was worth every minute to watch the others scramble up that hill. It just came alive. Talk about the Rifle Brigade. There must have been half the bloody division waiting there - and to think we had it all to ourselves."

CHAPTER 35

"See Naples and die, Harry," shouted Charlie above the roar of the engine as he negotiated the road skirting the Bay of Naples. The city was stretched out below them, the air clear of mist and the blue waters reflected the azure cloudless sky. Islands broke through the smooth sea, sheer cliffs stretching skywards, and in pride of place was the bay's most famous island, Capri. Its sheer cliffs looking, from a distance, like a barrier defying tourists to keep away.

Dominating the whole bay and reflecting its photographic image on the smooth waters Vesuvious belched smoke from its cone-like summit, clawing its way skywards and flattening out after a couple of hundred feet like a huge tablecloth. It was late 1943 and the silent mountain was about to erupt in protest at the folly of the war raging around its foothills, proving that nature could outshine any show that mortal man cared to put on. Charlie was overcome by the panorama spread out below.

"My God, Harry, it's beautiful. Francesca was right when she said I had seen nothing till I saw the Bay of Naples."

"Pity she didn't warn us about the pong," Harry muttered.

They pulled up onto the grass verge, the other two ambulances drawing in behind them.

"Christ, Charlie, what a stink," Harry complained again, wrinkling his nose and the two drivers standing beside him grumbled their agreement.

A faint zephyr of wind caused a ripple across the bay bringing with it even more intense fumes of the nauseating stench and looking directly below them they could see a large cemetery which had been shelled and bombed. Headstones that once stood in perfect symmetrical rows were cast aside at all angles, some smashed to small pieces. Skeletons with half rotted flesh hung from the low hanging branches of the trees, while skulls with perpetual grins and black holes where their eyes had been stared sightlessly down on the scene. One skull had been tossed high and caught up on top of a flagpole through one of its eye sockets, or had been placed there by someone with a macabre sense of humour.

A church stood in the centre, the focal point of the cemetery with its star of pathways leading in every direction. Rows of coffins lined the roads, makeshift coffins made from rough pine or any wood that the carpenters could find. Nearly all of them had the lids half open and relatives wandered from coffin to coffin, handkerchiefs across their noses and half blinded by tears trying to identify their loved ones. An anguished scream penetrated the still air, signalling the dreadful knowledge that hope had been shattered for the survival of a loved one. Harry covered his nose with his handkerchief.

"Bloody hell, looks like a scene from Dante's Inferno," he muttered.

All three ambulance crews were seasoned veterans. Some, like Harry, with three major campaigns behind them, but this was a sight that was to remain embedded in their memories for life. Harry tried to turn his head away but was fascinated by the sight of a skull in the gutter, strips of rotting blackened flesh and patches of hair sticking to it, a line of maggots parading through a decomposing eyeball. Then he turned his head away as more of the revolting sickly stench wafted up at him on a fresh breeze. They left in a hurry forgetting the tea they had stopped for. In fact they all wanted to puke.

The scene at the hospital was more reminiscent of old Victorian times and could be equally judged with the hospital at Scutari in the Crimea. Any minute Harry might have expected to see Florence Nightingale emerge from a ward carrying her famous lamp. The wards were so overcrowded that men and women were mixed together. Every available space was taken up with beds or stretchers where there was sufficient room to fit a bed, which made it almost impossible for the medical staff to attend to their duties. The befouled air was unbearable as the overworked staff had no time to minister to the patients' bodily functions, and most of the dressings were stained dark brown and in need of changing.

Large houses on the outskirts of the city had been commandeered and turned into emergency hospitals. The three ambulances had been sent to help with their evacuation.

Harry was detailed to help the British M.O. with the vaccines. The U.S. navy had flown in the serum and they had been allocated three days to carry out the work and return to their own unit. Three weeks would have been more appropriate and they worked around the clock.

"God, sir, If I ever see another hypodermic needle again I'll do my nut," Harry complained. "How many do you reckon we've done?"

The M.O. smiled at him.

"God knows, Jackson. I lost count the first day." He scrubbed his hands for what must have been the hundredth time. "You did quite well, Jackson, so I'll put in my diary 5,000. Do you think that will cover it?"

"Being a bit cautious aren't you, sir? I think we must have doubled that at least," he laughed.

"Well, at least you can get some sleep now. God, I felt sorry for some of those kids, they looked so scared and the blunt needles didn't help." He kicked the bucket of swabs and used needles. "At least we might have prevented that lot from getting typhus."

He got no answer. Harry had fallen asleep across the foot of the bed they had put at their disposal. He lay there for two hours before Charlie shook him by his foot.

"Come on, you lazy bastard, our job's finished here."

The division had been pulled out of the line for a rest, but all medical units were ordered to send in teams to Naples to handle an outbreak of cholera and help with the heavy civilian casualties, and with the possibility of the division returning to the lines only three days could be spared.

The sergeant in charge took the lead and, once clear of the city out in open country, pulled the ambulances off the road.

"Come on, lads, enough is enough. It's three days since most of you had a decent sleep and the drivers are dropping off at the wheel. If we carry on like this there'll be a bloody accident and, after surviving Dunkirk and a couple of years in the desert I don't relish the idea of ending up in a ditch here in Italy."

He examined his watch and went through the routine of shaking his wrist a few times making certain it was still ticking over, then held it to his ear. "It's 2 pm now. We're due back at six. That gives us four hours if we do oversleep a couple of hours. I can square that with the old man, but try and wake at six. Now go and get your heads down."

Most of them were completely exhausted and needed no second bidding. Charlie was almost asleep on his feet. He dropped onto the stretcher and immediately fell in a coma-like sleep without bothering to cover himself with blankets.

Apart from the short time on the bed Harry had been without sleep for so long he found it difficult to drop off. He stared at the plywood roof with unseeing eyes, his brain unable to record, but he must have dropped into a deep sleep for the next thing he knew the sergeant was shaking him violently by his foot. He sat up resting on one elbow. It was dark outside, his head was thumping and his bladder felt uncomfortably distended. He rushed through the back doors and stood at the rear wheels where he unbuttoned and let go with a sigh of relief. All signs of the previous storm had vanished and bright stars hung from the skies. The grey glimmer of dawn spread across the eastern horizon and a slight south westerly breeze blew in from the sea. For almost a week it had rained incessantly and the air was sharp.

The sergeant was performing the same job at the rear wheel of his ambulance. He strained his eyes to look at his wristwatch but there was insufficient light from the stars, and striking a match he gasped, "Fucking hell!"

"What's up, sarge?" Charlie asked.

"You might bloody well ask. It's almost four in the morning. We've slept the whole bloody night through!"

The sergeant dashed alongside the other ambulance, banging the flat of his hand against the canvas sides, his greatcoat wide open, flapping in the breeze. "Come on, you lazy bastards," he yelled, "out of those flea pits."

The butt of his cigarette fell from his mouth as panic stricken he slammed open the ambulance doors. The crew of the second ambulance was still fast asleep, their snores vibrating round the flimsy plywood interior and it was doubtful if even a hand grenade thrown in their ambulance would have disturbed them.

The sergeant jerked at their legs until they moved and then turning to Harry said, "Go and get that driver of yours into his driving seat. Drag him out if you have to."

Harry tugged at his driver's feet. "Come on, Charlie, the old sarge is doing his nut. It's four in the morning." But try as he might nothing would wake Charlie. "Balls to you then I'll drive myself," Harry muttered.

Two hours later when it was quite light Charlie struggled through the small door leading to the cab. He rubbed his eyes and stared at the wet road. "Has it been raining, Harry?"

"No, that's morning dew, mate. It looks like it's going to be a bright day."

"That'll make a change. It's pissed down every day since we arrived here. Do you want me to take over?"

"Doesn't matter, we're almost there," Harry replied.

Charlie lit two cigarettes and passed one to Harry.

"One of these days, Harry, I'll string your balls into a necklace. When you woke me this morning I was just about to mount my little Francesca again. You're a right bloody kill joy, you bastard."

Silence fell upon the small convoy broken only by the smooth humming of the engines. They passed over a small bridge where the faint splashing of the stream, overflowing from the constant rain, caused Charlie to look up. A flock of birds broke cover and flew across their path.

"Who would think there was a bloody war on, Harry?" Charlie sighed, marvelling at the tranquil sight.

"I would. God, I slept like a bloody log! When the sergeant woke me, I had a piss, a real tankful. Tell you, Charlie, if it had been petrol we could've got to Rome and back on it."

376

"You would have thought the miserable sod would have let us brew up before we left. My mouth feels like a sportsman's jockstrap," Charlie complained.

"Poor bastard was hopping around like his balls were on fire when he realised what time it was. He blamed me and all the others. Said one of us must have got up for a slash during the night and realised the time. If he's seen what I got rid of he would have known I didn't wake up," Harry said.

They stopped a couple of miles short of their unit while the sergeant called them all together. Charlie farted loudly, the second bomb blast that morning which was rather unusual for him! He always boasted he was a one fart man and after expelling his surplus wind first thing he was comfortable for the remainder of the day. He put this one down to tiredness and an irregular diet. The men around his sniggered.

"God, Williams, that was a shirt lifter!"

"Right, men, just follow me and don't say anything," the sergeant barked. "If any questions are asked let me do the talking. I still can't understand why one of you didn't wake up during the night. I have no doubt one of you did and said fuck it, let the sergeant carry the can back."

"Never mind, sarge, we're right behind you," said Charlie.

The sergeant nodded his head and clicked his tongue.

"Yes, Williams, that's what's worrying me, having you shower behind me. I would feel a lot safer with a battalion of S.S. at my rear."

He studied their faces each in turn by the dim light of the dawn. Murphy sat at his steering wheel his bleary eyes staring ahead. He was well known throughout the division for the amount of cheap red wine he could knock back and it was certain he would have been out of bed during the night frothing in a drunken stupor.

They reached the camp which was deserted. A mist shrouded the hedges. The ambulances and vehicles were spread well out across the open fields and, where possible, parked under any tree that offered protection from air observation. The sergeant waved them down and stealthily crept forward, his long greatcoat dragging in the mud. The guard was fast asleep, spread across a pile of empty ammunition boxes, and covered with his greatcoat.

A faint light showed through the flaps of the orderly room tent and the sergeant peered through. Corporal Sykes was fast asleep at the table his head resting on his arms. The sergeant sucked in his breath with distaste. Like the rest of the unit the sergeant couldn't stand the sight of Sykes and would dearly have loved to have taken this chance to put him on a charge for neglect of duty;

a golden opportunity he had waited for several years. Sykes was supposed to be Corporal in charge of guard and the sergeant let it rest like that, for the next morning Sykes would have some explaining to do for allowing three ambulances and crews into the camp undetected.

The sergeant moved from ambulance to ambulance his voice lowered to a husky whisper.

"Make as little noise as possible," he instructed, "the bastards are fast asleep in there. Let's go right round the back and drive through those hedges." He sniggered humourlessly, "That bastard Sykes will have some explaining to do in the morning."

Crashing through the hedges was more trouble than anyone anticipated with one of the ambulances soon firmly wedged in the soft ground. It took the efforts of the whole team pushing, and one of the other ambulances pulling, to tow it out and, all in vain for the unit was preparing with the division to move forward again and everyone was far too busy to worry about three ambulances being a few hours late.

Freshly shaven with a good meal inside them they were attached to an armoured car regiment. They moved out of the flat territory and into the mountainous country again and having done so set up their R.A.P. outside a deserted farmhouse in a small orchard hewn out of the mountainside. The roadway in front snaked upwards in a series of hairpin bends.

Strong rumours were flying around that this was to be the last action in Italy for the division, a rumour that was substantiated by one of the regiments pulling out and going back to the rest area with a Canadian regiment taking its place, but that was on another section of the line the division was holding.

Machine gun fire filtered through the still mountain air, too far away for the men sitting around the petrol fire to worry about. Armoured cars spread out across the orange grove sheltering under the meagre branches, small oranges clinging to them like golden balls on a christmas tree. The farmhouse had been abandoned at the first sound of gunfire.

Charlie bent over the petrol fire watching his brew can bubbling away with the crews of two armoured cars watching his every move. A German 88 sounded in the distance and the explosion rumbled round the mountainside like a clap of thunder, while the crisp cold mountain air forced them to turn up their greatcoat collars and wrap their hands round the hot mugs of tea.

"Not bad around here, is it, lads?"

Charlie sat down on an empty jerrican, his breath coming out in clouds of white vapour, his gaze wandering around the mist shrouded mountainside. Then he dug deep into his greatcoat pocket for his cigarettes but suddenly stopped dead as if he had just been struck by lightning. Casually he walked over to a sergeant standing under an orange tree.

"Don't look now, sarge, but I think we're being watched. Right above our heads where the road twists round are three bloody great Tiger tanks."

The sergeant burst out laughing and started to turn round but Harry restrained him.

"For fuck sake, sarge, I've just been watching them. The fronts of the tanks are overlapping the edge."

"Don't be a prick, Williams, there's no Jerry armour within four miles of here," the sarge snorted in disbelief.

"Any of our tanks in front of us, sarge?"

He shook his head. "Not so far as I know."

"Well believe me, sarge, there are three tanks up there and I should know when I see a Tiger tank or not. In fact if those tanks aren't Tigers you can safely say that your prick's a bloater."

Knowing that their every movement was being observed they moved unobtrusively towards the rear of the farmhouse. The back door was securely locked, so smashing a window they climbed in and rushed upstairs, and there hiding behind the flimsy, dirty net curtains the sergeant took Charlie's binoculars and studied the three tanks. He sucked in his breath sharply.

"Bleeding hell, you're right, Williams, they are Tigers. What the bloody hell are they doing up there?"

"Watching us down here, sarge. What I can't understand is why the hell haven't they blown us to pieces. They caught us with out pants down."

"I know," said the sarge, "it's because they can't depress the guns' elevation low enough, you prick, and I doubt if they would try and reach us as the road is only wide enough for one of them at a time. Wonder what their bloody game is?" He handed the glasses back. "I'll get Captain Larkin up here. If they make a move just yell."

A few minutes later Charlie was joined by the sergeant and Captain Larkin, who took the glasses.

"Some daft bugger has got it wrong. There's not supposed to be any armour about here. I wonder what they're up to?"

"Someone forgot to tell them to retreat, sir."

He gave Charlie a withering look. He hadn't seen too much action having joined the regiment at the closing phases of the desert war, although he had taken part in the retreat to Dunkirk. But the sergeant knew what was expected of him, and took the glasses again. A group of Germans stood between the tanks, dominated by a tall officer dressed from head to toe in black.

379

They were too far away to see with the naked eye, but close enough with their machine guns which, in the hands of good gunners could have wiped them out before they realised what had hit them.

"It's pretty obvious they saw us before Williams spotted them, sir."

Realising how close they'd been to a massacre sent shivers through Charlie. He felt a lot more comfortable with a thick brick wall between him and the enemy. Casually he walked downstairs. His luck was in - Harry was at the back of the house and nodded towards him.

"Come and had a shufti at this lot, Harry," Charlie said quietly, not wanting a mass exodus towards the house as this would rouse the enemy's suspicions.

Another officer had joined them and the three went into a huddle while Charlie kept watch on the tanks. The sergeant vanished downstairs again and soon reappeared with a short stocky sergeant who had rather long arms for a man of his size and walked with a gait more reminiscent of a trained monkey. He wore the crossed sabre of P.T. Instructor on his arm together with the badges of a crack regimental rifleman.

"Sergeant King how far away can you get to hit that German officer between the eyes with just one shot?" asked Captain Larkin.

The sergeant didn't need the glasses Charlie offered him and screwing his eyes he laughed, "I could take him from here, sir."

"Well let's hope you can because you might not get a second chance, mate. It's the tail one I want. He seems to be in charge."

"You mean the one with the Hitler moustache and the row of medals on his chest?"

"Christ, King, you've got good eyes."

The sergeant spoke to the rest of the group.

"Now one by one and not too close to the window. Take a shufti up the mountain." He pointed in its direction. "There's three Tigers up there."

The first man went to the window and in a long drawn out gasp whispered, "Fucking hell."

"Yes, that's right, you might well gasp. As you can see, there's a ledge running right under the road there, just below the tanks. It goes back perhaps five or six feet into a sort of cave. Now, if two of you can walk down the road a couple of hundred yards and climb to the ledge, as you can see it runs right round... then ease yourselves round till you're under the tanks and gently lob a few grenades up and over, Sergeant King and two other marksmen will take the crews from here the minute the first grenade goes off. With a bit of luck we can take them by surprise. The men below have been warned and are walking about casually. They'll run for cover at the first shot and pump as many shots as possible into the crews if they get a chance."

"I'll go along the top, sir," the other young officer said and sprang to attention. "I've done quite a bit of mountain climbing."

"I'll go too, sir," a quietly spoken Scot said, "I've done a bit of climbing in the Highlands."

Captain Larkin nodded his head in approval.

"Go out the back way and walk amongst the orange trees so they won't spot you. We'll have them under surveillance while you get to the mountainside and if it looks suspicious Sergeant King and his team can have a go from here. The ledge up there looks wide enough so I don't think you'll have any trouble."

Collecting a bag of primed grenades each, Lieutenant Prendergast and Trooper Steel made their way from the house and through the orchard. It seemed like hours before they drew level with the house but it was only just thirty minutes, the climb turning out to be much easier then they had evidently thought. Standing with his back as close to the mountain as possible Lieutenant Prendergast waved down to them.

"Stop taking a bow, Prendergast, and get on with it," Captain Larkin hissed between his teeth.

Prendergast made the climb look simple. Twice they had to press themselves close to the mountain wall as loose stones slid away from underfoot. Steel wiped the sweat from his forehead, and the men below held their breath as they watched the two men edge closer and closer towards the tanks, the slight overhang hiding them from the Germans. They stopped right under the tanks and fumbled about with their haversacks. The officer edged forward making sure he was in the right place, then he nodded his head to Steel and whispered, "They're right above our heads, Steel."

The circular metal turret door of the centre tank flew open and another officer all in black emerged and spoke a few words to the men and pointed to the orange grove below. One of the marksmen, his rifle resting in the fork of a tree, bore his sights down on him and a sergeant tapped his shoulder.

"Don't shoot yet," he warned. "Let Prendergast get the first grenade away." The remainder of the men walked around as if nothing unusual was happening, but they were ready to drop at the first shot.

"You, Hughes," the sergeant shouted to a man behind a tree, "put that bloody rifle down. You're the worst shot in the battalion. Go and sit round that fire with your mates."

Hughes dropped his rifle and grumbling went and took his seat.

"It looks like Prendergast is moving, get ready Sergeant King and don't miss." Captain Larkin spoke sharply as the tall officer walked towards the edge of the mountain. It was then that Lieutenant Prendergast moved forward, a grenade in his outstretched hand. He waited to the last minute and then hurled it upwards. But the officer had seen the hand and shouted. There was a mad scramble for the tanks but too late. The officer's hands went to his face, his knees buckled and he toppled over the edge, somersaulted and landed on the ledge beside Lieutenant Prendergast. He pushed the German over the ledge with the toe of his boot as he hurled the second grenade over. The body tumbled in a number of successive arcs hitting against the side of the mountain and bouncing off, and came to rest in the middle of the road, arms outstretched, legs twisted.

It wasn't the first time Sergeant King has proved in action that he wasn't just a good shot with the targets on the regimental rifle range. Before the men below got their first shot in he quickly reloaded and another German pitched forward, hands flung before him, his foot caught between two boulders. His body swung over the edge, his head and shoulders just showing in the cavern where Prendergast and Steel were about to throw out more grenades. He stared bewildered upside down at their heads, his arms hanging downwards. Steel tugged hard at the arms and sent him on his way down the mountain, while a bullet from below whizzed into the wall behind them and Steel waved his fist at the men below.

"Must be that bloody Hughes, sir."

A hail of bullets passed over their heads and four more found their deadly mark. Two of the tanks blew up, showering blazing fuel over the edge which fell past them like an illuminated waterfall. Some drained onto their ledge and Steel kicked dirt over it while a German, his clothes on fire, jumped over the edge screaming as he passed them, flames trailing behind him like some fireball.

Another man groped blindly about his clothes a mass of flames and Sergeant King, taking careful aim, centred a merciful bullet between his eyes. He slid gracefully over the edge and came to rest halfway down between the two large boulders.

Charlie watched every move through his binoculars and felt sick. He had seen many men die before but it always had the same effect on him. Then silence fell.

The centre tank still intact made no move and Captain Larkin whispered, "I hope we can get that third one intact."

As if in answer to his prayer a German waved a white flag and stepped forward. Captain Larkin smashed the window and, cupping his hands, shouted up to the Lieutenant but too late. The grenade he held in his hand was already arching towards the tank then the German, just as quick, kicked it over. It landed on the ledge. Steel quickly booted it forward and it exploded a few feet down the mountain.

Harry standing next to the officer said, "You ought to get that pair signed up for Arsenal, sir." Then he walked into the middle of the road and bent over the dead officer. A bullet had entered the centre of his forehead right between the eyes. There was hardly any blood just a neat hole as if it had been drilled with an electric drill.

Sergeant King joined him and stared down at the German. A moment later he moved the man's head round with the toe of his boot and said, "Strange isn't it? I've been killing the bastards all through the war but this is the first time I've seen a piece of my own handiwork."

Sergeant King started at the prostrate and motionless figure and placing his rifle in the crook of his arm slowly lit a cigarette as if he were a big game hunter studying his kill.

"Shall I bury him, sarge?"

"What else can you do with him? Stuff him and hang him over the fireplace back home?"

"Christ, sarge, you're a miserable bastard. Don't you care that the bloody man's dead?" Harry muttered.

"'Course I bloody care, and I care for the other two poor sods that I shot, and the dozens of others that I had to shoot at Dunkirk and in the desert and Greece. I also care about my mates that I left behind. I would much rather be shooting at some targets in Bisley, but don't you think he would have shot you if he'd had half a chance? Listen, son, we're not on some safari in Africa. This is no game. I would sooner think of shooting a lion or an antelope just to put its head on the wall of my house than I would of having to put my own dog down. When I was a kid I ran out of the cinema once when I saw an elephant shot. No, son, this is a case of kill or be killed and that's what ten years of training in the army has led up to."

"He's not very old, sarge."

"So what? A twelve year old boy is a man with a gun in his hands, believe me, and just imagine what damage that man can do with that bloody Tiger tank of his? Man, he could have wiped our lot out in a few minutes."

Harry pulled the dead German towards the orchard with Captain Larkin shouting orders all over the place.

"I want that remaining tank intact. You, Sergeant King, keep your rifle trained on that tank. If any man makes a move to destroy it shoot to kill. You, Melhuish, get up that mountain and see if Lieutenant Prendergast needs some backing and take Trooper Smith with you. You, Corporal Tennant, and you, Sergeant Patterson, get mounted on two cars and get up that road to those tanks and round up the prisoners."

Two more bodies were brought in and several men were detailed to help dig their graves, but the men couldn't dig down too far as after a couple of feet they hit solid rock. Harry swallowed his distaste and methodically searched the bodies and removed papers, any documents and the Germans' identity tags.

"He won't be needing these," he joked humourlessly and taking a packet of French Letters from the German's pocket passed them to Charlie who threw them at another trooper who stuffed them quickly in his own pocket, all the while grinning sheepishly at Harry.

"This one's only nineteen, Charlie," Harry sighed.

He felt like a scavenger as he searched the pockets, reading their papers and intruding on their personal property but the urge to know more about the man he had just witnessed dying drove him on. Fascinated he piled the papers beside him and added a few pictures. More photographs fell to the damp ground as he opened a pigskin wallet and he wiped them down his trouser leg.

One was of a fat homely woman with her hair neatly plaited and carefully arranged over her head, her face twisted into what resembled a slight smile. This was presumably his mother as it had a neatly written message across one corner. Another photograph was of a younger woman who bore a strong resemblance to the woman in the first picture, but here she sat on a chair with a soldier standing behind her. He was wearing a First War German uniform, his spiked helmet held proudly in the crook of his arm and his face sporting a thick moustache firmly twisted up at the edges. The young woman was beautiful, her blonde hair almost transparent under the photographer's strong light and Harry, comparing it with the other photograph, saw it was the same woman.

Another photograph was of a small boy with long blonde hair sticking out from below a straw sailor's hat. He wore knickerbockers and a sailor's tunic and clutched the woman's hand. It was again the same woman but now in the full bloom of womanhood. He studied the face of the boy and then that of the corpse. He couldn't be certain, not with that big bruise at the side and the blood over his mouth and chin, but he believed the boy to

384

be the dead German. There were further photographs, one of the soldier again with a black border round the edges, and more German writing; and another of the small sailor boy, but this time in the brown uniform of the Hitler youth, each picture telling its own story about the progress of the family.

Harry stood up. The regimental padre was standing beside him and he spoke a few words over the German before the graves were filled in. Then Harry handed over the men's personal papers.

"There's some more dead arriving, sir," Harry said. He had become curious about the photographs and tried to piece the boy's life together wanting to know more about him, fitting the photos together like a jigsaw puzzle. "Any idea what the writing is all about, sir?"

"I don't know a lot of German, Jackson." He turned them over in order. "Looks like his father was some kind of hero of the first war and was badly shot up at Verdun. He died of his wounds in 1926."

"Going to be a bit of a shock for her, sir, when she hears her only son has been killed."

"How do you know it's her only son?"

"Stands to reason, sir, if he had any brothers or sisters there would have been more photos of them in his wallet. Looks like there's just the three of them who kept to themselves."

"I suppose so, Jackson." The padre shrugged his shoulders and pulled a resigned face.

Harry looked at the mound of earth and couldn't understand why he was so concerned with just this one man, his enemy. He couldn't get him from his mind. Perhaps it was the pictures and the story they made up. After all he never thought of Germans having mothers, but how he wished he hadn't read the damn papers now. He was brought down to earth by one of the men driving the returning cars. Several prisoners carrying their dead walked in front of them.

"Better get up top, medic," he called out, "there's one of their blokes seriously wounded and bleeding badly. Two more have slight injuries. That Sergeant King when he hits them he makes sure they stay down. There are two more on top with neat holes between the eyes."

"Anymore Jerries up there, Corp?"

"Only one. We left him behind with the wounded man and he's shit scared. You've nothing to worry about there." He pointed at one of the prisoners. "That shit there is one of Hitler's bully boys. He wanted to wait till dark then make a rush for it and fight his way back to their own lines. The others were all for waving the white flag. They knew it was bloody stupid and wanted to jack it in. Not that bastard. He'd a real Hitler worshipper." Harry pointed to the graves.

"Well tell him he can dig three more graves for his pals and hope Hitler will thank him."

One tank remained intact. The other two were still burning, their metal outsides hot to the touch when Harry arrived with the ambulance. Lieutenants Prendergast and Steel sat on the undamaged tank a bottle of red wine between them and obviously pleased with themselves. Harry tended the man's wounds and they lifted him into the ambulance.

"Want a lift back, sir?"

"Not bloody likely. I'm waiting for the recovery vehicle. It's not often we get one of these in mint condition and this is one of their latest. I intend to guard it with my life."

"I'll try and get the News of the World to come up and take some photographs, sir."

This was the last action they saw in Italy. They returned to their own unit directly afterwards.

The R.S.M. stood in front of the parade. "Right men, this is as far as we go."

There were cheers from the men. He waited for the excitement to die down. It was almost certain that the division would be on its way back home, a rumour at last that hadn't gone wrong, for apart from the war in the Far East there was no other about.

"We're withdrawing to the other side of Naples, and today we're handing over our vehicles to a Canadian Division." So it was certain and another cheer went up.

"Alright, calm yourselves down," the R.S.M. ordered, but excitement ran high. Most of them had been out years. Was it really possible they could be seeing their families once again and so soon?

As the R.S.M. was talking a convoy of three ton lorries pulled up behind them. They collected their own equipment and personal papers and took their pin ups and photographs from the plywood walls. Charlie took down Francesca's photograph and smiled to himself as he sat in his driving seat for the last time and switched on the engine. It coughed out a little gasp in protest and then purred like a contented kitten, and the Canadian driver who was taking over smiled up at him. He was short and swarthy and spoke with a distinct French-Canadian accent.

"You 'ave 'ad it long?"

Charlie shook his head.

"No, but she's okay. Goes like a bloody rocket."

"Come on, Williams, kiss it goodbye and let's get out of here. I've seen all I want to see of sunny Italy," Captain Smithers shouted at him, lugging his own luggage towards one of the lorries.

Charlie patted the steering wheel and shook hands with the Canadian.

"She's all yours mate, good luck and keep your fucking head down." He didn't look back as he threw his kit in the back of the lorry and jumped in after it.

Excitement ran too high in the back of the lorry for anyone to worry about the new unit that had just relieved them. Soon they were all singing and stamping their feet on the metal floor of the lorry. Then it started raining once again.

CHAPTER 36

The small convoy of six tonners carrying the unit and their personal belongings wove its way south towards Naples, a route quite familiar to them, for only a few weeks previously the division had been battling over the same territory. Familiar landmarks loomed up and vanished just as quickly into the background. The drivers put their feet to the floorboards for everyone was aware the war in Italy, as far as the division was concerned, was now over. They crossed the River Volturno across a Bailey's Bridge. The American engineers were still working on a more permanent bridge beside it. The small village on the far side was completely ruined and filled with mountains of rubble making it difficult to drive over, shaking the occupants in the back of the lorries as if they were on a roller coaster in a fairground.

Mount Vesuvius loomed up belching out black smoke. Then they were coasting along a winding road skirting the Bay of Naples and moving towards the Sorrento peninsular. One of the men in Harry's lorry, already a keen traveller, and a graduate from Oxford with an honours degree in history pointed out all the interesting historical spots. It made a fascinating journey. But the men were tired and all hoping for a few days leave, so that uppermost in all their minds was the thought that, at last, they would be returning home.

Harry watched Charlie open his pay book and take out a piece of paper. It was Francesca's parents' address in Naples, and then to Harry's utter amazement Charlie tore the paper into small shreds and watched thoughtfully, as they floated from the lorry like confetti at a wedding. Just as Harry often thought of Sophia he knew Charlie's relationship with Francesca was deeper.

Charlie must have guessed that he was being watched for he didn't turn round but simply said, "It's an impossible dream, Harry. She was a great girl but it's over."

The streets of Sorrento were unevenly cobbled and twisted around in sharp u-bends causing great discomfort to the men sitting in the back. But the discomfort didn't dispel the gay mood the men were in, for the town square bore an air of festivity with its outside pavement cafes and the gaily coloured awnings. The local people too appeared friendly, waving and smiling at them. The war itself had all but passed them by. It was cold and crisp but the sun shone brightly overhead.

Charlie eased himself from the steel floor of the lorry.

"My arse is freezing, Harry," he grumbled.

The lorries pulled up outside a large building with a wrought iron balcony. Each side of the large doorway was a prominent panel of marble bearing the names of famous authors and stars of yester-year, and quite a few of them were well known English characters, for years ago the building had been a small but famous hotel of merit. Later used as a museum, now it was to be the unit's home till the division left for Britain.

With great relief the men formed up in front of the building in three ranks, for after the long journey most of them were suffering from cramp and were now intent on easing their aching backs. They were eventually allocated bed spaces on the tiled floor as there were no beds and only three blankets each. Yet there were no complaints, for they were all aware it would be their last stop in Italy, and the same thing was happening all over the town as the division took over every building of any size.

Daily routine was a bare minimum, after the cleaning duties were fulfilled there was little else to do. Trips were laid on to various historical sites, the idleness bringing its' problems. The wine was cheap and flowing freely, the booze artists amongst them having a field day and one man, after just a few days of over indulgence, was carted away with a serious bout of delirium tremens.

"Anyone for Pompeii today?"

Corporal Sykes squeaky voice echoed along the corridors, the inevitable clipboard in his hand, a stub of pencil poised above it. He sucked at the tip while he gazed around the room.

"Any crumpet there?" Charlie asked. Like the other men in the room he was busy sewing on his recently issued Africa Star ribbon on to his battle dress tunic.

"Yes, plenty."

Charlie immediately lost interest in his newly gained ribbon and stared blankly at Sykes.

"The only trouble is, Williams, what's in Pompeii has been dead two thousand years. I was on the trip the other day. The guide stopped at this large building. It was an old Roman brothel. The sign above the entrance was a pair of scales and balanced on one side was a set of family jewels, on the other side a bag of gold. It was the biggest plonker you ever did see, Charlie."

"That's buggered me up," Charlie answered. "If that's how you pay for it, with the size of mine it would take years to pay. Sod that! Anyway, it's not culture I want at this moment, it's a piece of the other. Any lorry going to Naples?"

"I'll put you down. I suppose your mate is going too. I tell you what, Charlie, it's worth a trip to Pompeii. In this one house there was a couple covered in lava. They must have been on the job when Vesuvius erupted. You should see the contented look of their faces." Sykes was trying to worm his way back into Charlie's good books after the incident in the desert when Charlie almost throttled him.

Charlie had placed his battle dress trousers between his under blanket and the floor. It saved him pressing them and it also helped to soften the bed.

Charlie stood admiring himself in front of the full length mirror on the landing because he knew it infuriated Harry.

"Plenty of fags and money, Harry."

He could see Harry's reflection through the mirror and laid it on good and thick. Then he lifted his chin and ran his hand round his smooth chin twisting and turning to get a better view.

"My God, Charlie," he muttered, more to himself, but making sure Harry could hear him. "You are a handsome bastard. Descend on Napoli, dear boy, and let those gorgeous senorinas feast their eyes on that wonderful profile." Grinning, he readjusted his forage cap.

It wasn't their first trip to Naples since they had arrived at Sorrento. They were familiar with the road leading into the town and Charlie banged on the cab roof as they entered the city.

"Don't forget, Williams, and you, Jackson, last lorry leaves at ten. Meet at that old castle down on the waterfront," the driver shouted as they leapt from the back of the lorry.

"Don't bother waiting if we're not there," Charlie hollered back.

"You bloody better be," the sergeant riding with the driver warned them, "or you'll be on a bloody fizzer in the morning."

"Bollocks," Charlie retaliated, but making sure the sergeant was well out of earshot.

Harry was a little puzzled as to why Charlie stopped so far from the city centre, but he didn't ask questions for he was sure Charlie had some motive. Then it suddenly dawned on him. The last time they'd come, Charlie had nodded towards a group of women with piles of washing bent over what resembled a long stone horse's watering trough. Quite common back home in many villages, they had been presented by some horse loving philanthropist. But out here they served as a communal wash tub!

They both stood on the corner leaning against a building watching the women, but it was a good fifteen minutes before anyone noticed them. Then one old cronie looked up and squinted her eyes till they became narrow slits, she nudged a young girl next to her. Bent over her washing she, in turn, nudged the next person to her, and she nudged the next person, until all ten women and girls were looking at them, giggling and nudging one another. Two of the youngest amongst them nodded towards Charlie and Harry. They both looked every inch a soldier in their well pressed uniforms. A far cry from their ragged turn out in the desert.

."Just look at that one, Harry, in the black dress. It's all wet and clinging tightly to her body." Charlie whistled softly through his teeth, "Take a shufti at those bristols! I wouldn't like one of those in my eye for a wart."

"No," Harry answered. "And I wouldn't like to be standing next to her when she turns round quickly. She'd knock you for a helluva six."

At that moment she looked at them. Her round face didn't have a blemish, her lips were full and pouting, and the sun bounced off her jet black hair. Then Charlie gave her one of his devastating winks that usually reduced a woman to a simmering mass of jelly, she giggled and bent over her washing, occasionally turning her head slightly to make sure he was still there.

"God, Harry, she's got me moving. I really fancy that one. Do you fancy the one next to her? I bet they're mates. They keep talking to one another."

"What? The old toothless one? You must be kidding!" Harry joked.

"No, you prick, the one the other side. Her with that big botty. If there is anything I like Harry it's a nice round arse. I reckon she must be about eighteen."

Indifferent to the remarks and giggles of the other women Charlie strode over to the wash tub, his forage cap under his shoulder strap. His blonde hair was starting to grow again after being close cropped in the desert, and looking closely at Charlie, Harry had to admit he looked handsome in his new uniform. It was no wonder women fell for him. He carried himself well, no slouching, his back straight and his chin pulled well in, and he could easily have been mistaken for a regular soldier with years of service. Harry was watching a master at work. Charlie didn't believe in wasting time.

"Get in there, Harry boy, the bleeding ship might get sunk on its way home," Charlie wisecracked, and started to talk to the girl in his stunted Italian with a smattering of German, French and Arabic for good measure.

He selected a cigarette from a packet and handed it to the girl. The other women stared at him, rubbing the tips of their tongue over their lips and he handed the packet round. That did the trick. They urged the girl on, and pushed the one with the rounded bottom forward as well. Still clinging to this mixture of languages he tried to ask them to come to Naples and help him find a restaurant, while all the other women stared at them all the time and gabbled away trying to interpret his words. The girl with

391

the rounded bottom was only too eager to go with them and urged her friend to come along, and gradually the language barrier lifted as once again Harry witnessed a master at work, for she had fallen for Charlie hook, line and sinker.

She bent to lift her basket of wet washing. But always a gentleman, Charlie waved her away and catching hold of the two handles he heaved. The basket wouldn't budge. She laughed and shooed him away, as if the basket was full of feathers with one scoop she hoisted it onto her head, balancing it as easily as a circus seal would balance a rubber ball! Then she grabbed Charlie by the arm and Harry commented, "Christ, Charlie, I bet she's a professional rugby player. She'll have to be a willing partner, mate. I wouldn't try anything on with her if I were you," and he burst out laughing.

They worked their way through a labyrinth of dirty narrow streets. Clothes lines, web-like, crisscrossed the narrow streets loaded with freshly washed clothes. More washing hung out on poles from almost every window, and still more washing hung from iron-latticed balconies. The noise was incredible.

People shouted from their balconies to their neighbours across the road. Children cried and the older children playing football, screamed at each other, all sounding as if they were in urgent need of hearing aids. A dog barked and a man dressed in just a vest and trousers, his lower jaw all lathered, waving a cut throat razor about, stood at the open doors leading onto his balcony trying to do a fair impression of the great Caruso. While further down the street another man was attempting a duet with him in a low baritone. Yet another man was giving his rendition of Neapolitan love songs on an accordion.

Another tunnel of dilapidated tenements, festooned with more washing, led onto a large cobbled square. This was dominated in the centre by a large circular fountain, long since dried up, and now a tip for unwanted rubbish, and from a great pile of paper, cardboard and tin cans and wine bottles rose a large statue of a nude man, with a large horn in his crooked arm from which, at one time, water must have gushed forth. Slogans had been dubbed on the bare buttocks, one buttock spelling out the virtues of Communism, the other the rewards of Fascism.

"Just take a shufti at that tool of his, Harry. There's enough space on there to write out Gibbons's 'Rise and Fall of the Roman Empire.'" A piece of stone had been chipped from the end of the statue's penis. "It's Jewish, Harry. It's been circumcised."

They stopped at a wide staircase leading up to the squalid tenements, and a wizened old man came down grabbing the hand rail for support.

"Hiya, Tommy," he greeted them, speaking English with an undoubtedly Bronx accent, and it wasn't long before he told them he had lived in America for a great number of years.

They had warned him in the hospital in New York that he had terminal cancer, and he had returned to his native Italy to die. That had been ten years ago, and he was still waiting, as his health had improved. He spoke to the girls.

To Harry and Charlie it meant little, but the girls and the old man kept them laughing then he turned to them and said, "This one is Carmen, and the other is Anita. Well, it's not quite that but it's the nearest you'll get in English. They'll take you to Naples and find a restaurant. But you must have cigarettes. They don't like your occupation money."

They told the old man their names and he passed the information to the girls, Harry forcing twenty cigarettes on him while they waited for the girls to get washed and dressed. The old man gave them a piece of paper with the necessary translations for a good night out.

A murky little wine bar stood in the far corner of the square, they sat down inside after the American Italian had made sure the two English soldiers wouldn't be robbed by the none too friendly proprietor. Also behind the bar stood a busy middle-aged woman, with mousy coloured hair that hung in long strands, and a face that would have put her in the big money if she'd taken up haunting houses for a living. A filthy smelling cigarette hung from her bottom lip and when she looked at them she had to tilt her head backwards to avoid the smoke.

Anita was the first to appear. Two other tables were occupied by elderly local men. They glared at Anita as she took a round tin of fifty Players from Charlie's breast pocket. The men licked their lips, but Anita tossed her head back defiantly and took out five of the cigarettes and gave them to the busy proprietress. An argument ensued with a flurry of gesticulating arms and a torrent of words that left Charlie and Harry speechless. All they could do was stare.

Carmen came in ten minutes later. Both girls were dressed in bright floral dresses, with their hair pinned back with bright ribbons, sitting down beside Charlie, Carmen placed her hand on his shoulder and smiled. He covered her hand with his own.

"Come on, Harry, let's get cracking," he said. "Who needs to speak their lingo? Let's see Naples before we snuff it."

It was all down hill to the great city. As they entered they passed Sykes sitting at a table at a kerbside cafe and his jaw dropped, he stared at them wide-eyed. Charlie deliberately put his arm around Carmen's waist and returning the compliment she placed her arm round Charlie. Sykes shouted as they passed,

"Don't forget, Williams, that lorry leaves at ten tonight and you had better be on it."

Charlie burst out laughing and shouted, "Bollocks!" At the same time putting his two fingers up at Sykes.

Carmen liked the word. It seemed to roll round her lips like honey, and no doubt at the same time thinking Sykes was a friend of Charlie's she turned and smiling broadly shouted at Sykes, "Bollocks!"

"Did you hear that, Harry?" Charlie said, pride in his voice. "We've only known them a couple of hours and she's almost fluent in English."

Every crowded lorry bringing troops into Naples for a day's leave slowed down as they passed, the troops in the back shouting words of encouragement, and at the same time warning the girls what to expect. Charlie looked round and saw the R.S.M., approaching in the front of a utility truck. He pulled Carmen closer to him and gave her a kiss on the cheek. She responded with eagerness and much to Charlie's surprise planted a wet kiss on his lips, knocking his forage cap to the ground.

"Put that bloody cap on, Williams," the R.S.M. shouted in passing and then turned to his driver and said loudly, "That bloody Williams is a right lucky sod. He could find a willing piece of crumpet in a virgin's retreat."

The driver was only half attentive. He had Charlie and Harry in his rear view mirror.

"I wouldn't mind screwing that pair, sir."

"Never mind that, Carter. Just you keep your eyes on the road. Anyway, you're a married man." Carter burst out laughing, almost choking.

"I'd swap any one of those two for mine, sir. In fact I'd swap her for anything going spare!"

Both girls felt at home straight away in the seafront restaurant. Carmen spoke to the waiter with some authority, obviously bartering with him on the price of the meal, for she kept pointing at the round tins of cigarettes bulging from Charlie's tunic pockets. Charlie winked at Harry and smiled, for they were getting used to the Italian way of life, all shouting and gesticulating and looking as if, at any moment, they would throw punches at each other. They were served a rich soup. This was followed by one of the tastiest meals they had eaten in a long

394

time. It even outshone the meals that Francesca had prepared for them that time in Tripoli. Then Charlie, never a man to bow down to etiquette, undid his tunic and slouched down in his chair sipping at his coffee and cognac.

The restaurant was superb, and must have been amongst the best in Naples in its heyday, the tables were well laid out with spotless white table cloths and crystal glassware. Across the busy road the waves lapped gently on the shore. Fishing boats were pulled up on the beach and fishing nets festooned the railings as far as the eye could see.

"This is the life, Harry, good food, good wine and two beauties."

"Better take it easy, Charlie. See the way she lifted that basket of washing, and you couldn't lift it off the ground? Don't try meddling with it, mate. She could make mince meat out of you."

"Don't worry, Harry, it's in the bag. She's been playing footsie with me every since we came to the table."

"Are you sure it isn't my foot, Charlie? My bird's been playing footsie with me." Harry looked under the table and could see Carmen's foot rubbing up and down against Charlie's leg and he burst out laughing. "You're safe, Charlie."

But the peace and comfort was shattered when Charlie felt a hand on his shoulder. He as first thought it was the waiter and he nodded towards his empty coffee cup for a refill. Then Charlie looked up into a fresh-faced one pip officer.

Harry was about to jump up and stand to attention but Charlie waved him down and shouted - it was more of a command,

"Can I do something for you?" Then he reluctantly added, "Sir?"

"Are you aware that this restaurant is reserved for officers only?" The young officer, just out from England judging by his white complexion, tried to put some authority into his voice, but it carried no weight with Charlie. He looked the officer up and down, the uniform was well pressed and his Sam Brownes glittered in the rays of the sun filtering through the restaurant window. He had pale blue eyes and a thin line for a mouth shaded over by a mousy moustache that must have taken months to cultivate and looked suspiciously like it had been darkened by the tip of a burnt match. He sported one pip on each shoulder and a red band on his arm. At first it made them think he was a military police officer, then Harry realised he was from G.H.Q. "I want you and those two sluts out of this restaurant this minute. I told you this restaurant is strictly reserved for officers."

Charlie drew in deeply on his cigarette and let the smoke out slowly, much to the annoyance of the officer.

"I didn't know that." Charlie let his eyes wander around the restaurant. "I thought it looked too good for us lowly ranks, but as you can see we are accompanied by two local women, who incidentally don't happen to be sluts. Carmen here - her father is a colonel in the Italian Foreskin Fusileers, and this one here..." He pointed to Anita, "her father is a general, he commanded the Italian Royal Standbacks and was responsible for their great retreat from Tripoli."

"Are you trying to take the piss?" The officer was red in the face as he blurted out the words. "It's in standing orders about this. You should be well acquainted with those."

Charlie was in a jovial mood, he'd drunk three glasses of wine, far more than he was used to. The girls had chosen the wine and knew what they were about. But Charlie had handled officers far superior to this jumped up twit. He didn't answer immediately but stared defiantly at the young officer till he blushed with embarrassment.

"Never read the bloody things myself. Harry over there, you had better ask him. He sometimes reads them. You did read them a couple of times when we were in the desert didn't you, Harry?"

Harry nodded his head.

"Yes, the last time was the night before we sailed for Salerno."

"Been out long, sir?" Charlie sounded convivial.

And before he realised what he was saying the officer replied, "No." Then realising his mistake blurted out, "Damn it, man, I was talking to you. Stand up to attention when I speak to you."

"Bollocks, sir, why the hell don't you sit down and enjoy your meal? We haven't got the clap or anything, and - who knows - if you have the misfortune to get to the front lines one of these days you might get knocked off. Enjoy yourself while you can." Charlie lifted his wine glass towards the officer in a mock gesture of a toast.

The officer, bright red with fury, was shouting at the top of his voice. The china and glass on the tables and shelves shook violently. The Italian civilians sitting at the other tables stared at the officer with amazement.

But Charlie remained placid and never raised his voice, just quietly said to the officer, "You should take it easy, sir, you might not get a chance of getting up to the front. The way you're carrying on you'll either have a stroke or die of blood pressure."

"Look, you two, I've just about had enough of you. Get out of here now and take those two sluts with you or I'll call the military police."

Carmen gave the officer a charming smile and said, "Bollocks," with her quaint Italian accent.

Charlie looked at the girl with growing admiration in his eyes. How the girl loved that word! It seemed to roll off her full rounded lips.

"Do you know, Harry, if this girl keeps it up I shall feel obliged to take her back home with us." Charlie ignored the officer, then after a long moment looked up at him. "Are you still there, sir?" He enquired, with a sarcastic emphasis on the 'sir.'

The poor second lieutenant was speechless. His training at Sandhurst had never taught him how to handle a situation like this, but then not many instructors at Sandhurst had handled many seasoned desert rats.

He strode, extremely flustered, towards the door and turning shouted, "Don't you two men move!" He stood outside the door a few minutes and then went in search of the police.

"Fucking nerve of the man, Harry."

Charlie sipped at the wine and nearly choked when Carmen said, "Fooking nairve. Whata fooking nairve, Charlee?" Her face a picture of innocence.

A new look of admiration spread across Charlie's face.

"My God, Harry, the girl is starting to speak perfect English." He patted her head and gently kissed her cheek. "Don't worry, sweetie, you'll know exactly what it means as soon as we find a secluded spot."

He gave Carmen his wallet to pay the bill but she shook her head and took the round tin of fifty Players from his tunic pocket. Once again she went into a long argument with the waiter, and the waiter picked up the wine bottles and first pointed at Charlie and then to the two bottles. It was easy to guess the fifty Players wasn't enough. Suddenly the waiter stopped arguing and pointed across the busy road. The officer and two Red Caps were trying to cross.

A fat Italian civilian who spoke English very well and had obviously been enjoying the torment of the officer said, "Give the waiter another fifty cigarettes and vanish out the back way. There's a narrow passage running the whole length of the street, and you can be miles away before they get across." The fat man placed his chair across the doorway and had his back towards it. "I will keep them out till you are well away."

After Charlie had quickly shoved another fifty cigarettes in the waiter's pocket, he hurried over to the restaurant window and jerked his two fingers up towards the officer and the Red Caps before following Harry, who was being steered by the now satisfied waiter to the back entrance.

Then the four of them, Charlie, Harry and the two girls ran as fast as they could along the passage behind a row of shops, until they felt it was impossible to run any further, crossing several side streets before they considered themselves out of danger. Then they crossed the main road and walked along the seashore.

But nothing could change the mood they were in, for the wine was stronger than they realised, and neither of them was used to heavy drinking. They had plenty of cigarettes and a full stomach, and the company of the two girls who, although not exactly beautiful, were rather pretty and would be, Charlie's instincts told him, quite alright.

Very soon he and Harry would be on that troopship and on their way home, not as if it meant much to Harry. There was no one there to welcome him. He would look up Victoria and a few friends at the hospital. But it meant more to Charlie as he would see his daughter again. He often told Harry he was worried if she would know what a father was. After all, she had only been a baby the last time he'd seen her and she would be almost four now. But the matron, good soul that she was, had kept him well informed on her progress and told her all about her father. His only hope was that when he reached home he wouldn't come in contact with his wife.

"She won't recognise me, Harry," he was always saying. But Harry would fob him off with,

"Don't worry, once she sees that ugly face of yours she'll know who you are."

They stopped at a photographer. There was a small queue of soldiers, but Charlie insisted on waiting.

"If I send her a photograph, Harry, my little girl might recognise me when I arrive home." With that the entered the photographer's shop. Charlie had a large photograph taken and Harry a couple of postcards. Then they had a photo taken with the two girls and left the shop laughing and singing, having been told to return in two hours. They sat on what little beach was available between the fishing boats to while away the time.

Two hours later they collected the photographs and Carmen insisted they take a ride on the funicular. She pointed to a lopsided tram gliding up the side of the mountain. With the incident at the restaurant completely blocked out of their minds, and on the tram Carmen started singing all the old Neapolitan songs. She had a pleasant soprano voice, and long before they reached the top all the people in the crowded tram were singing with them, for war or no war, the Neapolitans knew how to enjoy themselves.

Everyone was smiling at them as they left the tram. The women insisted on kissing them and the men on firmly shaking hands. The air at the top was fresh and clean and the view took their breath away. A slight mist had settled over the bay and the islands of Capri and Ischia penetrated the thin mist like some eerie spectres, while a gentle setting sun bathed the whole bay.

"You know, Harry, Francesca was right. The Bay of Naples must be one of the most spectacular sights on earth. Just look at it with the mist covering it like some gossamer tablecloth. No wonder the girl was bloody homesick," Charlie said.

It was obvious that Carmen was familiar with the area, for in no time she found two secluded patches of grass a hundred yards apart. Harry placed a protective arm around Anita. She snuggled up closer. Their warm bodies made contact and he gently lay her back, her deep brown eyes seeming to penetrate his brain, as if she knew exactly what he was thinking. She was resting on her elbows looking down at him, and plucked a blade of grass and sucked away the white part of the stem. Now he reached up and ran his fingers through the thick folds of her hair, then he gently kissed her. He lay back and stared at the blue sky and the black cloud of smoke rising from the broken crown of Vesuvius, her fingers traced round his ears and mouth until he caught her hand and kissed the finger tips. They were worker's hands, hard in places, and wrinkled with constant soaking in water in other places, at that moment he felt pity for her. Then he fell into a half disturbed sleep and woke with a shudder wishing he'd brought his greatcoat. It was just getting dark and the mist from the bay was clawing its way shorewards and up the mountainside. Anita moved in closer, almost on top of him. He put his hand in the large pocket of his battle dress trousers to pull out his handkerchief, and as it left his pocket a packet of three French letters went flying across the grass. He dropped to his knees and started searching. Anita burst out laughing, then started into a fit of giggles as she held the packet aloft. Then they both fell to the grass again, laughing. Harry could see why the Italians had no heart for fighting when they had such lovable and passionate women back home.

From Charlie's direction Harry heard loud giggles followed by Charlie's raucous laugh. He sat with his back resting against a gnarled tree with Carmen's head resting in his lap. A few minutes later Carmen ran past, waving Charlie's army issue braces round and round her head with Charlie in hot pursuit, his trousers round his ankles. He kicked the trousers off and gave chase and as he caught up with her she let the braces fly. And in front of Harry was the spectacle of Charlie on his hands and knees with no trousers and underpants searching through the undergrowth. Suddenly he held them up victoriously, Carmen tried to snatch them away, but they both fell to the ground. She looked seriously into his eyes for a few seconds, then suddenly placed a kiss on his half open mouth and without taking her eyes from him, Carmen stood up and lifted the shoulder straps from her dress and let it fall to the ground. She dropped to her knees beside Charlie and taking his hand placed it on her breast. Harry looked at Anita and smiled, for once again he had witnessed a real artist at work.

When they finally awoke the sun was just creeping up over the far horizon. Searchlights probed the fading darkness with their fingers of bright light. From a distance, on the silent air, they could just make out the faint rumble of gunfire. Harry lit a cigarette and with his head cupped in his hands he stared up at the paling skies, going over in his mind what had happened to him over the past years. Was it really three years since he'd sailed down the Clyde on that overcrowded troopship, so close to shore they could see the good Scottish people waving a sad farewell to them? Since then he had covered thousands of miles, perhaps more than many a sailor would see in ten years service.

He had had so many narrow squeaks, more so since he teamed up with Charlie, and he smiled to himself as he recalled that first meeting. He knew then they would be the best of friends. He remembered little Spag, that small dog who had been their constant companion throughout the latter part of the desert campaign, until Charlie had to shoot him. After that it was almost a week before Charlie spoke to anyone. Then there were all his friends he'd left behind, some in lonely graves miles away from civilisation. Would he every forget them? He doubted it very much. A flash of faces flipped through his mind. Then there was that man lying in the sand, burned beyond recognition and the revolver the sergeant threw down beside him, the black barrel emerging from the sand getting bigger and bigger.

He could feel the cold steel as he went to knock it away. Suddenly, as if his head would burst, there was this loud explosion. Would that nightmare ever leave him? He jumped with a start and felt the cold sweat clinging to his body. Anita stared at him, a puzzled look on her face, but she must have sensed something was wrong because she placed a comforting arm around him. And it seemed to do the trick for the more comforting memories infringed on his thoughts. Like the time they found the brothel in Tunis with that tall Australian taking charge. He had lived with all those beautiful women for almost two years. And the time Charlie found that blonde Italian girl and wouldn't go home with her because she hadn't a friend for him.

Harry had begged him to go, but Charlie remained adamant. Then there was Tripoli, with Francesca. She was a lovely girl, brilliant as well as beautiful, and he was sure if the circumstances had been different Charlie would have made a go of things with her. For after all this time Charlie was still speaking with fondness of Francesca, and Harry was certain that Charlie had felt real affection for her. And Sophia. Well, he almost shuddered.

Sophia was the real interpretation of a nymphomaniac. In days she had worn him down to a former shadow of himself. He told Charlie, "She did everything to me. I'm sure she could have mastered it standing up in a sailor's hammock."

But all Charlie did was collapse with laughter till tears ran down his cheeks.

Then there was that night they met the two pros. Harry didn't really fancy her and when he got to her room he sat on the bed and gave her the usual packet of cigarettes. She kept asking him if he was a virgin and tried to get him aroused. He dared not tell Charlie what had happened that night, because he knew he would never have lived it down.

Now the four of them, Harry, Charlie and their current dates, walked abreast down the hill with their arms around each other. The cold had finally got to them. Their breath came out in clouds of steam. They left the girls outside their tenement with the promise of a date the next day and then they set out towards Sorrento. It was a long walk, and the traffic was almost non-existent at this time of the morning. It was almost half an hour before a large American lorry stopped and gave them a lift. It dropped them in the centre of Sorrento.

Their luck held for the sentry was asleep, his rifle between his knees.

"What's going on, Bishop?" Charlie asked.

"Fuck all," he woke with a start and looked them both up and down. "Where the bleeding hell have you two been?" He glanced at the large clock just inside the building. "It's just gone six."

"Have we been missed, Bish?" Charlie enquired.

Bishop laughed.

"You kidding! Sergeant McNally's only just come in. His bird brought him home. You should see her, Charlie, a real good looker and what a figure." He shaped his hands into an exaggerated curve. "I don't know what she sees in that ugly, short-arsed bastard. He must have a nice sized plonker."

"Do I detect a note of jealousy in that voice of yours, Bishop?" Charlie enquired humorously. "You leave McNally alone. He's not a bad bloke. More N.C.O.s like him and I think I could enjoy the bloody army. Anyway, Bish, I'm knackered, so don't bother to wake me in the morning."

CHAPTER 37

For several weeks the division languished on the Sorrento peninsular. It was an idle time - no training, no vehicles to attend to, with all the sightseeing tours it could almost be called a holiday, except that the majority of men had been away for some years, and, almost certain now that the next trip would be home, they were growing impatient. But that didn't stop the rumours, for they plagued the soldiers with the persistent tenacity of the flies of the desert, flying around just as fast and furious.

The scorcher of a rumour that almost caused mass desertion was that the division was to be re-equipped with light tanks and embarked for India for jungle training for the war against the Japs. Gradually, when there appeared to be no move, it died a death, just like the others.

There was very little to do. Wine was cheap and plentiful and women seemed free with their favours. Security was quite content to let the rumours ride. The man who started the Far Eastern rumour was reputed to have been pissed for days on the outcome. His job took him to G.H.Q. frequently, with a glass of free wine in front of him he could boast of his close association with the general staff. However it was Charlie who finally came out with the truth that the only reason the man went to G.H.Q. was to take supplies of shithouse paper.

The unit itself was having it very easy. Their billet, an old museum, was cold and draughty, but what little work there was was easy. This in itself convinced Charlie that the next move would be back to England. Most days they were able to get away by ten, and never later than twelve unless it was their turn for cookhouse duties, and then they would make their way to Naples to see their girlfriends. When it was their turn for duty, the two girls came over to see them.

A couple of weeks after meeting the girls, Charlie managed to fix up one of the sergeants from the orderly room with a girl, Carmen's cousin, and by the looks of things she was just as much dynamite as Carmen, the sergeant made it his business to see that they were never picked for guard duty and would often cover for them while they spent the weekend at some second rate hotel or pension. Life on the whole had treated them well since the campaign finished in Italy.

Both girls were very proud of their country and its history, and took them to all the famous tourist attractions - Pompeii, Capri, Ischia, Amalfi and some of the attractions to which most tourists and troops dared not go. Carmen made it quite clear that she had been in favour of the fascist regime so they never talked about politics. As far as both Harry and Charlie were concerned, that subject was taboo.

The night life of Naples was gradually returning to some semblance of normality. As Charlie often remarked, "Harry, the Iteys might be an excitable shower, but when it come to survival they know all the answers." Which was true; deprivations and discomforts in every form and shape they may have suffered but they never lost their sense of humour, or the art of making money. Cigarettes were the main currency, they frowned on the occupation money issued to the troops, and their own money was hardly worth the paper it was printed on. Shady nightclubs and wine bars sprang up all over the place, and with the troops' unlimited supplies of cigarettes they were perfect and welcome customers. A little punch-up now and again at the more sleazier clubs only added excitement to the night.

The weather deteriorated, getting colder as the days passed, and Mount Vesuvius, with its smoking chimney getting more excited, throwing out great black clouds of smoke and shooting tons of red hot ash into the skies, night became a brilliant display as the millions of sparks descended and cascaded down the mountain side. The black cloud above the mountain glowed a brilliant red tinged with gold, like a giant halo round the mountain top. Thousands of people turned their eyes to the gigantic spectacular; by day it became a black cloud obliterating the sun. Then the people would go to church, some would fall to their knees in the open with eyes turned towards the angry mountain, crossing themselves.

"Alright you shower, on parade."

The sergeant's deep voice echoed along the darkened corridors, his heavy boots crashing on the red tiles. He switched on the light, the bare single bulb swung uneasily from its slender wire. Harry sat up on one elbow, the feeble light like a searchlight as he opened his eyes and closed them quickly. He winced as a bolt of pain shot behind them. He had to blink a few times before they adjusted to the light. He had only been in bed a couple of hours as he'd spent most of the night with Charlie and the two girls at some nightclub.

A blurry image stood at the open doorway. A faint wind whistled through the building. He blinked his eyes a few times before he could make out the unmistakable floor length greatcoat and the familiar face of Sergeant McGregor take shape. He sucked his dry lips a few times, he hadn't drank a lot of wine because it affected him terribly, but the couple of glasses he'd had left a bad nauseating taste in his mouth.

Charlie beside him hadn't moved. If he was awake he didn't show it and remained still with his head under the blankets. The sergeant walked round the room shouting at the top of his voice and stopped at the heap of blankets that represented Charlie.

"Give the bastard a nudge, Jackson."

There were eighteen men in the small room, that was including the small verandah outside where half a dozen men preferred to sleep.

When he was sure he had everyone's attention he bellowed, "Everyone get washed and shaved, then down to the cookhouse sharpish, then outside on parade in full marching order and with all your kit packed and have your bedding neatly rolled and stacked in the corner of the room, we are off on a nice sea voyage."

He waited for this bit of news to sink in, most of the occupants were still half asleep and a few of them were still suffering from the rigours of the night life, thinking they were still dreaming. There was a pause for a few seconds; first one man sat up rubbing his eyes, then another casually passing on the sergeant's orders, suddenly the news struck them like a slap in the face and a loud cheer shot the room. There was a mad scramble from the beds.

Above the din the sergeant shouted, "Everyone on parade, full marching orders, shaved, washed, and bellies full in half an hour, kit bags stacked outside and bedroll in the corner of your room."

He vanished down the corridor his mouth making as much noise as his steel tipped boots on the red tiled floor, opening each door as he passed and shouting the same instructions. "On parade everyone in half an hour, rise and shine. Eyes right arseholes tight and foreskins to the rear, stop playing with your puddings and get down below."

The news wasn't a great shock to them, everyone had been expecting some movement for days now. After all, there wasn't much sense in keeping a famous fighting division idle on some holiday parade. The bulk of their kits were already packed just leaving their small haversacks and personal items. Charlie had bought a small Italian doll for his daughter. This he made secure and well protected with his own clothing in the middle of his kit bag. As the news gradually sunk in that at last they were finally making their way back home, there was a mad rush for the wash basins and toilets which were far too few to go around. Charlie went to the verandah with his hands in his pockets. He rested his penis on the wrought iron railings and hands thrust deep into his pockets he pissed freely onto the garden below. He was joined first by Harry, then Chappie and Kelly. Soon there were ten men

405

lined up, each pissing and farting freely, trying to outdo each other.

"God, Harry, this bloody metal is cold. Get your lighter out and thaw the bloody thing out for me." He looked over the verandah, it must have been ten feet to the ground. "I thought it was dragging in the soil then!"

"Fucking bragging again, Charlie," said Chappie. Harry just shook his head, he'd heard it so many times before.

After along spell - he'd had a couple of glasses of wine a few hours before - he shook it, it looked enormous in the pale light.

"You wouldn't like that in your eye for a wart, eh Chappie."

"What about breakfast? I don't fancy that ride to Naples on an empty stomach in the back of a cold lorry. Knowing the bloody army it'll be hours before we get the next meal."

"Just like Ramsey, thinking of his bloody guts again."

Washed, shaven and fed, they stood in three ranks on parade outside their billet. It was dark, they stood there, collars of their greatcoats turned up round their ears. They came to attention and answered as the sergeant called their names. He held their board under a torch held by Corporal Sykes and counted.

"Alright, where the bloody hell is Humphrey?"

"He was pissed last night, sarge."

"Alright, so tell me something new. The bastard is pissed every night, he's been pissed since the minute we arrived here. Anyone know where he is now?"

"The last time I saw him, sarge, he was on his hands and knees crawling towards the shithouse."

The sergeant major came up behind the sergeant and took the board from him.

"Sergeant McGregor, take Lester and Williams," he paused, "No, not Williams, I've another job for him." He looked round the parade and picked out the tallest, heaviest man. "Take McKay, the three of you sort out that drunken swine and sling him under a cold shower, dressed or not. Whichever way you do it I want him down here on parade in ten minutes, sober, and God help him if he isn't, for the minute he boards that ship I will have him clapped in chokey and he won't get out till we reach home."

So it was going to be England after all. A loud cheer went up. The R.S.M. realised he had blown it and tried to correct himself.

"Or our final destination."

But it was too late, the men had guessed all along they were going home and now, unintentionally, the R.S.M. had confirmed it.

Humphries was fast asleep when they found him on the toilet with his trousers round his ankles. The door was locked so the sergeant eased himself up to look over the top and shook his head in disgust. Humphries had vomited down the front of his shirt. He tried to reach over for the bolt but it was out of reach.

"Alright Jock, put your shoulder to it."

McKay was noted for his strength. He pressed hard and the wood splintered with a loud crack like a rifle firing. The flimsy timber gave way and Lester grabbed McKay by his equipment and prevented the huge Scotsman from falling onto Humphries, but it didn't stop him from lashing out at Humphries and knocking him from the lavatory seat under a storm of protest.

No one had any love for Humphries, he was only kept in the unit because no one else would take him. Even in his sober moments, which were few and far between, his breath smelt of decaying cheap wine. Still protesting, but in a drunken stupor they dragged him along the corridor and tumbled him in a heap under the shower. McKay gave him the full treatment with the cold water. He screamed and tried to fight his way out but McKay pinned him by the shoulders and slung him back under the shower, and to make sure he had his full share, Lester found the fire hose and turned it on full blast. While the sergeant collected Humphries' kit, McKay and Lester grabbed his feet and dragged him along the corridor and down the stone steps, his head bouncing off each one and his wet clothes leaving a wide trail of water. They stood him in the rear rank, his wet clothes dripping water in the gutter while he stood, half stooped, a wet shivering mass.

"Right, Williams and you, Jackson, out here." They were the first called for detail and were soon followed by another four men and a corporal. "Right, corporal, take these details and load the kit into the lorry as soon as it arrives. You're to go straight to the docks and report to the R.T.O. The driver knows his way about." He pointed to Charlie and Harry. "Keep your eyes on these two oversexed bastards and don't let them out of your sight. They have a couple of bints in town and if they spot them, Williams will be like a race horse at a steeplechase, he will be over that tailboard in a flash. I think you had better try and squeeze him in the cab with you and the driver."

He handed the corporal a long buff envelope.

"Give these to the R.T.O. when you arrive. I want to see all that kit safely aboard. Understand, corporal? I am holding you entirely responsible for these two men." He turned as a series of dim lights were making their way up the road. "Here's the transport now." He turned his attention to Charlie and Harry. "Now, Williams and you, Jackson, the honeymoon is over for you two. Don't let me down, any bad reports and there's still time to

407

get rid of you, they are calling out for drivers here and only a few days ago we had a directive from the D.D.M.S asking for qualified medical orderlies and especially ones with your qualifications."

Harry shuddered, the thought of returning to a general hospital filled him with horror, he knew one day he would have to go back to one but at least not now while the war still raged. After all, he had enlisted and was trained as a regular soldier but he was still reeling from his last encounter at his previous hospital and would rather face a hostile enemy than the sisters and matron of a hospital, he thought it would be more prudent to remain silent and answered with a "Yes, sir," or "No, sir," as the occasion required.

The road stretching from Sorrento to Naples was all downhill, an hair raising experience with the road twisting and turning with numerous hairpin bends and a sheer drop onto the rock strewn seashore hundreds of feet below. Only a small stone wall separated them from sudden death and destruction. Harry was already fast asleep across the kit bags before they were halfway there. He gave implicit instructions to Kelly that he was to be woken when they reached the outskirts of Naples as he was hoping to catch a glimpse of the two girls, he knew they had to start work at first light.

Bert the old soldier sat unconcerned at the tailboard, unaware of the danger as the driver took tyre bends at breakneck speed, the tailboard hanging over the edges. He calmly smoked his pipe and each time the lorry took a bend he would spit a stream of brown fluid over the side, while the remainder of the men sent up a silent prayer for their safe deliverance from the suicidal maniac driving.

Kelly shook Harry as they came to the great city and the familiar places started to take shape. Any minute now they would be passing the washing trough. The lorry slowed down and came to a stop a few feet away, where the two girls were toiling at a mountain of washing. Bert the old soldier exclaimed, "Well I'll be fucked, that mate of yours has talked the Corporal and driver into stopping." He sent a stream of dark brown fluid over the tailboard.

The two girls were used to the army lorries passing and the soldiers shouting at them and making rude gestures, so they didn't bother to turn round when the lorry stopped. Seeing so many Allied troops the novelty had worn off, although it did make more work for them and higher wages, washing the troops' clothes. Charlie stepped lightly over and pinched Carmen's bottom. She turned round sharply with a wet shirt in her hand, about to swipe it across his face. Her anger changed to smiles as she threw her arms around his neck and shouted.

"You Charlie, you come out early, yes?"

It was surprising how much English she had picked up in such a short time. The wet cloth dripped down his back but he didn't notice it as she kissed him again and again, egged on by the men's cheers.

"Have a go, Charlie lad," they shouted, as his hands explored her round bottom.

Anita looked round for Harry. He swung over the tailboard and dropping her washing in the basket she ran towards him, her arms outstretched, her wet dress hugging every curve of her body showing it off to its full advantage.

Seeing all the kit stacked in the back of the lorry and both of them wearing webbing equipment, they guessed this was their farewell embrace. Tears welled up in their eyes and they held a quiet conversation. Harry emptied his pockets of money and cigarettes, forcing them on her. Charlie did the same. If either of them had realised it was to be their last night they would have made sure they were loaded with food and cigarettes the night before.

Although neither of them was under any illusion that the liaison would last, the four of them had to agree that the last few weeks were both enjoyable and pleasant, but as soon as they had said their final farewells it wouldn't be long before such enterprising and rather pretty women would find new protectors amongst the thousands of Allied troops.

"Come on, you pair of bastards, you'll get me shot," the corporal shouted from the cab. "Charlie, you bastard, I said just five minutes."

"Alright corp, as soon as I get her hands from around my neck." He raised his head but she pulled it down again and planted a kiss full on his mouth, her tongue darting out.

"Come on, Charlie, the fucking boat's waiting!" The men were getting restless now and shouted across to him.

Carmen shouted back, "Bollocks!"

How she had come to love that word. It rolled off her tongue and when she said it within earshot of other Allied troops it never failed to make them smile, and the more they smiled the more she repeated it. This time the men could hardly believe their ears.

"That's that bloody Charlie teaching her his King's English." Followed by a stream of dark brown spittle on the road.

Carmen stretched her arms tightly round his neck and kissed him passionately again.

"Give her some stick, Charlie," shouted one of the men. "She's got no bloody knickers on, you can see right through her dress."

His hand explored her rounded buttocks, trying to locate the telltale undergarments, but the man was right, she wore nothing underneath. He rotated his hands round the smooth dress, he knew this turned her on. She rotated her buttocks. The corporal could hardly believe his eyes and stopped shouting. The driver leaned over breathing heavily down the corporal's neck. Charlie forced her hands away and they both ran for the lorry where the driver had the engine running. The girls sobbed as Harry swung over the tailboard. Anita, overcome with emotion, sank to her knees in the middle of the road, tears splashing down her cheeks.

"Fucking hell, I wish my missus had cried like that when I left," said one of the men.

Old Bert packed the bowl of his pipe, stamped it down hard and then relit it.

"Your missus? That's sod all. I'm sure that old cow I married wrote to the war office and got me posted overseas."

"You never know Bert, with a bit of luck she may have found herself a nice Yank to take her off your hands," said Harry.

"I hope not for his sake. I wouldn't wish her on my worst enemy. Takes all her bleeding time to write, and when she does it's only to give me the bad news. Do you know all the time we were in North Africa she only wrote me three letters? The first was to tell me the finance company had taken my motorbike back."

He lay his head back against the canvas sides, puffing great clouds of smoke from his pipe and stabbing the air with the stem to emphasise a point.

"I'd only paid two instalments when I was called up with the first batch of reservists. I done my nine years with the Colours, six of them out in India."

He sighed. He could never forget his Indian service and never failed to remind the younger soldiers about it.

"I wish to fuck I had taken the bloody thing down to Tidworth with me when I was recalled. I could have put it in store for the duration, then the H.P. company would never have got their hands on it. The second letter was to tell me my dog had died, and that she had to sell my pigeons because she couldn't afford to feed them. And the last letter was to let me know our bloody house had been bombed and she was living with her sister."

Harry was still waving till the lorry turned a bend and the girls vanished from sight.

Bert said, "That Charlie is a keen bastard, you were lucky getting him for a driver. All my service in the army and I have

410

never come across such a keen bastard as him. He can find a bit of fluff anywhere." He tapped the tailboard with his pipe making the spit crackle in the stem. "Tell me, Harry, how many birds have you been with since you met up with him?

Harry scratched his head and looked a bit thoughtful. He started counting on his fingers, stopping only to search his pockets for a cigarette. Kelly rushed forward to light his and he inhaled, blowing the smoke out slowly, knowing he had their full attention. They went quiet.

"Fifteen, I suppose."

There were gasps all round.

"What!" Kelly's eyes almost jumped out of his head. The others whistled through their teeth. Old Bert laughed, he knew Charlie well. He also knew Harry wasn't given to exaggeration.

"Fifteen. That's between the two of you," said Kelly excitedly.

"Don't be a prick, Kelly, we don't share the women. That's fifteen each."

Kelly's face turned from one of excitement to one of disbelief.

"Hell, Harry, that's more women than I have spoken to in my life, never mind doing that to them. I tried it once, that was standing next to the dustbins at the back of our house. I didn't do it properly, she was wearing knickers. I kept asking her to come to the park so we could lay on the grass but she refused saying that if she did it laying down she would get pregnant."

Apart from few guffaws of laughter, no one was really interested in Kelly's near miss. They wanted to listen to the real thing, and none were more experienced than Harry and Charlie.

"Bloody hell, Kelly, by the dustbins? Wasn't very romantic, was it?" said Harry trying to smother a smile.

But old Bert and the others were growing impatient.

"Never mind that prick, Harry, I don't suppose he would know where to put it if she had laid down."

"We have had quite a few out here. Remember that time we were coming over the mountains. It was pissing down when we found this high class brothel. I fell down the hill and knocked myself out and Charlie carried me inside. When I came to I actually thought I had snuffed it and had woken up in heaven. They gave us both a bath and poor old Charlie, he accidentally knocked a bottle of perfume in the water, stank the ambulance out for days. Actually, the best time was when we pulled out of Tunis, picked up these two women, one was a teacher in Tripoli, spoke perfect English, almost without a trace of an accent. Spent a night with them, and again, when we had to pick up Captain Smithers we managed another night."

411

Kelly had led a sheltered life and was brought up with the idea that sex was a dirty word and, as he never swore, he asked Harry, "How many times did you do it Harry?"

"How the hell do I know? We never kept a score board. All I know is after three days I was knackered. My bird turned out to be a nymphomaniac."

"What, do you mean to say she drank as well, Harry?" asked Kelly innocently.

"Hit him, Bert." Harry tightened his lips to stop himself bursting out laughing.

Bert brought his forage cap smartly across Kelly's head.

"You prick, Kelly, Harry said nymphomaniac not dipsomaniac." Kelly still couldn't grasp it but not wanting to show his ignorance, decided to leave it for the time being.

Kelly was twenty-two years old but had a face that belied his age. He hardly looked eighteen and had led a sheltered life being brought up in a small country town in Hampshire. His father had vanished when he was two weeks old. Bert swore blind he'd done a bunk the minute he looked at his son's face. Kelly was then brought up by his mother and her sister. His life was spent behind a country bank counter, a visit to the cinema once a week and church twice on Sunday, first with his mother in the morning while his maiden aunt prepared dinner, and then evensong while his mother prepared supper. His girlfriend had been picked for him and always came to tea every Sunday. She too worked in the same bank and his mother and her sister were convinced that they saw enough of each other as work. She wrote twice a week, that was until a couple of months ago when her last letter informed him that she had been put in the family way by a Gordon Highlander who had been on manoeuvres in the area. As old Bert said, "She must have laid down in the fields."

He had been called up with the first batch of conscripts and had already seen service in Palestine and Greece where he just missed being put in the bag by the skin of his teeth. Then on to North Africa and Italy, yet he still retained an air of innocence.

Bert folded his arms and tapped his pipe on the tailboard sending a stream of dark brown fluid over the back; it was carried away on the slipstream.

"So that's where you pair of bastards got to. I was taking on bets you were kipping in bed with a pair of bints but I got no takers. I wish I had your bleeding luck."

By the time he got through their minutest detail of their experience in North Africa and Italy - much to the other men's satisfaction - they hardly realised they had pulled into the docks till they stopped and looked up at the bleak grey paint of a troop ship, its' steel walls towering above them, a row of faces peering down from the ship's rails.

The corporal vanished into the R.T.O.'s office, a small wooden shed perched on the dockside, and returned a few minutes later with an elderly major sporting two and a half rows of medals, most of them from the First War.

"Right lads, we haven't much time. We have two battalions to get aboard and a few hundred odds and sods like Engineers, Ordnance, Service Corps and Signals, and a couple of batteries of Artillery and so on. The ship sails at 2pm, shortly they will swing your gear aboard. Step lively and get aboard and sort it out on the deck, I want your unit down below as soon as they arrive."

"Where are we going, sir?" asked Kelly.

Everyone in the division had a strong feeling this was a homeward trip, but it had never been confirmed officially.

The major smiled and winked his eye. "You should know better than to ask a question like that laddie, they will be telling you as soon as the ship puts to sea."

Once on deck they set to sorting out the mountain of kit bags and officers' kit, placing it in neat piles awaiting their owners. A senior N.C.O. called them together and ordered them to follow him through a labyrinth of narrow steel passages, down vertical steel ladders and through endless doors. It seems as if they were going down to the very bowels of the ship. So far there were only a couple of small units aboard, no more than fifty men in each, and the ship was empty. The steel tips of their heavy boots resounded along the decks as if they were walking inside some huge empty shell. The N.C.O. was obviously a member of the permanent staff and quite at home aboard the ship, acting like some seasoned sailor. He never used the steps but stiffened his arms on the steel rails and slid down them, his feet a few inches from the rungs. The bars were so shiny they looked as if they had been silver plated.

It was a huge passenger ship of some twenty thousand tons, used before the war to carry passengers round the West Indies and America. Now denuded of all its finery it carried something like four thousand troops in squalor instead of six hundred pampered passengers in untold luxury.

They finished up in a large mess hall deep in the bowels of the ship, a converted cargo hold which was used to carry the baggage for the fare paying passengers, now converted to a mess deck for the troops as it was situated well below the water line. Hammocks hung everywhere; anywhere in the hold where two hooks opposite each other and six feet apart could be welded, a hammock was slung.

413

Underneath the hammocks, rows of tables were fixed to the floor with benches either side. They were allocated a section of the mess deck for their unit, but neither Charlie nor Harry relished the idea of sleeping in such a death trap.

"Can you imagine it down here, Harry, if abandon ship sounded? A couple of thousand men fighting their way to the deck? Balls to that, let's get on top and find us a nice sheltered spot before the rest of the shower get aboard. I was never one for sleeping in a hammock anyway." He slapped his hand across a canvas hammock and it swung freely. "I wonder what it's like to have a bird in one of these, Harry? I bet old Kelly couldn't do it standing up in one of these!"

They found a corner to park their kit and told Kelly to keep an eye on it. Then, taking their small pack and stowing what they would need for the trip, made their way to the deck again.

They had difficulty finding their way to the deck again, twice they took the wrong turning and found themselves back where they started. First they located the canteen, and then the galley, making sure they could find them easily, then set about finding some sheltered spot. If it was certain they would be returning to Blighty it wouldn't be very long before they were in the colder regions for it was the middle of winter with the worst still to come.

At least it wouldn't be the same distance or as long on their way out there when the convoy had to make the long tedious trip round the Cape and up the eastern seaboard of Africa. Both of them had made that trip in large ships with five or six thousand men crowded below in the sweltering, steamy heat.

They found a sheltered spot on the lower promenade deck, a recess some six feet square.

"Grab Chappie and Earley when they come aboard, this should be big enough for the four of us, make a nice card school to while away the time."

A large lifebelt locker was lashed to the bars of the cabin portholes some six feet away. They unleashed the ropes and pushed the locker in front of the recess and secured it to a rail.

"There you are, Harry, no bastard will even know we're here."

The only drawback to their cosy little nest was the fact that they would never be able to smoke after dark, but the compensations outweighed this little inconvenience and the canteen was only one deck down, directly underneath them, and Harry would always be welcome there as it sported a large well tuned piano.

They were issued with cork lifebelts and warned to carry them with them at all times. Harry was the more seasoned traveller, he pointed to the raft hanging in front of them.

"If we do get hit, Charlie, balls to the lifeboats, make a grab for this Carley float, it's not as comfortable but far more reliable, they never sink. Don't forget what you were told on the landing craft, if we go over the side grab your lifebelt with one hand and pull down hard from your chin and grab your balls with the other hand. A smack from that cork belt under the chin when you hit the water could break your neck. And we are higher up from the sea on this than that landing craft, so if you don't grab your marleys it will feel as if you have been kicked by a Welsh rugger player."

There was plenty of activity on the quayside with a battalion of troops boarding, each man carrying his own kit with his kit bag slung over his shoulder and weighed down with his full pack and rifle. There were wasting no time, another two gangways were slung on board, each one crowded with troops; Engineers, Pioneers, Signals, Medics, every corps that kept the fighting men in the field. Then it was the turn of their own unit. The R.S.M. looked relieved to see the two familiar faces smiling down at him.

At exactly two o'clock the ship's siren sounded. Harry jumped as the gruff sound was unexpected. The gangways were lowered on to the quay and the great grey hulk was towed into deep water. The tugs dropped their lines and she headed into the bay to join a convoy forming up. It consisted of several large transports and a dozen ships, all much smaller than their transports. A quick look round the assorted convoy convinced them it would be a slow laborious trip home. A convoy could only travel as fast as the slowest ship, and by the look of some of the smaller tramp steamers they looked as if eight knots would be their limit. The sea was choppy, the ships tugged at their anchor chains like impatient greyhounds tugging at their leashes.

Vesuvius was erupting, spitting out flames like a violent dragon, the cone glowing a brilliant red, reflecting on the underside of a black cloud of smoke hovering above the mountain. A couple of ribbons of red lava wound their way down its craggy sides, a thin film of lava dust covered the whole convoy.

Corvettes, destroyers and smaller naval vessels circled the convoy and in the distance, where the sea met the sky, two large capital warships took up their positions, their dark sinister outlines in contrast to the bright horizon. By late afternoon the convoy prepared to set out to sea. Signals flashed from ship to ship and ship to shore, shrill blasts from the naval ships and great grunts from the ships' sirens. The ship's anchor was winched aboard, the great metal links echoing throughout the ship as she headed for the open sea.

The glow of Vesuvius was with them throughout the greater part of the night. Next morning nothing was to be seen of any land and the supposedly blue Mediterranean was anything but blue. The sky was overcast with great heavy clouds that blotted out the distant horizon. The ship heaved up and down and rolled uncontrollably from side to side, the masts scribing out figures of eight in the sky. She plunged into deep troughs, then her bows swung upwards and upwards, then plunged down as if out of control. The passengers in the overcrowded hold vomited till their empty stomachs screamed out in agony. The only words of comfort from the crew were to be thankful as the rough seas made it harder for the U boats to have a crack at them.

Then the familiar coast of Africa hove into view. Charlie scanned the sandy coastline with his binoculars. Most of the men were thankful for a few days respite in a port, others were filled with nostalgia to see the familiar coastline. Harry was indifferent, while Charlie started a lucrative trade in cigarettes, lending out his binoculars.

They made directly for a port. A high concrete wall sheltered the huge cranes standing like sentinels along the quayside. Several large French Capital ships were tied up alongside the quay. The troopship made for the entrance and dropped her speed till only a slight wash lagged slowly astern.

A large French battleship cast off as the trooper turned into the narrow channel; there was little room to manoeuvre. The huge battleship, its' superstructure dwarfing the troopship, glided towards them. The men on the opposite side of the ship rushed over, much to the captain's consternation. Their combined weight was too much and forced the ship off its course. The narrow gap between the two ships shrank at an alarming speed.

Almost hysterical now, the captain on the bridge shouted through his megaphone, "Over to port, over to port."

He was wasting his breath. Confined below in those stinking, overcrowded mess decks for several days, seasick and hungry, they weren't in the mood for obeying orders, this was their first relief. Something was happening and they also hadn't the slightest idea what port or starboard meant. Two thousand blank faces stared up at the bridge, then down the narrow gap, those not on the ship's rail, pushed those in front almost over the side as the ships struck and glanced off one another with a grinding crash that put their teeth on edge. The captain's head sank into his hands. He groaned. The plates of the forepeak crumbled like a cigarette packet. Fortunately there was little structural damage to

416

hinder the workings of the ship. A few pipes ran from the temporary toilets on deck, through the mess deck and ran out the other side of the ship lower down. They fractured and the mess deck was afloat with a selection of well preserved turds. None of the men worried too much, after all it was only the sergeants' and senior N.C.O.s' deck.

CHAPTER 38

The damage to the troopship wasn't too extensive, and after urgent repairs, the ship was ready to put out to sea the next morning. From the calmness of Oran Docks she thrust her nose out to the ocean, the ship's bow raised up as if to curtsy to the enormous waves, and then it dropped immediately into a deep trough. Those still suffering from the hangover of the previous bouts of sickness ran to their hammocks or makeshift beds on the tables and benches, for many men couldn't get used to the idea of hammocks. But worse was still to come. That night they passed through the straits of Gibraltar without getting a glimpse of that formidable fortress and straight into the teeth of an Atlantic storm. The wind, on a direct route from the North Pole bit straight into the exposed parts of their bodies. Large Atlantic rollers picked up the bows of the ship and smashed it down into troughs so deep the ship's propellers lifted clear off the water sending a vibrating shock throughout the ship, and the decks were awash with foam and sea water.

For a few desperate moments Harry thought they would have to abandon their little hideaway hole, but a crew member saw their plight and found a few boards and a couple of old blankets. The boards lifted them clear of the deck and the blankets filled the draughty cracks where the life belt locker didn't fit flush with the walls of the ship.

Conditions below worsened. The captain ordered all portholes and hatches closed. The men became almost prisoners below and worse still, after a couple of days, diarrhoea broke out, the crowded mess decks made it difficult to get to the toilets in time. When the men did get there, great queues were waiting, the men bent double in torment, and the passageways and mess decks soon floated in a sea of vomit that washed backwards and forwards through the ship as it rose and fell.

One visit below was sufficient for Harry. He fought his way through the overcrowded passageways trying not to step on prostrate bodies writhing in agony and when he reached his own mess deck he found his kit almost afloat in vomit. Men lay helpless in their hammocks, swinging in unison with the ships movements. He willed himself to control himself from throwing up and rushed as fast as his legs could carry him to the open deck again and the comfort of their cubby hole. The fresh air rallied his senses and he was surprised to see that he had learned to master his walk to coincide with the roll of the ship. Then before retiring to his cubby hole he stood, legs apart, facing the wind, filling his lungs with the salt-laden air. It was the last time he went to the mess deck for the remainder of the voyage.

As the days passed there was no improvement in the weather. But the cubby hole on the promenade deck, where once only the rich could afford to walk, kept them fairly dry and sheltered them from the worst of the elements.

The smaller ships in the convoy - the escort of corvettes and destroyers - tossed up and down like toy boats in an unruly boy's bath, often vanishing for minutes at a time and sinking out of sight, only to reappear and shake themselves like small terriers. The riveted plates of the ship and woodwork protested at the rough treatment in no uncertain manner, creaking and groaning like an asthmatic old man.

On the fifth day, at about midday, they were roused by the sounds of muffled explosions. They struggled to the ship's side and stared at the heaving green waves, for apart from the rest of the convoy that was all that remained visible. Occasionally a small corvette or destroyer would rise from between the waves, only to vanish just as quickly. And at one time they thought they saw a huge spout of water reach skywards followed a few minutes later by muffled explosions.

"Depth charges, Harry. Must be U Boats lurking about. Bloody good job the weather is so bad. I don't think they will attack," Charlie said, and scanned the waters with his powerful binoculars. He dropped the glasses to his chest, but unfortunately at that moment a strong gust of wind caught them and swung on the strap around his neck, belting him under the chin. Salt spray mixed with the blood from a cut, he wiped it away with the back of his hand.

Once more in their shelter, Harry took a closer look at the chin. "That's a right beauty, Charlie, but I don't think it needs a stitch."

"Made me see stars for a few minutes," Charlie answered, touching the cut gently with the tip of his finger. They returned to the ship's rail.

"Don't you pongos get worried?" A crew member wanted to know as he fought his way along the deck, grabbing the ship rail to steady himself.

"No," replied Charlie, "the U Boats won't attack in this weather, it'll be dark very soon and we might lose them during the night."

Two sub-chasers came in closer to the convoy. All could plainly see what looked like dustbins arch over from the sterns, followed by a deafening explosion that rocked the troopship. Men came running up from below. Soon the ship's rail was crowded,

The men struggling for their life jackets, and Harry took the added precaution of placing his half bottle of brandy in his back pocket as he changed his heavy ammo boots for plimsolls.

For over an hour the sub-chasers kept up the attack. Then suddenly like some great wounded whale the sub broke through the waves nose first and rose half way up to her hull before she flopped down. Men jumped from the conning tower into the icy green water. The sub shuddered, started to roll to one side, then slowly went down stern first less than a quarter of a mile from the troopship, dead silence descended on the watching troops, until suddenly there was a loud cheer as the sub finally vanished beneath the waves taking its crew with it.

Harry shuddered. "What a bloody way to go, Charlie."

"Fuck them! That could have been us floating in that water. That was too close for comfort, Harry."

Scramble nets were dropped over the side of one of the corvettes and they counted twelve German submariners taken aboard. There was very little sleep for the men aboard the troopship that night, and those whose mess decks were below the waterline made sure they had temporary accommodation higher up the ship.

The weather continued to deteriorate after the attack, much to the delight of the crew, especially the catering staff who, so far, had only catered for the few hardy individuals. It became impossible to wander out onto the open decks and Harry and his mates became prisoners in their cubby hole. But they were grateful they had escaped the mess decks below.

"Be sure it is soon that we'll soon be passing the Emerald Isle," an Irish crew member trilled.

"Yes. I can smell the bloody bogs from here," Charlie answered. "Are you sure you don't shit all over them when you're there?" Charlie was lying down sideways at the time, his body and head propped up on one elbow, playing pontoon with three others including Harry and he didn't glance up from his game.

"Sure and it's better than that God forsaken hole they call England," the Irishman replied indignantly.

"Oh yes?" replied Charlie. "Then tell me why there are so many of you miserable sods living in England? My old man was in Dublin in 'twenty two and he said the best thing we ever did was get rid of you shower. You cause trouble wherever you go. The worst thing that happened when the British troops left was that you lot followed them home. Most of the bush rangers in Australia are from Irish stock and in America you have Molly Malones and Irish and Italian gangsters. Now back home all we hear from you shower is 'Danny Boy' and 'When Irish Eyes are Smiling'. Balls to you Irish! Troublemakers the lot of you."

The Irishman glared at Charlie seeming to calculate the size of the man, head and shoulders bigger than himself, Harry noted, and then shrugging his shoulders in disgust walked away muttering to himself.

"I gather you don't like Irishmen, Charlie," Chappie said, trying to hide the excitement in his voice. He'd just been dealt a royal flush.

"Take 'em or leave 'em, Chappie. I always take a man as I find him and don't give an arse whether they're Catholic, Protestant or just follow the band. Black, brown or candy striped there's good and bad amongst all of us. I just felt like an argument." The others sniggered.

Dawn was breaking when they woke the next morning. Harry lay on his back, his head cupped in his hands but it was a few minutes before he realised the ship wasn't rolling. He blinked his eyes, the glass on the promenade deck was laced with frost giving it a ghostly appearance, he sat up, the ship hardly moving. Harry struggled into his greatcoat trying not to disturb the other three men who appeared to be sleeping peacefully, sliding over the life belt chest to the ship's rails. A great grey mass loomed up in front of his eyes. There was no other ship to be seen. Gulls screamed around the ship's two funnels. He wiped the mist in his eyes and then realised it was real land he was looking at, not just the dark formations of cloud they had mistaken for land so many times on the voyage. The ship was sailing slowly. Then it turned to port and he saw that the other ships were in a straight line in front and behind.

"God, that really is land," he shouted and ran back to the locker. "Charlie, Chappie, we've arrived. There's bloody land all down one side!"

Someone from below must have been on deck for suddenly the weary seasick men scrambled onto the decks, taking there places along the ship's rails.

Someone cried, "Thank God, it's the first fresh air I have smelt since leaving Oran." He stood there, arms akimbo, breathing in deeply.

And two of the ship's cooks stood by Harry.

"Christ, Smiler, looks like we'll have to do breakfast for this lot," one complained and there was a look of the most utter desolation on his face.

"Shouldn't worry too much, most of them will be too excited to eat, and a lot won't have the stomach yet," the second answered.

He was right about excitement, for men were pouring up from below decks like worker ants around an ant hill, all of them trying for the most advantageous spot. Their rumbling stomachs cried out for food but they were too excited to go below.

Charlie studied the frost laden hills with patches of green grass visible here and there. The ship's siren screamed out followed in turn by the other ships as they made a turn to starboard, and now there was land on both sides. The convoy strung out line astern. Two corvettes raced along the convoy and received a cheer from every ship as they passed. Two destroyers and a heavy cruiser sounded their sirens, the shrill notes echoing against the mountains. Then they gave one more short blast as if saying goodbye, they turned and left the convoy, now in safe waters again. It had been a terrifying voyage and later they were to learn that the convoy had been shadowed by a pack of U boats since they left Gibraltar. Not one ship of the convoy had been lost and the Navy accounted for one U boat definitely, and probably another either sunk or badly damaged.

The convoy sailed majestically up the Clyde, a familiar sight to most of them who had left the same port years earlier. Great shipyards, the pride of Glasgow lined the great river, most with ships in various stages of building in the slipways, some just skeletons, others ready for fitting out or launching, and it was a sight to bring a lump to any Scotsman's throat, indeed, for that matter, to many an Englishman's throat. Workmen stopped working as the great ships lined with khaki clad troops passed raising their flat caps and giving a silent cheer, for the ships were still too far away from the shore to hear the voices. Then as the river narrowed Glaswegians amongst the troops shouted out familiar places and landmarks, for to a Scot no other country in the world could produce such beauty as the green hills sweeping down to the foreshore, while in the distance snow laced mountains created a breathtaking scene.

"Ever been to Scotland, Harry?" Charlie asked.

"Yes, three times, and always to Glasgow. I left here on three occasions and each time it was on April the thirteenth and each time from the same dock. The last time I thought, 'this is it'. No one could have that luck sailing from the same place three times and on the same date. Still, here we are. Mind you, this has been a terrible voyage. I've just heard that poor Kelly is so ill down below he hasn't been on deck yet, poor bastard. There's still quite a few below him who haven't moved as well."

Troops hung from every convenient spot on the ship to get a glimpse of their homeland. The mast and upper decks festooned with troops all eager to get a better view. A few older soldiers

422

had been away as long as eight years and Scotland, England or Wales, what the hell did it matter? It was home! To those ashore the fields may look drab in the heart of winter, less richly verdant than in summer, but to the homecoming troops after years in the desert and Italy it was a lush green Utopia, the distant patches of snow a cooling contrast.

They were closer inshore now, and the daily commuters stopped and walked right down to the foreshore to give the returning victorious troops a heartwarming wave. A Paisley bound tram stopped and passengers waved frantically. One of the men on the upper deck of the ship produced a set of bagpipes, and indifferent to the playful threats of the other troops played all the familiar Scottish tunes: 'Scottish Soldier,' 'Scotland the Brave,' 'Flowers of Edinburgh' and 'Cock of the North.' This was accompanied by the words of the soldiers' version. Many a moist eye was secretly wiped, but the air was electrified with emotion. Another man produced an accordion, several mouth organs and a saxophone player joined in, and an impromptu band was formed playing all the popular tunes, or at least they were popular when most of the men left the country.

Docking took quite a while as each ship dropped anchor waiting its turn for the tugs to take them to their berthing places. The ship swung round on its anchor and the men started going below for breakfast and to prepare for landing.

Harry and Charlie went below to get their kit together. Their kit bags still bore the stains of green vomit.

A few of the men still lay around the mess decks suffering the aftermath of sickness, aggravated by the hunger pains nagging at their empty stomachs, hardly daring to believe that the nightmare voyage had finally ended. Harry and Charlie lifted their kit and rushed to the upper deck again, just in time to see the excited men leaning over the ship's rail watching the gap between the ship and the shore. Then there was an almighty cheer and a gentle bump as the ship eased itself against the wooden pontoons, followed by another cheer as ropes snaked their way down to the quay and heavy mooring ropes followed.

The last of the seasick passengers staggered on deck, blinking in the pale January sunshine. Kelly was amongst them. His cheeks were waxen in colour, resembling those of a man suffering from acute yellow jaundice, and placing one hand on Harry's shoulder, he enquired, "Are we really home, Harry?"

"Bloody hell, Kelly, are you sure you're alright? I've seen better looking corpses than you. You eaten yet?"

Kelly shook his head.

"I couldn't, Harry. I feel too ill."

Harry nodded to Charlie.

"Go and get some porridge and a couple of slices of bread and a mug of sweet tea."

"I couldn't, Harry," Kelly protested.

Within minutes Charlie reappeared with a mess tin of porridge and although Kelly objected they forced food down him. He threw up at first, but gradually managed to keep the porridge down and a slice of bread and a couple of sips of warm tea. Then they forced a way clear to the ship's rail and, just in time, for up came the bread and porridge, landing much to Charlie's extreme delight, on top of a Red Cap's hat and shoulders as he stood below.

Charlie grinned down at the Red Cap and said to Kelly, "Bloody good job you didn't waste it, Kelly."

After a few more efforts on Harry and Charlie's part they managed to force more food down Kelly which kept down and by the time they disembarked he was able to walk unaided down the gangway to the tune of an A.T.S. band.

The unit went straight into the sheds by the jetty where a train was waiting to transport the unit and a battalion of Infantry travelling with them. Charlie found an empty compartment, and several men tried to blunder through but Charlie blocked their path till Kelly and his own mates secured their seats and seats for Chappie and his driver. Then Charlie and Harry took the corner seats which were the most favoured in the compartment. Everyone wanted a glimpse of the countryside although it was a bleak January day. The heaters on the train were at full blast and it wasn't long before they all removed their greatcoats.

"Looks good outside, Charlie," Harry remarked as he wiped the condensation from the inside of the window.

"If you're kipping, Charlie, let me have that corner seat." The familiar frame stood in the open doorway, his strident whine ringing round the small compartment.

"Piss off, Sykes. Let the great British public have a few more hours respite before they realise you're back."

Sykes pointed to the stripes on his arm. "You want to remember, Williams, we're back in England and I have a couple of stripes now."

Everyone in the compartment burst out laughing and Charlie sat up in his seat and examined two freshly sewn on stripes with contempt.

"So what? You have a couple of stripes. Big deal. You also have a permanent brown tip on your nose from sticking it up the officer's arse holes so often. But you don't boast about that, do you?"

424

"I could order you out of that seat."

"You could, and that would be right up your street, you selfish bastard. You don't give a damn for the comforts of the other men travelling in here with a bloody window missing."

Sykes looked at the windows and frowned. "I can't see any windows missing."

"There would be after your bloody big head went through it, you pimply faced little sod. Piss off, and close that door behind you."

"Fancy a game of pontoon, Charlie?" Chappie asked.

"Not now." Charlie snuggled down in the corner seat and closed his eyes. "Later, Chappie," he answered.

After a delay of twenty minutes there was a series of whistles accompanied by loud shouting and a man running up and down the platform. A loud gush of escaping steam and the train shuddered as it took the strain of the heavily-laden coaches. The coach shook violently throwing the occupants backwards and forwards according to which way they sat and slowly it left the station with the familiar clickety click as it crossed the points. This sound growing in momentum as it cleared the great city of Glasgow and moved out into the open countryside, the railside telegraph poles whistling past with monotonous regularity heading for the Scottish/English border. A thick frost quickly laced the outside windows, and the compartment grew hotter and hotter, and as the heat increased so did the speculation of their final destination.

Occasionally someone would recognise a part of the country and the information would pass through the train. It picked up speed and the carriages rocked from side to side, stopping only at the Scottish border to allow the crew to change.

Chappie spoke very little but leant over Harry occasionally and clearing the windows pressed his face against the glass. "Yes. I guessed we must be in Yorkshire. We should be passing through Leeds at any time now. It's a big station. I wonder if they'll stop and give us some grub? My guts are tearing apart."

Everyone expected the train to stop and stood at the doors, mugs in hand ready to jump out and be the first in the queue. Charlie lowered the window and the cold blast of air filled the compartment. He held his mug and Kelly's waiting for the train to stop. It slowed down, the men grew excited, and it almost stopped then just as suddenly, clear of the platform, it raced forward with the passengers on the platform waving a welcome. But the men were either too disappointed or too tired to wave back. A few of them who'd had a bit of foresight had written letters and they threw them to the platform hoping some Samaritan would post

425

them on, so letting their wives know they were back in the country again. Then the train clear of the station, turn eastwards and once more picked up speed.

One man, familiar not only with the area but who had worked on the permanent way before enlisting became very excited, pointing out the lonely huts at the side of the track where he used to have meal breaks or sheltered from bad weather, boasting that he was not only familiar with every inch of the track but knew every sleeper.

"It looks very much as if we are heading for Norfolk." The man lowered the window to get a better view. "We're coming to a set of points. If we turn - that's eastwards - we are definitely going towards Norfolk." The man was quite adamant and it looked as if he knew what he was talking about, so the men took greater interest.

Except for one man who couldn't give a damn where he was going and said, "If you don't close that sodding window, my son, you will be travelling due west."

But it turned out the man who'd lowered the window knew exactly what he was talking about for the train turned east. Then darkness fell, lights were dimmed and senior N.C.O.s came along the corridors shouting to them to pull down the blinds. Some of the men dropped off to sleep. Kelly complained he was hungry. Another complained when he opened his kit bag to get a fresh packet of cigarettes that someone had vomited inside it. The compartment came to life several times during the night when the train stopped abruptly and jerked forward again just as suddenly.

And so after a disturbed night and just as dawn was breaking they entered a large city. By now the men, wide awake, leaned up against the windows. Surely there must be food out here they told one another, and grabbing their mugs they waited eagerly at the train doors ready to jump out. Steam from the train billowed along the platform. As it cleared they could see long tables laden with plates of sandwiches and urns of steaming hot tea and coffee, the tables attended by members of the Salvation Army and W.V.S. They were home at last! Indeed it was only at this point that Harry and the rest of the men felt that they finally had arrived home. North Africa, Italy and the long sea voyage were memories that everyone wanted to forget forever if possible, and seeing those fresh faced English women and girls behind the tables weighed down with food was a reality. A joyful reality for every man present.

Harry could hardly take his eyes from the nearest woman and her young helper. She must have been about eighteen or nineteen. The men alighted from the train and formed up in threes, walked

426

slowly towards the tables, and the young girl handed Harry several sandwiches with the words, "Tea or coffee?"

"Tea, please."

Their fingers met. She smiled sweetly and blushed crimson.

"Sorry, miss," Harry stammered an apology, and walked on turning occasionally to make sure he wasn't dreaming.

Their kits were dumped along the platform. They sat on their kit bags eating the sandwiches, not giving a damn what was inside them, and even Kelly brightened up looking a damn sight better than he'd done for almost a month.

The unit formed up outside the station in full battle order with their kit bags by their sides. Crowds of civilians gathered to see what was going on, surprised to see bronzed British soldiers. For two years this part of the country had been the stronghold of American troops, mostly airmen and paratroopers. But the khaki and black berets would soon become a familiar sight.

The R.S.M. addressed them. "While we're waiting for transport I want to arrange a leave roster. Every man in the unit will get leave. The first batch will leave in the morning as soon as money arrives. The second party will go when they return." He took the lists from Sykes and quickly read down them. "I should say two thirds of the unit can go on the first lot. And it's only fair that we let the married men and those that have responsibilities go with them. Any objections?" He glanced around, always a fair man. "First we have Rogers and Walker. They've been away from home for almost seven years. They came to us from India. They could have come home a couple of years ago but decided to stay with the unit. Also Sergeant McKay has been away for eight years. I'm sure no one would object to him going first."

"Och, man, it dis'na matter, I hev no 'en. Let someone else away." He may have been away in Hong Kong, then Egypt, but he'd never lost his Highland accent, had the stalwart Sergeant McKay. He was a great favourite throughout the unit.

"Right, men," the R.S.M. bellowed, "married men step forward." He watched every movement. They accounted for less than a quarter of the unit. "What the hell you doing out here, Wells? You're not married."

Wells was a small man of about twenty eight or so, who always wore a permanent grin and this time his face almost split in two.

"I was living in sin, sir. She misses me, sir."

"That doesn't count, Wells! Get back to the ranks!" The R.S.M's eyes darted along the three ranks. "You, Williams, you're married. Take a step forward."

"That's alright, sir. I'll go on the second leave with Jackson." This suited him much better. He would be able to write to the matron of the home and prepare her for a reunion with his daughter.

Some card shouted, "He's found out it's the wrong week, sir."

Unaware of Charlie's circumstances everyone burst out laughing, except Kelly. He turned to Harry with a puzzled frown. "What's he mean, Harry - the wrong week?"

Harry shrugged his shoulders. "Should think any week is the right week for his wife after he's been away for a couple of years or more."

Kelly's naive eyes widened in astonishment and Harry stared at him in open mouthed incredulity.

Charlie was about to make some comment but Harry muttered, "Let it ride, Charlie. It's the age of innocence."

"Age of innocence be buggered," Charlie snorted. "The simple sod is twenty-two and it's about time he learned that he can do more than piss with it."

He bent over Kelly's shoulder and whispered in his ear, but Kelly looked more puzzled than ever after Charlie had finished. Charlie couldn't contain himself any longer and taking of his forage cap brought it down smartly on Kelly's head. "Idiot!" he growled.

"Alright!" shouted the R.S.M. "Quiet in the ranks! I'm trying to get this leave roster completed. If I were you I would bloody well enjoy it. Make the best of it. When you come back we're going into extensive training." His eyes quickly darted along the three ranks and fell on Harry. "You, Jackson, you had a stint in East Africa before you joined us, so if you want to go with Williams on first leave you can."

Thus it was all arranged. While Charlie went to see his daughter in the orphanage, Harry would spend a few days in London alone and later Charlie would meet up with Harry at the Union Jack club in Waterloo Road.

"It'll be our first night away from each other since the desert," Harry said, but his words were overheard by Jenkins in the row behind them.

"Oh, Ducky, Charlie will have to fix you up with a chastity belt," he hooted with derision.

"Don't stand for that, Charlie, put some sand in his vaseline before you leave," another man howled.

"Do you pair of prats fancy going home with a couple of black eyes?" Charlie answered, not bothering to turn around.

Just then the sight of the first of half a dozen three tonners rounded a corner in the station yard prevented a serious argument from developing.

428

With the leave period over they found themselves settling down to a dreary routine of barrack room life, quite tame after the African and Italian campaigns, but they soon realised it wouldn't last for long before training began in earnest for the invasion of Europe.

There was also the bitter English weather to contend with. In the middle of January the cold set in and it was so bad, in fact, the condensation in the unlined Nissen huts formed into spears of icicles. Windows frosted over and the single stove in the centre of the hut proved quite inadequate when they had fuel, which was short in any event. Parties scavenged the local woods but the pickings were bare. The units previously occupying the huts had stripped the dead trees of bark, so that exposed trunks were all that had been left.

Everyone accepted that the landings at Salerno had only been a rehearsal for the big one. The medical unit had taken over an old mansion that had seen better days, with a formidable drive. The mansion itself must have been great in its heyday. The large entrance was overshadowed by a wide carved oak staircase, once carpeted it now resounded to the heavy hobnailed boots of the army. 'The big house,' one man dubbed it. The name stuck, it was used for the officers and senior N.C.O's, as well as for administration.

But as the month progressed the cold became unbearable, scavenging parties became more desperate and farmers' gates and fencing posts vanished without trace. It was rumoured that the sergeant cook and his two cronies slept on the wooden tables in the kitchen just in case they vanished!

Charlie returned to the big house, a towel wrapped around his head and another around his neck tucked inside his greatcoat. The shower had been boiling hot and it was with some reluctance he'd returned to the Nissan hut. His bottom lip trembled as he kicked the Nissen hut door closed behind him. He flicked his towel at an icicle hanging like a stalactite from the steel curved ceiling and it fell on another man's bed, piercing the blankets like a bayonet.

"Let's go to King's Lynn tonight, Harry," he suggested.

"Anything to get away from this perishing hut. I've never been so cold for years. Let's see what's on at the cinema."

Charlie folded the drier of the two towels and placed them on the shelf above the bed. The other, much wetter, he hung from the window knowing that in the morning it would be as stiff as a board.

"The lorry leaves in ten minutes for King's Lynn, although I met Carter a few minutes ago. He's going to Norwich. What do you fancy, Harry?"

"Anything suits me, Charlie. King's Lynn, Norwich, Timbuctoo as far as I'm concerned. Anything to get away from this bloody fridge."

Carter was waiting at the big house with the engine of his utility running.

"Sorry, Charlie, my schedule's been changed. I've to go to Wisbech with the old man, but I can drop you off at King's Lynn. That might be better for you as the lorry leaves there every hour up till midnight. Knowing you pair of dirty bastards you'll soon find yourselves a bit of crumpet."

"King's Lynn suits us, Nick."

The orderly room which also served as the guard room was established in what used to be the stables in the mansion's heyday. Reporting to the corporal on duty they noticed the stove next to his table was red hot, his tunic was unbuttoned and sweat oozed from his forehead. He glanced up at them and entered their names in his book.

"Jackson, Williams, booking out. Be back by 12.30. Going to Lynn are you? Midnight the last lorry. See you don't miss it." His sentences were clipped.

"Sorry to see you suffering here, corp. Would you like us to bring you an ice cream back?"

"That would be very nice, Williams. But knowing you, your mind will be on other things, especially those wearing skirts."

Charlie put his hand on his waist in a feminine attitude.

"Why, corp, is the Highland Divi in town?"

"Piss off, you two." The corporal was smiling. "If there's one thing you two aren't that's a couple of pansies. But there is one thing I can tell you. There's plenty of Land Army girls in town."

"Great, corp," Charlie answered. "If them girls have been watching a bull on the job there's no stopping them!"

Charlie was pleasantly surprised to see a pile of blankets in the back of the utility and soon he and Harry made good use of them as the back of a utility isn't the kindest of vehicles to travel in at the best of times, even worse in the heart of a British winter on the East coast. Yet they were soon warm under a mountain of blankets and with the steady rhythm of the engine as they raced through the country lanes they soon fell asleep.

Before they realised it they were at the car park and old market in the centre of town.

"Right, lads," Carter dropped the tailboard. "Here we are and don't forget the driver!" He held his cap out. "The C.O.'s just

430

gone over to the pub. Said he wants some fags, more like a couple of whiskies."

"Where the hell did you get those bloody blankets, Nick?" Charlie asked, admiring the large collection in the back of the ute.

"Why? You don't think I want to sleep with you peasants in those ice buckets do you? With the canvas back flap of the ute down and half a dozen blankets beneath me and as many on top I'm warm as toast. I got a special mention from Captain Welsh. He asked me the same question. I told him I preferred sleeping in the ute in case anyone tried to nick it or steal the petrol. He thought it very commendable."

"Yes, but where the hell did you get them? All we've been issued with is three per person. I sleep in my greatcoat," Harry said.

Carter puffed out his cheeks. "Here and there. I've to take the old man round and sometimes spend the night with another unit. I tell them I have no sleeping roll. They usually issue me with a couple and then I forget to hand them back. I had a field day once. The Q.M. told me to help myself. Pity I wasn't driving a three tonner. I managed to fix some of the lads with a couple each."

"Christ, Nick, this is the first I've heard about it." If there was one thing Charlie disliked it was being left out of any racket that was going. "Here's me freezing my balls out in that Nissen hut and you going round dishing out free blankets." Carter burst out laughing.

"Free? You know me, Charlie. You ever see me giving away anything free? I flog 'em two bob a time."

"Well, put me and Harry down for a couple each." He looked over Nick's shoulder as he wrote their names down in his little black book. "Christ, Nick, what the hell's that list? It'll be spring before you get to our names. It gets so cold in that hut my balls are brittle and during the night when I go for a slash my balls play jingle bells when I walk."

"Alright, Charlie, you'll have me in tears. I haven't forgotten that time you fixed me and the sergeant up with those two Itey bints in Sorrento." He winked at Charlie. "I won't charge you two."

"Thanks, Nick. I met a couple of Land Army girls the other day and they invited us to a party at the end of the month. Fancy coming?"

Sadly Carter shook his head, looking nervously over his shoulder. "For heavens sake, Charlie, don't mention that. I'm expecting the missus down some time this week. I've got a room a couple of miles from the billet. God, man, she's a jealous bastard. If she saw me looking at another woman she'd castrate me. That's why she's coming down."

"Well, at least you're fixed up till we sail again." Charlie put a patronising hand on Nick's shoulder.

"You kidding? You haven't seen my missus! I'd pay Charlie to screw her and give me grounds for divorce. God, how I envy you two freelancers. A night with her and you'd never want to see another horror movie. I'm tempted to offer her to the film industry as a stand-in for Quasimodo."

Harry burst out laughing.

"Come off it, Nick, she can't be that bad. What the hell did you marry her for?"

"Had no choice. She wasn't too bad when she was sixteen and not sixteen stone. I was screwing her regularly and of course the worst happened. I put her in the family way."

"That didn't mean you had to marry here. You had a decent job in civvy street. You could have supported the kid."

"You never saw her father! Six feet six and that size around the chest. He could crack a coconut with his bare hands. And her two brothers made the old man look like a dwarf. They were the type that would punch your bloody head just for looking at them. When they went into a pub they would clear the bar, and what tempers those bastards had. Everyone knew them! None of the neighbours would have any truck with them."

"Wedding bells rang then, Nick?" Harry was trying to keep a straight face.

"Yes, and when the war started it was like a reprieve. Worse still it turned out she wasn't having a kid." Charlie patted Carter's back sympathetically.

"Never mind, Nick, we'll be away in spring."

"Poor bastard," Charlie said as they walked away and then turned to Harry. "Let that be a lesson to you, Harry. If you don't fancy it don't stuff it."

They walked into the railway station. It was warmer in the buffet and the pies were good and cheap. They sat by the radiator but every time the glass doors opened a cold crisp wind hit the room. After the third cup of tea they decided to brave the cold once more, pulling up the collars of their greatcoats. They stepped outside and made their way to the cinema. It was showing a double feature and quite dark when they came out. They had been shunned by two Land Army girls while they were in the cinema and they met them on the way out.

Taking another look at them in a stronger light Charlie muttered, "Christ, Harry, we could have ended up like Carter!"

432

The girls gave them filthy looks when both Harry and Charlie burst out laughing.

They were about to go into a pub for half a pint when they noticed a small cafe on the corner. Two girls had just gone inside and pulled the blackout curtain over the door to one side. They followed.

It was a small homely cafe with half a dozen tables, all covered with blue gingham cloths. An old but well polished piano stood in one corner. Harry sat next to the piano with his back towards the two girls who sat at the table in the far corner and he and Charlie ordered beans on toast from the frugal menu.

"Just as well give the girls a treat, Harry," Charlie said as he ordered another helping of toast and beans. They removed their greatcoats.

"Nice and warm here, Charlie."

Charlie nodded. It was the first time he had really taken notice of the two girls. They had both removed their hats and coats and admired their shapely figures, but they hardly noticed Harry and Charlie.

The lady at the counter must have been in her early forties and was quite attractive for her age, not fat but well built. In fact as Charlie would say 'nice and cuddly but very pleasant.'

"You boys just back from Africa and Italy with the armoured division?" She asked.

Charlie nodded and answered, "Yes, and finding it bloody cold."

"Yes, my old man's in the army. He's a prisoner in Germany, silly old fool. Did twelve years. Served in Egypt, China and India. Came home in 1938 but was called up in September and couldn't get away quick enough. Then in '39 they sent for him again. He was still on reserve. You should have seen his face. You would have thought he was going to one of them holiday camps. Then at Dunkirk he was captured, served the silly old fool right, at his age. I'm sure they would have found him a job at the depot."

"I don't suppose he had much choice. I'm a regular, Ma. They can send you anywhere they like," Harry told her. He glanced longingly at the piano. "Any chance of playing the piano, Ma?"

She looked at Harry for a few seconds, then took out a key from her cash till and gave it to him.

"It was the old man's. He used to play it regularly. It's not been touched since he went away. Go on, son, give it a go, or as my old man would say, 'tickle the ivories'."

Harry rubbed his hands together and cracked the joints of his fingers, then he rolled the back of his hand along the keys, and started playing the old Gershwin tunes. He loved Gershwin and had been playing for ten minutes oblivious to the other people in the cafe when he felt a tap on his shoulder. He looked around and then straight into the bluest eyes he'd ever seen. It felt as if his heart missed a beat.

"Would you play a tune for me?" The girl asked sweetly. Her voice soft and gentle with only a slight trace of the attractive Norfolk accent.

He couldn't take his eyes from hers and stared at her almost to a point of rudeness and blushing a deep crimson she tried to avert her gaze, but was forced to look back at him.

"What would you like, Miss?" His voice appeared to break and he could feel his pulse racing as he studied her face. It was round, with those deep blue eyes, she wore little make up and what she did wear had been applied with skill. Her hair was short, neatly combed back and she had a silken complexion.

He almost sensed her request, but was shaken when she said, "'Roses of Picardy'. I love that tune. My father always sings it and it seems to play an important part in my life. Do you know it?"

She hummed it gently but his hands were already on the piano keys.

His mind flashed back to that time in the desert when he couldn't rid his mind of the tune, and playing with one hand, he took hers and led her before him at the piano, enabling him to see her while he played, and never once taking his eyes from her. Tears formed in the girl's eyes and he stopped playing.

"Why are you crying?"

Her friend came and stood beside her placing a protective arm around her shoulder. "If you're playing requests would you mind playing 'A Small Hotel'?" she asked, as if she were trying to divert him from the tune he was playing.

He nodded, smiled at the second girl, finished playing 'Picardy' and went straight into 'A Small Hotel.'

Several more people walked into the cafe when they heard the music from outside, including a couple of Yanks and their girlfriends, more men from their own division and an elderly couple. All in turn requested some tune that reminded them of other happier days. The girl still stood behind Harry, her hands on his shoulders, swaying to the rhythm of the music and Charlie took his tea over and sat with the girl's friend. At times the people clapped enthusiastically and no doubt would have started dancing if the room had been large enough. Harry finished with a flourish, bowed like a professional and locked the piano. Then he handed the key to the owner.

"Listen, son, anytime you feel like coming in and playing the piano, be my guest," the cafe proprietress said with a smile.

The girl held her hand out. Harry took it and it felt small and warm.

"My name is Kimberly. Everyone calls me Kim."

Harry was almost speechless and stammered, "Harry. My name's Harry..." Then he led her to the table not completely surprised to see Charlie sitting there.

"Harry," he introduced his girl, "this is Kath." Harry took her hand and introduced Kim. "They're cousins, Harry. Do you think they look alike?"

But Harry was too interested in Kim to make comparisons and hardly taking his eyes off her, mumbled an incoherent answer.

The cafe emptied leaving just the four of them sitting with their fifth cup of tea. The owner yawned, a signal for them to leave, and led them to the door holding the blackout curtain to one side.

"Come again, lads. Anytime you like. Play the piano, Harry. Say next Friday. You and your friends will be very welcome."

Harry walked steadily along, his hobnailed boots resounding against the flagstoned footpath, and yet he felt he was walking on air. His throat and stomach muscles tightened. His heart thumped against the walls of his chest as if it were hollow, and he felt his knees tremble as if they were about to buckle under the weight of his body. 'God, I used to feel like this when I was about to go up the front line,' he thought to himself.

Kim didn't say a lot and when she did it was soft and musical as if she were speaking from afar. He could hear Charlie behind him talking to Kathy and thought to himself, 'Christ, I hope he doesn't cock this one up. Kath doesn't look like the girl that would stand any nonsense.' Harry had heard all that crap about magic in the air with some skepticism, and yet there was something strange about this situation. That tune for instance. It had rammed through his brain like no other tune. It had haunted him ever since Tripoli.

A new moon was slicing through the cloudless sky. They turned into a tree-lined street, the branches, leafless and covered in frost looked like spectres pointing skywards. Kim shivered. Harry took her hand and plunged them into the deep pocket of his greatcoat. He turned, but Charlie and Kathy were no longer following, and he could hear Charlie's footsteps gradually fading.

"It's alright, Harry, Kathy lives down that street. I live here."

They stopped at a low bricked wall. The house was double-fronted with a pocket-sized garden each side of a crazy-paved path. "It was a lovely night, Harry." Kim whispered. "I can't remember when I enjoyed such a night. And wherever did you learn to play so beautifully?"

435

"It's a very long story. I hope I can tell you one day."

"I hope so, Harry."

So she did intend to see him again. Her lips turned up a smile and he would have loved to take her in his arms, which would have been Charlie's tactics. But there was something so different about Kim. It was Victoria who had told him four years before, after he'd turned her down because the war was on, 'When you meet the right girl, Harry, the whole world will stand still.'

"What do you do in the army, Harry? I saw by that medal ribbon you are just back from Africa," Kim asked.

"I'm a medic and a kind of stretcher bearer. Charlie and I have an ambulance and we've just returned from Italy. We were in Africa before that."

They sat on the low wall for some time talking, until Harry made the first move to leave and stood up.

"I suppose this is where we say goodnight, Kim. Can I see you again?"

Kim nodded and sorted through her handbag until she found an envelope with her address on it and handed it to him.

"Tomorrow, then. Call for me here."

He'd only gone six paces when he realised he had no idea where the lorry pick-up place was, and he called her back just as she opened the front door.

"I forget the place where we're to be picked up and I don't fancy walking back twenty miles to the billet."

They both burst out laughing.

"What time is it?" Harry asked, after she directed him to the pick-up point.

"Just past ten."

He waved to her, turned and blew her a kiss and she responded, still laughing as she heard him drop into a stead trot.

Charlie was waiting at the pick-up point when Harry arrived out of breath.

"How did you get on, Harry?"

"Alright, Charlie. Nice pair of girls. How did you get on with Kathy?"

"No good, Harry. Her parents own a little shop. We stood outside for ten minutes and then she asked me how long I'd been married. Do you know, Harry, I could have fallen over! You didn't tell them when I went for a slash in that cafe, did you?"

"Come off it, Charlie, you should know me better that."

"Anyway, I told her everything. How I was married when we were both very young. How she left me the day I went into the army and placed our little girl in the home. In fact I told her

436

everything. More than I have ever told anyone else. I kind of liked her, Harry. Not quite like the girls we're used to."

"You can say that again, Charlie. Anyway, did she believe you?"

"I don't know. But did Kim tell you her brother was killed in North Africa? Apparently he was killed near Tripoli. He must be buried in the cemetery where we buried little Spag. It's all so strange, as if it was meant to happen. You meeting Kim and you telling me about the tune 'Roses of Picardy' that started haunting you at Tripoli. Then in that cafe Kim asking you to play it for her."

"She never said a damn word to me about her brother and I was telling her about the desert as if I was enjoying it out there. You must have had it bad, too, telling Kathy all about your life. It's more than you've told me in over two years."

"Don't you forget, Harry, don't get too serious. You're always preaching about getting too involved while the war is on."

Charlie was right, of course. Since the war had started he had done everything in his power to avoid a deep relationship. Harry took the envelope Kim had given him from inside his pay book. It was too dark to read and he would have torn it up there and then, but something stopped him. Her eyes haunted him. He must try and keep a level head. Like everyone else in the division he knew their next operation would be on the coast of France and that it would be no picnic. It was well fortified and the enemy would bring all its best divisions and seasoned troops to defend it. But he knew he would never eradicate Kim's face from his mind.

The pub facing the market was crowded with Allied troops. They started tumbling out onto the street. Several men sprawled to the floor. The American military police were waiting for their own men and tumbled them into a lorry. A member of the Rifle Brigade amongst them who had swapped his tunic and forage cap with an American, stood grinning as the lorry raced off, waving to the rifleman. Charlie and Harry helped the Yank across the road. They sat him on a bench where he went into a deep stupor, and they covered him with the rifleman's greatcoat that the landlord had thrown into the street.

Their own lorry turned up. It had called at several pick-up points. Several men were already inside in various stages of inebriation. One man couldn't make it and Charlie and Harry lifted him bodily over the tailgate and followed him in.

Then Harry wrinkled his nose and gasped, "What a bloody stink! Who dropped that one?"

"It's this drunken bastard here, Harry. He hasn't stopped dropping them since he got on at the last pick-up point."

"Bloody hell," the man gasped, "he's done it again."

437

Charlie recognised Smithy's voice in the darkness.

"I reckon something's crept up his hole and died. Shall we throw the bastard out and let him get the next lorry?"

Smith was answered by another voice from inside the darkened lorry.

"We can't do that. He was thrown out of the last lorry. We found him flat out on a park bench and he hasn't got a greatcoat. He'll freeze to death if we don't get him back to camp."

"I wish his ring piece would freeze up! Just see if he's shit himself, Harry, will you?"

"Piss off, Charlie. Throw the bastard out at the crossroads if he lets off another."

The lorry roared along the narrow country road the pale moon reflecting off its frost covered surface. The driver must have thought he was still out in the desert, taking the corners and bends at full speed, skidding around on two wheels at times. The men clung tight for their lives, hanging onto the cold steel bars supporting the canvas top and twice the driver was forced to slap his brakes down hard for some emergency, sending the passengers into a heap in the back. The lorry sped through the gates of the big house and screeched to a halt, leaving two black tracks in the frost covered path for thirty yards. Then the men tumbled out fuming and cursing.

"It can only be that crazy bastard Holden that's driving," Charlie said. He looked for the driver. "I bloody well thought so."

The men lined up in some sort of order in front of the duty sergeant's desk and the sergeant stared at the unsightly parade.

"What a bloody sight you shower look."

Although he felt a little sympathy for them, he tried not to show it. They hadn't been in England a month yet and it wouldn't be many more months before they'd be off again. "Right, I've got your names. Get to bed." They turned to file out. "Not you, Jackson, I've been waiting for you."

"Really, sarge, I didn't think you cared." Harry lowered his voice. "Not in front of the other chaps, sarge."

"Don't be a prick, Jackson. You have to report to the Orderly Room at seven in the morning. Get your breakfast and be outside the Orderly Room with all your kit including your bed roll."

Panic seized Harry and he stammered out a question.

"What's the idea, sarge, am I being posted?" He knew the unit was being sorted out and had heard from reliable sources that qualified men were being posted to general hospitals. 'God, no,' he thought to himself. 'If it's a hospital I'll volunteer for the paras.'

438

But the sergeant put him at ease. Harry had proved himself well and truly over the months and there was little chance of the unit being prepared to let him go.

"Don't worry, Jackson, you're going to a small L.A.D. Unit over at Dereham. They have no medic and the unit is too small to have an M.O. It looks like a cushy number - something to do with statistics. They want to find out how many men you can knock off before the invasion starts."

Harry chose to ignore the sergeant's sarcastic remarks, but was curious to know more. He didn't like the idea of being separated from Charlie.

"Will it be for long, sarge?"

The sergeant shrugged his shoulders.

"Who knows? Probably till we sail. You may have to go over with them."

"Will Williams be coming with me, sarge?"

"What the hell for? Do you want him to hold your nuts, Jackson? Shove off and get back here in the morning."

Charlie was waiting outside and was disappointed at the news.

"Never mind, Harry, you'll team up with me before we go on to the invasion."

They stood in silence as they watched the lorry turn round and head for the gates. Then Charlie put his hand to his mouth.

"Bloody hell, Harry, I just realised that that piss-arsed bastard is still in the back of the lorry! Poor sod, he'll freeze to death before he gets back here."

CHAPTER 40

Harry sat on his kit outside the orderly room waiting for transport to his new posting. Carter was already an hour late and Harry wasn't in a very pleasant mood, having spent a restless night wondering what would happen and whether or not his arrangements for the evening would be altered. There was no denying he had taken a real fancy to Kim in spite of his determination not to get too involved in a wartime relationship. His mind was on this track when the utility pulled up in front of him with a squeal of brakes that jolted him from out of his day dreams.

"Sling your kit in the back, Harry!" Carter shouted.

Harry sat down in the seat beside the driver with a thump.

"You're bloody late, Nick. Not like you to be late."

"It's my missus, Harry. The old cow turned up last night. I was in a right stew. I'd waited for that bloody train for a whole hour, so I pissed off back to the billet. Couldn't have been gone ten minutes when the train pulled in. She told a Red Cap and he phoned the company office. God, Harry, you should have heard the old cow. She gave my lugs a bashing right in the middle of the station when it was crowded with our chaps and Yanks. She's got a voice like a bloody fog horn. Then when we got to our lodgings she went for me hell for leather. Just couldn't satisfy the bitch. Worse than that bloody Itey bint you and Charlie fixed me up with in Naples, she is. She closes her eyes when we're on the job. I don't think she likes to see me enjoying myself. But there's light on the horizon, Harry. She's been called up and wants to go in the Air Force. Think she'll find her niche there, Harry, jump starting Wellington bombers."

The trees still laden with morning frost flew by and fortunately the country lanes were clear of traffic so Carter was able to make up time. They passed through a sleepy village breaking all speed limits, and a mile after Dereham they made a sharp right turn. Carter slowed down.

"It's around here somewhere. I've only been here once before." He turned up a driveway into a large farmyard.

"This is it, mate. Out you get."

Carter helped Harry with his kit into an ancient Nissen hut on the end of the drive. The hut itself, a relic of the First War was divided into three separate sections: one third was the M.I. room, the centre part was the waiting room and the end part the sleeping quarters for the unit cooks. The middle section was bare of all furniture with the exception of two wooden benches.

Harry dropped his kit in the centre of the M.I. room sighing deeply as he looked around it. The furniture consisted of one bed (hospital issue) with a pillow, two clean sheets and four blankets neatly folded. He felt the springs and they felt comfortable. A large cupboard, like a clapped out wardrobe, stood in another corner, and a worm eaten pine, glass fronted cupboard stood beside an old solid fuel stove. The only other furniture was a pine table on metal trestles and two chairs. The whole lot, including the army issue brown lino on the floor was covered in a fine film of dust.

Harry tapped the stove pipe rising through the roof of the hut and a cloud of soot fell into the room.

"Just take a look up there, Carter," Harry said. "There where the pipe goes through the roof. There's an inch of daylight all round. Bet it pisses through there when it rains."

"Shouldn't worry a lot if I were you, Harry," Carter assured him.

"Just take a shufti through the window this side. There must be ten ton of coal and coke there, you lucky bastard. All you want now is a lovely bint and it'll be home from home."

Harry stood at the opposite window watching Nick Carter vanish down the path into the road, then he set about cleaning the place but first he needed to light a fire. No problem. There were plenty of twigs lying around.

He'd just finished cleaning when there was a loud knock on the door and a cold blast as the door was flung open. A sergeant - he must have been all of six feet three - stood framed in the doorway.

"I saw the smoke from the chimney. I guess you must be the new medical orderly," he greeted Harry brusquely. "You should have reported to me on arrival."

Harry realised his mistake and had no intention of blotting his copy book on his first day. This situation called for a bit of bull. He snapped to attention.

"I'm waiting for my medical equipment to arrive, sarge. It should have been here by nine."

"That's no excuse. You should have reported to me," the sergeant reprimanded him.

"See you've cleaned the place up a bit. I was going to send a couple of men over to help you." He opened the door leading into the waiting room.

"I'll send them over to give this place a good clean up and see if I can find you some bloody paint."

He studied Harry for a few minutes, and his eyes seemed to pierce right through him.

"Wouldn't send us a medical officer. We have two hundred in this unit, but only about fifty here. The rest are scattered around in billets, so I hope you know your job. The M.O. comes twice a week. He's a moaning old bastard and always smells of stale whisky."

This sounded familiar to Harry.

"What's his name, sarge?"

"Smithers. What little hair he's got is ginger, sports a pale ginger moustache."

"I know him, sarge. A bloody good surgeon. He was out in Italy with us. He joined the unit in the desert."

Harry toyed with the idea of asking the sergeant if he could get away that night but decided to wait a while. After all, he hadn't got off to a good start.

"You a regular?" the sergeant asked Harry.

"Yes, sarge, six years almost seven."

"You must know something about it then."

"Yes, sarge, first class nursing orderly and an operating room assistant and I also worked on the V.D. wards so if one of the men gets a dose he knows where to come."

Harry hadn't the slightest idea why he said that, but the sergeant's attention was gripped, for he sat down on the end of the bed staring uncomfortably at Harry as he unpacked his kit bag and back pack.

"How can you tell when you have a dose, medic?"

"Easy, sarge. First you start pissing razor blades and broken glass and after a few days you get a discharge. Bloody uncomfortable. Or if you get a sore on the end of your tool, usually about the size of a shilling, that's bloody dangerous if you neglect if because it can send you round the bend. What's the matter, sarge?" Harry snorted with laughter but the sergeant's face remained sullen and Harry knew he'd touched a sore point.

"Anything I tell you, medic, can I have your solemn promise it won't go further?"

"You can stake your life on that, sarge." Harry had seen this all before. Usually in a friend with the signs and symptoms or a friend of a friend.

"Look, sarge, get if off your chest. You won't be the first with a dose and you certainly won't be the last."

For a long while the sergeant remained silent and stared vacantly at the floor.

"Like you said, medic, it's like pissing razor blades and now I have a discharge. But this is no ordinary dose, medic, I got this from the wife. I waited for the rest of the unit to have their leave. I've only been back a few days. Bitch. I very nearly killed her. I spent the last few days at the Union Jack Club in London and thought of throwing myself off London Bridge."

"Bit drastic wasn't it, sarge? Anyway, how do you know it's dose? It could be several things: bladder or kidney trouble, strain, cold in the water works division. Because you have a discharge it doesn't mean you have a dose. Honest, sarge, you people make me sick. You always think the worst. Drop your slacks and let's have a shufti."

The sergeant brightened up. He was like a man drowning in fast flowing water grabbing at a slender twig.

"You have a slight discharge there, sarge. Not a lot is it?" Harry said upon closer inspection.

"As soon as my medical kit arrives I'll take a couple of smears on the microscope slides and get them to the hospital. In the meantime find a small bottle and give me a sample. Make sure the bottle is clean."

"Will this be on official report, medic?"

Harry could see the distress in the sergeant's face. He could also see a way of working himself into the sergeant's good books. Here he was, miles from anywhere, and worse he was miles from Kim and so far there was no chance of getting away for the evening. His brain was working overtime. He'd heard there was a military hospital near the town and all he had to do was get there, then leave the rest to chance. But he must get transport.

"What about transport, sarge? If I could get the slides to a hospital there could be a chance of getting the lab assistant to test them on the quiet. I might have to drop him a couple of quid on the side, and should it prove positive I'll have to report it. But that's only for your own good, sarge."

The sergeant was in complete agreement and was feeling and looking far more cheerful than when he entered the room.

"I have an old ambulance in the old cow shed. Left here by the last unit, it was. I doubt if they'll be needing it as they're on their way to the Far East. I'll let you have a driver."

It was Harry's turn to feel jubilant and silently he thanked Charlie for teaching him to drive.

"No thanks, sarge. I can drive the ambulance and it's best that the visit should be between ourselves. Now I'll have to make a start for the hospital."

"Right, medic. But before you go let me fill you in on the routine. The mess is in the farmhouse. You just stroll up when you're ready. You can get away most days. The M.O. comes twice a week and if you want a new uniform just come and see me. I'll also send you down some tea and sugar. Milk you can get from across the road at that dairy farm. Anything else you want just let me know."

"Thanks, sarge, you pop back later and I'll fix you up. By the way, sarge, my name is Jackson."

The sergeant roared with laughter.

"Well, I won't forget that in a hurry! I'm Sergeant Jackson."

The medical panniers arrived within the hour and Harry hadn't unpacked them when the sergeant came rushing over and handed the small bottle to Harry.

"Right, sarge," Harry said, taking it, "let's get them slides done. I'll push off now. And don't worry, sarge, I think everything will be alright."

The ambulance was old but the engine was in perfect condition, reminding him very much of the first time he met Charlie with his wreck. But as Harry climbed behind the wheel he realised how the owner of a new Rolls Royce must feel when he climbs behind the wheel for the first time. Happily, he sang loudly to himself as he raced through the lanes, the wind whistling past the open cab. Tomorrow he would give the ambulance a thorough cleaning and if possible a lick of paint.

He found the hospital six miles the other side of the town hidden along a narrow country lane as if the authorities wanted no one to find the place. Having arrived he was directed to the laboratory with no trouble at all, and decided that this was too good to be true! 'Someone up there must be looking after me,' he mumbled to himself as he entered the laboratory and saw the corporal in charge, an old friend of his who had passed out at the training depot in the same squad.

He answered to the nickname of 'Bombardier', his name being Billy Wells, the same as the well known champion boxer. But there the similarity ended, for this Wells was five feet six with glasses like the bottom of jam jars, bow-legged, pigeon toed, and had a chest that would hardly measure up to the great Bombardier Billy Wells's neck. Harry was more than pleased to see him just as the bombardier was as astonished to see Harry.

"God, Harry Jackson! We heard you'd been killed at Tobruk, Harry. Glad to see that rumour was greatly exaggerated." He gave Harry a warm, welcoming handshake.

Quickly Harry gave him a brief fill in over the past years since they'd left the depot together, and soon their small talk led to the real reason for the visit.

"You know how it is, Bombardier. New posting. Got to get on the good side of the sergeant. He's in charge. Please run the slides through, then perhaps I can meet you in town one night - at least have a drink."

444

"Sorry, Harry. Me, I haven't touched a drop since I examined my first liver cut out of a dead heavy drinker. Tell you, mate, it looked like an old chamois leather."

"Anyway, I'll drop you a couple of hundred fags the next time I'm in," Harry said.

The corporal held his hand up in disgust.

"You kidding, Harry? Ever seen a pair of cancerous lungs taken from a heavy smoker?"

He didn't wait for Harry to reply, but pulled on a pair of rubber gloves and took the lid off a white enamelled bucket and threw a pair of lungs on to a zinc topped table. Then he cut them with a sharp scalpel, his pebble stoned glasses an inch from the offending organs as if he was about to smell them.

"See that black stuff, Harry? That's tobacco tar."

"Fucking hell, Bombardier!" Harry looked in disgust at the mass on the table.

"For heaven's sake, don't fart, mate, or you'll blow your ring away."

"Come back in the morning, Harry. I'll stain the slides. But you can have the prelim results straight away." The Bombardier placed one of the slides under the microscope and invited Harry to take a look.

"Why, the dirty little sods are screwing all over the place," Harry said as he adjusted the lenses.

"Looks alright to me, Harry. It's nothing serious."

Harry showed the corporal the envelope Kim had given him.

"Know where this place is, Bombardier?"

"Should do, Harry. I live in the next street. I was posted here soon as the war started. This place was taken over by the army. I met and married a local girl and I've got a couple of kids now."

Well, next stop Kim's. Harry didn't want to get there too early, or too late; for although the corporal's directions were specific it might be hard to find in the dark. Harry cruised around the town for half an hour stopping at a fish and chip shop, then he slowly made his way towards the house just as daylight was fading.

The house looked different in the diminishing light. It exactly resembled the whole ribbon of houses that stretched along either side of the road, and this was itself lined with young trees bared of leaves. 'Must look great in the spring,' thought Harry to himself. He guessed the houses were late Victorian or early Edwardian, lower middle class, belonging to a family that had probably worked through the Great Depression, but hardly wealthy enough to run a small car. The houses were double fronted with small front gardens each side of a crazy-paved path. In a couple of months time they would be a blaze of colour.

445

Charlie's advice came back to him.

"Always make friends with the mother. Concentrate on the old girl, the old man is a wasted effort initially. To him you are always a potential rapist intent on ravishing his daughter. It doesn't matter if she is a raving nymphomaniac, to him she's a vestal virgin reincarnate. Daddy's sweet English rose. Yes, nurture the old lady, and spend your last few bob on a box of chocolates. Nick a bunch of flowers from the local churchyard and agree with every word she says. Then once you have her eating out of your hand you start on the old man and the mother will support you. If he smokes a pipe you find out his favourite tobacco. Buy him a half ounce but, don't lay it on too thick to start - just half an ounce or ten Woodbines if he smokes cigarettes. Yet always bear in mind that to him you are a potential rapist so be constantly on your guard, watching every word you say." With Charlie's advice in mind Harry knocked on the front door.

He knocked again and heard a faint voice say, "Push hard on the bottom of the door."

Harry did as he was instructed from the unseen voice, the door flew open revealing a most beautiful woman standing before him, he could see now where Kim got her good looks from, the same short hair, the deep penetrating blue eyes and an elfin like face. She stared at him blankly, Harry felt uncomfortable, her eyes seemed to penetrate his body, the faintest of a flicker turned up the sides of her mouth.

"Damn door, it always sticks like that." The voice wasn't hostile, neither was it friendly, she showed him into the sitting room.

It was a neat room, a fire blazed up the chimney. With two heavy armchairs, one each side of the fireplace, a well polished piano stood on one side of the room, and a equally polished sideboard the other side, and a china cabinet, filled with glass and bone china and various mementos of holiday souvenirs, she indicated the armchair for him to sit down, she sat in the chair facing him.

"I understand you went out with my Kim last night?"

He smiled as he answered, "yes," but there was no responding smile from her.

"Yes, my friend went out with her cousin." He could feel a barrier coming down between them.

"Why is something wrong?"

"Of course you do know she is only seventeen, she won't be eighteen till another month and she is very innocent."

Harry stood up to leave the room.

446

"Madam, I was seventeen when the war started and I had been in the army over two years. And as for your daughter, what little time I spent with her I found her quite charming and I enjoyed her company, but I am not a damned rapist. Good day, madam."

He made for the door, but she sprang from her chair and barred his way.

"Oh, I am so sorry, I really didn't mean it that way. You see Kim is my only child now, her brother, my John, was killed in the desert."

She pointed to a large picture of a boy about fourteen in football gear. A nice looking boy who could have been mistaken for his sister's identical twin. He was holding a football under one arm and smiling broadly.

"When he died my world was torn apart and I have to be honest with you, Harry." She paused, and for the first time she smiled.

"It is Harry, isn't it. Kim told me you would be coming." She indicated to him to sit down again. Reluctantly he took his seat.

"You see, Harry, the last man I wanted to see come through that door was a man in soldier's uniform."

It wasn't the only picture of her son in the room, they were scattered all over, in football gear and cricket whites, swimming trunks and rugby kit. There was also a photograph of him that was taken in the desert, frayed shorts and wearing a Australian bush hat, and standing against a bren carrier with Harry's divisional desert rat on the front. She saw him looking at it and handed it to him.

"That was taken a few weeks before he was killed at a place near Tripoli, a place called Homs, do you know it?"

Harry nodded.

"Yes, I know the place very well."

"But, Harry, if you were in the war at seventeen and was already in the army for two years, what did your mother say about enlisting? You must have only been a boy. My John just enlisted the day after the war started, I broke my heart. My husband saw the last two years of the First War."

"I didn't have a mother, I think I was about two when she died."

"Oh Harry, I am sorry. What about your father, didn't he object?"

"I didn't have a father either. You just as well know the truth from the start. I was born a bastard and was brought up in an orphanage run by Quakers."

Her whole attitude changed. Her eyes softened. He thought he noticed a tear form. She leaned over and caught his hand.

447

"Oh I am so sorry, Harry, that must have been awful."

"No not really, what you never have you never miss. I suppose you could say I had about thirty brothers and sisters, it was a lovely home and they looked after us. Of course they were extremely annoyed when they found out I had joined the army, as you know Quakers are pacifists. Most of the kids there were orphans from the First War. We were smothered in love, the lady that taught me the piano wanted me to be a concert pianist. I ran away at fourteen and was roaming around London when I went into the recruiting office and joined the army. I was always big for my age and I told them I was eighteen. So there you have it, if you want to kick me out I will understand. It's not everyone that wants a bastard around the house especially if they have such a pretty daughter."

Once more he got up from his chair and pulled his cap from his shoulder straps.

"Now I have upset you, Harry. Do sit down, you make me nervous sitting on the edge of that chair and keep getting up. I will make you a nice cup of tea." She vanished into the kitchen.

Harry stood up and adjusted his uniform, then quietly walked out of the house. He was just pulling away in his ambulance when she came rushing to the door. He slammed the ambulance into gear and pulled away.

He returned to his M.I. room and made himself tea and fried himself eggs and bacon and two huge slices of fried bread, he was hungry, he hadn't eaten since leaving the camp that morning, but he couldn't eat. He sat staring into the stove sipping his tea and smoking cigarette after cigarette till his mouth felt sore and dry. Twice he took out the envelope with Kim's address, then screwed it into a ball and threw it into the red hot stove. He undressed and went to bed, but sleep wouldn't come, he just stared at the rounded roof of the Nissen hut, Kim's childlike face kept flashing before his eyes. Never before in his life had he felt like this about any women. He tried to blot her completely from his mind and substitute Victoria, the nurse he knew so long ago and thinking he would get a weekend pass and go down to London to see her, at least she would be good for a laugh. Victoria loved fun.

He collected the results of the slides from the laboratory the next morning, as he supposed, they were negative. When he returned the sergeant was over the moon.

"Go sick officially now, sarge. The old man will give you a course of pills, that should clear up in few days. And if I was you sarge, get the biggest bunch of flowers you have ever seen, go home and get down on your knees and pray for forgiveness from your wife. Personally I would kick your balls in if it was me."

448

And for the first time in twenty four hours, Harry smiled.

Three days later Harry pulled into his own unit for medical supplies. Charlie came out to meet him.

"What was the matter with you the other day, Harry? I met Kathy in town Tuesday night. Kim hasn't been to work since you walked out and will hardly speak to her mother, she blames her. Apparently they are both very upset. Kathy reckons she has never seen them fall out in their entire lives. She wants your address so that she can apologise. Will it be alright if I ring her up and give it her? What the hell happened?"

Harry gave Charlie the entire episode, leaving nothing out.

"You know how it is, Charlie, the old girl kept quizzing me, then I told her I was a bastard and walked out."

"That's sod all, I have been calling you a lousy bastard for a long time now, you don't take umbrage with me. Alright if I give her your address?"

"Please yourself. I am off down to London this weekend, I think I will go and see that nurse I was talking about. She doesn't even know I am back in England yet." He sat on the edge of Charlie's bed smoking.

"I have just come in for medical supplies. I am running out of aspirins, they are a pissy lot of bastards in this unit, that's all I am doing, doling out aspirins. The old farmer across the road from us broke his bloody leg last week, I fixed him up, put on a splint and took him to the local hospital. I can't seem to do anything wrong there. The farmer's wife keeps me supplied in bacon and eggs and I get fresh milk every day. The sergeant in charge of the unit has virtually given me the ambulance. I have a cosy billet with as much coal and coke as I can use."

"Well bring us a couple of sacks when you come down again, it's bloody freezing in here. Just look at the condensation in this place, the bloody icicles are dropping down like stalactites."

"That's no trouble, Charlie, you can have a couple of sacks tomorrow."

Next morning the M.O. was due for his weekly sick parade. It was pouring down when he arrived. He stood in the doorway and shook the rain from his cap. He stared at Harry,

"Morning, Williams."

"Jackson, sir, my name's Jackson."

Captain Smithers took the small leather bound note book from his top pocket and flipped through the pages.

"Oh yes, that's right, Jackson, the other mad bastard is Williams, is he still alive?"

Harry nodded.

"Strange, never thought you would make it the way he drives that ambulance."

He sat down at the table and looked around.

"Nice little billet, Jackson. How many sick?"

"Two, sir. Sergeant Jackson," he moved closer and confidentially lowered his voice. "He thinks he has a dose sir, but I think it just maybe N.S.U. perhaps overdone it when he went on leave and may have strained himself, he had been away four years. I bet he didn't have time to take his full pack off."

"Thank you, Doctor Jackson," his tone rather sarcastic. "Would you mind if I gave a second opinion? Call him in."

As the sergeant came through the door Harry winked and said, "Drop your slacks, sarge."

Captain Smithers lifted the sergeant's penis up on the end of his leather covered swagger cane.

"Much of a discharge, sergeant?"

"No, sir, very little."

"That's seen some active service sergeant." He tapped the end of the sergeant's penis with the tip of his swagger stick.

"Right pull them up."

He turned to Harry, "Get a couple of slides and a specimen and get them to the lab."

After the sick parade Harry said to the M.O., "The sergeant, sir. My mate is in the lab down at the hospital, will it be alright if I get them done on the quiet, unofficial like? The sergeant isn't a bad bloke and if this got round the unit - you know."

A flicker of a smile crossed the M.O's. face.

"You and that crafty bastard of a driver, still up to your old tricks I see. What you mean is you scratch my back and I'll scratch yours."

Harry helped him on with his trench coat and handed him his cap and leather bound cane.

"Alright, Jackson, get the official results through. Be it on your own head, I don't want to know, unless of course he does have a dose, then he will have to be reported. See you next week."

After Harry got the official results, which as he already knew were negative, the sergeant was overjoyed. He gave Harry his weekend pass.

"Stay another day if you want to, Harry, I will cover for you."

"That's alright, sarge. I will be back first thing Monday morning to dish out the usual aspirins. You certainly have a drunken lot of bastards here."

Harry managed to get a lift to the railway station and decided he would catch the midday train to London. He looked up at the large station clock, he still had an hour to go so strolled over to the book stall. He was flicking through the magazines when he felt a tap on his shoulder, he swung round and stared straight into Kim's face and stammered.

"What the hell are you doing here?"

Her eyes were red, he could see she had been crying, he softened towards her and gently touched her face, then led her to a bench on a quiet part of the station. It was several minutes before she spoke.

"I don't know what my mother said to you, but she was terribly upset when you walked out of the house."

"God, Kim, it wasn't your mother exactly, although the reception was a little chilly, I could quite understand that. You know, your brother being killed, I could see her point, she hardly welcomed another soldier in the house. It made me realise my own position, I just don't want a lasting relationship till the war is over. I saw all those photographs of your brother around the sitting room - it just wouldn't be fair on you, Kim."

"I think it's too late for that, Harry. That night in that cafe, I just couldn't take my eyes from you, and when you played that tune 'Roses of Picardy', there just seemed to be a message there, for months that tune has been haunting me. It just seemed to me that that meeting was meant to be."

"That's very strange. I haven't got that tune out of my mind for months. It started in a small town in the desert, a place called Homs, your mother mentioned it."

She gave an involuntary shudder.

"That's where John was killed."

They stared blankly at each other.

"Do you think..." But the rest of the words just would not come. Harry changed the subject, although he admitted to himself that it sounded more than coincidental.

"How did you know I was at the station here?"

"I have been here since seven this morning waiting for each train that's going to London. Charlie told Kathy you were going to London, so I just waited for you to turn up. I just had to see you again, Harry. Did you mind me coming here?"

"No." He just laughed it off.

"I suppose to tell the truth I was rather glad to see you."

He put a comforting arm around her shoulders. The mid morning London train came and departed again, so did the next two trains, they were still sitting on the same bench.

451

CHAPTER 41

Harry never went to London that night, they sat on the same bench for hours. It was totally dark when they left the station arm in arm and made their way back to the cafe where they first met.

The owner was delighted to see them again. Harry's piano playing had meant extra business last time he was here. As soon as they finished their meal, with a grin across her face, the landlady threw Harry the piano key. Reluctantly he took it, he would much rather have sat with Kim for the remainder of the evening, but Harry just couldn't refuse the plea in the owner's eyes. As soon as he sat at the piano and the music floated to the street outside the cafe started to fill. He played request after request, it was that time of the war when any music was at a premium, but by ten o'clock he had had enough and in spite of pleas from all over the small cafe he just shook his head, he walked Kim home. They stood at the garden gate.

"Won't you come in, Harry? Mother wants to apologise."

"Apologise, what for? It's me that should apologise." But the day had been so happy for him the last thing he wanted to do was meet the family.

"Look, Kim, it's better we should wait a few days. It's Sunday tomorrow, what say I meet you at the railway station, under the clock? We can take a train ride out in the countryside somewhere. Perhaps we may find some quiet pub and have a bit of lunch. Make sure you wear some heavy warm clothes."

Although she was disappointed he wouldn't come into the house, she was delighted with the prospect of spending a day alone and out in the country with him. They kissed, long and passionately, and she clung tightly to him. He waited as she ran down the garden path and the door opened, she turned and waved, just as the air raid warden shouted, "Put those lights out."

He made his way back to his billet. The first lorry that stopped dropped him to within a mile of the old farmhouse. Now that he had the complete use of the old ambulance, not a day went by without meeting Kim. His involvement grew deeper and deeper, all his resolutions about not getting involved in a deep relationship went by the wind. Kim, like most of the civilian population, was involved with war work and worked on different shifts, but he never failed to meet her from work. Sometimes she would be with Kathy but more often she was alone. Kim was everything Harry desired, pretty and shapely with a carefree spirit and an infectious laugh, and yet she would cry unashamedly at a sad picture. On one occasion, when out for a walk in the countryside, they saw a rabbit that had been killed by a motor vehicle. She cried, and made Harry bury it. But as the days passed they realised they had so much in common, liking the same music and enjoying the same films. But their greatest joy together was visiting old buildings and churches, with a morbid interest in reading the words on tombstones.

On one occasion they were sitting on top of a large flat tombstone in an ancient churchyard enjoying a picnic, when Kim said, "When I was a small girl I always wanted to be a nurse, but I can't stand the sight of blood."

Harry almost choked on the bottle of lemonade they were sharing.

"Lot of damn use you would be in a hospital. Some nurse, shedding tears over a dead rabbit. What would you do if you saw a dead baby?"

"I would faint." But she changed the subject.

"Do you think Charlie will ever meet Kathy again? It's a pity really, I know she is very fond of him, but won't see him because he's married. Do you think he will get a divorce, Harry?"

"It's not for the want of trying." He jumped down from the tombstone and lifted her to the ground.

"I hope this bloke under here enjoyed it as much as me." He read the name and the date. "Do you realise if this bloke had lived, he would be two hundred and twenty now?"

The next day Harry called into his own unit for medical supplies, this meant a further supply of aspirins and number nines, for those not drinking themselves to death were constipated.

He dropped in to see Charlie, who was as usual laid out across his bed covered with his greatcoat.

"Bag of coke and a bag of coal in the ambulance, Charlie. Get a couple of blokes to unload it." But he hardly got the words from his mouth when there was a mad rush to his ambulance. He shouted after them, "Make sure you clean the bloody thing out, or that will be the last."

He needn't have worried. While he had more fuel than he could use they had to scavenge around the woods for logs, and most of the farmers within a couple of miles radius were still complaining their five barred gates were missing.

"How's it going, Charlie, getting out much?"

"You kidding, Harry? Have you seen the Land Army girls around here? Randy cows they are. I think they must spend half their spare time watching the bulls and cows on the job. Went up to London last weekend with one. Pity you are so involved with Kim, I have arranged a weekend in London again with her this week, she wants to bring a mate and you could have made a foursome up."

"Not bloody likely, Charlie. Don't you fancy her cousin, Kathy, any more? She is what you call a real good looker. Listening to Kim, I reckon she fancies you."

"No good, Harry, I don't think she believes I am waiting for my divorce. I went to see the padre again. Frankly I don't think he gives a shit. When I went to see my little girl I called in to see a solicitor, he reckons it will take anything up to five years. Pity really, I think I could go for her in a big way. I suppose you know she did give me her phone number? I went to the phone box a couple of times and went as far as putting my coppers in, and thought, fuck it."

"Never mind, Charlie, I will put in a good word for you." He buttoned his greatcoat to face the cold. "See you later."

"By the way, Harry, the Div's on a big stunt shortly, it's going to last a few days, you are coming back to join me, we get the new vehicles later this week."

"That's good, and do me a favour Charlie, for heaven's sake don't get the name 'Mobile Brothel' painted on till we get out of the country. If I was out with you and Kim saw that she would throw a fit."

He returned to his unit and had only been in his M.I. room when the sergeant came rushing over.

"You better come over to the billet, Harry. Corporal Glover is in a bad way, you could fry an egg on his forehead and he's just staring into space, I can't get any sense out of him, he just keeps saying 'I'll be alright.' I gave him a couple of aspirins."

"I know Corporal Glover, sarge. Bloody nice bloke. Reported sick once or twice, keeps complaining of a headache, I told him to lay off the booze but he just smiled. Do you know, sarge, this is the worst unit I have been in for drunks."

"Well, to be honest, I don't think it's the booze in this case, Harry, you had better get over there now."

Harry took one look at the corporal.

"How long has he been like this, sarge?"

"Since this morning as far as I know, I have sent for the M.O."

"God, I hope the M.O. isn't pissed when he arrives here. I have been telling the M.O. I've been worried about those persistent 'headaches' but it's hard to tell, most of the men have been pissed out of their minds since we arrived here. I have ordered so many aspirins since we arrived the Q.M. almost accused me of flogging them to the local peasants."

Harry dropped to one knee beside the corporal's bed, felt his forehead and took his pulse and temperature.

"Better get a stretcher ready, sarge, and have a driver standing by, he'll have to be rushed to hospital. I think the best hospital would be Addenbrookes. Ring them and ask them to stand by, if it's what I think it is the M.O. will send him there. Just ask them to stand by in case."

"I thought something was wrong earlier. When I came into the room he was just staring into space, not like Glover that, can never stop the bastard from talking most of the time."

"Christ, sarge, I wish you'd told me before I left."

Ten minutes later Captain Smithers strode into the room looking annoyed at first, someone had been poaching his drinking time, as it was his breath smelt of stale whisky. He gave Glover a thorough examination. The sergeant left the room.

Harry said, "It looks like a tumour on the brain, sir. I saw a man in this state before."

The captain didn't answer but nodded his head as if in agreement. "When did he last report sick, Jackson?"

"A couple of weeks ago, sir, it's in my report. We gave him some tablets. I have notified the hospital, sir. I thought it best to report to Addenbrookes in Cambridge, they have better facilities there. The ambulance and a driver are standing by, sir."

There was very little doubt that the M.O. had complete confidence in Harry, for he neither agreed nor disagreed with Harry's diagnosis. Neither did he reprimand him for taking the action he did in notifying a civilian hospital. Cambridge was a fair distance away but it seemed the best decision to make. Four men were called into the room with a stretcher and they gently lifted the corporal into the ambulance. The M.O. walked beside Harry.

"Why haven't you been promoted, Jackson? It seems you know your job, you handled this case very well. I shall take this matter up with the R.S.M."

"I don't want promotion, sir, I'm quite happy serving on the ambulance, sir."

"Oh yes, I know." A slight smile flashed across his face.

"You and that other mad bastard, Williams. I have heard about the antics you two mad bastards get up to. I understand that your last ambulance was called the Mobile Brothel. Just be careful where you're putting it around, Jackson."

"Not anymore, sir, very little chance of that."

"Glad to hear it, Jackson. Now get that man to hospital fast as you can."

They reached the outskirts of the city in the dead of night and found a police car waiting for them. One policeman got out of his car.

"Follow me, driver. I will lead you straight to the hospital, no need to worry about the speed limit."

The driver was lapping it up, speeding through a thirty mile an hour limit. He turned and shouted through the communicating door into the back.

"Bit of alright this, Harry, it's like playing cops and robbers with us chasing the cops. I have always wanted to speed through a built up area."

Two porters were waiting at the door and wheeled the patient straight into reception. A probationer nurse was also there; she walked sharply down the corridor beside the two porters wheeling the stretcher.

Harry stopped at the reception, feeling strange to be back in the old familiar surroundings, for the smell reminded him of his training at that large hospital in London, and the military hospital on the south coast before the war. The same sounds, the same smells. God, he thought, has it really been three years since I left that hospital. He strode after the porters, his heavy ammo boots echoing against the shiny walls of the long corridor.

He waited in the sister's office till Glover was safely in bed surrounded by a competent staff.

"Take good care of him sister, the poor bugger has just returned from the desert and Italy, pity to lose him now."

"Don't worry, I can assure you he's in good hands." She smiled at him and showed him the door.

Back at reception he handed the young probationer nurse a slip of paper. She was a petite blonde with blue eyes and a small turned-up nose that wrinkled when she smiled. It was a smile that was infectious.

"May I have a signature, miss." She looked a little puzzled. "For the patient, miss. The army insists on a siggy for everything - a pair of boots, a pair of socks, even if you want a couple of sheets of army form blanks. So it stands to reason we must have a siggy for a sick man."

The petite nurse frowned again.

"Army form blanks, what are those?"

Harry burst out laughing and would have liked to answer - "shit house paper" - but to spare her blushes just said, "Never mind, miss, please let me have that siggy."

The nurse took the slip of paper and rushed along the corridor towards the ward, her stiff starched uniform rustling with every movement. Another probationer stood away from the desk, talking to the driver. They appeared to be getting along quite smoothly, both laughing and joking. The driver walked over to Harry.

456

"Eh Harry, fancy your chance with that little blonde nurse. I've got a date with the one I'm talking to, pretty ain't she? But she won't come unless we can make up a foursome. How about it Harry, we could park the ambulance some place."

"Sorry, mate, I have a date for tonight and every other night."

Then he heard the other nurse call over, "What time are we going out tonight, Zoe?"

Harry's ears pricked up and he said to the driver, "Did I hear that date of yours call that blonde Zoe?"

The driver nodded.

"Look mate, I can't make it tonight, as I told you. I can't make it any night, I am going steady, but there's my mate, Charlie. I could ring him up at our unit and ask him to make up a foursome. He can always borrow a motorbike so it won't be a problem getting here."

There was a public phone booth across the corridor. Harry sorted through his pocket for coppers and found three, but that wouldn't be sufficient as time would elapse while they sought out Charlie from the billet. The driver had two more pennies.

"Look, Zoe, I am sorry I can't make it, but I have a friend at the billet. A smashing bloke, six foot with blonde hair and very good looking. How about me giving him a ring?"

Zoe looked a bit hesitant.

"I don't know. I don't like the idea of a blind date." She looked at her friend who showed signs of disappointment for it looked as if she had taken a real fancy to the driver.

"I can tell you he's a smashing fellow, doesn't drink," - and that was the only true statement as he carried on - "all he does is sit around in the billet or goes over to the canteen. I know he would love a date with a nice looking girl like you." She smiled at that.

"He hasn't been out a lot since we arrived back in England in January, reckons it's too cold to go out. He'd sooner sit by the old stove in his Nissen hut."

He didn't think Charlie would turn the opportunity down, there weren't a lot of girls names beginning with Z. After a few minutes and a lot of blarney he finally won her over. He was overjoyed when he reached the phone box and at the same time felt a bit of a rat. The pretty girl looked so nice and innocent, he felt like some pimp, although he had the consolation of knowing that Charlie, for all his faults, would never do anything against a girl's will.

As he told Harry on many occasions, "It's no good, Harry, if you don't both enjoy it."

Sykes answered the phone sounding as if he had just woke from a deep sleep.

457

"Who the fucking hell's that?" He shouted down the phone. Harry held the earpiece a foot away while Sykes let out a volume of foul abuse.

"It's me, Sykes, your old mate Harry."

"You're no mate of mine, you fucking hypocrite. What the bleeding hell do you want at this time of night? Look, Jackson, first of all you know it's against regs to use this phone."

"No, look, Sykes. I want you to go and get Charlie for me." Harry spoke quietly.

"Sod off, Jackson. You dropped me in the crap the other day when I gave you a chit for tea and sugar, and you, you bastard, altered it to double the amount. I got a terrific bollocking from the Q.M., I should have had you on the fizzer."

"Look, Sykes, it's very important, it's not often I get out, it's no fun back at that M.I. room of mine, being there all alone twenty four hours a day. Go and get him for me, Sykes, my old mate."

"Don't be giving me that crap about being all alone in that M.I. room twenty four hours a day, you bastard. They are lucky if they see you for four hours a day. You're always with that bint of yours down at King's Lynn."

"Alright, Sykes. Get Charlie for me and there's twenty fags in it for you."

"Make it forty Players."

"Twenty Woodbines, Sykes."

"No chance, Jackson, twenty Players."

"Alright, Sykes, I will make it twenty Players and that's my last word." Harry raised his voice.

"I know if he don't get this message, Sykes, he will have your guts for garters. Twenty Players." He knew Sykes would do almost anything for cigarettes and also the threat of Charlie hanging over him settled the argument.

"Give him this phone number, Sykes, I'm running out of pennies."

It was twenty minutes before the phone rang.

"This had better be good, Harry, you have just woken me from a beautiful dream. We were back in Tripoli when old spotty dick woke me. Me and Francesca were going at it hammer and tongs. What is it Harry? And believe me, it'd better be good!"

"It is. I take is you still want to go through the alphabet Charlie. Well I have fixed up a date for you tonight with a beautiful nurse named, and listen to this, Charlie - Zoe! Yes, Zoe with a Z. I am up at Cambridge at this large hospital and me and a driver are chatting up these two smashing nurses. I tell you mate, if I hadn't been serious about Kim I would have fell for her myself. They want a date tonight. Can you make it?"

"Bloody hell, Harry, it's tough luck. Would you believe it, the old man has given me a few days pass to see my little girl. Perhaps you can fix me up with her another time, Harry?"

"Why don't you have a chat to her, Charlie? If you are going just for a few days - it's Monday now - you should be back by the weekend. How about Saturday?"

"Got this party Saturday, Harry, those land army girls. Mind you your offer is tempting. A Z - be lucky if I find another one of those."

The two nurses and the driver walked towards the phone booth. Harry cast a sidelong glance at the petite blonde, as pretty as she was she couldn't hold a candle to Kim.

"Look, Charlie, she's just outside. Have a chat with her, fix it up for another time."

Harry held the phone towards the nurse. She squeezed past him into the booth and put the phone to her ear. After a few minutes her face took on a blank expression, she turned a bright crimson, then slammed the phone down hard. She was livid, her eyes wide open. She stared defiantly at Harry as he held the door open, her face distorted with rage. Harry placed his hand on her shoulder, but she shrugged if off, slamming her foot down hard and bringing her arm round with all the force she could muster, her hand connecting with his cheek with a resounding smack.

"Very nice friends you have."

Her voice was raised in anger. The few people standing around the reception area looked at them. Harry rubbed his face; a red patch was already spreading across his cheek. She tossed her head, caught her friend by the elbow and vanished down the corridor.

"If that mate of yours has fucked things up for me I will kill the bastard." The driver raced down the passage after the two nurses shouting over his shoulder.

"Take the ambulance, I will make my own way back. And just warn that bloody mate of yours, if I don't get this date I will kill the bastard."

"I wonder what that sod said to her," muttered Harry to himself as he sat behind the wheel of his ambulance.

Dawn was just breaking when he left Cambridge. He felt tired, it was almost twenty four hours since he'd had any sleep. He pulled off the road beside a field of cows, and with plenty of blankets wrapped round him fell asleep in the back of the ambulance. It was midday when he woke. He filled his brew can and made himself tea over his petrol fire. This is the life, he thought to himself as he sat hunched up over the fire.

459

Charlie was fast asleep on top of his bed, covered with his greatcoat and his feet almost touching the side of the old pot bellied stove. Harry shook his feet. Charlie sat up, resting on one elbow and stifling a yawn. Forcing his eyes open, he looked at Harry, then dropped back on his pillow.

"You're a right prick, Charlie. Whatever did you say to that nurse?"

"Not a lot, Harry. I told her I would be back on Saturday and how would she like a date then."

"Come off it, Charlie, she wouldn't belt me around the face just for that. She shot out of that phone box as if it had just been invaded by a mob of mice. Then she belted me around the ear." He turned his cheek towards Charlie, it was till showing faint signs of the heavy slap.

"Did she do that, Harry. What is she a female wrestler or something? I am glad she turned me down, the vicious bugger, I can't stand violence in women, Harry."

"But you must have said something to her."

Charlie moved over and made room for his friend.

"I told you, Harry, we are having a party with those land army girls. I invited her to come, said she would have a great time. She said she had nothing to wear and I told her not to worry, none of us would be wearing anything by the time the party was over. I told her we were having an orgy, I don't think she knew what an orgy was, and after I explained to her, she just slammed that phone down in my ear."

"She certainly belted me. My lughole still feels as if it's on fire."

"Why don't you come to the party, Harry? I could meet you at the railway station. I will get one of the girls to massage your ear with her Bristols. That would be Naomi, she's fantastic. I think she watches those sheep and bulls all day long. Give yourself a break, Harry."

"Come off it, Charlie, you know how I feel about Kim, she's a great girl." Charlie sighed. "You're bloody lucky, Harry. I think I could have the same feelings about Kathy. I saw her out with another good looker the other day in King's Lynn."

"That's her mother. I told you before, both Kim and Kathy's mothers look very young, they could be taken for sisters. Did you speak to her?"

"No, I was just going into a shop for cigarettes. I looked through the shop window at her. Yes, Harry, Kathy would suit me down to the ground."

They sat silent for a few minutes.

"That big stunt is definitely on next week, Harry, you are coming back here. We get the new vehicles this week. I hope this damn cold weather improves. It's like a fridge in here, without that coke and coal you bring, I think we would all soon be down with pneumonia. Do you know we have to keep that fuel under the beds or the other huts would nick it?"

Harry prepared to leave, as he opened the door the icy wind whistled right through the hut, he turned and shouted to Charlie, "What price the desert now?"

And was answered with a chorus of, "Fuck the desert and close that bleeding door, you open arsed bastard."

A dusting of fine snow sprinkled the ground, the hedges were festooned with small icicles and snow giving the scene an aura of Christmas fantasia. Harry stopped the ambulance to clear the windscreen of ice and snow. As he climbed back into the cab he spotted a small sparrow pecking the ground for food. He crumbled a biscuit and watched intently as the starving sparrow attacked the crumbs and was soon joined by a flock of his mates. He stayed in his cab till the birds finished their unexpected meal, once more he headed to town. As usual he parked in the little used cinema car park.

Kim was waiting in the doorway of her office, sheltering from the wind and snow.

"Look, Harry, I am sorry but I must go home first, it's very important, then if you like we can go to the cinema."

He stopped at the corner. "Alright, I will wait here."

"Oh come on, Harry, it's like a blizzard here, you will catch your death of cold. Why don't you come home? At least let my mother apologise, she is terribly upset."

"It's not your mother that should apologise, it's me, I was being so damn stupid, and believe me I am so sorry for upsetting your mother."

"Well, do come on in. You will really love my parents when you get to know them. I think it was a bit of a shock when she knew I had met a soldier. She hates to see a man in uniform, she has never got over my brother being killed."

Harry knew he would have to face the inevitable one day, so it was no use putting it off any longer. Still reluctant, she held him by the hand and led him into the small but comfortable sitting room. The fire was blazing up the chimney and the blackout curtains hadn't been drawn, the flames cast dancing shadows on the wall giving the room movement. Kim drew the curtains and switched on the light.

"Mum and dad are in the kitchen. They don't like wasting electricity, not while the war is on."

She took off her heavy top coat, beneath she was wearing slacks and a tight fitting woollen jumper that accentuated her slim figure. The door leading from the kitchen opened and her mother came in, she looked at Harry and held out her hand.

"I was sorry about..."

But she was cut short by the icy stare from Kim. Harry had also seen the icy stare and smiled.

"You have no need to apologise, it was me being so damn stupid. To be honest we had only just returned and the cold was getting me down, and I had a bit of a job finding the house. However that was no excuse for my rudeness."

This seemed to please her, she smiled. Then Charlie's tips came back to Harry, 'Remember Harry, get on the old lady's good side, start making her laugh. Take no notice of her father, the minute you step over his front doorstep you are a potential rapist bent on ravishing his daughter. She may be a raving nymphomaniac, but to him she is a reincarnate of a vestal virgin' so Harry went straight into action.

"To be honest, I never expected Kim's mother to be so young, you must have been very young when you married."

She laughed.

"Oh my God, Kim. Where did you find Harry? I don't believe what he says, but my God, I like it. Anyway, you must call me Carol."

Just then the door opened again and Kim's father walked into the room. He wasn't a tall man, a couple of inches shorter then Harry, but he was well built and when he spoke it was with a strong Norfolk accent, he didn't wait for an introduction but gripped Harry's hand firmly and friendly.

"So this is the great Harry we have been hearing about for the past week or so. Pleased to meet you son. Just call me Jack and make yourself comfortable."

He indicated to one of the armchairs beside the fire.

Within minutes of the welcoming handshakes Harry wondered why he had delayed the meeting so long. Carol could not keep her eyes away from him. Every time he looked at her her eyes were upon him. At first he thought she was trying to weigh him up. Was he good enough for her one and only child, or was she comparing him with her son? For as she looked at Harry, her gaze would go to the large photograph of her son above the fireplace. But altogether the atmosphere was warm and friendly and the evening passed all too quickly.

"Don't you dare stop away again, Harry," Carol said as Harry stood up to go, she kissed him lightly on his cheek.

He had learned a lot about the family, and he had no need to worry about Kim's father, he had the potential of turning out to be a good friend.

462

He was in a great mood when he went to collect his ambulance. It was covered in snow, but Charlie had tuned the engine for him and it started at first go. Halfway to his billet it started to snow heavily, but nothing could deter him from the jubilant mood he was in. He started to sing at the top of his voice what had become both his and Kim's signature tune, 'Roses of Picardy'.

His visits to the house were daily. If Kim was at work he would sit for hours talking to her mother. Every day he would leave the billet at noon, for Kim had arranged with Marti, her aunt, and Kathy's mother, to leave her phone number with the sergeant, if Harry was wanted urgently he could phone. It was if the house had now become his base. In Carol's eyes, Harry could do no wrong and one night, it was unexpected, she asked Harry, "Will you play the piano for me?"

Kim, half open mouth, looked at her father and he stared back at her, for apart from cleaning, the piano hadn't been touched since John was killed. Carol shed a tear as Harry took the seat, intertwined his fingers and pressed them forward till the knuckles cracked, then ran the back of his right hand across the notes, exactly as her John would do the minute he sat down to play. The piano playing became a nightly ritual.

One night he was still playing when Carol said, "Do you know it's nearly twelve, Harry?"

Still playing he said, "No, not really, if you hum it I will play it."

"Bloody fool," she answered. But when they went to the door the snow was more than a foot thick, and the ambulance was shrouded in a white blanket.

"Harry, you can't drive through this weather, the ambulance will never make it."

Harry laughed.

"You kidding. These things are made to move, the one Charlie and I had, served three years in the desert, they can go through two feet of loose sand, so I should have no trouble with a bit of snow."

But Carol was insistent, although Harry tried to tell her he was the only medical orderly at the unit.

"So, all you do is dish out aspirins you told us, let the drunken devils suffer, you are not going back in this."

She turned to her husband. "Go and stuff a couple of hot water bottles in John's bed, Jack."

A deadly silence fell over the room. For John's room was a shrine. They had been surprised when Harry had been allowed to play the piano, but to use John's room, it was unheard of.

463

She virtually dragged Harry back into the room and forced his greatcoat from him. "You are staying, no if's or but's about it."

Kim couldn't say a word, she just stared hopelessly. This was greater than she had ever expected, at last her mother was about to break that shell she had put around herself, and these last few days had almost been like the old days when John was here, now Harry was playing the fool like John used to and her mother was enjoying every minute of it.

Kim showed him inside the room. He stared round and whistled through his teeth and whispered, "You are right, Kim, it is a shrine."

She whispered back, "This is the first time I have been in here since John went away." She picked up a silver trophy, one of the many round the room, tears came into her eyes. "I remember the day he bought that home, he won it for swimming and made me clean it every week."

The room was covered in posters of his favourite football team, Norwich, and there were photographs of sports stars, footballers, rugby players and a shelf of trophies.

"I would have loved to have met him, Kim, he was my type of man."

"Yes I know, Harry, you two would have got on fine together, you both had the same warped sense of humour."

They sat on the bed.

"Well, are you going to get into bed with me or are we both going to sit here for the rest of the night?" he joked. She blushed a deep beetroot red. He led her to the door.

CHAPTER 42

The great black cumulus nimbus hung low from the sky, hugging the flat landscape like a large theatre curtain bellowing in the draught from the wings. It was so close to the ground it was impossible to tell where the clouds finished and the flat landscape began. Dawn was breaking and the division, all quiet, stretched along the shore like a coiled spring waiting to be released. The men, sitting in their vehicles, muffled up to their ears in thick scarves and balaclava helmets, shivered as the merciless wind blew in from the North Sea forcing the high waves to crash relentlessly on the beach.

Charlie sat behind the wheel of his new ambulance and Harry, brought in for the manoeuvres, sat quietly beside him. He was well protected from the cold with the collar of his greatcoat turned up, and wearing a scarf that Kim had knitted and balaclava helmet, his hand thrust deep into his pockets and two army blankets wrapped round his knees. Both of them were wearing steel helmets as instructed and Charlie had, as usual, chewed on the chin-strap. Neither of them were in a very good mood and had hardly spoken since Charlie picked Harry up at his M.I. Room.

They had experienced bitter cold nights in the desert, but always with the comforting knowledge that the sun would soon be scorching their eyeballs out. The lowering sky was only heralding what the rest of the day would be like.

A battery of twenty-five pounders opened up with a roar firing a salvo of blanks. A few seagulls flew away in disgust, and the local inhabitants, now getting used to these schemes, pulled the blankets over their heads and turned over and went back to sleep.

At the same time it started to rain, not a downpour but a steady drizzle mixed with sleet that found its way through every crack of the ill-fitting side screens of the ambulance. Platoons of infantry stood around, formed in lines, their ground sheets wrapped around their shoulders. Before the day was out the fine rain and sleet would penetrate the ground sheets, their greatcoats and uniform, and finally their underclothes, making it uncomfortable to walk.

Scout cars moved forward, followed a half hour later by heavy tanks clattering away into the thick mist, their wide steel tracks stripping the tarmacadam from the roads. At times the tank tracks cut into the grass verges, tuning them into quagmires of freezing mud, thus adding difficulties to the lines of infantry trying to walk single file along them. The infantrymen cursed and swore, turning the air blue, but struggled along worn down by their heavy equipment, rifles and bren guns. But they had more to swear about when the umpires came into action with their great wooden rattles simulating machine gun fire and forcing the men to drop flat into the mud. By mid-morning every man was reduced to a wet soggy mess, shuffling along on heavy boots that no longer kept the water out.

"This is it, Charlie, our first stop."

He pointed to an old deserted barn that had been set up as a Regimental Aid Post. Charlie parked the ambulance outside and rushed in, but they might just as well have stayed out, for the barn was almost roofless, and what corrugated sheets remained on the rafters were riddled with rust-bored holes. However in one corner, partially dry, stood a large pot-bellied stove a relic of a previous century, and beside it a huge pile of coke and logs, and with the aid of a tin of petrol its flames were soon racing up the chimney. Men jockeyed for position trying to dodge the drops of water from the roof, steam in great white clouds rose from the men's rain-sodden uniforms. Yet no one spoke for no man was in any mood for conversation, even the latest round of filthy jokes.

Wrapped up in a thick travel rug and from the warmth of his staff car, a passing general sent in his aide with orders for the aid post to move up half a mile. He had been attracted by the smoke pouring from the chimney.

The new station was set up in a corner of a field with a canvas sheet spread out from the three tonner. There was no sign of habitation for miles around, and the bleak wind cut through the exposed position. With some difficulty they started a fire and brewed tea and the men gratefully clasped their hands around their hot mugs. Rain filled the canvas lean-to which drooped lower and lower as the canvas stretched. Harry found a dead tree branch and it took the combined strength of four men to hoist the rain filled canvas with it. Unfortunately just at that moment a brigadier chose to cut behind the lean-to and caught the full torrent of the water. He couldn't be certain it was done deliberately, but the M.O. - new to the unit - took the full verbal lashing.

"You stupid bastard, surely you heard me coming? Why the hell did you allow them to do a stupid thing like that?"

The brigadier's hat had become misshapen with the weight of the water, and the rain ran down his face shooting off the end of his hooked nose like a miniature waterfall. "Now get out of here!" he bellowed, while Harry and the men struggled to keep straight faces.

466

"But this is our position, sir. The general sent us here," the M.O. said and unfolding his ordnance map, pointed to the cross the general's aide had made.

But the brigadier was in no mood to listen. He brought down his leather-covered swagger stick with a loud smack onto the ordnance map, ripping it in two and dashing it from the officer's hands. "You damn poultice wallopers, go on, move out from here!"

"What's to be our new position, sir?" the M.O. asked nervously.

"How the hell should I know?" The brigadier bellowed, removing the last drop of rain that had been suspended from the end of his hooked nose. "Just get away from here, and don't cross my path on this exercise. Is that understood?"

The M.O. called the men together.

"Alright, get ready to move," he told them, but the sergeant held his hand up.

The officer, fresh from medical school and his basic military training at the R.A.M.C. depot was without any real military experience.

"Hang on a few minutes, sir," said the sergeant and watched the Brigadier walking across the fields. "When he gets back to his car, sir, we won't see the bastard again. He's a pain in the arse at the best of times. He needs to go on about poultice wallopers! If it hadn't been for Jackson here, that old prick might have lost his finger, if not his arm." He turned to Harry. "Remember, Jackson? He had that septic finger in the desert all swollen up like a kid's balloon. Jackson cleaned it and dressed it every day, sir. The old bastard almost shit himself every time Jackson cleaned the bloody finger up." They watched the Brigadier's car vanish. "Don't worry, sir," the sergeant assured the M.O., "we won't see the old prick again."

They had to make this exercise as authentic as possible and orders came to dig and sleep in slit trenches. There was little point in digging two trenches so they decide to share. Harry took the first turn with the spade, but as soon as they went down two feet in the soft dark brown earth water seeped in, and within minutes it was six inches deep.

"No kipping in the ambulance, Williams. Anyone found asleep in their vehicles can be sure of seven days' jankers. We'll be carrying on inspections throughout the night," a whining voice added to their discomforts.

Charlie was digging, his steel helmet pushed to the back of his head, and in spite of the bitter cold he could feel the sweat mingling with the rain and sleet. At the precise moment that Sykes spoke Charlie held a shovel full of a muddy gooey mess.

467

With one scoop he pretended to slip forward the shovel swinging upwards, and the contents flew straight into Sykes's face. He wiped the sleeve of his overcoat across his face making his eyes stand out like white organ stops. Harry burst out laughing and Charlie apologised profusely.

"Bloody hell, corporal, I'm sorry," he said, trying not to laugh at the same time.

"You bastard, Williams, You did that on purpose."

"Piss off, Sykes, it was an accident. Isn't that right, Harry?"

Harry nodded his head in agreement.

"Your a right pair of bastards! Just you watch it the pair of you. I'll be round all night at frequent intervals and what's more I intend to bring another N.C.O. round with me."

The six inches of water Charlie was standing in seeped through his gaiters and into his boots. Rain ran down his back soaking his underclothes and the chin strap of his helmet was soaked and rubbing the underside of his chin raw. He let the strap hang loose, straightened his back and leaned on the shovel.

"Sykes, I am browned off. I am wet through. I am bursting for a crap. The grub they brought round wasn't sufficient to feed a pigeon and what's more it was bloody cold. I would like a smoke, but every time I try to light up the fag gets soggy and I can't even light the bloody thing. I had a date tonight with a nice redhead and to sum it up - I'm hungry, wet and fed up and worse of all bloody mad, so the best thing you can do is sod off, or I will, and let me emphasise those two little words, I will ram this spade right up your rectum. Then, while you are attempting to extradite the shovel I will knock you fucking teeth right down your fucking throat, so piss off!"

Suppressing a snigger, Harry didn't look up and just resumed his digging.

This exercise was played by the book, for the division had been brought up to strength. Many of the officers hadn't seen real active service, so their enthusiasm knew no bounds. Harry scrounged around and lined the bottom of the trench with branches, and they retired to the back of the ambulance where two more men joined them and they soon had a card school going. It was half past nine when Sykes, together with a fresh officer came round and ordered them into their slit trench. As they dropped into it there was a loud crack like the sound of breaking glass. The bottom of the trench was covered with an half inch of ice making it impossible to lie down, and it felt like a huge electric shock as their boots filled with ice cold water.

They crouched at each end of the trench, but soon cramp set in and as the rain quickened, Charlie was the first to climb out, taking minutes to straighten out his legs.

"Sod this lot, Harry," he grumbled. "Open the back doors of the ambulance and let's sit just inside. You get in the front, make up a bed across the seats and the spare jerricans. If that bastard Sykes comes around let's hope he only looks in the back of the ambulance. You have a couple of hours first then I'll have a snooze." It was pitch black. If anyone were to cross that field they would have to use a torch and he would see it for miles.

With unlimited blankets Harry made a comfortable bed across the front seats and petrol cans, but no matter how many blankets he covered himself with he just couldn't get warm. His feet felt like blocks of ice, but he was afraid to remove his boots and massage his feet in case he couldn't put them back on again. He just lay their staring out of the windscreen, thinking of that huge fire in Kim's house, and dreaming of her fell into a doze. The next thing he knew Charlie was shaking him.

"Come on, Harry. Roll on France. At least out there they won't give a damn where we sleep."

The next day wasn't much better. The rain and sleet continued without the slightest signs of any let up, and the aid post handled over a hundred mock casualties and three genuine ones. Men seeing the red cross reported with the most feeble excuses. Harry hadn't seen so many sick parades since some idiot started a rumour that many of them from the division were going out to India and the Far East.

"Some stupid bastard can't read a map, that's for sure," an infantry sergeant said, as he came into the aid post his arm, or rather what was left of it in a bloodstained sling. Every second word was an obscenity. The man's forearm was hanging by a couple of tendons.

"I could kill the stupid bastard responsible for this. Two years on the Indian Frontier, through Dunkirk and Greece, North Africa and Italy and I have to come home and within a dozen miles of my home town I have to lose a fucking arm."

Making the exercise as authentic as possible a mortar section had been told to stonk a position near an advancing platoon. There had been the usual cock up with someone misreading the map, and a bomb fell short. Fortunately no one was killed.

"Bleeding winged in my own back yard! The lads at the pub won't stop laughing when they hear about this." And for the next ten minutes the sergeant swore in an exotic mixture of foreign languages.

Harry was hoping they would be chosen to evacuate the sergeant to the military hospital and both he and Charlie could sneak off to Kim's for a bath and get their clothes dry. But their luck was out. Neither were selected for the next casualty, a member of a tank crew had jumped from his tank to relieve himself and he was still shaking the drips away, when the tank rolled back a fraction and crushed his foot.

The greatest shadow of the exercise took place the next day when a driver from their own unit, obliged to drive a motor cycle during the exercise, was taking a bend at a crossroad, the bike went into a skid throwing him against the side of a loaded tank transporter, reducing him to a misshapen heap of flesh and bones. He was an old member of the unit and a great friend theirs.

So the days dragged on wetter and colder than previous ones, so wet they had given up any idea of drying out or washing, the men moved around like zombies. They did manage to get a couple of hours sleep each during the day. But the exercises didn't seem to be serving any useful purpose and from the highest rank downwards everybody appeared to be fed up with it.

"Charlie, if you don't pack this stupid lark in there'll be no one left to go to France. Those that survive injuries or getting themselves killed will die of pneumonia or any other bloody lung infection." Harry searched the skies for a break in the clouds and received a faceful of sleet for his trouble.

To everyone's amazement the show was called off at noon. They had some kind of inkling when a D.R. rushed up, coming to a skid beside a bunch of men and splattering them with mud. Normally they would have cursed him, but as they were already covered in mud it didn't matter a lot. He winked his eye at the sergeant and handed him a long buff envelope. The sergeant handed the M.O. the envelope and he lost no time in telling the men it was all over. There was a loud cheer. Harry went over to investigate and came running back.

"It's over, Charlie. It's been called off."

For the first time in days, Charlie's face brightened.

"What's happened?" He enquired, hardly able to believe his ears.

The stunt had been planned to last at least another thirty-six hours, or two more long nightmares, whichever way you looked at it.

"I'm buggered if I know," Harry answered. "They said pack up and that's what I intend to do. I bet some poor General has just stepped out of his staff car into a pile of cow shit and took the shine off his boots. I couldn't care less, Charlie. They said pack up and I'm not standing here waiting for confirmation."

The canvas lean-to vanished before they had time to pack away their brew cans. The M.O., N.C.O.s and men had the canvas down folded neatly and stuffed into the back of the lorry in record time.

"Christ, Harry, remember that time in the desert when we were nearly put in the bag? I thought we got away smartly then but this lot beats it."

They were flagged down at the crossroads, where the R.S.M. poked his head out of the side window of the utility.

"Right you pair, any dry clothes?"

They shook their heads.

"Well, get back to your billets as fast as you can. Drop Jackson off at his own unit, then you, Williams, report back to ours. You needn't join the convoy. Make your own way back." He unrolled their map and pointed to their present position. "Don't waste time."

"What's the show been called of for, sir," Harry asked.

"Don't ask me, Jackson, your guess is as good as mine. I don't know why they started the bloody thing in the first place. No one is any the wiser for it. I suppose some bloody wanker at G.H.Q. thought it up."

The R.S.M. as usual showed concern for his men. He knew the show had been one large charade. In their section alone they had suffered five casualties and a fatality, and that from his own unit. There would be no telling what the cost would be when details of other sections came in.

Harry hadn't the slightest intention of returning directly to his M.I. Room. He was a keen map reader and took it from Charlie.

"Look, Charlie, we can avoid all this traffic. Take the side turning into Wisbech then straight to King's Lynn and Kim's. I've got a change of clothing there and I can let her know it's all over. We can stop for fish and chips at Wisbech, then have a bath at Kim's. You can dry your clothes, well, your uniform at least. I have a couple of shirts there. Then, you can take me to my unit to pick up my old ambulance."

"What if we get to her house and no one's at home?"

"Her mother is always at home. She hardly ever goes out. And should she go out she always leaves her front door key under the mat. We can go straight into the house."

"Bloody hell, talk about getting your feet under the table. She should be charging you billeting money."

They pulled up outside the fish shop, and looking like tramps, with three days' growth of beard and mud spattered uniforms, they were a sorry sight as Harry ordered two large servings of fish and chips. The lady behind the counter felt pity for them, for not only did she pile the paper with extra helpings of chips and the largest two pieces of plaice she could find, she refused their money.

"You two men look beaten. Would you care for a pot of tea? I haven't a lot of sugar but you're welcome to what I have." She spoke with a smooth southern Irish accent.

Charlie grinned back at her, his white teeth flashing against the mud spattered face, and he adopted a thick Irish accent.

"To be sure it's a fine Christian woman you are, be Jasus. May ye be blessed with many fine upstanding sons and daughters."

Her husband bent over the bubbling frying pan gave a little laugh but she gave him a withering look. "Sure and not if I can help it, sonny."

Harry gave her the soot stained brew can. She held the wire between her finger and thumb and wrinkled her nose in disgust, but she made no comment as she took it in the back room and filled it with boiling tea.

They sat in the back of the ambulance for their meal, then made their way out of Wisbech, taking the narrow back lanes towards King's Lynn. Charlie negotiated the twisting roads like a racing driver tackling a familiar race track taking the bends, on occasions on two wheels. Harry hung on for dear life but had all the confidence in the world in Charlie's driving. Neither of them was in the mood for talking and it wasn't till they entered King's Lynn that Charlie complained of his feet feeling like blocks of ice.

"Never mind, Charlie, when we reach Kim I'll rub some meths into them and after a bath and a rub in meths you'll think the bloody things are on fire." He handed Charlie a lighted cigarette. "Better slow down, Charlie, we're getting near their road."

"Get a load of this, Harry." Charlie stopped the ambulance and nodded towards four women who had their backs towards the ambulance. Harry recognised the four familiar figures at once. It was Kim, Kathy and their mothers.

"Lovely, Charlie. Lets stop and chat them up. see if that old charm is still working."

Charlie cast a glance at his mate. "I thought you were going straight, really serious with that bird of yours."

"Just stop a few yards behind them and see if you've lost that golden touch."

Kim swung round as Charlie stopped as instructed, her face wreathed in smiles, then a look of disappointment took the place of her smile. It wasn't Harry's ambulance, for although it was spattered in mud she could see it was new. She couldn't see who was sitting in the front seats. The dense clouds were low and threw their reflections on the flat windscreen, it acted like a one way mirror - those outside couldn't see in, but those inside had a perfect view.

Harry dropped from the cab, his face twisting in pain as his ice cold feet came in contact with the road, sending a heavy electric shock through his body. He hobbled a few feet, then rested with his hands on the bonnet of the ambulance.

"Why, you lousy bastard, Harry, you recognised them straight away," Charlie hissed through clenched teeth.

Harry would have smiled but the freezing cold was enough to crack his face if he did and was sending convulsive shivers through the whole of his body. Kim ran straight towards him and threw her arms around his neck. Then she stepped back aghast.

"Why, Harry you're soaked right through." She clasped his hands which were ice cold. "You look as if you've been sleeping in the fields for a few nights. We weren't expecting you back for two more days at least."

He forced himself to smile and hobbled along a few feet to rest against a lamp post.

"You're right, Kim, we've been sleeping in the open. It was murder. I doubt if I've ever felt so damn cold in my life." Rain ran down his face leaving three white tracks and his eyes were sunken from lack of sleep.

"You're not driving in that state are you, Harry?" Her face was a mixture of pity and wonderment that any man could drive in such a state.

"No, but the bloke that is driving is in a far worse condition. Go and take a look. Take Kathy along with you. I doubt if she'll recognise him in his filthy condition."

Her eyes opened wide and her mouth split into an impish grin, Harry hobbled back to the ambulance while Kim led Kathy forward. They still hadn't recognised who was sitting in the driver's seat. This was the moment for which Kim had been waiting, for like Harry she was just as anxious to get Kathy to see Charlie again. Harry had told Kim the whole story, or as much as he knew about Charlie's matrimonial problems. She also knew how Kathy felt towards him and when she saw Kathy recognise him this time, she knew she was right, for Kathy greeted him with concern and pity.

"Hello, Charles, how are you?"

"Right now, Kath, I'm cold, wet and miserable, but all round I'm not too bad. How are you?"

"Just fine, Charles." She held out her hand and winced when he held it, his hands, like Harry's, were frozen. "I see what you mean,

Charles. You should get out of those filthy wet clothes. If you don't watch it you'll both go down with pneumonia."

He stepped down from the cab, his face twisted with pain as his feet made contact with the ground. They were joined by both the girls' mothers. Kathy introduced him.

She took his hand. It gripped her's firmly and she studied his face keenly. Through the film of mud she could make out his firm cut features, a square jaw, and eyes that looked directly at her face while a slight smile lifted the corner of his mouth. A smile that displayed two rows of regular white teeth, and like most women in Charlie's company she took to him immediately.

"So you are the great Charles I've heard so much about." He threw back his head and burst out laughing, although the pain from his legs and feet would have made it easier to wince.

"Don't you believe it. One of these days I'll sue Harry for slander, or is it libel? I always get those two mixed up."

"This is Kim's mother."

Charlie took her hand and kissed the back. Harry almost choked, but Charlie tossed his head back and laughing in an off-hand manner said, "I saw Clark Gable do that in the movies the other night."

The women laughed and Harry smiled. Yes, the old technique was working again. Get the mothers on your side and the old man's viewpoint was secondary. Harry studied their faces. Kim couldn't take her eyes away from Kathy's face, while her mother closely watched both of them.

Harry felt sorry for his friend, for when he looked at Kathy closely he could see, almost feel, why Charlie was so attracted to her. She held her head high and her back straight, her clean cut features very like Kim's, and Harry thought both of them were the most beautiful girls they had ever met. When she spoke her voice was soft with just a trace of an East Anglian accent - far different from Charlie's West Country drawl.

Since Charlie's marriage had split up, as he often told Harry, women had meant very little to him. They were just partners to work off his biological urges on. This was with the exception of Francesca, but there were now a few thousand miles separating them and it was doubtful if they would ever meet again. Besides she was also ten years his senior which may have meant that a permanent relationship was doomed to failure.

Charlie was staring at Kathy to the point of embarrassment. She reddened and quickly turned away.

"What I can't get over is how young you four look. You were either child brides or it's the air around here," Charlie smarmed and Harry squirmed, for those words were exactly the ones he'd said to Carol.

"You know, Carol, I really like this boy," Marti stepped forward to hug him, but his clothes were soaking and so she settled for a kiss on his cheek.

Harry could hardly keep a straight face. 'Here it comes,' he thought. 'In five minutes Charlie has the old lady eating out of his hand. Same old technique every time. Get them laughing and the first stage of the battle is well and truly over.' Harry loved listening to the charm being switched on. The look on the women's faces told the rest of the story. Harry had seen this happen countless times, and it didn't matter if they couldn't speak English. It happened several times in North Africa and Italy and it was succeeding here.

CHAPTER 43

The key of the house was exactly where Harry expected to find it, under the mat outside the door.

"Push the bottom of the door, Charlie, the bloody thing always sticks."

Forgetting the agonies and the pain of his feet, Charlie gave it a heavy kick. The pain shot through his body like a gigantic electric shock, he yelled with pain as every shock penetrated his system, he leaned back against the door in agony, the door gave way and he hurtled inside the passage adding to the torture, Harry, in spite of the pain he was going through could hardly contain himself seeing Charlie sprawled out along the passage and burst out laughing.

There was still a bit of a glow amongst the ashes in the fire-grate, Harry stirred away the dead ash and threw on a pine log and several lumps of coal, in minutes the fire roared up the chimney.

"Christ," Charlie said, as life returned to him as the blood pumped through his veins once again, "you certainly know your way about the house, talk about getting your feet under the table".

It fell on deaf ears. Harry was concentrating on removing his wet boots and socks, gasping and sucking his breath as they clung to his soaked, frozen and wrinkled feet, looking for all the world like dressed tripe in a butcher's window. Covering the easy chair with newspaper to prevent soiling it, he sat down heavily and stretched his feet towards the fire and closed his eyes, as the circulation started, so did the pain, his toes were bleeding beneath the nails.

The four women returned and stared incredulously at Harry's feet. Kim dropped to her knees, stifling a sob. She was about to lift his feet into her lap, he pulled back sharply.

"Don't, Kim. Please don't touch them for a while." His hands shook as he went to light a cigarette. "Just nip into to the ambulance. In the back is two boxes, one of them holds the medical kit, you will find a bottle of meths and cotton wool. Will you fetch them?"

A few minutes later she returned. Harry lifted Charlie's feet and gently massaged the meths into them.

"There you are Kim, now you have seen me do it, be bloody gentle the pain is unbearable".

Carol led Charlie upstairs to the bathroom and filled the bath with hot water.

"Step in there, Charlie, and throw your wet uniform out."

She left the room and returned in a few minutes with a dressing gown and pyjamas. "Use these till your own clothes dry."

Under normal circumstances Charlie would have made some suggestive joke, but he was in no mood for joking. Up to his neck in the hot water, he was almost asleep when Harry came in.

"My shaving gear is here, Charlie, help yourself, and empty that bloody bath, I am not getting in there after you, its ten to one you have pissed in it, and it looks like mud."

Charlie lifted the plug with his toes and let the water drain away, leaving a muddy rim along the top.

"A nice shave, Harry, and I will feel like a new man"

The hot bath and shave performed miracles for Charlie, his face shone with a reddish glow and the blonde hair, now grown since his return to England, had a persistent wave in the front, reflecting in the light. No wonder women fell for him. It wouldn't do for Charlie to know he was admiring him.

"I can't for the life of me think what women see in you, Charlie."

"It's my fatal charm, Harry. I told you several times, I am like that Greek prick, Adonis. I reckon I must be his reincarnation or something."

"You look more like a reincarnation of Popeye to me. You know what they say, Charlie, self praise is no recommendation. What's that you have clenched in your hand?"

Charlie unclenched his fist to reveal a part packet of French letters.

"There's only two in that packet. Where's the other?"

"Remember the second day of the exercise when I stopped at that farm house for milk and that young blonde took me to the milk shed, well, it had to happen, didn't it?"

"For heaven's sake, Charlie, you hardly spoke to the girl and you were in that cow shed for fifteen minutes."

"Yes, pity really, I was just about to start again when her old man walked in the shed".

"Well get rid of the bloody things, flush them down the karzy or something, you can't go downstairs with those in your hand".

"I can't, Harry. I have flushed them several times but they keep bobbing up to the top of the water again, they are bloody indestructible!"

There was a small screwdriver on top of the wall cupboard. Harry eased out the side panel on the bath and placed the offending Durex behind it.

"I will get rid of them tomorrow."

Still limping slightly but greatly refreshed, they entered the sitting room, it wasn't quite dark, the room was dappled with fragments of light from the blazing fire. All eyes, except Kim's, turned towards Charlie, his flawless skin giving off a radiant glow accentuated by the bronze glowing reflections on the walls. Harry saw the love and tenderness in Kathy's eyes. Like his own, Charlie's fate was sealed. Kath, without her heavy winter coat, sat on the edge of the dining table, her slim figure with the curves in the right places moved uncomfortably as Charlie turned and saw her staring at him. He winked that certain wink that could turn any woman's legs to jelly. Kath poured his tea and wandered slowly towards him, the cup and saucer in her trembling hand spilled slightly into the saucer. Harry knowing Charlie, his constant companion for almost two years, sensed that from now on no other woman would mean anything to his friend.

Harry broke the silence. Still wearing John's pyjamas and dressing gown he sat at the piano. It was open, he had forbidden Carol to lock it again. Marti was astonished to see him interleaf his fingers, stretch them forward then roll the back of his hand along the keys just as her nephew John would do as he sat at the piano. He started with what had become his and Kim's signature tune 'Roses of Picardy.' He was still playing two hours later when Jack silently entered the room with Kathy's father, Wilf.

Wilf appeared just as pleased to see Charlie. His handshake was firm and friendly, leaving little doubt he had felt for his own daughter, tearing her heart out, so attracted to Charlie, but undecided whether to form a serious relationship. He took an immediate liking to him as he had with Harry.

Jack wasn't in the least bit worried about his dinner being late, he was overjoyed to see his wife falling back into her old ways and he had to thank Harry for that for within days of his first visits, she changed dramatically. Perhaps it was the similarity between Harry and his son John. What ever it was he was getting his wife back. She no longer objected to him wearing his Home Guard uniform in the house. She was coming out of the shadows, she had been almost agoraphobic just in case when out she should meet a serviceman outside.

Jack nodded to Wilf. They went outside, unnoticed by the other members of the family gathered round the piano and singing. Fifteen minutes later they returned with arms full of fish and chips wrapped in newspapers. They all sat round the fire not bothering with plates but eating them direct from the paper.

The impromptu party broke up at midnight with Jack protesting he had to be at work at six. They changed into their clean and pressed uniforms. Carol took her farewells at the door, hugging both of them in turn. Harry with his tongue out made a show of fighting for breath. Tears in her eyes she kissed him goodnight.

Driving along the country lanes it was a moonless night and the shielded headlights were insufficient to light their way. Charlie drove slowly and concentrated on the road, it was almost an hour before they spoke and the speed was down to ten miles an hour. Twice he hit the verge. Harry lit two cigarettes and passed one to Charlie,

"Well what do you think, Charlie?".

"Harry, you are the luckiest bastard alive. You can't do a thing wrong in Carol's eyes. You bastard, you could fall into a barrel of shit and come up smelling of roses. They are a real lovely family, salt of the earth. Why the hell don't you get a transfer to a General Hospital at home? With your qualifications you shouldn't have any trouble."

"And who the hell is going to look after you on the other side? Now you have met Kathy you don't think I would let you loose on your own with all those French bints."

"That's all over, Harry. I am meeting Kath again."

He didn't stop singing the praises of Kath and her family for the rest of the journey.

"One thing worries me, Harry - those bloody Land Army girls. I have been knocking them off like bloody skittles and have made arrangements to go for the weekend. She works as a sister for a medical specialist in this big house. The family will be away this weekend, she has a friend and with her sister that makes five of us, I was hoping you would come, but after seeing the performance tonight with you and Kim I should say there is no hope of that. Anne told me her sister is better looking than her and is red hot."

"Why don't you tell her you are on duty, doing guard or something like that?"

"No, Harry, I will have to see her. She is always in King's Lynn and I may be out with Kathy one night and bump into her, then there will be ructions, that bloody temper of hers will get her into trouble one day and I don't want to be the cause of it. No, it's better if I go and see her and break it to her gently. Surely you won't help us out for the last time, Harry?"

"Not on your life, Charlie, this is one load of shit you have to get out off by yourself. Why don't you tell her the truth, or at least say you are married and sorry what has happened?"

"Can't do that, Harry, I have already convinced her I have an unhappy marriage and I'm waiting for a divorce."

"Well, tell her you have made it up with your wife for your little girl's sake."

"Harry, do you want to see me without my balls? I told you she has a vicious temper and she has already told me how her and the farmer go about castrating the young bulls."

They parted at the entrance to Harry's billet. Harry waited till the sound of the ambulance engine faded. The Nissen hut was cold, the old iron stove filled with cold ashes, it was blazing when he left it almost three days ago. He set about cleaning it out, then with the aid of a pint of petrol and filled up with coal and coke, in minutes the blaze was rushing up the iron chimney.

Sick parade was well attended the next morning - most of the men complaining about their feet and pains in the back. The sergeant arrived and detailed a man to light the fire in the crowded waiting room.

"Bloody stupid exercise," the sergeant complained, "haven't got half the men to carry out maintenance duties."

Captain Smithers arrived, stepping from his utility Harry could see he wasn't in a very pleasant mood. Cane under his arm and his hands thrust deep into his trench coat pocket he barged straight into the M.I. room and threw his hat and cane on the bed.

"Brass monkey weather this, Jackson." He scanned Harry's medical reports. "Fifteen, eh Jackson? Bloody load of pansies. Out for a couple of days strolling round the old English countryside and take a shufti at them, a sick list as long as your arm. Right, Jackson, wheel the first man in."

Harry placed a mug of hot tea under the M.O.'s nose. It improved his mood slightly as the first man stood in front of him.

"It's me plates of meat, sir. I have seen pigs' trotters in my old woman's boiling pot look bloody healthier." He slipped off his plimsolls.

The M.O. whistled under his breath, "You are right laddie, they look a fucking mess, I have amputated healthier looking feet. Give him some meths, Jackson, and a few pots permang crystals then tell him what to do. NEXT MAN."

"Its me feet and back, sir. The pain in my back is bloody awful. I think my kidneys have jacked it in. My missus always complained when she was pregnant about pains in her back, I bet they wasn't as bad as these." He straightened up and winced with pain.

"Right, laddie, shirt off and bend over." He prodded the back. "Well you're not pregnant. Give him a bottle of embrocation. Get one of the boys in the billet to rub this in hard and take these tablets every four hours. Excused duty for four days, and lay off the booze while you are on the tablets. If the pain gets worse report sick again."

The sick parade continued. Now that one man was excused duty for a few days, most of those that came complaining about their feet had suddenly developed back trouble.

"See they keep warm, Jackson. Tell the sergeant to keep an eye on those bastards. Are you alright, Jackson?"

"Yes sir, could have done without that exercise all the same, didn't learn a bloody thing." His voice took a more serious note. "You know we lost one of our own men sir?"

"Bloody hard lines, been with the unit some time I believe, long before I joined the unit, or should I say after that ride with you and that mad bastard of a driver of yours, I nearly didn't join the unit. Still alive is he?"

Harry smiled, "I have to agree, he is a mad bastard, but a good driver, sir."

"That's your opinion." Relieved the tedious medical was over, the M.O. initialled Harry's report. "Keep your eye on this bloody shower." He took his hip flask from his back pocket and took a long drink, he belched loudly, filling the small room with obnoxious fumes, wiped his hand across his mouth and rushed to his utility.

Harry walked over to the farm house to give the sergeant his report and met a girl from the Land Army with her hand held across her chest, she waved with the other. He stopped and waited.

"Harry, I cut my hand a couple of days ago, it's started swelling, have a look at it, please."

She gave him a smile that verged on daring him to refuse. He took her by the elbow and propelled her towards his M.I. room, receiving cat calls and wolf whistles from the men gathered round the farmyard attending to their vehicles. Several shouted out warnings not to go in there alone with him,

"He'll have you on that bed in minutes, Mary," someone who obviously knew her shouted. It didn't offend her for she just smiled. He removed the soiled bandage with some difficulty, the wound was red and inflamed.

"Have you been injected, Mary?"

"Not by you, Harry."

He playfully slapped her bottom.

"I mean, have you had an anti tetanus injection just recently? Working with those animals a deep cut like that could be dangerous. Roll your sleeve up I will give you one now."

"What, right here? Now, wouldn't it be more comfortable for you with my jodhpurs off and on the bed?"

"You are a mucky sod, Mary. Why do you always twist my words?"

"The jumpers too tight to roll up my sleeve." Without hesitating she stripped of her tight woollen jumper, then she removed her shirt.

"Look Mary if you are trying to turn me on, forget it, I have a girlfriend. Jack it in or I will use a blunt needle."

"I bet your needle isn't blunt, I heard what you buggers got up to in Africa and Italy, and I bet your girl friend hasn't a nicer and bigger pair of tits than these."

"I wouldn't know, I haven't seen them yet, and I am in no hurry. Come on hold your hand on your waist."

"Shouldn't I lay on the bed and you stick the needle in my buttock." She tantalisingly started to undo her jodhpurs. She lifted her eyes to study Harry's face, her eyebrows lifting slightly.

His face was without expression as he looked at her bare chest, she was well proportioned and any other time he would have had her on that bed, but even now he felt slightly guilty. He grabbed her arm and plunged the needle into it, she didn't feel a thing, or if she did she didn't show it.

"Get dressed, Mary, before I fetch a couple of the lads in to service you."

She wasn't going to give in that easily.

"Harry, you don't know what you are missing."

He bandaged the injured hand. She caught hold of his, "You have lovely smooth hands, Harry, I wished you had put that needle in my bum, your hands are lovely but cold."

"You been watching that randy bull of yours, Mary." He opened the door. "Come on. Bugger off. See me in a couple of days time, or better still go to the hospital."

She turned and kissed him passionately on his lips. "Let me pay you in kind, Harry, I will pop round tonight and sleep with you."

"Piss off, Mary, and keep that bloody hand clean."

She ran across the farmyard to renewed cat calls and remarks and as Harry left his M.I. room he was met with a chorus of suggestive and abusive remarks.

"Had it away, Harry? That Mary knows how to wriggle her arse. Don't stand for it, she will kill you." Just a few of the remarks.

One of the men was servicing the ambulance. "Well away there Harry lad, that Mary is a hot piece of stuff."

"Jack it in, Wright, I only gave her an injection."

"Oooo," Wright pursed his lips, "I don't blame you, Harry. I would give anything to get her in my bed and give her an injection." He gave him a wink that suggested a page from the Kama Sutra.

"Don't be a prick, I gave her a tetanus injection, she had an infected cut on her arm."

"I bet she has." He replaced the engine cover and patted it. "That will get you another few thousand miles, Harry. If you like I could get a bloke to weld one of those stretcher runners together to make a double bed."

Smiling, he jumped into the cab and only did a few yards when he felt something was wrong. He stopped and walked round the ambulance, he should have known. Someone had written in beautiful signwriting as would be seen over a shop window, 'If the bulls can do it, so can Mary and Harry'. And underneath was a cartoon of a girl in Land Army uniform with her jodhpurs round her ankles, and exaggerated breasts, on top was a man in soldier's uniform. Harry knew instantly who the culprit was.

"You wait, Bennett, you won't get a sharp needle like Mary, I will bash it on the wall before you get it." Bennett was their unit signwriter, he was hanging out of the farmhouse upstairs window with a few of his friends, all grinning like Cheshire cats.

"Everything comes to he that waits, Bennett. We will be off soon. Believe me you will get the bluntest needle I can find when it's your turn to be injected." But Harry soon lapsed into a better mood as he drove along the familiar country lanes.

CHAPTER 44

A week after the exercise, Harry entered the Nissen hut back at the main unit. The men lay around the beds still complaining about their feet.

"It's alright for you," they moaned, "you've got a bloody cosy billet, and us poor sods only get enough fuel to light up at night."

"In that case, you miserable bastards, now you do get an issue of coal you don't need these sacks of coal and coke I brought you."

Bad feet forgotten, there was a mad rush for the ambulance and four of the men, barefoot, dragged in the two sacks of fuel.

"God, Harry, if you wore bra and knickers I would bloody well kiss you," gasped Parker, under the weight of a sackful of coke.

Harry sat on the edge of Charlie's bed. Charlie was talking to Fogwell.

"I don't know what you are getting so het up for, Foggy. She's done you a good turn," Charlie was saying to Fogwell who looked down in the mouth.

"What's the matter with him?" asked Harry.

"It's his missus, she's fucked off and left him," Charlie replied.

Foggy started on Harry. "It's not that, Harry, she'd pissed off with the A.R.P. warden. It's me fucking pigeons. I've asked for compassionate leave to make some arrangements for me pigeons. The selfish bastard Harry, that's all she does, think about herself all the time. What about me pigeons? I went and asked the old man and all he did was laugh his bleeding head off. They're good pigeons, Harry, cost me ten bob each before the war. I would have raced them but this war started. I tell you Harry, if those pigeons snuff it I'll kill that selfish bastard."

Foggy moved off further down the hut to foist his grievances on some other poor suspecting soul, leaving Harry and Charlie trying to suppress their laughter.

Harry shouted to the other men in the hut, "I hope you untidy sods have cleaned the back of that ambulance out. One speck of coal dust and that's the last fuel you get."

Charlie laughed.

"I don't know how you do it, Harry, what with bringing it here and you with that stove going twenty-four hours a day. Where does it all come from?"

Harry winked his eye.

"They dropped me another ton today. It's that sergeant, Charlie, he thinks the sun shines out of my arsehole. I hardly eat in the mess there. The cook corporal has stocked my cupboard up with tea, sugar, bacon, sausages and bags of slices of roast beef. In fact anything I want I just have to ask." He lit a cigarette. "That's not what I came to see you about. How you getting on with Kath?"

"Great, Harry, I didn't know such women existed. Last weekend was also my last fling. I never thought I would ever say it Harry, but Kath is just the girl I have been waiting for."

"What happened the weekend then?"

"I told you, we had that date with those Land Army girls. We had to take Foggy to make up the third man. He's a real prat, make no mistake. We get to London and the three girls were waiting for us. They looked so different in real clothes and not that standard uniform. Well, I told you her sister worked in this big house and the owners were away. Well, there was a change of plan, the family were at home. So we all troop to this hotel, it was bleeding hilarious. Then we went to the theatre. Foggy tried to grope this bird, but she wasn't having any of that in public. So there he is, kissing and smooching, he almost raped her on the seat. This old chap behind him taps Foggy on the shoulder. You know what a gate Foggy's got, he tells him to wait his fucking turn. The old boy tells him, 'I'm a Brigadier.' 'So fucking what,' Foggy answers. I can tell you I could hardly stop laughing with all the shushing going on. Anyway, we get back to the hotel and Foggy want us all to get into one bed. None of the girls wanted that. Then, halfway through the night, what happens? There's a bloody air raid and they evacuate the hotel. There's Foggy running down the hotel corridors trying to pull on his trousers with his tool hanging out and, my God, does Foggy have a tool, demanding his money back and the three girls killing themselves because it was them that paid for the hotel. They evacuate us to the cellar with Foggy moaning all the time and demanding they put the lights out so he can carry on groping." Both Harry and Charlie were chuckling to themselves. "But that's definitely the last time, Harry, I'm glad it went off with a bang. I saw Kathy last night. There's only one thing I wish, Harry, I do wish she would call me Charlie. She does insist on calling me Charles."

"Seeing her tonight, Charlie?"

"I shall see her every night. I used one of the units motorcycles."

Foggy returned, still moaning.

"I am worried to death over me pigeons, Harry. You get on alright with the R.S.M. Could you put in a good word for us, Harry?"

"He won't take much notice of me, Foggy but I'll try." Harry hesitated and looked rather puzzled. "I thought you had a couple of kids, Foggy?"

"Oh they're alright, she's taken them with her. They've been calling him dad for two years or more, since I've been away. Fuck her and the kids and that bleeding warden, it's me sodding pigeons I'm worried about."

"Well that's your answer, Foggy. See the padre, tell him you're worried about the kids and you want compassionate leave to get them fixed up. Give him a real sob story, then you can go and fix up your pigeons and at the same time give that warden a kick up the family jewels."

"You're kidding, Harry. Why should I be the only one to suffer? He's welcome to the selfish cow."

"You need to talk, Foggy, after that weekend. By the by, Foggy, did the hotel give you the money back?"

"No, Charlie. They threatened to call the police if I didn't shove off." With that Foggy left the hut in a hurry, a smile across his face as he approached the small room the padre had set aside as a chapel to hear the men's grievances.

"If for any reason I can't get down, I can phone Kathy. But you want to see that phone box along the lane, there's always a queue. Marti laughs blind when she sees me turn up at the house with me greatcoat, leather jerkin and steel helmet. I'm taking her shopping in Kings Lynn on the back of it Saturday. I tell you that Marti is a game old bird. I wish my wife's mother had been like that, the miserable old bastard. I had her and Kath and the old man playing pontoon last night. Marti won four pence off me, but when I put my overcoat on she had put it back in the pocket. My mother-in-law would have gone out and bought a pint of beer with it." Charlie sounded in a joyful mood as he related to the previous night's experiences.

Harry took his leave. He inspected the back of his ambulance. It had been scrubbed clean. They'd made sure they wouldn't be deprived of their welcome fuel.

The roads were covered with a layer of ice, and frost clung to the trees. He took it very slowly. Twice the ambulance went into a skid, then the rain started, quickly turning to sleet. He switched on the windscreen wipers. They made a half hearted effort, moved a couple of inches, then stopped completely. He swore under his breath, jumped from the cab and tried to clear the windscreen to get the wipers started but they wouldn't move.

"Having trouble, soldier?" He spun round, for he hadn't heard anyone approach and found himself looking directly into the faced of a beautiful blonde in Land Army uniform.

"Yes, the damn wipers have packed in."

486

She examined the windscreen and the wipers. "That's your trouble, soldier. Your windscreen was frozen and the wipers stuck to it. Looks like a fuse has blown. Where's the fuse box?"

He shrugged his shoulders.

"I don't know, all I know about this tub is it has four wheels and an engine. If the engine ticks over the wheels go round, once you put it into gear."

The girl appeared to know what she was doing. She traced some wires and finished up at a black box smiling triumphantly. There was half a dozen spare fuses in the lid of the box, and in two minutes the wipers were working perfectly.

"For that, you can give me a lift into King's Lynn."

Before Harry could answer she was already seated in the cab. She opened a silver cigarette case, offered him one, then selected a cigarette and lit it, taking in a deep exaggerated drag and letting the smoke filter slowly between her lips.

"I know a fellow who drives one of these things. He calls it a blood tub."

Harry froze, knowing immediately who she was going to talk about. She removed her hat and her blonde hair fell across her shoulders. Her firm breasts burst forth in her tight fitting jumper when she undid her topcoat. Charlie had described her to him so many times there was no mistake. The ambulance picked up speed and the wipers continued their steady to and fro motion. He tried to concentrate on the road, wondering what was coming next, but he almost choked to death when she came out with the next statement.

"I'll kill the bastard the next time we meet. Name of Charlie Williams, I don't suppose you know him do you?"

Her eyes searched his face. He swallowed hard and let her continue while he thought up a good answer.

"We've had a couple of parties together and I saw him over the weekend, but he hasn't turned up since. I suppose the bastard has met someone else."

What could Harry say? His brain raced. Charlie had just told him all this was over and he believed him. Ever since that night in the cafe when they met Kim and her cousin, he had been telling Kath that Charlie spent lonely nights in his billet. If Kath learnt about this it would all be over. He had to help him out. If the position was reversed Charlie would do the same for him. He knew Charlie was serious about Kath and he had been hoping it would turn out this way so they would be able to make up a foursome.

"Oh yes, I know him." And that was the only piece of truth she was going to hear. He had to get him out of this mess, for one day

Charlie may be out with Kath in town and meet the girl. "Yes I know him, he's a real karzy wallah, a pig of the first water. Since we arrived back in England he's had more women than he's had hot dinners. I don't know why, he had a smashing wife and a lovely daughter." Harry felt like cringing with embarrassment as the lies poured fourth.

She gasped. "Why the lousy bastard, he told me he wasn't married, wait till I catch up with him again! I'll castrate the bastard."

Harry winced at the thought of listening to Charlie's voice another two octaves higher, and the pain he would have to undergo being castrated without anaesthetic. He would have to lay it on thick to get his friend out of this mess, for by the looks of the girl she really meant business.

"Yes, his wife is a sweet kid. They were very young when they were married." He suddenly remembered how young Kath looked. "To see her you would never believe she had a child. He told me he thinks she's in the family way again, poor kid, it's her I feel sorry for." Harry shook his head sympathetically. "You want sod all to do with that karzy wallah, miss."

"Anne," she answered. "My name is Anne." She gave him a sweet smile, wondering if it was all the truth or if he was really making a play for her. "Do call me Anne."

Her hand went across and started smoothing the inside of his thighs. Harry pulled over with the wheels on the grass verge. He wanted to make sure she had everything right. Although he wasn't left in any doubt that she thought he had pulled over for something else. She squeezed his hand.

"He's a bad bastard that one, Anne. Let's make sure we are talking about the right man. Six feet tall with blonde hair, a bit wavy, and blue eyes, nice looking bloke. When he carries his gas mask and steel helmet it always hangs down from one shoulder and not across his chest."

"Yes that's him alright. Anyway that's his name, Charlie Williams." She squeezed his hand, almost certain now he was making a play for her.

"You're not likely to see him again, and if you do it's best that you ignore him. His wife came down two days ago. A beautiful girl. He was just the same in North Africa and Italy. A woman in skirt passed by and it was like a challenge to him. One time it was rumoured when we were in the desert that he took one of the unit's motorcycles and dashed back to Cairo, a distance of over three hundred miles, just to spend a night with some A.T.S. girl in a sleazy hotel. And what that bastard got up to in Italy is beyond belief, you'd call me a liar if I told you."

"I wouldn't, you know." She moved across the petrol tins towards him. "That swine doesn't deserve a decent wife."

"I know that, Anne," and wondered why he had never taken up dramatic art at the orphanage. "All the same, I would hate to see his marriage break up. You should forget him, Anne, he isn't worth it." He tried to reassure her with an extra squeeze of her hand. This she misconstrued. Thinking he was making a pass at her, she put her arm around his shoulders. He felt the blood rising and his face reddened. "Don't worry."

She was whispering soothingly into his ear, her hand all the while stroking the inside of his thigh, her voice husky and the breath hot. "If I do see him out with his wife I won't even bother to speak to him. But should I meet him alone, I will spit in his face after I've kneed him in the goolies."

He sighed inwardly with relief, but her hand moved slightly across.

"A girl needs a bit of comfort."

Charlie had described her as a bit of a nympho but never told him she was such a fast worker. She took her arms away and went to open the small door leading into the back. His throat dried. He licked his lips, they felt like sandpaper. For once since meeting Kim, he felt sorely tempted. Kim's face flashed before his eyes. He knew he could never betray her. He shook his head.

"I am sorry, Anne, I have a steady girlfriend."

"So what you were saying about Charlie Williams was the truth? I thought you were making a play for me." She shook her head in disbelief. "You don't know what you're missing, soldier."

Harry dropped her off in the centre of King's Lynn. Snow was falling fast, laying across the ground, and the clouds hung heavy. He burst out laughing. "That's another bloody mess I've got you out of Charlie," he said to himself, happy in the knowledge that if Charlie and Anne ever met she would ignore him completely.

When he arrived at Kim's house he was still smiling to himself. The welcoming fire was blazing up the chimney and Carol sat alone, half asleep in one of the armchairs, her feet across resting on the opposite armchair. He gently lifted her feet and rested them in his lap as he sat down. She moved slightly but remained asleep, and with the warmth of the fire it wasn't long before he fell asleep himself, and they remained like that till Kim arrived home.

Carol playfully smacked Harry across the head. "You little bugger, why didn't you wake me up?"

"Well, you looked so beautiful when you were asleep, it was a shame to disturb you." He winked his eye at Kim.

"Alright, Harry, cut the blarney out," Carol said as she rushed out into the kitchen to prepare dinner.

That night Charlie and Kath came round, and Carol and Jack went round to Marti's house leaving the four of them alone. Soon the playing cards came out and Kim was learning the intricacies of three card brag (army fashion) and pontoon.

At ten Kim brought out the sandwiches and made tea. Harry sat down to the piano and the four of them sang the next two hours away. "God," Harry thought, "if only life could be like this all the time."

Charlie picked up his motorcycle and was soon roaring along the country lanes, while Harry and Kim had a prolonged farewell at the garden gate.

February soon led into March, with the worst of the weather over, an occasional gale now and again, but the bitter cold weather seemed to have subsided. Then one day Harry turned up at the main unit to see Charlie preparing his kit for a weekend pass. In the past few weeks his whole attitude had changed, with every night he met Kathy a new experience.

"I am off to see my little girl this weekend, Harry. They've moved her nearer. Unfortunately I have to take two trains as I have to change. I am off Friday and the R.S.M. said I can return on the Monday."

"Bloody hell, Charlie. Kathy won't like you being away for three nights. Kim was telling me she worries herself to death when you're late."

"She doesn't have to mind me being away for three nights, she's coming with me."

For a minute Harry remained speechless, just staring at Charlie.

"Close your bloody mouth, Harry, we're starting to get plenty of flies around here." But Harry remained speechless. "Oh don't worry, Harry. When I told them where I was going, it was Marti who suggested I should take Kathy."

Harry found his voice at last. "I don't believe you, Charlie. Are you staying at an hotel together?"

"Not really. I phoned the matron at the home and she said I could get a room at the pub in the village. When I told Kath we could get a room at the village inn, all she said was O.K. so I'll have to play it by ear."

Harry was still speechless when he left for Kim's house, and that night he never mentioned it to Kim and she never spoke about it to him. In fact, she remarked how quiet he was that evening.

490

On the following Monday, Harry phoned the main unit three times before he learnt that Charlie had returned. Sykes answered the phone.

"Yes Charlie Williams has just reported in, I think he has been shacked up with some bint from King's Lynn."

"If I were you Sykes, I wouldn't let him hear that. Remember that throat of yours out in the desert. Just say he has had a nice weekend away."

Harry was desperate to know how the weekend fared, and soon skidded to a halt outside the Nissen hut. But he still had to wait as Charlie was over at the big house taking a shower. It was still a bit fresh outside and Harry stood with his back to the red hot stove till Charlie returned. They were alone in the hut.

"How did it go, Charlie?"

"Well, Harry, you can kick my arse if you like. I never ever thought I would feel like this about any woman."

"Well, come on then, did you share a room?"

Charlie smiled.

"If anyone else but you had asked that question, Harry, I would have knocked their bloody block off. The answer is yes, we slept together. Let me tell you what happened."

"We arrived at this sleepy old village, I don't think you can actually call it that. A church, a butcher's shop, a village store, and the quaintest little pub you ever saw. The pub was closed when we arrived so we knocked on the side door. The pub was called the George and Dragon. A large woman came to the door. You should have seen her, Harry, built like an outside shithouse with arms like the branches of a tree. We asked if she had any accommodation and she asked, 'One or two rooms?' Then, like a flash, Kathy said, 'One room of course,' and showed her hand. She had turned her signet ring round to look like a wedding ring. I was bloody paralysed. The woman vanished. I said to Kath, 'If this is the George and Dragon, I wonder what George looks like!' Kath could hardly stop laughing.

The old bird returned in a few minutes and when she told her we had to come to see our little girl, she couldn't do enough for us. She took us up to our room and in the middle was the largest four poster bed you ever did see. Kath fell in love with it straight away. That pub was old, Harry, it must have been built in the fifteenth or sixteenth century. The floorboards were polished so you could see your face in them and there were half inch gaps between them, they were so old. And the bar itself, Harry, solid oak beams, you were expecting Dick Turpin to come smashing through the doors at any minute.

But I very nearly put my bloody foot in it. The old dear, who turned out to be an angel, served up a roast chicken dinner in the corner of the bar, in front of this large open fire which had an enormous log burning on it. She said it had been burning for three days and I could well believe her. Anyway, she makes this home brewed wine and serves it up in old French wine bottles. Kathy picks a bottle up and starts to read out loud in perfect French. Of course, prat that I am, I said, 'I never knew you could read and speak French, Kath.' Well, the old girl gives me an old fashioned look. I mean to say, any husband would know if his wife spoke French."

Harry was laughing, but still unable to believe that Kath has spent three nights in a room with him.

"But surely Charlie, it wasn't her that suggested you have just one room, I can't believe that."

"I told you, when that old dear asked us, Kathy showed her her hand with the ring on. But the best is still yet to come. When we were going to bed, all the locals told us the place was haunted by one of the late squire's sons, a bloke named Roger. It seems he was a bit of a randy sod and liked the village women. He had this large bed brought down to the pub from the big house so he could frolic with the local girls. The men laughed and reckoned half the bloody village was related to him. It turns out he was killed during the Napoleonic wars and comes back frequently to his old room and bed. So when we did get to bed, Kathy was shit scared and snuggled up close to me. Harry, I tell you it was heaven, and what's more there will be no more pissing around for me. Kathy is the girl I have been searching for. As soon as my divorce comes through you will be hearing wedding bells and you are definitely my best man."

"What about your little girl, Charlie, how did they get along, her and Kathy?"

"Like a bloody house on fire, she kept calling her Mother. Kathy loved that. We had her out all day and went for long walks. You should hear some of the things that kid comes out with, laugh, it brought tears to our eyes." Then Charlie changed to a more subdued tone. "You know, Harry, I don't think I have ever been so happy in my life, and I owe most of it to you, because without you I doubt very much if Kathy would have believed me."

"Forget it, Charlie, you would have done the same for me. But I must say this pub and village sound good to me."

"You would love it, Harry. Every Saturday they have a chap who plays the accordion and another plays the drums, and the old dear that keeps the pub plays the piano. I can tell you, it's a real rave up. They haven't seen the war. Some Jerry plane came down about half a mile away and they have the plane's prop over the fireplace. But that's about all. We were in the bar on the Friday night and they were gently taking the piss out of my west country accent. When I told them I came from near Bristol there was a fucking argument as to where Bristol was, till the old lady took out a map and showed them. I tell you Harry, talk about being cut off from civilisation, I'm sure they still think Gladstone's a prime minister!"

"I must come and see this place one weekend with you, Charlie."

"Yes, bring Kim with you. They have a couple of rooms, but you definitely can't have our four poster."

"Don't be a prick, Charlie. I couldn't ask Kim to share a bed with me. She will wait till we're married and I don't suppose Kathy will tell Kim and her family what happened."

Charlie laughed. "She tells Kim everything, and I mean everything. She already told me that she had told Kim she was going to sleep with me and she said Kim wasn't the least surprised. When it comes to women, Harry, you are still bloody innocent. Haven't you ever wondered what women talk about amongst themselves?"

Still puzzled and a little bewildered by what Charlie told him, they walked together over to the dining room to have dinner. Half the unit was still away and the food was good and plentiful.

"By the way, Harry, I haven't thanked you for getting me out of the shit with that Anne. She met Foggy and told him all about it, and he'd guessed what you were up to and confirmed your story. She has threatened to spit in my face and knee me in the goolies if she sees me out on my own."

"Yes I know, that's what she told me. She was real upset."

"She can't be all that upset, she's fixed up with Nick Carter. His missus has gone to the Air Force and he kept that room on and they go there every night. That won't last long. She'll kill the poor sod off. You should see him, Harry, he's just a shadow of his former self."

When he arrived at Kim's she threw her arms around his neck and kissed him.

"It's not so cold tonight, Harry."

"Cold enough for me." He went straight into the sitting room and removed his heavy boots. "That's great." He stretched his stocking feet towards the blazing fire. Kim sat opposite him on the edge of her seat. It was obvious she was waiting to ask him something.

"Have you seen Charlie today, Harry?"

Harry nodded.

493

"Just left him at the billet."

She tried to sound unconcerned.

"Did he tell you he spent the weekend with Kathy. They went to see his little girl."

"Yes, he told me."

He leaned back on his chair waiting with baited breath for the next question, but it was a long time coming. Kim fidgeted about in her chair and leaned forward as if she wanted to ask him a confidential question, but instead asked him if he wanted a cup of tea. Harry was enjoying this cat and mouse game and shook his head. She lay back, staring at him and no doubt wondering if Charlie had told him about the weekend he had spent with Kathy, and if so, just how much he had told him. But to all outward appearances Harry remained completely relaxed while inside he was all tensed up, just waiting for her to make the next move. She came over and sat on his knee and whispered so confidentially in his ear.

"Did you know they slept together?"

He sat up and put his arms around her to save her falling off his lap and gasped, "No."

She shook her head and whispered, "Yes."

Then he returned to his relaxed position.

"Well it's none of my business." He touched her small turned up nose and whispered, "And it's none of your business."

"I know, Harry, but her mum and dad know and they don't seem to mind. I just can't understand it."

"Well she is two years older than you and twenty. Quite old enough to realise what she was doing." He could have enlightened her with the skills of Charlie as a smooth operator. As with any woman, he would have Marti eating out of his hand at their first meeting, and it didn't take long for Kathy herself to succumb to his charms, but he decided against it as he knew Charlie really loved Kathy. "I know one thing, Kim, Kathy will never find a nicer or more kind hearted man than him. Only yesterday he told me, the minute his divorce comes through he will marry Kathy the first chance he gets."

Kim's mother and father had taken their usual stroll round to Marti's house, a habit they had got used to over the past week or so, leaving Kim and Harry on their own. It was midnight when they returned.

"Did Charlie tell you he took Kathy to see his little girl the weekend, Harry?" It was obvious Carol was fishing, just to see how much Charlie had told his best friend.

494

Instead, all he said was, "Yes, apparently she got on very well with Amanda. She was calling her Mummy before the day was out."

He immediately changed the subject. "I shall be away for a couple of days next week. This unit I'm attached to is doing a stunt. They're a tank recovery unit and they're going out for a bit of practise. I don't know why, they've had almost three years of the real thing."

Outside, standing by the ambulance Kim said, "I will miss your visits next week, Harry."

"Well, you had better get used to the idea. It will be April in a couple of weeks and if the weather improves we will be doing more exercises. It certainly can't be worse than the last one."

CHAPTER 45

Harry could hardly believe what was happening, this was nothing like the prewar army days. A nice clean comfortable billet, unlimited tea, sugar and fresh milk, and rations, bacon and fresh eggs and occasionally a chicken, things the local civilians dream about in these troubled times. There was unlimited fuel, enough to keep his hot stove going day and night and more to spare, which he often dropped in at Charlie's Nissen hut. But the most important item of all, his own vehicle had sufficient petrol. Sometimes he would think he was just dreaming expecting at any time to wake up and be back in some mud hole back in Italy. In the sergeant's eyes Harry could do no wrong and was of the opinion the sun shone from Harry's bum.

It was exactly the same at Kim's home. Her mother treated him as her own son. It was this that worried Harry. For, sitting in what had now become his armchair, when she thought he wasn't looking, she would stare unashamedly at him and from time to time cast a glance at her son's photograph above the fireplace. It was as if she was comparing them. She would insist on washing his clothes every week and press and sponge his uniform, fetch his tea and wait upon him hand and foot till the position become embarrassing. Most evenings she would, with Jack, go out, if not to the cinema, then she would visit a relative, something she had hardly done since she lost her son. Harry felt as if she was throwing him and Kim together. The time came when Charlie was going to the village to see his daughter with Kathy, Carol suggested Harry should take Kim. At first Kim reddened at the suggestion and put up a mild form of protest, at the same time watching Harry for his reaction, but stone faced, all he could say was, "It's up to Kim." But Kim nodded her head in approval, still blushing.

After a very restless night, it was the rain belting down on the corrugated iron roof of the Nissen hut that woke him fully the next morning. He stoked up the fire and wandered around the M.I. room in the old dressing gown Jack had given him. He made a fresh pot of tea and set about cooking himself egg and bacon, although this morning he had very little appetite. The sergeant came in and sat himself on the edge of the table.

"That lab bloke of yours, Harry, how much do I owe him?"

"Forget it, sarge, he did it as a favour. There isn't much I can give him, he neither smokes nor drinks and he's married with a couple of kids, how he managed that God only knows. I think he only farts when there's the letter F in the day."

"Holy Joe is he, Harry?"

496

"No not really. What I might do, sarge, is ask that farmer to sell me a duck or a chicken. Give him that, he's not a bad bloke. I suppose he gets a bit worried, it must play on his nerves sometimes. He sees all kinds of things in that lab, cancerous lungs, dodgy liver and kidneys. That reminds me, I wonder if he's a fucking vegetarian?"

He drove into his own parent unit. Corporal Sykes came out to meet him, it was still pouring down and Sykes's waterproof groundsheet wrapped round his shoulders looked as if it had absorbed the rain.

"Hello, Sykes, my old son," Harry shouted out in greetings.

"Don't you old son me, you crafty bastard. Where's that twenty Players you promised me, and not so much of the old son."

He pointed to the two stripes on his tunic sleeve.

"Corporal now, and don't you forget, Jackson."

"How the hell am I supposed to see two stripes on your jacket when it's covered with that groundsheet?" Harry reached behind his seat and threw him a packet of twenty Players.

The men in Charlie's hut were already waiting for him when he arrived there, and without asking, rushed to the rear of his ambulance and humped out two large sacks of coke and coal. Harry sat on a bench in front of the stove, his greatcoat over his shoulders like a cape. They were alone.

"I shall be coming down to the village this weekend, Charlie." Charlie hardly blinked, he just stared at the stove.

"I know, Marti told me."

"How the hell could she, I didn't know myself till last night."

"She phoned me here, got Sykes to get me to the phone, said she was my mother and the message was urgent. He pratted about a bit and gave her some shit about not being allowed to receive personal calls. But you know Marti, she had the prick eating out of her hand in five minutes."

"How we going to arrange it, Charlie? Will Kath sleep with Kim and us share the other room?"

Charlie looked at Harry as if he had gone mad or something.

"Piss off, Harry! You know I am not kinky, having two girls in my bed, and sleeping with you, you must be kidding."

"But, Charlie, it's not fair on Kim. She's not that sort. I don't know, Charlie, I think I will give it a miss. I doubt if I could ever face her mother again."

Charlie shook his head slowly.

"You prat." He stared at Harry and repeated, "you prat. Don't you know this was all Carol's idea. It was her that suggested it. I don't think you really understand, Harry. She is substituting you for her own son, Marti told me that, she reckons you two are so

497

much alike. Even Marti thinks there is a resemblance. Frankly, Harry, if Kim came back in the family way I don't think Carol would give a toss. You had better get used to the idea, Harry, you are up to your neck in it. Bang goes your resolution, no wartime romance for you, and you are in so deep there is no turning back, for if you said goodbye to her tomorrow it would be worse than not coming back at all. Kim's a great kid, just be gentle with her. No one was more surprised than me when Kathy suggested she should come and spend a weekend with me. Do you know what they call Kathy at work. The iceberg. And it was her that took the initiative when we went to the pub and asked for a double room."

This left Harry thinking. It was still bitter cold when he went to Kim's house but was greeted warmly by Carol with, "Looking forward to your weekend this week, Harry?"

Just as if he was taking Kim out for a day's outing to the countryside. That night, the weekend was hardly mentioned again and fortunately for Harry, the next day he would be on a three day exercise with the small unit he was attached to. This would save him the embarrassment of meeting the family till at least Friday, so he arranged to meet Kim and Kathy on the railway station half an hour before the train departs.

The exercise consisted of loading and unloading tanks, replacing tank tracks that had been deliberately removed, but the main task was tank recovery.

"What the bloody hell for, sarge?" Harry looked fed up after the first day. "Surely you had enough practice in the desert and Italy? This is just a bloody waste of time."

"It's not me, Harry, I can assure you I could do without this. I told you I have managed to rent a little cottage just by the farm and the wife is down here now."

Then a thought suddenly struck him.

"Why the hell don't you bring Kim down one Sunday? The wife is all alone here, I would like her to meet some of the locals."

"I might take you up on that, sarge. I would like you to meet Kim."

So the exercise dragged on and on, fortunately there were no restrictions about not sleeping in the ambulance. Harry had found an old Valor stove in the farmhouse. It became quite cosy at night, for the sergeant and two of his cronies had made the ambulance their headquarters. The only trouble with the Valor stove was they could only get kerosene that was used on the farm and it gave off a smelly and greasy vapour. The first morning they woke up the inside of the ambulance was covered in a sooty greasy substance. Harry wasn't too troubled, it had been warm all night and they all managed to get a good night's sleep and he certainly had the day to himself to give the ambulance a thorough clean through.

On the third day the men took to shooting rabbits. The 303 cartridges made a mess of them but they roasted what was left of the rabbits over an open wood fire, what's more they tasted real good. The weather stayed pretty good, it rained slightly on the second day but by mid morning the clouds had cleared and gave way to a crisp but dry frost.

"What time are we jacking it in, sarge?" Harry asked as he finished off his tenth cup of tea that day, for as far as he was concerned, the exercise had been a complete waste of time, not one man had even got a tiny scratch and he had come to the conclusion that the ambulance had only been brought to use as sleeping quarters for the sergeant and his cronies. When Harry told him this, the sergeant just burst out laughing.

"I don't give a toss," Harry answered, "so long as I get back by Friday night, I have to be at King's Lynn station by eight on Saturday morning."

"Don't worry, Harry, I will personally drive you there."

And the sergeant was as good as his word. Not only did the sergeant have him at the station with half an hour to spare, but promised he would pick him up at the assembly point on the Sunday evening.

"Don't worry, Harry, if you are not there I will have guessed you were staying another day," was his parting shot.

The station was almost deserted, a few regular commuters but hardly any troops going away for the weekend. A few minutes later Charlie came rushing into the station,

"I will kill that bastard Sykes before long! That bastard stuck me on guard duty last night and I didn't get out of the house till past seven. I had to get Reynolds to run me out here. I am sure that bastard must have been one of those dare devil riders you used to see on the fairgrounds before the war."

Charlie's mood changed when they saw the two girls enter the station. Kim waved, and they quickened their steps, Kim stood on tip toes to kiss Harry, he took her small weekend case from her. They still had ten minutes to spare before the train pulled out.

The journey was uneventful. Kim hardly spoke and turned a deep shade of red when Charlie mentioned the pub, she could hardly look at Harry. There was a ten minute wait while they waited for a branch line train. Harry wanted to be alone with Kim and ask her if she had changed her mind. Unfortunately the compartment was in one of those old type carriages with no corridor. They stepped onto the platform at the village station and were enveloped in a cloud of steam from the noisy steam engine.

The pub wasn't open so Charlie knocked on the side door. Rosie, the proprietor, welcomed Kathy and Charlie with open arms. She looked at Kim.

"So this is your cousin, Kathy? You didn't tell me she was so young. It must be me getting older, for all policemen and brides are starting to look younger."

Rosie's thick arms and twenty stone body enveloped Kim till she could hardly breath. Then it was Harry's turn, and in a tight clinch all he could gasp out was, "Hello Rosie."

"I suppose you will want to clean yourself up." She led them straight up the narrow staircase, which screamed in protest as Rosie stood on each step. The upstairs passage, polished to the brilliance of a prewar guardsman's boots, was so old there was an half inch gap between the boards. A small window at the far end bounced its light the whole length of the passage. She opened the first door. An enormous four poster, heavily carved, took up most of the room. Kim gasped in amazement. She stepped inside the room and traced her fingers through the heavy carvings.

"It is the most beautiful thing I have ever seen in my life." She sat on the bed and almost sank down, for the mattress was made of feathers. She invited Harry over.

"Come and sit here, Harry."

"Well I am sorry my dear, this is Kath's bed. Your room is further down the passage."

"No, Rosie, I think Kim can use the bed tonight. Like me, I see she has fallen for it."

She turned to Kim. "Just one night, Kim, no more, this is a special bed. Am I right, Rosie?"

Rosie seemed to be enjoying herself watching Kim, for Kim at this moment was just like a little girl with her first dolly.

"Yes, it's very special. Round here all the property belongs to the Bellamy family. They live up at the big house. The old lady up there, I was her personal maid. My Ernie was the colonel's batman. The old colonel was killed in the war, during a gas attack. My Ernie was badly gassed, so when he came back from hospital madam let us manage this pub. We have been here twenty five years this year. Now the story about this bed, Kathy has heard it before so if you want to go to your room, Kathy, that's alright."

"Rosie, I wouldn't dream of it, it's one of the loveliest stories I have ever heard." She made herself comfortable on the bed and pulled Charlie down beside her.

"Carry on, Rosie."

"Well as you can see, the bed is almost the size of the room. It belonged to the big house. In the late eighteen century the master had two sons, Roger (at the mention of Roger's name, she bent her knee in a slight curtsy as in reverence) was the eldest. A fine man, he loved this pub, but best of all he loved the local wenches. This pub then was the centre of life for the locals. They do say that Dick Turpin and Tom King stayed here, so did Henry Fielding. Before the railways arrived this was an important route to London, so there was always plenty of life here. But it was Roger (slight knee bend) that gave this place character. He was good to the locals. He had that large wall built around the estate just to give the locals work. Sceptics say he did it to keep the men busy while he kept their wives and daughters busy. I wouldn't be at all surprised if half the population roundabouts here were all related to Roger (another slight knee bend) but he was dearly loved, no one ever went hungry round here. Then he went off to the Napoleonic wars and was killed at Waterloo. He had several of the locals serving with him and they brought his body back all the way on an old farm cart. He is buried in the church next door. You will see his tomb when you come to church in the morning."

At the mention of church Harry stared blankly at Charlie, but apparently it was the done thing. Charlie had never mentioned it to him.

"Don't mind them, Rosie, carry on with the story," Kathy said and gave the two of them a look of disgust.

"Well, they had to bury him straight away, the body by this time was over six weeks old, but the next night all the locals swore blind they saw Roger (slight knee bend) standing by the bar. No one was scared so on the anniversary of Waterloo, everyone toasts him and the vicar comes in and blesses the pub. Well you tell me, how did they get such a big bed into this room. The stairs hardly takes my size and just look at that window, it's not much bigger than a ship's port hole, and the mattress, it's all feathers and when I take it out for an airing it takes four men to lift it from the bed. Just look at the carving on this bed and the head, you can make out the R. and a G, carved in amongst the leaves and vines. Don't ask me what the initials are, Roger (there goes that knee bend) never married, but even if he had it couldn't have been his wife's, for the bed was already over two hundred years old when it came here. Now Kim, just lay on the bed and look into that big mirror on the wardrobe at the foot of the bed, see how bold the initials stand out."

Kim's eyes widened as she looked through the mirror, for although the initials were reversed, inside the initials were the

501

same initials in reverse that made them stand out the right way in the mirror.

But Rosie was well into the story now and Harry himself had to admit he was fascinated.

"Roger's (knee bend) presence is still felt in this pub. I know he watches over this, his favourite place, I can feel him near me. Couples all around here always book this room for their wedding night, because this is a lucky room, and a lucky bed, and without a doubt they always fall pregnant within a year."

Harry stared at Charlie, shaking his head from side to side.

"They say if you stare at the initials on the headboard through that mirror and they turn into your initials it's one hundred percent certain you will become pregnant."

Harry jumped from the bed as if he was on fire, but Kim burst out laughing.

"Don't you worry if you see Roger (knee bend) he's a lovely man and he won't do you no harm."

Rosie left the room with Charlie and Kathy.

"Makes you laugh, doesn't it, Kim? They are all the same, these lonely country villages. No history, so they make it up as they go along. I bet that story has been doing the rounds since Roger died (he made a mockery knees bend). They have sod all to talk about in these lonely dumps so they make up stories, most of them frighten the kids when they misbehave. I hope it didn't frighten you, Kim." He put a comforting arm around her shoulders.

"No, Harry, I loved the story and I certainly loved Roger, he must have been a real rogue. You can say what you like, Harry, but this place has character."

When they went to the bar that evening it was crowded with the locals, they all knew Charlie and Kathy by name. They took Charlie to the far corner on his own, no doubt to hear the latest dirty jokes going the round back at the billet. The bar itself had a low black beamed ceiling, in parts Charlie had to duck down. There was a large open fireplace against one wall, so large, two people could sit comfortably inside. Names were deeply carved into the black beams on the ceiling and the black oak timbers on the walls and around the fireplace. Two sets of initials had two small picture frames over them, the initials of Dick Turpin and Tom King.

One end of the bar had been set up as a small stage with an old but well polished piano, complete with brass candlesticks and ornate marquetry on the front panels.

"I wonder if old Dick played that," Harry said to Charlie, who had left the locals and returned to his own party. Rosie set out a meal for the four of them and about nine, the local musicians took up their positions on the stage, a drummer with no teeth who, when he grinned his mouth almost cut his face in two separate portions, but he could play, as could the man with the piano accordion and everyone joined in the singing. Rosie was at the piano and finished with a flourish.

"Come on lads, all out, it's closing time."

Ernie, the landlord was behind the bar sitting on an upturned beer crate and holding his hand against the bar to steady himself as his chest wheezed up and down as he fought for breath. Harry gently tapped his back.

"It's the gas, Harry lad," he wheezed and fought for breath.

"If Jerry gets desperate, Harry, and uses gas and you get a lungful, for Christ sake, Harry, shoot your bloody self, twenty-seven years this lot, and every day torture, I would have finished myself years ago if it hadn't been for my Rosie." The old man shook his head.

"You have a lovely girl there, Harry, don't you come back like me, son, she looks as if she is the kind that would stand by you so don't torture her and yourself, Harry. I wished I had gone with Colonel Bellamy. I wasn't just his batman, we were friends, served with him in India on the North West frontier, then Egypt and straight into the great war. Mrs Bellamy has taken me over to France a few times to see his grave. I look at all those rows and rows of white stones and honestly, Harry, I wish my name was on one of them, right alongside Colonel Bellamy."

"Bellamy, Bellamy, I seem to know that name, where the hell have I heard it before." Harry was almost thinking out aloud, and so, he departed to the bedroom with Kim, with the name Bellamy ringing through his brain.

Halfway through the night Harry grew restless, he came out into a sweat, he grabbed the sheet hard and twisted and turned, suddenly the room went dark, he was back in the desert behind the blazing lorry, then he was standing at the front of the dying man, beside the man's head the muzzle of a revolver came out of the sand like some huge black snake emerging from a hole. The barrel of the gun pointed menacingly at him like some enormous black eye socket, he bent to pick the revolver up, but his body didn't seem to work, the next thing he knew he was gripping the revolver, it pointed at the man's head, there was a loud explosion and a big black hole between the man's eyes with blood pouring out like some huge fountain, he called out. Kim shook him and he woke with a start, the room was bathed in light.

"My God, Harry, whatever is the matter? You are drenched with sweat." She put her arm round him, Harry was shaking.

503

"Were you having a nightmare or something, Harry? Just look at you."

Harry jumped from the bed and rubbed himself down with a dry towel. He took out a cigarette from his tunic and sat on the edge of the bed still shaking. Kim didn't say anything but slowly stroked his back. After his second cigarette, he drank a glass of water.

"I shall be alright now, Kim, I just had a bad dream."

Kim held him tight.

"This is not the first time, Harry. When you have stayed at our house I heard you call out before, what is it?"

"Don't worry Kim, it's just something that happened a long time ago, its just one of those things." He took down the blackout and lay awake for the remainder of the night, pleased when he saw the first rays of daylight coming through the window.

Rosie made them an enormous breakfast of ham, eggs, sausages and fried potatoes, for the four of them there were enough rations to last a whole family a week of breakfasts. Kim was helping Rosie to adjust her new hat when Harry came down.

"Are you ready for church, Harry?" Kim said without losing attention from adjusting Rosie's hat. Harry groaned, he hadn't been to church since the last compulsory church parade at the training depot before the war and was rather sceptical about religion since witnessing the horrors of war. But he was ready to sacrifice anything for his beloved Kim.

Charlie and Kathy went to the home to fetch Amanda and Kim was seated by the side of Roger's tomb when the three of them came in. It was the first time Kim had seen her and she could hardly believe how beautiful she was. The service hadn't started and Kathy lifted Amanda into Kim's arms, they took to each other immediately, then Kathy asked Kim to move along.

"She always sits there, Kim."

As Kim moved over Amanda immediately stood on her chair and kissed Roger's marble face. This seemed to amuse Kim and the congregation near the tomb. Rosie leaned across towards Kim.

"See what I mean, Kim, everyone loves dear Roger, even the children."

In the few hours Kim had been here, she, too, was thinking there was something extraordinary about this village legend. There were so many stories told about him and treated with reverence, Rosie for instance, doing that slight curtsy every time his name was mentioned. Also the way Rosie always paused at the top of the steps and stared towards one position. She made the excuse she was winded after the climb. And the villagers, as

504

they passed the tomb always touched Roger's forehead, over the years one spot had been rubbed so often there was now a slight dent in Roger's forehead.

Harry was about to say something to Rosie when his attention was drawn to an army officer who had just entered the church. In full military uniform with a well cut greatcoat with an empty sleeve tucked inside the pocket. A dark patch over one eye, a deep scar ran from below the chin and under the eye patch. An elderly lady with snow white hair, dressed in black, with a black silk blouse that fitted tightly around her neck, she held on to the officer with one hand and steadied herself with a black mallacca cane. The congregation stood up as they passed.

"My God, it's Captain Bellamy." Harry's voice was hushed, just above a whisper. But in the gloomy silence that gripped the church, the captain heard him and looked around, he faltered in his steps, and nodded his head.

"Did you see that, Charlie? It's Captain Bellamy. Did you know he lived around here?"

But Charlie looked far more surprised than Harry.

"No, it's the first time I have seen him. I never would have thought he would make it home, looks in pretty good shape to me apart from that nasty scar."

"The state we picked him up, I doubted if he would have had much face left. They made a good job of it."

"Did you know that officer, Harry?" Kim asked.

"I say, we picked him up he when he was wounded out in the desert." He shook his head slowly.

"I never thought he would make it, Kim." Just then the service started.

"Tell you all about it when we get out."

After the service the officer was waiting outside with the vicar. He touched his hat to the ladies.

"I was surprised to see you two lads here. What are you doing in this neck of the woods?"

"Williams, sir, his daughter is in the kids' home up here, he comes down almost every weekend. I am pleased to see you have recovered from the wounds, sir. I must say you looked in a very bad way." Harry could hardly take his eyes away from the officer's face.

"Yes, Jackson, and I believe I have you to thank for it." He lifted his head and showed them a small round scar in his windpipe.

"There you are, mother, this is the lad that made that emergency tracheotomy." The old lady looked at Harry, her eyes misted over as she took Harry's hand.

"My son has often told me about you two lads, it was extremely good thinking on your part, Mr Jackson."

Harry smiled to himself, it was the first time he had been called mister since he enlisted, in fact he couldn't remember if he had ever been called mister, for he was only a boy when he enlisted.

"Thank you ma'am." Then he changed the subject.

"I see you are a major. Congratulations, sir. I remember now, you were made a major after that raid. I will always think of you as captain, sir."

"Some raid that, eh lads? That dump certainly went up with a bang. Do you ever get with the old regiment? I suppose you lucky devils are getting ready for the big day?" He suddenly remembered the women were with them.

"Why, hello, Rosie." He held out his good arm, she gave a slight bend of the knee, just the same bend as when Rogers name is mentioned.

"Good to see you about again, sir." Then Harry introduced first Kim then Kathy.

"You two girls look much too young to be married to this pair of ruffians. Do look after them, these are the type our army could do with." Just then a carriage pulled by. A pair of grey horses stopped outside the lych-gate.

"You say your little girl is up at my house, Williams, and you Jackson, I will expect you for tea this afternoon. Three o'clock prompt." It sounded more like an order than an invitation.

"Bring the ladies, Jackson." He touched his hat again and led his mother to the open carriage.

Back at the pub Rosie couldn't get over the fact that they knew the captain, round here he was still called captain. Ernie had cooked the dinner, slices of lamb half an inch thick and soaked in a strong mint sauce, roast potatoes and several other vegetables.

"Yes, Ernie, it was Harry that saved the captain's life when he was wounded," Rosie said.

"Come off it, Rosie, I just did what any other medic would have done."

"Don't be modest, Harry, you did better than anyone else would have done." She turned her attention to Ernie once more.

"Yes, and these two were on that long raid behind enemy lines to blow up that dump. He was decorated for it. It was in the papers round here. Captain Bellamy led a raid deep into enemy territory with sixty men, they blew the largest dump in North Africa and released thirty British and Allied prisoners. They lost very few men and shot down two enemy planes."

506

"Pack it in, Rosie, you know how the papers exaggerate." He turned to Charlie.

"There was nothing like that, was it, Charlie?"

But Charlie said nothing and just smiled. Rosie vanished from the room and five minutes later returned with a newspaper wrapped in brown paper, she opened it up and placed it before Kim and Kathy.

"Just read that and judge for yourselves, it's all there, the whole story, how they used captured Italian armoured cars, and how they passed through a line of Italian artillery."

It was here that Charlie interrupted Rosie.

"They were a battery of anti aircraft guns. Come on, Rosie, they don't want to read that crap." He had seen the looks of despair on the girls faces.

Alone with Harry again, Kim became very worried.

"You didn't tell me anything about this, Harry, I thought you just took the wounded back to the hospitals out there."

"Well someone has to do it. Do you mind if we leave the subject now, Kim?"

They walked slowly back to the big house, Amanda holding Kathy's and Kim's hands.

"Bloody strange, Charlie, Captain Bellamy owning this house and your girl being here. Rosie said the old lady gave part of the house over to the children's home to be used for war orphans. When Rosie mentioned Bellamy last night, that name flew around my head, I just couldn't put a face to it. I never made the connection. It looks like the name Bellamy is well respected round here. Did you see the way they all stood up when they came into that church?"

They had the usual crying session when they handed Amanda over to the matron, she in turn handed her to a young nurse. Amanda looked over the nurse's shoulder, eyes full of tears and waving till she passed through the small door at the far end for the conservatory was massive, perhaps sixty feet long, the floor made up of mosaic marble. Much the same as they remembered when they went round the ruins of Pompeii. In the centre of the floor was a large mosaic compass, at each point of the compass a leading Roman god, and the smaller points of the compass the lesser gods. The rest of the floor was covered in an assorted mosaic of entwined flowers and plants. The conservatory was maintained at an even temperature to preserve the assortment of tropical plants in tubs around the large glass fronted room. The matron noticed the interest Harry showed in the plants.

She said, "Yes, all these plants were brought by generations of Bellamys from around the world. They are a great soldiering

507

family." She pointed out several plants from India and China, Australia and the Americas.

The matron led them up a wide oak staircase, richly carpeted. Life size portraits of the family lined the staircase walls. Along the wide upstairs passage were more portraits, many by well known artists of the time, in between the paintings stood suits of armour and weapons. Mrs Bellamy received them in a large sitting room, furnished with superb antiques. Kim held her breath as she gazed at the wide ornamental marble fireplace. A large pine log blazed merrily. More paintings of the ancestors, one that took Harry's attention was a painting of a colonel in the khaki uniform of the first world war, a very distinguished looking man. The old lady watched Harry admiring the painting.

"That was my husband, he was killed in the First War, fine looking man, isn't he?"

She led them to two large sofas, one each side of the fireplace with a long marble occasional table separating them. She pulled a bell rope beside the fireplace and a few minutes later a maid, of about middle age, came in with a tray, a teapot, cups and saucers and biscuits. She set them down.

"Shall I pour, madam?"

"Doesn't matter, Lucy, you can go home now, it's getting very late, and thank you for staying behind." The old lady poured the tea and handed the biscuits round. At that moment the captain came in.

"So you made it, lads. Mother looking after you?"

His major's crown was quite prominent now. He was still in uniform not the wartime battle dress, but the prewar khaki, similar to the one on the painting of his father. He wore several decorations.

"Are you still in the army then, sir?" Harry asked.

"Oh yes, I am on the general staff. You are not going to get rid of me as easy as that, for these few scars. As a matter of fact it's pretty certain I shall be going over to France with G.H.Q, unfortunately I won't be playing any real active service parts, but at least I shall be there egging you lot on. Mother's family has plenty of influence in the war office. Her brother is also in the war cabinet. So I may see you over there." As expected, the conversation turned to war. It was getting dark when Harry looked at the clock.

"Well we really must go now, sir, it's been so interesting, with a bit of luck we may meet in France." He held out his hand, "Goodbye, sir and good luck."

He shook hands with the rest of them.

508

"Don't worry, Williams, I will keep an eye on that little girl of yours, she's very pretty."

He looked at Kathy. "So is her mother." He led them downstairs.

"Sorry I can't take you to the station, petrol, you know, it's all strictly rationed." He waited at the door of the conservatory till they were completely out of sight.

CHAPTER 46

Hand in hand the four of them walked slowly back from the mansion. It was a typical warm spring day, the trees eager to burst their buds, the hedges alive with daffodils and bluebells trying to break through the soil. While Charlie and Kath broke away and headed towards the woods, Harry and Kim stopped at the gate watching a flock of sheep with the young lambs springing innocently over the grass. Harry, rested one elbow on the wooden gate, and put his other arm round Kim's shoulder. He sucked on the white stem of a blade of grass like some old farmer. The silence was broken only by the birds amongst the woods.

"I always feel sorry for anyone not born an Englishman. There is no sight like the English countryside in the spring. I think that is what I missed the most while I was abroad. Try looking at oceans of sand for a few months and then you really appreciate this."

Harry took her hand and steered her towards the woods, in the opposite direction from Kathy and Charlie.

The sunlight filtered through the trees the shadows in a million fragments, the birds flittered through the woods breaking into a thousand sounds. Kim rested her head on his shoulder.

"God, Harry, if only this moment could last forever."

He swung round to face her and they both sank to their knees without uttering another word. A young rabbit scurried away, time overtook their emotions. They heard the soft sound of a train whistle in the distance shattering their dreams, Harry jumped up straight and holding Kim's hands pulled her gently to her feet.

"Sorry, Kim, we must be on our way, that train will be returning in less than an hour's time."

Completely out of breath they ran into the pub from the side door and rushed upstairs to pack. Harry crammed what little kit he had into his small haversack while Kim neatly packed her small case. Rosie was laughing when she heard them rush downstairs.

"Don't worry, you two, the train will wait. When the train rounds the bend the driver will blow his whistle. Old Ted is outside, he will have a slow walk to the station and the driver will hang on for a few minutes. Where have you two been?" A kindly knowing glint in her eyes. "Kathy and Charlie returned half an hour since. They are upstairs."

Harry's eyes met Kim's, there was a slight flash of amusement between them, for a few minutes ago they had both been upstairs and Kath's door was firmly closed and the room deadly quiet.

510

It was a tearful parting, Rosie and her husband were treating them like the children they never had. To soften the blow Rosie had prepared each a parcel for them, eggs, bacon, thick slices of home cooked boiled ham, but the most wonderful thing, a bag of onions which were in short supply in war torn Britain, so short they became a complete luxury.

They heard the sickening warning whistle as the train took the bend. Rosie hugged each one in turn and made them promise to return as soon as possible.

"You just try and keep us away," Charlie said as he planted a firm kiss on her lips. "If I had met you twenty years ago, Rosie, Kathy wouldn't have stood a chance."

"Twenty years ago your mother was still changing your nappies no doubt, now go on the lot of you."

Kim and Kathy hugged old Ernie, he gave a coarse wheezy laugh and gently patted their heads.

The train screeched to a halt filling the small sidings with steam, a couple of carriage doors opened then slammed shut. The guard threw a couple of boxes and sacks from his van, then blew his whistle. A few quick bursts of steam and the train slowly chugged away, they waved to Ted as the train left the station.

Emotions ran high for the first half hour of the journey, neither of them spoke a word. Kim, always emotional and not in the least comforted by Harry's arm round her shoulders, sobbed inwardly, her eyes moist with tears. Kath reached over and put her hand on Kim's knee.

"Did you enjoy the weekend, Kim?"

Kim turned towards Harry, their eyes met, dancing with amusement, as if they were sharing a secret unknown to the other two, her voice lowered to a subdued whisper, "I will never forget it as long as I live. That four poster bed, it was too wonderful for words."

Her eyes still retaining that jovial look, she grasped Harry's hand and wanted to shout from the top of her voice how much she loved him, but was much too modest to even whisper the words. How she wished that Kathy and Charlie had found another compartment in the empty train, then she could have had Harry to herself for another hour at least.

The remainder of the journey was uneventful, when they changed trains they had to wait for nearly an hour and when it eventually arrived it was packed with troops returning from a weekend's leave, mainly men from their own Division. There was a group from their unit, including the R.S.M.

"Evening Jackson, Williams. Still not wearing your hat, Williams?"

Charlie removed his hat from the shoulder straps and adjusted it on his head, a slight sarcastic smile towards the R.S.M. silently saying, 'Is that better'. The R.S.M. like the rest of the men cast an envious eye over the two girls, and no doubt wondering what two perverts were doing with two nice girls like that.

There was a mad rush for the doors in an already packed train. They eased themselves along the corridor.

"Come on, lads, make room for two young ladies, move over, Smedley, or stand up."

"Piss off, Charlie." Smedley didn't look up from the book 'Men Only' he was deeply engrossed in, his next door neighbour nudged him and his eyes fell on Kim. "Sorry, Charlie, I thought you was having me on." He stood up and held his hand towards Kim, she sat down trying to avert her eyes from the rest of the men in the crowded compartment who were staring at her unashamedly.

"Did you get on the train in London, Todd?" He was sitting next to Smedley, he nodded. "Well, it's about time you stood up and let the lady sit down."

He stood up and Kath took his seat. The men in the compartment stamped their cigarettes into the floor. Collins and Blakney sat opposite the girls trying their hardest not to look at the girls' knees. Collins attempted to read a magazine averting his eyes, occasionally they would slip back, Charlie was standing by the door.

"Look, Collins stop trying to shufti my wife's knees." Collins became confused and stammered, "Sorry, Charlie, no offence, I couldn't help it." He stood up. "You had better have my seat, Charlie."

Charlie took the seat with a grin. Anderson was in the next seat, Charlie nudged him, "I think you had better let Harry have that seat. That's his missus opposite and you know what a jealous sod Harry is."

Anderson shuffled in his seat, red with embarrassment, then stood up and let Harry sit down, thankful the girls were with them, for if they had been on their own the men in the train would have thrown them through the window. Kath's eyes when they met Charlie's were full of good humoured anger as much to say, 'You just wait Charlie Williams till I get you alone.' He winked at her and she just melted.

Harry was absorbed in the magazine he bought at the last station for he was sure if he just looked at Kim he would burst out laughing.

"Charlie Williams, I was never so embarrassed, I felt so sorry for those two men."

512

Charlie answered with a deep laugh.

"You had a seat, didn't you? And don't worry, they will have forgotten it by now. Don't rush to the barriers yet, there will be panic stations in a few minutes. Just bide your time and see what happens."

They moved closer to the exit, a crowd was gathering. The first man went through jerking his thumb over his shoulder, the ticket collector tried to hold him, then jerked his thumb towards a kiosk, "Wait there." The second man went through and also jerked his thumb over his shoulder, this happened a dozen times - "Travelling on group warrant". This was repeated on every occasion. The twelfth man went through and gave the man just one ticket.

"What about the others?"

The man, a corporal shook his head in mock surprise, "What others?"

The collector looked round and where the dozen men had been standing was just a blank space with a dozen men running in all directions. The corporal shook his head, a feigned look of astonishment on his face.

"They are sod all to do with me, mate, never seen them before."

The old collector yelled across the station for the station master. He must have been prepared for this, he came running and leaned against the gate.

"They have done it again, station master. They are all over the place. I will be glad when they have all pissed off to France or wherever they are supposed to be going. Let's have a bit of peace and quiet. I thought you said the military police would be here when the London train arrived?"

"They were, Maurice, but the train was late and they couldn't stay all night. Don't worry they will be gone shortly then you can get back to the old routine."

"Thank God for that, when this is lot is over I can get down to my retirement and pension, I should have retired three years ago if it hadn't been for this bloody war. I was in the last sodding do, never bargained for this." While he was talking his eyes never left the remaining crowd and watched them like a hawk as they filed through one at a time. "Who told you, station master, they would be away shortly?"

The station master rubbed his index finger up the side of his nose in knowing gesture as if he had been let into a military secret of enormous proportions. "Don't worry too much about that, Maurice, they won't be with us long."

Harry was alongside the exit gate and heard every word that was spoken and took notice. When the troops moved south, as they would surely do, it would be a mammoth task involving several divisions and would take some organising, something that couldn't be done over night. It had taken several long trains to move their own division from Glasgow to the east coast and apart from the British divisions there would be the Americans to contend with, so it stood to reason if anyone should know, it would be the railways.

When they arrived at Kim's house, Harry was relieved to see that her father was out with the Home Guard although there was no need to worry. Carol welcomed them with open arms, firing question after question, "Did you enjoy yourselves?" and "How was Charlie's little girl?"

"She is adorable, how her mother could have abandoned her I should never understand. Charlie adores her, so much so, that I am certain if Charlie had to decide between Kath and his daughter, as Dad would say, Kathy would be a non starter."

She told her mother all that happened and when they took Amanda to church and she kissed Roger's tomb.

"And that pub, Mother, so very old with everything smelling of beer and furniture polish." While she talked her eyes sparkled with excitement, she soon got carried away. "There was this large four poster bed in the bedroom, it was the most beautiful thing you could lay your eyes on and Kathy insisted we use it for the night." Then she realised what she had said, blushing a deep crimson to the roots of her hair, her hand went to her mouth. She attempted to continue the conversation but words seemed to stick in her throat. She stammered and stuttered, saved only by her mother's deep understanding, for she loved Harry as if he were her own son. In her eyes he could do nothing wrong and watching Kim's utter confusion she bit her bottom lip to prevent herself from smiling. There was only one thing for Kim to do to relieve the tension, she gave her mother the parcel of food Rosie had sent her.

They were having tea and Harry just sat down at the piano when there was a loud banging on the door and then the door pushed open and Charlie and Kath walked in.

"Come on, Harry, we have to make that lorry at ten, then I have to take you on my motor bike to your flea pit."

While Charlie walked on Kim took her farewells at the gate.

"Thank you, Harry, for the most wonderful weekend I have ever had. Will I see you tomorrow?"

"Yes if your father doesn't kick me out. It's a bloody good job you have an understanding mother. You very nearly put your foot in it when we arrived back, I mean, telling your mother about the four poster."

Kim gave a little laugh.

"She isn't a fool, Harry, she knew that Charlie and Kath slept together, it wouldn't take her long to guess the rest. One day I will let you into a secret that I have never told anyone, not even Kath." To stop further questions she kissed him full on his lips, turned and ran indoors, still smiling.

He caught up with Charlie, who clapped his hand on Harry's shoulder.

"Now can you believe it, Harry? Aren't they the loveliest girls you ever did see? For the first time since I enlisted I felt like deserting. What a time we had. And that Rosie and Ernie, aren't they the greatest? I don't know how that Ernie keeps it up with his lungs full of mustard gas."

But Harry was in a world of his own.

"Charlie, it's all a dream. I will wake up at any minute and find myself in some bloody slit trench in the middle of the desert. I could hardly believe it when Kim practically told her we slept together and her mother didn't say a bloody word, she just smiled. I am sure if Kim told her she was in the family way she would jump for joy. She fussed over us like a mother hen with her chicks. I was pleased her father wasn't in when we returned, I could never have faced both of them at once. Look, Charlie, I would never say this to anyone but you, so don't breath a word. Just before we left the pub we were alone in the bedroom, I know you were in the other bedroom, I never took precautions, I am bloody worried."

Charlie laughed as he usually did when Harry had a serious look on his face, but he had never seen it so serious as now.

"I thought you couldn't conceive the first time." Pausing steadily then "She was a virgin, wasn't she?"

"Of course she was, and that's a fallacy about virgins and the first time. It wasn't the first time, I used something before but there is only three in a packet and I wasn't sure if I was going to use them."

"Poor old Kim, you certainly put her through her paces, I shouldn't worry too much if I were you, Harry."

"It's no joke, Charlie. I will be worried for the next few weeks, then how the hell am I going to ask her if she is alright. I bet I don't sleep tonight, it is a lot of crap about the first time, a woman can conceive at any time although there is a safe time during the month, let's hope it was this weekend. I know we have had some women but this time it was different. Kim isn't like our usual pick ups, and Kathy, too. How could we possibly compare them to anyone else we have been with?"

"Francesca wasn't so bad and I notice you didn't refuse her mate's advances. I didn't mind Francesca one bit, although I have to agree she is nothing compared to Kathy. I know when my divorce is through and this war is over you won't see my arse for dust, King's Lynn first stop. I didn't tell you, did I? Kath is looking for a house, I hope to hear about my divorce at any time now."

Harry knew better, divorce takes a very long time even with a decent lawyer acting for you, but in the army and away most of the time it will take years.

"Stop disillusioning yourself, Charlie, don't rush things, once you get the divorce you have to wait twelve months or more before you tie the knot. I made it clear to Kim, there is no chance of marriage till I am safely back home and this bastard war is over."

The leave lorry was full as usual and hardly anyone spoke, some too drunk to speak, others still smarting after leaving their nearest and dearest after a weekend's leave. The lorry weaved and swerved along the narrow country lanes, deserted of all traffic and the driver doing his best to break all records to get back to his warm bed. Charlie borrowed a motor cycle and took Harry back to his own billet. The evenings were still cold and the sergeant had detailed someone to light Harry's stove, the tiny room was like a hot house.

"Bloody hell," Charlie gasped. "What the hell did you do for that sergeant? He certainly looks after you."

Harry smiled. The sergeant was eating out of Harry's hand, but there was no way he would divulge the sergeant's secret, not to Charlie or anyone else. "I just look after him, Charlie, a few hard to get tablets for his old lady and something for his stinking feet, they sweat blind," he lied.

"Pity you couldn't do something for that Sykes' pimply face. It's worse since we arrived home. I could tolerate him if he were more pleasant, but his personality matches those repulsive spots."

"There is only one sure way to get them of his face, cut his bleeding head off."

"Don't tempt me, Harry." He sipped at the freshly made tea, then spat the tea leaves against the red hot stove, "I must be getting off, Harry, it must be at least 2 am."

Driving to King's Lynn the next morning Harry noticed there were heavy troop movements. The vehicles wore divisional signs Harry wasn't familiar with. It looked like an Infantry division, apart from a few Bren carriers there was no armour. It was easy to tell by their attitude, singing and shouting and the slogans scrawled on the sides of their vehicles that the impending invasion was the first time in action for most of them. He waved and some bright spark shouted, "You're going the wrong way, mate!"

Harry poked his head through the side panel and retaliated with, "No, you are," at the top of his voice.

Kim and her mother also remarked on the unusual heavy amount of troop movements, real concern in Kim's voice when she asked, "Have you heard anything yet, Harry?"

And dreading the answer, for she knew the happiest days of her life were drawing slowly to a close. For every time she saw Harry she wondered if it would be the last day. Harry just shrugged his shoulders.

To soften the blow he said, "I doubt if it will be for a few weeks yet, it's just the first week in May, they will wait till the weather is more settled, I am not anxious to go out but the sooner we go the faster we return home."

On his return to his billet, the sergeant informed him he had to report back to his own unit for a three day exercise. The sergeant allowed him to use the phone.

"That's too bad, Harry, Kathy phoned Rosie this evening to make arrangements for the weekend. Will Charlie be with you?"

"Yes, hasn't he told you yet? I think he has a bit of difficulty getting into that phone box near his camp, there's always a queue or the damn thing has broken down. Tell the girls not to worry. If we get back in time we'll meet them at the station, if we are not there tell them to go ahead. Charlie and me will come down on my ambulance. Cheerio Marti, and thanks for everything. You know what I mean." Harry was convinced that Marti had a hand in the previous weekend. Not as if Carol needed much coaxing, Marti just made the going easier.

Fortunately the weather was warmer for the whole three days, the usual boring exercises, setting up dressing stations, handling mock casualties, advancing or retreating, whichever took the C.O's fancy, all and sundry heaved a sigh of relief when it finally came to an end.

"What a load of bullshit, sir," Charlie's final comment to the R.S.M.

"You may have done it for real, Williams, very many times, but remember we do have new members in the unit who at this moment can't tell their arses from their elbows. Believe me, Williams, I didn't ask for this and I certainly didn't enjoy it. Unfortunately it has to be done. By the way, where is that mate of yours? Find him and tell him you can both have a week's embarkation leave starting next week. I shall be sending a man to take over his duties."

"That will please him, sir, he's bored to tears out there on his own."

"Bullshit, Williams, it's the cushiest job in the unit. Don't you think I am aware where he pisses off to about ten every morning after he's finished his sick parade? The way you two put it around I find it hard to believe you have the strength to lift any stretchers, and those nice girls you were with on the railway station, what the hell they see in you two perverts I shall never know."

"It's my fatal charm, sir, I find women cannot resist me."

The R.S.M. shook his head in disgust and walked away. Charlie joined Harry sitting round a petrol fire with half a dozen men. He broke the news to him.

"We didn't have all this bullshit at Dunkirk," one of the new members of the unit was grumbling. "No time, pick up the wounded, down to the beach and back for more," he boasted.

"Well believe me it will be the same on the beaches when we land, but once off the beachhead we have to create a line of evacuation for the wounded. Believe it or not this unit has seen plenty of action." A sergeant, who had served with the unit since its formation, spoke up.

"What, playing sand castles in the desert? Nothing like Dunkirk, mate."

Charlie who had sat down next to Harry while the man boasted, looked at the man, red with temper as his Jewish friend Solly's face flashed before his eyes, together with Mundy and a dozen of his other friends.

"Sand castles, you prick! The only sand castles we made were on our mates graves and believe me there were plenty of those." He stood up. "Come on, Harry, before I hit the stupid bastard."

The exercise finished on the Friday night, both exhausted, much too tired to shower and drive to King's Lynn, Charlie rang them and promised to meet them at the station at nine the next morning.

Harry picked up his pass, pay and railway warrant with the hope that he could convince Kim to spend a few days in London. She was thrilled at the prospect, but when they arrived at the village any planning went to the wind, for the village and roads leading to it for miles were packed with troops and army vehicles. In the field directly behind the church a regiment of artillery was camped, lines and lines of twenty-five pounders. Under the trees that lined the roads, were army troop carriers all covered with camouflage nets, and crowds of men standing round fires brewing up.

"It's been like this for a few days. Regiments come, then overnight they pack up and leave and the next day another convoy takes its place. Where are they going, Charlie?" Rosie asked.

"I suppose they are heading for the south coast."

"It's been hell here, as soon as the bar opens they crowd in, I have run out of beer several times and I haven't a cigarette in the place. They are all fighting to get to the bar."

Opening time and Charlie organised the drinking. Since war started Rosie had locked the door into the bar because of the blackout regulations. Charlie opened it and Rosie made a makeshift curtain from an old blanket.

"You, Rosie, Kim and Kathy serve behind the bar. Call a couple of N.C.O.s in, Harry. They can stand at the door and let the men in half a dozen at a time, they can take their drinks outside. Harry, help Ernie to fetch up a few empty crates and put them outside. As soon as the men are served I will let them out and see no one pushes in, a kind of one way system, they will all be served and no panic stations."

The first two Harry let in were a staff sergeant and a sergeant major.

"Look, son," the R.S.M. protested, "I object to being ordered about by a private. I have this crown on my arm, I will do the organising."

"Not in my pub, you won't!" Charlie intervened, winking his eye at Rosie. "Frankly I couldn't care less if the crown was on your bloody head, see the men come in orderly and you will be kept in booze all night, if you don't like it, give him a pint, Rosie, then get outside." He fell silent and for the first time since the troops arrived they had an orderly pub. After a while Harry sat down at the piano while Charlie enjoyed throwing the orders about.

Rows of pints lined up along the piano, men asking for their favourite tunes and plied him with pints, Charlie passed them down to the 'door orderlies' as he liked to call them and the sergeant major was knocking them back as fast as they were lined up. After his twelfth pint he was spending his time walking unsteadily to the toilet door. He finally collapsed in a sitting position a stupid smirk on his face. Charlie dragged him to one side while another N.C.O. seeing he was getting free beer joyfully took his place. The one way system worked perfectly, there were one or two minor squabbles but as soon as Charlie arrived and they saw the size of him, no one wanted to argue.

"Not much beer left, Charlie!" Rosie shouted over the din.

"Ration them to half a pint each, Rosie, then if you run out of that, serve that wine of yours, one glass of that and they will storm the beaches alone."

Kim and Kathy were enjoying themselves. It was their first time as barmaids. Several times they were chatted up and the bolder ones asked to meet them in the woods but as soon as Kathy nodded towards Charlie and said, "Ask my husband." It always did the trick.

Closing time came around and they had one barrel left, not sufficient for the Sunday opening.

"I know it's Sunday tomorrow, Rosie, see if we can get in touch with the brewery, tell them we have a crisis on our hands."

The sergeant major, legless with a stupid grin on his face remained sitting with his back to the wall, with an untouched pint of beer by his side. Two of his own men carried him out. The next morning he was found stripped naked with a ribbon round his penis, bound to a yew tree in the churchyard, saved only by the parson a few minutes before morning service. Quick thinking and with no other clothing available the parson gave him one of his own surplices, then quickly pushed him in with the choir just as the first congregation arrived, but with his early morning shadow and drink bleary eyes he stood out like a pineapple in a bowl of cherries - much to the amusement of the crowded church filled to its capacity by the influx of the sergeant major's own troops.

Once again, the girls insisted that they go to church. Charlie was informed that the captain and his mother would bring Amanda from the home. She greeted them with a wave from the horse drawn carriage. She stayed with them for the day and in the evening the captain collected her on a large black stallion. She gave Charlie a cursory wave as he stood with the others outside the pub, she shouted "bye" then turned to the captain and ordered, "Make him gallop."

Harry was unable to contact Kim or her family for two days, for as soon as he returned to his unit he was, with Charlie, posted on a two day course. The only phone box he found was out of order, so he was unable to contact Marti to pass on a message.

He had been informed officially that he would be travelling with two hundred infantrymen on an old tramp steamer, acting as their sole medical orderly. From the steamer, the infantryman would be landed on the beach from small landing assault craft and were now on a two day course learning to negotiate scramble nets. The nets had been hung from a high brick wall, specially built for the job with a rail along the top similar to a ship rail. But on the second day his medical services were needed. One of the infantrymen had caught his equipment on the netting and fallen twenty feet to the concrete ground below with his leg tucked under him, breaking his femur.

"Ain't that just like you, Clegge?"

The marine sergeant instructor bellowed down the injured man's ear, his mouth just a few inches from the unfortunate man's face.

"I've told you till I'm blue in the face. Over the rail, get a firm footing on the net, then grab the net with one hand, thrust your arse out and grab the net with your other hand. Thrust the arse out more then slowly descend." He looked round at the anxious faces and bellowed, "Arse well out!" He glared at the men to see if it had sunk in. "Well out - leaving your equipment free from the rope." He pointed to the man writhing in agony on the floor, and said with complete indifference, "Medic, take care of this twot." Then he carried on training, bellowing at the top of his voice.

Harry splinted the man with Charlie's help, then with the help of two men from the squad lifted him into the ambulance. It was also Harry's chance to contact Kim and he asked the nurse at reception at the local hospital if he could use the phone. She nodded and pointed to the phone on her desk and, with Charlie standing close behind him, Harry managed to get through to Marti straight away. He explained the situation.

"Be back on Friday, Marti. I saw the sergeant at my unit and he said we would be alright to get away for this weekend. Let Kim and Kath know we'll be going down to Rosie's. So, if you don't mind would you give Rosie a ring and let her know we'll be down?" He then handed the phone to Charlie.

There was no one using the scramble nets. The sergeant had them form up in a three-sided square. Harry guessed it was a lecture. The sergeant was bellowing at the top of his voice, treating the N.C.O.s and ranks alike, but taking into account the size of the man no one dare argue.

"You stupid lot of bastards," he bawled, "I've told you again and again, over the rail, get a footing on the net then grab the net with the other hand, thrusting your ring piece out... Then, just for starters, come down the net slowly, we can speed it up once you've mastered the art of descending. For at the end of two days you'll be down that net faster than if you had a rattlesnake down your pants. You'll be down in one minute flat, and by one minute I mean fifty-five seconds not one minute and five seconds. IS THAT UNDERSTOOD?"

He stared at the parade of blank faces and then to Harry's surprise sank to his knees. His mood changed and his voice dropped to a loud whisper. He clasped his hands together as if in prayer, and piously gazed skywards.

"Oh God, Oh Lord Jesus," he whispered, "thank you, thank you... " He shook his head. "So you do remember me at last, Lord? I was that lad Ronnie that prayed to you when I was ten years old. My daddy had bought me a large box of soldiers, Lord. I loved those little lead soldiers, Lord. I lived in Rosemary Street at the time, dear Lord. Then tragedy struck, Lord. I lost those soldiers. I think it was the little bastard Nigel Smith from Emily Street that nicked them. I prayed to you for three days and three nights. But, Lord," he shook his head slowly from side to side, and real tears rolled down the marine sergeant's face, "I never found them, Lord. I thought you had forsaken me. But after all those years, Lord, you finally managed to find them for me, and I thank you from the bottom of my heart. All I want to know now, Lord, is why have you made them so FUCKING STUPID?"

He rose to his feet, brushed the knees of his trousers with his hand, took a large handkerchief from his pocket, blew his nose, and wiped his eyes as if nothing unusual had happened. Then he bellowed at the top of his voice, "Right, let's see you up there and over those ropes, and God help any man that doesn't stick his arse out!"

The parade was stunned. Silently, the men looked at each other. Some shrugged their shoulders, others looking quite dumbfounded, but all remained speechless except for one man much braver than the rest who shouted, "It's alright for you, sarge, you're a marine, and it's common knowledge that you marines stick out your ring pieces for the sailors aboard ship."

The words had hardly left the man's mouth before he regretted his remarks. The sergeant's eyes stood out like a patient terminally ill with thyroid trouble. His face turned a pale plush red, deepening gradually to crimson. He crooked his forefinger at

522

the culprit, and without a word pointed to a spot on the ground less than three feet away. The man slunk forward, and the sergeant pointed to another man carrying a bren gun.

"Go and swap arms with your comrade out there, that one with a wide grin like a Cheshire cat. You give him your rifle then both return here. So, you think all marines are beef bandits, eh? And you, you thought it a huge joke? Well, take up your arms, raise them above your head and run around that ambulance three times. Now, the ambulance is a hundred yards away - that should make it six hundred yards. You can have a rest then by going up onto the balcony and down that net. Then, after that you can repeat the performance until I tell you when to stop or you drop down exhausted. Now," he addressed the parade, "any more tomfoolery and you lot will be doubling round the ambulance."

His voice took on a more serious note. "Right, gents, let's start again. Believe me, you'll get down those nets in less than a minute or die in the attempt. You haven't been sent here because you're bored. This training session could save your lives. You'll be on the initial landing, and that ship of yours will be under constant shelling, so as soon as you can get into those assault craft the safer you'll be, for an assault craft isn't such a large target as the ship you go over in. Now come on, no more sodding about, let's have a little co-operation all round."

By the end of the two days, the men could get down those nets like well trained commandos in well below a minute. The sergeant stood at the gate of the camp as the convoy of lorries came by, and as each vehicle passed him he was greeted with a shower of good natured abuse. For although it had been a hard couple of days they realised it was for their own benefit.

As soon as Harry arrived back at his own unit his sergeant told him he could get away immediately as his relief was staying there till the Monday.

"Better make the best of it, Harry. Doubt if there'll be many more weekends." And it was apparent he knew more but changed the subject. "How did the training go down, Harry?"

Harry laughed and told him about the antics of the marine sergeant.

"Yes, Harry, I know that bastard," nodded the sergeant, "big burly sod with a row of medals. Commando. He's been here a few times. Mad as a bleeding March hare. He was in our mess a few weeks back. I've never seen a man knock so much back. He must have guzzled a full bottle of whisky and ten pints, then he gets on the table and recites the filthiest rendition of Eskimo Nell I've ever heard."

Harry realised the sergeant may have heard something so he pressed home. "How long, sarge, before we push off?"

The sergeant glanced nervously over his shoulder and lowered his voice. Of all the men in the unit Harry was the only man the sergeant would confide in.

"Not more than a couple of weeks, Harry," he whispered. "All vehicles have to be prepared by the end of the month, so at a guess I should say about June the fourth, or thereabouts. But not a bloody word, Harry, not even to Kim. If this should get out they will have my fucking guts for garters. You're the only man I trust, Harry, so keep it to yourself."

At last he had something to go on after all the rumours that were doing the rounds had sent him into a spin. This could be his last weekend together with Kim. He would try and get through to Marti and see if they could get away that night. He rang her from the sergeant's office, and, by a fluke Kim answered.

"Can you get Kathy away tonight, Kim?" Harry asked. "I'm off till Monday. I can ring Charlie and let him know."

"Don't bother, he's just phoned. He can't get away till morning. Still you and I could go with Kathy then Charlie can come up to us in the morning."

"Great. If we can catch the four-thirty from Lynn it means we'll have an hour to wait at the next connection."

"That'll be alright, Harry, you were lucky getting me now, we finish at three today. So I'll have to move. Just hang on there while I talk to Kathy." She returned a few minutes later. "Kath's in the bath," she said. "She says she would love to come down with us. Will you let Charlie know?"

They met at their usual place at the railway station and were soon on their way, a compartment to themselves.

"Charlie was upset he couldn't get away," Harry apologised. "He got caught for guard duty and no one would change with him, but he said he'll be on the first available train tomorrow."

"How did the training go Harry?" Kath asked. "Enjoy yourself?"

"You must be joking!" Then Harry told them about the marine sergeant and how he'd prayed in the middle of the training ground, and before they reached the other station Harry had them roaring with laughter. Kim asked him what he was supposed to be doing on the course. Harry evaded the question. This made the two of them suspicious and off-handedly he said, "Something to do with landing craft." They didn't pursue the matter.

The three of them were pleased when the journey came to an end for it seemed to have taken ages. Then, a girl on each arm, Harry walked proudly from the station under the admiring glances of a company of engineers who were unloading stores from the train, for once again soldiers crowded the village.

"It's been like this all week, Harry," the landlady greeted them. "We've had three convoys through here since Sunday, and we have several camps around here. It's not a bit of good opening the pub, for no sooner do the brewery send down a truck load of beer than it's sold in a couple of hours. There was almost a riot Wednesday, and we can't get enough cigarettes for love nor money. I had to ration them to one packet each. I think they were trying to stock up before they go." Rosie frowned. "Where the hell is Charlie?"

"Got stuck for guard duty. He'll be here in the morning," Harry answered. "Will you be opening tonight, ma?"

"Just for a couple of hours. We did manage to get a couple of extra barrels." She changed the subject. "I suppose you and Kim will want the four poster tonight then?" She laughed as she said it, for she knew that Kim envied her cousin sleeping in that bed.

Before Harry could answer, Kim said "Yes, please," her voice almost childish. Kathy laughed and just nodded her head.

Rosie was right. Well before the official closing time she'd sold out of beer and put out the lights. If the men saw the lights on they would forever be banging on the door to let them in.

"We'll clean up in the morning," she said.

They sat talking in the kitchen for another hour, but it was inevitable the conversation would turn to the war.

"This place looked more like Aldershot during the last war," Rosie said and Ernie nodded his head in agreement.

"Those four Red Caps come in here most nights. They help to keep the place in order. Must be another convoy due during the night they're on duty. Where the hell are they all going, Harry?"

"I suppose towards the south coast. This is happening all over the country, Rosie. You can't move for the Yanks around Norfolk, can you, Kim?"

Kim shook her head.

"The only good thing about it, Rosie, is that it'll soon be over. I might come and get a job here as a barman. Any chance?"

"I can't see bar work suiting you, Harry, but you don't know how near the truth you are. Me and Ernie has had quite enough, and Ernie's chest isn't getting any better. Now, I don't want to offend either you or Charlie, but I had a talk with madam up at the big house and we're going to ask you, Kathy, and Charlie, if you would like to take over. This is a grand village and all the people like the four of you. But honestly, Harry, I think Charlie would be more suited to taking the pub over. What do you think, Kathy?"

525

But Kathy just stared at her speechless. "I just don't know what to say," she stammered. "Ma, you just don't know how the idea appeals to me, and Charlie would be over the moon. He can't get down here quick enough." She turned to Kim, who looked as delighted as she did. "You'll be able to come here as often as you please, you and Harry, and every time you visit we'll relinquish that four poster bed for you."

Harry was overjoyed. "That's a great idea. You're right, Rosie, running a pub is out of the question as far as I'm concerned. It doesn't appeal to me at all. And don't think I'm saying that to make you feel at ease. No - when I finish with the army I want to take a course and become a chiropodist. But tell me, Rosie, where the hell are you going to live?"

"Don't worry about that. There's a small cottage up near the house. Madam said we can have it as long as we want. My Ernie can sit in the garden all day if he wants to. And you can visit us as often as you like, and that also goes for you girls when Charlie and Harry are away. Don't you stop visiting. Bring your parents down any time you like." Rosie yawned a signal for bedtime. She kissed the three of them. Kim and Kath kissed old Ernie and he laughed, his chest sounding like a deflating tyre.

Harry held Kim's hand as he led her to the bedroom and the four poster. "I wonder if we'll see old Roger tonight, Kim?"

Kim shuddered.

"Please don't joke about it, Harry." She rubbed her arms and Harry held her tight.

"You're not frightened are you, Kim? Surely you don't believe that rubbish about seeing Roger's ghost?"

"No, I'm not in the least frightened but, yes, I do believe Rosie. I believe if a person loves a place so much it stands to reason his presence can be felt. Or if you love someone so dearly they never leave you. I often feel that our John is standing in our front room. It doesn't frighten me one bit. I love him and never done him no harm. It's the same with Roger. He must have loved this pub. Rosie feels his presence everywhere and it doesn't frighten her. Why should it frighten me?"

"Well, I must say you are a cool customer, Kim. Any girl your age, and even older, would be scared to death. I'm certainly going to marry a level headed woman." He held her tightly. "I want to be serious now, Kim. If anything should happen to me, don't mourn too much and should you meet someone that will be good to you and you can show him as much love and affection as you have shown me, for heaven's sake, marry him."

"Harry, I could never marry another man. Our love is sacred. Do you honestly think I could share my bed and love with any other man? Should you not come back and I pray to God every night to keep you safe, you've given me the kind of love that'll last me a lifetime. They say time dims the memories - but, Harry, I shall always remember you as we are now, sharing this lovely four poster. But don't talk like that, let's get to bed."

Next morning Kath went to pick up Amanda and they waited for the train. Harry helped the brewery man to unload the barrels of beer and store them in the cellar.

"I should have packed this lark in years ago, you know Harry. I only kept going for Rosie's sake. She loves it here. I doubt if she would have ever left if it weren't for Charlie taking over. Do you reckon he will take over the pub?"

"You joking, Ernie? Ever seen a rat refuse a lump of cheese? Funny. Only the other day he was talking about a pub. You haven't been bribing him on the side have you, Ernie, you crafty old sod?"

Ernie made a supreme effort to laugh. But his chest failed him and wheezing and coughing he held his hand against the cellar wall. Harry brought forward the old backless chair Ernie kept down the cellar to him and made him sit down. "Take it easy, my old son," he said and gently patted Ernie's back to help him to breathe.

"That's that bloody mustard gas, Harry. I shall be alright shortly. Twenty-seven years it's been," he gasped, "and I would've ended it long ago if it hadn't been for my Rosie. You look out for yourself out there, Harry, it's not going to be any picnic. And, if they use gas when they get desperate and you should get your lungs full, shoot your bloody self, Harry. Don't suffer like me. Kim will soon get over it, lad." A theme he had repeated many times over the months.

That night, the pub full of beer, and the old piano going, turned out to be one of the best nights, except briefly when one local came in and protested that the locals 'wasn't getting any beer, just the soldiers.'

"Now bugger off, Tom Reddy," shouted Rosie, "you'll be having more than your share when these lads are on a hostile beach." She pulled a pint. "Now get that down you, Tom, you miserable old bugger, and let these lads get their drink down them."

There were quite a few of the soldiers at church the next morning and Amanda sat next to Roger's tomb kissing the cold stone every time she stood up on her chair. This amused the soldiers around her. The vicar blessed the troops and asked for a special prayer for the Allies, "Who would be taking on the stupendous task of driving the enemy from our front door."

527

And he also asked the congregation to pray for the airmen who would be watching over the invasion forces and the navy, escorting what would be the great Armada. At the word 'Armada,' Amanda stood on her chair and shouted, "Yes!" in the ultra quiet church, thinking the vicar had called out her name. Kim burst out laughing. Harry and Charlie were doing their damndest not to laugh and Kathy was trying to calm Amanda down, but ripples of laughter circled round the church, and Amanda having captured an audience, tried to struggle along to the vicar in his pulpit.

"Shows you up blind," Charlie said as he left the church hand in hand with Amanda and Kathy. He tried to apologise to the vicar.

"Don't worry, Charlie." It was 'Charlie' now, like the rest of the village who had welcomed the four of them into their tight-knit circle. "It brought a little relief into the sermon." He shook hands with Charlie. "Good luck son, be back with us soon."

While Kathy went for a long walk Charlie strolled up to the house. Madam wished to see him. He came out all smiles and after finding Harry, told him, "It's all fixed, Harry, Kathy and I will be taking over the pub when the war's over. So, come on, Harry, I want a machine gun on the front of the ambulance and a rear gunner to help finish the war quickly. Let's show them what we can do."

But neither Kim nor Kathy saw the funny side of his joke.

"You just be careful, Harry," Kim admonished him.

The departure was long and drawn out, for everyone had that feeling it would be a long time before they were together again. Rosie was crying openly, and sobbed on Harry's shoulder, "I shall miss you four, you're like the kids I never had." She crushed him against her ample bosom. "Take great care of yourselves you two. I know this pub'll never be the same without you. And you, Charlie..." She pulled him close to her. His tongue dropped out as if she was choking him, and he made believe he was gasping for breath. "That bloody table of mine you danced on with those damn hobnailed boots, you make sure you get back here and sand out those marks."

Then it was Kim's and Kath's turn. "Don't you two neglect us while they are away," Rosie said, trying to hide her feelings.

"Of course not, Ma. I shall be down nearly every week to see Amanda, and Kim will always come with me, won't you, Kim?"

Kim nodded her head. She couldn't answer, her shoulders going up and down as she sobbed silently, her eyes flooding with tears. Finally she managed to gasp out, "Yes, Ma," and threw her arms round Rosie's neck. "I love you, Ma, we all love you. Thanks for everything."

They hardly spoke on the return journey. Harry sat with his arm around Kim, brushing his lips across her soft hair. Kathy was laying across the seat with her head in Charlie's lap for the first part of the journey. But the second part turned out differently. The train to Lynn was crowded with troops returning from the weekend leave, most of them from their own division, and quite a few from their own unit. And of course the talk, much to their dismay was soon turned to the impending invasion.

"Alright you lot, cut it out. You know we're not supposed to be talking about troops movements," Charlie said. They were in a compartment filled with men from their own unit.

"We all know one another, Charlie," one man complained.

"That's not the point, Griffiths. This lady here," he pointed to Kathy, "is the late Mata Hari's daughter. And Kim here is her decoder and wireless operator. Right. Joke over, now cut it out." He would have loved to have added, "in future keep your bloody mouth shut." But to Harry's relief silence remained supreme for the remainder of the journey.

There was the same mad rush for the barrier as there was every Sunday night, but the old ticket collector was waiting.

"Take it easy, lads, you're not going on leave you're returning, so what's the bloody rush? One at a time." He looked round at the four Red Caps standing near, making sure he had reinforcements in case they pulled off the old warrant gag.

Charlie and Harry, with the two girls, waited for the crush to ease down. It was then Kathy realised how popular the boys were with the division, for they must have said cheerio to at least fifty men, several stopping for a chat.

It was past midnight when Harry left Kim. The farewells were well drawn out, Kim lingering at the door with him. He should have been at the lorry pick up at ten, but rightly guessed with so much troop movement on the roads he would soon get a lift.

"We haven't heard anything yet, Kim. They usually place us on forty-eight hours stand by when we move off. Then after that it's twenty-four hour stand by, so don't worry, you should see me here tomorrow." But Harry wasn't certain whether she believed him, or thought he was just softening the blow.

But he did manage to get away for another two nights. He was certain on the Wednesday that it would be the very last night he would make it. All day the unit was preparing to move off, and he was told by his parent unit to have his kit packed and stand by. But it was Carol that assumed he would be moving out. By this time she knew what his divisional sign was and had noticed columns of the divisional vehicles moving off.

"There was a large column of ambulances and several lorries going towards Cambridge, Harry," she said and he had to admit that he was on stand by and this could be his last night here.

"Oh, Harry, I am so sorry," Carol murmured. Kim burst into tears and Jack looking very worried said, "Harry, before you go there is something Carol and I would like to give you. It'll be a constant reminder of the happy hours we've spend together, here." He handed him a small square blue velvet box and Harry's hand trembled. He had a shrewd idea what it was. "You can open it, Harry," Jack coaxed.

Just as Harry thought, it was a large silver pocket watch suspended on a thick silver chain. He flipped it open, and inside the lid was some engraving, but he couldn't read the words. His eyes blurred over. He would have liked to have said, "Would you keep it for me till I return." But that would have defeated the object, for he realised why they had bought the watch. They had probably asked Kim her thoughts on a gift, and as she had told them about the nightly nine o'clock tryst and answered, 'a watch.' Well, a watch it was. The largest Harry had ever seen. He loved it straight away, but what would Charlie think? He wouldn't have a watch on the ambulance for, of all his stupid petty superstitions wearing a watch was the most stupid. But Harry recalled Charlie's words when first they'd met. "Every medic I've ever lost was wearing a watch. I hope you don't wear one, Harry." Well, he had one now and there was nothing he could do about it, so the best thing he could possibly do was to keep it tucked well away in his large webbing pack.

He shook hands with Jack then kissed Carol. "It's lovely. Every time I look at it I'll think of both of you and Kim. This has been more than a home to me."

Carol wiped a tear away. "Come on, Jack, let's get round to Marti's. We're playing cards tonight." Jack gave his wife a rather curious look. Then he looked at Kim and realised why she had said it.

"Oh, that's right," he hesitated, "we promised, didn't we?"

And so the night drew on with Kim alternating between crying and making love to Harry. "Life won't be the same until you return, Harry. I'll pray for you every night, love."

He wanted to say 'You prayed for your brother John every night, but he's lying in some lonely grave out in the desert.' Yet he settled for just saying, "At least we'll be together for a few minutes every night. When you do think of me, Kim, will you be in your bedroom? Then I can picture you lying there."

530

He waited for her parents to return before the last farewells, he didn't want to leave Kim alone. She was still crying when they stood at the doorstep and said goodbye to one another. Far down the street he turned back and still saw her standing in the doorway.

Fortunately he didn't have long to wait before he managed to hitch a lift on one of the lorries from his own unit. Charlie was heavily asleep when he went to rouse him, and the Nissen hut was in a mess, the men's kits already packed, for they would be leaving the next day.

"Get a motor bike and run me back, Charlie," Harry pleaded.

"You're a bloody nuisance, Harry, I was in a deep sleep then," Charlie grumbled as he slipped on his trousers. "I had a bit of a job with Kathy tonight. Her and Marti cried all evening and I was glad when I had to come back. I left there at eight, made some excuse I had to get back early. God, Harry, I hope this bloody job don't take long. I had a chat with the padre today. He said my divorce should take another twelve months. Fucking nuisance, isn't it?"

It was cold on the back of the motor bike, for Harry had no greatcoat. The sergeant had fixed him up with an electric ring in his room, so he made them both a cup of tea, and they sat talking for most of the remainder of the night.

"Heard the latest, Harry?" Charlie asked. "Carter is over the moon. You know he told us his wife is going into the air force? Well, it appears she met this chap, massive bloke, a gym instructor and they've both done a runner. Now Carter is running round like a cat with two backsides. He was thinking about sending the bloke a letter of sympathy, but thought better of it. 'Let the poor bugger suffer like I have for the past few years,' he said. He also said that if he could stop laughing he would feel sorry for the bloke."

"Any other news?"

"Yes, remember that chap you told me, you had to rush him to hospital, thought he had a brain tumour? Well, one of his officers came to the unit said he was alright now, being medically discharged but he came to thank you personally, said you saved his corporal's life. That pleased the old man."

"It pleased me as well, Charlie. It's very rare that we hear what's happened to them once they are out of our hands."

CHAPTER 48

Harry jumped up in bed. Someone was kicking at the door and it sounded urgent.

"Come in, it's open," he shouted from a sitting up position in his bed.

"Hello, Harry, get out of that flea pit, you should be ready to go by now, kit packed."

"What the bloody hell for, Carter? I haven't been told anything. Christ man, it isn't light yet. When I heard you kicking the door like that I thought someone had had an accident."

"You'll have an accident if you don't shift yourself. I have to get you down to Tilbury docks before noon. I took Foster and Lawson last night, they are on the same job as you. When I came round last night there was sod all about. I found the cook, and he hadn't the faintest idea where you were. Don't you read standing orders?"

Harry shrugged his shoulders and extracted himself from between the warm sheets.

"First I have heard about it, and you ain't getting me in that bloody truck till I have had my early morning cuppa. Fancy one yourself?"

"Don't talk crap, Harry. Ever seen me refuse a mug of char?"

Harry was thankful for that electric ring that Jack had given him some time ago, when the weather had become too warm to light a fire. While the kettle was boiling he washed and shaved.

"Make that bed up, Nick, fold the blankets. There's an old frying pan in the wardrobe and plenty of bacon and fresh eggs, we'd better have a meal before we leave."

Carter didn't bother to fold the blankets and threw them on a heap at the head of the bed.

"Where the hell did you get this bacon and eggs, Harry, and bread, where the hell did it all come from?"

"From the farm across the road, there should be a jug of fresh milk there, too."

"Bloody hell, Harry, you certainly live it up here, sure you haven't got a housemaid and butler, no wonder you don't want to leave here." Carter's voice carried a touch of envy.

"You are right there, Nick. The sergeant let me have that old ambulance when I arrived, I get down to the girlfriend's every night and most weekends. It's been almost six months of sheer heaven here."

"Yes, I saw you and Charlie at the railway station one Sunday night. Have you been screwing that little chick one, Harry? She's bloody gorgeous."

Harry wasn't pleased with Nick's off-handed manner and the way he talked about Kim.

"Nick, if you and I want to stay friends, please don't talk that way about Kim. She's an angel, and as soon as this lot's finished we are getting married."

"No offence, Harry mate, with the reputation you and Charlie have built up since you joined the unit, I never realised you could get serious." Carter realised he had blundered and turned the conversation in another direction, he sniffed the air.

"That bacon smells very good, Harry. What are you doing with the rest?"

"Help yourself, Nick, take that and the ham and those eggs."

The roads were crowded with military vehicles of every size and shape, and it didn't take a military genius to realise what was happening. And the same thing was being repeated all over the country, to assemble the largest invasion force the world has ever seen.

"It looks like it's going to be some show. I understand that you, Lawson and Foster will be on assault ships. Bleeding good luck to you, sooner you than me."

Harry just nodded, the journey was becoming tedious, never exceeding twenty-five miles an hour. Carter was well acquainted with the area, being a long distance driver at one time, and tried taking short cuts through the back lanes, but they were just as crowded and to make matters worse, all the sign posts had been removed at the start of hostilities. He got lost on two occasions. But nothing could dampen Carter's jovial spirits.

"I suppose you heard about the missus, Harry, joined the air force? Well, she pissed off with a P.T. instructor. She must have been too much for him, he gave himself up after three weeks, now he's in the glasshouse doing fifty six days. She has been confined to barracks for fourteen days. Unfair, Harry, she should have got the glasshouse and the instructor a medal as big as a dinner plate. I received a letter from her yesterday asking me to forgive her. She must be barmy, it was the biggest break I ever had. I stopped her allowance. I won't be going home after the war, so her father and brothers, as far as I am concerned can all go and get stuffed. I will be shacking up with that blonde land army girl, Harry, she's a corker."

"Yes I know, Carter, I have met her. Nice looking girl, too."

Harry never realised how big the docks were. Two Red Caps and a civilian policemen stood at the main gate and directed him to the right dock. Ships of all sizes lined the quays and all painted a dull wartime grey. He reported to the R.T.O., an old major with several rows of medals that stretched back to before the First War. Harry stood to attention and saluted.

"Is that all the kit you have, medic?"

"Yes, sir. I was told to report in battle order, my large pack and kit bag are still on the utility outside. He has to take them back to my main unit, I understand they will follow."

The major looked at the long list on his desk and stopped half way down the paper.

"Jackson, that's right. You are on the 'Major McClaren', she is the third ship along the quay. You are the medical orderly?"

"Yes, sir."

"Right then." He wrote something on the chit and handed it to him.

"Cut along, give this to the military policeman at the foot of the gangway. Have a nice trip and good luck."

Harry saluted and turned. The major gave him an admiring glance and no doubt wished he were a young man once more. For the major, like most of the old retired officers, who had served in India for years cursed their fate, for being too old when the war started to take an active part, and out of sympathy in most cases, finished up at railway stations and docks, anywhere where there was troop movements, to act as R.T.O.s.

Harry stood at the gangway and looked up at the ship.

"Rust bucket," he thought, "would be the more appropriate term." Patches of red rust like cancerous growths clung to the sheer sides of the ship and superstructure like lichen and moss clung to ancient tombstones in a churchyard.

Four derricks had been welded to the decks, and from each a flat bottomed assault craft hung. Harry rightly assumed that there would be another four on the other side. Handing the slip of paper the R.T.O. gave him, Harry asked the Red Cap, "Does she actually float?"

"Well, you will soon find out, won't you? No kit."

Harry shook his head, it was no good telling him it was an assault ship and none of the men would be carrying full pack, all would be in just battle order, but he sarcastically said, "My batman will be bringing it shortly." For, like Charlie, he hated the Red Caps.

As Harry climbed the steep gangway the Red Cap shouted after him, "You will be sailing tonight and the weather forecast is bloody awful."

The Red Cap laughed aloud and this only proved to Harry, what he had always thought about Red Caps, they were recruited for their sadistic tendencies.

Harry was greeted at the top of the gangway.

534

"Welcome aboard, I am the ship's chief steward, and medic. But don't worry, I am the only steward, we only carry a crew of twenty. I was a petty officer steward in the Royal Navy, but was invalided out two years before the war. One of my officers took pity on me and got me this job. His father owns the line, about twenty of these ships. But calling myself a chief steward allows me to wear a uniform with a couple of gold stripes and I can get my own back on some of my old oppos from the navy when I meet them ashore, and I often get a salute from the pongoes and airmen. The old man here kills himself when I go ashore in a officer's uniform." He was obviously anxious to put Harry at ease.

He led Harry to what looked like a steel box, twelve feet square, welded to the aft end of the deck.

"This is what we call the lazarette, it's the sick bay." He opened the steel door. The lazarette was spotlessly clean inside with two beds, a large glass fronted cupboard and above each bed a steel cupboard. Two large medical panniers lay between the beds.

"They delivered your medical supplies this morning."

"Bloody hell!" Harry said. "They must be expecting another Battle of Jutland."

The steward burst out laughing.

"We had to tell you, before you go ashore one of the assault craft has to take it and leave it on the beach. But I must warn you, we pass through the Dover straits and will be under the guns of the Jerries from the French side. So you might need them." He showed Harry how to bolt the porthole shutters into place.

"My advice is to keep that door open after you put your lights out after dark. Should we get hit, the doors are inclined to buckle. And another warning. After we get there, the Navy takes over this ship. The holds are filled with concrete, they are going to beach it, along with a few others to make a break water, I understand a prefabricated docking pier is going to be erected for the main force to land. I tell you, mate, it will break the old man's heart when we hand this ship over."

He pointed to two old men leaning on the ships rail watching what was going on the quay side, both the men's blue suits were well worn and threadbare at the elbows.

"That's the old man, the shorter of the two and wearing the bowler hat, he's the captain. The other one in the greasy peaked cap, that's the ship's engineer. The old man started on this ship when it was launched towards the end of the last century, started as a boy and worked his way up. The engineer came on at the same time, both boys together. They retired both of them a few months before the war started and sold the ship to the breakers. Then war started and the ship and them were brought out of retirement, and ever since we have been a supply ship for the Navy. Mostly up the east coast between Pompey and Scapa, but occasionally we go up the west coast. We had a bit of a scare in '42, a German U boat surfaced. She wanted stores and was preparing to board. One of the dinghies was half way across, when out of nowhere a British plane came over. That bloody U boat went down like a lead balloon leaving the Jerry officer and two men on top, but they did get a shot in before they went down. It hit just below the bridge." He pointed to a slab of steel which had been welded to the side of the bridge.

"We took the three Jerries prisoner. Cocky little bastards, we hauled them aboard and they wanted to take the ship. The old man threatened to heave them over the side. I know when the Navy takes this ship off him, it will break his bloody heart. Well, you can kind of say, they grew up together."

Harry walked around the ship alone making a further inspection. The steel decks in part had been eaten through with rust, steel plates an inch thick had been welded to the deck where the rust had been bitten right through. He touched the rusty parts on the superstructure, it crumbled away in his hand. The whole of the ship was covered in a fine layer of soot, for the ship still burned coal. He went back to the sick bay and unpacked his medical supplies, keeping ample supply of sea sickness tablets handy. Having taken a look at the cramped quarters for the troops, experience told him if the sea kicked up rough, the tablets would be in fierce demand.

He lay on the bed writing to Kim before he was disturbed by the activity below and went to the ships rails. Squads of sailors were being detailed to each ship in turn - eighteen aboard the 'Major McClaren'. Two to each landing craft and two P.O.s. Shortly afterwards, the army assembled on the quay all in battle order, composed of four squads of fifty men, their ranks as straight as if they were still on the parade ground. Then they filed aboard to their quarters, but it wasn't long before they were back on deck complaining about their cramped conditions.

"Like fucking cattle," was the usual description. Harry smiled to himself, typical army, two minutes aboard and having grievous complaints.

"What about grub? Where the fuck are we to eat?"

"Trust you, Metcalfe. Always bloody moaning," the R.S.M. bellowed out. "What you do, is take your mess tin to the galley, he will put some grub in there, then you find yourself a nice cubby hole or spot on the deck and sit down and enjoy it. I suppose the most you will be aboard is three or four days, so make the best of it."

Harry returned to his bed to finish his letter and searched his haversack for the watch. He checked the time; half past four, it seemed later. It had been a hard day, twelve hours previously he'd been aroused from his comfortable warm bed. It seemed such a long time ago. He finished the letter and was half asleep when he felt the ship vibrate as the engines came to life. He went to the ship's rails, but they were crowded with men and he heard the ship's captain shouting orders.

"Let go for'ard."

There was a pause.

"Let go aft."

Harry jumped on the top of his sick bay and watched the ship's propeller churn up the mud. The gap between the ship and the quay widened, the whistle shrieked, and black smoke belched from the single funnel as the ship made its way towards the middle of the river. Two more ships of the same design and size followed suit. The dockers on the quay stood motionless as if they were watching a funeral procession, one of the men gave a solemn wave and slowly the ships edged down the river towards Dungeness and the open sea.

A small naval ship headed the small convoy as darkness fell. The chief steward brought Harry a large dinner plate, with a slice of lamb a half inch thick and mountain of fresh potatoes, cabbage and fresh garden peas, the whole lot smothered in mint sauce that penetrated the small sick bay.

"We have a naval officer aboard, Harry. We should be passing through the straits about midnight, don't forget what I told you about keeping that door half open, there is a chain on it. There are two Red Caps on deck to see that no one smokes during darkness. We should be out of the danger area by first light, the only thing to worry about then is the German E Boats, but they operate mostly at the other end of the channel. Still they may twig what's going on and get them up here."

The night passed peacefully enough, there was a little mist at first, but by eight it cleared, although there was a slight sea flowing causing the ship to heave slightly, and a queue for sea sick tablets formed. Much to Harry's pleasure, and many more men on the ship, the small convoy hugged the coastline. Several men had binoculars and occasionally a man familiar with the coastline would recognise something and give a shout, and speculation grew as to their destination. One bright spark started a book, with Portsmouth and Spithead the odds on favourite, and Plymouth a real outsider. Just past Brighton, three more ships joined the convoy, one larger then their own, the two others smaller. They were escorted by two small naval ships. The merchant ships formed two lines ahead with the three naval ships on the outer flank, waiting to deal with any trouble.

At first there was a slight drizzle and a slight wind blowing up. But by tea time it had turned to a downpour with the sea starting to whip up. And passing Littlehampton more ships and naval escorts joined the now substantial convoy and the speculation increased.

"You watch. By nightfall, this convoy will turn and head straight out across the channel, we will be right in the front of it."

"Fucking hope so," one man said, "I have got ten to one we won't stop anywhere and head straight across the channel."

But he was wrong, the convoy was only just moving with enough speed to make headway and by nightfall they were still hugging the coastline.

Harry turned in, and soon fell asleep, but was rudely wakened at midnight by the ships anchor chain rattling through the hawser holes. Putting on his greatcoat he went to the ships rails, but could see nothing, it was pitch black outside, not even a star was showing, for the clouds were heavy and overcast. The ship tore at its anchor chain like a anxious dog pulling at its lead. And every time it jerked a shudder went straight through the ship.

Excitement had gripped Harry and he could sense that old feeling returning. His muscles felt as if they were eating the insides of his legs away. Drink never offered him any solace, but he had an urge to help himself to a tot of brandy from his medical chest. He poured a liberal dose into his white enamel mug. The fiery liquid bit into his mouth and throat, but after a few minutes it appeared to do the trick and he felt relaxed. He smiled to himself and, wondering if he had drank too much, he belched and felt the fiery liquid rise up in his throat. He closed the steel door and made sure the port hole covers were in place. He felt a romantic mood coming on and took out his pencil and started to write to Kim, omitting to tell her that on the first night he had completely forgotten their nine o'clock tryst.

He dropped off to sleep sitting up with his back against the steel wall of the sick bay, pencil still in his hand, while his writing pad fell to the floor. He was awakened by the commotion outside his door at first light.

He went to his door, his greatcoat round his shoulder, and gasped, his eyes stood out like the stops of the great organ in Winchester Cathedral.

"My God, I don't believe it." The ship was anchored between the Isle of Wight and the mainland, but the sea was covered with ships of every size and description. Huge pre-war luxury liners, large ferries, tramp steamers, cargo carriers, tankers, cable layers

538

and naval ships from small torpedo boats to several capital ships and aircraft carriers. Small launches darted in between the vessels carrying messages and stores. Tug boat were still pulling the larger ships into their rightful moorings. Signals flashed from ship to ship and from ship to shore.

One man amongst the crowd said aloud, "I saw the Naval Review at Spithead, but believe me it had nothing on this."

Another man pointed to a massive concrete block with several anti aircraft guns mounted on top, being towed by two tugs. It created a lot of speculation amongst the assembled troops.

"What the bleeding hell is that?" a man said aloud as he scanned the apparition through his powerful binoculars."

"Must be some kind of secret weapon," a man answered. There was neither derision or argument over his remark.

The sea whipped up stronger and the tops of the waves frothed up, and as they did so the ships tugged at its heavy anchor chain making it difficult to stand unaided on the wet steel deck. The men keyed up for the invasion became lethargic with the inactivity and heavy bouts of sea sickness set in. A queue formed up outside the sick bay. Harry's supply of anti-sea sick tablets were running short.

The steward, who was now calling Harry by his first name, came down with a plateful of ham and eggs and tomatoes, another plate of white bread and a large pot of tea.

"Get that down you, Harry. See you have plenty of men with the old sinking tummy feeling. How's your guts?"

"Nothing the matter that that breakfast won't put right. Is there any chance of getting a message ashore? I am running out of anti-sea sick tablets."

"I should think so, one of those P.O.s that came aboard is a signal man I will get him to flash a message to Pompey dockyard." He set the tray down on Harry's bed, much to the envy of the men not suffering the pangs of sea sickness. Several of the men standing near the door took one look at it and ran to the ship's side.

At midday a small naval launch pulled alongside the ship, skillfully manned by three female naval ratings. A line was thrown down to them and a small waterproof bag hauled up. One of the sailors handed the bag over to Harry. This was his chance, he took out several bottles from the bag and quickly tucked in three letters he had written to Kim during the voyage round the coast. He threw in several coins for the postage and pinned another note to the outside of the bag to let the girls know there was something inside, but to make sure, as the line was lowered, he cupped his hands and shouted, "There's a tip in the bag for you."

The girl below laughed and waved. Like the dozens of others that had been smuggled ashore, they would be posted as soon as the armada was on its way.

But the day passed slowly with more ships joining the fleet. Most of the late arrivals were tank landing ships. Harry wondered if some of his own division would be on them, or if Charlie had got away and what Charlie's new medic was like.

A sergeant and two corporals came into the sick bay with a pack of cards and they played till well into the afternoon. The school was broken up when the steward came in with a tray of sandwiches and a pot of tea for Harry.

"No signs of movement yet, Harry, the old man has been ordered to keep steam up, but reports are coming in that the sea out in the channel is bloody awful." The steward looked towards the ship's rail and out over the sea, the Isle of Wight was obscured by mist.

"If a pack of U Boats got in amongst this lot they would have the time of their lives."

"What do you make of those bloody great concrete blocks steward?" Harry asked in an off hand manner.

"We have been trying to figure that one out since they started to arrive. The only conclusion I can make of it is, I told you they are beaching this ship and several others, I think it may be that prefabricated pier I was telling you about."

"Could be, steward, very well could be, now you come to mention it. Wouldn't fancy cruising across the channel on top of one of those buggers. Do you reckon we will be going across tonight chief?" one of the corporals asked, helping himself to a mug of Harry's tea."

The steward shrugged his shoulders. "You know about as much as we know, all I can do is repeat myself, the old man has been ordered to stand by with steam up. The bleeding stokers down below are kicking up hell."

"Not as much as our lads down below in their cramped quarters, it's bleeding hell down there," the sergeant retaliated, "and the bloody food is awful."

"What do you expect? The galley is designed to cater for twenty men, its no bigger than an ordinary kitchen back home. Yet we are supposed to cook for over two hundred. And those two army cooks they sent to help out are bloody useless, they are both sea sick and they overcrowd the galley. How do you expect three men to work in a galley made for one cook?"

"Yes I suppose you are right, chief," the sergeant apologised.

"These cramped conditions doesn't help to boost morale."

"Never mind, sarge," one of the corporals sitting on Harry's bed sarcastically said.

"Get a message sent ashore, chief, for two hundred helpings of fish and chips, and make mine plaice, I can't stand cod."

Harry pulled out his heavy silver watch and looked at the time.

"Almost six. Come on lads I will have to show you the door. I have my letter to write and my reports to write out. Perhaps we can have another game of cards tomorrow, can't see us moving with this sea whipping up." As he opened the steel door to let them out a fine spray of salt water and rain struck at his face.

"Heaven help a sailor on a night like this," he gasped.

"Fuck the sailors, if there is any help going let heaven throw it this way. I have never been a bloody good sailor." The corporal said, buttoning up his tunic around his neck and making a dash for his own quarters.

Alone, Harry sat on his bed with his writing pad on his knees and his pencil in his mouth. He wrote on the top of the paper.

"No address as yet." Then he put the date, June 5th 1944. At first he hadn't the slightest idea what he would put down, but he took out the snaps they had taken at the village. His stomach churned as he looked at Kim's smiling face and he wondered if he would ever see her again. He started writing furiously. This might be his last chance, for the steward said he would take any letters when the navy took over and he was shipped back to England. He watched the fingers of the silver watch laboriously transverse the face. At ten to nine, he put the paper and pencil away and lay back on his pillow to clear his mind. The watch had been synchronised with the clock on Kim's bedside table, and at exactly nine a picture of her face came clearly into his mind. He felt close to her, as close as if she was lying alongside him. Then, just as he felt he could communicate with her, someone banged against the steel door.

"Can I have some sea sick tablets, medic? I have just been terribly sick."

"Why you b..." But Harry pressed his lips together to prevent him abusing the man.

"Come in, it's not locked."

The man was a forlorn wreck, his face a waxy colour and his hair wet and bedraggled. At once Harry felt sorry for him for he was well acquainted with sea sickness himself.

"Go on, mate, lay on that bed for a while." He gave him a tablet and half a mug of water. "If you feel you want to be sick again, get out of here fast."

But within minutes the man had closed his eyes and was fast asleep. Harry finished his letter, then dragged on and on. The steward brought on deck a large bucket of cocoa, as only the navy could make, thickened to a constituency of liquid chocolate. The men on deck took one look at it and snarled. A few, a lot braver and not suffering from the deadly pains of sea sickness, scooped out mug-fulls but found it much too sweet. They continued to stare out to sea.

"It's just past midnight, Harry, there isn't a lot to see for another four or five hours," the steward said, looking at the bucket of cocoa. Harry didn't want to hurt the steward's feeling, he scooped up a mug of cocoa and beat a hasty retreat to the sick bay.

He woke with a start, the grey light of an early dawn spilled into the sick bay through the half open door. It wasn't the light that had disturbed him, it was the talking outside, men's voices, very excited. He sat up and heard a soft drone, like a swarm of bees working a hive. It grew stronger and stronger, throbbing, louder and louder, turning into a continual roar and the ship vibrated from stem to stern drowning out the ships engines. Grabbing his overcoat he ran outside. The convoy plodded on beneath an umbrella of planes. Fighter planes, bombers, transports, planes towing gliders, literally hundreds and hundreds of planes.

One man pointing out the gliders said, "Fuck that for a lark, sooner them than me."

Gradually the planes vanished towards the French coast. The light allowed them to inspect their own situation. The Armada stretched in every direction. Battleships and battlecruisers with menacing guns pointing forward, cruisers, frigates and small corvettes. Merchant ships of every description. It looked like the admiralty had scoured every dock and breakers yard for any type of ship capable of carrying troops or stores. Tramp steamers, tankers, pre-war luxury liners. Long lines of tank landing craft, and larger infantry assault craft. Their own ship was placed almost central in the fleet with six more ships of similar size ahead of them.

"It's certainly going to be some bloody war, Harry."

Harry jumped, he was so engrossed in the scenes unfolding before his eyes he hadn't heard the steward come up behind him.

"Yes." His voice almost inaudible,

"I was at Salerno, but compared with this lot it was sod all."

The steward was admiring the destroyers.

"I used to be on destroyers, lucky bastards, those smaller ships were always happy ships. Couldn't be otherwise, you lived so close together it just didn't pay to fall out with your mess mates. In a rough sea they buck worse than a wild west bronco."

He sounded as if he was still on a destroyer. Harry guessed how he felt, for he would be feeling the same if the unit had left without him. There had been times when he was with Kim that he had felt like asking for a transfer to a job in a general hospital, with his qualifications it wouldn't have been a problem. Harry placed a sympathetic hand on the steward's shoulder.

"Never mind, chief, at least you have had the satisfaction of coming this far."

He gave Harry a smile and fingered his weather beaten nose. "I suppose you're right, Harry," he sighed deeply. "But I would have given a year's wages to fire those guns at those bloody square heads." He vanished below.

The men were silent now, eyes scanning the horizon buried in the mist, for a view of the impending enemy shore line. Harry returned to his sick bay, surprised to see the man he had allowed to sleep on the spare bed still fast asleep. He shook him, the soldier sat up and looked stupidly around the small steel room.

"Where are we, medic?"

"You have to be joking. The whole of the R.A.F. and most of the American air force flew over the fleet a few minutes ago. Do you mean to tell me you have slept through that lot? You should go and get a fresh battery in that hearing aid of yours. At this moment we are heading straight for the French coast, but you can't see it yet, there's too much mist around."

The man sat up and cradled his head in his hands. "I have got a bloody thick head, medic. Do you think it will be long before we land?"

Harry could hardly believe his ears.

"Are you serious? Land, what do you mean land? This is not a bloody ferry you know, we won't be docking at some port. We will be running up a beach with the enemy pouring shells into it, and believe me I don't mean sea shells. Believe it or not but you will be amongst the first assault troops to land. What are you, a rifleman?"

"No I am a bren gunner."

A look of despair spread across Harry's face. Was this man true or was he just stupid? Harry was convinced the man was quite unaware what was laying in wait for him, and it was obvious he hadn't seen action before.

"Look, mate, the only advice I can offer is when you go in on the assault craft and you see the front drop down, make a rush for the shore. You will probably have to run through two or three feet of water. Keep close to your sergeant or corporal and when you see him drop, that's when you drop. Haven't you had training going down the scramble nets and into the assault craft?"

"Oh yes, we had two days with the marines."

"Well thank heavens for that, well just remember what that marine instructor told you, and for heaven's sake when we do hit the beach get away from the craft as fast as possible. Now piss off and get your gear together, I have to finish packing."

He pushed the medical pannier outside.

"You are on assault craft four, medic, leave those panniers here, they have to go on number one."

The soldiers started to return to the deck, all dressed in the usual battle order. Then the cooks bought up several trays of fried bacon floating on a lake of grease. Another cook laid a tray of white bread on the deck. Several men took one look at the bacon tray and rushed to the ship's rails. Others who felt hungry but knew the penalty of stuffing themselves with greasy bacon settled for several slices of dry bread.

Ships continued to flash signals to each other. The old tramp steamers and several more in the convoy poured out black smoke, covering the men and the decks with a fine film of soot. Harry strained his ears forward. Was that the familiar rumble of gunfire or was it a thunder storm in the distance? He stared hard forward and saw pin point flashes through the early morning mist, followed a few moments later by a long drawn out rumble.

"Sounds like a thunderstorm, medic," the man who had shared the sick bay with him the previous night said.

Harry coughed out a laugh, choking on a mouthful of dry bread, he swallowed hard. "Yes, some bloody storm," he answered. "But instead of rain this storm lashes out red hot metal. No, they are just starting to soften up the beaches."

The battleships and cruisers moved up fast. The mist rose revealing a long stretch of what looked like black cloud. The battleships opened up with a roar, flashes of light spat out from the darkened land, it was impossible to see in this false light whether it was the enemy guns firing or the shells from the warships landing on the coast. The men crowded on the deck looked anxiously forward, it was here at last, they had been training for four years just for this moment. As the tramp steamer neared the shore the navy men prepared to unleash the assault craft and prepare them for landing. Scramble nets, rolled up like gigantic tubes were stashed, one below every landing craft, with one end lashed to the ships rail, when they closed in near enough to the shore the one end would be thrown over the ship's side.

Harry checked his small pack for the last time, making sure the silver watch was wrapped in a waterproof dressing and stowed deep down in his pack, together with the photograph of Kim and her family. He checked his field dressing and his army issue knife,

544

leaving it half clasped and ready for emergencies. He tightened the straps on his gaiters, then realised he was finding unnecessary jobs to do. He felt his jaw tremble slightly and bit his lip to take control, his intestines seemed to be wrapping themselves round his stomach. It was too late to go to the toilet and he smiled to himself wondering if that's why they issued khaki trousers. He returned to his sick bay and swigged down a full glass of water, then walked to the ship's rail. The foreboding shore line was much plainer, he could see the continual flashes of the enemy guns and the ship was just about to come into their range. At first glance he thought the shore line was on fire but it was the shells landing from the heavy naval bombardment.

The steward came and stood by him.

"Can anyone live through that lot, Harry?"

Harry shrugged his shoulders.

"Don't worry chief, when we hit that beach there will be a reception party waiting."

N.C.O.s were shouting orders all over the place, the men were at the ready, all fully armed waiting for orders to scramble down to the assault craft. Harry stood by his sick bay, the steward and the cook looking anxious accompanied him, the cook wiping his hands on his once white apron. With a sigh of resignation the cook took off the apron and with a defiant gesture threw it overboard. The steward was in his best uniform with the gold braid on the sleeve. He held his hand out to Harry.

"The navy is just picking us up now, Harry. I will post those letters for you as soon as we arrive home. Good luck, son." He gave Harry a slip of paper. "That's my address, let me know how you get on." He turned sharply and joined the old captain and the rest of the crew at the stern end of the ship. A corvette was just pulling up and more naval men scrambled aboard. The ship's captain didn't bother to turn round and take a last look at his doomed vessel.

A shell dropped close by, the ship rocked slightly and a jagged piece of metal tore through the hull. The ship was drifting towards land.

"Prepare to land." The order bellowed through the ship's tannoy.

CHAPTER 49

Silence settled over the assembled company as they formed up for the assault craft and, as if they were still under instruction by the marine sergeant, they clambered over the ship's rail exactly by the book.

One thing the sergeant had forgotten to tell them. Instead of clambering down the scramble nets onto dry land, he hadn't mentioned dropping into the craft in a heaving sea. Consequently men were falling into the assault craft from various heights, and it wasn't long before Harry's services were needed. He had just settled into the heaving craft when a sergeant poked his head over the ship's rail and shouted, "Medic!"

Harry looked up to see the sergeant beckoning him to come aboard again. He laboriously climbed the net, panting as he clambered over the ship's rail.

"Get down to number one craft, medic, a silly bastard's fell from the net and broke his sodding leg. One of the best mortar men I had. See what you can do for him."

Harry scrambled into number one assault craft. The injured soldier writhed in agony at the bottom of the boat, and a quick examination revealed that he had suffered the identical accident which had occurred on the training ground.

"How is he?" a young officer asked.

"Well, let's put it this way, sir, there is no way that man is going to land on the beach. I will give him a temporary splint and the best thing we can do is get him over to the hospital ship; there are a couple laying off."

"That's fucked it," the chief petty officer said. "I have to lead this lot in. How long do you thing it will be before they fix him up?"

"All bleeding day if you keep talking here. Get the boat towards the hospital ship now and I will try and put the splint on as we go along." Harry gave the man a pain killing injection and, with the help of two of the men in the boat, managed to splint the leg.

The chief petty officer continued cursing as he turned the craft towards the hospital ship.

"Give it all you've got, Spider," he shouted to leading seaman Webb, in charge of the craft's engines. He turned to Harry.

"If they get the order to go in while I'm away I will really be in the shit."

"Well don't blame me. If you were so bloody important why the hell didn't you transfer to number two? Anyway I don't think they need you to hold their hands."

Harry tried to make his patient comfortable and to write out a casualty card. The petty officer brought the assault craft under the lee side of the hospital ship which, from sea level, looked enormous. A platform was lowered and the man was soon hoisted on board. Harry gave them a wave and the craft turned to join their own small fleet.

The P.O. sighed with relief when he saw the small flotilla circling the mother ship, waiting for instructions to head for the beach. It was over an hour before the order was given. The craft heaved and bucked. Already the bottom of the boat was awash with vomit and sea water. As the square nosed bow rose sharply, the vomit and sea water rushed to the stern, and as the bows lowered and the stern rose it washed forward, splashing against the sides and the men's knees.

Shells dropped all around them, the water danced to the tune of the shells. Hot jagged lumps of red hot metal skimmed across the sea burying themselves in a tormented wave. Harry lifted his head to see how far off the shore was. A dead body passed by, swirling in a whirlpool made by an exploding shell. The dead man half rose from the water, arms dragging by his side, spun round, then dropped face down, his arms outstretched.

A shell exploded not six yards away, and a large piece of shrapnel tore through the flimsy steel, taking a man's pack from his back before carrying on across the boat, hitting another man's steel helmet and shooting harmlessly over the side into the sea.

The man took off his helmet and inspected the large dent.

"Now you know why they issue you with steel helmets. Let that be a lesson to you all, always wear your steel helmet. Nigger Brown would have had his bloody head blown off by now," shouted the sergeant. But hardly a man was listening. Most of them were still suffering the pangs of sea sickness, a few no doubt wishing the shrapnel had hit their head without the steel helmets.

A destroyer rushed past at full speed sending the flat bottomed craft spinning in its wake. The men grabbed at the sides, their knuckles white, half expecting the flimsy craft to turn at any minute. The helmsman steadied the boat but the extra swell brought on more sea sickness from those that had escaped the agony.

"Do you reckon we will make the shore?" asked Harry of the C.P.O.

"Of course we will, you prat." It was the last words he ever spoke. He rose to his feet to give the helmsman his orders, when a piece of shrapnel skimmed across the sea, lifted over the boat and took half the chief's face and side of his head away. His knees buckled under him and his blood spattered over the men crouching beside him. Harry, his sea sickness temporarily forgotten, caught him in his arms.

"Is he dead?" asked a young one pip officer.

"Yes sir," replied Harry, and with the aid of two men, lifted him to the stern of the boat.

They were within fifty feet of the shoreline when disaster struck. A high explosive shell scored a direct hit on the ramp and exploded. The craft appeared to split in two as the helmsman shouted, "Jump clear!"

Men scrambled to their feet adjusting their Mae West life preservers. A few of them stood on the side of the boat blowing a final lungful into their preservers before leaping from the side, their sea sickness a thing of the past. Harry threw his medical satchel into the sea and jumped, but as he hit the water the webbing strap holding his pack caught on a jagged piece of metal taking him down with the boat. It hit the bottom, raising the silt in a dense cloud, swirling around in the water. As he looked up, large silver bubbles of air sped upwards, breaking with a flourish on the surface. Pinching his nose, with his free hand he tried to tug the webbing strap away. It wouldn't give. His fingers dug into the bottom sand as he tried to gain leverage to give his strap another tug. His inflated life preserver was pulling him away from the sunken craft and tightening the web strap, holding him firmly in place.

He felt his lungs were bursting and tried not to panic. All sorts of stupid thoughts raced through his brain. Drowning men were supposed to see their past lives flash through their minds. In spite of his predicament he couldn't help but smile at the prospect as the last two years had been the most exciting of his life. Then Kim's face flashed before him, giving him renewed energy.

He reached for the strap holding him to the craft and his fingers made contact with his army issue knife. Thank heavens that he always kept it as sharp as a razor and had left it half clasped. He grabbed the knife and turned it sharply, cutting the lanyard holding it. Then, without panicking or rushing, he cut through the webbing strap. Like a child playing with his rubber duck in the bath and holding it under water till he released it, he shot to the surface.

His small pack, still held by one strap and filled with water, tried to force him down again, but Harry was a strong swimmer and struck out for the shore, gulping in great lung fulls of the clean fresh air. He bumped into the headless body of a sailor, a crewman from his own boat. The body spun round and the last spurts of blood oozed from the headless body, staining the sea around him a deep crimson. At last his feet came into contact with the shingle bottom, he dragged himself ashore on hands and knees.

With his feet still in the water he lay flat, completely exhausted. A small crackle of bullets from a spandau burst a couple of feet from his head threw up fountains of sand. A body lay a few feet away. From where he lay he could see the man's chest had been ripped open. He sidled along towards the body, hoping it would give him a little protection. Sightless eyes stared at the clouded sky. He recognised the man, the same one who had shared his sick bay the previous night. The basic training Harry had been taught some years ago came into practice. Snake-like he crawled slowly up the beach, his small pack full of sea water seemed to weigh a ton. He would have ditched it onto the beach but it held what few precious possessions he owned. Shells burst all around, machine guns chattered and the rolling sing song of mortars moaned as they tumbled through the air. His mouth felt dry; he licked his salt laden lips, it added to his agonising thirst. A dead body lay nearby, a water bottle attached to its belt. Harry moved over to get it and as he did so a single snipers bullet thudded into the sand where his head had been a few seconds earlier. He cut the water bottle away with his knife.

"Time you wasn't here, Harry lad," he gasped.

Men were pouring from assault craft all along the beach. Some never made more than a few yards before a man's arm would fly into the air, his knees buckle and he would lie on the wet sand. One man clutched his chest, then his hands dropped to his sides, dangling there and, as his legs gradually gave way, he kept walking on bended knees, his mouth wide open and staring towards the sky, just like some long-armed hairy orang utan in a circus, for there was no dignity in death. Another man was hit and as his rifle fell to the sand, he clutched at his abdomen and walked around in circles before finally dropping to the sand, pausing on his hands and knees for a few minutes, then buckled over.

A medical man lay stretched out on the sand, his medical satchel beside him. Crouching low Harry ran towards him. He was still alive.

"Where you been hit, mate?"

"My legs, I think it was a Jerry machine gun. I think the bastard was waiting just for me, I hadn't taken more than a dozen steps from the boat. I'm bleeding cold, we had to wade through about four or five feet of water, it was almost chest high. Just have a shufti at my legs."

Harry cut away the man's blood soaked trousers with his knife and removed the lanyard the man had used as a tourniquet on one leg. The blood spurted out. He held the pressure point with his thumb and with his free hand took out an issue tourniquet from the man's medical satchel and applied it.

"Well at least one femur and a femoral artery has gone on one leg, the other isn't in too bad a shape. There isn't a lot I can do and you won't be using your medical gear so I will take that. Before I go I will give you a jab to ease the pain. If I see the bearers I will let them know. Sorry I can't stay, mate. With a bit of luck you should be back home tomorrow."

"Forget it, I'll be alright here. Good luck mate."

All fear left him, once more death had become his constant companion. He had walked side by side with it for so long it was no stranger. He spurted across the sand, over a road and straight into a drainage ditch, dropping beside two men manning a bren gun.

"Keep your fucking head down, medic, there's a Jerry machine gun over in the far corner of that field." The machine gunner touched his companion's shoulder.

"Let's move, Brum, we may get the bastard from the other end of the field." They crawled along the ditch till they were completely out of sight, both cursing with every step they took.

Harry watched an officer spurt towards the ditch. He dropped close to Harry and looked at the medical satchel.

"You a medic." It was neither a question nor a statement, just a few clipped words. He didn't wait for an answer but said, "That's good." He started to remove his tunic, his face distorted with pain. "I have taken one in the shoulder, I can't use my arm, it's bloody useless."

Harry cut the tunic away and then the officer's shirt.

"No bloody wonder, shrapnel or a bullet has gone straight through shattering your shoulder blade, you have got a lot of shit round it. The best thing you can do is get back to one of those assault craft and over to a hospital ship. It's a bloody bad wound."

"No time for that, medic, there's a bloody machine gun round here and it's kicking up a hell of a stink on that beach. I intend to get that square headed bastard."

"What, with just a revolver, sir?" Harry laughed.

"It's over in that far corner, two of our chaps have just gone after it. Don't worry, medic, I have also got a couple of hand grenades." He held his revolver in his good hand and followed the ditch round.

Harry thought the ditch was a good place for treating the casualties. He called the stretcher bearers several times and dressed the wounds of six walking wounded. He lost all sense of time and gave his hunger pains an off-handed shrug. He emptied his sea soaked small pack onto the ground and picked up the small parcel wrapped in waterproof material, shook the watch and held it to his ear. It gave a steady, loud, tick tock, and he sighed with relief. If the watch was alright the photographs wouldn't be touched. Kim smiled back up at him. Then there was one of Kim and her mother and father, and several more of the four of them taken in the village and more taken with Amanda. Harry sorted through them and could hardly believe that it had been less than a week since they were all together. He felt it had been more like a week since he fought for his life at the bottom of the sea.

Deep in his thoughts he hardly looked up when a stoutish medical officer dropped beside him.

"Found yourself a nice little cubby hole here, orderly." He must have been a regular medical officer, for only regulars called them orderlies, and it wasn't long before he proved Harry right.

By Harry's standards he was pretty old, late thirties or early forties, with a gut that showed he must have spent most of his service in front of the mess bar. He sat panting beside Harry, then pulled out a slim packet of cigars.

"Almost got the bastards wet coming ashore, I tripped and fell in the ogging."

Harry shook his head.

"Don't use them, sir."

The M.O. took out a flat bottle of brandy from his hip pocket and offered Harry the bottle. Harry had just tipped out his small pack and his white, but chipped, enamel mug lay beside him. The M.O. poured brandy into Harry's mug, and Harry filled it with water.

The M.O. shook his head.

"If I knew you were going to waste it I wouldn't have give it you. Water, that's only fit for washing. I haven't touched water since I left India in '38. Ever been to India, orderly?"

Harry shook his head.

"Damn fine place, served with the Bengal Lancers for six years, fine body of men." He stared into the distance as if he was back beneath the burning sun on the north west frontier and muttered to himself.

"A splendid bunch of men as you would meet anywhere." He took a long drawn out swig of brandy and inspected the few casualties.

"Nice work, orderly. I will just toddle down to the beach to see if we can get these men evacuated." Then, as if he was taking a morning stroll through Hyde Park, he casually walked across the shell and bullet strewn beach towards a small assault craft and mustered several stretcher parties.

"God, he's a cool bastard," said one of the casualties.

Several times Harry was called from the ditch to attend the wounded and often, for the lack of bearers, he was forced to carry them back over his shoulder, and was soon covered in mud, sand and blood.

"This your first time in action, medic?"

If the question hadn't been so stupid, Harry would have laughed.

"You've got to be joking. I dare not tell you how many times I have been in a situation like this, you would never believe me." He lit a cigarette. Then more out of habit, lit another and passed it to the man, at the same time staring at the devastated beach and the sea shore and the damaged craft, crewless, banging up and down with the waves and smashing against the shore.

"Do you mean to say a man can actually go through this lot more than once. When I get back, medic, I shall play on this wound, they won't get me back here if I have to work metal polish into it." Metal polish worked into a slight wound was an old trick used by soldiers in the First War. Unfortunately it sometimes had fatal results, it could drive a man insane. He tried to lift his arm.

"Can't move my fingers, medic. Do you reckon this is a bad wound?" His face lightened up. "Do you reckon I will get my ticket?"

Harry had already dressed the wound. He let the smoke drift from his mouth.

"Don't worry, mate, it's bad enough, I doubt if you will be coming back here." For, like the officer's wound earlier, a bullet had smashed through the man's shoulder, splintering the shoulder blade.

"You are lucky it didn't do any internal damage. It was within inches of your lung, a few inches lower and it could have proved fatal."

The man shuddered.

"Thank fuck for that, I don't fancy being buried out here. Apart from French birds, I can't say I am very partial to France or the French. Why you can't even understand what the hell they are talking about, and without using their bloody hands they would be dumb." He laughed and flicked his cigarette end across the road.

A padre dropped in beside them.

"I see you have everything in hand, medic. They have set up an aid post about five or six hundred yards along the road. They're very busy as you might well imagine."

552

"I think I will stay put here, sir, we are getting quite a few casualties. I just had an M.O. here and he told me to carry on. My orders for when I landed were to make myself useful. I don't know if any of my own unit have landed yet sir."

"Well it looks like you are doing fine. Just take a look at that lot." He pointed to a flotilla of assault craft heading for the beach amongst fountains of dropping shells.

"It reminds me of a few lines of Shakespeare's Henry The Fifth: 'And gentlemen in England, now abed, shall think themselves accursed they were not here.' Yes, that Shakespeare certainly knew how to weave words."

"Not me, sir," said one man, "I feel myself accursed now for not being in bed with my missus and getting my leg over."

"We had a chap in our unit in the desert, sir, and this man could quote any chapter or verse from Shakespeare," said Harry.

"Lucky man, what university did he attend?"

"None as far as I know, self taught. Didn't do him a lot of good though, he was killed just outside Tripoli."

Another medic dropped in beside them.

"We have just had Major Dempsey in the aid post, he told us we would find you here. Get your gear together, you have to report to the aid station we have set up. Come on, get a move on."

"Sorry, lads," Harry said to the casualties.

"Stay here and keep your heads down, someone will pick you up shortly."

He followed the other medic along the ditch for several hundred yards, across a road still under small arms fire.

"There's a couple of snipers got this place covered. I will dash first; give it a couple of minutes, then you make a dash," the other medic said, his eyes darting along the road. He pulled his head in quickly as a single bullet spat by.

"See what I mean, mate." He took a runners stance, held his breath, then sprinted across the narrow road. Two bullets hit the tarmac in quick succession. Harry followed at the fastest pace he had ever run, throwing himself across the hedge on the other side. Once under cover of the hedge they ran as fast as possible to the aid station, a tumbled down house. A large red cross was displayed on the crumbling facade.

Someone threw a white gown at him.

"Ever worked in a theatre?" a surgeon said, not bothering to look up from operating on a wounded man.

"Yes, sir," said Harry, coming to attention.

"Well cut that crap out and start work. How long have you been ashore?"

553

"Five, maybe six hours, sir, it's hard to tell. I have been working on casualties further along the beach."

"Yes, I have heard about that. You can work alongside me."

Darkness was descending when Harry was relieved. Exhausted he walked away from the room being used as a temporary operating theatre. Sitting with his back against the wall he sucked in the fresh night air. It looked like the enemy were respecting the large red cross on the outside of the shattered building, for although the beach was still alive with falling shells and small arms fire, none landed less than a hundred yards from the building. He saw an army greatcoat just inside the house. Harry picked it up and, still sitting, pulled it over himself. Within minutes he had dropped off to sleep.

And so he continued for another three days, working in the makeshift aid post. Ambulances had been landed making it easier for the bearers. The Infantry gained ground slightly, pushing the enemy back, with every inch paid for dearly. The division's heavy armour had already been in action and fighting its way towards Bayeaux, whilst other columns were making towards Caen. Several times he saw tanks with the familiar desert rat emblem on the front.

On the third day, an ambulance drew into the aid post and he heard his friend Chappie's familiar voice. He ran outside.

"Tell them you have been sent to fetch me, Chappie."

"What the hell do you think I am here for? Get your gear, you are wanted back at the unit, the old man wants you urgently. The 1st Tanks have already been involved. Charlie's ambulance has landed and he lost his medic, that's why they want you back. I think your mate is pining."

"Don't be a prick, Chappie, I will get my gear." He reported to the staff sergeant in charge who dismissed him straight away.

"What's this I hear, Charlie, you have lost your medic?" Harry greeted Charlie who was sitting at the wheel of his ambulance.

"Don't mention it, Harry, poor bastard. We came down the ramp of the landing craft. First I got bloody stuck in the wet sand and a bloody tank pulled us free. We got onto the road. I said to this little prick - it was his first time in action - 'If you hear the shells scream over don't jump from the ambulance, in fact don't do anything till I give the word.' Fucking shells were dropping all over the place. One dropped a few feet in front of us and before I could stop him, he had baled out and gone straight under the tracks of a tank. It cut him in half. I just couldn't believe it Harry. Right across his guts. I lifted his head, he was still alive, sheer terror in his eyes. Then suddenly he calmed down accepting the inevitable. He gripped my arm and in a voice as clear as I am speaking to you said: 'Tell my mum I am sorry. If you can, Charlie, go and see her when you get home.' Then, as calm as you like, told me I could have his wristwatch. Believe me, Harry, if I had known he was wearing one he would never have been on that ambulance. I tell you, that episode shook me."

Harry didn't say a lot and dared not tell Charlie he had that silver watch packed away in his haversack. He changed the subject immediately, telling Charlie about the episode underwater and the tough time on the beach.

"Bloody snipers had a go at me twice. First on the beach and then crossing a small road just away from the beach. Then a bloody officer, who couldn't use one arm, and a couple of blokes with a bren gun, went after a German machine gun. I didn't hear from them again, but the Jerry machine gun was still at it when I left."

Harry reported to his own R.S.M. and, as expected, was sent to Charlie's ambulance and straight down to the beach with a load of casualties. The sand had been churned up by the heavy armour and transport which was still arriving, so they pulled up on the road itself and the bearers carried the wounded down to the assault craft. Many of the casualties were pleased to get away from the man-made hell, although they still had the nerve-racking experience of running the gauntlet between the heavy shelling. They were lifted into the waiting craft without ceremony, the walking wounded sitting between the stretchers.

So it continued throughout the next few days, ambulances dodging in between the assortment of vehicles, a constant stream of DUKWs (amphibious lorries), and landing craft of every variety unloading men, stores, fuel and ammunition, the beach itself taking on the form of a large ordinance depot. Captive gas balloons floated above from ships and the beach, to deter low flying aircraft. Although the enemy retaliated by random raids at night trying to bomb the area, as the beachhead widened the raids became less and less, and the shelling decreased, although an occasional shell still arrived from enemy batteries that held out. They heard that Bayeaux had fallen, and commandos were engaged south of the town. Resistance was building up, but as yet without any enemy tank units.

German prisoners were streaming in, some mere boys.

"I doubt if the poor bastards have left school yet, Harry."

"Put a bloody rifle in their hands and it doesn't matter much how old they are." Then to their amazement, amongst the prisoners were two Japs.

"Just take a shufti at that, Harry. I know the bastards went through Burma like a knife through butter, but someone should have told these two men when to stop."

With the first week over they expected some respite. The bridgehead had widened daily but they were back to house to house fighting as the villages grew closer and had to be cleared of the enemy before they could advance. They reached Villers Bocage. The country wasn't quite right for tank fighting. The farmers hadn't cut their crops and the Bocage country was covered in waist high bracken giving plenty of cover for the German Tiger tanks. The fighting came so close and the divisions shoulder to shoulder, it was inevitable mistakes would be made. Our own troops were strafed by allied planes and, to make matters worse, the division was converging on the Americans who were already on the outskirts of Gaumont; the Americans reported not having much opposition.

German spandaus opened up in the village. Shells were dropping all around, and to add to the noise of the battle came the sound of shattering glass and buildings collapsing as the Germans pressed their attack home. On the road to Caen there was more heavy fighting, but this wasn't like Bocage country. It was open farming land broken only by a few hedges, but with plenty of villages. This left the ground wide open and the enemy had plain views of the British and Canadian advance, and casualties grew heavy. Minefields had been laid by the enemy in the hope it would slow down the advance, but the pressure was kept on, and neither Harry nor Charlie minded one bit, for the sooner this lot was over the sooner they would be home.

Then one day the unit dispatch rider caught up with them.

"Where the fucking hell have you two bastards been? I have been chasing you around for over five weeks." He searched in the two bags on the sides of his back wheel and pulled out two bundles of letters and several parcels. He threw one bundle of letters to Harry and the other to Charlie. Then placed half a dozen parcels in the ambulance.

"They are all for you two, sort them out yourselves. Got a brew on the go, Charlie? My mouth feels like the bottom of a parrot's cage."

Harry was sorting the letters out in order of posting. He nodded towards the brew can hanging beneath the back step.

"Help yourself, mate, the making's in the back."

"Thanks a lot you pair of unsociable bastards." But he didn't hesitate in getting the brew cans and a petrol fire blazing. He filled both their mugs.

"Should be in Caen anytime, Charlie. Be alright with the French bints. Won't take you pair long to sort a couple out." He nudged Harry and winked.

"Bit different from the gyppo bints eh!"

"You can have my share, Matthews," answered Charlie, still trying to sort his letters out.

"Fucking hell, Charlie, don't tell me you have seen the light?"

"No, Matthews, just found someone who is worth a thousand foreign girls." He waved the bundle of letters in his hand.

"By the looks of this bundle she must have wrote every day. If I mean that much to her surely I can play straight. Piss off, Matthews, you can have my share, I want to get on with reading this lot."

He handed Matthews a pile of letters, still unopened.

"Hand these to the old man for censoring, and don't you read the bastards else you'll get my foot up your jacksie. Want your letters posting Harry?"

Harry didn't look up, but handed Matthews half a dozen letters tied up with string.

"Next time don't keep us so long, try and find us a little harder."

"Thanks for the tea, you miserable pair of bastards. I liked you better when you were footloose and fancy free."

The largest of the parcels was from Rosie. Two square biscuit tins, one filled with homemade cakes, a bit stale now but still edible. The other was filled with cigarettes.

"These are from me and Ernie and all the customers. We have a collection every Friday (some of the miserable buggers don't turn up that night, so we catch them on Saturday). But they all send their best wishes, and, Harry, they all miss the piano sessions. Keep away from the French girls and Ernie said when you get around Arras and Vimy Ridge and all those places and you see anybody in their twenties that looks like him, it's sheer coincidence. (It had better be!) Cheerio, lads. When you get back we will have the biggest party you ever did see. Love Rosie."

There were socks and a balaclava helmet from Kim with more cigarettes and the same from Kath and her family.

Kim's letter read: "My darling, how I miss you. We ring Rosie up every week and every time I cry when I think of the lovely time we spent there. We have been to see her twice since you went away. We took mother and Aunt Marti. They loved it and said no wonder you were always there. We shall be going there for the August bank holiday." And so the letter went on and on, giving him every small detail of her daily life and activity.

557

That night Harry went over to the aid post. Someone had rigged up a wireless there using a car battery. He waited until just before the nine o'clock news from the B.B.C. then walked well away. His large silver watch had stopped many days ago, and he hadn't the accurate time, and he dare not bring it out into the open while Charlie was around. So now, during the lull in the fighting, he would try and make some mental contact with Kim. He couldn't confide in Charlie, he would think the shelling had got to him and he was going off his rocker.

It was still night, broken only by the sporadic gun fire in the distance. That night the stars shone with a brilliance he hadn't experienced since they left the desert. He looked for the North Star, and found it, and worked out the direction where he supposed Kim would be. Then at nine even the guns seemed to have stopped, for the distant roar had become familiar and fainter until there was total silence. He tried to picture Kim's face in front of him; he could almost hear her speaking. Was it really working? He didn't know, but he did know he felt closer to her than ever before. He must have been concentrating really hard for he fell asleep with the picture of her child-like face in his mind and didn't wake until the early morning, and only then when the cold really got at him. He felt at ease as he walked slowly back to his ambulance.

"They must think we are going to be here for the winter, Harry, sending us all those woollies. We had better answer Rosie's letter. Have you written to her since we have been away?"

"Yes, twice, and I wrote to Kim a dozen times at least and yet she says she received only two in one of her letters. She received those I wrote on the boat, but the steward posted them for me. He said he would as soon as the landings were over. But it's very difficult finding something to say. I mean, how can you say, we were shot up by a couple of Jerry planes this morning - or last night was terrible, they shelled us from arsehole to breakfast time. Kim would never sleep."

"She certainly wouldn't if you used those words."

"Don't be a prick, Charlie, you know exactly what I mean. Look, Kim, sorry I buried half a dozen of my mates today, one of them had been with the unit since the desert. That would go down faster than the Titanic. She must be cheesed off with me telling her we had a wash in a muddy stream this morning - or some such stupid talk."

But the small talk and the letter writing came to an abrupt halt when the sergeant ordered them to prepare to move off.

CHAPTER 50

By the second week in August the division had made rapid progress across rich agricultural land. Scattered German graves bore testimony to the heavy fighting that had taken place, as did the dead cattle laying around, bloated cows, their skins filled with gas and stretched to bursting point, their heads to one side and their legs pointing to the skies. The stench of rotting carcasses filled the air. A badly wounded cow tried to struggle to its feet as the ambulance passed.

"Hang on, Charlie, look at that poor bastard, look's like it's paralysed in its back haunches."

Charlie unclipped his rifle from its rack and slid a bullet in the chamber.

"Let's put the poor sod out of its misery."

The shot echoed round the quiet countryside, the cow's legs gave way and it sank to the ground.

"Wonder why no one saw it suffering like that, Charlie?"

"It was over in the corner, you could see the way the crops had been flattened, right across the field where it dragged itself. Shame to see all that beef going to waste, but I don't think I could fancy it knowing I had shot the poor bastard."

Harry shuddered.

"Neither could I. Seeing all these cows stinking and laying around is putting me off meat altogether. I think I might become a vegetarian after this lot."

The track, which could hardly be called a road, they were travelling was a foot thick in dust. Worse still, the heat was oppressive and several times they had to jump out of the ambulance and wipe down the windscreen.

"Makes you think you're back in the desert, eh Harry?"

"Strange you should say that, I was just thinking the same thing myself, except for these crops and the stinking cattle."

Early that morning they had left their parent unit to relieve the ambulance crew attached to an infantry regiment which had seen some heavy fighting. Now they were to witness some of the enemy's atrocities, for no sooner had they entered a village occupied by the regiment than weeping civilians pulled them to the rear of a building where several civilians lay in a heap, shot by the retreating Germans.

"Tell you, Harry, the bastards are desperate. The nearer we get to the German border the harder they will fight, but I doubt if there is any reason for this."

They were welcomed at the regimental aid post; no strangers to the regiment.

"We are not getting very many casualties in and we keep advancing so I hope that engine of yours is in good nick, Williams, you will be going backwards and forwards to that main medical unit several times a day, and I hope you can read a map. Twice that last ambulance lost us, each time after he took casualties to the rear we had moved. We don't unpack a lot in case we have to move fast."

"Suits me, sarge, the sooner we get this lot over with the sooner we get home," answered Charlie.

The sergeant, a wide grin on his face said, "Why, don't you like it out here, Williams? Some of you chaps are never satisfied. You, Williams, moaned like hell about the flies and the sand in the desert, you moaned about the mud and the mountains in Italy, and here you are having a Cook's Tour round the continent and you are still moaning. One of these days you will look at this lot with nostalgia."

"Yes, sure, sarge," Charlie's tone was sarcastic. "One of these days I will look back and think to myself, Charlie, you prick, you actually volunteered for this lot. No, the first thing I'll do when we get back is go to a bloody head shrinker and find out what made me do it. Have you ever sat down and thought it out, sarge? Since I joined I have been in two invasions, three campaigns and, at the last count, twenty-two battles of any importance. Harry here has been on five campaigns, twenty-seven battles, and one evacuation, but don't you think the odds are stacked against us?"

"Don't be fucking morbid, Williams, just get a meal going. If we are going to snuff it let's go with full bellies because once you go it will take hours for them to decide whether you will be going upstairs or downstairs."

The first casualty arrived just after noon. From a distance Charlie looked through his binoculars and watched a jeep coming towards them with stretchers laying across the bonnet.

"Come on, Harry, let's go."

In a few minutes they had caught up with the jeep. The injured man was quite conscious, he lay on the stretcher his trouser leg ripped away from the wound. It looked like the fleshy part of the thigh has been cut straight down with a sharp knife. Harry doubted if a good surgeon could have made a cleaner cut, but there was very little blood. Harry turned on the driver and his mate.

"Why the hell didn't you cover the wound? All this bloody dust flying around! When did this happen?"

"About twenty minutes ago, he was on a twenty-five pounder and a shell landed a few yards away. He was the only man wounded and we had sod all to cover the wound with, his field dressing wasn't big enough."

"What about a towel? You could have covered it with that."

"We didn't have a clean towel," the jeep driver answered. Harry was beginning to lose his temper with the stupidity of the two men.

"Clean towel! Anything would have been better then laying the wound open to all this dust! You want your fucking heads seen to."

"Who the hell do you think you are talking to? I happen to be a sergeant. I want your name and number and which unit you belong to," shouted the driver.

"Fucking marvellous how you made sergeant! You wouldn't have made shithouse wallah in our mob." Harry placed a temporary dressing over the man's wound. "Give him my name and number, Charlie," and to the sergeant he snapped, "When I report this our M.O. will have your balls."

They lifted the stretcher into the ambulance. The sergeant didn't take the argument any further. They raced the casualty back to the aid post and the M.O. lifted the gauze covering.

"What happened, son, did you run into a bloody bacon slicer?" The man, although in a state of shock, could hardly help but laugh, then became serious.

"Will I lose my leg, doc?"

"You have to be joking, when they've finished with you back at base you will have a scar from the knee to the groin, and when you get home you won't be able to flash it around without showing your bollocks, but apart from that you will be alright."

"Won't go back to Blighty then, sir?" The man looked very disappointed.

"Of course you will, but the wound isn't too serious. It's big, mind you, but no bones shattered. In few months' time you will be running for the regiment."

They hung around for another couple of hours waiting to see if any other casualties turned up and were ready to push off when a D.R. roared into the aid post. He handed the M.O. a long buff envelope.

"Right, Jackson, get that casualty back, we are moving up." He spread out a map. "We shall be there." He stabbed the map with his finger, then circled the spot with a pencil. "Keep on this track for five or six mile, then turn on to this sunken road. Now make sure you get it right, we have been notified there are pockets of resistance about."

561

Finding the main unit was much harder than they expected, the front had advanced so quickly and the division was all over the place. They stopped a three tonner.

"Yes," the driver said. "I passed a Red Cross unit back there a couple of miles, whether it's your mob or not?" He shrugged his shoulders, "don't ask me." He didn't wait for an answer. "Cheerio mate, can't stop, I have to get this ammo up a bit sharpish."

As luck would have it, it turned out to be their own unit. Sykes came rushing out, his steel helmet at a crazy angle, and the inevitable clipboard in his hand.

"What you got aboard, Williams?" And before either Charlie or Harry could answer, Sykes shouted, "We are just about to move up, we can't take casualties."

"Don't be a prick, Sykes. What the hell are we supposed to do with them?" Harry jumped from the ambulance, his leg gave way under him and the pain shot through his body. He limped to the orderly room tent.

"What's the matter with you, Jackson, been wounded?" asked the R.S.M.

"No sir, a touch of the cramp, but we have a casualty aboard and Sykes said you can't take him. What shall we do, sir? Carry on to the C.C.S. or Field hospital?"

"No, transfer him to Jock's ambulance, but mind he doesn't see Brummie's face, it may frighten him."

Harry hadn't been to his parent unit many times since he landed on the Normandy beaches.

"Don't tell me you brought them over here with us, sir?" said Harry, a look of disgust on his face.

"We had to, Jackson, no other unit would have them." The R.S.M. turned his back on him hiding his joke. For in spite of their nefarious ways they were a competent and trained crew, used to taking the rough end of the stick, otherwise the R.S.M. would have got rid of them.

While at the main station they replenished their petrol and rations, then made their way towards their regiment. They stopped at the last place they had seen the aid post. Harry took out his ordnance map, Charlie looking over his shoulder, and pointed to the spot the officer pointed out.

"No, Charlie, it was there," Harry argued, and pointed to another spot. Soon an argument started over whose responsibility it was to have marked their map with the destination.

"Right, Harry, tell you what we do. We travel for five miles, or six, till we get to a sunken road, we travel up there for another five miles. If we don't hit anything we turn back and get on this road." And so it was agreed.

Charlie watched his speedo till he had counted five miles.

"Righto, Harry, start looking for the sunken road. Don't bother, here's one." Charlie made a sharp right turn.

"You should have turned left, Charlie."

They stopped and Harry took out the map. "You see, two miles back there was a fork, you turned on the right fork so when we hit this road we should have turned left, not right."

"Have you lost your marbles, Harry, that wasn't a V road, that was a track up to a farmhouse."

Harry didn't bother arguing further. Charlie drove on, but only for another mile. A dead German lay in the middle of the track. Harry jumped form the cab and turned the man over.

"He's still warm, Charlie. I don't think he has been dead more than an hour, probably not that." He straightened up. "Christ, Charlie, here's another." He walked forward. "And another. Jesus, Charlie, there must be at least ten." He looked up at the ridge above his head. "I bet one of our patrols from up top caught them, you can see everyone has been hit on the top of his head."

They walked further along the road until they came to another road crossing it, a large barn on the corner, the gate still open with another dead German just inside. Harry examined the body, a bullet had passed downwards through his shoulder and into his chest.

"Look, Charlie, he had enough strength to run this far, or he's been dragged by his mates."

Charlie pointed to a scramble of footsteps in the dusty ground, they led straight on. "Come on, Harry, it's time we wasn't here." He pointed to the footsteps the Germans had made. "And we won't be going in that direction."

"I don't like this, Harry, it's too quiet."

But there was no need to tell Harry, he felt that tingling feeling creeping up the insides of his legs, and his guts twisting into knots.

Instead of going forward and following the Germans' footsteps, or turning right round and heading the way they had come, Charlie made a sharp left turn. The front had to be that way, he calculated, but inwardly he knew he was hopelessly lost, and Harry had drawn the same conclusion.

"Right, Harry, give it three or four miles, if we see sod all we turn back and go past those dead Jerries."

It was no good arguing. Harry knew that when Charlie made his mind up nothing would deter him. Charlie dropped his speed to a crawl. The track was dusty and he was leaving a tell-tale column from behind if he went too fast.

"Here we are, Harry, life at last." They passed an orchard, ahead near the farmhouse they could see several half tracks and two lorries. A man was crouched between the trees, his trousers round his ankles, reading a newspaper. Charlie turned into the wide path leading to the house and suddenly stopped dead.

"Fucking hell, Harry, they're bleeding Jerries!"

At that moment a bullet hit the metal supports of the windscreen. Charlie swung round fast and drove madly between the apple trees. His engine roared and the man doing his business between the trees stood up and looked around. Bullets were flying all over the place. The ambulance hit the German sending him flying through the air and landing on the lower branch of a tree. Another bullet thudded against the back stop and yet another ricocheted off the steel runner holding a stretcher in place.

Harry poked his head out to see what was going on behind them, men were kneeling with rifles to their shoulders.

"Get into the next line of trees, Charlie! Start weaving around!"

Instead Charlie swung the steering wheel round and crashed through a small hedge and back on to the track. Above the din they heard a half track rev up.

"The bastards are after us." He roared down the dusty path. The barn loomed up in sight. "Hold tight." He swung over and down the path where the dead Germans lay. He ran over the legs of one body and almost crashed into a small scout car. The half track was no longer following, possibly they knew the fate of their comrades down that sunken road. Harry saw the reconnaissance regimental sign on the armoured car and, stopping the ambulance, went over to talk to the sergeant.

"We just ran into some Jerries, a half track followed us but gave up the chase when we turned down this road."

"What was the strength, was it an artillery regiment?"

"We didn't stop to ask any questions," Charlie interrupted.

"There were about six half tracks and a couple of lorries, didn't see any 88s. We did kill a Jerry, though. He was sitting down between the trees having a crap, the last we saw of him he was hanging from an apple tree."

"Report it to your C.O. You should get a fucking medal."

But Harry ignored the sarcastic remarks and pointed out exactly the spot the Germans were holding.

"Felt sorry for that Jerry having a crap, all the same. If there is one thing I hate, it's being interrupted while I am on the bog. I don't think he had finished."

"Well in that case I will have a shufti and let you know when we catch up with them. Cheerio."

With Charlie's help, Harry pulled the dead Germans' bodies inside a field, a burial party would catch up with them soon. An hour later they caught up with the regiment. The sergeant came out to meet them.

"Sorry, lads, we gave you the wrong location. After you'd gone we heard there were some Jerries around so we sent someone after you but he couldn't find you, and at your own unit they said you had already left."

"Yes, sarge, we know you had ballsed things up, we ran into those Jerries alright." He took the sergeant to the ambulance and showed him the bullet marks and the long groove along the stretcher runner. "We were very nearly put in the bag, a bloody half track came chasing after us."

"Oh well, lads, you have to expect that, this is what they call a fluid front."

"Yes, and I know why it's called a fluid front, I very nearly pissed myself!" answered Charlie. Then he turned to Harry. "It was my skill and dexterity at the wheel that got us out of that mess, right, Harry?" Charlie went back to his old self again, taunting Harry in a jocular way.

The advance continued for the next two weeks with the division fighting over the old battlefields of the First War: Somme, Arras, Vimy Ridge, Lens Lille. The men knew they were fighting on hallowed ground where some had lost their fathers, uncles and other near and dear relatives. They were men that they had never grown up with, but knew their surviving families talking about them, or seeing their names on the local war memorials. Now they were doing a repeat performance over the same ground that was supposed to have seen the war to end all wars. Long rows of white stones marked the lasting resting places and men gasped when they stood at the large cemetery near the Somme. Some went in search of their father's or other relatives' graves. It brought it home to one and all exactly what they were fighting and suffering for.

"You just can't believe this, can you, Harry?" Charlie's voice was subdued. They walked slowly along the rows of graves, everything was so quiet, even the birds failed to sing.

"My uncle served with the Warwicks round here, he used to tell me about the men they lost on the Somme. It's only now I realise just what he meant. Tears welled up in his eyes as he talked about it. His regiment was well represented here, Harry."

"You're wanted urgently back at your unit, Williams," the sergeant ordered when they reported back to the aid post.

Charlie was greeted by his R.S.M. on their arrival.

"I think you must read this letter, Williams." He handed him a long, official looking, buff envelope. Charlie slowly opened the letter. He had been expecting the worst, but his face lit up.

"I don't believe it, I don't believe it." He handed the letter to Harry.

It was from the police in the West Country.

"Dear Sir, we regret to inform you that your wife, Mrs Christine Williams was involved in a road accident. She died later in hospital. Under the circumstances you are now serving, I and my fellow officers of all ranks offer you our deepest sympathy." The letter went on for a few more lines, but Harry didn't bother to read it. How Charlie must have hated his wife, for Harry hadn't seen him so happy since they had left the east coast.

"Look, Williams, I know your circumstances." The R.S.M. turned to his clerk. "Right, Sykes, stop ear holing, get off that idle arse of yours and find something to do." Harry turned round to leave the lean-to. "Not you, Jackson, you stay." He turned to Charlie. "Now that girl of yours, Williams. She is in a home. Leave has started in the division for those with urgent business or with compassionate grounds, so I am giving you fourteen days so you can go and sort things out. Go and see your girlfriend in King's Lynn, make sure things are alright between you and her."

Harry shook hands with Charlie. "I know I shouldn't say anything against the dead, Charlie, but I know you will feel better after this."

"You needn't shake hands with him, Jackson, you can pack you gear and go with him, half a bloody ambulance crew isn't any use to me. I have seen the C.O. Your leave starts officially in two days time. That will give you time to get down to Calais. I can't find transport, there's a big push coming on, but there is plenty of traffic about so you will have no trouble getting a lift. Now get your gear together and hand over your ambulance to Redgrave, he's a new lad in the unit." He shook hands with both of them. "I suppose you will be seeing that pretty little girl of yours, Jackson?"

"No need to ask, sir." Harry realised what a thoughtful and understanding R.S.M. they were lucky enough to serve under.

One of their ambulances took them as far as Bethune, another place whose name would go down in history for having seen some of the fiercest fighting in the previous war.

"Sorry lads, have to report to second echelon, can't take you further," the driver said.

They threw their kit from the ambulance and with full pack and kit bags over their shoulders, they walked along the road.

566

"Bleeding turn up for the books, Harry. Who would have thought less than four hours ago that we would be on our way home? I bet the girls will be surprised to see us."

"Bloody shock will kill them when they see us walk into their houses. Kim will think she is seeing a ghost."

"Just a minute, Harry. See what I see?" He pointed to an airfield. "Come on, sonny boy, let's see if we can get a lift back in a plane. Bloody hell, am I glad I kept that letter from the police, let's take advantage of someone's sympathetic nature."

There were two men from the airforce regiment on guard at the high barbed wire gates.

"I wonder if we would have a word with your transport officer, corporal?" Charlie was on the point of shedding a tear. He showed him the letter.

"Hang on here, mate, bloody sorry to hear about this, mate."

The sergeant came to the gate and read the letter.

"What do you want us to do about it, soldier?"

"Well, sarge, if I could see the transport officer, perhaps he could get us a lift. You see, I have my small daughter to make arrangements for, she's in an orphanage. I thought you could have a plane going back to England I could scrounge a lift on."

The sergeant rubbed his fingers round his chin, stared hard at the pair of them in their filthy uniforms, then read the letter again.

"I am sorry about the wife. I will go and see the C.O."

He returned a few minutes later and handed the letter back to Charlie. "Follow me lads." They stood to attention in front of the C.O.

"This is very unorthodox men. You were supposed to be going to Calais."

"I know, sir." Charlie looked dejected. "But I would like to see my daughter, without her mother there it will be very hard for her."

"Right, son, hang on there, I will see what I can do for you. And your friend, why is he going?"

"Well, sir, we are an ambulance crew, been here since D-Day. The R.S.M. said the unit will soon be starting a leave roster. He said an ambulance crew is no good without a driver so he had better come along with me and take his leave at the same time."

The airforce officer picked up his field telephone and spoke to the operator.

"Give me that American airbase, I wish to speak to Captain Maddox." He hung on there for a few minutes. "Paul, my old friend. Fine, Paul, yourself?" There was a pause and the officer laughed. "Look, Paul, can you do me a great favour? One of our boys, a front line medic, has just heard his wife was killed. Any chance of getting him back home on one of your Dakotas?" There was another pause. "Two hours time? That's great, Paul, I will get them over straight away. Thanks, Paul, I will buy you another drink when I see you. No, not warm beer, Scotch on the rocks. Cheerio, old son."

He put the receiver down and his face beamed up at them. "I see this letter was from the police in the west country, they have a Dakota going to Norfolk in another two hours to pick up supplies. You will have to make your own way across to the west country from there. Sorry lads, but that's the best I can do."

"That will be fine, sir," said Charlie, trying to keep a straight face. "Norfolk will suit us down to the ground, train to London then across the country." Trying to convince him that they would head for the West Country. "Thank you, sir, for all your trouble. You don't know how grateful we are."

"That's alright, son, just get yourselves sorted out and good luck. Once again I am very sorry to hear about your wife."

"That's alright, sir, there isn't a lot I can do about that and they say time heals, but it's my daughter I'm worried about."

"Right, sergeant, lay on transport for these two lads, take them over to that American air base. Ask for Captain Maddox and see them safely away."

Safely aboard the plane, Harry looked at Charlie. "You bastard, I nearly curled up in that office, you certainly laid it on good and thick. Do you realise you almost had me crying in there."

"Balls to her, Harry, that's the best good turn she has done me since she deserted my girl. If you are asking me to get emotional about her, forget it, she was a cow and the only thing I would like to do is piss all over her grave. There's one thing I'm thankful for, if I should get killed she won't get that bloody widow's pension. I used to lay awake at night thinking about that and shuddered every time."

A top sergeant came aboard and shook hands with them. "Make yourselves comfortable, lads." He threw them a couple of rugs each. "You are our only passengers today, we'll have you safely back home in less than two hours, it looks like we have a tail wind. The rest of the crew will be aboard any minute. What's it like up front?"

"Not very pleasant," answered Harry, but the rest of the conversation was drowned out as the engines roared into life.

The plane shuddered, the noise was incredible. The sergeant placed their seatbelts into place and shouted at the top of his voice in Harry's ear. "Keep them on all the time, these planes aren't meant for passengers really." The plane taxied towards the runway, paused for a while, then the engines revved up. Harry thought his eardrums were about to burst as the plane raced skywards, then, as it levelled out, the noise died down a little. A few minutes later the sergeant returned with a flask of coffee. Harry hated coffee but forced it down, he didn't want to upset the sergeant and crew who had shown them so much courtesy. Then, before they realised what was happening, the plane started to descend. Harry felt his ears pop and clear themselves. The plane bounced on the runway a couple of times, then ran a few hundred yards before coming to a stop. The doors swung open and a ladder was brought up to the opening.

"Thanks, sarge." Charlie held his hand out.

The rest of the crew came along and shook hands, and the plane's pilot said, "Sorry to hear about the wife, hope things turn out alright for you."

They reported to the office and found out they were less than thirty miles from King's Lynn. Charlie hadn't decided if he would try and phone Marti or just drop in and surprise them all.

"What day is it, sir?" Harry asked the officer behind the desk.

"Thursday." He was rather surprised to hear the question.

"Where the hell have you been, soldier?"

"Well, sir, up there it's hard to tell one day from another. Unfortunately the war doesn't stop for Sundays, it's no respect for a man's religion, you lose all sense of time."

"How long have you been out there?" He scrutinised their filthy uniforms.

"Since D-Day, sir. It was a bit rough, it's kind of calmed down a little since then. Two days ago the division was fighting its way towards the Belgium border, that's when we left."

"It must be tough out there." He called for the sergeant. "Any transport out there, Sergeant, get these lads home?"

"There's a jeep going to Wisbech, sir. Where do these lads want to go?" The officer looked at Charlie.

"We want to get to King's Lynn, sir, Wisbech would be fine." The officer looked at the large map on the wall behind him.

"God damn map, King's Lynn is just a few miles further on, tell the driver to take them there. Isn't that where Levinski's broad hangs out? Let him take them."

Outside Harry said, "Fancy a C.O. like that, Charlie? Levinski's broad lives there, let him take them home." Harry mimicked the officer, but not arrogantly. "Imagine one of our officers if we wanted to go to the east coast to see our girlfriends, they would send us to the west coast deliberately. Seems like these Yanks can't do enough for you, remind me in future not to take the piss."

"Thanks, buddy," the driver greeted them. "You have managed to get me a day's furlough." He rubbed his hands together. "Come on Irene, get those bloody pants down, Stevie's on the way home and that's not a beer bottle in his trouser pocket, it's just that I am pleased to see you."

He slammed the jeep into gear and roared from the base, waving to the sergeant of the guard as he passed the gate. The sergeant shouted after him.

"Be back on base by 7 am, Levinski."

"Up yours too, sarge," he shouted back.

If this man was in training for the Monte Carlo rally, Harry wouldn't have been the least bit surprised. He roared down the narrow lanes, forgetting the main roads, taking the corners on two wheels and the brakes screeching like banshees. Both Charlie and Harry hung on for grim death.

Twice they had to stop at road junctions and each time Harry said to the driver, "Would you mind if we wait to get back to the front before we terminate this earth."

The driver laughed and tried to go faster to prove a point.

"I can find my way to King's Lynn with my bloody eyes shut, just relax, I will have you there in just over an hour."

It was with relief that they were dropped off at the corner of the street. The American shook hands with them and threw their kits to the ground.

"See you buddies, and good luck." He roared away. Charlie slung his kit bag over his shoulder.

"I will drop round tonight, Harry. Just wait till Kathy hears the good news. I shall be down that registrar's office first thing in the morning."

"Good luck, Charlie, and don't forget I am best man!"

CHAPTER 51

Harry still couldn't take it in that he was back in England and about to walk down the same street where he had found so much happiness in such a short time. Less than twenty-four hours earlier he had been in amongst the heavy guns sitting in a muddy stinking slit trench, and the uniform he was wearing bore testament to that. He hesitated at the next corner, wondering if he had made a mistake dropping in on them so unexpectedly, perhaps they should have phoned from the American air base. The C.O. had offered the use of the phone, but Charlie just laughed.

"It will be a bit of fun just dropping in on them, Harry." But that was Charlie, anything for a laugh, he always treated life as one big joke.

He picked up his kit bag again and heaved it on his shoulder. Too late now to do anything about it. The street was deserted, as if the neighbours were anticipating the surprise and didn't want to spoil it. Once more he hesitated at the garden gate where Jack's rose bushes were a blaze of colour. He dropped his kit bag at the front door, then with his field knife cut a red rose from the nearest bush; Jack wouldn't mind on this occasion. He knocked hard on the door, there was no response, he knocked twice more and was about to bend down to see if Carol had left the key under the mat, when he heard footsteps down the passage. He felt someone wrenching the door, as usual it was stuck, he put his foot against it and pushed, it flew open. Carol was wiping her hands on her apron.

"Sorry, I was just..." But the words faded on her lips as she looked up and saw Harry. She stared dumbstruck at Harry's face, unable to move or speak, and for a few stupefied seconds remained rooted to the spot. When the words finally came all she could say was, "What the hell are you doing here?"

He burst out laughing.

"Thanks a lot! Is that all you can say?" he mimicked her, "What the hell are you doing here?"

She stepped outside and threw her arms round his neck.

"You were the last person I expected to see standing on the doorstep." She held out her hands. "See my hands are trembling." She wiped her hands across her forehead. Harry thought she was about to faint and held on to her.

"Don't tell me I look that frightening." But he wouldn't have been surprised if she agreed, for he was still carrying the mud and filth of the battlefield.

He threw his kit in the passage and was soon sitting in his usual comfortable armchair.

"I suppose Kim is working." It was the first time they had mentioned her daughter. She stammered and became confused.

"Er, no, as a matter of fact she has gone to the doctor's."

"What's the matter, is she ill?" He sounded concerned.

"Nothing much." She patted his shoulder.

"There's nothing to worry about, a little run down I suspect, she will tell you all about it herself, she's due back any minute." She made an excuse and hurried from the sitting room saying, "I'll go and make you a nice cup of tea." Harry immediately sensed there was something wrong for by nature Carol was an inquisitive person and so far she hadn't asked him the most important question, 'Why had he come home so unexpectedly?'

He looked around the now familiar room and could hardly believe it was four months since he left. Nothing changed, everything was just how he left it, except for one additional item. Above the sideboard was a large picture of himself and Kim, taken a few days before he left. He was looking at the photograph when Carol returned with a tray with teapot and cups.

"Do you like it, Harry? Jack had the photograph enlarged and framed for my birthday. It's exactly the same frame as my John's photograph." She sat on the opposite armchair and set the tray down between them on a small occasional table.

"Oh it's so good to see you, Harry." Then the questions started to roll, in Carol's straight forward way, fast and furious, for as far as she knew leave for the troops in France hadn't started.

"Why are you here, Harry?" she asked, with plenty of emphasis on the 'why.' He couldn't prevent himself from bursting out laughing.

"Now that I can get a word in I will tell you the good news. Charlie has come home to marry Kathy. The police notified him that his wife was killed in a road accident. The R.S.M. said I might just as well go with him as half an ambulance crew is no use to him. Frankly I think they were glad to get rid of us. But leave is starting in earnest in a couple of months for everyone."

"I know I shouldn't say it, Harry, not with his wife's death, but Kathy will be over the moon."

"Don't waste your sympathy on his wife, she did desert him. I think after a while Charlie would have accepted that, but deserting their baby, he just couldn't handle that."

As he was talking to Carol he could sense all was not well. Every few minutes she would look at the clock, then turn her attention to the door. Twice she got up from her armchair and looked through the window.

572

"Something worrying you, Carol?"

"Not really, I was just thinking Kim should have been home by now." Then as an afterthought. "Perhaps she decided to carry on shopping, she hardly goes out now, not since you went away." She made small talk till she heard footsteps coming down the garden path. Carol vanished into the kitchen as the front door banged open.

"I'm home." But Kim's voice trailed off as her eyes fell on Harry's kit stacked up in the passage. She pushed open the sitting room door.

"Harry."

Her voice was a hushed whisper, she leaned against the door frame for support. If she was surprised to see him, it was nothing to the shock he was about to get. He stared unbelievably at her. His mouth opened to say something, he couldn't move. Finally words came.

"Why, you're pregnant." His throat was dry and the words sounded like two pieces of sandpaper being rubbed together. She knelt beside him, he ran his fingers through her silken hair.

"Why didn't you write and let me know?"

"I had an idea before you left, Harry, although I wasn't absolutely certain. I couldn't tell you, you had enough to worry about. Mum and Dad stood by me, Dad is over the moon."

"What else did you expect from parents like yours?" Harry didn't know whether to cry or burst out laughing.

"But there's one thing for certain, Kim, tomorrow we will go down to the registrar's and get a special licence."

She sat on his lap and he smoothed his hand round her swollen abdomen.

"I wish you had told me before we left, Kim, I feel a right bastard leaving you in this condition."

She smiled back at him.

"It did take two to make the baby, Harry, I did play a part in it you know, and always remember, Harry, they were the happiest five months of my life." She whispered in his ear.

"There's only one thing I'm sorry about. When I was a little girl I always dreamed that one day I would walk down the aisle all dressed in white on my dad's arm and with four bridesmaids. I would lay in bed and fantasise. Then after we met I would see you waiting at the altar. But now I wouldn't have it any other way than at the registrar's."

"That last bit is a fib, Kim, and I know why, you're just trying to put my mind at ease. Don't worry, as soon as the war is over we will have that wedding, we'll go to the church and have the

573

marriage blessed. We may even take our little girl as a bridesmaid."

"Hang on a minute, I hope the damn war isn't going to last that long." Then for the first time she frowned and gave him a rather suspicious look.

"You haven't told me yet how you have managed to get here. Did my mother write and tell you about my condition?" At that moment Carol entered the room and Kim gave her an admonishing look.

"No she certainly didn't, and I blame her as much as I blame you for not telling me. I have come for Charlie's wedding." Then he told her the whole story and how they finally arrived.

"Well Harry, how does it feel to know you are about to become a father?" Carol returned with another tray of tea for the three of them. She set the tray down and went over to the chair and kissed him.

"Congratulations, Harry, I couldn't wish for a better son-in-law." By her attitude Harry couldn't help but think things had turned out with her connivance, it was something she had wished for all along. Was this pregnancy a blessing in disguise for her? For during the time he was here before D-Day, never once had Carol objected to Kim going away with him.

"I guessed there was something the matter when I arrived, you were acting like a cat on a hot tin roof. You kept looking through the window. At first I thought maybe you had a boyfriend and I'd arrived at an inopportune moment. When you said Kim was at the doctors I never realised for one minute she was suffering from Egyptian flu."

Kim and her mother, wondering what the hell Harry was talking about, looked questioningly at each other.

"What do you mean Harry?" asked Kim. "Egyptian flu, I don't even have a cold."

"Egyptian flu, you are about to become a mummy."

The three of them fell about laughing and Carol playfully slapped him across the ear.

"And another thing Carol, what do you mean, son-in-law?" Harry looked over Carol's shoulder and winked his eye at Kim, then gently pushed Carol away from him.

"What son-in-law, she will be lucky if she gets five bob a week from me."

Kim joined in the act straight away and fell to her knees clasping Harry round his legs.

"Oh sir, I am ruined, a poor innocent girl, you forced yourself upon me and robbed me of my virginity, and now you are about to desert me, what's to become of me? I knew nothing of life till you forced yourself upon me and had your wicked way."

"Forced, forced," Harry became melodramatic and threw out his arm. "What do you mean woman, forced. Was it not you that paid for the hotel?" He made another exaggerated gesture pointing towards the door. "Go, and never darken these doors again."

"But sir, what is to become of our child, I am cold and hungry and there's a blizzard outside."

"So go easy on the snowballs."

By now Carol was creased up with laughter and flopped down on the easy chair. Wiping the tears away she gasped, "Harry, this place hasn't been the same since you left."

"Right, in that case let's liven the joint up a bit. By the looks of Kim you should be a granny by Christmas." He picked up the rose he had taken from Jack's garden and sat at the piano with the rose between his teeth. Carol had obeyed his orders; he had forbidden her to lock the piano. He played with one hand as Kim rested on his shoulder. He handed her the rose.

"Sorry it isn't from Picardy, Kim, we should be there in a couple of weeks and the first rose I see I will save for you." Harry felt her hands tremble slightly.

Kim whispered in his ear.

"Damn the rose, just you be careful, I would go mad if anything happened to you and I think it would be the end of Mother."

"Don't be so stupid, Kim, I want to marry you now more than anything in this world, I don't want my child born without a father's name. I don't know if Jackson is my real name, but I do know what it's like to be brought up a bastard. So if anything should happen to me, you and Carol must keep your heads. Without a father will be bad enough, but without both parents would be a tragedy. Just promise me that."

She shook her head as if she didn't want to hear those words, and clutched him tightly round the neck.

"Please come back, Harry, please come back." She sounded a child again.

So within days both Charlie and Harry took their wives to the usual place, Rosie's. She was so pleased to see the four of them together once more that she laid on a reception in the bar. The table stretched the whole length of the black timbered bar, covered with a snow white table cloth and weighed down with food of every description. Slices of freshly boiled ham, half an inch thick, bowls of hard boiled eggs, homemade pork pies and cakes, bowls of pickled onions (Charlie forbade Kath to eat them), and pickles of every description. Three huge barrels of beer were arranged along the bar, and everyone was to help themselves for the whole village had been invited. When they stepped off the train the whole village had been there to greet them.

"I knew you buggers weren't married the first time you were here. When Kathy picked up that French bottle I made my homemade wine in and read the label in perfect French, old loud mouth here," she pointed to Charlie, "said I didn't know you understood French, Kath. Now I ask you, they were supposed to have a three year old daughter, that means they must have been married for at least four years, and he didn't know his wife was a French scholar."

They all started to laugh but Rosie kept a straight face and pointed to Kim.

"You needn't laugh, the minute you stepped over that doorstep I knew you were still an innocent little girl. I watched you as you went into that room." She laughed inwardly and her shoulders shook, her enormous breasts heaved up and down like two huge sacks half filled with live worms.

"I bet old Roger (there goes that slight knees bend again) was laughing his blooming head off, and I wouldn't mind laying bets that was where this was conceived." Rosie patted Kim's protruding abdomen.

"Come on now, go and get ready and let's enjoy ourselves, and I don't want to know when you are going back, not tonight anyway."

It was well into the next day when the laughter and music finally died down with even the vicar and the local bobby joining in the merriment. Although the vicar, slightly the worse for wear, insisted that the four of them came to church the next day to have the marriage blessed.

Charlie and Kathy stayed till the following Sunday, while Harry and Kim extended their stay till the following Wednesday. Rosie said her goodbyes at the pub, giving Kathy and Amanda an extra hug.

"You take care now, Amanda, be good to your mummy and daddy." She pressed Charlie hard against her.

"Goodbye, Charlie, take care son, I want you back here to take this pub off our hands, it's about time me and Ernie retired. Goodbye son." She patted his back, her face wet with tears as the train pulled away from the station. Charlie leaned out of the train window till the village was completely out of sight.

Harry and Kim spent most of the next few days walking the lonely countryside, sometimes watching the farmers reaping the fine harvest. In the evenings they would spend the time round the darkened fireplace talking to Rosie. Most nights Harry would play the piano for them. The pub was rather quiet during the week with perhaps one or two farm hands dropping in for a pint. To Harry and Kim it was the idyllic life, but alas it all ended far too soon, for Wednesday, the day they had promised to return and spend the last few final days with Kim's parents, came with the speed of lightning. Even then they left it till the very last minute and instead of catching the mid morning train they caught the evening one. Their farewells to Rosie and Ernie were long and tearful, and before Rosie would let them go Kim had to promise she would be down to the pub the first weekend possible. Rosie was still dabbing her eyes with a snow white handkerchief as the train pulled out of the station in a cloud of evaporating steam.

On Saturday night, Carol threw a farewell party. All the relatives came down and most of the neighbours, for Kim was a very popular girl, and most of the crowd had already made friends with Harry and Charlie. Harry was kept busy at the piano with Kim standing behind him, her hands firmly on his shoulders.

Occasionally she shed a tear and would whisper to Harry, "I wish they would hurry up and go, Harry." But it was well past twelve before the last guest departed.

Alone at last, Kim sobbed the night away and it was partial relief when Harry heard Charlie banging on the front door.

"Come on, Harry." He was greeted at the door.

"We have just half an hour to get that London train."

Kathy had already brushed past Harry and made her way into the sitting room to sit with Kim who was still in her dressing gown. Harry had a quick shave and a hurried cup of tea. Both Charlie and Harry insisted that the farewells should be at home.

"I hate station partings, Kim." They clung together for the last few desperate minutes. Harry kissed Carol who immediately burst into tears, then grabbing their kits they both dashed from the house.

They walked in silence to the railway station and, with just a couple of minutes to spare, caught the London train. It was half empty, not like the days when the division was billeted round the town. Harry sat staring through the window, smoking cigarette after cigarette.

"I couldn't take too much of that back at the house, Charlie." But Charlie didn't answer, he just nodded.

They took a taxi across London and were halfway to the coast and the ferry to take them across the channel before Charlie spoke.

"Well, Harry, it's done now, I wonder if we did the right thing?"

"I would rather have waited myself till the war was over, but you saw the condition of Kim. When I saw her come into that room I very nearly died. Why the silly little bugger didn't tell me before we left for D-Day I shall never know. I still can't take it in that I shall be a daddy."

"Well how about Kath? She's a ready-made mum. God, Harry, I am pleased about that, at least Amanda will have a more settled life. Kath's father will spoil her, you should see him, Harry, he takes her everywhere, and her mother idolises her; she laughs blind when Amanda calls her nanny. At least I'm returning more settled than since the war started."

The ferry was crowded with troops, some returning from compassionate leave, others reinforcements for various regiments. Most of them couldn't have been more than eighteen and nearly all eager to get into the fray before the war ended.

"Well at least they don't lack enthusiasm, Harry, the stupid cows." Charlie sat down with Harry behind a sheltered partition.

The sea was kicking up a bit rough, the mast carving figures of eight in the cloudless sky. Mid channel and the ship heaved and bucked like a mad mustang. The ship's rail was shrouded with a line of khaki backsides as the men vomited and retched over the side. But it was just a short trip and the sea was patrolled by several corvettes and sub chasers. Unfortunately, at times they came in too close to the ferry at full speed, causing a heavy wake throwing the ferry around as if it was a cork. It was with relief that the ferry ran into the sheltered waters of Calais. Several lorries were waiting to whisk the troops away to their respective locations.

They reported to the R.T.O. at the dockside. He gave them a keen look, then stamped their passes.

"Seventh Armoured Division outside, we have a lorry going to Second Echelon. Had any food on the way over, or did you throw up over the side?" There was a slight smile on the major's face.

"No, sir." Harry answered. "But it was more luck than judgment, took a real bollocking in mid channel and the navy kept rushing past in those tin kettles of theirs at full speed, I think the buggers were doing it on purpose."

The trip back on the lorry was long and tedious. There were another dozen men in the back with them. Twice they stopped while the driver brewed up for them and they tucked into the doorstep sandwiches the R.T.O. had supplied. They passed mile after mile of wrecked vehicles, both British and German. It was the first time most of the men in the lorry had seen a German tank and they grew quite excited. They passed isolated graves with the white crosses; later the bodies would be removed and placed in larger war cemeteries. Then the men gasped when they saw two large war cemeteries from the First War. Rows and rows of white stones stood sentinel, warning that no man had heeded of the futility and stupidity of war. One man, a little older than the rest, came and stood at the rear of the lorry, grabbing the overhead steel bar for support.

"My old man is buried somewhere out here. He was with the Warwicks, killed on the Somme in 1916."

"That will be further on then mate, it will be another couple of hours yet." Charlie pointed to the larger of the war cemeteries.

"That's nothing yet, you'll be passing those cemeteries every few miles later on. Do you know which one your father is buried in?"

"Menin Gate, I think that's nearer Belgium."

Then the occupants of the lorry fell silent, some tried to sleep, others were showing signs of nervousness. The steel floor of the lorry became harder and colder, and the roads became rougher.

Divisional headquarters was settled in a large chateau with thick stone walls and surrounded by a dried up moat. Harry was the first to jump out but his legs gave way under him as he was suffering from intense cramp, he groaned as Charlie helped him to his feet.

They spotted an ambulance, it was from their own unit. Harry hobbled over to it, Charlie carrying both their kits.

"Hallo, Jonesy," Charlie shouted inside the ambulance. The driver stirred from the stretcher and gazed stupidly at Charlie.

"What's up, Charlie?"

"Not a lot, Jonesy, just back off compassionate leave, anything happened while we've been away?"

"What do you mean, 'we'. Don't tell me they sent your mate with you to hold your fucking hand. Some bastards have all the luck. We've had a few casualties while you've been away. Little Sergeant McGregor caught it and we've lost two medical officers. Remember Captain Smithers? He caught it. That will send a couple of whisky distillers in Scotland in the shit. Then we had more casualties. Barnes got a bad face wound, and Morgan, that Welsh chap always bloody singing, I think he may have lost a leg. I tell you, lads, there's some real shit flying around. I suppose you two pricks want a lift back to the unit. Just hang on, I'd better let the M.O. know."

Twenty minutes later they were back in their own ambulance. The first thing Harry did was pin Kim's photographs on the plywood wall of the ambulance. Then he placed the new balaclava helmet and gloves that Kim knitted in the wooden ration box. In a few weeks time they would be needing them, already the trees looked barer out here than they did at home. They reported to the R.S.M.

Harry handed over his new marriage certificate.

"I sent him home to get things sorted out, Jackson, not for you to get yourself spliced. I hope it's that pretty young thing I saw you out with in King's Lynn one night."

"Yes, sir."

The R.S.M. wasn't in the least surprised when Charlie handed him the new marriage certificate, for he knew more about Charlie's circumstances than any other man in the unit.

"I hope you managed to get things sorted out, Williams, and got that little girl of yours settled down."

Charlie nodded.

The R.S.M. continued, "I suppose you have heard we have had a few casualties while you were away, so I want you to work here for a few days till you get back into your stride. The division moves up again tomorrow. Bloody trouble is the Jerries are leaving small isolated pockets of resistance behind to slow up the advance and you never know where the next shells are coming from. Most of them are young fanatics, should be in bloody school."

He heaved his shoulders in resignation.

"Still, behind a bloody 88 they can be just as deadly as a seasoned veteran. Right, sod off the pair of you, I will get these papers straight away."

He handed them a parcel of letters each.

"These came while you were away, I suppose the news is stale now."

There was also a parcel for each of them, an old tin box wrapped in brown paper and filled with goodies from Rosie and the people of the village.

Taking the dates they were posted, Harry placed the letters in chronological order. Then they both sat on the back step of the ambulance reading them, but as the R.S.M. said, the news was quite out of date.

The next morning they moved up towards the front line with their own unit and it wasn't long before they came within the sound of heavy gunfire.

"Just listen, Harry, they're playing our tune."

But Harry ignored his mate's remarks. He was sitting on his usual seat with his legs stretched forward and his feet pressed against the dashboard.

580

"I wrote to Kim last night and told her we had caught for a cushy number back off the lines, so don't you get writing to Kath and telling her otherwise."

But the conversation came to an abrupt end as casualties arrived. Harry rushed to the operating theatre to lend a hand. They worked throughout the day, dressing the wounded and evacuating them to the rear. Twice they had to take the ambulance forward to the A.D.S. to help evacuate back to the M.D.S. as the regimental ambulance couldn't cope alone. It didn't take long for them to fall into the old routine.

"Nothing much changes, does it, Harry?" said Charlie as they lifted a dead body into the ambulance. As they did so a corner of the blanket caught on the stretcher runner and pulled it away.

"Bloody hell, Charlie, look who it is! He didn't get to see his old man's grave after all." It was the man that travelled up with them to Second Echelon.

"He could only have seen a couple of days action, poor bastard." And that was all Harry could say, he was truly getting hardened with the war.

The division gained ground, advancing a few miles, then stopping to consolidate the ground. They were both enjoying working with the M.D.S. but it wouldn't last for long. The ambulances out with the regiments were taking a real bashing, the division had a fanatical S.S. regiment ahead of them desperately fighting a rear guard action.

They were sitting on the back step of the ambulance when the new orderly sergeant came over carrying a large ordnance map.

"Sorry, lads, I have to send you out at first light, the ambulance up with the Hussars has just caught it, smashed to pieces and both the driver and the medic are dead. That's Nichols, the medic, I don't think you knew him, he's only been with the unit a few months. Ever met him?" They both shook their heads.

"The driver was Perkins, joined us in Norfolk to replace the man we lost on that motorbike near Swaffam. Not a bad bloke, trouble was he was also a booze bandit. He was a sergeant before he came to us but got knocked down to a driver, pissed as a cricket, smashed a three tonner and got fifty-six days in the glasshouse."

"And now he's got a wooden cross, pity he didn't lay off the booze, he would still be back in Blighty. Some bastards never learn, eh sarge?"

The sergeant spread the map out on the grass and told them to get closer.

"We are here." He stabbed the map with a grubby finger, the blackened nail tracing a route.

"Turn left at the gate, then follow this road. At the first crossroads make a sharp right turn, the road winds round here."

He marked the map with a pencil. "Now here is another dirt road, it's been battered around a bit and they say the verges are mined, so whatever you do, don't wander from the road. You can't miss it, it's lined each side with tall poplars and a couple of miles inside there's a burnt out farmhouse. Don't get looking for eggs or spuds, the engineers haven't searched it for booby traps yet."

"That's sodded it then, sarge, you can bet your bloody boots if the ginger beers are going in to de-booby trap it there will be sod all eggs or anything else left."

"Never mind that, Williams, just try and keep away from the place. Now about four, maybe five miles along this road you will come to a T junction. Sharp right here and you will see the armoured cars, you'll just have to find your own way from there."

"What about this road here, sarge. Surely if we took that it would be nearer?"

"Don't be a stupid prick, Jackson, that's like a boundary line, like the counties we have at home. Over there and you're in Picardy, so in your next letter home you can tell them you're in Picardy, you know, like the old First War song, 'Roses of Picardy' - surely you've heard it?" The sergeant started to sing the song that Harry knew so well, in a fine baritone voice.

"Don't worry, sarge, I doubt if I will ever forget it, it's my wife's favourite." But somehow Harry had the most unpleasant and yet the most comforting feeling run through his body.

That night he took the heavy silver watch from his waterproof wrappings and, without letting Charlie see it, walked away from the ambulance. At exactly nine o'clock, alone, he lay back on the grass staring at the millions of stars above his head. Never before had he felt so close to Kim, he could almost feel her warm breath on his neck. After an hour he rose from the grass and walked over to a small copse. For the first time since he'd left the orphanage he prayed in deadly earnest - not for himself, but for the safety of Kim and his unborn child, for deep down inside him he knew he had an appointment with eternity.